D1193452

A Fragile
Respectability

HELEN TURNER

NIMBUS PUBLISHING

Nimbus Publishing Limited
P.O. Box 9301, Station A
Halifax, N.S.
B3K 5N5

Design: Steven Slipp, GDA, Halifax
Printed and bound in Canada by Best Gagné Book Manufacturers

Cover: *Portrait of Alice 1929* by J. Frederic McCulloch
Photographed by Neil Steinberg
Permission to reproduce painting courtesy of Alice McCulloch Sutton

Canadian Cataloguing in Publication Data

Turner, Helen, 1906-

  A fragile respectability

  ISBN 0-921054-99-8

I. Title.

PS8589.U76F72 1991   C813'.54   C91-097641-4
PR9199.3.T87F72 1991

Dedication

For Violet and Graham Young, Dr. J.I. Askins, and
the late Herbert Mendelson.
With special thanks to Violet who, time after time,
literally saved my life.

Acknowledgements

Through writing this book I was priviledged to meet
Dr. John F. Godfrey, to whom I owe a special debt; without his
encouragement and generous help I would never have finished it.
My thanks to Sylvia Moir of 'Ship's Bell,' Chester, who read portions of
this book some four years ago, and whose continuing interest and
support have meant a great deal to me.

1

Nova Scotia, December 1939

I am swathed in mink. My careless hat, and how carefully I chose it, is just the right contrast of neutral-dark felt to accentuate my white skin, my scarlet mouth, just enough brim to shadow my eyes. My cultivated façade, and how I have worked to perfect it–and even in my dazed misery, I'm aware of it–is making its usual impact: when I stepped on board, the rough-loud voices of four or five lumberjacks, sole passengers on this backwoods train, dropped to an obsequious murmur, involuntary tribute to a lady.

Expeditiously, the conductor snaps the bag from my hand, flings it to the rack above my head. He squints at me through steel-rimmed spectacles. Though it is barely six o'clock, it is dark outside. The center string of grimy ceiling lights are on. Winter's night. December night. Vaguely, through the frosted double windows I can see the heavy, white-shadowed trees.

"Look, there's a bad draft. Don't take your coat off. These fellers won't keep a door closed. Brought up in a barn. The coach will warm up when we get under way."

"Thank you." Ponderous, dandruff on his faded blue uniform, he's a replica of all the conductors I used to know. But I don't know him, I've been away too long.

He pulls the heavy gold watch (I know it's a Hamilton, that it keeps perfect time, that he's proud of it) from his vest pocket, studies it. "We seem to be running a little late."

Running a little late! Now and then, in summer, that train runs on time, but in winter, with the excuse of bad weather and time-and-a-half for overtime for the crew, at the earliest, it's two hours late. Pa once said if the Edgeville train came in on schedule, the people in two counties would think they were having a mass hallucination.

Pa. He's dying. Is he dead? And of my own volition, I am on the Edgeville train. Who in Edgeville would believe that "Papa's pet" deliberately is not hastening to his death-bed?

Undemonstrative, he never kissed me and he never told me he loved me, Pa was the strong root that fed and restored me when my childish hopes

1

were crushed. Until Flora's daughter, Vera, his first grandchild, was born I had no rival for Pa's affections. He was the one person, aloof but not remote, who taught me, and without sentiment or prejudice, something of the meaning of life. Theoretically, he taught me the triviality of my ambitions and fears. Theoretically, because, although I understood his words, they were but the beginning of knowing the reality; away from him I lost his perspective. Pa tried to show me myself against a large background: the almost invisible–the mostly unstrung–thread I was spinning in the global tapestry, where the achievements of the great were woven in unbreakable strands of selfless beauty.

Beauty. He never called those achievements "beautiful." How he laughed at that word. Debased, through popular misuse, he refused it. Satirical, uncompromising in his hatred of the pretensions of the ignorant to a capacity for discrimination in matters beyond them, in which they had limited experience, I can hear him now: "In the land of the blind, the one-eyed man is King."

And it was heavy going when I tried to convince him that the reality of beauty could not be debased. I had to explain "reality." I thought I knew, but I could never convince him. I never dared admit that I longed for beauty. I was ashamed to tell my father that I read poetry; that I worshipped Keats; that I identified with him, his words; that John Keats, as the apogee of Edgeville, meant more to me than Pa's "common man." How would I dare? Knowing I was lulling, self-deceiving, emulating Pa's ludicrous fools, I kept my shabby copy of Keats secret-hidden in the hayloft. And Pa never found out.

Illusory images playing over the paralyzed thing that is me. I am paralyzed with grief. I walk. I talk. I make sense. I hear what is said ... What has the conductor been talking about?

"As I say, I've been railroading for thirty years, and I've only been on this run a few months, but I can still tell them a few things. Here, I'll just turn that seat for you." He turned the back of the seat in front of me to give me a double space. "We don't get many visitors up here this season of the year."

My cue. He expects me to identify myself. Then he'll know my life history. Everyone around here knows everyone. But if he finds out who I am, I'll have to listen.

"How far you going? What station?"

"I ... I'm going home ... Christmas. My husband has the tickets. He'll be along in a minute. If you don't mind, I think I'll rest." Rudely, I turn my head away from him.

2

"Why ... Sure, you do that. You rest yourself."

I've embarrassed him. He hesitates, walks away.

I am going home.

Since I married Dick, my relationship with my family is ... extraordinary! That childish rivalry for "place" is ended. No one now contests my place; I am an equal. They love me at last. As Flora says, "We are adults now."

And yet, approaching Edgeville, I am haunted still by the echoes of my childhood: the mockery, the cruel laughter, the hostility. In coming home, and it seems I am helpless to avoid it, my senses go rummaging in that turbid mass: the garbage of my childhood. My larynx clamps shut. I choke. Against my will, I disinhume that buried atmosphere of emotional violence.

Relax, I say to myself. Take it gently; relax your throat.

"Darling, are you all right?"

Startled, I look up. My handsome husband is leaning over me. No need for him to worry about his perfect façade. Born to wealth, sheltered and protected by it all his life, he wears it as casually as he breathes. But he has not caught me out. Nothing shows on my disciplined face, and Dick is automatically spouting the amenities. "Kitten, I *am* sorry about this train. But you do understand? I couldn't risk getting stuck in a snowbank."

"Y-yes. Yes. Of course I do." Understand! All I had to say was, "Go ahead. It's safe." For I know the road, and I know the people. Completely responsible, they would never send us out if the road was impassable. I know quite well that the road from Otter to Edgeville is open. And I know quite well that taking this train will delay us about three hours.

"I suppose the car is safe in that garage? Ye Gods, what a one-horse town." He sits down beside me, squeezes my hand. "Kitten, how they ever produced you up here is a miracle."

"Dick, you did get through to the house? Is Pa ... Who did you talk to?"

"Don't worry. I'll get you there in time. Your father is still alive. But it took me ten minutes to persuade Central, as the local yokels call her, to ring your house. She didn't want to disturb them. I told her they'd be more disturbed if their ewe lamb had to wade through two miles of snow to get home from the station. Actually, I talked to Martha. She'll send a sleigh for us. How are you, Kitten? I'm glad you're not taking it too hard. I hate weeping females. But go ahead, if you feel like it. Cry."

Cry. Lean on him. Be weak. Drench him with tears so he can touch me, comfort me. Tears excite him ... roll me into bed. Bed is the place to heal all wounds, get rid of my scabby notions; restore sanity.

And of all my insane notions, the maddest was my latest one, a month or so ago, to leave him–when it was too late, when I should have left him years ago–for of all things, a principle: unrequited love for Clay, a man who had just announced his intention to marry someone else. Of all my foolish, my amusing aberrations, that came the nearest to wrecking us.

But my husband knows what's best for us both. He knows me far better than I know myself. A simple case of: "The grass on the other side of the fence is–face it–greener." He talked me out of it. Why go away to suffer alone, leave him to suffer? For he'd be lost without me. Even if I didn't love him–but he was sure in my heart I did–I didn't want to hurt him, did I? I had enough affection for him, didn't I, to stay and take care of him, let him keep his home? He was satisfied to keep me without love. Even without love, sex is good for you.

And then, think of our families, his and mine. How would they feel if we broke up? My father, ill. The news would kill him. What would it prove to make everyone miserable? In the end, he persuaded me to "see reason."

He must have been terrified that I would leave for there was a sudden honeymoon attitude; gifts. But I'm a far more expensive item now, than when we first married. I have extravagant tastes.

My unexpected revolt, my absolute refusal to accept his dictate of sensible dress, that rotten accusation I made against him of cheeseparing. That hurt! Was there anything I needed that I didn't get? I needed a winter coat, but did I have to have mink? Ostentatious! That mink almost broke him. But never mind. Tolerant, he would indulge my vulgar taste; he happened to have enough money to do so.

So, everything is fine now, for, in staying, did I not admit him right? Poor Dick. He never found out that even after the coat, unable to go on without another glimpse of Clay, despairing, knowing it was too late, I went to see him.

"How well you look," Clay said, coldly. "And how very beautiful."

"Yes," I said. "I have a lovely new coat. It's a bribe, I intended leaving Dick, at last. But ... Clay, I betrayed you." For although he had never said it to me, he had told the Volkhovs that he loved me and that if I went back to Dick, after Spain, it would be over between us.

"You haven't betrayed *me*."

That stopped me. How right he was. I'd betrayed myself: loving him, I stayed with Dick to prove to Mother that marriage made me worthy of her respect. What good does it do to think about it? Especially, now! But why had Clay never told me that he loved me?

Why do I suffer? For my shoddy behaviour? For losing Clay and my father? Losing the two I love with a deathless love, and losing them together and within months? I'm all mixed up. I don't know for whom or for what I suffer. All I know is that beneath the surface–smiling, attentive, wife–I carry a lethal wound.

"Ye Gods. Damn! Darling, why didn't you remind me? I left the flask in the car. I could stand a drink. You must need one, too. Are you thirsty? I can get you a drink of water. That is, if I can stand up in this antiquated hunk of machinery they call a train. Does it always shake like this? Lucky you're not pregnant."

Perhaps if he'd have let me have a baby ... But I'm glad now he wasn't ready for a child. I haven't the strength. And every cent I can scrounge out of him these days must go to the Volkhovs. How jealous he is of my love for them. They are my only link, now, with Clay. Is he well? Happy? In spite of everything, I believe Clay loves me.

"Well, don't answer. I know you're feeling miserable. Cigarette? Here, I'll light one for you. This lighter is running out of fuel. Don't think I've got a match. Just a minute, Yabbit."

Yabbit! I'm his "bed-rabbit!" I'm his "Kitten," his "Cat," his "Skunk-weasel." I'm his "Crazy coot." I looked that up once. Coot: a duck-like bird, stupid, slow in flight; not classed as game bird.

He's right. I'm his Crazy coot.

"Why don't you put your head back Darling? Rest. No pillows on this benighted train. I must say, you are primitive. Here, lean on me. I guess it's all right to kiss my wife in public. You poor angel. All right, don't lean on me if you don't want to, but lean back. Go to sleep if you like. My God, the back door! Kitten, did you remember to lock the back door? The last thing I told you before I got the car out. Try to think! Did you do it? You did? Are you sure? Well, all I hope is that we don't get back and find it swinging on its hinges!"

The back door? To hell with it! For all I know, it's wide open. For all I care, it can swing on its hinges till doomsday. A fine attitude. Yet one that's easy enough to conceal. So simple. Dick is convinced I'm telling him, and how agreeably, everything he's saying himself.

Yet I can't shut it out, his constant nagging; it trickles in. Chinese water torture. How can he say that he loves me? He wants attention.

This constant silent vilification of every word he speaks. He means well. How kind he has been to my parents. What a shock I got when I heard him describe Pa to his mother! "You'd like Philippa's father. The nearest description that would fit him is that he dresses like a New England farmer."

Pa? What fantastic lack of insight. Or are New England farmers ... I've never met one ... all intellectuals? Of course, Pa's careless. How long since he's bought a new suit—or worn one? But Pa has more brains in his big toe than Dick has in his head. But then, if Dick wasn't stupid, he'd never have married me. And I? How clever of me to marry him. Stupidity? We're a pair.

"Yabbit? ... You know? I'm not at all sure that this was the moment to give the servants time off, but perhaps you were right. As long as we had to put Sugar in the kennel. You know I'm right about that dog; he's getting out of hand. It's the breed. All Alsatians are treacherous. I just hope he doesn't take it into his head to get loose!"

Sugar, how suddenly he changed. And how he picks up my emotion. Was I shocked or delighted the morning after that insufferable night, after I consented to stay, when Dick leaned down to kiss me, and Sugar bit him! The look on Dick's face! Well, as my beloved husband says, why pussy-foot around it? It was funny. I was delighted.

What's he twaddling about now? I simply can't take any more. I must shut him up. "Dick, darling." Christ! "Will you be offended if I don't talk?"

Tenderly, "Why, no. Of course not. Not another word out of you, Cat. Shut your eyes."

I shut my eyes.

"Take off your hat."

I take off my hat.

"Darling, would you please take ..."

"Heavens, Dick, I was almost asleep."

"I just want It to take off Its old glove. I just want to hold Its hand."

I pulled off my gloves, gave him my hand. I shut my eyes. God, I prayed, You don't exist, but would You please give me five minutes peace? Why has he dropped my hand? Why is he fidgeting?

"Piglet, look, what's this? All wrapped up in Its handkerchief?"

Wrapped up?

I pretended not to hear. Wrapped up? For a second or two I couldn't imagine what he was talking about. Wrapped up? God! I jerked up in my seat, snatched ... "Give it to me!"

He held the little bundle out of reach, unfastened the safety pin. "Uhn, uhn, not till I find out what you're hiding."

The pills! They could be traced to me. "Dick!"

"Well, what do you know? A mystery, no less. What's this? You taken to dope?"

His greed to possess me. To possess every last thing about me. He

6

forbids me a private thought. I didn't dare let that little bottle out of my sight. And how deal with him? Unless with an axe ... Be sugar-sweet, playful, cozen him; baby-talk him into ... "Dearest, it's an itty-bitty secret, a girl-secret." I could vomit. "Give it to me."

"Uhn-uhn! No secrets. Come on, 'fess up, what are they, Yabbit? Love pills so you don't lose me?"

'Fess up! Damn his soul, I ... what a shock if his ittsy-bittsy Yabbit opened her mouth; what a shock he'd get if he could read her pure little mind. Careless, stupid! Why didn't I get rid of them?

"Come on, now. What have you been gobbling up behind my back? You'se a bad little mouse. Tell me what they are and I'll let you have them if I think they're good for you."

Tell him? Flick it off with a joke? Or with the truth? "Your wife, my dear, is a walking paradox: she ennobles murder; prepared to kill but too moral to allow the blame for stealing to fall on an innocent." A dozen people on that ward had access to the poisons, and I couldn't steal them and place suspicion on any one of them.

The dreadful trouble for those hideous pills. Me–leaning against that barred window, the drug room–innocent, looking old Mr. Bernard straight in the face. How lucky that my nursing record was irreproachable. Me–pretending conscientious distress: "Oh, Mr. Bernard, I'm so sorry! I was visiting Ward Seven, helping Loretta ... uh, the Supervisor, with the medications, she went to the ward and the orderly came in suddenly and startled me. I upset a whole bottle in the sink. Can I pay you for them?"

"Why no, Miss Jerrold. Of course not. Thank you for reporting it. Most of these nurses are so careless, they forget I have to account for every grain. But not you. I hear you got married. Will you be coming back?"

"Yes. Uh ... no. You *are* kind, Mr. Bernard. Thank you, but are you sure you don't want me to pay for ..."

"No, no, of course not. Here's a full bottle. Now just forget it."

"Dick, I'm too tired to play games. I've had no sleep. Give me that bottle."

"It won't tell? It'll be sorry. It's a good thing Its husband isn't a nasty old man who would spank Its bottom."

I could strangle him. I hesitated, then turned away and didn't answer. He hated that.

"Okay. If that's the way It wants it. I'll find out for myself. I'll eat one and see what it does to me."

"No! How dare you steal my things! Since when have you taken to searching my handbag?"

"Well, now, look! You don't have to insult me. And I wasn't searching your handbag. My lighter won't work. I was looking for a match. You always get so mad. What is this stuff, anyway?"

Easy, easy, watch it. His wolfish need to dominate might lead him to ... I sighed. "Dick, dear, it's not like you to be inconsiderate. How can you be so silly? What do you think it is, poison? Really!"

"No, but Yabbit, what are these pills?"

"Well, what do they look like?" What do they look like? Saccharine! "They're nothing. Oh, all right, if you must pry into my little vanities. Give them back and I'll tell you."

"No you don't! You tell me first."

"All right, you dummy. They're saccharine. Now, are you satisfied?"

"Saccharine! So, that's what It's been hiding. Slipping it into Its coffee behind my back. I thought something was going on. No wonder you're so thin. Well, I'm just not going to let you have them. If anyone needs them–I'm the one who's getting pudgy–I do. I'll keep them."

"No!" My voice cracked. "No! Give them to me! At once!"

"Look, Kitten, will you please control yourself? I don't want to complain, but people are looking. Look at yourself; you're shaking."

"Give them to me!"

"Temper, temper! You don't have to tremble when I speak. I'm not a great big woof."

"Give them back!"

"Oh," sulky, "if you feel like that about it. You know, you're only doing yourself harm. All right, you can have them. Here, take them."

I took that lethal vial and dropped it in my purse. I couldn't stop shaking. "Dick." I held out a propitiatory hand. "Don't be cross. You're stronger than I am, and when you bully me ..."

"Bully you! Who touched you? You just have no funny bone!"

"Please, Dick! I'm really tired. I'm sorry I shouted at you, but I can't ... I ... Honestly, I can't take any more. Will you please let me alone!"

"Let you alone! Oh, sure, you say anything you please to me, and it's all my fault. It's always my fault!" There it was, his underlying resentment, breaking through the veneer, directed openly at me.

"What about me? How do you think I feel when you jump all over me? All right, all right, forget it. Go to sleep. And you don't have to hang on to your purse till your knuckles turn white. No one's going to snatch it."

Now he'll sulk for the rest of the night. The hell with him. No, we're almost home. "Oh, you silly!" I managed a light laugh. Hysterical? But he wouldn't notice. "Don't be ridiculous. Here, let me rest my head on you,

8

then perhaps I'll sleep." Tense, alert, eyes closed, I forced myself to lie back against him. Sustained agony. The train stopped, started, shunted, bumped–masking, I hoped, my intermittent and involuntary trembling.

"Edgeville! Edgeville!"

"Kitten? Surely you can't sleep through all this. Are you awake? We're here."

"Edgeville!"

"Can I help you folks with your luggage?"

"Thank you, if you'd just take this case. All right, Darling, we have the luggage. Don't you worry about a thing."

Clutching my handbag, I followed them to the end of the car. Dick turned to smile at me. Then the anger beneath his public–one must be patient with idiots–face.

"Here! Hell's bells, I do have to look after you! I'm sorry, Darling, but I had to pay for it. Go back to the seat. You forgot your hat."

2

That constant part of the heart's deep wish-recall of home: the improbable lustre that embellishes the ugliest. Old George, crabbed, churlish, was standing beside the sleigh. I loved that old man. I threw myself at him. Stiff-armed, embarrassed, he held me off. But his voice was kind.

"Your Pa's still alive, Pill. It's a sad homecomin'. Get in. I got the bear rug for you."

I stood beside the sleigh and I couldn't lift my foot, so I leaned against it, trying to get my breath, waiting for courage. The Edgeville station ... half buried in snow. When I was a child, the romantic point of departure for the great-big-exciting world that I would live in one day. Once, at thirteen, expecting any minute to turn into a famous author, writing my first story, it was the Edgeville station I had in mind when my heroine, me, eloping, left a note for the family: "Don't worry, and don't come after us. We're down at the station taking the train for South America."

"What is it?" Dick asked. "Don't stand there mooning, or you'll freeze to death."

I got into the sleigh.

Martha was in the kitchen, standing beside the red-hot iron range. Running to me with open arms, heavy, flushed, she smells of laundry soap. "Well, you're here!" she said. "At last. I was havin' fits!" Muscles like a day labourer, she hugged me; she almost broke my spine.

She pulled a handkerchief from her apron pocket, wiped her eyes, and blew her nose. "What on earth happened? Why you so late?" She peered into my face. "You look like the wrath of God. All the way from New York, drivin' like crazy, I suppose, and nothin' to eat.

"Why you standin' there? I'da thought wild horses couldn't keep you from your Pa. You're famished, that's what. Well you can't eat now; it ain't decent. The doctor's there. Hurry! Go on up!"

"Dick, give me a cigarette."

"Cigarette! Oh, no, now, stop it. Stop it, I say." She was scandalized.

"You think that becomin? Smokin' at a time like this? What you think the people in Edgeville will say when that gets out! A good thing it's me in this kitchen."

Dick put a lighted cigarette in my mouth.

"Pill! You crazy? You got no respect for yor Pa? It's not nice. Nervous is what ... You always was. Well, I know you don't mean no sacrilege to your Pa, and I don't want to start harpin' at you, but at a time like this you got to show some respect."

"Kitten, shall I go up with you?"

"No. Martha, get Dick a cup of coffee. Dick, Martha will give you whatever you want. Go into the sitting-room."

Pa would be in the big front bedroom and I thought, cynically, it would take me two seconds longer to get to him if I went up the back stairs. So, I started up that way.

With everyone home, I should have anticipated finding someone in our old playroom, but I didn't, and I stopped in sudden panic when I saw my mother–completely out of character–lying in the bed. I turned my head away. In all my years I couldn't remember that I had ever seen her lying down.

"Philippa?"

I forced myself to look at her.

"Yes?"

Her face was bloodless, paper-white against her disordered gray hair. I walked over and stood beside her. Only her sunken, dry eyes had colour. They were threaded in scarlet. I hadn't seen her in more than a year, but neither of us made the conventional move to embrace.

"Philippa. You're late. Did you have to take that train? The road's all right."

Her voice was hesitant; she had failed. I couldn't look. I said, "Yes." I turned my back on her, went out of the playroom, through Geoffrey's bedroom and opened the door to the upstairs parlour. The family were all there, Geoffrey and Edna, Flora and Edward, Sue and Elliot. Geoffrey came over and kissed me. "Where's Dick?"

"Pa ... Is he ..."

"I made Flora come out of there for five minutes, for Christ's sake," Geoffrey said. "She's all in. The doctor's with him. I spoke to him, but you're too late. He's unconscious."

I went to Flora, bent down and kissed her cheek. She looked utterly spent. Her hair, generally so neat and tidy, was stuck in little wet curls to her forehead. She was slumped in a chair with her feet on a pouf.

"I can never repay you," I said. "I shall be grateful to you for the rest of my life, for taking care of Pa."

Tears started to her eyes. Her lips began to tremble.

I crossed the hall and opened the door to my father's room. I hesitated, listened. Stertorous breathing ... I stepped inside and closed the door behind me. Dr. West had his back to me. He didn't turn his head. I went over and stood beside him. I didn't notice until later, when he made me put it out, that I was still holding my cigarette.

There was a towel shading the bedside lamp, but I could see my father's face. I recognized his condition. My father would never open his eyes again. I need never again tremble in uncertainty, in doubt that he might look at me in fear.

And standing beside him now, it seemed utterly improbable that he was dying, that all his passion could be thus snuffed out. He was the quintessence of all that is civilized, fine: great. It was his right that he depart life in majestic ceremony, in triumph. How was it possible that he could drift away in this forgotten corner of the world? In obscurity. In Edgeville. For except for us, his family, the Wests were the only ones who could appreciate, or begin to understand him.

Like my father, Dr. West is a law unto himself. He is no man to conform to the respectable. In unexpected contrast to his slow, somewhat heavy manner of speech, his mind is sagacious, acute. It is his habit to "get down to cases" and, without ceremony, to strip a patient of his covering veil of "decent" pretence. "How else can you wake 'em up? If I don't tell 'em they're ignorant, they'll never find out. This way, it gives them a chance to improve."

But it never crossed my mind that at that moment, standing beside Pa (could Pa hear?) talking as though he were already dead, Dr. West would, with one sentence, smash the barrier of civilized reticence between us. "Tell me, Philippa," he said, "how did you intend to do it? Your father said, 'one of my children is willing to die for me.' He didn't say which one, but I knew. It was you."

Shocked, frozen with fear, I stammered, tried to summon my dead wits to evade his questioning. His appalling curiosity! What were my intentions? The details? The method?

Pa! Had he been delirious at the end? What we knew should have been held inviolate between us. Yet, Pa had confided in this man. "S-surely," I said. "Y-you misunderstood. Uh ... I ... You don't really think, I ..."

I was reprieved, finally, by the doctor's instinct not to destroy me.

12

He took one last look at Pa. Then he turned away from the bed, opened his bag, and handed me a sleeping pill. "Take this tonight," he said. "That's an order." He snapped the bag shut and left the room.

He would keep them talking a minute or so.

My head close to his face, I said, "Pa! Pa! You do know there is nothing on earth I would not do for you."

Did his lids move? Tremble ...

Geoffrey opened the door and came to stand beside me. Flora followed him. We waited silently while each gasping breath became critically far apart.

I was standing at Pa's head, Geoffrey next to me, Flora next to Geoffrey. Sue was not in the room when Pa's laboured breathing stopped. Geoffrey put one arm around Flora and one around me and pulled us—tried to pull me—to him. But no human force could have moved me from my father. Rigid, I did not budge from my place.

I had no need to be comforted at the moment my father died. My only need was to comfort him ... Had the soul, the spirit of my father died with his body? Or did it linger still? Whatever new element the spirit encountered at death, so far as I could penetrate that element, I would go with him; he would enter this new sphere sustained, supported, by love. I put my hand on his forehead. I spoke soothingly, comforting him as though he were a child. "It's all right, Pa. I'm with you. I'm here."

"Stop it, Philippa," Geoffrey said. "Papa's gone. You're touching his dead body. Come away."

Flora started for the door but she didn't reach it. She collapsed against the wall, piteously staring. Her round-china-blue eyes were full of tears. "I'm all right; I won't cry," she breathed. "I'm faint. Smelling salts."

Geoffrey caught her by both arms, held her, kept her from sliding to the floor. "Philippa!" he ordered. "Get them. On the sitting-room table."

I found the smelling salts, opened the bottle as I ran, and held it out. Geoffrey snatched it and put it under Flora's nose. I waited till she recovered and I followed them out of Pa's room. And then I don't know where they went. They disappeared. I suppose Geoffrey put Flora to bed. But where I expected them to go, and where they didn't go, was to Mother.

But ... they must tell her, at once. Sue? Was Sue with Mother? I was certain she was not. Did they expect me to tell her?

I opened the door to the playroom. She was alone. I walked over and sat down on her bed. She raised her head.

"Mother ..." But I didn't have to tell her.

"Charles ..." A keening, thin, animal whine. She threw up both hands in a helpless gesture. I caught them. They were like ice. I held them, then placed them together, one over the other, and slipped them under the covers. I stood up and tucked her in. "Look," I said, harshly, "it's over. You're exhausted. Can you sleep?"

Her face! The hard-tight lines, encircling the slack little bits. She looked up at me, dry-eyed, red-eyed. Her head went back and forth like a mechanical doll. "No."

"Will you try to sleep?"

I could barely hear her.

"I'll try."

"Do you want anything? A drink? Smelling salts? Are you faint?"

"No, nothing, no. I'm not going to faint."

"I can give you something to make you sleep." I placed my fingers on the pulse at the side of her head. She was all right.

"I hate that stuff. It makes me sick." She dropped her head on the pillow, turned it away from me. She said, faintly, "I'll try to sleep."

I put my hand on the counterpane over her hidden hands, just for a second. Then I turned and left her.

With the house full of people, I went to find a bed for Dick. I found him asleep on the couch. I threw a blanket over him, tucked him in. He didn't wake up. Geoffrey came along and gave me another yellow capsule. I now had five of them. Then I discovered the others had taken the bedrooms. I found a rocking chair.

In the middle of the night–indifferently, for who cared? Not I–I stood in the bathroom trying to decide which pills to throw in the toilet. I said "Eeny-meeny-miney-moe" standing over it. It came out three times for Pa's, so I swallowed all the yellow ones for sleep and flushed Pa's lethal tablets down the drain.

I spent the night in the rocking chair, not with Pa. He was alone. Dead. I meant to go and say "Hello" to him, but once I sat down I couldn't get up. Those pills don't make you sleep, but they immobilize you.

The light–silent, relentless, brutally insensitive–lifting the dark; unmasking day. I huddled in the rocking chair, my eyes wide open; the eyelids in tight recoil, despite my night-long effort to force them shut, despite the primitive, animal-need of the wounded for the dark. The light, the splitting light! I lifted my numb hands to my torpid head. How massage the brain? Coffee.

14

Mother was in the kitchen preparing breakfast. She looked haggard, ill, but as usual, every hair in place.

I said, "Where's Martha?"

"I sent her away. She talks too much. Don't tell me you slept in that dress! Look at your hair!"

With a vague notion of comforting her, I touched her shoulder.

"Comb your hair! Do you want Dick to see you like that?"

She was back on her feet, her reaction to adversity or sorrow always the same, a violence of physical activity. Whatever else, I thought, she's a gallant woman.

She handed me a cup of coffee. I took it, then put it down. The walls were sliding ... The floor lifting ... I started for the bathroom. I said, "I'll come back and help with breakfast."

Geoffrey was sitting at the kitchen table filling out a paper and I was sitting beside him, my absent eyes following his pen.

Name: Jerrold, Charles Alexander.

How Pa laughed at 'Alexander.' He claimed he'd been named for eight popes or perhaps, since his father had infinite regard for the church and worshipped indiscriminately, for Alexander VI: the whoremaster.

Age: Seventy-six.

Race:

"Caucasian," I murmured. I'd filled in lots of those things for the interns in the city hospital.

Cause of death:

My heart started pounding; this was Papa's death certificate. A hand, disjoined from me, picked up the certificate. Another took Geoffrey's pen from his hand. My voice, a conspiratorial whisper, I said, "I'll do that." I held the certificate before my eyes. Cause of death. The words blurred, jumped and then fell into focus. It was filled in. Angina Pectoris. What did I think it would say? Murder? A murder I hadn't committed? I had to fill in the blanks or Geoffrey would be suspicious. Words, words, ordinary words and the blanks ... but in mental paralysis I had no idea what the words meant.

Time of Death:

"Time of death," I murmured. "What shall I write?"

"Here! Give it back." Geoffrey took the death certificate away from me.

During Pa's illness, Flora and I, both trained nurses, were equally competent to care for him. But never mind my promise to kill him that had kept me away from him. I could not have taken care of him. I was prostrate at the thought. My mental processes with regard to him were so confused by emotion that I no longer trusted my judgement, nursing or otherwise. I believed my presence would be unnerving to him; if I offered him a cup of tea or a medication, how could he be certain of my intention? With that, I could not have watched his physical deterioration or suffering without violating that so-important tenet of the nursing profession: never reveal apprehension for a patient's condition. I stayed away. Flora took care of him. And I came to realize that in caring for Pa Flora had disclosed an innate generosity and compassion. For with Pa's death–after a lifetime of estrangement between us–now seeking me out, she poured into my ears, bitter words and tears intermingling, a torrent of shocking facts about Pa: Pa had tortured and terrified Flora all her life!

Preposterous, I thought. Pa: kind and just and impervious to or uninfluenced by my bad reputation in the family; Pa, who had treated me, as far back as I could remember, as an equal, that very same Pa had wronged Flora dreadfully. I sat, horrified, listening to Flora's bitter monologues.

"When I was a child ..." Flora's cheeks rosy-pink with suppressed emotion, Flora's little-blue-eyes-opened-wide, pleading with mine for an equal and just censure of Pa. "When I was a child of six or seven, lying in bed at night, when I heard Pa in the kitchen rattling the silver, getting something to eat, I thought he was looking for the butcher knife and was coming upstairs to kill me."

I couldn't speak. An incredible, malevolent accusation, I thought. Silently. "If you talk," Pa used to say, "you hear one voice, your own."

I said, mildly, "Flora, I don't understand. Pa never raised a hand against any of us in his life. How could you be frightened of him?"

"People don't have to hit you to hurt you," Flora said. "They have plenty of other ways to make you suffer."

True. How true. But terrify a child? "What did he do? How did he hurt you?"

Flora, hesitating ... Flora's eyes, appealing; anyone who didn't believe those innocent eyes was a liar. "I ... I don't know."

I learned it as a nurse. If people hesitate before answering, the answer is generally contrived. "You must have done something Pa didn't like."

"No! I did not! All I know is, I was always terrified of him because I never knew what he might do."

What he might do? He never did a thing. Sat around and read a book.

16

What did Flora fear? His anger? Yes, Pa's anger was truly monumental, but rare. I saw him angry only a few times in his life because so few things could rouse him to anger: the corrupt, man's exploitation of man, cruelty. Yet, come to think of it, he had a chronic, local anger against affectation or stupidity. Pa: an enormous, independent, intellectual vitality. But physical violence? Never.

Then why, as a child, did Flora think Pa wanted to kill her? And how account for this, our diametrically opposite view? Pa, to me: judicious, calm, denouncing irrational force. Pa, to Flora: intimidating. Terrifying.

Pa, to me: amusing, sometimes very funny. Always–when I could get his attention away from his book–ready to talk, humane, warm. Pa, to Flora: intolerant, inhuman, glacial.

Pa, my archangel. Flora's archfiend: the archetype of the prurient mind, knowing all lewdity and seeing it everywhere.

As a child Flora thought Pa wanted to kill her. As an adolescent, Flora felt Pa had such a dirty mind that she was ashamed to invite a boy to the house. "Why, if a boy walked home with me after a party, there he was, waiting!" The minute she stepped inside the door, she was confronted with Pa's indecent suspicions.

"Oh, come now," I protested. "The only time Pa ever accused me of anything, he had very good reason. And Sue had boyfriends from the moment she stepped foot in Edgeville and he never said a word–not even when she took off on the back of a motorcycle with that boy!"

"You just don't remember. It's true. He was awful! By the time you and Sue came along, he changed. I got the worst of everything because I came first. He had a filthy mind. He really did. And he took it all out on me."

A filthy mind? Pa? He had the most innocent eyes I'd ever seen. His filthy mind must have been an expression of extreme solicitude: no amorous fondling for his daughter with the Edgeville swains. He didn't trust her. I said, "You misunderstood him. The only time to fear Pa was if you were morally at fault."

"Oh, poof! He didn't care what people thought. All right for him to detach himself from society. When he spoiled things for me, he just laughed. D'you think he cared?"

Pa. Callous? Brutal? Never. And to think I used to envy Flora, popular, running around with the girls and boys. I had no idea that when her friends got anywhere near Pa, they took one look and were on their way, leaving her–pride trampled, bitterly ashamed of him–to suffer.

But tender-hearted, vulnerable Flora, had had a bleak time of it.

And, unlike me, she had never escaped. She, too, had dreamed of leaving Nova Scotia for that blazoned Mecca of the ambitious poor: the States,* but New York had shocked and disappointed her. Flora could not exist in a heartless environment. "Who knows, or cares who you are?" she exclaimed. "In the city, unless you have money, no one notices you. Or if they do, they have no respect! Why I was looking in a shop window one day and this well-dressed man walked right up and stood beside me. 'Oh, you kid,' he said, 'follow me and you'll wear diamonds!'"

I had to laugh. "Heaven's. Weren't you flattered?"

"Flattered! To be taken for a cheap ... You ... I guess not!" Flora came home to stay.

Worse, her marriage was not what she had anticipated. Edward, through his early life as a bus boy in a commercial hotel, and later as a sports writer and broadcaster, had acquired a few habits that upset Flora. Careless of money, he gambled and drank and, no matter her complaints, refused to mend his ways.

And now Flora, always the glamorous one who, from the day of my birth, had taken the lead, bossed me around and thrown me whatever she didn't want, was–by what trick of doltish fate?– brought low. I was rich; she was poor. And now she was generous enough to acknowledge that her arrogant behaviour towards me, while growing up, had been childish. Generous enough to say (that shook me): "You know Pill, we're exactly alike. If anything should ever happen to me, I want you to take Vera. Promise me that you will."

Vera! Her only child. The light of her life.

For a moment, I held my breath. I couldn't believe it. Trust Vera to me: the liar, the twister, the whore? I shook my head. Then I laughed. "You're joking."

"I'm not! Promise me you'll take her."

"But ... why me? I should think you'd want Geoffrey to take her." Geoffrey and Flora had been allies all their lives.

"No! I don't! He ... He's not what you think. Promise me."

"What's wrong with Geoffrey?"

She was trembling in righteous anger. "He's not fair!"

"But Geoffrey loves you."

"That's what you think! Remember when you came back from Paris and married Dick?"

"Go on."

* The U.S.A.

"When you sent Mother the ring and the thousand dollars?" She stopped again.

"That had nothing to do with Geoffrey."

"You think! Well, instead of dividing the money equally, because he has two children and I have one, he took two-thirds!" She burst into tears.

They took it? Mother's money! Bloody hell! When the Volkhovs had been facing war in Paris and no tourists. Those two greedy bastards! ... Still, when it came to the test, when Pa needed someone, who was there? Flora. I said, "Don't cry, Flora. It's not worth crying about." And with Pa gone, I thought, no matter her seeming control, Mother would be lost for Pa was her strength. She would need Flora. That burden was already hung about Flora's neck. "Flora ..."

"Not only that," Flora interrupted, wiping her eyes. "I worry about Sue. Married to an older man. And the way she picked him up!"

"What! She didn't, he picked her up! I mean they were stuck on a sand bar. Elliot saw them from his yacht and pulled them off."

"Well, she didn't have to marry him. A widower with two children. He's too old for her."

I said, "For God's sake, Flora, Elliot is barely ten years older than Sue. Mother was eighteen and Pa was thirty-six when they married. D'you think that was a mistake?"

"Well, I guess they were happy, but Sue is stepmother to those two awful children. And what about his family, what do *they* think?"

I had to laugh. "When they first met, Elliot's mother asked him 'how a girl brought up on the outermost edge of civilization had acquired such poise.'"

"How can you laugh! What did he say?"

"He told her the moment we're born in Nova Scotia we're taught two things: poise, and how to build an igloo.

"Flora, Sue loves Elliot, she loves New York, she loves sailing, she loves shooting in Africa and India, and she loves everything else in her life. Sue's fine. Perhaps you should worry about yourself. This has been a dreadful time for you and it seems to me you're overwrought. How can I help?"

"You mean it?"

"Of course. What can I do?"

"Well if you really mean it, I've been dying to try on some of your clothes."

We were sitting in the kitchen. I took her upstairs and gave her what she wanted. She loved my diamond and sapphire engagement ring and tried that on as well. I couldn't give it to her but later, asking Sue and Geoffrey to share some of the cost, I sent her a large opal surrounded by diamonds that had belonged to the late opera singer, Madame Shuman-Heink.

Papa had asked to be cremated. That meant taking his body, by train, to a crematorium in the nearest city. Geoffrey and Edward had arranged to accompany the body. But Flora insisted: "If there's one thing I'm sure of, Philippa must go, too. Pa would want her."

I opened my mouth to object, then shut it; it was easier to go than to talk about it.

"And with Philippa going," Flora looked at Edward, "you can stay here. You don't have to ..."

"As long as Pa's this side of the grave," Edward interrupted, "I'll stick with him. I'm going."

Out of my splayed vision, Edward came sharply into focus: black hair, black eyes, neat bow tie, neat brown suit, shiny brown shoes. Edward ... Devoted to Pa?

As clearly as though he were standing beside me, I heard Pa: "Edward? What a philosophy! Gad! 'Everyone has an angle.' He 'wasn't born yesterday.' He's a baby, with as much idea of what's going on in the world as my foot. But give him credit. He's honest, he has a quick mind and he never had a chance. It's possible he'll listen to me. I'll try to teach him."

"Edward's so-called mind," I declared rudely, "is occupied solely with local news and noise." I was thinking of the radio. He read through it, ate through it. Did he turn if off when he went to bed? Once, despite Flora's warning look–Edward was reading the paper–I turned it off.

"Jeee-sis Christ! Now, can you tell me just why you did that? What's wrong with you? Don't you like music?"

"You mean those revolting popular songs delivered with static?"

"Hey! Wait a minute! Everyone else likes them. Now, why the hell don't you? Would you mind telling me why? Go ahead. Tell me."

"Edward, I just ..."

"Okay, go ahead, the explanation. I'd like to know."

"I just told you. Sound is distorted on the radio and then the sentimental drooling, the repetition; the continuous blah, blah, blah is extremely unpleas ..."

"Blah! Blah! Blah! Will you listen to who's talkin'? If anyone goes blah, blah, blah around here, it's you. What are you and your family, anyway, a bunch of nuts?"

"Edward, bright?" I said to Pa. "Considering his opinion of you, I

20

shouldn't think anything you might say would carry much weight. Edward thinks you're a nut."

Pa said, "What? You mean to say that nincompoop says I'm not sane?"

"Keep your shirt on, Pa. Not you, exclusively. He's convinced all of us are *non compos mentis*; Well, not all."

"Gad! You mean he actually said that?"

"He got it across," I confessed, "in his own subtle fashion. If you promise not to throw a fit, I'll give you a sample:

"'Look, would you mind giving me a little information? No hard feelings, mind you, I'm curious is all. Can you tell me what makes you fellows tick? Now Geoffrey, there's a guy. I like him all right, and he must have brains or he wouldn't be a doctor, but get him in a card game, b'Jee-sis, and a kid could take him. And that's all he ever wants to do when he gets down here. Play cards. Lose his money.

"'Your old man? Jee-sis Christ! Innocent? He's exhibit A. Some hobo walks in he never saw in his life and gives him a hard luck story, and Pa hands over the till. I don't say Pa's got nothin' on the ball. There's no subject you can mention he don't know all about, its history and all, but when it comes to living in this world, nothing clicks. Your old man is a sucker.'

"What's that funny look on your face, Pa?"

The expression on Pa's face turned from an astonished glare to mirth. "A sucker? Well, well. That little jackass. But so long as he's no sucker, that may be fine for Flora. She won't starve to death."

"Cheer up, Pa, we're not all hopeless; he admires your wife."

"Mother? Now there's a smart woman and don't you forget it. No flies on her."

Pa was pleased. "You see? I told you he was bright. He's got sense enough to admire Liza. Go on, what else?"

"You've heard it all," I said. "The rest would be blah, blah, blah."

Edward ... "As long as Pa's this side of the grave, I'll stick with him."

Was I hearing things?

The four of us were on the train. Geoffrey and Dick had disappeared. Alone at the end of the car, Edward had pulled up the drop-table between the seats and sat, elbows on it, staring into space. I walked down the aisle and sat beside him. "Edward, thank you for not drinking. I must apologize for Geoffrey. I think ... I think Pa's death has knocked him off balance. Maybe ... The Irish hold happy wakes. Look, can you get the whiskey away from him?"

21

Edward said, "Oh, Jee-sis, I don't know. Your brother is a tough nut to crack." Edward's black eyes were full of pain. "You ever try to convince Geoffrey of anything? Jee-sis Christ. I don't hold out much hope, but okay, I'll try. You know Flora thinks he's the top, but Flora wouldn't like this."

"But you, Edward, I know now. You liked Pa."

Edward turned away from me. He stared out of the window at the rushing snow. "They don't come like him around here. I must say, when I first met him, I didn't think he was so hot. He yelled at me, mocked me. Insisted I use my head. I never met anyone like him in my life. He taught me a lot. I loved Pa."

It was dark when we arrived in the city. We'd been on the train all day with nothing to eat. When we got to the hotel, Dick suggested that we have dinner but no one listened.

Geoffrey had made reservations for us. We walked into an ornate, white and gold sitting-room. "What is it?" I asked, surprised, "The bridal suite?"

"I told them I wanted the best," Geoffrey said, "but for what they're charging, I could have bought the joint."

Geoffrey ... still in his overcoat, striding around the room, his congested eyes, his plethoric phrases an indication of the amount of alcohol he had consumed, kept insisting that we "get the hell out. Edward," he demanded, "this place is headquarters for your pals, isn't it? Get hold of someone. They'll know some dames."

"You nuts?" Edward said. "This time of night? Anyway, it's not like the States where no one knows you. I have to live around here. I'm a married man."

"Jus' doan you be nervous, honey," Geoffrey giggled. "No one's gonna tell Flora an' I'll see to it personally that you don't get raped. We're not gonna sit an' mope all night, so go on, call someone."

What drove Geoffrey to such excess? Dispassionately, I considered him. Was he expressing grief in a primitive-savage way; in the face of death, a reassertion of life? The people of France copulating at the bloody foot of the guillotine. Or did he dread going to bed to lie awake, suffering?

"Okay, I'll try." Edward picked up the phone and asked for a number. He put his hand over the mouthpiece and turned to us. "Jee-sis! He's still there! Hi, Pal, don't they ever let you go home? What you doing in the office this time of night? Just a minute, just a minute, someone wants to talk to you. Hang on."

22

"Aren't you lucky," Geoffrey said into the phone. "I'm calling for a gorgeous dame and she wants to see you. Find a couple of girls and come over. We'll have a party. Make it fast. Just a minute, I'll let this one talk to you." He handed me the phone. "Get him over here."

I hesitated. He couldn't be alone: that enormous energy must be dispersed or the slightest incident would trigger him into a brawl. I said in a sugary voice, a silly imitation of French-accented English, "Allo? You are free? Please, you come to see us? We love to 'ave you."

"Hello ..." the man hesitated. "Really? All right. We've finished work. I'll bring my secretary. Her sister's here, too. Where ..."

I handed the phone to Edward.

Shortly afterwards, this man arrived with two girls.

Perhaps I should have foreseen Geoffrey's sottish behaviour, the schoolboy smut, the snickering obscenities. They had barely arrived when Geoffrey pushed or followed the girls through the bedroom into the bathroom.

Giggling, scuffling. Screams!

Was he undressing them?

Edward ran to the bathroom.

Hat in hand, unhappy, the man stood, looking at me. "I'm sorry," he said. "I didn't ... I must go."

The bathroom door was flung open and the four of them, yelling and jostling, erupted into the bedroom and ran for the elevator. The man ran after them.

I went to the bathroom. The white-tiled floor was yellow, flooded with urine.

I could hear Geoffrey shouting in the corridor, "She's willing ... just the wrong time."

And the man, "Go to hell! Bernie's. You'll get it ... Bernie's!"

"Quick," I said. "Stop them, Dick, or we'll be put out of the hotel."

I heard the clatter of the elevator. In *vino veritas*? Here the real Geoffrey? Had Pa given life to this clown? This loutish brute who would dishonour him while he lay in his coffin?

Geoffrey and Edward came running back. "C'mon," Geoffrey said. "Let's go."

"Dick! Get my coat. If Edward starts to drink, they'll end up in the gutter!"

"It's all right, Kitten. I'm coming, too."

There was a cab in front of the hotel. We got in.

23

"Bernie's," Geoffrey ordered.

"Oh, no," the driver said, "not with the lady. Not me."

Geoffrey, belligerent, loud: "I'll tell you where to go. You just drive."

The chauffeur twisted his head, looked at me. "Lady, you want to go with these men?"

"I'm with my husband," I said, "and my two brothers."

"All I can say is I wouldn't take no wife or no sister of mine. Look, lady, I don't advise it."

"You've delivered the news," Geoffrey said, with drunken, weighty sarcasm. "Now we know all about it, so you can get goin'."

The driver kept his eyes on my face. "I'll get going if and when the lady gives the word. You wanta go, Miss? It's up to you."

"Where are we going, Geoffrey?"

"Oh, hell, nowhere. Have a little fun ... a roadhouse. Pay no attention, this guy is crazy."

"All right," I said. "It's all right, driver, go ahead."

"Look, Lady, it's none a my business but that's no place for you."

"Thank you. I want to go."

"Okay I told you. If you wanna go, whadda I care? It's your funeral."

My funeral.

We drove through the city, through the half-seen, half-sensed slum area, out into the snowy countryside. The cab pulled up at a shabby, small house, a lonely house. Except for a light on the first floor, the place was dark.

"Is this joint closed?" Geoffrey asked.

The driver was surly. "Open night and day. Go round back to the kitchen."

The kitchen. Why the kitchen?

"Wait for us."

"No, sir. I ain't spendin' no night in this place. Not me. I got my living to earn."

Geoffrey got out of the cab and reached for his wallet. Comtemptuously, he threw a handful of bills at the driver. "That ought to hold you."

Largess, and Geoffrey drunk.

The driver examined the money, looked up. "Okay, I'll wait," and then, grudgingly, "Sir."

Through the snow, along the path, around the house and back to the kitchen. Geoffrey pushed open the door, and we all went in. The kitchen, irredeemably soiled, dimly lit, half-warmed.

A young man, fat-faced, little blue pig-eyes, was sitting at a rough wooden table playing cards and drinking beer with a sluttish girl. Her heavy breasts sagged under a cheap housedress, a dirty pink sweater. Our host and hostess.

The man turned his fat red neck and his eyes slid over my face. He picked up a kerosene lamp and stood up. "You men come with me."

I started after them.

"Not you."

"Where?"

"You wanta go to a men's bar?" He stood aside while Geoffrey, Edward and Dick walked past, then he slammed the door in my face. I was left standing in the kitchen.

"They'll be half the night, maybe," the woman said. "You like a beer?"

"No, thank you."

"Sit down, if you like."

She whistled. "Holy crow! That's some coat! You buy that here? What kinda fur?"

"Yabbit," I muttered. "Just plain Yabbit."

"What? What did you say? I bet somebody paid somethin' for that."

Pa, I thought, lying in the railway yard, in the freezing freight car, in his coffin. My funeral. Pa ... What kind of roadhouse was this, anyway? "Where have they gone?"

"Whaddaya mean?"

"I mean, where are the men?"

"Huh, cute, aintcha."

A moron? I'd better keep my mouth shut.

"Look. You kiddin'? You new to it? Look, in this business, well, it's nonna my affair, but yer too thin. Where you frum?"

"What?"

"Look, you frum around here?"

"What?"

"How you get mixed up with them sports? I mean, how come they bring you here? With that kinda fur on your back, you can't kid me. You got a place of your own."

A place? The truth began to percolate in my thick head.

The door opened and Dick came in. He put out a hand and took mine. "Don't worry," he said. "Geoffrey and Edward will be along in a minute. They're not staying."

"Dick, where are we? What is this place?"

Dick smiled. "It won't offend this young lady, I guess, if I call a spade a spade. You are ... uh ... you are now standing ... uh ... in one of your Canadian centers of learning and culture."

"What? Where?" But I knew. Pa! Pa, waiting in the freight car, in his freezing coffin, to be cremated, while Geoffrey ... He was dead, of course. He couldn't know. It couldn't hurt him. Pa ...

"Oh, shit." Our hostess' voice was full of venom, of disdain. "What's wrong with that one? He a friggin' nancy-boy? You're in a cathouse."

3

We buried Pa's ashes in Edgeville, high on a hill. There was an eternal–immortal quality about that day; it was the most glorious day: crisp sun on a dazzling world of snow. Death was unreal.

How casually–coldly I had agreed to kill him: that dispiteous acceptance between us when I agreed to take his life. ... It was over. He was gone.

... "*Mordre wol out,*" Chaucer said, "*that we see day by day*" ... still rattling in my head. It was over! He was dead! And not by my hand. Above the weight of numbed agony, my spirit soared. I wanted to throw off my hat, lift my face to the sun, take a deep breath. Free! I am free of murder! Of patricide!

And in that crowd of villagers who walked with Pa to his grave, I saw only old George. And that's because he came and took my hand in his. His rough, bare hand. He had no mittens and my hands, too, were bare. Old George, his lined brown face expressionless, tears streaming down his withered cheeks, looked into my eyes but did not speak. And risking the embarrassment of the community tongue, he kept my hand fast and safe in his and walked down the snowy hill with me.

We took the six o'clock train out of Edgeville on the day following Pa's funeral. Sugar had not escaped from the kennel, but he had indeed changed. No one, now, could make any sort of quick move toward me. Bringing him home from the vet, I stopped for gas and the garage attendant put his hand through the window with my change. Sugar had that wrist between his jaws before I could move. "Your pleasure?" those dog eyes demanded of mine. "Shall I kill him?"

Yes, Sugar had become a one-woman dog. My dog. Glued to my side when we got home, he did not greet Dick, but in an attitude I can only describe as patient insolence, he stood quietly, his eyes on me, and allowed Dick to make a fuss of him.

And taken aback, furious that Sugar had rejected him, Dick blamed me for the dog's dislike of him. "You've turned the dog against me!" he exploded.

Good old Dick, in his usual form. I said, blank voice, blank face, "yes, dear, it's my fault."

That stopped him. For after saying, "Yes, dear. It's my fault" for years, Dick had finally noticed. It had become a joke.

"Oh, well," lamely, "nobody around here pays any attention to me. You spend all your time with him."

We entertained as usual that winter and were entertained. The chit chat, as usual, came easily to me. The bright look of attention, the amused laugh– all mechanical, all without interest. And on the surface, I suppose, there was no significant sign of my inner struggling attempts to orient myself. No one–certainly not Dick–noticed that, really, I wasn't there.

For my mind, except to recall, refused to function. No matter with whom I was talking, no matter my occupation, my head, like an erratic movie screen, carried on a life of its own. At any time, at any place, it reflected a medley of pictures and words: the past.

There he was, again, Geoffrey, the brother I had adored and admired, in that hotel, the bathroom floor flooded with urine. I was back in that kitchen ... "How come you get mixed up with them sports?" I was back in that whorehouse while Death, triumphant, merciless, waited with Pa in his coffin. Death walked with me. Since Pa's funeral, Death, a formless yet precise horror, beset me, dominating my helpless mind. Unable to throw it off, nervously and physically exhausted, I began to think I could not go on without complete solitude and rest. I pleaded with Dick to allow me to be alone at night. But I could give him no logical reason for this request. For how explain to Dick that if I were to be well again I must have time to exorcise Death?

And so, despite my desperate, reiterated plea for help, for solitude, Dick refused me a single night alone, a single night without sex. "Just one of your foolish notions. I won't have you sleeping in another room. Separate rooms! That's the start of the breaking up of a marriage. I guess I know what's best for my Yabbit. You're going to stay right here with me."

And what fantasy, I wondered in despair, did he build in his mind about love? How could he believe that the smile he demanded, the empty look that he forced from me, indicated my full and loving attention? "Ours," he informed me, "is an ideal marriage, because we can talk to each other."

"Yes, dear."

But as week followed week, I could no longer force myself to be civil to him. I could no longer sit through a meal with him. I would swallow a few spoonfuls of soup, wait for the entrée to be served and leave the table.

28

"Come back here! Sit down at your place. Look at me! Look at me when I speak to you!"

Resist? Try again to make him understand? To oppose him would do nothing but initiate another blasting harangue. "Don't tell me what you think. I know what's good for you."

It was easier to dissemble. Easier, in pretended interest, to keep my blank eyes on his face. But because of his total disregard of my wishes, everything about him was becoming more and more repugnant. I was beginning to hate him.

Sugar. As the days went by it became more and more obvious that Sugar expressed my hidden antipathy. Forbidding, on guard, he never took his eyes off Dick's face. He was ready, ready ... I knew that with a nod from me Sugar would attack Dick.

And in that year of Hitler's growing aggression, Germany imbruted; the Nazi slaughter was an ever-present background to my personal unhappiness. The world crime was my crime. I ... We ... The world weak or unwilling: complice to human butchery.

For I might have done something. Dick's name would have launched me, and solidly, into politics. I had joined that body of women seeking political education: the League of Women Voters. But my enthusiasm was not whetted by facts but blunted by them: the world was too heavy. The idea that I might prevail against the mass mentality was unreal. Thinking of the enormity of that task exhausted me.

Reform the world? Far from knowing how to make others happy, I wasn't happy myself. I must come to terms with myself. My moments of peace were rare, I no longer read poetry, and peace came only when I could lose myself in colour. Since I had encountered the masters in The Hermitage, I had wanted to paint. I had endless material: a lifetime of hidden emotion to be expressed on canvas.

The undistinguished days rolled over my head. I had three hunters to keep in condition that winter and weather permitting, with friends, I was almost constantly in the saddle, Sugar with us, running with the horses. But with spring, cubbing first and then hunting, we started riding to hounds and Sugar had to stay home. He was dangerous. I considered locking him up. Then I decided, away from me he would have no cause to harm anyone.

But with all the exercise, I could not sleep or rest. I was driven by a pointless urgency. Even in the saddle I could not escape the pressure of my locked-in emotions and I could not be rid of that punishing spirit: Death.

Death rode with me, a following horror, accelerating when I galloped to escape, mocking–courteous, acceding to my wish to slow down when I walked my horse. Death attended me, waiting for night, for that unprotected time between waking and sleep, that fearful moment when I must let go. Then, shackled to Death, I would wander, lost, in a dread, unknown space.

And so for some six months after Pa's funeral, living the lucky life: "You have everything!" Dick reminded me. "Husband, friends, horses. What a lucky woman." Bright, cheerful, tearless, I lived banished from love, in a fraudulent and arid imitation of life.

"Tasha Volkhov phoned while you were out," Dick said. "She wants you to call back. Your boyfriend, Clay, is getting married in a few days."

"How nice," I said, indifferently. "Sorry I'm late. I must get out of these clothes. Could you ... I'd like a drink." I went to the bathroom, trembling. No more, I begged the wall. No more, I can't take any more. My separate pains blurred together, overpowering me. I felt faint. I slid to the floor, reached up and bolted the door.

"Come get your drink." Dick's footsteps in the hall ... "Kitten?" He turned the doorknob, banged on the door. "Good God! Honestly, you crazy loon, there's only me in the house. One would think you were afraid of me. Hurry up, or I'll drink your martini."

The following day Tasha telephoned me. "Clay got married today. I'm not sure how long it will last. That girl's not in love with him and, well ... I rather expected you'd call me back the other evening."

"Yes," I said. "I thought about it but with Dick hanging around my neck, I couldn't talk. Why do you say she doesn't love him?"

"She's in love with his brother."

"What! Oh, Tasha, please."

"It's obvious. And he's still in love with you. He came here late last night in a fever. He had too much to drink and ... are you alone?"

"Yes."

Tasha laughed. "We had to prevent him, by force, from phoning you. We took the telephone away from him."

Why? Why? Didn't Tasha understand my dreadful need to hear his voice!

"Philippa, are you there?"

"Yes."

"When are you coming to see us? We miss you."

"Very soon," I said. "Tomorrow, perhaps. Tasha, I hear Dick's car in the drive. Forgive me, I must fly." I replaced the receiver hastily, ran to the bathroom, and locked the door. Sugar whined and scratched at the door. I let him in and locked it again.

Dick couldn't walk in the house without yelling for me. That constant demand for my presence.

"Kitten? Kitten? Where are you?"

"I ... Sugar!" Sugar was growling, scratching to get out. He'd attack Dick. I pulled him back, made him sit, but I couldn't stop his growling.

"Kitten?" He was outside the door. "What's wrong with that dog!" He twisted the knob. "Look, I know you're there. What's the big idea of locking yourself in the bathroom? Yesterday and again today! Let me in!"

I couldn't, wouldn't let him touch me. "Can't I go to the bathroom alone?"

"Open the door. Look, can't you control that animal? He's pathological! He must know who I am. Will you unlock that door or do I have to break it down?"

"Dick, please ... I have to talk to you."

"Through the door? I'm trying to be patient, but you make it ... "

"Patient!" I shouted. "Is it too much to ask for five minutes alone? Go away! I want to go to my room. I need rest. I want to be alone. I haven't slept in ages."

"Oh, Cat, I'm sorry, I really am. I know you miss your father. But it's not good for you to keep thinking of him. That's why ... "

"Oh, God!"

"Kitten, answer me. Let me in."

"Dick, why don't you believe me? I need to be alone. I need rest."

"Look ... Well, all right. I don't approve, but you can take a sleeping pill tonight. Now will you please unlock this door?"

Sleeping pill! How many had I taken? They were useless. Useless and ... Why attempt to withstand that crushing ego: Dick's single-minded determination to have his own way? He would go roaring around the house. And the only way to end it ... let him paw me. Throw me into bed.

If only I could get drunk. But since Pa died ... Since Geoffrey ... alcohol made me sick. But perhaps it was better to be drunk and sick than ... If I got drunk enough or sick enough perhaps I could let him near me. It was useless trying to get him drunk. He must have an incredible tolerance for alcohol; he never got so drunk he forgot sex.

"Kitten! Please! Are you all right?"

All right! "Dick, Sugar thinks you're attacking me. If I open the door he'll remove your arm or leg. Look, I've been thinking. You're right.

What I need is to get my mind off everything. Let's make a night of it. Go make some brandy and champagne cocktails and I'll comb my hair. I'll be right out."

"Oh, Cat, you're coming to your senses. Good. I'll tell Ernest to bring the Beluga caviar and to leave dinner ready. What about it? Do we need them? Shall I tell him and Jessie to take the night off?"

"Yes. Fine. Do that."

"My silly coot! You're almost pretty tonight. You're an angel. Yum, yum. I want to eat It."

I pushed him away. "You're drooling drunk," I said. "Stop! Stick to the business at hand. Open another bottle. Pour me another one."

I don't remember going to bed.

What woke me in the middle of the night, in rigid, sweating terror, was the screaming. The screams came out of the hostile night. Harsh, wild, someone was screaming, "Pa! Pa!" Screaming, "Pa!" Screaming ...

"Stop!"

"Oh, darling, stop. Kitten, don't push me away! Kitten, you're with me; you're safe. Oh, what can I do? Ask me, I'll give you anything, anything, only please, please stop screaming."

Screaming? Me? I stopped at once.

Dick said, "You're out of your mind. Absolutely crazy. I know I said I'd give you what you want, but we settled this before. I'm not going to give you a divorce; that won't solve any problems, and that's final. All right, you've got your own way; you've got your own room and I haven't touched you in two days. It's up to you when you come back to your own bed. I'm there, waiting.

"Look, you were awfully drunk the other night. That fit of hysterics. I've been thinking you'd better go and get yourself straightened out.

"I hate to say this, Kitten, but these past few weeks, you've not been yourself. If you insist on this divorce, I think you ought to see a psychiatrist."

I said, dully, "I'd go like a shot if I thought there was anything he could tell me that I don't know. But I know what I need. I need a rest. That's why we have to get divorced."

"Look, you've got your own room. What more do you want?"

I turned my head away. I couldn't look at him. The exhausting, ineffectual efforts to force him to stop brow-beating me. "Dick, what's the use of talking when you won't listen? You're hopeless. I get in that room and two minutes later you bang on the door. For years I've pleaded with you to stop nagging, and now I'm too tired. I can't go on."

"Oh, Cat, now honestly, can't you try to be reasonable? I know I nag. I admit it. But how can I help it if that's the way I'm made?"

I said, sharply, "You can't help it? Of course! You've never been weaned! You're the one who ought to see a doctor. Very well, to please you, I'll see a psychiatrist, but on one condition–you go, too."

He gaped. "How can you possibly sit there with a straight face and tell me I ought to go to a psychiatrist? I'm not the one who wants a divorce! I'm not crazy!"

I refused to talk to him. I refused him his marital rights. I locked myself away. Dick went raging round the house furious, sulking. He was drinking heavily.

Our house was a considerable distance off the highway and surrounded by a wood. When the servants went off, no one could hear, and then he shouted at me. I kept my hand on Sugar. Hackles bristling, he growled whenever Dick approached me. But when I didn't give in after a week, Dick phoned a psychiatrist and made separate appointments, the first for me and the second for himself.

"Why have you come to me?"

"My husband thinks I'm crazy because I want a divorce."

"Why do you want a divorce?"

Doctors don't tell. I was safe. Words poured from me like water from a burst dam. I hurled them at him: "I'm tired. Nerves on edge ... Every word exasperates, grates ... My fault perhaps, I love another man, but different ... I do love Dick, or did, but no more. He's cruel! Drives me to a frenzy!"

"Deceive me? Oh, never. He's honest, but possessive. He's impossible: hates me and loves me in one breath, won't let me out of his sight. Tells me what's in my mind! I can't persuade him he's dreaming it up. Drives me mad."

"Sex? He keeps a book. Doesn't want to spoil his record. A day off ... I didn't go to bed when my father died. Other than that, sex every night. Says I'm frigid, undersexed. Am I? ... But he ... baby-talk. At a nursery level. I can't respond."

"And the wrangling! Terrible, I hate it and I can't control my rage. I started jumping horses, bad ones. I decided to break my neck. Rows! Appalling and a waste. I couldn't make him ... He can't change."

He raised a hand to stop me. "Don't you object?"

33

"Object! Me? Object! Do cats or coots or kittens object? It's like colliding with an omnific ... "

"What?"

"An omnific mule!"

The doctor began to laugh. I had to laugh, too.

"Oh, my," he said. "An omnific mule. I never met one. Omnific? I'm not sure what it means. Now where did you pick up a word like that?"

"Oh," I said, "perhaps ... Pa." I turned my back on him and put both hands over my twisting face to hide my gasping breath. "I can't take anymore. I refuse, I'm tired."

"Tired?" the doctor said. "You've expended more energy roaring around this office in the past half-hour than I use in a week. Shall I make another appointment for you? Do you want to see me again?"

"Should I?"

"Perhaps. Yes. Come back tomorrow."

But the next day when I went to his office he wouldn't talk to me.

"Where did you get that hat?" he asked. "Yes, it suits you. Um, yes, well, I've thought about it. There's nothing wrong with your mind. Go home."

Dick had an evening appointment. He came home late, his face was expressionless, white. He was ominously still.

I hesitated. "What did the doctor say?"

"He said you can do as you please."

"What?"

Dick began to shake. "He said for me to let you do whatever you want to do. 'If you want your wife,' he said, 'don't touch her with a ten-foot pole.' What are you going to do?"

"Oh, God," I said. "What a relief! Forgive me, I'm going to divorce you."

"Can't we talk about it—some alternative?"

I shook my head. "Not now. Later."

I leaned up and kissed his cheek. He didn't put his arms around me. He stood like a stick.

I said, "Good night. I'm going to bed."

Sugar at my heels, I went to my room, hesitated, turned the key in the lock, fell on the bed. Sugar jumped up and pressed tight against me. Dick ... I could feel him—his rage—through the door. He'd sit half the night drinking, waiting for me to relent.

Tense, I got into bed, expecting his knock. I was frightened of him!

Nonsense, he wouldn't come in–not tonight. I put him out of my mind. I must sleep. I was drowsy. Sleep.

Sugar on my bed, his weight pressed hard against my legs, reassuring. I turned off the light, shut my eyes and settled myself for sleep.

Half asleep, it came again. Death ... and that weird sensation. I can leave my body. A part of me dissolves, is being pulled from me by the cold enveloping horror ... I am jolted awake.

I sit up in bed. Dick! Where is he! Outside my door? ... silence ... I turn on the light, hold my breath ... silence.

Sugar yawns, stretches, and I breath again in relief. Dick is nowhere near. Anyway, what nonsense, afraid of Dick! I must try to sleep. I turn out the light, lie down and shut my eyes. The room ... the windows are tight shut, and yet I feel that strange cold draught in the empty room. Cold ... On the edge of sleep ... Death ...

4

T he dog kept whining and licking my face and I couldn't brush off his dead weight. Flora was wrapping her money in Vera's skirt. If I could sprinkle water on the money it would rot and Flora would be free. I couldn't move my right arm so I took the watering can in my left hand and ran after her. "Flora," I called.

She turned, saw me and screamed, horribly.

I ran and ran after her; and Geoffrey was running from me in terror. He raced into the great, gray stone house and up to the balcony over my head.

I stood on the soft brown earth and lifted the kitchen chair and the legs grew and grew until, eclipsing the distance, they imprisoned Geoffrey between them and the graystone wall behind him.

He was forced to face me and he shook with fear.

At last his trembling admitted his forever denied guilt. I was ripe with contempt for him. And joy. I knew a satisfaction more complete than I have ever known and I turned away, happy.

Sue was standing behind me, her accusing eyes full of tears. "You hurt their feelings."

"Sue!" I screamed, "Sue! I ..." And then the space came into my head, the space you hear on a telephone when the receiver is off the hook and there is no one on the other end of the line. And then a confusion of velvet thick and smothering nothingness and I, struggling, screaming without a voice, "Sue, I ... "

The dog kept scratching and licking my face and, half awake, I pushed him off my arm, slid my bare feet to the floor and then, without dispelling that clinging aura of despair, I remembered I could never convince Sue of Geoffrey and Flora's hostility.

I stumbled down the narrow back stairs to the kitchen, reached for my coat, slipped my feet into the heavy rubber boots and threw Martha's scarf over my head. I snapped the leash on my dog and unbolted the door.

It was day time. Gray. Freezing. I gasped with cold. Fish raced down the back steps and I ran with him. Fish. What a name! I call all my dogs Fish. They speed from the cod liver oil on their food to lick me and when I say, "Fish!" they love it and the name sticks. This one's an accident: I found him.

He's a calico absurdity, patches of chestnut on white and except for a feathered tail, he's short-haired. A stunted whippet. And so insecure because of his precarious past that when I call he wriggles, staggers in circles, bumps into me and flops on my feet.

The factory whistles are blowing. Is it morning? Noon? Five o'clock? I don't know. There's been no sun for days and I've lost track.

Up on the sidewalk high above my sloping backyard, my neighbour, the plumber, passing, stares down at me. I am abruptly conscious of my bare feet in the heavy lumberman's rubbers, the inches of nightdress showing beneath my coat, conscious of my uncombed hair under the faded scarf and of my bare and freezing hands.

The wind rattles the bare branches of the old trees, it whips the tears to my eyes. The dog jerks at the leash and I follow, slipping in the icy snow. He runs, hunkering against the bitter gusts. I pull him to the shelter of the cellar wall. Absorbed, snorting, sniffing, he digs at the frozen trash. I wait. Shivering.

Months ago, when I left Edgeville, when I first came here–before the snow–I meant to clean up this yard, to cart away the charred remains of garbage, the tin cans, the rotten, fallen branches. But I have not had time. Well, not that. There was plenty of time but … If I had not had the dog, and we both have to eat, I would not have stepped outside the door.

I have never lived in a factory town before. This is new. The house I have taken here is just another sagging frame house in a slum neighbourhood, built in that period before gingerbread when the fireplace gave way to the more efficient iron stove. But it has been modernized. The wood-burning stoves in the kitchen and living room–there's no heat upstairs–have been replaced by gas and there's a bathroom of sorts, but the old privy still stands back of the house in a tangle of menacing brambles. Rotting fences on three sides, old lilac bushes, more brambles and the ubiquitous self-sown apple trees isolate this property from its neighbours. When the house was new this must have been a fine shady street. The big elms and maples are still here, but when spring comes their slender green will not conceal the waiting death.

Still, for the moment, it suits me to be here, despite a few weird telephone calls which forced on me the realization that the impulse to criminal mischief, the seemingly common lust inherent in the weak to bully the helpless, might easily be gratified. The front door is flush with the sidewalk and it has no lock. Anyone could smash one of the small panes of glass and draw the bolt. It's not that I fear death, but how awful to die at the hands of some lout for the sake of a few jewels.

But I imagine things. Who, in this place, would guess I have jewelry? Whoever might force his way in would expect only a few dollars and the release, through the enjoyment of another's pain or fear, of a primitive emotional tension.

In any case, I have hidden my trinkets. My mother's engagement ring, my beloved pearls, my diamond clasps, the emerald ring and watch, and the heavy diamond neck-piece Dick's mother gave me are thrown together in a paper bag and stuffed behind the store of canned food I laid in when I first arrived. And Fish would warn me. He has taken possession. When there are loiterers near, he barks.

I am aware, suddenly, that I am up to my knees in a snow bank and that my feet and legs are bruised and aching. Lately I find myself losing myself. I come to, as it were, to find myself sitting or standing rigidly, lost in some futile speculation. I've been in a trance these past months, living in a dream, existing without purpose. It is almost as though in running from life I have banished it: committed myself to a timeless present that precludes a future. And for some unaccountable reason, I'm always drowsy. Unaccountable because I have been an insomniac all my life and, despite my desperate searching, in all my rapid and disturbed years (except in the lunatic asylum when they gave me chloral hydrate) I could find no drug to counteract it.

I must get warm! Did I ever thank Martha for the rubber boots? I thought she was mad when she threw them into my car when I left for New York.

"Fish! Come!"

I slammed the kitchen door behind me, pulled off my boots and lit the gas. Then I remembered there was no coffee. I would have to go to the store. Was it morning or evening? The winter light was dull and heavy. Someone left a clock in this place. I found it in a pile of rubbish when I first came. The empty house is a sounding board and I hear it ticking upstairs and down. But it doesn't tell me if it's day or night.

I pulled Fish to my lap and wiped his cold wet feet. Then I shut him in the kitchen and, barefoot, ran up the back stairs. It was brutally cold and dark in my room and when I snapped up the old green blind, I saw the crazy disorder: the unmade bed, blankets thrown on the floor, the dog's basket, his scattered toys, books and clothes strewn all over the place. Disgusting! In a fury of impatience with myself, I reached blindly under the bed, found a pair of shoes, shoved my feet into them and stood up. Damn! High heels. And no stockings. But it was getting late. Never mind …

I found my lipstick in a tangle of soiled handkerchiefs and stockings on the bureau and slapped it on by guess, my hands and face numb. There's no looking-glass in this house and I've mislaid my compact. I pulled my sack dress off the hook in the musty, lime-damp closet. I've lived in that thing since I've been here. I bought it in Rome and lucky I did. It covers me in a hurry. It's a simple black wool, expensive and elegant. I do know how to dress.

I ran downstairs, threw on my coat and checked my purse: car keys, license, money. It was getting darker. Evening. I would have to hurry.

"Behave yourself, Fish!" I hugged him, gave him a push and shut the door in his protesting face. I ran to my car. The wind was bitterly cold. I must get a hat. I'd forgotten my gloves. One of these days I must take a driver's test, get a local license. I'm still using my African license. "It's good for a year," the man at the motor vehicle bureau said, but when? How long ago? I got in my car and sat there breathless, shivering with cold and tension. If I didn't need coffee and dog food, I'd have gone back. I turned on the ignition.

The supermarket was open but about to close. I grabbed a cart and hurried from aisle to aisle. I was picking up horse meat for Fish, hesitating over the frozen food bin, when I felt someone behind me. I held my breath. Eyes boring into my back! All I need, I thought, is to begin imagining things. Still ... I could feel the eyes, insistent and oppressive and I stood like an animal frozen in fear. I turned swiftly.

There was a shabby old woman waiting for me to move. I breathed again. Why do I get so upset? People always stare at me. I hold myself well and ... But watch it, I cautioned myself, this is no place to fall into another stupid reverie.

I went through the checkout in a hurry, paid my bill, found my car and threw the groceries on the front seat. There was so much traffic it would be easier to walk across the road for Fish's cod liver oil. I bent my head into the wind.

The warmth in the drugstore brought the tears to my eyes and I stood near the door sniffing and cursing myself for an idiot because I didn't have a handkerchief. I wiped my nose and eyes with the back of my hand. There was an old man ahead of me and the clerk was leaning over the counter shouting, "This is the one you want."

"How's that?" He was deaf. He looked poor and furtive. This is a sad neighbourhood.

Someone opened the door, touched my arm and spoke. "Hi." The dismal old woman from the supermarket had followed me!

My heart thumped and pounded in my throat. My knees shook. I was standing on two wavering columns of ice water.

"It's awfully nice to see you again, after the bus," she said mildly.

She was wearing a cheap rusty-black coat and had a soiled black hat tilted foolishly on her scraggly yellow hair. The centre of one brown eye was opaque. She was half blind. She'd mistaken me for someone else. "S'sorry," I stammered, "I'I wasn't on a bus." How stupid to panic.

"Why yes you was, Dearie. You was too on the bus. I recognized you right away. That lovely black hair and that funny coat!"

The funny coat? Sue brought me this coat from Paris. It's a Balenciago and it must be unique in this factory town, but to the local eye, I suppose it looks like a bag. Anyway, I haven't been on a bus in years.

"I wasn't on that bus," I said, flatly, and turned away from her.

She took my arm, leaned on me and nudged my ribs, hard, with her elbow. She spoke close to my ear. Her confiding voice had the saccharine and lugubrious overtones of the beggar and yet, implicit in it, the assumption of an understanding between us.

"I hope you don't mind bein' mistook for someone else, Dearie," she said, "I sure know what that's like. Dreadful. But you and me, we met before."

I jerked out of her reach and stepped behind the old man, but she pushed between us with her back to him and leered up at me. Hogarth! I thought. But the faces he drew from the half-world were transcended by his essential innocence. Her's was an obscenity. Her stale breath stank of alcohol and her sallow skin was coated with dirty white powder.

"I bet you a dollar it was you," she said, "but a person can make a mistake, of course. There's a woman around here everyone takes for me. Dreadful! You know why?" She winked and her voice dropped to a hoarse whisper. "She runs a house."

Good God! What a rotten old ... My eyes flew to the clerk but there was no expression on his face. Perhaps he hadn't heard. Was she talking about herself? Oh, for God's sake! No. She was just a dreary old wretch.

The clerk handed the old man his change and looked at me. "You next?"

"Yes," I said. I pushed past her to stand at the counter.

"What can I do for you?"

"Uh, I'd like ... " What did I want? She ran a house! The old whore! "Yes?"

"I'I ... I think, uh ... " What did she want? What in hell had I come for? My mind was a blank.

The old woman leaned on the counter and stared at me. "You was goin' to get kleenex, Dearie," she said, lovingly. "It was you on the bus, wasn't it?"

"K'kleenex," I stuttered.

"Anything else?"

The old drab put her hand on my arm and rubbed it back and forth, caressingly.

I was speechless with shock. I took a bill from my purse, threw it on the counter, grabbed the kleenex and ran.

"Your change!"

I turned. The clerk was staring at me. Was there pity in his eyes? What for? For me? Was I going mad again? I slammed through the door out on to the sidewalk. Strings of coloured lights were flashing up and down the street. Blinded, I stopped. Which way was the supermarket? Where was my car?

"Well, Dearie, you told a little lie, didn't you?"

The old woman! The leech! The old man of the sea! "Go away!" I shouted, "I'm in a hurry." I started away from her at a good clip but she grabbed my sleeve and held on.

"Not you, Dearie," she said, "You're not in no hurry. Excuse me for sayin' so, but you got no place to go."

The colossal nerve. The brazen ... The whole thing was absurd. But why create a scene? I forced myself to stand still. I forced a quiet and reasonable voice. "Look, don't be a nuisance. I never saw you before in my life. Now, please stop. Look, I'm mixed up. Which way is the supermarket?"

"The supermarket? Which way! You sure are mixed up. Or a couple too many. Not that I mind if a girl takes a drink." She turned and pointed. "You left your car over there."

My car was under a light. I was looking at it. "Oh, you *are* kind. Thanks." I tried to free my arm but she held on and, irrationally again, I began to panic. "Please let me go!"

"Nuts!" she said. "Take it easy. I'm comin' too."

"What!" I jerked free of her and turned to run and a woman bumped into me and dropped a whole load of packages at my feet. She was pregnant and so heavy she could hardly bend. I stooped to pick them up for her but I couldn't hold on to them. They kept slipping out of my hand and she thought it was funny! I dropped my kleenex and got the packages back in

41

her arms and finally, she went off, laughing. I stood there panting.

"You know what I'd like, Dearie? A nice glass of gin."

My voice went completely out of control. It was loud and shrill. "Well, go and get one!" To hell with the traffic! I was running, dodging the cars, running across the road. Brakes squealed, a man shouted, cursing me. I tripped on the opposite curb, ripped the heel off my shoe and went sprawling on the sidewalk. My purse flew in one direction, the kleenex in another. I crawled along in the snow on hands and knees and grabbed my purse. I got up, lurched, and fell again. Then I got up carefully and ran on tiptoe. I snatched the car door open, shoved the groceries off the driver's seat, and started fumbling through my purse for my keys.

The old woman panted up beside me. "Say! Listen, what's the rush? You see? You fell. You should wait for the light, like me. Don't be crazy, Dearie. You think you can fool me? You're in trouble. I'm right, hanh? What? I bet you got to spend this Christmas season all by yourself. Now that ain't necessary. I got this house and a couple of rooms and you can trust me, an' ... "

Christmas? Was it Christmas again? Christmas! All of a sudden all of it, everything I've been through these past months, these past years caught up with me. If I hadn't managed to half fall, half crawl into my car, I'd have been sobbing and howling on the street. Where was my key? I put my hand on the ignition. The key was there. "Go away!" I shouted through my tears. "If you don't leave at once, I'll call the police." I turned on the motor but I forgot to release the brake and the engine stalled.

"The police! You dirty tramp. You wouldn't dare." The scurrilous voice was raw with contempt. "I never said a word. It was you, come after me! Who do you think you are, hanh? What are you crying for?"

She was hanging onto the open door and it took all my strength to pull it shut. "Get out of my way!" I shouted. The motor was running again and I released the brake. I slammed my car out into the road. What am I crying for? By good luck, I didn't hit anyone. The answer was shrieking, beating in my head. My mother! My mother! I'm crying for my mother! I saw the red light but I went straight through it, right beside the traffic cop. He yelled at me and, automatically, I jerked to a stop. But there was a stream of traffic between us and he made a gesture of anger and waved me on.

Then I got lost. I went up one street and down another. This place is a rabbit warren. I couldn't find my own street or any landmark I recognized and with all the traffic, I didn't dare turn or stop. By the time I was calm enough to drive rationally, I was on the edge of town. I pulled over to the side of the road.

That gruesome old woman! She took me for a tramp! That predacious predatory ...

What did I look like? A whore? Me? Impossible! But I had been living in such a state of apathy, sluggishness. Are my clothes wrinkled? Perhaps. Soiled? I hadn't sent anything to the cleaner's for months!

But why try to evade the obvious? If she could approach me like that, there was something terribly wrong. God! I was wrecked. I longed for my bed. How could anyone mistake me for a ... I must *look* like them! The sisterhood of the streets! And all that stupid panic! I turned on the engine. I would have to ... I would have to stop somewhere and look at myself.

There was a drugstore in the shopping center with a long looking-glass on the side window. I pulled up near it and parked. I got out of my car carefully, jolting along on one heel.

I think my heart stopped completely when I saw myself. I mean when I recognized myself because, for a second or two, I didn't know it was me. My reflection wavered and shook. The wind had blown my hair into a crazy black haystack. My lipstick was crooked, smeared on my lips like a clown's. My face was dirty, streaked with dirt and tears. When had I washed it last? There was a button missing on my coat, the threads were hanging down, and I had buttoned it askew; my collar was up one side and down on the other. The hem was ripped out of one side of my coat and my bare legs were blue with cold and splashed with dirt. There was blood on one of them. And to finish it I was wearing, scuffed and soiled and dotted with rhinestones–I had bought them for a masquerade and had been wearing them around the house–red satin evening slippers with spike heels, or rather one spike heel. I looked as though I had been on a six-month drunk. I looked as though I had just crawled out of a gutter.

In those few seconds while I stood and stared, I was beyond shock. I went past it and came out on the other side. It was as if I had been struck by lightning and burned clean in a flash–down to the bone–and survived. For the first time since I'd left Edgeville, I was starkly sane. My eyes were clear and steady and so was my head. I got back in my car and started for home.

I was sober, sober, sober.

5

T he wicked flee when no man pursueth ... " So sayeth the book. Yet how often it's the other way, the innocent fleeing in dread; fleeing the obtuse, fleeing the brutal insensitivity of the mass.

I am innocent and I run.

My whole instinct last night was to go to earth: hide. And from whom? A vicious old whore!

But I should be grateful. Because of that obscene encounter, I am no longer sleep-walking. My eyes are open, my mind is alert and lucid. I know, and with a basic logic absent these past months, that I must take stock of myself and my situation.

I reached my own backyard last night, floundering through the snow on one high heel–clutching that enormous bag of groceries–and I don't know who was more eager to see the other, the dog or I. The house was dark. When I shoved open the door, Fish's delirious welcome caught me off balance. My ankle turned, the groceries crashed and I crashed on top of them, flat on my face.

I must have suffered a complete collapse for I couldn't fend off his furious attack. I covered my head with both hands and sprawled across the door sill. I lay there gasping and laughing with my tears dripping on the floor.

I got my breath at last, held him away, got up and pulled off those ridiculous evening slippers. I found the light, shot the bolt on the door, and gave him a biscuit.

And then, deliberately, I went to take a look at the house. My eyes were open all right and I began to wish they were shut. There was no single cluttered room that did not reflect a sick mind: my mind. For the second time in my life I was facing disaster.

I wanted to weep, to shriek, like Balaam's Ass, and with the Ass's question in it, I wanted to open my mouth and bray: "What have I done unto Thee that Thou hast smitten me?" For I knew it could happen again.

"The Bible says," my father used to say, "*Laborare est orare*: to labour is to pray." An atheist, it was his chronic joke to send me to the Bible for an answer to a problem. Last night I prayed. I lit gas under the ancient

44

water boiler, heated pails of water and scrubbed the whole night through.

At noon today, I drove into town and dropped a load of clothes at the cleaner's. I bought a full-length looking-glass and a couple of thick, lined exercise books. Then I came back and telephoned Sue. I told her I was working and I promised to be with her either before or shortly after Christmas.

I know I must come to terms with my past: evaluate it calmly and then refuse it significance in my present life. To keep my sanity, I must never again be thrown into the kind of depression I have just experienced.

I have pulled the heavy kitchen table close to the stove and set up a place to write. And without quibbling or equivocation, I must write down everything relevant that has brought me here. I must think!

But I can't think! I don't want to think! To think is to face confusion, and confusion has its dangers; I dare not risk my grasp on sanity. The landmarks in that treacherous swamp–the muddled wastes that lie between normality and abnormality–are familiar to me. They have no fixed place, they shift with a glance and their directions tell no truth. Once lost in that nebulous space, there is no sure way home. Why travel a path that may end behind barred windows and locked doors? Yet how avoid it? Unless I am content to rot here, I must think.

... It's a mistake to brood on the past. Here I sit, huddled over the table, lost in that rat-cage I call my mind. And I'm shaking. I can't do it.

My mother used to say the story of her life would make a book. My own life, not haphazardly but logically, step by step, added up to insanity. It, too, would make a book. My own case history.

Yet even if I wrote it, who would accept "truth" from a maniac? For the stigma, no matter how long you've been out, sticks. And could I do it? Hold us up in shame for the world to see? For I would name my family as complicit. Yes, I must hold others, as well as myself, as accessories before and after the fact of my madness.

God! The accepted "truth" about the mad! They can't face reality; the first ones they turn against are their nearest and dearest; there must have been something wrong with them from the beginning: a flaw.

A flaw? Throw a pearl into a handful of pebbles and bang them around for a few years. The pebbles will survive–unflawed. The pearl may be completely destroyed–unreconstructable. I believe the sane and the insane differ only in their degree of sensitivity to shock: put on enough pressure and we'll understand each other.

Do the mad ever write their own case histories? I've never read one. There must be many who are literate and capable of it. There is so much mumbo-jumbo that might be dissipated. Insanity on the films is a stereotype and the fiction is just as bad. The mad always suffer amnesia. That's absurd. One may live in two worlds simultaneously and remember everything in both, as I well know, from my own experience.

In England, when I landed in the admitting room of that ancient charity hospital, when I saw the heavy iron keys, the barred windows, the grim, defaced walls, I knew at once and in lucid and hideous clarity where I was and why I was there: people who talk to the dead are crazy. I was crazy!

Ah, but why think of it now? All that happened years ago. I got better. I got out. And I found out how to take care of myself. I've been constantly aware and constantly prudent. So, where did this start? ... My mother! Her legacy to me!

I shoved the table aside and stood up. I snapped the leash on Fish, yanked the door open and started to run.

Perhaps I needed the shock of the icy air for something happened: I stopped, suddenly calm. Standing there, stock-still, up to my knees in snow, I was somehow unburdened: relieved of ignominy; freed of guilt ....

Perhaps during my mindless months in this place, I have paid my dues. For the first time since her death–since Sue handed me her jewelry– I thought of my mother without hurt.

I can breathe again!

I'm freezing! "Fish! Back to the house!"

I'm sitting in front of my first exercise book and I can't move my foot. Fish is sleeping on it. And my mind is a blank. I cannot write into space. To whom shall I write?

To Mother.

I cannot stop the tears.

How begin? Pledge myself to write the truth–but with love. No matter how emotionally sterile I feel, I still believe in love–that living force that has lain covered and denied in my heart–and in its counterpart, justice, for beneath the gimcrack superstructure we build up in our breasts, there lies captive in each of us the inarticulate and deprived heart that needs to be fulfilled through love.

My mother's death had brought me from Africa to Edgeville, that small village where I grew up for, strangely, she had made me, her least-loved child, her principal heir. Not only had she left me the Edgeville property but without even a keepsake for Sue or Flora, she had left me every scrap of her jewelry including her precious diamond and ruby engagement ring. She had kept that magnificent ring through all the hard times and I knew how much it meant to her.

After a lifetime of anger and indifference toward me, why had she changed? Was it because I had shown her how little her beloved son, Geoffrey, cared for her? It was that. For with her bequest to me I realized, in horror, that what I had told her about Geoffrey had caused her to disinherit him.

I had just been released from the asylum and had been staying in New York with Sue when Geoffrey dropped in. He had come to the city to see his lawyer and to make his will. We were finishing lunch.

I said, idly, "I hope you have a good, big insurance policy for Mother. What have you left her?"

"Why, nothing," he said. "In the normal course of events she'll die first."

I was stunned and then in a rage! Mother's fair-haired boy! Geoffrey flies his own plane; he drinks, and not infrequently, at the same time. Less than a year ago–a surgeon–he had almost lost his right arm; had narrowly escaped death in a motor accident. The incident, no doubt, that had driven him to make his will. I turned to look at Sue. She was frowning, staring into her cup. I started to speak, then stopped. No matter what I said, Geoffrey wouldn't change.

A few days later, home in Edgeville, I was having a leisurely chat with my mother.

"How is Geoffrey," she asked, "and Sue?"

"They're both well."

Then she repeated something that has annoyed me for years, something she's been saying all her life. "I have such wonderful children. You're the best children in the world."

I was in a rage again. "No," I said, coldly. "We're not wonderful. We're bastards. But not Sue."

Red suffused her face. She stared at me. She looked shamed, as though caught in a lie. Then her eyes filled with tears and to my astonishment, she breathed, "Yes."

"As for Geoffrey," I said, still enraged, "He's just made his will and left you out of it."

Harsh! How smooth that over? I couldn't, I didn't care. I felt sick.

She turned her head away. Then she said, "I guess I'm not surprised," and reached for my hand.

That was a strange experience. There has been tension and friction between us since the day I was born. I could never bear for her to touch me.

But from that moment, incredibly, and for the first time, we were at peace. During the two weeks I stayed with her, I was closer to my mother and she to me than we had ever been in our lives.

But uneasy about leaving her, thinking about her on the plane to New York, I was filled with misgiving. Geoffrey was the pride of her life. What had I done to her?

Flora lives in Otter, thirty miles from Edgeville; I rang her from the airport. "Look, will you please get over to Edgeville? I told Mother about Geoffrey's will. She must be suffering agon ... "

"I know all about it!" Flora's voice was frosty with contempt. "You were hardly out of the house when she came rushing over to give me an earful. But you needn't worry. I said you were lying, as usual. She knows Geoffrey wouldn't do any such thing."

"Thank you, Flora." I hung up. I was vastly relieved. Mother is a brilliant woman but with a great capacity for self-deception concerning her wonderful children. She would believe Flora.

And my reputation as a liar, with Geoffrey, Flora and Mother doesn't bother me. At any rate, not now. I was sure it had saved both Mother and me a lot of grief.

But on my way back from Africa after she died, when I met Sue and Elliot in Rome, and Sue handed me her jewelry and told me the Edgeville place was mine, I knew I had destroyed her: nothing but unbearable disillusion would have caused her to disinherit Geoffrey.

I've had long experience in hiding my feelings so I accepted the jewelry and the legacy without comment, but with morbid dread.

Sue said, "Look, Pill, she wanted you to have it all, but ... "

"What?"

"Mother. She wanted you to have everything, but Flora had given her a cameo and a gold chain and she wanted them back so I gave them to her."

"Of course. Were you with Mother when she ... "

"Geoffrey, Flora and I were with her the evening before. Geoffrey and Flora left, I stayed. That's when she made me promise to give you her jewelry, all of it, but we had no idea she was dying. She died alone in the night."

Alone ... surrendering to death in bitterness at Geoffrey's neglect? Geoffrey a doctor, Flora a nurse, they must have known her condition. Did Geoffrey distance himself from her, as he did from me when I asked him about *my* condition, with 'It's not my field?' "Sue, are you sure Geoffrey didn't know?"

"Yes. She had a high fever but she was vivacious, laughing, I couldn't believe ... "

"I must go straight home to Martha!"

"Yes, but look, stay over for a day. I need some clothes. Unless you're going back to the Cape, or you're going to stop in New York, you'd better get something here."

Simonetta, the brilliant Italian Couturier, had just returned to Rome after a successful show in New York—which Sue had missed—so we went to her atelier to see her fall and winter collection. I bought some very beautiful clothes and, later, accessories and boots and shoes. Shopping did not detract from our grief for Mother's death, but Sue hid her distress as did I.

Sue and Elliot were en route to East Africa on safari. I dined with them at the Hassler, took a night flight from Rome and picked up a car in New York. That trip was one of the worst in my life. I couldn't sleep on the plane or in New York. I was distraught: my thoughts and emotions ungovernable. Added to my grief at Mother's death was the agony of remembering my senseless cruelty in exposing Geoffrey to her. And, unable to control it, the unreasoning pain and worry because of my lifelong failure with my family.

These past years living and painting in Africa I'd been happy. I had left Edgeville well behind me, buried the past with its mistakes. With this legacy it was uprooted: the mental and emotional turmoil were back. A manic depressive must live without obstacles, or lose control: go back to the asylum. The biggest obstacle is depression, which to me is concomitant with guilt. I knew it was essential that I survive this onslaught of emotion.

It was after midnight when I stopped my car in front of the house. Martha was waiting for me. Martha and I grew up together. She was kitchen skivvy for Mrs. McCarthy, our housekeeper, at the age of thirteen. My age. The odd ones in the house, we spent considerable time together and notwithstanding my puerile efforts to correct her vulgar speech and my everlasting demands on her time, there was and there remains great empathy between us.

Now, sitting in the kitchen drinking tea, despite my unbearable fatigue, I could not escape hearing every detail of Mother's last days, of her funeral. I must hear what Geoffrey, Flora and Sue said or wore, what the minister said. About the people, the flowers, the letters. And then—to my astonishment—"Your mother made me promise to take care of you."

In shock, I couldn't speak. Ever since Rome that nagging question: was it a death-bed repentance or had Mother made me her heir in disgust at Geoffrey? I dropped my head. I couldn't hold it up. I was suddenly exhausted. "Martha, let me get to bed, we'll talk in my room."

"All right. You look terrible! But it's true. She said it over and over, 'You must promise to take care of Philippa.' That's a tough one, Pill, but I promised."

"That's great. I'll hold you to it."

"Well, a promise is a promise. Anyway, what else would I do? Look, have you et? I suppose not. Go up. I'll bring you some dinner."

Martha expected me to live in Edgeville and it occurred to me that I might do that. It would be easy enough to arrange shows in New York.

If I knocked out a wall between the two north bedrooms and put in a skylight, I'd have a fairly decent studio. I called old George who is knowledgeable about construction and we started.

But ...

She was always near. She was dead and buried, yet Mother's presence in the house was so pervasive, so persistent that no matter when or where I was, I expected at any moment to turn and face her.

I was incredibly tired. In the long, restless village nights I turned and twisted on my bed trying to sleep, and when I did the dreams began. I was not really surprised one night when I woke to see her, a ghostly white form, leaning over my pillow.

I lay there paralyzed. I couldn't speak. Then I reached for her. She faded as I touched her. I screamed, "Mother! Wait!" I tried to get up. I was trapped, tangled in the bed clothes. "Come back! Wait!" I couldn't stop screaming. Did she know how sorry ... Did she know I loved her? I had ruined the last days of her life and she had left me. I was alone with my devastating guilt.

It was raining, lightning and thunder. I got rid of the bed clothes, stood up and threw on a sweater and slacks. I half fell, half ran down the back stairs, found a coat and rubber boots, and headed for the woods. I ran, stumbled, fell, picked myself up, ran, fell, ran ...

I came home at dawn and woke Martha. "Get me some coffee and help me pack. I'm leaving for New York."

"My, God, Pill! Soakin' wet an' runnin' off to New York! You're crazy! Get them clothes off—go change before you catch your death! Coffee. What about breakfast?" And then, bitterly, "I might of known. You won't come back."

"Martha," I took her hand. "Don't be stupid. You know I'll come back." I was freezing, shaking. "In the meantime, for God's sake, marry Lester! And hurry up. I'm in a hurry."

"Change your clothes! You can have your coffee but you don't leave here without breakfast."

I had to sit and eat with her. She pushed me aside when I tried to pack. I let her take me back to bed because I was dead on my feet.

It was dusk and still raining when she finished loading my car. She had repacked my wardrobe trunk and several suitcases and because I refused to eat again I had to wait while she made sandwiches.

I was standing by the car waiting to kiss her goodbye when she took the old scarf from her head and put it on mine. "You just ain't got the sense God gave geese! Do you have to get soakin' wet again? Maybe this'll remind you to take some care of yourself. Get in that car!" Then she said, "Wait a minute! You're not going off in this weather ... I know you! You'll be off in the woods in mud up to your neck!" She ran in the house, came out and threw the rubber boots into my car.

Around midnight, half sick, meandering along the deserted back roads, my headlights picked up a muddy lump in the middle of the road. I hesitated, then stopped and got out. When I realized it was a dog I was panic-stricken. I could have killed it. I squatted near it and called, "Fish!" He was in such bad shape he could barely crawl and he was soaking wet.

I took off my heavy sweater, wrapped him in it, carried him to the car and put him on the seat beside me. When I fed him Martha's sandwiches he licked my hand and I wept. I wept for the cruelty to animals, my cruelty to my mother and the savage cruelty in the world. He was shivering. We were both shivering. Mud and all, I pulled him to my lap.

I drove all that night. The next day I stopped for gas and for food for Fish, but I didn't want to stop. I couldn't eat and I couldn't conceive of getting out of the car to go to bed. I wasn't sleepy; I felt I would never sleep again. I drove through the second night.

The route to New York City is as familiar to me as the Edgeville woods, yet the closer I got to the city the less I wanted to be there. What I needed was to be alone—to hole up in some nondescript motel, catch my breath, get my senses back. That was nonsense; I had the keys to Sue's house, I would be alone there.

I drove all the way into the city to 64th Street and stopped in front of Sue's house but I couldn't get out of the car. The servants were there and Jet, her labrador. I knew I couldn't stand the talk. I drove back across town to the East River Drive, crossed the Triborough again and headed for the Connecticut Throughway.

Coming into Bridgeport there was construction. I was forced to detour and, through lack of sleep or attention, I got lost in a maze of back streets and couldn't find my way to the highway. I hadn't slept for two nights and three days and I was tired, dirty and hungry. It was late in the afternoon when I happened to turn into a quieter street. There were huge old trees.

I slowed down to check my direction, stopped and saw the "For Rent" sign in a dusty window of an old house. I got out of the car to walk Fish. I thought, why not? I would be alone. Why not? I was trying to make up my mind when a woman ran across the road with the key. The house had just been vacated. The gas and electricity were still on. I gave her money and she brought clean sheets, a loaf of home-made bread, coffee, and food for Fish.

6

This has been a most pleasurable day. I woke at six serene and relaxed; I felt wonderfully well. Unpacking my trunk, I found Martha had put in, carefully wrapped and stuffed with tissue paper, my Italian clothes and accessories as well as the winter suits I had left in Edgeville when I went to Africa.

Feeling human again, and vain, I chose a white wool suit with ermine hat, white gloves and white leather boots. I didn't stop for breakfast but showered, pulled on my beautiful, fresh clothes, checked myself in the looking glass and took Fish for a long run.

I've been thinking of leaving these past few days. This place is anathema to me. I won't go to New York until I've finished writing, but there's no reason I can't go somewhere else–to Lottie and Reg. I thought I had better let my landlady know, so I stopped in to see her on my way home. She's been kind and I've been rather putting her off. She's an odd woman for this neighbourhood; a spinster, whimsical, with Victorian manners.

This morning she greeted me, smiling, and took my hand. "How elegant you look, Mrs. Bentham. I'm glad to see you well again."

"Thank you. Yes, I've been rather ... "

"I know it's inappropriate but I can't resist telling you that I was much concerned for you when you first came. I assumed you'd had a great loss."

"Yes. My mother."

"Oh! My dear! You could have come to me. I was so often tempted to ask you for tea, to talk, but I did feel you preferred being alone."

"Indeed. I've been very sorry for myself. And you've been most considerate. But I want you to know how much I've appreciated your kindness since I've been here. The shopping when I first came and the home-made bread. And now I've come to tell you that I shall be leaving in a week."

"For Christmas?"

"Permanently. If you want to rent to someone else until the end of the month, that's quite all right."

She leaned over and kissed my cheek. "Take care of yourself. I feel you've had a bad time. I shall miss seeing you and the little dog."

I stood for a moment without speaking. I was touched, almost to tears.

I fed Fish, changed my clothes and had breakfast. While I was married, I had entrée to a rather exclusive Lodge in up-state New York. Isolated on a lake at the end of an old woods road, deep in the forest, it's open all year but not to the public. It's nameless, just a telephone number, and run by an astonishing couple from Switzerland, Charlotte and Reggio. I'm looking forward to staying there, perhaps until Christmas, and to some decent food! At this time of year the place will be almost empty.

If I want to leave in a week, I shall have to organize my time. Today I want to write. I'm glad I started digging into my past. As the French say, "*Tout comprendre, c'est tout pardonner.*" In retrospect, I see my early misfortunes with my mother in a very different light. The reason for my lifelong reluctance to have her touch me is no longer obscure. The antagonism between us started early. She was harassed and ill and in an incongruous relationship with me ... she thought me incorrigible, if not delinquent, so her occasional kindness seemed hypocrisy. Finally, it is not only that my bitter memories are dissipated, but that I can truly sympathize with her.

I had finished packing my car and was just about to walk out the back door when I stopped. In all conscience, I could no longer put it off. The phone was still connected. I picked up the receiver and dialled the operator. "Martha?"

She was so mad, she was sputtering. "SSSis about time! Not a word! Do I care if you're dead or alive? You start off like a crazy woman in the pouring rain and that's the end of it. Not a word. You wait. You go away some day." She was crying. "When you get back, I won't be here!"

"Oh, Martha, I'm sorry. Please! I couldn't help it. It's not just you. I haven't talked to anyone. Please don't cry. Why didn't you call Sue?"

"Oh, sure, Sue! Gallivantin' half the year in some God-forsaken country. She just got back two weeks ago. Look, I'm not foolin'. Your ma's gone so I might as well go, too."

"What! Don't talk rot! What's wrong? Did you talk to Flora?"

"Her! You think Flora gives a damn? She ... "

"Martha, stop it! If you don't want to talk to me I'll hang up."

"Well, I wanted to, but where were you? You could be dead and buried for all I knew! Look, Pill, Lester wants to get married."

"That's great! That's wonderful! When? What did you say? Does he know what he's in for?"

She began to giggle and her giggle was infectious. "I told him I might. ... In June. But, Pill, where will we live?"

"That's easy. If you move out I'll kill you."

"Oh. I knew you'd say that, but what about Flora and Geoffrey?"

"The house belongs to me, for God's sake. What would I do with an empty house? If you left I'd have no home. Do you need more money?"

"No, but I don't want to get married all alone. Will you come home?"

"I'll have to, to make sure you don't run out on him."

"Well, I had to be sure. That's all I wanted to know."

"Martha, you know I'm pleased for you both. Lester's getting a great woman. Bossy, but ... "

"Yeah, well I guess you'd know about that! I thought I'd ask Mrs. McCarthy to stay awhile."

"Give her my love. If there's anything you need ... Wait. Don't do anything about your dress, Sue and I will get it in New York. I'll be at the Lodge until Christmas. The number is under "L" in your book. Look, it's beginning to snow and I'm driving. Give Lester my love and take care of you both."

It had taken me a whole week to prepare myself to face civilization, and driving away from that house with Fish draped over my knee, leaving behind the mind-destroying events of those desolate months, I felt I had come into daylight after a long, malevolent night. I was so glad to be free of that place that I stopped for a spectacularly expensive lunch and then I dawdled, taking secondary roads so I could let Fish run.

It was dark now and snowing hard but the road to the Lodge was just ahead. I got out to take a look at it. There was a lot of snow and no tracks, strangely; it hadn't been ploughed, and Fish was in a snow bank up to his neck!

I cleaned him off and we started again. Snow-laden fir and hemlock on either side, tight against the narrow road. I crawled along. We were driving through a speckled white and black magic tunnel and Fish was barking his head off. My spirits lifted. I began to feel happy. Carefree!

The Lodge was blazing with light. Lottie came running out to meet me. "Philippa, you're late! Reg was getting ready to go out to look for you. That road."

I said, "You must forgive me, I left too late to find a phone. How are you, Lottie? No coat? You'll freeze! What's going on? A party?"

"No, no, nothing. I'm checking the rooms for the New Year and we're still working. There's someone waiting for you."

"Really? Who?"

Lottie opened the door and Fish and I got out of the car. I leaned over and kissed her and she put an arm around me and gave me a hug. "He's in the south sitting-room. William will take your car. He'll put your luggage in your old room." She took Fish from my arms. "I'll feed him."

"Thank you, who ... "

But she was gone.

The main lounge was deserted. I started along the corridor to the south sitting-room. Without Fish, my hands felt empty. Who on earth was waiting for me? My ex-husband, Dick? But, no, married again, he was safely out of my way. In the Bahamas, likely. I opened the door and stopped. Greying hair, tanned, a handsome man. I knew him.

He stood up and came to meet me. "Let me take your coat." He slipped it from my shoulders. "Your gloves?" I pulled off my gloves.

"Thank you." What *was* his name?

He turned and stared at me. "Yes," he said, "it's you. We were about to go out and rescue you. How did you get through the road?"

"The road wasn't bad. I enjoyed the drive." He was still staring at me. I turned away.

"Come to the fire. You must be cold."

"Not at all."

"I don't know any other woman who'd attempt that road alone, under these conditions, but you're from Nova Scotia so perhaps your roads ... "

"You've been there? Then you know. Yes, our roads prepare us for everything." Who the hell was he?

There was a huge log burning in the fireplace and a silver ice bucket with a bottle of champagne cooling in it, beside his chair.

He said, "We'll have a drink and Lottie will let us have dinner here." He pointed to the chair by the fire, opposite his.

You can always spot them, the privileged; the ease and the authority. Everything arranged without bothering to ask me. Would it upset him if I decided to dine alone? He seemed to know me, but for the life of me I couldn't think of his name or where I'd met him. I said. "How kind of you to suggest it. But I'm having an early night. I'll eat in the dining room." I turned to go.

"Wait!"

"Yes?"

"The dining room is closed."

"Closed? Why?"

"It's always closed in December. The Lodge is closed."

"But Lottie didn't ... "

"Your wire didn't include a return address. She couldn't let you know, but she's very happy to have you here."

"Oh. In that case ... "

"Yes. Please sit down." He pointed to the chair near the fire, opposite his.

I sat down. I looked up. He was still standing there, looking at me. Expectantly. And then he smiled and our eyes met with an eerie, light-headed, instantaneous recognition of ... intimacy? ... consanguinity? And I remembered where I'd met him. I turned my head away and forced a light laugh. "The Greenwich Hunt."

"Finally! But I'm not flattered. I'd have known you anywhere, but then I'm interested in you."

I felt a rush of heat. I'd been alone too long. I'd lost my instinct for the predator; the man was chatting me up! How could I be so naive. I said, coldly, "Really! Why? Were you hurt? Or your horse?"

"No, of course not, but you disappeared and I was concerned; you see I saw you before the Hunt. I saw that horse erupt out of the stable with a groom on either side, hanging on to the bridle, trying to stop her, but you were up and running before I could interfere."

"Grand Emma. What a magnificent horse! My mare, Rocket, had thrown a shoe and the stable let me borrow her, but they sent her out with a bar bit instead of a curb. I had trouble holding her. I was too close when I saw the red ribbon on your horse's tail.* I must apologize."

"Nonsense!"

He had been riding a big bay. I was trying to pull away from him when his horse started kicking and backed into us–slid against Emma's rump. She reared and came down in a hurry ready to take off. I kept twisting her head, trying to keep her from bolting, and we ended up cutting circles around each other on that narrow woods path. It struck us both as funny and we sat on those heaving, gyrating animals laughing like fools.

"They should never have put you up on her. I lost track of you during the Hunt, and when I looked for you at the Hunt breakfast you'd gone."

"I couldn't keep her off the Huntsman's heels and after two hours my hands were so bruised I couldn't hold her, so I took her back to the stable."

---

* A red ribbon signifies the horse kicks.

57

"Grand Emma belongs in the first flight, you should have let her go."

"I was a guest. I did want to be asked back."

"You've a good seat."

I laughed. "A friend told me my horses deserve medals for life-saving. I manage–if the horse knows what's going on."

"That helps." He twirled the bottle in the ice. "Is champagne all right or do you prefer something else?"

"Champagne's lovely." I began to relax. There's something about horse people that tends to remove barriers. A sort of camaraderie or pleasure in our mutual love of horses and our enjoyment of the hazards of the Hunt.

"I hope you're not rushing off again."

"But if the Lodge is closed?"

"Lottie's been looking forward to seeing you. I think she would like you to stay." He wrapped the bottle in a napkin, popped the cork, poured the wine, tasted it, then poured a glass for me. "The widow's wine," he said. "I hope it pleases you."

"Very much. We drank it in Rheims before the war."

"We," he said. "You and Dick?"

Not Dick. Clay! I could never forget Clay. But I thought of him now in a very different way. I said, "Do you know Dick?"

"He was a year behind me at Yale. Interested in publishing or some such." He leaned over and touched his glass to mine. "Cheers."

"He was, but he changed." Damn! My hand shook and I spilled my champagne.

He said, "You're cold." He handed me an immaculate silk handkerchief. "Wipe your hand."

"How awkward of me. I've had a long day." I'd been in Africa too long, away from all this.

"Now I'm curious. What does Dick do?"

It came out sharply. "He's in the Senate, now."

"Senator Bentham? That's Dick? I didn't realize. Well, enough of ancient history. Finish that and I'll give you another and we'll drink to our future."

That sudden reminder of Dick. I couldn't sit still. I put my glass down and stood up. I said, abruptly, "I must see about my dog. He ... He's never been away from me."

There was a knock. The door opened and Fish shot across the room and up into my arms.

William said, "Good evening Mrs. Bentham, welcome to the Lodge. He wouldn't eat so I've brought his food."

I took the food and placed it on the floor and stood up to shake hands. "How good to see you, William. I was afraid he'd be nervous, he's on unfamiliar ground, but he's house-trained."

"He'll be fine here, but what about you, Mrs. Bentham? The Countess sent me to ask if you'd like something to eat right away?"

"I'll wait for dinner."

He glanced at my host and then at me. "It's been ordered for eight-thirty. Does that suit you?"

"Perfectly."

William shut the door behind him.

My host said, "Let me fill your glass."

I held out my glass. I was all right again ... considering everything, it was ridiculous that I was still fond of Dick. I wasn't afraid. It just hit me every once in a while.

"What were we talking about? Dick?"

I still didn't know this man's name but after all his questions, I thought I'd take a shot at him. For all I knew, he might be a bachelor or homosexual but I said with great assurance, "You have a very beautiful wife."

"Had," he said. "We separated shortly after I met you. I didn't know you knew her."

Met me? "I don't, really. That is, just casually. And now?"

"And now we're divorced. I know you discarded old Dick, too. I really looked for you."

I laughed.

"Don't laugh. I pursued strange females on the street, I ... "

"Do go on."

"Never mind. Now, you tell me. What's been going on in your life since you left Dick?"

"Nothing."

"I see. By the way, do you believe certain events are foreordained? Why do you think we're the only two people to show up here this evening?"

"There's no one else?"

"The Lodge is closed."

"Lottie couldn't stop me, but why did she let you come?"

"Oh, that. I think she likes me, too."

I stood up. "Thanks for the drink. I must take Fish out, and I must wash my face before dinner."

He took Fish from me. "I know a sheltered spot. I'll take care of him." He opened the door for me and I went up to my room.

My luggage was in my room so I took a shower and changed. Lottie brought Fish and we sat and talked. She assured me I could stay as long as I wanted.

Lottie's presence is sustenance for the weary spirit; I love her. I'm always the better for seeing her.

A little before eight-thirty, I went down to dinner. I was very much aware of my host but I had no inclination for talk and he, too, was withdrawn. But after my tormented months this interlude–all of it, the attractive man, the wine and the superb food–gave me intense pleasure. With almost no talk, we were at ease and happy together. Still, from the moment our eyes had met, I had an uneasy feeling that if I stayed, I'd do something that, in my sorry mental condition, I had no intention of doing: I'd get involved with him.

After dinner, over brandy, he asked, "How long are you staying?"

"I leave in the morning."

"No," he said, "I think not." He crossed the room and pulled aside the heavy draperies.

The wind was howling and flinging hail and snow against the huge windows.

"With thirteen miles of private road and the Lodge closed, it will be some days before anyone gets out of here."

But surely they had a snow plow! But ... Did I really think this man could subvert my will? I had intended to stay and I wanted to. I yawned. "If the road's not open, then I suppose I must stay. Good night."

I went upstairs thinking I would fall asleep before I reached my room. I was deliciously drowsy after the wine, the food and the open fire. But the moment I fell into bed and turned off the light, I was wide awake. I was back in Edgeville thinking about Mother. If only we'd had more time. I had a sudden deep need to be near her. I got out of bed, opened my case and slipped her engagement ring on to my finger. Then I went back to bed and fell asleep.

Fish woke me. He was in a frenzy, scratching and whining. I couldn't remember where I was, couldn't orient myself. Things kept falling past the window. The whole house was shaking. All of a sudden the wind and the weight of ice broke a limb from one of the old trees. It hit the roof with an unearthly, crashing, splitting sound: a continuous moving sound as wood, ice and snow settled or slipped off the house. The window! Any minute it would blow in! I jumped out of bed and grabbed my robe and Fish.

Lottie knocked and opened the door. "Philippa, get your slippers and come with me."

It was cosy in the kitchen, the wind was coming from the other side of the house. I held Fish in my lap. I was still sleepy.

"Coffee or cocoa?" Lottie put a plate of toast in front of me. "Reg and Johnathan have gone to check on the girls."

"Coffee, please. Johnathan?"

"Your host last evening."

I still didn't know his name. "Lottie, if the Lodge is closed how come he's here?"

"He owns this place." She hesitated. "Look, Philippa, Johnathan's charming, but ... " She was standing at the stove looking at me and I sensed a certain constraint, unusual between us.

I said, "But?"

She handed me a cup of coffee and sat down opposite me at the kitchen table. "Don't misunderstand. You could put your life in Johnathan's hands and you'd be safe but he's not serious about women."

"He doesn't like women? He could have fooled me!"

"Oh no, not that! And you must forgive me for meddling but I think you should know. With Johnathan there's always some woman but no matter how kind or attentive he is, even to his ex-wife, at heart he's indifferent; he's not serious about them. And Reg and I, we're fond of you."

Quick tears pricked my eyelids, my childish reaction to kindness. I lifted my head abruptly to stop them.

"Let him have your toast."

I pulled Fish out of my plate and fed him the toast. I said, "It's kind of you to warn me but really, I can't think why."

"How well do you know Johnathan?"

"Not at all. That is, I saw him for about three minutes ten years ago."

"I see."

Lottie must be close to sixty. She has great presence and she's discreet. I'd never heard her make a derogatory or personal remark about anyone at the Lodge since I'd known her. It would be a rash act to question her veracity or judgement. I said, "Lottie, what's going on? You must have a very good reason to talk to me about him."

"Perhaps. I'm not sure. You see the day before yesterday he had to get back to Washington. He was in the helicopter, packed and ready to leave when the boy brought your telegram. He turned around and unpacked. Johnathan never stays when we have guests. Never. That's totally out of character. Philippa, if there's anything in your past you don't want him to know, please be careful."

"My past! Heavens!" My past! If it had come to that point I'd have killed my father! Did I destroy my mother's last days with my careless tongue? My past! Did my face betray my wretched memories? I hoped not. "Uh, well, of course my past isn't blameless, but nothing criminal."

"You married Dick in Russia. Could it have anything to do with that?"

"Why would that concern him?"

"I don't know. I'm guessing."

"Lottie, do you trust me?"

"Absolutely. You know I do. But who knows if by chance you know someone or something ... "

"There's no possible reason, political or otherwise, for him to be interested in me. But since you've gone this far, is he in covert services?"

She shook her head. "If he is, I don't know about it. But during the war he risked his life over and over. He was supposed to be stationed in England but, however he managed it, he organized an escape route for Jews and others from Nazi Germany. Reg and I were his liaison in Switzerland. This estate was private then and until they were established–after we got the refugees out of Europe–they stayed here. You see, for many of us the war is still close. And December is reunion time here. We close so that whoever wants to may come.

"Your telegram saying you would arrive alone just at this time was unexpected. And Johnathan's behaviour, asking that he see you alone, was extremely odd. You see Reg and I have known Johnathan since he was born and under every sort of condition, good and bad. There's no formality amongst us; we're closer than family. And I know you well enough so that, as with the refugees, you would have joined us."

"Of course! But Lottie, I've been in Africa and I had no idea the Lodge was ever closed. Does he think I'm involved in some devious plot? Really! I'll leave at once."

Lottie reached across the table and took my hand. "No. No, you won't. You'll stay as long as you wish and as our guest. I can't tell you how happy I am to have you here. And since you're sure you're not involved in anything devious," she smiled, "I must assume Johnathan's interest in you is personal." She hesitated. "But unless he's had a serious change of attitude, I'd question his intentions." She dropped my hand. "Philippa, if you think I am betraying Johnathan, try to understand. I had to chose between saying what I have said or seeing you hurt again."

Hurt again? I was shocked; I felt somehow exposed. "What do you mean? I'm not sure I understand."

Lottie laughed. "I haven't been eavesdropping or reading your mail, but hotel and inn-keepers see a great deal. Until the last few years you came often with your husband, and very often you and I sat and talked, always about nothing. But, Philippa, when you see a couple and one face is blank–a very beautiful face, but blank–then you know the marriage is one-sided."

Tears again, threatening to spill over. I'm getting soft. I would never have guessed that she knew. "Is that why you are–have always been–so kind to me?"

"Not at all! You didn't wear a blank face when you were talking to me. We always enjoyed having you here. I haven't had a chance to find out how things are with you these days, so ... "

We heard the men pounding their feet, shaking off the snow on the porch. She took my hand again. "Philippa, you must listen. Johnathan can charm birds out of the trees. If you're not certain, don't make the same mistake twice. They're here." She stood up to take their coats.

Johnathan took them from her and hung them up.

Smiling at me, Reg said, "Hello, Philippa," and came to kiss my hand. "I see Lottie pulled you out of bed." And then to Lottie, "There's no damage to the cottages but we'll have our work with the fallen trees. The storm's moving off. We'll be out of it in an hour or so."

Fish jumped out of my lap and ran to Johnathan and he picked him up. His eyes on me, he said, "Since the storm's coming from Canada I assume it pleases you."

"It leaves me cold."

For some reason that was funny. We were all laughing when he started across the floor, I thought to sit beside me, and automatically I pulled out a chair for him.

He stopped and lifted my hand. "Rubies? They're magnificent! Are you engaged?"

"Secretly. Just ... "

He dropped my hand and turned away from me. "I think I'll turn in." And still holding my dog, he left the room.

I said, stupidly, "I was about to say, just for tonight." His departure left me deserted. No matter that Lottie had warned me of his charm and his indifference to women, it did not change the reality: I was deeply vulnerable.

I got up and kissed Lottie. "Thank you for everything. Good night."

When I got to my room the door was open, the light was on and he was sitting in the rocking chair with Fish asleep at his feet.

My knees were shaking. I leaned on the wall. "Are you sure you're in the right room?"

"Yes." He stood up. "We must talk."

I didn't move. I couldn't. If I wasn't careful I'd make a complete fool of myself. I said, "Another time."

He crossed the room. Without touching me he put a hand on either side of me, against the wall. He said: "I did but see her passing by. Yet will I love her 'till I die." Then he kissed me, lightly, on the forehead and went away.

I couldn't breathe. I felt as though my heart had been ripped out of my chest.

I couldn't go to bed. I couldn't sleep. I couldn't think. I sat in the rocking chair and hugged Fish. I wanted him to come back. But because of that mindless interlude, because it might happen again, because ... because ... Until I had sorted everything out, I could no more allow him near me than I could fly. I would have to leave.

And then I was angry. Why run? I would stay! I would dissociate myself from him. Completely. I had to get on with my writing. Sanity depended on it.

And with that decision I felt a burden had been lifted from me and, with a strong feeling of balance restored, I put Fish on the floor, found my exercise book, turned on the desk lamp and turned to a clean page.

7

When my mother was happy she sang and her untrained voice had the authority, the richness, the beauty and the range of an opera star. When she was angry and when her quick temper did not assure her our immediate obedience, she reminded us that we were lucky to have her, that she had had no mother to care for her, and that her life had been "ruined."

The woman who "ruined" her life–my grandmother–haunted Mother all her days and her "ruined life" was an ever-recurrent theme when things went wrong, but with all her pride of ancestry that story, except to us, was never told.

My mother was born out of wedlock in Vienna, on Christmas day in 1881, to a family for whom such a birth was a dishonour, and she was disowned: sent to a remote village and placed in the care of an old servant, retired, and living out his last days as the village butcher.

Grandpa Lauber, illiterate, couldn't teach her to read or write or to speak a civilized tongue, but when he was dying, although he'd been bought off and sworn to secrecy, he told her where she could find her family.

At seventeen, Mother, the darling little aristocrat who had been allowed by her peasant guardian to rule the house and to run wild, travelled to Vienna to confront her mother. At the entrance to the estate, banging on the great bronze gate, she shouted for the gatehouse keeper to let her in. A lifetime family retainer, the gatehouse keeper knew the family secrets and he recognized her. She was a replica of her mother. Just as I, to a startling degree, resemble mine. He opened the gate.

At the house, an immense block of stone, she had trouble getting inside. There was alarm and confusion when, claiming herself a daughter of the house, come to see her mother, she stubbornly refused to go away. An ancient man-servant was called. He took her in, gave her a chair and told her to wait. With rude disregard of that instruction–"I'd waited long enough!"–she followed him up the grand staircase and along a stone-walled corridor. He scratched on a door.

"When it opened I pushed in front of him, but the woman in cap and apron who stood there wasn't my mother. The room was as large as our

65

entire cottage and glittering with silver and glass. My mother was standing, dressed in some kind of flowing white, hanging on to the back of a chair. I crossed the room. She was young, her skin dead-white. Face to face, our eyes met and held. I was looking at myself! She turned away. She shrieked at the servant, 'Bebel! How dare you! Get her out of here!'

"He started towards me and I raised my fist to him. I had never been so angry in my life! I said, 'No! Not me, Bebel! You! You! Get out!' I pointed to the maid. 'And take her with you!' He hesitated, then he took the maid's hand and they backed out of the room and closed the door.

"When she refused to admit I was her daughter, when she refused to tell me my father's name, I wanted to kill her. I swore she'd tell the truth or I'd choke it out of her. I had her by the shoulders, shaking her, when her husband came rushing in."

Fighting and kicking, mother was locked in the servants' quarters. Although she no longer remembered it, this was not the first time she had been hidden there. Born in December, she had not left the house until August when Grandpa Lauber had been relieved of his duties and sent away.

Unlike her family, the servants were well-disposed towards her: they greeted her with respect and love and tender sympathy. She was a child of the family, her mother all over again. How could they throw her out? Her wet-nurse stared in disbelief and joy, her lost baby had survived.

Then her ill-fitting country clothes disappeared and in their place, mysteriously, fashionable coats, dresses, hats, underwear, stockings, slippers, shoes, gloves. Enough to fill a good-sized trunk. Her hair was trimmed and she was taught to dress it.

Ten days later, the major-domo who accompanied her on board ship, inspected her small cabin and spoke to the chief steward. "Miss Liza Lauber–very well connected–was to be shown every courtesy." When he left, Miss Liza Lauber found herself with a one-way ticket, bound for another continent.

She raged. She hated her cabin, she hated the ship and everyone on it. She was too furious to be seasick, she stormed around the deck, her eyes shooting fire at anyone who dared look at her. She was noticed: what a charming creature!

The handsome young man who managed to get her attention fell in love and proposed marriage on that long voyage. He didn't speak her language and she didn't speak his but they understood each other. He had no idea that Miss Lauber was penniless but that didn't matter, he'd have money of his own–some day. They became engaged, formally, with a special dinner at the Captain's table.

In sight of land, Miss Lauber accepted that she was now permanently and hopelessly alienated from her mother and home. She had been shipped off to an obscure port city: Saint John, New Brunswick on the Canadian coast. The middle of nowhere.

Having arrived in this foreign land, Miss Lauber expected to meet her fiancé's parents at once. At the same time her fiancé realized his parents might not be as happy as he, about his proposed marriage. He found a boarding-house for Liza and suggested that until she learned the language, there might be some slight difficulty with his family. But he loved her. He would teach her English, himself. To prove his good intentions, he presented her with an engagement ring–a large ruby.

Although she wasn't completely sure that she was engaged to the right man, Miss Lauber accepted the ring. When it came right down to it, she wasn't too eager for another confrontation with anybody's family.

But she was alone and restless and running out of money. She had to find a way to earn her living and she started out briskly to do that. Two confused weeks later, although she knew how to ask for work, for the most part she had no idea what her prospective employers were talking about. She didn't get a job. But she kept looking.

At dusk one day, wandering around on the outskirts of the city, she stopped near a very large building–some sort of factory. There was an office at one end with a shining, black enamelled door and carriage lights on either side. It was getting late. She was turning away when the door opened and a handsome old man came down the few short steps. She turned to look at him.

He raised his hat. For one split second, he was back in London. This elegant, fashionably dressed, striking beauty was not of the neighbourhood. He asked, "Are you lost? Are you alone? What are you doing here?"

"I want to work here."

"What! Not in this place! Where are your parents? Come! I'll take you home."

"I have no one. I want to work."

In the end, he understood. He took her to his office and called Bert, his foreman. "Miss Lauber will be coming to work. Teach her to weave. She is under my particular care; no one is to speak to her or bother her. I shall be watching."

So, Mother found work at last where there was no need for her to talk–as a weaver in a textile mill in the city slum. And because it was almost dark, he drove her to her boarding house.

The handsome old man–my paternal grandfather, Francis Xavier

Jerrold, was born of landed English gentry who, by the law of primogeniture and in an unbroken line from father to son, had maintained their estate for more than three hundred years. They were Catholic at the time of Henry VIII and despite the cost in material things and the loss of prestige incurred by hanging on to a possibly lethal theological argument, they remained Catholic.

Early in the nineteenth century, dispossessed of his home when his elder brother inherited, grandfather emigrated to Canada to seek his fortune. And just as his family had refused to bow to the Crown in matters of religion so, in the new world, he refused to bow to English policy. The colonies were looked upon as markets for English goods and Royal Governors were adjured to discourage rival factories. Nevertheless, Grandfather was rapidly successful in establishing a textile mill in the province of New Brunswick, and as quick thereafter to establish himself, socially, as a man of substance.

He married an English woman, Flora, I don't know her maiden name, and with success he built the very conventional mansion of his time. It had a full complement of magnificent rooms: conservatory, ballroom, billiard room, bedrooms with bath and dressing rooms, dining room, breakfast room, sunroom and what have you. The french windows in the great rooms stretched from the floor almost to the ceiling and were veiled in real lace curtains and covered heavily and darkly with french brocade draperies. Faucets and doorknobs were solidly of silver. There were carved, marble fireplace mantels throughout the house and here and there, appropriate to the time, stuffed animal heads: caribou, deer and bison. In the entrance hall of this grand house, sloping up from a carrara marble floor, a wide mahogany staircase flaunted two bronze Graces holding gas lamps. The servants' wing was in the rear, adjacent to the stables.

My father, Charles Alexander Jerrold, the first of Flora's three children, was born into this rigidly conventional Catholic family in a period of industrial as well as social revolution and at a time when man was fashionably intent on abolishing God. I suppose he had some sort of formal education. I do know that in the tradition of his family, he cut his teeth on a solid and Catholic assortment of theological volumes. But rebelling early against his father's religion, he went on to read what he pleased: everything he could lay his hands on against all religions.

My father lived abroad for many years. He spoke French and German and he was conversant with European history and the then modern ideologies. He detested prejudice against nations or peoples: "Man is one family, it's the idiot who is not competent to cope with a single individual who is eager to expound the despicable mores of an alien tribe."

But while he declared his contempt for Chauvin's nationalism and rejected Imperialism, at the same time, he admired the English character– that is, except in his own family. Visiting England, this brash colonial did not get on with his father's family any more than he did with his father. He was revolted by a narrow orthodoxy: the Holy Catholic Church had all but got him by the coat-tails and when he saw it coming, he ran a mile, protesting. The antipathy must have been mutual, for our English cousins dropped out of sight.

Pa rarely spoke of his mother but now and again, talking of his early life, he mentioned his father in a tone of quasi-humour-quasi-contempt: "The old man was a pious hypocrite; he believed in God and Money. God with a small "g" and money with a capital "M." Except for contributions to charity and an hour in church on Sunday, he was exclusively occupied in the time-honoured business of acquiring wealth. But his ancestor's religion was deeply inbred: to save his immortal soul, he'd have had me a priest! Can you imagine me in a Roman collar? Gad!"

So, there was no demand in our family for God-worship or money-worship and, most emphatically, none for ancestor-worship. Pa approved Mr. Jack London's dictum that no man–rather none of his children–should "walk on dead men's legs."

Darwin and Huxley were Pa's substitutes for God, yet he laughed at Darwin's gentle scepticism and when Huxley invented "agnosticism" he scoffed: "It's his courteous concession to convention." He admired Gustave Flourens, the nineteenth-century French atheist and revolutionist, but he modified Flourens' statement, "Our enemy is God. Hatred of God is the beginning of wisdom. If mankind would make true progress it must be on the basis of atheism," by saying, "How hate a fictitious character?"

Pa was an atheist. He was also, theoretically, a socialist which was what the early communists called themselves. With Marx, he claimed the capitalistic system, based on greed, "the exploitation of the common man for profit," contained within itself the seeds of its destruction. Given time for the gap to widen between rich and poor, and with the inevitable reduction of world resources, the economic order would collapse. He insisted capitalism was doomed and therefore he wanted nothing to do with Grandfather's business.

Whatever hope Grandfather may have had of establishing a commercial dynasty in Canada was cut short by Pa's fatuous ideas. Yet, bound by tradition, Grandfather had no alternative but to leave him everything in the hope that forced into the business to maintain his accustomed way of life, with age, Pa would come to his senses. To that end and to hasten the process, when Pa was thirty-six years old, Grandfather pleaded ill health and sailed for England leaving him, temporarily, in charge of the business.

Well, Pa didn't believe in God and he didn't like the Mill, but every now and then he had to send off a report to keep the old man out of his hair. In the late afternoon–he spent the night reading and needed his sleep in the morning–he would turn up at the Mill, grab the foreman and take a quick trot through the place. Usually with his eyes shut.

One day fate pried them open. Across the Mill floor, a long blazing shaft of light shone through a high window directly down on an angel. There she stood in a halo of light. Never mind that he didn't believe in angels, he'd been brought up on them. "Bert," he yelled. He had to yell, the Mill was noisy. "Who's she?"

The foreman's eyes followed Pa's pointing finger. "Oh. Er. Uh. Well, that's Miss."

Miss? Who ever heard of calling the hands, Miss! "What's her name?"

"Nuthin'. I mean, she's Miss. Your Pa said so."

"What! How long has she been here?"

"Seven or eight months. You seen her before."

"Never. Who is she?"

"Who? I dunno. Immigrant-Polish-French, I dunno. One of that lot." Bert caught Pa's sleeve. "Sir! You call 'er Miss, Sir. Don't insult 'er. 'Er name's Lobber."

"Lobber?" Maybe he was going deaf. He took off in a hurry and managed to get across the floor without knocking down the looms in spite of keeping his eyes solely on target. He was in a hurry to find out, which is why he forgot to call her Miss. "Who are you?" he yelled.

Miss Lobber had stopped her loom and was tying weaver's knots rapidly and expertly in the rough canvas. She glanced up swiftly, looked back at the canvas and kept on tying knots.

She was, Pa noticed, radiantly beautiful. She was also radiantly clean, but that exquisite face looked extraordinarily stubborn. Pa touched her arm. "Listen, I asked you your name."

Miss Lobber looked at his hand on her arm and until that moment, Pa said, he'd never noticed the inherent ugliness in a man's hand. He yanked it off her arm.

Miss Lobber switched the power back on her loom and began to weave.

For some reason, Pa suddenly remembered he hadn't changed his underwear. He also remembered, suddenly, all about allowing the working man his dignity. "Would you be kind enough to give me a moment of your time? ... Uh, Miss?" He waited.

Miss Lobber kept on weaving.

Pa turned to Bert who had appeared beside him. "Turn off that machine!"

The power went off and Miss Lobber turned the same look on Bert that she'd turned on Pa's hand.

Bert started waving his arms. "Look, Miss, no offense, this gent's got a right to know.'Ee owns the place. Now, Miss ... "

"Never mind all that," Pa yelled, "She'll give me the information. What's your name?"

Miss Lobber's face turned bright red. Then she said, "I'm Liza Lauber."

"Lauber. Oh. Where are you from?"

"Austria."

Pa spoke to her then in German. "Who are your people?"

"What!" She glared at him.

Pa took a step back. There was no mistaking her contempt for him. Then she flung him a word that "knocked me back on my heels."

"Butchers!" she shouted and switched the power back on.

My father stood there like a fool, ashamed of his rude intrusion on another's privacy. Dismissed by a factory hand. He turned away. But he hadn't crossed the floor before he was roaring with laughter at her cheek! Miss Lauber had handed him some of his own equal rights medicine and he hadn't known how to swallow it. And he felt fine.

Then a terrible thing happened. He got home, sat down, picked up his book and the words didn't make sense. All he could see was Miss Lauber's hand flashing back and forth on the canvas and, ... there was a ruby on it! He jumped up. He had to get back to the Mill. He was at the door when he heard the Mill whistles. The place was closed.

The next day Pa discovered that it was one thing to get up at the crack of dawn and get to the Mill and another to make the girl talk. "She wouldn't utter." But the ring was there, on her left hand.

For the next week or so, it was not only that Pa couldn't read, he couldn't sleep. If he happened to fall into uneasy slumber, he would wake sharply in shock: "Visions of angels floating in my head and the word 'Butchers' shattering my ear drums."

At a safe distance, late one afternoon he followed her home. He started taking solitary walks. His favourite was up and down in front of Miss Lauber's boarding-house.

One evening, she appeared walking arm in arm with ... "A callow youth! And she was laughing! Gad! Did she imagine for one moment that she was going to marry that imbecile?" Pa knew him, a banker's son, recently home from Europe. Where had she met him? "The girl had no sense!"

Pa had once asked a girl to marry him. He thought she had plenty of brains–an essential, in his opinion–but she turned him down, "with a feeble excuse." She preferred horses: if there was something wrong with a horse, she didn't bother to let Pa know. She stood him up. Then she married a friend of his. "That poor feller's life was spent in the stable." That settled it for Pa. What an escape! Gad! What if you got married first and then found out! He'd never risk matrimony again.

The next evening, Pa was waiting outside the Mill for Miss Lauber. "Would she allow him to walk along with her for a moment or so?" He had a few things to say for her own good. The Mill was on the river and they were half way across the bridge when Pa stopped her and proposed.

Without preamble or ceremony, Miss Lauber gave him a flat "No."

Then she made a fatal mistake. She pulled off her mitten and stuck out her hand–the one with the ruby on it–and informed him she was engaged to marry someone else.

Pa took the hand, removed the ring and threw it in the river. "Not any more," he said. "That's over."

After that, things for Miss Lauber went from bad to worse: Pa was ready to help her make some sensible arrangements concerning her future. Miss Lauber found herself out of her boarding-house and in residence with a nosy old Scottish couple who wouldn't allow her to be alone with her fiancé, so that she might explain that it wasn't really her fault that she had lost his ring. "He thought I stole it! He refused to believe that the old man who owned the Mill stopped me in the middle of the bridge, pulled the ring off my finger and threw it in the river."

That was because, her fiancé knew for a fact, the old man was in England.

The engagement was off.

Miss Lauber couldn't believe the kinds of fools she'd met in Canada: one fool threw her ring in the river and the other fool called her a liar because she expected him to believe it.

All that happened about the middle of January 1901. In March of that year, Miss Lauber accepted an engagement ring with three large, pigeon-blood rubies, set in diamonds and a wide gold band and married my father. He was thirty-six years old and she was eighteen.

Off-hand, I'd say that a loaded gun in the hands of a madman is less dangerous to love's survival than marriage. But love does happen: the love between my father and mother was never compromised, no matter the never-ending clashes of temperament. Perhaps love survived their marriage because they kept it a priority, for it could only be through the miracle of love that such disparate beginnings could be transmuted to lifelong trust and regard.

Except for their passionate interest in each other, which persisted for their lifetime, my parents, even in dress, were ill-matched. Mother was always meticulously groomed and she had a flair for fashion and elegance. Her wedding dress of heavy ivory satin had a high neck–a three inch dog collar–and a lace-covered yoke with tiny twisted silver ornaments.

As for my father, six feet, two inches and handsome enough, he had light brown hair, blue eyes, a fair complexion and, for the time, a conservative moustache. Elegant at his wedding, down to the carnation in his button hole–someone else put him together–except for weddings and funerals when mother inspected him, he appeared that way less and less often. His mind occupied with matters of urgent importance, his collar crumpled, his tie half on and half off, he wore his clothes as though he was about to shed them.

Grandfather returned to Canada to meet the woman–some bluestocking atheist, no doubt–that Charles had got himself tied to. He worried: "Think of it, if neither were religious, Charles might well go to his grave unaneled."

The moment he saw Liza, he remembered her. He was shocked. He had to think about it. But they were married. And she was a beauty; a ravishing pink and white complexion, delicate features, perfect teeth, raven hair. She looked and walked like a duchess. She had enormous poise and dignity. No matter her background. She was quite suitable. Incredibly, Charles had made a superb match. Reassured, Grandfather went back to England. A few months later, he died.

Mother, still frustrated by her mother's rejection of her, was further frustrated by Pa's extraordinary ideas. Surrounded by every luxury, eager to embrace the world and to be embraced by it, she found herself tied to a man who was solely concerned with considering the evils of society and how to cure them. Pa spent most of his time reading and talking about reform; how to better the lot of the working class.

When mother, who could not read or write her own language, asked what it was all about, she thought him insane. Brought up with the working man, she had no precious notions about him. As far as she was concerned, he could take care of himself–and if he didn't, he deserved what he got.

Pa thought parties bourgeois or boring. If mother pleaded for company, he invited sexless old fogies, of both sexes, to dine and, while she yawned, they sat far into the night talking incomprehensibly.

As for family, Pa's sisters looked down their fine noses at the illiterate mill-hand Charles had married. With considerable kindness and charm, they brushed her off.

But Pa adored her. Outside of frivolous company, he gave her everything she wanted. And her joyous fervour for every aspect of her new life: the house, the horses, the clothes, astonished and delighted him. It never occurred to him to try to dominate or change her. But her ignorance exasperated him, so he hired a tutor to teach her English. Once she was familiar with the language, he was sure, "She would acquire a true perspective on society as a whole." But he wasn't really bothered. With the house, servants and money, she was well off. And he had never been so happy in his life.

When Pa was thirty-seven years old, he inherited his father's estate. And he promptly began to give it away. Because of his father's adherence to the law of primogenitor, he believed that his two married sisters had been deprived of their just due. So, he gave them two-thirds of the property. For his own portion, he kept the house and, "In order to ameliorate the hard lot of the working man," the Mill. And because his sisters refused it, he also kept the farm.

He knew what he had to do with the Mill. He raised the worker's wages, allowed them an unprecedented amount of time off and installed a library for their use. And for a time, he kept his eye on the place–until everyone got used to the new regime and then, well ... The staff knew the business better than he did. They were always right when it came to production and sales, and it took up his time. So, he left it to them.

He kept his father's office but, except to sign things, no one bothered him and gradually the office turned into a library. An inviolable sanctuary.

In 1902, Geoffrey was born. And the following year, Flora arrived. It was about this time, that the Tutor, with whom mother had no patience, got lost in the shuffle. Three years later, just at the time when money had ceased to flow from the Mill as generously as before, I came along.

8

I have not tried to write for three days. It is easy enough to remember incidents, but how recall the emotional atmosphere of a child? Inevitably the years colour and distort the view.

But there is a trick I use when I want the solution to a problem that baffles me. I put the question to my sleeping mind. In the morning or within days I have the answer, for the subconscious, it seems, is a repository where all that we know and have experienced is stored. When I left off writing, I resorted to that method of dissolving time.

There was no sudden transition the following morning from the void of sleep to the fullness of waking. The two states had merged. I progressed from a dim consciousness, thrashing and struggling in my bed, to a fuller and then a full realization of my position: I was struggling, dream-glued, in a hostile and breathless world, no longer a distinct entity but by some weird concrescence an integral part of it. And I fought to the limit of my strength and in desperation against what was happening. Because through me and that world–that amorphous extension of myself–there was a noisome flow that engulfed and threatened to destroy me: I was empty and being filled, resisting but unable to prevent that interfluent horror.

I feel it now! It goes in and through me, ceaselessly ebbing and flowing and there is no moment of peace: I am still there, plastered against her. In rebellious and somehow shameful union, as though by an infinity of silken threads that bind me from head to foot, I am enmeshed with my mother.

I have not been able to shake off the proliferating horror that I have surfaced from the depths of my mind. Now, reliving that blind and mindless struggle against irresistible and destructive odds, reliving my time in her womb? My first months? My first years? I stand appalled before that ironic revelation of my heretofore interred bondage, for I cannot escape it. I am, and out of all proportion, still involved. To be free of my mother I cannot, simply, as the psychiatrists say, cut the cord. There is a major operation involved. I must cut through the whole of our intermingled lives, from the beginning.

The atmosphere clings. And like corn in a popper, incident after incident has been jumping in my mind. I can reconstruct, and almost from

75

day to day, the first years of my life. The faces are blank, featureless, but I remember, particularly, sounds, scent and colour. I remember our clothes. I remember the weather. I remember, distinctly, the first words I heard my mother speak.

"Take the child, Bertha."

There was a quick sharp pain of disbelief when my mother left. My mother walked out of the house and stepped into the waiting carriage and the carriage drove away.

I threw myself into the street and ran after the wheels. The wheels were high and thin with gray rubber bands. They rolled round and round, faster and faster; they made crunching noises on the gray cobbles. The street began to stretch out between me and my mother. I ran, agonized, gasping.

Bertha grabbed me from behind and I hit the road flat out, holding on with my hands and knees, grasping at the cobbles. Above the back of the seat, the flowers on my mother's hat bobbed up and down. The carriage turned a corner and the flowers disappeared.

I opened my mouth wide. I tried to shout, "Wait. Wait for me!" Tears ran down my face but my breath wouldn't come.

"Uh-uh," Bertha panted. She swooped, she swept me off the ground. I was rushing through space on my back. The houses hung over me, the sky was miles up. I kicked, I clawed with both hands.

Her beautiful face, ebony and ivory, blotted out the sky. Tears rolled from her eyes. "You hurt me!"

My hands and feet stopped. Transposed by her tears to my world, Bertha was me: deserted, desolate, crying for comfort. I flung my arms around her neck and held her tight.

"My baby," she said, "my good, good baby." She rocked me in her arms till my breath came back, she carried me through the great open hall, she sat me in her lap and wiped my face with a warm, wet cloth. "Wait," she crooned, "you jus' wait. Your mammy goin' come back. She goin' bring you a bran' new baby."

Bertha was black. I felt it; I knew it consciously. Black is compassion, black is love, black is safety in sorrow. I was almost three years old.

Was it that day or weeks later that the coachman came?–impatient to take us away. The horses wouldn't stand. I screamed, pounded his legs and tried to bite his knee: if we left the big house, my mother would never find me.

"Sho, sho, child, we jus' goin' out to play. Geoffrey an' Flora comin' too. The horsie goin' take us to the farm an' Philippa goin' sit on Bertha lap all the way."

Terror subsided when Bertha touched me.

In terms of Canadian history, my father's farm was very old. It had been established at the time of the American Revolution by a family of loyalists, English aristocrats, who had fled the rage of the American rebels: "That handful of treacherous beggars, that murderous riff-raff, who were pillaging, burning and destroying the property of their betters." And at that time and in that stretch of wild country, along the Bay of Fundy, where men built rudely and of wood, the stone house was unique. It was a manor house and it had been built by slaves. Half a mile back of the house–separated in death as in life by a railing of iron spikes–generations of bones, master and slave, lay dust in the family cemetery.

When my father inherited the property, there survived of the original family, a very old woman, and by a clause in Grandfather's will–had she been his mistress?–he had to care for her for the rest of her life or, failing that, legally renounce his claim: cede the entire property to her.

The old lady had her quarters upstairs and she rarely left her great black-carved four-poster bed. But via some mysterious grapevine–was it Andros, the Greek, who grew up on the farm?–everything was known to her and she could not accept the new regime.

Pa, concerned about money and hoping to be independent of the Mill, had fired the servants in the big house in the city and intended living for most of the year on the farm. But blind to immediate and practical issues, he had left Mother to oversee the farm. Since Mother would not allow the old lady to supersede her authority, there were periodic tempests of rage, but now pregnant and ill, Mother was in hospital a long ways away.

And three months went by.

There was the great, gray-stone house sleeping in the sun and the world was made of sun and grass. That was the farm. Geoffrey and Flora were always together and they wouldn't play with me. I ran and ran, chasing them. I could never catch up. "Mama!" I shrieked, "Mama!"

Bertha left the flapping white sheets and caught me in her arms. She put a warm black hand over my eyes. Then she brought the elephant and the cart and took me to the top of the hill. Away below, she pointed out the gate. "When yo' Mammy come home," Bertha said, "she goin' look right up an' see you. She goin' come that way."

So, I stayed on the hill watching for my mother and when Bertha came to get me, she left the elephant to watch. "Dat el'phunt, he goin' tell you. Even in the middle of the night. He goin' come right down to your bed and tell you if you' mammy come back."

But all the nights went by and the elephant didn't come. And all the bright dewy-wet mornings when I raced up the hill and shook him to make him answer me, the elephant wouldn't speak. I ripped him to pieces to find out when my mother was coming home. The stuffing came out but the words stayed inside him.

I was running in the field up above the great house. Running, running in the field on top of the hill. The field was full of high grass, so high that it switched my face as I ran and fell and ran and fell in it. The sky was raw gray and the grass was gray and the world was big and empty with gray wind in it and the heavy smell of grass. The memory is sharp and clear. Around the edge of the field there was a path with bubbles of water on it. I threw my head back and ran full out, round and round. I was waiting for my mother.

Bertha came up the hill shouting, "Philippa! Philippa! Yo' mammy, she heah."

Down the hill and through the kitchen, running, running, and into the dark red and black parlour.

There was a tall, hard, sharp lady with a frill of lace at her neck standing there. I was going so fast I couldn't stop. I ran full into her hands and her heavy rings hit me on the face.

"Philippa ... "

I turned, shot past her and back to the kitchen. Bertha was coming in the door. I caught her by both knees and the pan in her hand went straight up. "Bertha," I shouted, "where's my mother?"

"Why she standin' right behind you."

I turned to throw myself at my mother, and the lady reached for me with her hard, malevolent hands.

In blind retreat, I clutched at Bertha's legs. "No!" I screamed, "No, not you!"

For I knew my mother. I saw her all the time: the image of my mother that I carried in my mind was neither nebulous nor intangible. What I saw, I saw solidly. There was a drift of black hair, a blank, white smiling spot that was her face, and below it a heavy, curved body in a soft, pink wrapper. The figure was seated on an armless, low, brown-cane rocking chair.

I tried to dodge but she caught me and I screamed, "No! I want my mother! No!"

She clamped my arms tight against my sides, she shook me. "You foolish child, hold still! Hush! Look at me. Who do you think I am?"

"Bertha," I cried, "Get me!"

"Get back to your work, Bertha. Listen! Listen to me! Will you shut up! I'm your mother."

Then the rings hit my face. "The faster you find out who I am, the better for you! I'm your mother all right and I've had enough of your nonsense. Get in here!" She dragged me, kicking, to the parlour. "Hush! Come, look at the baby, look at your little sister, Sue."

The baby was ... blurred ... in a woolly basket.

I struggled, I kicked, I pushed, I got away from her and breathless, from my vantage ground, the door, I shouted, "My mother is coming home and she's bringing a baby too!"

The lady sat down on the big, black-carved red velvet chair and my father, who was standing behind it, put out a hand and touched her hair. "Liza," he said, "she's only a baby."

All of a sudden her voice went straight up in the air, straight through my head. An elemental, searching-piercing cry that hypnotized: held me waiting and wary. "My God, Charles, I'm going crazy!"

"Liza! You've just got out of a hospital bed. What are you trying to do–go back? Control yourself. You'll be ill again. You've been away three months. That's a long time in a child's life. And you've changed. I suspect she's waiting for a fat woman. Let her alone and she'll come to you of her own accord, you can't expect ... "

"I can't expect anything," the lady interrupted, "not from my children, as far as they're concerned, I might as well be dead. The other two took one look at me and ran. They're sorry I came back! Where are they? Where's Geoffrey?"

"Andros is making him a fishing rod, they're going fishing, I guess they're in the barn."

"The barn! Flora? Flora in the barn with those men? Bertha! Find Flora! Bertha! Where's that idiot? I'll go myself."

"Liza–Gad!" he pushed her back in the chair. "Andros is there. Besides, there's not a man on the place who would harm Flora, or any of the children."

"That's what *you* think. A lot *you* know. As for that one ... "

She was looking at me and I shivered.

"Look at that rag she's got on for a dress! Is that a dress? I've never seen such filth in my life! Look at her hands and feet–she must have been rolling in mud, and she's soaking wet! I suppose that thing in the kitchen let them all run wild."

She turned her head. The blank white face lay flat against the crimson velvet chair. "How can a child forget her mother? Charles? It's not natural, it's not possible! Don't worry, she knows who I am all right!"

I caught hold of the doorknob and held it tight. She was talking about my mother. Did she know where she was? I wanted to ask, but ...

"Philippa!" she commanded, "Come here, come to me!"

I edged away from the door into the hall.

"Look at her, just take a look, trying to get away! A child that age and I can't control her! It's the God's truth, Charles, she's been nothing but trouble since the day she was born!"

"Gad, Liza, do be quiet. Give the child a chance, she'll get used to you. There's nothing wrong with Philippa. A little dirt won't kill her. Bertha took good care of the children; they had plenty to eat and they're strong and healthy. What more do you want? Gad, don't get so excited."

"Excited? Who wouldn't be excited? A lot you care! You wouldn't notice if they were naked! They're a disgrace!" She struck his hand away and stood up. "I must ... I feel weak," she said. Then her foot slipped and she fell. The chair went over with a crash and Pa got down on his knees and picked her off the floor. Both her hands hung down. He pushed past and knocked me against the door. He carried her through the hall and up the stairs. He was going to keep her!

I ran to the foot of the stairs and stopped. I stood, suspended in space, re-hearing her voice, that shrill, shrieking confusion of sound was still in my head. Where was my mother? I wanted to look for her but I couldn't move. I stood at the foot of the stairs, rigid in fear, until long after dark–until Bertha found me.

I sat in the crib and watched Bertha. The yellow kerosene light shone on her and she lifted her arms and pulled off her dress. I was surprised to see a big woman take off her clothes. I thought they stayed in them. Underneath, except for a white thing tied with a string around her neck and full of ragged holes, she was all black, a shiny, rich, black. The black colour of Bertha was the loveliest colour I had ever seen. "Bertha," I pleaded, "When is my real-Mother coming home?"

Bertha put on a kitchen dress with the arms gone and got in her big bed. She put her hand on the lamp. "Go to sleep, now. Bertha right heah. This mammy you real mammy. You young and you fogit. Lay down now. I got to get up in the morning, I got work to do."

Bertha didn't know. I saw my real-Mother, pink and soft and plain as day, sitting in the rocking chair. Where was she? Out on the grass? Yes! I tried to climb out of the crib but Andros had put on an extra bar.

"Philippa!" Bertha groaned. "Land o Goshin, Philippa! What you doin' theah? What goin' on? Is you asleep?"

I held my breath, then let it out, "Uh, huh. Sleep."

"Den who rutchin' aroun' in dat crib? Unh? Lawd, I done in. Lawd." Bertha moved and her bed creaked. She sighed, groaned, "Chile, you wanna come in Bertha bed? Doan move. Doan move. Set still. Wait, now. I come an' git you."

Geoffrey was seven years old, Flora six and I was three when this-Mother came with the new baby. I was sitting in the sun with my back against the warm rain barrel, trying to tell them she wasn't the right one.

Flora gave my foot a good kick and my ankle hit a rock. "You're crazy," she said. "She's the same mother who went to get Sue, and everybody but you knows it."

Geoffrey was throwing stones. "You're crazy!" he yelled. "Crazy! Crazy!"

A stone hit my chest and they laughed and held hands and ran away.

I didn't move. They wouldn't play with me.

This-Mother came out of the house with a comb in her hand. "Come, Philippa." She picked me up and stood me on the chair beside the rain barrel.

I was trapped. If I tried to get away, she would hit me with the rings. My legs were stiff, my feet rooted in fear.

This-Mother was quick and the comb was hard and my hair tangled. The longing for my real-Mother grew worse when this-Mother hurt me. "Bertha," I whimpered, "Bertha."

This-Mother jerked my hair. "Shut up, or I'll give you something to cry about." She held my hair tight in her hand, hurting, pulling me backwards.

"Bertha! Bertha! Get me!"

This-Mother yanked my head around, shoved her face into mine, and screamed, "I'll teach you to yell for Bertha! I'll teach you a lesson you'll never forget!" She slapped me, she hit me with the comb and then she lifted me up and threw me, head first, into the barrel of rain water.

When Mother dropped me into the rain barrel that day, she had an unexpected success. I stopped crying. Or, if tears betrayed me, I ran and stayed away, hidden, until I could face her—face them all—with dry eyes. And when this-Mother told the story, I listened: mute. I watched my real-Mother, solid and pink in her brown rocking chair. Her chair stopped rocking and she sat quite still, and the brightness that shone on her was erased. Beneath that cloud of soft black hair two crystal tears rolled down her blank white face.

The farm was bounded on one side by the Atlantic Ocean and the house lay a mile or so inland on a tidal river. Geoffrey and Flora were fishing off the end of the wharf. The row-boat bobbed and bumped. I climbed into it and sat in the narrow prow. "Look!" I yelled, "Look at me!"

Geoffrey threw down his fishing rod, shoved me off the seat, and they both scrambled into the boat. Then Geoffrey cut the mooring rope with his new jack-knife.

Oh, the soft, dark, lifting water, the gentle sliding boat, the lilting ... This-Mother! Running along the bank, splashing into the water wading–she couldn't swim–shrieking. All the muddy water curling around her starched white bosom, shrieking. Her chin, her hair in the river, then the white hand lifted through the thick, brown soup and caught the trailing rope and pulled us back to shore.

Oh calamity! The thing I did this time was the worst I had ever done. That sound! My chest twisted, yanked, gyrated. Anchored in a stone of misery, a core of pain, that corrugated series of shrill shrieks and desolate moans pulled my chest all out of shape. I shook all over. This time no one was safe. Those angels of beauty, Geoffrey and Flora, were in trouble. And Bertha and Andros, too.

"Where was Andros when the children were in danger?" (The old woman had sent him to the cemetery to trim the graves.) "That old witch thinks more of the dead than she does of us! He got there all right. He heard me scream. But when?" Bitterly, "When it was too late."

"And Bertha," this-Mother screamed, "where was Bertha?" Bertha was flat on her back, snoring. "Oh she can sleep in the middle of the day while the children are all being drowned. I swear it, Charles, if I stay another day I'll do something you'll be sorry for!"

Her ungovernable rage defied his attempts to calm her and Pa was frightened. She'd been ill. She'd been shocked and her health was endangered. The farm was too much. And no matter that he thought the farm was the answer to his problems, he felt obliged to cede it to the old woman. And that was why, when we left, we never went back.

When we got to the city, Bertha tied a white rag around her head, lifted me hard against her face, put me down, picked up a big bundle, walked out and never came back.

I couldn't believe it. I went all over the house looking for her. Shouting for her. When she didn't come, I started looking for the other one, my real-Mother–shouting for her. Then I shouted for both of them.

She slapped my face with her rings.

I couldn't shout at the top of my lungs any more so I went around shouting in a whisper. The rings! My face stung from the rings. But that didn't stop me. I wanted them back. I had to keep looking, so I kept my mouth shut and shouted in my mind. But who knew if they could hear?

One day I went out behind the stable and hollered again loud and hard and with all my might.

She ran out of the house, hit me, yanked me by the arm, dragged me in and all the way up the stairs.

She couldn't stand it anymore.

She shut me in my room and locked the door.

What if they came and couldn't find me? I had to get out! Pa! Paa! Papa! Paaa!

Pa never knew what was going on under his nose. Living with the wonders of the future, blocked off by books and theories, he was immune to the present, immune to the practical and–what luck!–blind and deaf to the family contempt for me. Pa didn't know I was bad.

When Geoffrey and Flora fought me, when this-Mother slapped my face, having denied myself tears, my emotion could not be contained and I shrilled like the fairy who foretold death: I howled like a Banshee: "Pa! Pa! Paaa!" Though I knew he was miles away, I screeched for Pa, my island of safety.

"Scream your head off!" this-Mother blazed, "your father's listening, but not to you and not to me. When we're all in the Poor House, your father will be listening to some imbecile preaching about 'the necessity of leisure for the working man!'"

We were on our way to the Poor House.

It wasn't that business in general was bad. The country was growing and flourishing. It was simply that there was something going on at the Mill and Pa couldn't get to the bottom of it.

"A few years ago," Pa said, "I went all over that place: office, warehouse, inventory, the lot. And despite the die-hard opposition of those iniquitous old men, I succeeded in improving conditions."

But now, well ... The warehouse, for example, when grandfather died, he remembered distinctly, had been stocked to the rafters. Yet recently, considering the possibility of a quick sale to get some ready money, he'd gone to inspect it and found the mill running full blast and the warehouse empty. Where was the money? Had he spent all that? The books, he must examine the books! Then he discovered that the office records for the past five years, those old ledgers, had disappeared.

His old bookkeeper was crushed. "Surely, Mr. Charles could not suspect him of fraud!"

And, of course, he didn't ... not fraud. Well, that is ... those hard-headed old men would stay within the law ... for why, when he'd done everything possible to help them, would they want to swindle him? It didn't make sense. Thieves in his office? He wouldn't believe it. He wouldn't insult them ... and he didn't want to be hasty: before he started accusing people—probably innocent of everything but carelessness—he must think about it.

He tried to talk things over with Liza, but for all he loved her and he loved her dearly, she had no vision. All he got from Liza was a tirade on his laziness and his inefficiency. She, clearly, had no understanding of the need for the emancipation of the working man from "the immediate intolerable conditions." But as much as he believed in the future ameliora-tion of those conditions—so much Liza distrusted and despised the working class.

What she couldn't understand was that man's greatest need was leisure: time to study and understand himself and the world. And with this new era of machines, it was possible. It would come. We were approaching Arcadia.

But Liza was incapable of abstract thought. The only thing she could understand was what was happening here and now—and to her. With Liza, everything came down to personalities.

"Do you think they'd have dared with your father?"

"They wouldn't, of course, but who wanted to be like the old man?"

"They know whom they're dealing with, they know you're soft. With all your talk, they're stealing you blind!"

It was possible she was right. But the immediate necessity was to be constructive not destructive. The workers were powerless. It was up to him to educate. But at the moment ...

Economy was the thing. He'd begun but there would have to be more. And now things were really bad. The wages to meet. The household bills. Things were all tangled up. And even after he'd mortgaged the house, the bank was still after him. And on top of everything, the insurance was due on the Mill. He could mortgage the Mill until things got better but he'd have to consider that. Finally, just when he decided he must investigate, without a word to Pa, his Executive Secretary left the country. He went off to a Spa in Germany—for his health.

If he paid the wages, Pa thought, and the household bills, he might

84

just scrape through, that is, if he didn't pay the insurance. After all, the Mill had never burned yet so let the watchman earn his wage. "Drop it," he instructed the insurance agent, "next year, we'll see."

This-Mother was dressed–starched white shirtwaist, long tight navy blue skirt, her coiffed, shining black hair framing her ivory-white face–all ready for the day. But there was something wrong; she was shaking. She woke us in the middle of the night. We had to get dressed and go downstairs and sit in the big dining room in the old black-carved chairs.

The Mill was on fire. A smoky-red blaze filled the midnight sky. We could see it through the great high windows. The shacks were gone and half the city was in danger. We were ruined. We had to be ready to run.

She took a silver bucket out of the sideboard, brought ice and a bottle of wine and put them on a silver tray with glasses and sandwiches.

We heard the buggy. Pa came in. His clothes were black, his face and hands grimy, he smelled like smoke. She would never put up with that.

When she threw herself at him, I screamed.

His big black hands made marks on her white waist.

I jumped, grabbed her, tried to pull her away. Then I let go. She wasn't mad at him!

He dropped his hands and she just stood there.

"We've lost everything."

"Charles," she shook her head. She began to laugh. She kissed him.

I stared. She was transformed. Was she my real-Mother? I grabbed her skirt again. She looked down and pushed my hand away.

Then she threw her arms around him again. "No matter, my love, we have each other."

The Mill burned to the ground.

The destruction of the Mill, and the loss of the mansion and her comfortable life must have been devastating for Mother. She must have been deeply depressed and discouraged trying to cope, for when we left the city, we were truly poor. We were living close to and on the wrong side of the railway tracks about two miles from Saint John in a shabby little house, one-in-a-line of all-the-same drab, gray-brown houses.

Each house had a little backyard and above them, high on a cinder bank, the trains went by all day long and all night. White men, covered black with dust, sat on the open coal cars. When children went up on the tracks to "pick coal," the men threw shovels of coal on to the tracks for them.

One day, Geoffrey and Flora went to pick coal. I followed them. On top of the railway bank the world was wide open and the sky went for miles. Line after line of shining rails stretched out into thin air. From up here, the houses looked sad and old and full of patches–all but one.

On the black earth just below me, between the tracks and the road, there was a house made of glass! The whole house was made of glass and full of flowers! A man was standing beside it, smoking a pipe. When the tracks began to shake and the man began to shout and wave his arms, I turned to look. A long way off and covered with smoke, a roaring train came rushing down the track. The man ran up the bank on his hands and knees. I started to go to him but I tripped and hit my head on the rail.

Mr. Henderson carried me home. Mr. Henderson was like Bertha, only white.

When the lump on my head got better and when this-Mother let me out, I ran down the road to find Mr. Henderson and the glass house. I went every day. Mr. Henderson would never let me touch the flowers. But even outside, I could smell the damp, sweet, spicy smell. There were heaps of black earth around the glass house and lots of pots–some broken. There were bits of worn-out flowers with brown edges. I could pick them up, wipe off the dirt and put them against my face to feel the real feel.

One day, Mr. Henderson took me inside and let me look at the flowers one-by-one until I showed him the one I liked best. He said, "It's my favourite, the white carnation." Then he picked it and gave it to me.

I held the flower in my hand. The full, damp, living, flower. It was so beautiful I didn't know what to do with it. I held it till all the petals got soft and then I kept it to sleep with.

What we lived on now was Pa's mistakes. He'd lent everyone money, but unless he asked for it, we couldn't eat. But would he do it? No.

So this-Mother did. She wore her handsome clothes and she walked two miles to the city and got the money. When she was dressed to go out, she was so beautiful I couldn't look; my throat ached.

Pa was trying to do something too, no one knew what, he went out every day.

There was a new thing in the city called cinematography. Instead of cameras, there were cinematographs. When the pictures were thrown on a lighted screen, they gave the illusion of motion. Large houses were turned into places where you could look at the moving pictures and because it cost a nickel to go in, they were called Nickelodeons.

This-Mother had been collecting money and her feet hurt so she went into the dark Nickelodeon to sit down. When the light came on, she saw Pa. They came home together. They came into the kitchen and she opened the cupboard and began to throw dishes at him. They crashed against the wall. I tried to pull him away but he stood there and laughed. Then she sat down and laughed, too. I ran to hide. She wanted to hurt him.

Right next to our house was Renee and George's house. They kept a pig. He lay on the ground and covered himself with wet, black mud. When the sun dried him, I could help him scratch off the mud with a stick through the fence.

Renee and George's mother always carried a string of beads. They were white with knots in between them and a white cross hanging in the middle. I wanted to touch them but I didn't want to get too close because I didn't like her smell.

One day, the pig broke the fence and Renee and George and their mother went chasing after him. I crawled under the fence and went into their house. The beads were on the kitchen table. They slid, soft as silk, in my hands. I took them.

After that, I didn't dare go near Mr. Henderson or the glass house. Renee and George's mother told everyone on the road that I was a sneak and a thief. I didn't want to go out, even to scrape the pig, but this-Mother made me.

Mr. Henderson came to the house to see me but I ran. When he called to me, I ran faster. I didn't want him to call me a thief.

No one will play with a thief. Everyone chased me away. "Yah! Yah! Yah! You sneak!" It was Geoffrey behind me. "Holler for your real-Mother! She's a big fat, old washer woman by the name of Mrs. Pineapple. Old Mrs. Pineapple left you on the steps."

Flora yelled, too. "You're crazy! You're crazy! You don't belong with us. When Mrs. Pineapple comes, we'll give you back!"

I tried to fight them. They were too big. They hit me and ran. I ran after them screeching and yelling. I tripped and fell. When I got up my pants were wet. I was too old for that.

"Now what!" this-Mother said.

I said, "I didn't do it."

"No? Who did it?"

The only one who wet her pants was Sue. So I tried it. "Sue."

"She's not only a thief and a liar," this-Mother said to Pa, "she's stupid as well."

"She's not stupid," Pa said. "You're harsh with her and she has no recourse. At her age, what alternative does she have but to tell a lie? Actually, she's older than her age."

When I heard that I was nervous. Didn't Pa know Sue couldn't get in my pants? Was Pa stupid, too? How can you be older than you are?

I'd asked him before, but he would never listen. He was reading. "Pa! Where's my mother?"

"What? In the kitchen."

"I don't mean her. I mean my real-Mother!"

"Gad! How old are you?"

"Five."

"Five! Gad! Who would believe" ... He put down his book, took both my hands in his and looked at me. "Do you believe what I tell you?"

"Yes."

"Then listen well, and don't forget. Liza is your real mother. But you need never ask. Look in the glass. You're the image of her. What started this?"

"Nothin'," I said. "I was only foolin'." I ran to the brambles to hide. I did belong to the family. She was my real mother.

Coming home from kindergarten, the man at the vegetable stand sometimes gave me an apple. One day, I copied some words off the sidewalk, on to my slate, and I stopped to show him how smart I was.

He grabbed my slate and rubbed off all the words. "They're bad words," he said.

How could a word be bad?

"Run along," he said, "and do as I say. Don't write them again."

I never stopped to talk to him after that because he spoiled my words. I had to write them all over again.

What made words bad? I loved the sound they made. I went around mouthing them–the kindergarten words and all the ones from the sidewalk and the walls: cat, rat, fat, fukk, lukk ... I tried them out singly and in combination, on children, on cats and dogs. I ran up to two old women sitting on a porch. "Rat!" I shouted, "Cat! Fukk! Sukk!"

"Beat it, you brat! You hear? Don't come around here with your filth! Father's outa work. Mother's a foreigner. What a sight with her clothes! Where'd they come from? The minute he's out of the house, all dressed up and into town. I can guess. An' them starvin'. How are decent people supposed to bring up kids in this neighbourhood!"

I yelled again, "Fukk, Sukk! Rat!"

"Go home! I give you a couple on your backside you won't sit down for a week. Go home! That one, yesterday, down the road with two dogs, you know, hangin' on an' hollerin' for everyone to look. She knows more'n me when I got married."

I shouted, "You big liar! I never hurt those dogs. I was tryin' to pull them apart. They were stuck!"

"Will you go home? You smut! Or do I have to come after you with a stick?"

On Sunday, Mother washed me clean and put on my starched white cambric dress. I begged to stay with her but she sent me outside. I had no one to play with and no place to go. The sun was hot. It had rained and the road was inches deep in mud. I went out to the road, leaned down and touched the soft, black mud. A lovely, rich black. Bertha was black. If Bertha were here, she would hold me. I lay down in the mud in the sun, hugging it and then I turned on my back.

Mother and Pa came out the front door.

"My God! What did I do to deserve that!" She ran into the road, jerked me to my feet and slapped my face. "One thing sure, she doesn't take after me. She's no child of mine!"

Not hers? Where was my real-Mother?

"Liza," Pa sighed. "It's the Austrian peasant who says 'hit her on the head so you won't lame her.' If you must punish the child, don't slap her face. Talk to her."

"Talk!" This-Mother said, bitterly, "Talk! A lot she understands. I can hit her till she's black and blue and she just stands and looks at me. The other children have feelings, but not this one." She gave me a push. "Get into the kitchen and don't move till I clean you up. I'll never put a white dress on you again."

And she never did.

That afternoon, I was in my room in my old dress when Pa came in and took me out. We walked all the way to the park and he showed me the big brown hole where the bears slept all winter. Then we stood behind a lot of men shouting to another man who was talking to them.

"Socialists," Pa said.

If you blink your eyes at the sun, you can see all colours of carnations; splashes of red, and white and yellow on black. I was lying in the brambles doing that when Mr. Henderson floated through my mind. "If you want the flower," he said, "you must plant the seed."

"Pa! Pa! Pa!"

" ... Uhn?"

"Carnations. I want carnation seeds! You're not listening!"

This-Mother came into the room. "My God! I can hear her all over the house. What does she want? What do you want?"

"Nothing."

"Well, get out of this house. Go out and play."

I caught hold of Pa's sleeve and pulled.

"Look at her. She goes to you. She knows better than to come to me. The sneak! Get her out of here before I ... "

My father threw his book on the floor and stood up. He was six feet tall and he looked like a giant and his voice came out like a lion's roar. "Sneak? Gad! Liza! You have no idea what you're saying. Never let me hear you call her that again! Never!" He turned to me. "All right, Philippa, tell me, exactly, what do you want?"

I mixed some of the pig's mud and some water and the carnation seeds Pa brought, in an old pail and stirred and stirred. Then, Sue grabbed it. I hit her, hard, scraped it up, put it back in the pail and added more mud and more water–too much–so I poured some off and put in more mud. But nothing started to grow, so I watered it again.

Sue yelled so hard because I wouldn't let her help that this-Mother came out, dumped the whole thing on the ground and gave her my pail and stick. There was a pot in the brambles without a bottom so I scraped everything up on a board and poured it in that. And I stirred that hothouse and watched it and watered it for weeks but the carnations never grew–not one sprout!

When she puts me to bed I try to stay awake, for if I fall asleep, I am in that place again. I am running, running on the grass in the brilliant sun and the green grass turns gray ... I am in the tunnel.

I am pushing, panting, pulling, trying to run and my legs are rigid. I am pushing, panting, pulling my useless feet and I am running again–hopelessly. For I know what will happen: I am crouched, squeezed under the ground in a narrow, damp tunnel and the earth falls against me, falls in back of me, falls in front of me. I am trapped. I am tearing at the earth, the airless, brown earth that is crushing me. I am alive, suffocating, struggling, fighting, tearing at the earth, screaming, screaming, screaming ...

The dream comes all the time.

But they know why I wake them up. I will not sit down and eat a meal like the other children. I eat too much, or not enough. I gulp my food and run. I will never listen and I will never behave and no one can tell me a thing. And what makes me scream in the night, Pa says, is indigestion. She is not to give me heavy food at night.

But the dream doesn't stop.

Pa went down to the docks and he got a job carrying things. He came home at night with streaks of sweat and dirt on his face. His clothes looked empty and he didn't wear a hat and he brought money, but not enough. One Saturday, he came down the road carrying a big yellow and brown stalk of bananas. I started to run to him but this-Mother pushed me away.

And suddenly the sun and the air and the dust on the road all stood still for she spoke in the strangest voice I had ever heard. "Charles," she said. And she repeated his name softly and tenderly, "Charles, what is to become of us?"

I rushed to the brambles to hide my throat-full of tears: the lump that pushed up and tried to spill out of my eyes. Was she my real mother? I didn't know. Whomever she was, I was lost for I loved her and she didn't love me.

Our speech was unintelligible, Pa said. We were running wild; running all over the place with hoodlums, scum. He couldn't face seeing us grow up in squalor, in a city slum. He had made up his mind to move to the country where it doesn't matter if you're poor. And, "most opportune," there was a village in the wilds of Nova Scotia with a single store and the family who owned it "had a monopoly on the trade." And three old men, Mr. Simms and two others, said they needed a competitor and if Pa would consider it, they would set him up in business, in a general store. In time, he could buy them out. They had a house for us and land. There was plenty of that.

And that was why we went to live in Edgeville.

9

The village of Edgeville comprises about two and a half square miles and lies on a plateau. The country around is all forest: spruce, fir, hackmatack, beech, oak, maple, and birch. It has three roads that meet at a Corner. There is a Corner Lake and two miles to the south, a South Lake. Two miles to the east there's a mill-pond with a saw-mill on it. The railway station is situated two miles from the Corner on the West Road. There are two stores, a post-office, a school and four churches: Baptist, Methodist, Catholic and Church of England.

The population, including our family, numbers three hundred and forty-two, plus a family of Indians who live outside the village on the South Lake. Here is a people so upright they refuse spiritual compromise: each reclines safe in the bosom of the only true church, be it Baptist, Methodist, Church of England or Catholic. Everyone goes to church. I exclude the Indians and Pa.

Our store is about a quarter of a mile from the Corner on the East Road. It is a two-storey building, rectangular in shape. The narrow front has two big show-windows, one on either side of the entrance. When you enter, you are in a long room with counters along both sides and rows of shelves on the walls. One side is for dry goods, the other for groceries. There is a big iron stove in the centre of the store and, in line with it, towards the rear, a wide oak staircase that leads to the second floor. The office is back of the stairs on the right. Left of the stairs, through a heavy, sliding door is the rough, cold unfinished storehouse. The ceilings upstairs and down are made of sheets of pressed tin, patterned in squares and curlicues and painted white.

The store is full of everything: barrels of tamarinds and molasses, salt pork and kerosene oil, big round cheeses and spices and canned salmon, vegetables and jam. There are middlings (cow feed) and oats, flour, men's work pants and boots. There are pots and pans, pails and Po's (chamber pots). Dress goods, "rats" for the women to make rolls, when put under the hair—flannelette with roses on it and muslin and gingham and Dr. Denton's coveralls for children to sleep in. And best of all, there is a big glass case filled with all kinds of candy.

Initially Mother went to the store to help Pa, who never knew where to put things and could never find things. Pa was so inept, that she took charge of the store and as a storekeeper she was unique: she never opened her mouth. Moreover, she was so easily shocked that people came for miles to tell her things, just to see the look on her face. Mother could hear twenty identical stories from as many people over the same number of years and look, at the last one, as startled as a virgin doe. After a few years, she knew everyone's business, including their sexual and medical histories, from one end of the county to the other. And no one knew hers, or anyone else's from her. She was respected and admired.

Pa also got on fine in the village. Since all he talked about was what was wrong with the world and how to fix it, no one (except Mrs. West) paid any attention to him. If, by mistake, the barber or the station master showed an interest, Pa would load him up with as many large volumes as he could carry; books that–if he recognized the content–no respectable member of the community would be caught dead with. Pa never missed them once he'd read them, but if anyone was fool enough to return one, Pa would ask his opinion of it. People were a little wary of him.

Pa did his part in the store. He got up early in the morning, made the fire, swept and cleaned everything, opened boxes, sorted things, carried in enough wood for the day, and then left. Once home, he sat down at the table, with a book, to eat breakfast, stood up still reading, bumped his way from the dining-room to the sitting-room, lay down on the sofa and left Edgeville.

Our house is more than a hundred years old and it sags. It is on the dusty East Road, a long city block from the store, and it stands between two fields. There is a big barn behind it with nothing in it but hay and, back of the barn, a swamp that runs down to the wood. The poor little wood, the scrubby airless, thick-growing, shade-maimed wood, stretches out and out beyond the eye. At night, the swamp mist jumps with burning flies and the trees creep closer.

It is summer. The sun is hot and the fields are full of daisies and strawberries. There is a strip of grass in front of our house. Just the spot to grow carnations. By the time I got it dug up, Pa would have the seeds. The first thing I ask for in Edgeville is a hoe.

I was working in my garden. Two little girls came tripping up the sidewalk and stopped in front of me. I stopped digging.

"What's your name?"

"Philippa."

"I'm Loretta and she's Gladys." Loretta and Gladys stood tight together and stared at me. "We've got new dresses." They were starched shining clean.

I replied, "My mother is going to buy me a new dress." A lie! When the words came out of my mouth, my stomach jittered. I took a quick look around but there was no sign of Flora or Geoffrey. I breathed again.

"What grade are you in?"

"I don't know." I had never been to school.

"You don't know what grade you're in? You're crazy!" They doubled up and howled with glee. "She don't know what grade she's in!"

It was awful how everyone knew, right away, that I was crazy. I stretched my mouth into a false grin.

They collapsed: one fell flat on the grass and the other fell on top of her. Finally, they stood up. "Are all your family like you?"

"Yes ... Uh ... " I lost my breath. What if Flora and Geoffrey heard that! "Uh ... No. They're not. I mean NO!"

"Don't you know?"

"No!" Was that what I meant? "I mean, yes! They're not like me."

"No?" they shouted, "Yes? Don't you know? Don't you know anything?" Abruptly, clutched together, they rushed down the sidewalk. They stopped under the big willow tree.

I must run! Hide! Too late, they were coming back. I braced myself, waited.

They rushed me. Each put a strangling arm around my neck. "We've decided," they shrilled, "to be your two best friends."

I stood between them, shaking.

Mrs. McCarthy was our housekeeper. She only stayed because she got used to us, but "anyone else," she said, "who wanted to work for us should take a fool's advice and stay away. If I had known the day I came what I was in for, I would never have took off me hat!"

Every Sunday when Mrs. McCarthy took the day off, Mother walked into the kitchen and had hysterics. Nothing was where she'd left it, everything was upside down and the groceries had vanished. (Mrs. McCarthy always borrowed a suitcase full of food to take to her daughters.)

Mrs. McCarthy's wages were ten dollars a month. After twelve years, she asked for eleven.

Mother couldn't believe her ears. "That old thief!"

But Pa thought it just; and later on, when she was "absolutely useless" and Martha ran the house, Pa, "out of his mind!" gave her fifteen.

94

Except for Mother–who made her so nervous she couldn't speak–as a family, there were things about us that Mrs. McCarthy couldn't "abide." Careless of my presence (she ranked me with the furniture) she voiced her disapproval to Mrs. Porter, her bosom friend.

Mrs. McCarthy had no confidence in Pa with "his unnatural habits! When every respectable man is out doing a day's work, where is he an' what does he want? In the parlour!" Mimicking him. "'A pot of tea, Mrs. McCarthy, an' a extra pot of water. An' slice the lemon.' Lemon yet! Who ever heard about putting lemon in tea? Can I give him a decent cup of strong tea with milk and sugar? Oh, no! Not Him!

"An' the other one, the doctor's wife, that stuck-up Mrs. West, comin' in to drink tea with him. They gabble like lunatics. There's a pair for you. An' that lovely lady in the store, what do she know? Nuthin'! She don't turn a hair! I tell you, Annie, there's more to it than meets th' eye."

Mrs. McCarthy was one of my chief sources of information. She knew something about everything and everything about everyone. Also, and this in common with Mother, she had my "true interest to heart." But whereas Mother was apt to slap my face and let it go at that, Mrs. McCarthy was always willing to give me any number of indications as to how to change my "natural character to something human."

Other people's opinions were all right. Words slipped from their lips and disappeared into thin air, leaving no trace. Something happened to mine. Once voiced, they were there to stay and they hung, crude and naked oddities in a suddenly sulphurated mist–smelling of things unchurched. In our house by the railway tracks, George and Renee had informed me that the devil was black. With memories of Bertha still close, I proceeded to proclaim my undying affection for him. This unsettled Mrs. McCarthy.

Mrs. McCarthy could smell the brimstone on me. "If I go stark-ravin' crazy," she declared, "an' I expect to, they can come and get me!"

But the religious debate took second place when the unwed girl next door had a baby. No one would tell me where Cynthia got the baby and Mrs. McCarthy's conversation with Mrs. Porter did nothing to solve the mystery. First, they agreed it didn't have a father. Then they wanted to know who the father was! But how the ants got into it, as far as I was concerned, took it into the penumbra.

"Tch, tch," said Mrs. McCarthy, "that Cynthia. I warned her. Runnin' out every night. Tch, tch! Another baby without a father. Annie, if anyone was to ask, I'd say Annie Porter would know. Tell me, Annie, who's the father of that child?"

"Minnie, you ask me? Minnie, you set yourself down on an ant heap, you ask which ant bit you?"

I had such trouble trying to find out where Cynthia's baby came from and why it didn't have a father that I had almost ceased to bother when it occurred to me I hadn't tapped the original source of wit and wisdom. He was a half block ahead of me on his way to the store.

"Pa!" My voice suitably pitched to attract his attention. "Pa! Why do some babies have fathers and some babies don't?" He turned around. I ran to catch up with him. "Hey, Pa, why do some babies have fathers and ... "

"All babies have fathers."

"No, they don't. Cynthia's baby ... "

"Oh, that." He was talking to something back of my head. I twisted my neck to look. Nothing. Trees. "It's illegitimate. No, it's legitimate all right. It's illegal."

"What?" Of all the nerve! Right in the middle of the conversation, he was gone. I stook there and howled: "Pa, Pa!"

He turned again. "Now what? I just explained it to you. Cynthia's baby has no legal father."

"No father? But you just told me all babies ... " He was gone again. Everyone said I was crazy. Was he crazy, too?

The more I thought about it, the madder I got. Once and for all I would get to the bottom of this baby business. I went back to the house.

Mrs. McCarthy was bending over the dishpan having one of her mumbling fits.

I heaved myself up on the edge of the sink. "Where did Cynthia get her baby?" I demanded. "Can I get your teeth?" Her teeth were to talk with. Mother gave her tea the first day she came and she took them out and put them on the saucer. But she has good manners; she asked first, "Would you mind if I take out these dirty teeth? I had them in me mouth the whole mornin'."

"Git off me sink!" She pushed me with her elbow.

I held on. "Mrs. McCarthy! Where did Cynthia get her baby?"

"Git!"

"Where?"

"Git away! Runnin' loose in the woods. Git down!"

They kept telling me it was dangerous to play in the woods. "Can I get your teeth?"

"Git off me sink!"

"Will I get a baby? If I play in the woods, will I get one?"

"You'll git one awright y'do what Cynthia did!" She pushed me with her elbow.

"What? What did she do? Tell me!"

"What they all do!" She glared at me. "Slept with men!"

"What!" If sleeping with a man was enough to get a baby, it might be dangerous to walk down the road near one! "Do you only get them near men? Can you get them near women, too? How?"

"They catchin'. Go 'way! No!"

"What? Catching! Who did Cynthia catch hers from? A woman? Is that why it hasn't got a father?"

"Go 'way! Nobuddy! Git!"

"But you just said ... Why hasn't it got a father?"

She gave me a good push and I fell off the sink.

"Out of me kitchen!"

"Why is it worse if they don't have fathers? Did Cynthia get hers from a mother?" But she was after me with the dish rag. I had to run. But the whole thing was clear at last. Cynthia's baby didn't have a father because she caught it from a mother! Outside of Edgeville, the settlements were full of girls who had babies without fathers. They caught them from each other like chicken pox. I told myself, frantically, to remember to stay in the village where babies without fathers were fairly scarce and never to go to the settlements where they were thickest.

Not long after this, Mrs. Porter, who generally tried to get rid of me, turned into a real friend. "Pill," she called. Her chest was hanging out of her front window. "Yoo-hoo, Pill, come here. Go 'round back of the house. I got something for you."

She was waiting at the back door when I got there.

"You cross your heart and hope to die?"

"Yes, Ma'am." I crossed my heart. (I crossed my fingers on the hand behind my back. Die later–not today.)

"Now don't you let on to Minnie McCarthy, the old bat! Ha! Ha!" She gave me an entrancing wink. "Or I'll be taking her jaw for the rest of my natural days. Look in the woodshed."

It was dark in the woodshed and for a minute or two I couldn't see. Then I saw them. Kittens! "I'll take them." I gathered them up in my arms.

"Here!" She started unloading me. "You wanna get us both scalped? You know Minnie's opinion of cats."

Mrs. McCarthy's opinion of cats was no secret: "Cats attract rats."

"Oh, but ... "

"You can have one. And if I ever hear a word out of you, about where you got it! You promise? You found it. Hear?"

"I'll never, never tell. I promise Ma'am. Gee, it's like magic. I always wanted a cat." I took the one crawling on my neck. I couldn't get it loose. "I'll call her Magic." I could hardly wait to get home.

"Magic!" shouted Mrs. Porter. She snatched the kitten out of my hands. "They's no such name! You call that varmint Maggie, an' get it out of here. Just a minute!" She turned Maggie upside-down. "I knowed it! Another batch before you can say spit!" She dropped Maggie on the floor.

And in almost no time, Maggie turned into a cat and had a batch of kittens. I asked Mrs. McCarthy if she was liable to have any more.

"Any more! Any more! That varmint will go on havin' kittens every five minutes for the next fifteen years!"

She was right. In the grasp of inexorable fate, Maggie kept on having kittens. One litter hardly dry before she had the next, and she always wanted me to help her have them. Persistent, yowling, she followed me around until I went to the playroom with her. She had a nest there.

Maggie would get up between kittens and dig her claws into me. I kept a lot of dress between me and the claws. Her kittens arrived in soaking-wet-white cotton wool and, sitting on the floor with her, pulling it off, helping her to dry them and trying, as Pa said, to 'reason it out,' gloom settled on me. I couldn't forget Mrs. Porter's story about the lady who had a baby with a pig's head. All she did to get it was feed the pigs.

I got much closer to Maggie than that and I couldn't help but be upset. What if I got a baby with a cat's head or a cat with a baby's head? I kept hoping that if I got anything, it would be a plain cat so I could give it to Maggie and no one would find out.

Someone knocked. "Philippa." Johnathan stood in the doorway.

I glanced at my watch. Almost five o'clock. It would soon be light. I had been writing for hours.

He said, quietly, "You haven't slept."

"No." I could feel my heart accelerating, pounding.

"I've been watching the light under your door." He pushed the door shut behind him and started across the room to me.

In the half-light from my desk lamp, I could see him looking at my left hand. I had a feeling of déjà vu: like Pa, he was about to rip off my ring and throw it away! I said, hastily, "It's my mother's engagement ring. Leave it alone!"

He stopped. "What! Do you think I'm about to rob you? I intend to marry you."

I began to laugh. "Uh ... Really? Oh, dear ... " I couldn't stop laughing. "Th' th' this is ... Heavens! This is so sudden!" I was about to have a laughing fit I couldn't control.

"Sssh! You'll wake the house."

"S'sorry!" I caught my breath, stopped for a moment. "S'sorry. I can't ... "

Fish woke up and jumped in my lap and I shoved my face against his furry neck. If I didn't stop laughing, I'd begin to cry. "W'What's your name?"

"My name! It's Milford. Johnathan Edward Milford. I thought you knew."

"No. No, I didn't. But it's good of you to enlighten me. Actually, I never heard of you." I was laughing again.

"No matter. My name has nothing to do with it."

"What?"

"You hadn't been in this place five minutes when you knew that."

I took a deep breath.

He was staring at me.

It was pointless to lie. I was as aware of him as he of me. But ... it would be ruinous for me to enter into any sort of relationship. If he found out I'd spent six months in a mental institution that would finish it. I said, "Yes."

He crossed the room and took Fish out of my lap. "God! How could you do that to me!"

"What?"

"That ring!"

"What!" But that was howlingly funny. We were both laughing.

"You're mad!"

Away from me, he sat down on a chair. "Would you prefer ... "

"That you be more circumspect? Yes."

"Would you prefer to talk now and sleep later?"

"I was just about to go to bed."

"Right. I'll tell the kitchen not to disturb you. I'll keep Fish." He carried him out and shut the door.

I stared at the closed door. He moved like a shadow; silent and swift, with the hidden strength of a ballet dancer. I'd noticed it before. He exuded power.

Lottie hadn't lied. I knew the truth about him. But that truth wasn't for us–for me. He hadn't said it but I knew ... not love, perhaps, but something primitive between us. Compelling. But just for tonight–today– I'd pretend we were in love because I was so incredibly happy.

10

Half asleep, I pushed and pounded at the door–a revolving door, whirring over my head–when I opened my eyes, it was still there ... a helicopter. I didn't want to wake up. I lay in a cocoon of warmth, of happiness. I felt sixteen again. Johnathan!

I got out of bed and pulled aside the heavy draperies. The storm was over and the sun was shining. The world was a sparkling, dazzling universe of white. I could hear voices, dogs barking, the heavy drone of machinery; power saws, snow ploughs. The helicopter had landed on the cleared tennis court.

I glanced at my watch. Three o'clock. I'd slept eleven hours! I felt wonderful! Coffee. I got back into bed and rang for the maid. What heaven to be in a civilized house. The helicopter ... Johnathan's? Perhaps not.

Lottie knocked at my door and came in, smiling. "You slept well? Good. Cook's sending your breakfast."

"Thank you. The best night's, uh, day's, rather, that I've had in years."

She sat down on the bed and took my hand. "You're happy?"

"Yes, but ... "

"Forget the gossip ."

"You talked to Johnathan?"

"I believe he's set the date for your wedding. So tell me."

"That's nonsense. There's nothing to tell. I didn't even know his last name until this morning."

"Go on."

"About Johnathan? This whole business is ridiculous! I have no intention of getting married–to him or anyone else. Look, have they cleared the road to the village?"

"We don't bother in December. We're self-sufficient here, so there's really no need. We have the greenhouses and Johnathan flies in and out. You know, Philippa, we had no idea yesterday that you'd attempt that road. We were expecting you to call from the village. And, at the moment, what with the storm and the high winds, it will be impassable. You won't get through. Voila! Your breakfast." Lottie stood up to leave.

"Wait! There's a helicopter out there. Can I get a ride to New York or somewhere?"

"It's Johnathan's. He's about to ... "

We heard the engine start, heard the helicopter lift off.

"There he goes now. I promised I'd keep you here 'till he gets back but I want you to stay anyway, for me."

"Oh, well, thank you. I mean, I'd like to stay. I wanted to stay until Christmas. How long will he be gone? How long before they clear the road? Lottie, what shall I do?"

She began to laugh. "Not capricious, I think, but a trifle irresolute. Eat your breakfast. Put on warm clothes and we'll take a walk. And don't worry. He's on his way to France. We'll be alone for days now."

Lottie and I went a long way around the lake. There's something magical about this place. Lottie behaved like a kid, knocking me down, running to avoid me, laughing when I caught up and shoved her over. We shrieked and yelled and fell and got up and threw snowballs. The big dogs have adopted Fish and they all ran with us and jumped all over us. Just what it took to restore me to good solid sanity. But I got a fright on the way back. It was almost dark when we heard the helicopter.

"Johnathan?"

"Don't worry. I'm sure not. He'll be in France in the morning. One of our neighbours, perhaps, they fly over now and then for a drink."

But it wasn't the neighbours. It was the florist with white roses for Mrs. Bentham. No message.

What flashed through my mind was that ridiculous Victorian painting of a half-naked girl leaning against a bronze door, autumn leaves falling all around, entitled: *Love Locked Out*. For I have decided: my life is on hold until I find out why–after six perfect years–I slipped over the edge. The answer lies in my past, and I must see it objectively before I make a move. Which means that I must go on writing.

———————

Impelled to solitude by my fear of pregnancy, I had to wait so long for an empty road that very often I was late for school. One day I was tearing along so fast, I didn't see Mr. Simms until he stood in front of me. I swerved, lost my balance and skidded into the ditch.

He said, "Oops! Are you hurt?"

I pulled my dress over my scraped knees.

He had a globe of colour in each hand.

I pointed. "What are they?"

"Love apples," he said, "or that's what we used to call them. We thought they were poisonous and grew them in the flower garden. They're tomatoes." He put one into my outstretched hand. "You may eat it," he said. "You're the little Jerrold girl, aren't you?"

The taut, sun-warmed, Christmas-red fruit had a dusty green star on top and a musty-ripe smell. "Yes, I'm Philippa. Have you any more?"

"Why ... all you want. I had no idea you'd ever tasted them. Very few people cultivate them. Look, you're late for school. Quick, be off!"

My treasures clutched to my bosom, I fled. But I had no thought of eating the tomatoes. I wanted, greedily, to look at them.

Mr. Simms lived in a faded-brown frame house behind a big, green hedge. His head was haloed in light; his hair and beard snow white. He was a widower, the father of Miss Simms, an old maid who owned a black Spitz. He would stop almost every day to talk and to give me tomatoes and flowers. Then he disappeared.

"He's sick in bed," Mrs. McCarthy informed me.

"Oh! Then I have to see him."

"You have to see him!" Mrs. McCarthy mimicked. "The brass of it! You think Dr. West will leave a seven-year-old snot to run around in the old gentleman's sick room? Hmff!"

I hung around on the sidewalk in front of the house. I wanted to go in, but Mrs. McCarthy said they didn't want me. People went in and out. Dr. West came out on the porch with Miss Simms. His head went up and down and he didn't smile. He was mad at her.

The Spitz yapped and she smacked him. Dr. West hurried down the path and stopped. He put his hand on my head for a second. I know why dogs like it.

Then Mr. Simms died and they were going to bury him. I had to see him. If she wouldn't let me in, I would go away and then come back and crawl in the window. I went up the path to the door and knocked. I was frightened of her.

Miss Simms opened the door.

"Ma'am, I have to see Mr. Simms."

She stood and stared at me. Then she grabbed my shoulder marched me in, shoved me into the parlour and left.

Mr. Simms was all alone in a black coffin. The blinds were down and there were candles burning. He had on his best black suit and a black tie. His face was white–dead white–like his hair and beard.

"Mr. Simms." I waited. Could he hear? I wanted to touch his hand but it was covered. I touched his face. Then I jumped back because it was damp and hard and cold. But I knew I had to tell him.

In the end, I put my fingers on his cheek and held them there so he'd know I didn't mind how cold he felt. I wanted him to know I liked him even if he was dead and not just for the tomatoes and flowers.

They buried him but I kept expecting to see him. I'd go to the cemetery, hang on the gate and look in.

One day the fat woman who lived in the house across the road came and spoke to me. "You're here a lot," she said. "Are you looking for someone?"

"Mr. Simms."

"Oh, my uncle. I loved him, too." She took my hand, led me across the road to her house. "I take him flowers." She was going to have a baby. When it came she wanted me to see it, and I was to call her Aunt Augusta.

One morning Mrs. McCarthy told me the baby had come, but Aunt Augusta and the baby were both dead.

I didn't believe it, I ran to her house but so many people were going in and out that I didn't dare go in.

The next day people were still there in a long line and I couldn't wait any longer. I stepped in to the middle of the line and followed a lady up the steps, through the front hall and in to the sun room on the left.

Surrounded by white flowers, Aunt Augusta was lying with her babe on her arm, on a white satin pillow. And loving her, I had no feeling of sorrow or loss. And no feeling of haste. I stood staring at her unbelievable beauty. And slowly, slowly, the heavy white lids lifted and I saw her eyes fully revealed; the luminous, round brown iris' fully defined. Her eyes looked directly in to mine, held them a moment or two and then slowly, slowly, the lids descended. Her eyes closed again.

How long in retrospect did I watch them? I woke one night screaming. Aunt Augusta! They had buried her alive! What if she woke in her grave? Her fear! Her agony! I should have told somebody. I had murdered her!

I couldn't go the cementary again. I couldn't talk. I didn't know what to do with myself.

And then that bewitching image of flower perfection, still in my head, became an obsession: if I did not have a real carnation, I couldn't stand it any longer. I would die.

The carnation seeds came the following spring and I planted them all, but I watered so heavily and the sun was so hot that the earth turned to baked, cracked clay. Nothing grew.

103

Pa ordered more seeds. And the next spring, when the seeds arrived–I was almost nine years old–I studied the back of the package. I read about soil, about staking them up and about watering after the sun went down. And now I was cautious. I divided the seeds into three lots for plantings. I was determined to have carnations.

I planted early and there was no frost. They grew. One morning, I found them pushing through the soil. But at noon that day when I got home from school, Pa's hens were scratching in my garden. My carnations were gone.

Pa had a dozen hens. Mrs. McCarthy prepared their food and he fed them because he liked to stand and watch them eat. I didn't want to hurt his feelings so I didn't say anything hateful when I told him what his hens had done. I just asked him to mend the wire so they couldn't get out of the pen.

I planted again and we had good weather and again the seeds sprouted. And again, I came home to find the hens in my garden. I got down on my knees and sifted the earth, carefully, through my fingers. I didn't find a single sprout. I dropped my books, stumbled down the path to the back of the barn, fell on my face and wept. After a while, I wiped my grimy hands and face with meadow grass, got the last of my seeds and went to see Pa.

As usual, he was flat on his back on the sofa, reading. "Pa, listen! I want to talk to you. Pa!" He always said he could hear just as well reading as looking at me, but I had to make sure. I grabbed his shoulder and shook him. "Pa! Pa! Are you listening?"

His eyes kept sliding back and forth over his book. " ... Uh, ... certainly."

"Well, listen, I'm sick of it and I'm not foolin' either. Look! My carnations are gone again. This is twice and I've only got a few seeds left. It's your fault. It's the hen-pen. The wire is full of holes. Look, if your hens eat my carnations again, I'll kill them. All of them. Do you hear? Pa! Do you hear me? I'll kill your hens."

Silence. His eyes kept going back and forth over his book.

"Did you hear me?"

"Unh."

"Did ... "

"Quite right. Go ahead."

"What? Do you promise? Are you going to fix it?" I snatched at his book. "Pa, did you hear me?"

"Let go of my book." He frowned at me over his spectacles. One of the sides was broken–he was always sitting on them–and he had them tied around his head with a piece of string. He hung on so I couldn't pull the book out of his hands.

"Pa, listen to me. I'm serious."

"Confound it! Can't I have five minutes … "

"I just told you! I … "

"Go away, Uh … "He got that resigned, sarcastic look on his face. "Philippa! Do me a favour, tell me next week."

I hung onto his book. "Will you promise? Will you lock up your hens so they can't get out? Did you hear me? I told you, I'll kill them. All of them. Are you listening?"

"Of course I'm listening. Good-bye."

I let go of his book and his eyes started going back and forth again. I didn't know if he had heard or not, but I knew he wasn't going to listen anymore. I went out and, dreading to part with them, I planted my last carnations seeds. But wary now, I brought sticks and built a fence around them.

And one evening about ten days later, I found a few gray-green shoots. I hung over them and though I wanted to–they were so delicate– I wouldn't allow myself to touch them.

The next morning on my way to school, clutching my books, I ran to look at my garden. The hens had knocked down the sticks and were digging in it. I dropped my books and threw myself at them.

Fighting the one I caught, all flapping wings and dirt and scratching feet in my face, I lost my anger but I did not lose my resolve to kill it. I got into the kitchen and I got a sharp knife and, outside again, I sawed off its head and threw it as far as I could throw, into the swamp. Then I washed the blood from my hands and clothes, picked up my books and went to school.

I paid no attention to the hen-killing taunts flung at me that day because I was occupied with an impossible problem. I had told Pa I would kill all his hens. Now I must do it. But how? How to endure again that helpless, terrified white-sliding, vulnerable-tender feathered flesh? How?

Pa was sitting on the counter swinging his legs. There was no one else in the store. I went in after school to get some candy. He kept looking at me, but he didn't speak until I put my hand on the door to go out.

"Did you tell the Baptist Minister to kill my chickens?"

I let go of the door, walked over and stood in front of him. "Yes."

"That's what he said."

"I thought Mr. Lovatt was a good one to do it because he's thin."

"Thin? Just what exactly did you tell him?"

"I told him he could stand a little more food. All I said was I noticed your hens got in his garden, and when he caught one there, he was to kill it and eat it. Has he killed them all?"

"Not all. Three. He came in to thank me for the chicken dinners. He thought I knew."

"But you did know. I told you I would kill them all. Did I have to do it myself?"

Under the peculiar smile, Pa had a funny look on his face. Shamed? Sad? Hurt? "Don't you remember, Pa? You said you were listening."

I turned and left the store. He hadn't listened, of course, or he'd forgot. And now to keep my word, I had to kill the rest of his hens.

I threw the candy in the ditch and ran for the barn. I couldn't kill anymore hens. My knees were shaking but I got to the barn. Things were going round in circles. I was dizzy. I couldn't stand the pain in my heart. Had my heart been bashed in? I threw my anguished body to the ground, and sobbing, writhing, convulsed, the hot tears running down my face, I lay there biting and chewing at the grass, tearing the earth with my nails.

The carnation seeds that came to the store early the next spring stayed there for years. No one bought them and I didn't touch them; my heartfelt need to grow carnations had somehow been displaced.

11

F lora was the prettiest girl in the village–with the charm of an angel–she was so popular that where she led, Geoffrey and half the kids in Edgeville followed. But not me. Flora made no secret at home or abroad that she considered me the family misfortune.

I was harassed by two fatal emotions: I loved my sister and I delighted in her conspicuous success but at the same time, to avoid absolute serfdom, I had to fight her to a standstill. In infinite frustration, time after time, I saw an argument between us elevate Flora to a shining spot amongst the saints and drop me to limbo. If I persisted in declaring my right to be my own boss to Pa, all I got was, "I have yet to hear the other side." But since he never asked the other side to report, how bring her to account?

There was something wrong with me: I was different. And in desperation, finally, I decided I'd be like everyone else if it killed me: I would listen carefully, remember how everyone talked, and tell the absolute truth about everything. I told Pa I had decided to reform.

"It's a sound decision," Pa approved, "astute, and it would be just as well to keep it a secret between us; further, with the wisdom of the ages at your disposal," he gestured towards the book cases, "it should be easy."

I started taking Pa's books to the hayloft to search out the answer to my permanent dilemma–how not to be me–but they were heavy going. I kept coming back to Pa. But he was on the same old track, he'd never get down to the case in hand or make a personal judgement. It was always, "The Bible says 'Fret ye not for the evil-doer.' King Solomon says ... "

Moreover, my passion for truth did not better, to a noticeable extent, my family's opinion of me. The only result of my insisting on "Truth" was that I got in more fights than before and fought more violently than before.

I even went so far on the stony path of honesty as to alienate the affections of my two best friends. Those happy intervals when Loretta and Gladys and I were on speaking terms grew rarer in number and shorter in time.

The rifts between us could not be kept secret. And just as popularity breeds popularity, so the opposite breeds the opposite. Except for a few old people, and cats and dogs, everyone in the village knew, and I knew, too, that I could never be a beloved part of Edgeville. Indeed, I was hard put to appear indifferent to the dislike or ridicule of those whom I loved and admired.

I put on a bold front. I developed an exoskeleton. I shut all the seething, boiling confusion and pain. But I teeter-tottered in fearful indecision. My fault? Theirs? Who right? Who wrong? The pressures within me built up, built up ... and exploded in shrieks of rage, in foolish laughter. My pain at rejection was expressed now in increasingly erratic and excited behaviour. Mother kept telling me I was so nervous I was driving her crazy. She had the right idea but the wrong people. I was the one who was going crazy.

I found solace in secret dreams. I took refuge in solitary excursions, but I was a rude child, loud, unstable, desperately lonely and with that very real physical pain in my left breast–my heart–that never left me day or night.

It was Sunday morning, sunny, and Mrs. McCarthy had just driven off in the buggy to visit her daughters. For some unusual reason, Pa was in the kitchen in his shirt sleeves, shaving. He had placed a small looking-glass on the window sash. He soaped his face with a brush and stropped his razor.

"Pa, let me shave you."

He turned, hesitated, looked at the long blade, handed it to me and sat down. "Be careful. One false move and you'll be an orphan."

"And where will you be?"

"Me? In heaven. Playing chess with the angels. Stop laughing! You'll cut me."

I put the blade carefully against his cheek. "Pa, am I crazy?"

Blood came through the soap. "Ye Gods! I cut you!"

He took the razor from my hand, stood up and looked in the glass. "It's nothing. A scratch. I'd better shave myself."

"Pa, am I crazy? Everyone keeps saying ... "

"Gad! Everyone!"

"Yes, but ... I mean ... "

"Everyone? You exclude me? Good. Listen, Philippa, a staggering proportion of the citizenry of Edgeville ... " He started sliding soap and stubble off his face. "Uhn ... their mentality, characterized by a smug infatuation with inherited misconceptions ... a strangle-hold, isolating the brain, incapacitating thought. That, combined with mythomania makes 'everybody's' opinion something less than worthless. If you listen ... "

"Mythomania? What's that?"

"Don't parade your ignorance. You're too old to ask questions. Look it up."

"Oh, Pa, why don't you just tell me?"

"And have you missing my more important words of wisdom? No. Find out for yourself. If you live in a country, you should speak the language. Mythomania, yes, I suppose it's universal: a mass disease."

"All right, I'll look it up but all the same, everyone says ... "

"Everyone! Phah! Everyone has a Pinchbeck philosophy. Don't tell me you never heard of Mr. Pinchbeck!" He stopped shaving and gave me a dirty look. "Look him up, too. Everyone! Gad! Everyone is oblivious to anything outside of Edgeville; oblivious and living in oblivion. As far as Edgeville is concerned, the printing press need never have been invented. Edgeville! Nothing but ... sanctimonious claptrap. You know what claptrap means?"

"I could guess."

"You'd be wrong."

"Oh, PA! You're awful! I ask you a question and you never say a thing! Why does everyone say I'm crazy? Why?"

"Why? Simple. You weren't born here."

"But they only say it about me."

"It makes us all suspect, liable to odd notions and unaccountable behaviour. But the other children conform ... You think about trying it. Look, I'll tell you something that may clarify it for you. Take the word 'barbarian,' the name given by the early Greeks to foreigners. The word is probably onomatopoetic, meaning it imitates natural sound. To the unaccustomed ear, a strange language sounds like uncouth babbling–bar-bar–and so, 'barbarians.' You know, the Romans were included in the term. The word soon assumed an evil meaning, becoming associated with the vices and savage natures of which they believed their enemies to be possessed. In Edgeville, not only your speech but your manners are different: you are a barbarian."

"No, crazy. Is it my manners?"

"Local idiom. Same thing. If it makes you feel any better, Diogenes, the Cynic, said, 'Most men were within a finger's breadth of being mad; for if a man walked with his middle finger pointing out, folks would think him mad; not so if it were his forefinger.' Does that answer your question? Does that satisfy you?"

"I wish I knew how to change."

"Try to understand. You're mature for your age. You have a

considerable capacity for independent thought. No one will lead you by the nose, but that makes you unacceptable to the majority who refuse to accept anyone different. So ignore them. Ignore the invidious bleating. Ignore mob morality–immorality, more like. Ignore mass opinion. You will find it's generally uninformed. One day, you'll leave Edgeville and you'll discover an enlightened world. Look, put these things away for me, will you? I'm late and I promised your mother we'd take a walk."

I started cleaning up. What he said was ... what was wrong was that my speech was different and my behaviour. How could I change my speech? But I could change my manners. Strange, I'd never thought of that before.

It was noon, the village dinner hour. We sat at the table, each with a book propped in front of us. No one talked. We were all reading, but I was watching Pa. No one in Edgeville read at meals but Pa did and I was sure he had good manners.

Mrs. McCarthy came into the dining room and put a plate with meat and vegetables–all piled up–on the table in front of him. He looked at it, dropped his book, picked up the plate, turned slightly and threw it, dinner and all, out of the window. Our dining room windows looked out over the meadow.

I knew why he did it, of course–either the plate had a crack in it "a breeding place for germs"–or, as he'd explained to me, he was sometimes "overcome" by Mrs. McCarthy's presentation.

"Mrs. McCarthy."

"Yes, sir."

"Bring me some eggs."

"What happened to your dinner?"

"Don't worry about my dinner. Bring me some eggs."

"There won't be a whole plate left in the house," Mrs. McCarthy grumbled. "Nor a cup nor a saucer! Everything has to be examined with a magnifying glass for fear it's got a scratch on it, or it goes out into the meadow. I've et out of pots all me life and what happened to me? Nothin'! I'm fine. What was wrong with his good dinner? Try and find out! Eggs, yet, in the middle of the day!"

I wondered ... perhaps Pa's manners were only good for a big city? He wasn't too popular. I'd better shift my sights. Everyone loved mother. I'd go help her in the store.

I leaned against the counter, listening. Yes, she really had manners. Wonderful. All harshness muted, soft, concealed. Hers, a voice through a veil.

"Gracious," she said. "My goodness, Mrs. Marvel, how awful for you."

"As true as I'm standin' in front of your two eyes, Mrs. Jerrold." She glanced at me. "Little pitchers ... Well, you know, it was me time ... "

"You poor woman," my mother murmured. "What you went through. It makes my blood curl."

Would she never learn to speak English? "Sst!" I jerked her dress. "Sssst!"

"What is it? Let go of my dress."

"Curdle," I whispered, "curdle."

"Curdle? What are you talking about?"

"Your blood."

"My blood!" Mother began to laugh but she was mad. "Really, Mrs. Marvel! This child!" She turned so that Mrs. Marvel couldn't see her face and all her manners fell off. "Get out of here! And stay out! And don't come back!"

Whenever I tried to improve anyone–or myself–all I got for my trouble was more trouble!

"Ittsy-tittsy-too," Flora minced around the room, pursing her mouth, "it's too, too, toot. That's you, Pill, you Pill! You sure have changed all of a sudden. Company manners! Smeared all over the place. Sickening. You sure are crazy!"

And it wasn't just Flora, all the kids in Edgeville were in an uproar about my new manners–tormenting and mocking me. And I was getting nowhere with Pa's books. Macaulay's *History of England* didn't help. The English and Scots were crazy about religion. They murdered each other at the drop of a hat. I was desperate. I began thinking out loud.

"Them as keep talkin' to themselves," Mrs. McCarthy said, tapping her head, "will end up in the looney-bin and sooner than you think. And don't think you're different from the rest, for you ain't."

Was I really crazy? Is it crazy to talk to yourself? I couldn't get to sleep at night; I'd wake in the middle of the night in a delirium of fear: they would send me to the asylum. Then one sleepless night, in sudden anger, I decided I wouldn't hang around and let them send me anywhere. I had my bank. I would go to Mr. Sherwood, a bachelor friend of Pa's who spent several weekends with us every year.

The next morning, I got up early–the train left at six–wrote a note to Pa, bought a ticket on the train, and took off for the other end of the province.

It was quiet and peaceful in Mr. Sherwood's house. We talked and

111

we went for walks. When he was out, I stayed with his housekeeper. But after a week, when no one came for me or wrote, I had to go home. Now they'd be sure I was crazy! I couldn't even stay away! But when I got home, no one said anything. Not even Pa. No one noticed that I'd been gone!

I was moping around the house one day with nothing new to read when Mrs. West dropped in for a talk and tea with Pa. "Dear child," she said, "run over to the house. The doctor has a good library and so have I. If he's not there, take what you want from mine."

That was when I discovered the novel. Mrs. West read everything: good, bad and indifferent: Jane Austen's *Sense and Sensibility*, Scott's *Waverley*, Fielding's *Tom Jones, The Vicar of Wakefield, Rasselas*, Brontë's *Jane Eyre*, Thackeray's *Vanity Fair* ... Trollope, Kingsley, Hardy, Meredith, Dickens, and dozens of later novelists down to the sickly, sentimental, badly written, Ruby M. Ayres. And from then on, I did, too. And then from my father's library, my mentor, Epictetus, Greek slave to the Romans. And, of course, Keats. I read and re-read Keats.

In the spring, Mrs. Lawson came to stay with us to sew our summer dresses. And this year, we could choose the colour we wanted. Flora chose a pretty plaid and Sue wanted pale blue, with ruffles. It was my turn ...

Mrs. Lawson stared at me and all the wrinkles under her glasses got bigger. She was angry. "No little girls have black dresses," she said, "not any. Have you ever seen a little girl in a black dress?"

"No."

"Tell me, just tell me," Mother demanded, "where will you wear a black velvet dress?"

"Everywhere. All the time."

Mother raised her hands in disgust and started for the door. Flora giggled, Geoffrey hooted. Mother came back from the door and stood over me. "Mrs. Lawson, that child drives me out of my mind." She was ready to shake the life out of me but she was holding it in.

"Shame on you!" Mrs. Lawson pushed me roughly away from her sewing table. "Why don't you behave? No other girl treats her nice mother like you do."

"She's crazy," Geoffrey said.

Mother said, threatening me, "I don't know where she gets these ideas! You've been reading some book again. If your father don't take those books away from you, I'll break his neck. What are you reading?"

" ... Uh ... nothing. History."

"Whoops!" Geoffrey hooted again. "You bet! Why don't you ask her what she was reading in the hayloft yesterday? I bet that wasn't history."

Keats! If they took him, I would die. Get him out of the hayloft! Hide him! Where?

"Why are you always running off to the hayloft to read? Why can't you read in the house?"

There was the danger signal in Mother's voice. The furious impatience which meant in a minute she'd slap me. Run? Epictetus would hate that. I didn't move.

She slapped me hard across the face.

When mother was angry, it upset Sue. She was squirming now in her chair.

Flora, as usual, looked important. She'd known all along I'd get it, and I certainly deserved it.

"Tell me! What are you reading?"

If Geoffrey would only keep his mouth shut. But he was right. I was lying. It was plain justice.

Mother grabbed me by the hair and jerked my head sideways. "You stupid fool, tell me what you're reading!"

Not Keats. Not Epictetus. She'd take them away. "Mrs. Corelli."

"What? What's that?"

"Mrs. Corelli," I mumbled. My speech couldn't have been intelligible. I was trying, against odds, to stand in a dignified manner as Epictetus would expect, and at the same time to excuse myself for the lie.

"You get it," Mother jerked my head and with every jerk she slapped me, "and throw it away and never let me catch you reading it again!" She flung me from her and left the room. I held my hand tight behind my back. I knew my face had bumps from her rings but I wouldn't touch it in front of them.

"That'll learn you," Mrs. Lawson said, satisfied. "Now just you come over here and pick a pretty dress out of the book like the other children."

"I'm going to have a black velvet dress," I mumbled through bruised lips, "quite long and with a low neck." And then I got out.

Martha was waiting for me in the hayloft. "What makes her so mad at you?"

"I don't know."

That evening, I went to get Maggie from her nest in the playroom. If she was in bed with me, I could sleep. I was picking her up when I heard them downstairs in the kitchen–through the stove pipe that came up through the floor.

"What's wrong with her now?"

"She wants a black velvet dress."

Pa laughed and laughed, very loud. "Well, give it to her."

"At thirteen? Don't be a fool. She's been reading some trash again. Why do you let her have those books?"

"I'll let her have anything she wants to read."

"Someone she calls Kowelli?"

"Marie Corelli?"

I thought that book must be all right because Pa was laughing again. I thought he was going to choke. After he stopped coughing, he said, "Gad!" and laughed some more. Then he got mad. "Gad, Liza, she's no fool. Give her the black dress and let her alone."

Mrs. Lawson told everyone in Edgeville that Mother couldn't do a thing with me because Pa went along with my foolishness. She was mad because she had to make the dress. She didn't ask me to turn when she fitted me; she pushed me around. She kept putting her knuckles hard on my growing breasts. The pain was like fire, but I didn't change the look on my face or open my mouth.

I was wearing my black velvet dress one evening, when Cecil Atwater came down the hill. Cecil was the milkman's son and in winter, when we were little, he used to haul me to school on his sled.

"Hi."

"Hi."

"Where you going?"

"No place."

"Let's go down to the pond."

It was dusk. We started along the sidewalk together, Cecil carefully on the outside.

"I like your dress."

"It's not made right. Mrs. Lawson never made anything right in her life. But I love it; it's so black."

Cecil put out his hand and touched my dress. "It's nice and soft. Why don't everybody else wear one like that?"

I said, "I can't imagine ... I'm crazy about black. They didn't want to give it to me but I had to have it. I wish there was something to do. I wish I could write a book. But what would I write about? Nothing ever happens around here. I wish something would."

"I bet we could write a play," Cecil said. "Come on, let's. We could act it out down in the Hall."

"About what?"

"Oh, cowboys or somethin'. Cowboys."

My own inclination, based on Mrs. Corelli's predilection for grandeur, was to write about a countess and a distinguished diplomat. Put them in a drawing room under a crystal chandelier ...

I said, "They always have love scenes but no one in Edgeville would stand for that."

"I know."

It was almost dark. Cecil stepped in front of me. "I know," he said, again. "But I don't care. Pill, let's write the play and let's play the love scene first." Then he leaned down and kissed me.

The tender words, the gentle touch betrayed me. The stranglehold on tears that I had maintained for longer than I could remember suddenly cracked. Cecil put out his arms and held me and I began to cry.

12

The Lodge, Upstate New York, December 1947

I can't believe that a week ago I was sitting in that slum! I've never felt so well in my life. We've just brought the horses back from a tremendous ride. Helga, the housekeeper, woke me with coffee at six to tell me the men were riding out to assess the damage to the road. Lottie was going with them. If I cared to go, there were riding clothes in the store-room.

Helga found me a pair of breeches, a vest and jacket, and I discovered a Cavanaugh that fit my head and I had long johns so I was all set.

I'd ridden here before but not with Lottie. I was astonished to see she still rode sidesaddle. It was difficult going; there were places where the snow reached the horses' bellies. We waited while the men carted away the fallen trees. It took a long time but, on the whole, there was nothing really serious. When we finally reached the village, the men took the horses to dry them off and Lottie and I followed a raucous group of skiers into the village café.

We were barely seated when one of them, an attractive young man, came to our table, bent low over Lottie's hand and lifted it to his lips. "Countess! What a pleasure!"

"Hello, Denys, when did you arrive?"

"We followed the storm. But I have only one day. I must get back to New York."

"And your mother?"

"She is in Barbados and happy. Or at least ... "

"I understand. It will be better for her in time."

She turned to me. "Mrs. Bentham, may I present Count de Maur?"

I nodded. I was sitting across the table from him so I didn't offer my hand.

He chatted for a few minutes with Lottie and kept glancing at me but, when she didn't ask him to sit down, he went back to his friends.

It had sounded strange to hear him give Lottie her title. Lottie and Reggio were "Count" and "Countess" when I first knew them. They had come to the USA with their staff, directly after the war. All co-conspirators against the Nazis, several in the Resistance, they had been made honourary

116

citizens, and they had dropped the titles. Now, more American than the Americans, they were Lottie and Reg to the cook, the housekeeper, the maids, the gardeners, and the children.

About three years after the war of 1914-18, echoes of the disturbance caused by the younger generation's mutilated morals penetrated the village slumber. Flora, infected with the new disease, sophistication, and looking spiffy, came home from college for the summer holiday. When Flora left Edgeville, barely nine months before, she had naturally curly, fluffy hair. Now it was shingled–cut in back like a boy's–and her round, innocent face was outlined with seven soaped-stiff, cardboard-hard, but madly passionate, spit-curls.

Flora's skirts, which had hit her ankles with a bang at fifteen, were now, in electric tension, zipped up to an inch below her knees standing, and three inches above sitting. Beneath her dress, her camisole had been exchanged for an almost flat band that, a decade later, Edgeville pronounced a braz-iere, and beneath a wisp of silk petticoat she called a slip, she was wearing that shocking, immoral–no pants at all, just a band you could unbutton–lace-trimmed, crêpe-de-Chine creation, the step-in.

So great was my awe of such magnificence, I had a lump in my throat just looking. But for all the attention she bestowed on me, I might be sitting on the moon. Still, I was of some importance in Flora's scheme of things. I stared, listened and admired; I added a tittle to the adoring family audience.

It was a bright day, too bright: sultry, glaring.

"What are you reading?" Flora took Mrs. West's book firmly out of my hand. "Oh, good. I started this yesterday and then I couldn't find it. You do something else. And look, bring me some apples; I'm going outside to read."

I stood, chagrined. Did she think I was her lackey? But she was just home. It was no time to start a fight. If I was good to her, things would be different; she might even introduce me to one of her fabulous college friends!

It was June and the apples were shriveled, but I found a few good ones and took them to her. Flora, propped up on her elbows, was lying on a blanket under the pear tree reading my book. All leg. What gorgeous legs, and what fashionable extravagance for Edgeville, she was wearing silk stockings! I hesitated, suddenly shy, "I've brought the apples."

117

"Well, give them to me. And don't stand in my light. Go away."

It's a reflex action, I thought, morosely. She gets what she wants and kicks me out of her way. Nothing to do. Hot. Geoffrey had the Ford. I got my bathing suit, walked two miles to the South Lake and went swimming. I stayed in the water a long time. It started to rain.

I decided to walk home through the woods and enjoy the greeny-gloom. I put up my face to feel the drops, leaned on the rough, wet trees, smelled the black earth; I found a few stalks of late trillium. When I got home at dusk, I was soaked to the skin. And I barely had time to change my clothes before Pa came in and sent me to work in the store. Then he forgot to relieve me, so I didn't get home until ten o'clock.

Flora had gone out and I couldn't find Mrs. West's novel. I made an exasperated, systematic search: kitchen, dining room, sitting room, parlour, pantry, bedrooms. Where had Flora put it? I looked out. It was raining hard and I had no place to go and nothing to read. I ran to the barn and dug Keats out of the hay. I would memorize a few delicious lines.

"Find it yourself," Flora said the next morning. "It's right here, somewhere. Don't bother me."

Two days later, I found my book soaking wet, sticky and swollen double under the pear tree. I examined it in despair. Mrs. West would have a fit!

"Flora! Flora! Yoo-hoo Flora. Look, you left Mrs. West's book out in the rain. You'll have to go and tell her you spoiled it."

"You're crazy. I never touched her book."

The audacity. I couldn't control my rage. "You left her book outside in the rain and you know it. You're going to tell the truth!"

"Shut your big mouth. I never touched her book." And then, contemptuously, "A lot you know about truth!"

I screamed, "You'll tell the truth. I'll make you!"

"You'll make me! I'd like to see you try. Go ahead. Just try!"

At supper that night, I raised the roof; no one could read for my screeching. Flora lied when she said she hadn't left Mrs. West's book in the rain and now Flora was sitting there calling me a liar!

"What a bore," Flora said. "She's boring me, Mother. Can't you shut her up?"

Geoffrey kept giggling. His derisive laughter, a more potent insult than any words, enraged me further. I wanted to slap his face. If they weren't so big, I'd kick the living daylights out of them. But I knew my rage was useless and screaming didn't help; I was licked before I started: Mother agreed with them before they opened their collective mouth.

"All right," I said, quietly. "I'll stop boring her. But Flora will tell the truth about that book or I'll never speak to her again."

Silence now.

I stood up and left my untouched supper.

It seemed to me I'd been truthful and honest for years. And my situation at home was not better but worse. I was fifteen years old and as always, except with Pa, I was an ignominious joke.

Flora was right, everyone said, and I was wrong, but as week followed week, and Flora refused to admit her lie and I refused to speak to her, they became more and more disturbed and increasingly angry with me.

My desperate and silent waiting took its toll. Terrifying, out of nowhere, time after time, I had the strongest impulse to destroy myself. Go to the lake. Swim out. Die. I longed to be at peace. Finally, I decided, if I talked to Pa and got things straightened out, it might help. I was sure Pa believed me. But did he? He hadn't said so. If Pa didn't believe me, I would kill myself.

"Pa! Pa! I hope you know I'm not lying!"

"What? About what? *Now* what's going on?"

"I mean about Flora. I hope you know I'm telling the truth. She ..."
He had that weary look on his face. He found me tedious.

"If you're telling the truth, that should be sufficient. No need to try to convince anyone else."

"If! Don't you believe me?"

"Tell me, do you lie?"

" ... Yes."

"Do you lie to me?"

"Sometimes, but not this time."

"You expect me to believe you."

"Yes."

"Well, Liza tells me you are a trouble-maker and I'm blind. She says Flora insists she is telling the truth and you are lying. I don't know anything about it. She may be right."

"But Pa, I just told you ... "

"How can I judge? I don't know the facts. I'm not going to interfere. Fight it out between yourselves."

I couldn't let him see my consternation. I turned away. But when I could control my face and voice, in concealed panic, I went back to him. "Pa ... "

119

"Ahh, Gad," Pa said. "If it's any more about you and Flora, I won't listen. How can you go on with anything so childish? Let it drop."

I was ashamed of that terrifying impulse to kill myself. I wanted him to know. But how tell him? What would I say? He'd made it very clear that he didn't want to talk to me. But I was in agony and I decided to go to him one last time–calmly. "Pa, I'm serious about this. I've admitted that sometimes I lie, but now I am telling you the truth. Do you believe me?"

Pa lifted his spectacles and looked at me. "If you are innocent, why worry?"

I couldn't help screaming, "I'm sick of that! Why won't you say you believe me? I tell you Flora is lying. Do you believe me?"

"I refuse to listen to your childish quarrels."

"All right," I said. "I won't bother you again. It doesn't matter. I won't talk any more."

"Now look here!" He was impatient. "You must learn how to deal with people, and now, while you are young. This is your training time. This may teach you to think twice before you accuse your sister or anyone else of lying. It's hard on Flora and, to say the least, it's not politic. When you go out in the world, you'll discover that, as the Bible so succinctly puts it, 'I send you forth as sheep in the midst of wolves: be ye therefore wise as serpents and harmless as doves.' It's good advice. Heed it. Now go away and don't bother me again. Forget it. Go read something."

I was perpetually close to tears. I never knew when a word would start them pouncing on me. I never knew how much more I could take. Mealtimes, I sat out the insults with a book protecting my blank face.

"Wacky!" Geoffrey sneered. "Crackers! Going around hurting Flora's feelings. What she needs is a damn good kick in the ass! She's crazy!"

"How can you be so mean to Flora?" Sue asked me, with tears of sympathy for Flora in her big blue eyes. Indignantly, "It's not fair!"

Mother, increasingly impatient, kept hounding me. "What kind of crazy notions do you get in your head, anyway, that you refuse to speak to your sister? You go straight to Flora and apologize!"

Flora flourished. Her air of suffering martyrdom added daily to her stature. My attitude of callous indifference to that suffering detracted daily from mine.

There were moments when, dizzy again, I doubted my memory. Was I right or wrong? I must repeat the whole thing to myself. Flora ... taking the book out of my hand ... the apples ... the swimming. I would go to the looking-glass and stare at myself. What a mess! Sloppy, countrified; in comparison with Flora I was a cipher.

I started hiding, so I couldn't hear them. It was more than two months since Mrs. West had lent me the book. I'd avoided her; if I had to speak to her, I'd die of shame. And yet, one day I would have to face her—return the remains of her book.

I began, again, to think of the lake. What a relief it would be to end it there. Die. I walked to the lake and stared at it. Then I waded in, shoes, clothes and all. Up to my neck in water I stood for a long time. Drown myself? Let them win? When I was right? And no chance to vindicate myself—not ever—especially to Pa.

I waded back and lay down in the water with my head on the shore. I thought of Pa. I had begged for his trust but I was wrong. Pa was just: he would never allow his feelings, his affection for me, to influence his decision. He couldn't be on my side, because, at times, I'd lied to him; and now he couldn't trust me.

I thought of Epictetus. No one knew his real name! As a boy, he'd been captured by the Romans, made a slave. He was lame and in poor health, but he was brave and wise. He listened to the Stoics, who endured all with indifference.

I thought of Keats—I thought of him as John, because I loved him—nursing his tuberculous brother, Tom, exhausted and writing the most magnificent and beautiful words and then dying of the same disease at twenty-six. What deprivations, what humiliations they had endured; yet, not one of them had tried to kill himself to avoid pain.

I thought of Carlyle. "Where thou findest a lie that is oppressing thee, extinguish it."

How could I extinguish Flora's lies? Martha knew Flora was lying. She had seen me give her the book but she didn't dare open her mouth. If she did, she'd be in trouble with Mother and Mrs. McCarthy would kill her.

It was long after dark when I got up and, my shoes squelching water, found my way home through the woods. Martha's light was on and I crawled through her window. Martha could always cheer me up. She shut the window behind me. "Shit, Pill, I could knock that bugger Flora's head off! D'you want some cocoa?"

Mrs. West was behind the house on her knees, weeding her flower garden.

I held out the pulpy, swollen book. "It's spoiled," I said. "I'll pay for it. Can you get another one? How much did it cost? I'm sorry. Oh ... I'm sorry."

She stayed on her knees, glanced at the book, then looked at me. "Dear child."

The tender words unnerved me; the lump came in my throat, the tears ... The book trembled in my hand.

"Philippa, my dear, what's wrong?"

I couldn't bear it! I threw myself at her feet, my face in the loose soil, my hands clutching, clutching at her skirt. I couldn't stop the tears, the dreadful sobbing. I blurted it out, I told on Flora! And then, appalled, I pleaded with Mrs. West to forget what I'd said: "Please, please don't tell. Please excuse me."

"Don't worry," she said, "you have my word. I'll never tell. These things happen to all of us. Flora is a nice girl. You'll see, in the end, she'll admit she was wrong. You must believe that. You wait and see."

I was cheered. How had I dared lose faith in Flora? Poor Flora. She, too, must be suffering–in attrition–as Mrs. West said; it was simply a matter of time and Flora would tell everything. So, believing now, expecting any minute, any day, that Flora would throw herself into my arms and say she was sorry, I waited. But nothing happened.

We were standing at the foot of the stairs near the door in the front hall. "You fool!" my mother said. "It's three months since you stopped talking to your sister! Do you realize? Flora came home in June and this is September. What do you think you're up to, anyway? Flora goes back to college in a week. You speak to your sister. Do you hear me? At once!"

Flora must have heard us. She came down the stairs and stood a few steps above me. Her round, blue, innocent eyes were swimming–visible but unshed–tears. She said indignantly, reproachfully, as though I had done her a grave injustice: "I think it's about time you spoke to me."

I stared at her eyes. No shame, no vestige of deceit, just righteous indignation and sorrow.

"It doesn't matter anymore," I said. "That's funny, isn't it? It just doesn't matter. Yes, I'll speak to you."

How strange. My anger dissolved, no feeling left. How very strange. I was so tired, I couldn't stand up. I went upstairs and threw myself on the bed. I didn't want to eat or be with them, but I went down to supper. We sat at the table waiting for Martha to bring the food.

Vindicated, victorious, Flora looked around the table. She giggled. "I guess now you know which one of us to believe. Philippa admitted she's the liar around here. She spoke to me!"

Guffaws from Geoffrey.

"Now, now, children," Mother smiled, tolerant. "No more talk. Everything's settled."

I got up and smashed my chair against the wall. "No!"

"Will you sit down and shut your mouth?" Mother said, grimly. "Will you ever let us have peace around here?"

I looked at Pa and he was looking at me. That cold, speculative look in his eyes. I was horrified. Was it possible that he, too ... ?

"Sit down! Charles, if she doesn't sit down at this table, I won't be responsible for what I do to her!"

"Enough of your foolish behaviour," Pa said. "Sit down and eat your supper."

Foolish, I thought. I'm a fool. He's right. I spoke, and in speaking, I had proved, irrevocably, Flora's innocence; proved my guilt. I turned and walked out.

The days went by and they were all alike. Nothing to do but go to school. I had no need to study till the end of the year when, concentrating, I would race through the books, memorize everything overnight, write the exam and then forget everything within a week. There was nothing I could force myself to do. I couldn't read, I wasn't interested. Nothing mattered. And I felt rushed, pushed, in a hurry. I had one idea in my head, to finish school and to leave Edgeville. But, I was no longer frantically thinking of suicide. I was too tired to care. Sloppy, half-washed, half-dressed, no more manners for me. I loitered along the sidewalks, the roads, I wandered through the woods. If I went at all, I was always late for school.

I met Mrs. West one day after school.

"Philippa, come home with me and have a cup of tea. Do you know how long it's been? Weeks! Did you enjoy the books?"

"I haven't read them. I haven't had time. They're home, in the bureau drawer. I'll bring them back."

"You haven't read them? Never mind, I have. Keep them. You'll read them later. Sometimes one likes to talk. Sometimes I get hungry for it. I often go to the house to talk to your father. You're a lucky girl to have him for a father. Excepting the doctor, of course," she smiled, "he's the only civilized man in Edgeville."

How was it that I got on so well with Edgeville's unpopular people? There were all sorts of rumours about Mrs. West. Everyone said she took drugs, that the doctor didn't even care; he gave them to her. She was abrupt with people. Edgeville called her "highfalutin'" and compared to Edgeville, she did have some odd ideas. Her vegetable garden, for some obscure reason, was on the front lawn, the flower garden at the back of the house. But I was at peace with her and I understood that oddity when I went to see her. We took tea on the wide back porch. No one could see or hear us, and the garden was silent and brilliant and fragrant.

Mrs. West talked about everything: books, music, metaphysics–did the spirit survive death? She theorized that since the spirit of man was incredibly stronger than his physical body–not part of it, not material–it could not perish when the physical house decayed.

There were thin slices of brown bread and butter; there were little cakes. It was pleasant and easy, and nothing hurt. Mrs. West never mentioned a soul in Edgeville. It was so lovely, that every afternoon after school I ran straight to her house to see the garden and enjoy the tea and talk.

"What's this Mrs. Lawson tells me about you?" Mother was furious. "Why are you running to the doctor's wife every day? Why don't you have friends your own age? What's Mrs. West's interest in you? She's an old woman. It's not healthy!"

I began to think that Mother would go to Mrs. West and complain about me. She would embarrass Mrs. West and tell her about me, ruin my reputation. So, I stopped going there.

It was examination time. That year, I hadn't opened a book at home and half the time I hadn't gone to school; even when I had, I couldn't listen.

Algebra. I didn't even know how to begin. Well, start a question and try to figure it out.

That afternoon, we had History. I hadn't opened my book since I'd read it through at the beginning of the term for the story. I glanced at the clock. I had seven hundred pages of *British History* to memorize in three-quarters of an hour.

Was Mrs. West right? Did the dead live? I shut my eyes. I could see them. The spirits of my ancestors. They were wispy, white shadows floating in front of my closed eyes. "All right," I whispered, "If you're here, help me." Then, at random and three times, I opened my *British History*.

When I looked at the examination paper–prepared and sent out by the Provincial Board of Education–three of the ten questions were those I had just read. The other seven I knew. Was it true? Was it possible? Did man's spirit survive death? If not, what a coincidence!

And what a pity I thought, a few months later, when the letter came from the Board of Education, that I hadn't remembered my ancestors earlier. The History was marked 98, the Algebra 23. For the first time in my life, I'd failed an exam.

"Just as well," Pa said. "I can't send you to college because I haven't the money, and you're too young to leave home. You can go back to school for another year."

I was relieved that he didn't care. But ... he didn't care? Had I been wrong about his liking me? Geoffrey and Flora could go to college but there would be no money for me?

No. It was true about the money. I knew all about the big bills. I still spent a lot of time in the store. Pa's bank account was flat. Flora couldn't go to college next year, either. It was all he could do to keep sending Geoffrey. Geoffrey had to have a profession, Pa said, because he'd have to support a family. "You girls will marry."

Still ... Flora would have had two years ... Couldn't he have saved one year for me? But when it came to something we wanted, Flora got it. No, she was oldest, that was all. He liked me best. I was sure. I understood Pa. He used the money for whoever came first until it ran out. That was all there was to it, and I would never doubt him.

Flora! I heaped all the blame for my unhappiness on Flora. Why did she lie? Why was she so unfair? Why didn't she like me? I was obsessed with Flora, tormented by her callous behaviour; I would never get over it. I brooded night and day. I went around in a fruitless and burning fever, trying to understand.

And then, one unprecedented morning, I woke suddenly, calm and empty. Flora's face hung, as it had hung for months, before my waking eyes. Her red cheeks shone. To improve her complexion, summer or winter, Flora washed her face in ice-water. I saw her eyes, round, innocent and blue. That pretty face. And for the first time in my life, I saw it without its blinding charm.

Unclouded by my love, my longing, I saw that those eyes–so quick to shed tears–concealed the crafty twin sisters, self-pity and self-love, and I understood her. Flora's tears were not alone tears of hypocrisy. They were tears of weakness. And now I knew that in a show-down Flora would always and knowingly destroy me to save herself.

And strangely, I didn't care. Remotely, I was sorry for her. The beloved face had altered: it's charm gone forever. And of her two faces–the pretty one and the one I saw now: naked, and selfish–the second was the one I would see, sometimes with anger, sometimes with pity and sometimes with love, for the rest of my life.

125

13

My father believed in the innate dignity and honesty of man. He gave everyone his due, particularly the underdog, and a little over for good measure. At the same time, he could not read a book or a newspaper without discerning therein all sorts of lies and treacheries.

The 1914-18 war, he said, had been a struggle between the great powers to maintain and guard their possessions and to acquire new ones. He saw no difference between this war and the civil war in Russia, where the peasants were fighting to throw off the rule and seize the property of their masters. Pa refused to condemn the Russian peasant for behaving in the same way and for the same purpose as the world's great statesmen. "If murder for property is to be condoned," he said, "let us not distinguish between murderers." And if sympathy was indicated in either case, he was inclined to bestow it upon the untutored peasant who had been deprived of, and was fighting for, his basic needs.

It occurred to me to wonder why Pa had not joined actively in the fight against capitalism. Why wasn't he a Bolshevik?

Challenged, he maintained he had been "imprisoned by circumstance." He had to feed us. Nevertheless, he insisted, hope for man's future lay with the proletariat.

I was staring out of the kitchen window one day, waiting for Martha to bring tea and thinking about this when I noticed old George, fully clothed, sweating in the afternoon sun, chopping our fire wood.

I stuck my head out of the window. "Yoo Hoo! George! C'mon in an' I'll give you a cuppa tea."

I took him into the parlour. "Look, George, may I ask you a few things? What's your philosophy?"

"Me what? Come again, Pill. Don't throw them big words at me."

"Oh, I mean, what is most important to you? I mean, in life. What rule, what purpose, uh ... what motivates, I mean in life ... "

"Oh, life! I see. That's diffrunt." George settled himself comfortably in Pa's chair. "My, it's nice an' cool in here. Well, now, that's easy. Like me Pa sed, 'live an' larn, live an' larn.'"

Just like Pa.

"Yup, live an' larn. An' then, yuh know what 'appens? Yuh die an' fergit it all. Ha, ha, ha!"

At that moment, Pa walked in for his tea and the easy, warm atmosphere became immediately uneasy and cold.

George stood up, hitched up his trousers and removed his hat. "Sir, I wuz jest tellin' Pill here a coupla things about life, but I gotta go."

"George! Your tea!"

But he was gone.

"What's all this!" Pa demanded. "What's that cretin doing in this house?"

"Pa, for heaven's sake, he'll hear you! I asked him in because I wanted to find out what he thinks. I like him."

"If your likes lead you to consort with people at that intellectual level, you picked the right specimen."

"But what's wrong with George? He's got a brain!"

"Indubitably, but it has one slight local defect, it's atrophied. What makes you think that slack-baked oaf has anything to say to you? I should think his very presence would be offensive. I can smell him!"

"Pa! He was sweating, that's why!" I'd never heard Pa talk about anyone like that. He must be furious.

"Don't Pa me, and keep him out of here. Or if you must persevere in your investigations, do it in the woodshed."

The proletariat were admirable, but the local proletarian was another kettle of fish. Never mind; I promised myself: one of these days, I'd become a Bolshevik.

Meanwhile, I had other troubles. I spent three quarters of my time examining my defects in the looking-glass. I was fifteen years old and certain I was the ugliest girl in the village; my black hair was so slippery I couldn't keep it out of my eyes. I had plenty of eyelashes and my eyes were all right, but the rest of me! My wrists were so thin, they made my hands look like feet. And my feet were gunboats!

The boys chased Loretta and Gladys, but nobody looked at me. Of course, they thought I was crazy. If it hadn't been for Cecil, my social life would have been nil. As usual, I went alone to the weekly dance at the Hall. I looked a mess. I'd made over my dress half a dozen times, and it still looked awful. I picked a chair against the wall and sat down on my big feet. If Cecil was coming, he was late. Then he was there, grinning at me.

"Oh, hi, Cecil."

"C'mon," he said, "let's dance."

I stood up in relief.

When the music stopped, we were standing beside Loretta. She was with a tall, dark-haired stranger.

Cecil said, "Hi Loretta."

Loretta didn't answer. Her partner turned and looked at me ... directly into my eyes. The music began. He dropped Loretta's hand, lifted Cecil's hand from my shoulder and held out his arms. I stepped into them and we began to dance.

"You're the loveliest girl I've ever seen."

"W' What?" I stumbled and he held me.

"Is he your beau?"

"Cecil? Ye Gods! No. I have no beau."

"Listen to me." He held me a little away from him and I saw his solemn face and his very beautiful brown eyes and dark hair. "I've found you and from now on, I'm your beau and no one will ever take you away from me."

Dancing with him, safe in his arms, I knew it was true.

Where I lay the next morning, back of the barn in the open meadow and hidden by the tall grass, the sun and the wind beat down on me. The sun, the wind, the hard damp earth, the tall grass–the world–was part of me. It breathed in and with and through me. In that one shocking second when I looked into his eyes, the questioning, the aloneness, the unrelenting torment had ceased. The secret of belonging is to love! Everything was significant, reborn, tender, vital, brushed with light ...

"Philippa!"

I stopped breathing, and the world stopped with me.

"Philippa, answer me!"

I stood up. She was standing under the pear tree. Reluctantly, I approached her.

"What's this Mrs. Lawson tells me about you? The whole village is talking."

"What! Why? I didn't do anything!"

"Oh, no? You spent the whole evening dancing with some idiot from Otter–a drunk!–with a terrible reputation!"

"What! He's not! He was ... "

"Sober, I suppose. As if you'd know. Is that why he kept pawing you all evening? If you think I don't know."

I turned and ran.

"Come back! Get into this house! You silly fool, I can't trust you anywhere. Other girls have some respect for themselves."

I stopped. I must never run. I turned back, got past her, and went into the dining room. Pa was eating his breakfast. Maybe he'd make her stop. "Pa. I didn't do anything. We ... "

One hand holding his book, Pa looked at me over the rim of his spectacles. His eyes were cold. "All right, Philippa. Your mother is right. That boy is no good. He drinks. Heavily. Don't have any more to do with him."

Mother said, bitterly, "The whole place is talking about you. Don't you ever see him again."

"But Loretta ... If he's so bad why did Loretta ... "

"Never mind Loretta! You heard your father."

Bill. No good. How did they know? Who told them? Mrs. Lawson, of course. She could hardly wait. That old ... But if Pa said ... Pa would never tell a lie. Could it be ... It must be true. Bill!

A bubble hung before my bewitched eyes. A shiny empty crystal globe. It shattered. Waves of too-bright light from the open window. The sun on the too-white tablecloth, the scattered crystal dust ... blinding. I sat down. I couldn't stand.

My voice came, hard and cold. "Mrs. Lawson, poof. She talks about everybody."

My mother's angry words–a blurr. They were both looking at me; I could feel their eyes, their untrusting eyes, all over me. I spread butter on bread, lifted it, hesitated against the sudden nausea, shoved it in my mouth. I would have to give him up. Not for Mother; for Pa. I sat there. Stunned. Finally, I got it out. "All right, Pa. I heard you."

He looked up but he didn't speak.

Otter is a small town about thirty miles from Edgeville. Bill's letter reached me two days later. He'd pick me up Sunday afternoon, he wrote, we'd go driving and have a picnic somewhere.

I hid his letter in the hayloft. Ten minutes later, in terror, I couldn't find it. Then I found it. I pinned it to my camisole, unpinned it, pinned it there again. I jumped at every sound. Food made me sick: I must run from the table, hide, talk to Epictetus, beg him for help, beg him to control my helpless tears.

And Sunday came nearer and nearer. Saturday, waiting, I stayed up in the hayloft all day. Outside the open door, rain fell. The gray rain: tranquil, muted drops, a curtain of mist, struck the wooden roof of the barn and slid past my eyes. The living, vibrant air was full of a strange beauty, a limitless tenderness, an unbearable sadness.

On Sunday, towards noon, for fear of being seen by someone in the family, I walked to the corner to wait.

Bill opened the car door and I jumped in quickly.

A couple of lumberjacks gawked at us but there was no one else on the road. But I couldn't hope to escape notice, not in Edgeville. I said, breathlessly, "Bill, please turn around. Let's go to the South Lake."

Eyes fixed on the road ahead of him, Bill leaned towards me and his cheek brushed mine. And, overwhelmed, I glimpsed it again, that unbelievable, that miraculous world where undreamed depths of tenderness and love were promised; granted with a touch.

He swung the car around. Two miles outside the village at the bottom of the long hill, Bill drove the car off the road and stopped. "Come," he said. He took my hand and pulled me out of the car and quickly after him, through the pine grove till we came to a cleared pasture. It was out of sight of the road, but we could see the lake through the trees.

The sun was hot on the dried grass and tree stumps. We stood for a moment searching each other's eyes. Then he sat down and pulled me down beside him. He still held my hand, my fingers twisted in his. I looked at the grass, at some ants crawling through the grass.

He said, "Philippa" under his breath.

I didn't look at him. I put out my free hand to touch the ants.

"Philippa, do you love me?"

It was as though my body had ceased to exist. There was no feeling in it, no sensation. Suspended in nothingness, I heard my voice. "No."

"Philippa ... " How lonely his voice. Neither of us moved. "Philippa ... "

I looked at my feet. My hand in his was paralysed. "Philippa. Do you like olives?"

"Yes."

"Didn't you have to learn to like them?"

"No."

"Do you think you could learn to love me?"

"No."

Still holding my hand, he jumped up and started back to the car. I stumbled behind him. He opened the car door, dropped my hand, threw it away from him. "Get in."

Driving back, it didn't matter who saw us. I sat, staring at him,

130

learning by heart his set, expressionless face. I longed for a word, a glance, but he didn't speak and he didn't take his eyes from the road. He stopped in front of our house, leaned across me and opened the door. I got out and stood on the road.

He whipped the car around. The skidding wheels flung the dust high about me. I could feel the skin tighten over my forehead. I could feel my throat muscles stiffen till I must open my mouth and gasp in the filth-laden air. Now, I was twisted to nausea inside. His speeding car, the dusty road, rolled in front of my eyes. I turned and ran for the barn. I fumbled my way up the ladder to the loft. I threw myself on the hot, dusty hay. I had no tears. I was sick.

It was still light when Martha came calling me for supper. When I heard her climbing the ladder, I hid. After a while, it was night and I wanted to stay in the doorway leaning against the stars and the cool, dark sky. But it was late. They'd start looking for me. I could slip through the front hall past the sitting-room door and call out to them that I was going to bed, that I'd had supper with Gladys.

I must continue to hide that constant and bitter undercurrent of pain beneath a put-on indifference. Daytimes, I hid it. At times, absorbed in a book, I forgot it. But it lay waiting and sleep uncovered it.

I would wake sharply to the tense beauty of the country mornings. The soft sunny mornings and the dull rainy ones, the dead cold or the brilliant ones. I would wake painfully in fear and dread. Music came from the meadow and wood. Muted summer sounds, or brittle or windy. Pain and beauty inextricably mixed. Sometimes the beauty and love of life were so strong that the pain was dulled. Sometimes the beauty intensified the pain.

I would bury my head in the pillow and count the minutes and months until I would be grown up and could go away. Away from the family, from Edgeville, from people who considered privacy a shameful hiding and whose delight was to expose every wished-for, secret, hidden thing to public speculation, to mockery and contempt. Outside in the real world, the interesting world I read about, and that Pa knew and talked about, people were different.

In less than a year I'd be sixteen–the age at which Flora had started college. I would not be allowed to go to college, but I'd be gone. I told them that on my sixteenth birthday I was leaving home.

Mother stopped speaking to me, but she didn't try to conceal her distaste; she referred to me as "that girl." "That girl is so nervous she's driving me crazy. If she's so set on going away, let her go. She'll find out she can't behave with other people the way she behaves here. No one will stand for her."

Pa said, "If you wait until you're eighteen, perhaps I'll have enough money to send you to college."

"If you don't give me permission, I'll run away."

Each year before Flora left for College, Mrs. Lawson spent the summer getting her ready. She had a trunk full of new clothes. No one bothered to call Mrs. Lawson for me, so when I left I wore what I had: a gray flannel skirt, a white cotton blouse and a gray sweater. I didn't dare touch the good luggage but I had a handbag that Flora had discarded and I found a battered suitcase. Pa gave me my fare and a hundred dollars and four twenty-five dollar cheques. I was going to Boston.

The train left at six. Martha came to my room at four-thirty to wake me. She sat on my bed while I packed some underwear, a night dress, a couple of skirts and blouses, and an extra pair of shoes.

"Now, Pill," she warned, "You look out for them city boys. It's a different thing entirely from around here. Don't you believe them, no matter what they say." She hugged and kissed me. "Remember the time we ran out of gas and hadda walk six miles?" I was glad Martha talked, because I couldn't. She took my suitcase, carried it downstairs and stood it by the door.

We heard the horse. Mrs. McCarthy was washing dishes and my mother, who was busy at the stove, turned around, walked over and kissed me.

I was astonished and embarrassed. I picked up my suitcase and ran to the sidewalk where old George was waiting in the buggy. I shoved it in back and got in front with him.

They were standing in the doorway when I left. Martha throwing kisses, Mrs. McCarthy, her arms folded, with that look on her face that meant she was expecting the worst. When we started, my mother ran halfway out to the road and–I couldn't credit my senses!–tears were streaming down her face.

When we got to the store, I told George to stop. Pa was standing on the platform waiting for me. I got out of the buggy and went over and kissed him on the cheek. He turned his head away. He was shy. I had never kissed him before in my life.

"Take care of yourself, Philippa," he said. "Write to me. And don't forget, in a city, the police are there to take care of you. If you get in trouble, go to them at once. And don't forget, hotels are public. If you're lost or frightened, go to a good one–the best one, be sure–and don't worry about money. Wire me. I'll send it at once."

I said, "Yes." But I knew Pa needed money for Geoffrey. I could never ask him for money. And the minute I could, I would send back the cheques and the hundred dollars.

I ran back to the buggy.

"Pill," old George said, "You're going out into the world and they's somethin' I gotto tell you before you go."

"Yes, George, I'm listening. Go on."

"Well, there you are, you see. You hear what's said. Now I just want you to know that we all know that you don't get on too good in this place. And that's because they can't see past their noses. I've sawed these peoples' wood all my life, but just because they own a few acres of timber and can hire and fire as they're inclined, I ain't good enough for them. Their kitchens, yes, but not their parlours. Now I ain't never forgot you asked me in for tea. I want you to know these stuck-up people don't cut no ice with us. All of us in the east settlement think good of you. Now be a good girl and behave yourself and don't forget, they's some of us is good friends."

"Thank you, George. Say goodbye for me. Gee, I guess I forgot my hanky. I ... Never mind. It's down my neck."

All the way on the train to Yarmouth–where I would take the steamer to Boston–I considered my future. From now on, no matter the circumstances, no stupid behaviour. No one would ever treat me as brutally, as unjustly, as I had been treated at home. No one would ever get close enough. I had watched my mother. She treated everyone with great kindness and charm, but no one dared be familiar with her. She was a lady.

I intended to do something of importance in the world. I intended to be a Bolshevik. To prepare for it, I would have to learn to be a lady.

14

Grimy, dingy Boston. How different from the big city–the scintillating, glittering big city–of my imagination. The cluttered dock, the sooty railroad station. Trains roaring overhead in the narrow, dirty streets. Torn newspapers blowing in the wind. The Traveller's Aid sent me to a boarding-house for working girls.

When I got to the house, I found I would have to share a room. The landlady took me upstairs and opened a door. I stepped into the room and the landlady shut the door behind her. A girl was sitting on one of the beds. I took a good look and turned my head away. I didn't want to stare. Then, I couldn't help it, I had to look again.

She had bright yellow hair, bright brown eyes and her eyebrows were navy blue. Her eyelashes were clotted with a heavy blue paste. "Well," she said, grinning, "when you get your eyes full, fill your pockets."

I put my suitcase on the floor and sat down on the vacant bed.

"You from the country?"

"Uh ... Canada. The backwoods."

"Oh? No foolin'." She laughed. I could have guessed. What you doin' here?"

"I must get a job."

"Doin' what?"

"I don't know."

"A secretary, maybe. You got brains?"

"No ... No."

"No brains, huh? Or no chance."

"No. I ... that is, not much of either, I suppose, but anyway, I don't want to be a secretary."

"Shop girl?"

"I could do that."

"I'm out of a job myself," the girl said. "Maybe we could get something together."

I had a moment of panic at the thought of stepping out on the street in broad daylight with those blue eyelashes! I dropped my eyes so she wouldn't notice. When I looked up, she was looking the other way but the silence that hung in the room was not good. I said, tentatively, "What do you do?"

"I'm on the stage," she said. "The chorus, The Green Peacock. I mean I was till the fuckin' show went bust."

I was shocked. I hadn't heard that word since I was five; since we lived near Renee and George's pig. "I ... Uh. That must be ... It's hot here."

"It ain't the country. What's your name?"

"Philippa Jerrold."

"Sounds like a high-tone stage name. What's your real name?"

"It's my real name."

"Oh? Well look, I'm Millie Davis. If you want to room with me it's okay. Look, you're green, I'll help you." She pulled a newspaper off the rickety table. "We can look in the 'Help Wanted.'"

I hesitated. Then I moved over to sit beside her on the bed. "I'd like that very much."

Girls! To solicit advertising over the telephone. Must have good speaking voice. Apply for interview by telephone.

"Not me," said Millie, "but I bet you sound great on the phone."

We ran downstairs to the house telephone and Millie got the number for me and I asked for the job.

The man told me to come in the next day.

The ship had been cold and damp and I was so tired my bones ached. I never had a headache in my life but now my head felt transparent with every sound, rudely intrusive, banging through my eyes. For weeks before I left home, I hadn't been able to sleep. I was terrified of going away from home, alone. Now ... I had to get out of my clothes.

Millie watched me unpack. "I guess you're poor," she said. "Ain't you got no good dress?"

I began to shiver. "I'll get one after I get work."

"Gee, look, are you all right? I got bread and stuff. I'll make a cup of tea."

"Millie, d'you mind if I get into bed? I hate to in the middle of the day, but ... " I pulled back the coarse sheet, slipped off my skirt and blouse and, still holding my night dress, fell into bed. "Millie," I mumbled, "would you mind if I just go to sleep?"

Millie took me to the Herald-Traveller Building in the morning. "Don't worry if you don't get it. There's plenty more."

I found my way through the crowded building and upstairs to the employment office. I was dizzy. I didn't imagine that I'd get the job. My throat was swollen tight shut.

135

"Eighteen-fifty a week," said Mr. Raymond. "You're sure you'll get your voice back? I remember your voice on the phone. Perfect diction. You're not from Boston?"

"Canada."

He said, "You'll do. Come in when you get your voice back."

Millie was waiting on the sidewalk. "You get it, kid?"

I nodded. I was dizzy and felt faint. I had no idea it took such effort to apply for a job. I grabbed her hand.

"Geez! You're on fire!"

She got me to the bus.

Our room was oppressive; dusty, airless, hot. I couldn't breathe. I was dying. I couldn't croak anymore so I whispered. "Come ... " I handed her my money. "For us." Then I blacked out.

I had pneumonia and I was ill for almost two weeks. Millie called the doctor. She also washed my sheets, fed me, ran upstairs and down. Still, I had an uneasy feeling that someone from Edgeville would drop in and tell me she was no lady. I hated the room. "Millie," I complained, "It's awful here! No air."

"We cawn't leave," Millie said. She'd begun to imitate my voice, and she was an incredible mimic. When I was first ill and half-conscious I thought she was Sue. "You're too fussy. I'm out of a job and it's cheap and your money won't last forever. What did you expect? If you don't like it why did you come?"

"Oh, shut up!"

Millie was illegitimate. "I suppose you have a father."

I hesitated. "I have a father but ... but no mother."

"She dead?"

"Uh, well, uh, not really. She's fine, and living at home."

"Geez! You nuts?" Millie was irresistible when she laughed and very pretty, make-up and all. I forgot about our poverty and my aching, broken heart and laughed with her.

Millie thought I ought to learn how to dress. A skirt and blouse had no style, but she would teach me. Her dresses were bright with sequins. They looked very pretty in that drab, dusty room. I tried one on. "A pity," I said, staring into our half looking-glass. "All I can see is the dress. I can't see my face."

"There's something wrong, that's for sure, but your clothes is so dull!"

My speech fascinated her. "Teach me to talk like you."

She was all grace practising dance steps in our narrow room. "Teach me to dance and I'll teach you some grammar."

I thought Millie was stupid when I first met her, but I rapidly changed my mind. She was intuitive and fast to learn. As a child, she'd lived in the worst part of Boston. "I knew the pimps and prostitutes, the sick old men and women and I hated it. My mother beat me. I had to get out." At fourteen a social worker had placed her in some sort of Mission House where she lived for several years. "I always wanted to dance and I got my first job in the chorus when I was fifteen."

I went to the office every day, except Sunday. We sat, a dozen or more of us, in front of a long table. We wore headphones and we dialed hour after hour, day after day, business firms, boarding-houses, hotels, begging advertising for the newspaper.

I had intended doing something of importance in the world and now I felt caged. I read and re-read the "Help Wanted" and a feeling of futility grew in me. I had no special training and I hadn't been to college. It seemed there was nothing else I could do. And life in Edgeville had not prepared me for the young man who sat next to me. While I was on the phone, he'd pull at my arm, touch my hair, or put his hand above my knee. Coming up in the elevator one morning, he pressed tight against me in the crowd. I could feel his genitals hard against my thigh. He was immune to insult. When I spoke contemptuously to him or ignored him, he laughed at me. "Quit yer kiddin'."

Millie gave me some advice. "Kick him! Hard! And you know where!"

I was shocked. No lady ... How did girls manage these things? How would Flora stop him? Light dispersed gloom. "Millie," I said happily, "there's a better way. I can cry."

"Christ!" She eyed me with respect. "Say, you're not the dope I took you for."

I went to the office next day prepared to weep my head off, but I didn't have to. Mr. Raymond had fired him.

At noon, with a half hour to eat, we rushed to the street, pushing and hurrying. We ate soft, sweet, over-spiced or fried food smelling of cheap oil. Food thrown at us by careless men and women in soiled aprons. I saw vacant stares, tired eyes. I heard the brainless wise-cracking all around and somehow it filled me with shame. And then I began to see my own unhappy face reflected from a hundred city faces and I was frightened. I must never become one of them.

But I need not have worried; because my speech differed from theirs and because I refused the abrupt familiarities, my co-workers mockingly and derisively renamed me "Lady Jerrold." But I was getting ads and, for the moment, I would stay. It was relief each night to get back to Millie.

I tore up the four cheques Pa had given me and sent them to him. I wrote, "I have a job soliciting advertising over the telephone. There's a nice girl rooming with me; her name is Millicent."

The Green Peacock reopened and Millie got her job back. We worked every evening after the theatre. Millie was quick to imitate my speech during the lesson but she forgot to go on with it when we stopped. I pounded at her: separate your words, repeat, repeat, memorize. It will soon come. You must read. When she couldn't take anymore, she'd give me a dancing lesson.

Now that I was away from it, Edgeville was dear to me. I was homesick for the sun, the woods. Coming home from the movies one night I stopped, startled to see the moon, incongruous, above the city roofs. The old mixed-up pain that had to do with my love for the family nagged at me and every tall young man on the street was Bill. One day, I was sure I saw him step into a taxi. I ran after it, calling his name ...

On Sundays, Millie and I walked through the quieter streets. At dusk, lonely, we watched the lights come on. We stared at the lighted windows. Families dining together. The light made them look safe and warm and happy. Other people's houses.

Millie said, "People like you and me isn't meant for that kind of life. We're stuck where we are."

It shocked me to hear Millie classify me with herself, but then I thought, of course, we're the same: we're working girls. Only until then I hadn't thought of myself as that.

"It's no home and no money," Millie said.

One Sunday afternoon, walking along a spacious avenue, we stared at the great, quiet houses. Although it was broad daylight, blinds covered the huge, blank windows. We stopped in front of one.

"I can't imagine it," said Millie. "I wonder why the blinds is down?"

"Are down, Millie. Several blinds. Plural."

"It must be heaven."

Footsteps behind us. We turned. A young man had stopped and was hesitating there. He looked at me. "Uh ... I heard you. Come in, if you like."

I stared at him and his face turned red.

"I beg your pardon," he said in embarrassment, and started for the door. He had keys swinging from a gold chain.

138

"Wait!" said Millie. She ran after him. "Wait, could we really come in?"

The young man stopped and looked at her. Then he looked at me again. He said, "The family's abroad. There's no one here. Come in if you like: I'll give you a drink."

Carried on the tide of Millie's daring, I followed them into the house.

From the big hall, we could see an enormous room. Light shone dimly, through the ivory blinds. Lamps, tables and chairs were shrouded in white dust covers. We followed him up a wide staircase and down a long wide corridor to a small study. Leather-covered desk, leather chairs, a wall of books, sporting prints. The desk was covered with books and papers. On a side table, a decanter of whiskey and glasses stood on a shining silver tray. The glasses sparkled in the light. We stared.

"Do sit down."

Millie kept walking around, touching things. I had stopped noticing when we were alone but now I was conscious of and uneasy about her eyelashes and her brassy yellow hair.

"It seems to interest you–the room."

"We're burglars" said Millie, "casing the joint."

There it was again: Millie's irresistible charm!

We all laughed. And we were suddenly at ease.

"Scotch and soda?" He poured drinks.

The glass. A crystal tube, fragile. I'd never seen ... a delight to hold in my hand. I sipped the whiskey.

We sat and said nothing. No one minded the silence. He kept looking at Millie's eyelashes. When he spoke to her, his voice was gentle. He said, "What do you do?"

"Me? The chorus. The New Green Peacock."

"Oh, yes, I've seen it. And you?"

"I solicit advertising for the *Herald-Traveller*."

"Look here," he said, "I have some work to finish," he waved his hand at the desk, "and I'm alone. Eat with me tonight."

Neither of us answered. His face began to get red again. "I assure you... " He leaned a little forward on his chair, his mouth open.

It was ludicrous. We knew he was harmless. We all laughed again. He said, "My name is Henry Austin."

He wrote our names and address in a little leather book. "I think I know where it is, I'll find it. I'll pick you up around eight."

When Millie got dressed, she was beautiful. The too-bright sequins suited her. I had tried one of her dresses again but it was no good.

... Henry ushered us into the restaurant. I stopped. Here was the glittering Boston I'd dreamed of: a dozen tables with starched white tablecloths and gleaming silver. Benches running the length of the tables were covered in red velvet and the small gold chairs facing them were upholstered in the same material. There were tiny red-shaded lights on each table and a soft red carpet under our feet.

Millie and every other woman in the place had bare necks and bare arms. I knew my blouse and skirt looked countrified and woefully out of place.

"What would you like to drink?" Henry was looking at me.

Pa drank cognac after dinner but I had no idea ... "What are you having?"

"A dry sack."

"Falstaff's drink! Oh, good, for me, too." I forgot my clothes. I could barely wait to taste it.

"Not me," said Millie. "A martini. Dry."

Pink, crisp baby clams on cracked ice. Scarlet grilled lobster. Golden bits of crisp potato. Fresh green lettuce tasting deliciously of pale and darker green. Still white wine, cooled in a dewy silver bucket, wrapped in a stiff white napkin. A lemon ice. A runny cheese, delicately, deliciously rotten on small dry biscuits.

We laughed and laughed all through dinner.

The following evening Henry was standing on the sidewalk when I came out of the Herald-Traveller Building.

"Come along," he said, and took my arm. We walked across the Common and sat down on a bench. It wasn't necessary to talk to Henry; to cover silences with talk. I turned to smile at him and my heart contracted in fear. He was looking at me with contempt.

"My God, Philippa, why do you hang out with a bag like Millie?"

But last night he had liked Millie. I fumbled for an answer but I couldn't think. I wanted to hit him–hard! I found an old limping childhood taunt. "Your face is dirty," I said, but my voice was trembling.

He flushed. "All right," he said. "I was only trying to help you. You can tell by looking at her what she is."

"I know what she is."

"You don't know much or you wouldn't be seen with her." He moved closer to me and slipped his arm around me. His fingers circled my breast. I shoved him away. I thought, in panic, he thinks we're the same! I jumped up and started running across the Common.

140

He ran after me. On the sidewalk, he caught my arm and held me for a moment in mute apology, then he called a taxi and gave the driver some money. He opened the door for me. "Take this lady home," he said.

We were doing Millie's lesson the next Sunday when the landlady called her to the phone. She ran all the way down the stairs and all the way back up. She whirled into the room, dancing.

"Food!" she yelled. "Food! Come on! Get dressed. It's Henry."

I hadn't told her ... She had no idea ... I hesitated. He'd called her because he knew I'd not accept ... or because he was sorry? And to let me know? Yes! I jumped off my bed, snatched my towel and ran for the bathroom. I was starving!

The three of us went out often. Sometimes to the first restaurant, sometimes to others. Then Millie began to be silent when Henry called and Henry began to look at Millie in a strained way. The dinners became less gay.

"That guy's got me, Pill," Millie told me. "Christ, I wisht ... "

"Wish," I said, "And leave Christ out of it."

"Wish," said Millie, and stopped.

But I knew what she wished. "I think he loves you, Millie. Maybe he'll marry you."

"Marry me! Never!"

The life I was leading in Boston was disappointing; the hard voices in the office, the careless conversations, the lack of reticence, the little rivalries astonished and sickened me. I'd been in Boston seven months. Christmas was near. I was homesick, longing to go home.

Millie broke down and cried. "Christ, Pill! You won't come back! I know. And you're different. Decent ... Henry says," mimicking him, "'She's that rare being, a lady.'"

A lady? I'd done it!

"It ain't my luck ... " she hesitated. "It ain't ... I mean, it isn't ... "

We laughed. Millie was beginning to remember her grammar.

Then she said in a slightly stilted but absolutely charming voice, "I shall never meet anyone like you again."

We laughed.

And then we threw our arms around each other and wept.

More white roses this morning. I'm of two minds whether to wait for him or run.

Sue and Elliot are back from safari. I talked to Sue briefly a few days ago. Today I called her again. She's happy about Martha and Lester.

"There's a stack of mail for you. A dozen letters from Africa amongst others. Millie Austen telephoned yesterday. The last she heard, about six months ago, you had a picture in Africa's National Museum in Cape Town. You didn't tell me."

"I forgot."

"She and Henry are having some sort of celebration this Christmas and want you there."

"I'll phone her. No hurry about the mail." Almost as an afterthought, I said, "By the way, do you happen to know a man called Johnathan Edward Milford?"

"Good grief, Pill, you're doing it again!"

"Doing what?"

"Reading my mind!"

Every now and then Sue reminds me that I'm crazy. When I was in the asylum I could tell what was in her mind before she opened her mouth. "Oh, that. You're lucky it's me. So?"

"We were just talking about him."

"What! Do you know him? Who's we?"

"No. That is, I've met him. He was sitting next to me in the Garden* at some horse thing, a long time ago. Someone introduced him to me but it was dark. I wouldn't know him now if I fell over him. Why do you want to know?"

"He owns the Lodge. I'm curious. If you don't know him, why were you talking about him?"

"Is he at the Lodge?"

"No."

"So, why are you interested?"

"For heaven's sake!"

"Now I'm curious, why d'you want the dirt?"

"Oh, go on, Sue. Who were you talking to? About what?"

"Well, all right. You remember Ann Marie? She just walked out the door. It seems that for some years Mr. Milford has been romancing a friend of hers, an Italian actress, and suddenly there's discord in heaven. He's called it quits and she's weeping on every available shoulder in Washington and has just now transferred herself to New York where she's having a nervous breakdown on Ann Marie's neck. So, why do you want to know? Is he having a breakdown, too?"

"Uh ... It's possible."

---

* Madison Square Garden, New York City.

"Have you met him?"

"Briefly. He left a day ago."

"Well, be careful. Ann Marie says he's unbelievable, charming but an idiot, and that he was married to a Nazi. Elliot knew him at Yale. Elliot says he's in the State Department and if he's a Nazi or an idiot he's a changed man. Much money, frivolous, much joie de vivre, one of the most brilliant students in Yale and a genius in languages, so take your pick. Is that enough? When will you get here?"

I felt as though I had been kicked in the stomach. "I'll let you know." I hung up.

It is obvious that the staff is fully apprised of Johnathan's interest in me. Helga brought me a cable with my early morning coffee and she stood for a moment before handing it to me. "Philippa, it's from Johnathan."

"Yes?" I hesitated.

She gave me a brilliant, conspiratorial smile. "You'll want to be alone."

"Thank you, Helga."

How can I tell them that, when Johnathan finds out I spent six months in a lunatic asylum, any idea he may have of marrying me will be rapidly rejected? I feel trapped; it is not only Johnathan that I am deceiving, but Lottie and Reg and everyone on the staff.

I opened the cable. Two words. "Please stay."

Lottie knocked, came in and sat down on my bed. "Johnathan will be home in about ten days. He's bringing a guest; a woman who is very close to us."

I caught my breath. My cup rattled in the saucer. Was he romancing every female in sight?

Lottie reached up to steady my hand. "Are you all right?"

"Who is she?"

"You'll love her. She's charming and beautiful and a heroine of the Resistance; we must show her special respect."

"What did she do?"

"She ran a brothel."

I came sharply out of my depression. I wanted to laugh. "Comfort to our gallant boys?" I sounded derisive and I hadn't meant to.

"No. Comfort to the enemy's gallant boys. Officers."

"My God! How frightening!"

"Yes."

"Lottie, we've talked of the war before now. How is it that you've never mentioned your part in it?"

"I refuse it. But this month it's close, impossible to block out and at times I'm in hell. I go to Helga or your chamber-maid, Elsie, or to the gardeners. We all need to talk, to know it's over. I stay away from Reg. It worries him when I suffer."

"Tell me about the woman."

"The woman! You don't feel you should say a few kind words to comfort me?"

"Oh, Lottie! I think there are no words to comfort you. I know now that you were in a dangerous situation, rescuing people from the Nazis. Under similar circumstances I would not have survived. During the war, far less than that destroyed me. I made an attempt, but actually, I did less than nothing to help."

She took my hand. "Philippa, you are unique. I don't think you were destroyed. If so, you've made a remarkable recovery. If you did not help in the war, I think circumstances prevented it. Now, about Alethea ... "

I choked on my coffee.

"Are you sure you're feeling well this morning?"

"I ... I had a friend named Alethea." In the asylum! "It can't be the same ..."

"I suppose not. Well, she's an English woman of a somewhat renowned family who, ten years before the war, married a German industrialist. He wasn't Jewish but he hated the Nazis and when they attacked Poland, he plotted with several others to assassinate Hitler. He was betrayed and murdered and his property confiscated. Alethea was next on the murder list, but Johnathan got her to us in Switzerland and we were about to get her back to England when it was discovered that, unknown to the Nazis, her husband had owned a most exclusive officers' brothel. And since drunk and amorous Nazis might be useful to us, we decided that one of us should run it. Alethea was secretly returned to Germany to take over."

"You mean ... "

"I mean that brothel was an important listening post and that one of the most cultured and gentle women of our generation was the listener. The entire place was bugged. Alethea was ensconced in the attic where she remained during the entire war. In emergencies that attic also concealed resistance fighters and others who had need of secret shelter."

"It must have been a continuing horror for her."

"It affected her health. There was so much that was hideous, that by the end of the war she was an emotional wreck. Fortunately she has recovered. But enough, you'll meet her soon and I predict you'll love her as we do." Lottie stood up. "I must fly! You look a trifle off-colour, get some rest."

"I have a lot of writing. I'll stay in today."

When Lottie left I got out of bed and headed for the shower. I couldn't stop thinking that with Johnathan I seem to be reliving my first love, with Bill. I had loved other men and with passion, but never like this. With Bill, innocent, never having known physical passion, I knew only the spirit of love. I am reliving this experience with Johnathan. I know this is nonsense. Yet no other man, even Clay, whom I considered the love of my life, has affected me like this.

I kept my word to Pa, I did not see Bill before I left for Boston, but when I returned to Edgeville I wrote and asked him to meet me.

It was dark when he drove up and late. I'd been walking up and down in front of the house, my heart pounding, for a good half-hour. When he stopped the car, I jumped in quickly. There was a strong smell of sour alcohol inside. He did not greet me, nor I him. Perhaps he was conscious of the neighbours, for he slammed into gear, hastily.

In the dim light from the dashboard, I could see his face. It was set. Sulky. I put out my hand and touched his sleeve. "Bill, I had to see you. I thought you would want to see me, too. I love you."

He didn't turn his head. "I know you love me. Why didn't you tell me that a long time ago? Why did you lie? Did you expect me to beg?"

"I couldn't. My father ... Oh, what difference. I'm telling you now. I've never stopped wanting to be near you."

"It's a little late."

We were a mile or so out of the village. He raced the car and then, recklessly, swung it across a frozen ditch and into a field. He switched off the motor and lights. He turned to me. We were in each other's arms. We clung to each other. I could smell his whiskey breath, but it didn't matter. But he was cracking my ribs. "Bill!"

His face was pressed tight against my cheek. It was wet. His tears or mine? "Please. I can't breathe."

He let me go. I dropped my arms but I sat as close to him as I could. "I need a drink."

I was shocked. "No!"

He pushed me away from him. "Yes!"

"Bill!"

He leaned back, took a bottle off the back seat, jerked out the cork and handed it to me. "Drink?"

"No." I watched him, his head thrown back, the bottle held to his lips, silhouetted against the night-white field of snow. He put the cork back in and threw the bottle on to the back seat. He put both arms on the steering wheel and dropped his head on them.

"Bill ... What is it?" Silence. "Bill ... "

"What's the use," he said, "I'm going to be married."

I was sick with sudden and desperate loneliness. "No ... No ... "

"Yes, soon. Any day now."

"But, you love me!"

"I love you. Yes. It doesn't matter."

"Once," I said, "I thought it didn't. Now I think it's the only thing that does matter."

"For Christ's sake!"

I jumped at the violence.

But when he spoke again his voice was soft, blurred with tears, "I have to marry her."

After a second, I tried to comfort him. I touched his bent head. "Bill, it's all right. Bill, I understand."

"Don't touch me!"

"What?"

"It's bad enough this way."

I moved away, against the door of the car.

After a long time and still without raising his head, he said "I'll take you home."

No! Not yet! But he was right. I couldn't stay. "I'll walk home."

He didn't move.

I opened the door and jumped out of the car. But I couldn't leave. I was in love with him and he with me and he had never kissed me. But, like him, I wouldn't beg.

His voice was muffled in his sleeves. "Goodbye."

"Bill ... "

He didn't raise his head. "Philippa, goodbye."

Vanity had sent me out in sheer silk stockings, pumps. At every step I stubbed my toes against the ploughed earth. There were hummocks of grass under the crusted snow and I kept falling through. I stumbled across the icy ditch to the road. Waited. There was no sound.

On the crest of the hill, I stopped. His car, it's shadowed blackness dissolved in the white-gray night, had disappeared.

146

Ten days later, the village was joyously lamenting the scandal: Bill had got a girl in to trouble and deserted her. He'd run away.

"He'd have done the same thing to you."

"Yes, Mother."

"I told you he was no good."

What equals the self-destroying passion of unrequited love? My refuge, my vivid inner life, failed me now. That fabulous, glowing world beyond Edgeville, the shining beckoning light that all my life I'd watched, waited for, followed, did not exist. Or not for me. The light was but a reflection of my own desires: my hopes, my ignorant will. There was no light. Now darkness reflected darkness.

Dr. West had a saying which he quoted frequently, "Men dig their graves with their teeth." His habit, when called to attend the ailing, was to suggest that they give up eating.

Mother took me to see him. "She won't eat."

"Good. Good."

"And she just sits around all day and mopes."

"Nothing wrong with that."

"It's not natural."

"How old is she?"

"Sixteen."

"There's nothing wrong with her."

"But, Doctor!"

He pulled out a long, narrow box; took my blood pressure. He mumbled, "Well, now, it's low. Abnormally low."

My mother said triumphantly, "Oh? Well, I knew it. I told you."

"Hmm."

Mother wanted him to give me something for it: a tonic. He shook his head.

"Hmm. No." He was staring out of the window. Then he made one of his non-medical remarks that made him the joke of the Village.

"Is she in love?"

"In love? With who? She was fine when she got home from Boston," Mother laughed, disdainfully. "In love! With someone around here? Nonsense!"

"Well ... It's possible."

I could feel his eyes on me. "Are you?" he asked.

Those hated tears were in my throat and I couldn't speak. I kept my eyes on the floor. At last I got it out. "No."

He didn't give me anything to take because there was nothing wrong with me, but I didn't get better. And working in the store, I was more trouble than I was worth. I kept forgetting things. I dropped a brand new pair of lumberman's rubbers into the barrel of pickled pork and left them there over night. I was too tired to take them out.

"Philippa," Pa said, "you failed grade ten and now you must repeat it and I want you to take grades eleven and twelve."

Three years!

Millie had moved in with Henry. He was at Harvard. I didn't want to go back to Boston, get another stupid job and spend my Sundays looking in other people's windows for vicarious comfort. And my life was over anyway, so what else could I do? "All right, Pa."

I repeated grade ten, passed grade eleven and went to the Colchester County Academy in Truro for grade twelve. A young college boy from Halifax, whose name I no longer remember, swore he loved me. I wasn't interested but, just to prove someone liked me, I brought him home with me for the Christmas holidays, where he promptly fell in love with my darling sister, Flora, also home for the holidays.

Things were happening for Millie. She wrote about once a month. She was still living with Henry, but doing all sort of things, buying all sorts of wonderful clothes. As well, she was taking lessons for voice, speech, acting and make-up.

I had to get out of Edgeville!

After two years of college, when Pa's money ran out, Flora had gone to New York to train for a nurse. With her R.N. certificate she had returned to Nova Scotia, had become a Victorian Order Nurse and was working with the miners' families in Cape Breton. Gladys and Loretta had decided to become nurses as well. I thought about it. I was eighteen years old and my empty life–meaningless without Bill–stretched endlessly ahead of me. Why not dedicate it to suffering humanity? As a trained nurse I would be of some use in Russia. I had Flora's hospital address in New York and the name of the Director of Nurses. I wrote to her.

15

H ot, tired and careless of my dress, I was sitting on the bare cement stairs with my feet propped up on my suitcase. Loretta was leaning wearily against the wall, blowing wisps of yellow hair out of her baby-blue eyes. At the last minute, Gladys had decided not to come.

We had been ushered into the Nurses' Residence through the service entrance and were waiting for the housekeeper. Carol Jenks, the girl assigned to room with us, kicked off her high-heeled pumps and rubbed her cramped toes.

"Jesus! What I'd give for a smoke."

In shocked contempt, Loretta's eye caught mine.

I returned her look wall-eyed.

A door opened and a pillar of starched white flowed in. I recognized her from Flora's description: Miss Carver, the Director of Nurses. She glanced past Carol and Loretta and her eyes rested with cordial and welcoming recognition on me. "Well! Miss Jerrold!"

I stumbled over my suitcase to take her out-stretched hand. "Uh ... How d'do. Uh, you must be ... "

Gracious, smiling, she interrupted. "You've come to follow in your sister's footsteps."

"Whose? Flora's? Well, no ... I ... "

Abruptly, frigid in disapproval, she dropped my hand. "Your sister is a fine nurse."

What I meant was that I intended making tracks of my own, but I had no chance to explain. I was facing her banishing back.

Loretta, admirably poised, was doing Edgeville proud, mouthing the correct nothings.

And Carol, in her shoes at last, shaking in them, a forced smile hard and false on her face, was waiting to shake that petrifying hand. But she never shook it, at least not then.

Miss Carver, perhaps by an exercise of faith, looked straight through her to the fat woman who'd materialized behind her. "Uh, Mrs. Roy, Mrs. Roy is our housekeeper. She'll show you to your room." And she left.

Mrs. Roy weighed two hundred pounds and every ounce fluttered.

A girlish frizzle of gray hair escaped the confining hairnet that encircled her baby-pink forehead, but there was nothing girlish about her command: "Okay. You're in the army now. Pick up them suitcases and follow me."

We followed her up five double flights of back stairs and along a dark-brown corridor. She opened a door. There were three uncompromising beds squeezed into a very small room.

"Here at the Nurses' Residence," Mrs. Roy informed us, panting, "you start at the top and work down. Ha! The supervisors' rooms are on the first floor and Miss Carver, bless her heart, has a suite there."

I shoved my suitcase under the nearest bed and went to the window. I'd seen the hospital on my way to the Nurses' Home. It was a thousand-bed city hospital, a great grayish-black octagonal block behind a long curved cement drive. We were in back of it. Our window faced several shabby buildings.

Mrs. Roy pointed a fat finger past my nose. "That's where they keep the poor, crazy ones; that's Psycho, that is. Don't pay no notice when they start to scream. It don't mean nuthin'. They can't get out. And the building next to it, that's Isolation. It's for typhoid and meningitis and all them things."

Two nondescript buildings guarding fever-tortured bodies and lost minds: symbols of unknown horrors. I was terrified.

She turned away from me. "Now, you three, you do as you're told and you won't have no trouble." The door closed behind her.

The first week we had nothing to do but worry. "They" were watching, with the object of "weeding us out." Supervisors made unexpected rounds. We might be awakened at dawn or at midnight by a flashlight probing our pillows. Uneasily, we searched the bulletin board. Then one day there was news for us, we were on probation. Our uniforms, coarse blue cotton, covered by a starched white bib and apron, with stiff white collar and cuffs, were ready. After three months, if we passed the exams we'd be allowed to wear the school cap.

We sat, the new class of probationers, self-conscious in our new uniforms, in the auditorium. Mrs. Graves, Supervisor of Nurses, immaculate in starched white, faced us at our first official class meeting.

"For the first two years," she said, "your training will be in the main hospital. Later, you will go to the isolation and psychopathic wards." She paused. "Today, I am going to take you through the main hospital. I must ask you not to touch anything, and while you're there to make no comment on what you see. Questions later. Rise, please, and line up, two by two."

We followed her down the stairs and out into the open court, where the big white ambulances were drawn up outside the emergency rooms. The city police who drove them were lounging and smoking in the sun. They looked us over critically as we went by–the new probationers.

In the first emergency room a nurse was stripping a bloody sheet from a high table and laughing with an intern. The smell was human blood! In sharp recoil, I stopped.

"Keep going, please."

Loretta caught my hand. "What's wrong?"

"Let go." I breathed lightly, unwilling to inhale that nauseous air.

We moved past the emergency rooms and past the admitting rooms. Through the open doors of the clinics, we saw the charity patients, row upon row of men, women, children and babies waiting for the doctors. We continued past the shut-in telephone exchange, past the record rooms with their tier upon tier of locked steel cabinets, past the queue of yawning, gossiping nurses waiting at barred windows for white-coated chemists to fill prescriptions.

A cement tunnel took us underground to the great dim cave centered beneath that massive block. And we were deafened; monster furnaces sucked out silence and roared their voluminous blasts through our bodiless ears. Soapsuds on cold stone floors, porters with clanking pails, utility rooms, kitchens. At the end of the tunnel, wide cement steps led back up to the great open corridor of the main hospital. We walked through ward after ward. Men's wards and women's wards. Surgical, accident, gynecological, chronic disease wards. Forbidden entrance, we stared through glass doors into the maternity ward and the children's wards.

Loretta pinched my arm. Smothering giggles she was whispering. "Pill, ask her to show us the lunatics."

The lunatics. A peep-show for Loretta? I pushed her out of my way.

Back in our room, Loretta was sulky. "What was the big idea? Shoving me!"

"That was nothing. What I wanted to do ... "

"Look, Pill, you'd better learn how to behave. You're not home, you know. You're crazy!"

At first, I saw the patients in the mass: helpless, infinitely deserving of my love and care–and loathsome–I was aghast that the human body could be so marred and ravaged by disease. And it was not excessive zeal that made me first to take any and every job, but my determination to deny my feeling of disaster at having chosen this profession. To scamp this work would be criminal. On the wards, driving myself, I schooled myself to show

151

no sign of distress, but inwardly I shuddered away from the festering flesh and the human excretions–running to the utility rooms to vomit my revulsion.

For whatever else they were hospitalized for, fifty percent of our white patients had venereal diseases, either acquired or hereditary. And with our black patients who, for some uncanny reason, were so dear and close to me, the percentage was nearer ninety. It was routine to take a Wassermann on each new patient.

After three months, we were given the school cap, and we became full-time student nurses. I was still not conditioned to my work; I suffered for and with the patients and I wrote verse:

> *Dead light from the high ward windows*
> *Cold on the bodies, row upon row, diseased ...*

And then, in class one day, Loretta, who very often copied my notes, opened my book at the wrong page. She was furious. "Anyone who feels that way about the patients shouldn't be a nurse. No one can take care of patients if they hate them."

"I hate the condition, Loretta, not the victim."

"Don't try to kid me! I know what you think of them. We all do. If I were you I'd be ashamed to show my face on the ward. Go home."

Loretta called a special class meeting. The class refused to report me. But at our first meeting, having been elected president, I was now demoted to vice-president. Loretta walked out.

She was waiting for me when I got back to our room and perhaps she saw the misery in my face. She took my arm, gently, coaxing. "Pill, go home."

"What's wrong? Do I cramp your style?"

In frustrated anger, she pinched my soft underarm. "I'd be ashamed, if I were you."

"Pinch me again," I shouted "and I'll break your neck!" I ripped off my collar and cuffs, pulled off my uniform and kicked it out of my way. "I'm staying!" I declared. "But not today!" I threw on a street dress and grabbed my purse.

"But Pill ... " Loretta stood in front of the door.

"Get out of my way!"

"But you can't skip the ward, or classes; they'll kick you out!"

"That should delight you. Come on, move!" I grabbed the doorknob,

152

swung the door open and ran. She ran after me. "Pill! Pill! What'll I say if they ask me where you are? What time will you be back?"

I stopped and looked at her. "You stupid ... Tell them, thanks to you, I've gone out to jump in the lake." I ran down the back stairs, slid past the dining rooms, through the empty reception room, and banged the street door behind me. I was blocks away, still running, when I remembered I hadn't signed out. The damn book! The hell with it.

A gray day, heavy clouds shrouded the housetops and trees. There were few people on the street. I ran. The heavens rumbled, lightning flashed, the sky darkened and it began to rain. The rain poured down and I lifted my face to it. "God," I said, "wash me clean."

It was still raining when I got back to the Nurses' Home. It was pitch-black outside and I was soaked to the skin. I eased the front door open and listened. There was no one in the reception room. I took off my squelching shoes and tiptoed across the carpet. The dining rooms were empty; the maids were clearing the tables. I raced up the back stairs and opened our door. Loretta was alone.

"Pill! Where were you? Honestly, I've been having fits! My God. You didn't really jump in the lake, did you? You look like a drowned rat."

"You're an ass!"

"You're just crazy enough to do something foolish," she laughed. Then she began to cry. "I hate this place! I wish I was home! Gee, Pill, your good dress. You're really ... "

"I know," I interrupted. "Crazy. Look, I'm starving. Is there anything to eat?"

"Get into the bath tub; I'll go swipe something."

Loretta went down to the maids' dining room and brought back a bowl of stew. "Mountain-goat," she said. "That's all they had."

I hesitated. The hospital food was bad but the stew was revolting, the meat tough and slippery with an odd flavour.

"Oh, Pill," Loretta wailed, "I went all the way downstairs ... "

"Don't cry," I comforted her. "I can't swallow the mountain-goat but I'm really hungry, I'll eat the bowl."

We sat over our books silently that evening; neither of us wanted to talk. We were glad Carol was out. At nine-thirty, I couldn't keep my eyes open so I got into bed. Loretta crawled in beside me, put both arms around me and held me tight. We were half asleep when, as usual, without the ceremony of a knock, the door opened and the light clicked on. I blinked and sat up in bed. Mrs. Graves! What was she doing, making rounds?

"What are you doing in one bed?"

"W'what?"

"Get to your own beds!"

"W'what?" I stuttered again. "B'but, Mrs. Graves ... "

"You, Miss Jerrold, you're back, I see. you left the hospital today without permission. Be in my office tomorrow at ten." She was furious. "And never let me ... if I ever hear of you sleeping together again, you'll be expelled!" The door slammed behind her.

"She's nuts!" Loretta complained, crawling back to her cold bed. "The whole place is nuts!"

I was baffled as well. Pa had given me lots of information about the big world, but he'd missed out on the Isle of Lesbos.

Mrs. Graves appeared strangely unconcerned when I came to her office the next day. She was examining a paper and she didn't look at me. "Where did you go yesterday afternoon?"

"For a walk."

"In the pouring rain?"

"It did rain, yes."

"Why did you leave the hospital?"

"Uh ... for a breath of fresh air."

"I see." She dropped the paper and started flipping through a notebook.

"I won't do it again," I volunteered.

She sighed. "When we assign you to a ward, we need you there. Do you understand that?"

"Yes."

And then she looked up at me and smiled.

Why, she's young, I thought, astonished, just a girl!

"I confess," she said, and laughed, "I've wanted to do the same thing–and more than once. It's a great change coming to a city hospital. One can't help but feel overwhelmed, at times. However, a good nurse learns to control her emotions. You'll be glad to know, Miss Jerrold, that I have excellent reports of you. Look, next time you need air, ask me for leave. Now run or you'll be late for Dr. Thomas' class."

In class, Dr. Thomas offered his usual greeting: "I see you're all here–physically." Then he posed a question. "Suppose," said Dr. Thomas, "that Mr. X has turned on the gas. You come into the room and find him lying unconscious on the floor. What do you do?"

There were titters, starched rustlings and giggles around and behind me. I turned my head. Damn. Mine was the only hand in the air.

"Well, Miss ... uh ... what would you do?"

The answer that leapt to my mind was automatic and idiotic, any fool would ... but it was too late. "Open the windows," I said.

The doctor's eyes, owl eyes behind thick glasses, widened in surprise. The laughter increased while he stared at me. He raised a hand for silence. "I've put that question to every class of student nurses for the last ten years, and this is the first time I've had the correct answer. What's your name?"

"Jerrold."

"We have a genius with us," the doctor observed. "Now, for the rudiments of artificial respiration. I'll need help." He eyed me, coldly. "Come up here."

And I'm a genius, I thought, at making an ass of myself as I climbed the stairs to the stage and prepared to resuscitate our victim–a six foot black man made of rubber–stretched flat on his back on the floor.

As my practical nursing skill increased, so did my recognition of the patients' conditions; the various diseases, heart, lung, liver, kidney and glands, wrote individual signatures, visibly, on bodies and faces. Studying the chart and observing the patient, I began, automatically, to perceive his ills. And now, too, as I learned to care for them, I lost my repugnance for the diseased body; the flesh, whatever its condition, was but the covering for the spiritual man.

Here in the hospital there was a constant battle against dirt and disease; for here were the poor. They came in pain, in helplessness and in fear. They looked to the hospital, to the doctors and nurses, for hope. And, seeing them, I saw myself: I saw man, alone and naked. I gave to the meanest of them my heart and my strength. For their ignorance touched me. They did not know–as every nurse knew–that their lives depended on our honesty: unwashed hands or a slip in technique could be a major crime. Death stood, a possible victor, beside each white bed.

Now and then that first winter, walking across the open, disinfectant-scrubbed, brick court, I remembered Nova Scotia. The clean snow and the sound of sleighbells in the crisp, sunny air. I remembered the damp woods and the cool lakes. But these things were no longer real; they were as remote as a once dreamed dream.

There is an unwritten law in hospitals that anyone may be ill, except a nurse. Between 1920 and 1930, probably beyond, nurses had twelve-hour periods of duty with a half-hour for lunch and for dinner and a two-hour "recreation period." If a nurse went off duty for illness, other nurses had to do her work. Only a poor nurse allowed others to take on the extra burden. Only a poor nurse slowed up, or rested during her menstrual period. We swallowed codeine and aspirin and stayed on our feet.

The incidence of tuberculosis among nurses in city hospitals then was fairly high. The incidence of immorality was fairly high, too. To an extent, we looked on life as soldiers look on it. Each day we faced an enemy. This invisible enemy was powerfully present; a germ is as deadly as a bullet. Because we saw before us, constantly, the precariousness of life, we wanted to live each moment as fully as we knew how.

And, in the hospital, the facts of life were not veiled in mystery; they lost their taboos. "When the spermatozoa enter the vagina, they are alive," the obstetrician told us. "They swim up through the opening in the cervix and how they can swim!" Here, sex was a natural function. "Women are ready to bear children when they begin to menstruate. It is unnatural to suppress the sex instinct for years. Women should conceive and bear children while the cartilages are still soft."

I had a swift recall of my childhood fear that pregnancy was catching, that someone would brush past and leave me pregnant and I smiled.

"That delights you, Miss Jerrold?" the obstetrician asked.

The whole class tittered.

It had been a long, hard day and I was tired and trying to study. I had worked my two months in the emergency rooms and I was in despair of the fragility–and the idiocy–of the patients. They came in an unending stream; burned, mutilated, strangled and beaten both physically and mentally. Careless of life or enraged with it, they destroyed their own and each other's minds and bodies. I'd gone from emergency to the men's tuberculosis ward. And now, endlessly running through my head, lines from Keats' "Ode to a Nightingale":

> *Here, where men sit and hear each other groan;*
> *Where palsy shakes a few, sad, last gray hairs,*
> *Where youth grows pale, and spectre-thin, and dies;*
> *Where but to think is to be full of sorrow*
> *And leaden-eyed despairs ...*

Keats, too, had walked the hospital wards and, before he wrote those lines, had nursed his brother, Tom, and watched him die of tuberculosis. But Keats ...

"I wanna be raped!" Lying on her back, hands behind her head, feet in the air, Carol was endlessly repeating, "I wanna be raped! By a plushy guy.

A guy with plushy balls. I wanna plushy guy ... "

"Carol, shut up."

"You want to be raped by a guy with plushy balls?" parroted Loretta.

"For God's sake be quiet."

"Philippa," Carol observed, "if you'd get out of the books and into the sheets it would improve your lousy disposition."

"I'm sick of you."

"You can do it without sheets, you know."

They were both screaming with laughter.

I slammed my book shut. "How can I work! Wait ... Listen! Listen!"

It was the women. Distantly through the night, in the hospital stillness, we heard an increasing hubbub; screams of protest, of terror.

"The nuts in Psycho." Carol yawned. "They're all right 'till one starts, then they all start. They must be admitting a new one."

I thought, I'll never be a nurse. I was ashamed of the gooseflesh on my body and my sudden weakness. I said, "Let's get out of here. Let's go downtown."

"You're nuts!" Loretta said. "It's almost ten o'clock. But if you're so anxious to go out," she rolled off her bed and reached for her purse, "run over to Happy's and get us some chocolate ice cream and some cupcakes."

"You'll weigh a ton if you don't stop eating."

The women were in a frenzy. Shrieking. I stood up, banged down the window and drew the curtains.

"Now we'll suffocate. Say, Jerrold, what's wrong with your boy friend, ain't he got no love?"

"Don't be crass." I went out now and then with the brother of one of the nurses and Carol knew him. He was a bore and a bad dancer.

Carol said, "Honestly, Jerrold, my Jimmie's got a friend. He's a good sport and plenty of dough. Why don't you come out with us?"

"Don't waste your time on her, Carol. She's never had a boy friend in her life. She wouldn't know how to act."

The trouble with me, I thought, is that I want something I'll never get. "Good sport and plenty of dough" was Carol's dream and she was living it. I'd been wishing all along for a very different life. It existed, I was sure, yet how remote from me. Meanwhile I, prim and priggish, sat on the side lines.

"C'mon, Jerrold, it'll do you good to get out."

"Don't take her, Carol, she'll ruin the party. I know her!"

"Carol," I said, "maybe I'm under-sexed."

They were screaming again. Carol cupped her hands below her breasts, shut her mouth and puffed out her cheeks. Her eyes rolled idiotically at me.

"I suppose I have enough," I said, laughing, "but they're just decorations."

"They're decorations all right! Look, Jerrold, some man must have given you an awful crack."

"I had an upright upbringing," I said. "Didn't I, Loretta?"

"You were brought up the same as me," Loretta said, "so don't try to pretend any different."

"All right, Carol, I'll go."

"Pill," Loretta persisted, "they don't need a stick-in-the-mud! Stay home!"

Why didn't Loretta want me to go?

"That's it kid," Carol said, "I won't let on you're Jesus' little sister. I'll tell them you're one of the nurses."

The next day I went out and bought a dress: a straight tube of black velvet, cut high to the neck with narrow white collar and cuffs.

"Why do you always dress like a nun!" Carol protested. "That sure needs perking up! If you want, I'll lend you my red beads."

"Thanks, I won't risk it. Beads make me nervous. I might pull them off."

"I told you, Carol. She's nuts!"

There was no one around. Carol slipped out of the front door and I followed. It was still light. I stopped. Where were they?

"Hey! That's them. That car on the corner." Carol began to run.

Car? Long, black, shiny, opulent. Good God, I thought, it's a hearse: he's an undertaker! No. Not the right shape. Carol jumped in the back seat. So, my date owned that magnificent ... He was rich!

"Hurry up!" Carol yelled at me.

Even if I wanted to, I couldn't run. My skirt was too narrow. But I was in a trance. Strange that no one got out to hold the door. Rich, tall, dark, handsome; no matter. I didn't dare look. I kept my eyes on the sidewalk till I was opposite the driver's seat. Then I stooped and looked in. Damn Carol!

"Pill! You waitin' to be introduced? Jesus! Get in before some damn supervisor catches us."

Catches us? They were married!

"Take it easy, Carol. If a lady likes to look a guy over before she falls in his lap, it's okay by me."

And middle aged!

He put a fat hand on his tie; orange, patterned in circles of green. "I'll introduce myself," he said. "I'm Harry and if you don't soon hop in, another pretty little nursie will come along and grab me."

"S'sorry," I got in the car. "I-uh-that is-uh-" I was overcome. "Uh, I was admiring your tie." Thank you, G.B. Shaw for, with you, I do appreciate the easy social lie.

It was the most luxurious car I'd ever been in. Sitting back on the lush upholstery, it rested every part of me. But Harry had been a shock. And now, fattish, self-assured, slick, he hastened to tell me he owned a string of small, popular stores. "Comfortable, kid?" He put his hand on my knee.

I picked up his cuff with the tips of my fingers, handed it back to him and moved away.

He stared at me, appraisingly. "Carol promised me something different. She's quite a girl."

I returned his stare. "I'm sure you wouldn't want just anyone."

He threw back his head, opened his heavy mouth and laughed. His front teeth were backed with gold. He peered into the mirror on the windshield, watching the reflection of the couple in the back seat. "You two, back there, behave yourselves! Can't you wait till we're out of town?" His voice was rasping, aggressive, vulgar.

"What about a drink?" Jim suggested. "Carol's attacking me. I need help for Christ's sake! Gimme a drink."

Harry lifted a flap on the car door and pulled out a flask. "Help yourself." He handed it back over his shoulder. "It's the best," he boasted loudly. "Hey, wait till we pass that cop!"

They drank and then Carol touched my shoulder. "Have a swig."

"Thank you." I took the flask. This is life? What a boy friend! After more than a year on the wards, I didn't need a crystal ball to tell his fortune: one wife, four or five kids, and two diseases. No, no disease. He was smart enough, or he wouldn't be out with a nurse.

Well, I'd asked for it. Life. I was going to eat a slice. I tipped the flask and drank straight rye whiskey. It was the best, perhaps, but it was raw. I held a mouthful for a moment, my eyes watering, then let the burning liquid slip down my throat.

Harry took the flask out of my hand. "Leave some for the chauffeur." He took a quick drink and handed it back to me.

I tipped up the flask and took another drink–slowly. This time, I was prepared for the best.

"Where we goin', Harry?"

"I thought we'd go up to Greene's Palace," he paused, "and get a steak."

They laughed. No mistaking the implication! This shouldn't shock me, I thought, shocked.

"Why so serious?"

I wasn't going to explain that I was worried because I was still sober. How much did you need to drink before you got drunk? I had no idea. Nor did I then know that I was to discover that you can drink a pint of straight whiskey and remain completely sober for twenty or thirty minutes until your shocked, tense stomach muscles relax and pours it into your system. Then you're drunk! Dead drunk!

Harry patted my knee and then squeezed it. Over his shoulder he said, "Little Pill here needs another drink."

"If you can't loosen her up," said Jim, "no one can."

We drove out of the city, along the Hudson River and turned on to a bridge. We were on our way to New Jersey.

Harry pinched my thigh. "Feelin' good, girlie?"

I thought of Millie. Christ! I'll break his damned neck! No, I admonished myself. None of that. Life!

There were woods now on both sides of the road. We had passed the last lights several miles back. It began to rain.

Jim leaned over the front seat. "Slow down. It's along here somewhere."

We turned off the main highway on to a narrow unpaved road. The heavy car bumped on the uneven surface.

Panic hit me. I put a hand on the door. I could jump out and run back to the main road. Carol was giggling in the back seat. It was raining hard. I sat still. I'm a fool, I thought. But I won't let him near me. It was dark, now. God alone knew where we were.

In the stillness, through the woods, we heard saxophones, a piano. Our headlights picked out a cleared space. Dozens of cars were parked in a field. Back of the clearing, surrounded by trees, stood an enormous white barn with Green's Palace in neon lights running across the front.

A boy ran up with an umbrella. "Park your car, sir?"

Harry flipped him a bill and got out.

I felt cold sober. Maybe I couldn't get drunk?

Inside, the smoke was so thick you could hardly see through it. The

160

music blared. Dozens of tables crowded the small dance floor. A brown girl, naked except for a narrow loin cloth and bra, was shaking and writhing, jerking her bushy black head, beating the air with her hands; stamping out an orgasm in the glare of the spotlight.

"Hot!" approved Harry. He stood behind me with both arms clasping my waist and pushed himself against me. He bit my ear, released me, and pushed me. "You girls run upstairs and powder your noses. I got to see the boss."

In the dirty washroom, I snatched at Carol's arm.

"Carol, I don't like it! I'm leaving!"

A manufactured blonde stopped painting her wooden face and turned, her compact in mid-air, to listen.

Carol jerked her arm away. "What's wrong with you?"

"Where are we?"

"Are you drunk?"

"No."

"Well, where the hell do you think we are? It's a roadhouse."

"I'm getting out of here."

"Getting out? Listen, don't pull this Sunday-school stuff with me. You knew damn well where we were going!"

"But those men! I can't go through with it!"

"What are you trying to do? Spoil the party?"

"They're so cheap!"

"They're damn nice boys," said Carol, furiously. "You're the cheap one, coming out and acting like a fool."

"Carol, I can't ... "

"Who asked you to do anything? Keep your mouth shut and act human!" She was shaking with anger. "I should've known enough not to bring you!"

The blonde, who had stepped nearer to listen, looked at me, opened her mouth, hesitated, shrugged her shoulders, shut her mouth and went back to her painting.

In the glass above the stained basin, my eyes looked back at me, shamed. I powdered my nose, quickly, and turned away. After all, it was a public place, there wasn't much he could do. There must be a telephone. I could call a taxi. Thank heavens I was sober.

The "boys" had a table next to the dance floor.

"I told you," Carol bragged, "Harry's a friend of the boss."

The floor show was over, people were dancing. The rhythm of the drums was exciting. There were double whiskeys on the table. I picked up my glass. Two ounces of whiskey. Well ... I raised it to my lips and slowly, steadily, I drank it. My mouth hurt. My throat burned all the way down.

"God!" said Harry, "No soda? No nothing? Let's dance. Come on Babe." Harry pulled me out of my chair. "Order my girl another drink."

He was very strong and I couldn't hold myself away from him. We danced cheek to cheek, his knees pushing between mine.

"You're okay," he said. The arm that held me rubbed up and down on my back. I tried to force him away. He laughed. Then ... Damn! My knees were trembling! I could hardly stand! He supported me. Was I drunk? I was dizzy.

"In just a minute, Babe, we're going to see if they got that room ready."

I tried to control my voice, to make it casual, reasonable. "I'm sorry, Harry, I'm not leaving this room."

"Why not? Don't you want it?"

"I shouldn't have come out with you. I didn't think ... "

"Don't worry. I'll make you want it." His saccharine voice unnerved me. He pressed his cheek hard against mine; the bristles hurt my face. I could hardly breathe. His arm was like a vise around me.

"Please!"

He released me suddenly, so that I staggered and almost fell. I clutched at him.

"What you need, Babe, is another drink." He turned me around and, hands on my shoulders, pushed me to our table.

I sat down quickly. I was dizzy, muzzy with drink, but he pushed a highball into my hand. "Drink up, sweetie," he urged. "Look, I wouldn't hurt you for the world."

We were alone at the table. Carol and Jim were dancing. He pulled his chair close to mine and put his arm, heavily, over my shoulder. I could smell the awful hair oil on his head. I turned my head away.

"You're a grown up girl," he said. "Look, tell me, what's wrong with me?"

I'd like to tell you, I thought. You ... You Neanderthal ape. You missing link. But I still had enough sense to keep my voice down. I looked into his eyes. They looked soft and gentle in the half light. I said quickly, trusting him, "Harry, you see, I haven't been out like this before. I ... "

I saw his eyes change, harden. He didn't believe me! "I've met babes like you before. Playing innocent! Who do you think I am? Some kind of sucker?"

162

Carol came off the dance floor, laughing. She sat down at the table and put an arm around Harry. Harry took her hand. "Hello, Hon. Give me the dope on your friend. She got morals or is she on the take?"

"Who's on the take?" Jim came up behind me, put a rough hand on either side of my face and forced my head back. He leaned down and tried to kiss me on the mouth.

"No!" I dodged, but he held me. I bit him. Hard.

"Christ!" But he let me go.

Carol and Harry hung together, laughing.

"Christ! How long have you had her up at that hospital, anyhow?"

"God!" said Harry, "You just kissed the virgin Mary."

"I didn't," said Jim, "but I'm going to!" He caught both my wrists, held them in one hand and took hold of my back hair with the other hand. "You bitch!"

"Carol!" I said, desperately, "Carol!"

Harry put his hand on Jim. "Okay Jim, let go. She's mine. I'll handle her."

Jim dropped my wrists and hair. I staggered to my feet. "I'm leaving!"

Harry grabbed my arm. "Sit down!"

I jerked away from him. I half fell. I started off between the tables bumping into chairs, my eyes blurred.

Harry had my arm. "Don't be dumb. You're miles from the city and it's pouring out."

"Call a taxi. Taxi! Taxi!" I hurried, tried to shake him off. I could hear my voice–through a cloud–"Waiter! Get me a taxi!"

Carol had me by one arm, Harry by the other. "For God's sake shut up! Relax! No one's going to hurt you. Pill. Listen, Hon," his voice was gentle, coaxing, "don't break up the party, we just come. If you'd sit down a minute, I'll take you home myself. I promise."

"No!"

"You're drunk, you fool!" Carol was furious.

A man in evening dress approached us. "You asked for a private room, Sir?"

"Yeah!"

"Come this way."

"I won't go! Waiter! A taxi! Waiter!"

Carol pinched me. "Shut your mouth! If we're caught we'll be kicked out of the hospital. Both of us."

They manoeuvred me past the tables. When they started up the stairs, I tried to pull back but they gripped me, painfully. We went up two flights of stairs and along a narrow corridor.

The man in evening dress unlocked the door and threw it open. He handed Harry the key. "Here you are, sir."

It was a large, whitewashed room with a bureau, a double bed and a couple of painted wicker chairs. The pink spread on the bed and the pink upholstery on the chairs were stained and soiled. A small hanging ceiling bulb and two green-shaded, iron, standing lamps gave out a cold light. Stale cigarette smoke hung in the dead air. A bare french window stared out on blackness. A bottle of whiskey and four glasses stood on a aluminum tray on the bureau.

Through a half-open door, I saw a black and white tiled bathroom floor, grimy-stained.

"Jesus, Carol!" Harry said. He kicked the door shut and turned the key in the lock. "Phew! What we need, after that, is a drink!" He opened the bottle and poured half tumblers of whiskey.

I stood with my back to the door. I had to get out! I was drunk!

"Now," Harry carried glasses to Carol and Jim, and then came to me, "take a drink, Pill and let's be sensible. You could have got us in a lot of trouble. You want to get Carol kicked out and you, too? That's a fine pal!"

"I'm leaving!"

"Okay, okay, but wait till we have a drink. We're all leaving in a minute. Come on, sit down, kid, I won't hurt you." He put his arm around me and led me to the bed. We sat down together.

"Here," he said, pressing his glass against my mouth. "Have a drink."

"No!" I shoved the glass away.

"It's all right! You're going home in a minute. You can take a drink with me, can't you?" He pushed the glass against my mouth again. It began to spill ...

If I didn't want it all over my dress ... I opened my mouth and drank.

Jim said, "There's an awful lot of light in this place." He dumped Carol, giggling, on the floor and got up and switched off all the lights. The room was pitch black.

I sat quietly on the bed with Harry. I was dizzy. He said, "I've had a drink too much, myself. Better wait till it wears off before I start driving back. That's a new car." He pulled me back on the bed with him. "Lay down," he said. "Relax."

I was exhausted. I lay back.

We lay side by side. It was still raining. I could hear it beating against the windows. The room rolled, expanded, collapsed. Then it was still and I was floating in it, whirling up and down, floor to ceiling in a wide arc. I held on to him, trying to steady myself.

Harry was kissing me on the cheek. He was holding me, one hand on the nape of my neck. He was strong and gentle. He was stroking my breast, back and forth, back and forth. My body was solaced, wanting to be solaced. It was right when he opened the neck of my dress, touched my bare skin. Holding me, holding my breasts, he rolled me towards him, my body flat against his. He kissed my mouth. He began to move gently against my thighs. One hand moved down and rubbed my knee. It slid under my dress on to my bare leg.

"No!" I jerked away from him, but he followed me and the room carried us both around and back.

"Relax, sweetie! I won't hurt you." Rolling, one hand on my bare leg, the other on the nape of my neck, he was kissing me on the mouth. I forgot about pulling away. I wanted the kisses; they were part of the dizziness.

"God! How I want you!" He took his hands from me. He was fumbling at his belt.

I was alone and suddenly conscious of the heavy breathing in the other corner of the room. Conscious that I was being seduced by a man I despised, in a cheap soiled bed. The door was locked and he had the key in his pocket. I sat up, jerked past his reaching hands, rolled over and fell on the floor. I scrambled for the french window, fumbling in the dark for the handles. I found them, twisted and pulled. A wave of cold, wet air hit me.

He had me by the shoulders, the waist. I strained away from him, trying to fling myself into the blackness outside. The rain beat in on me. I fought him, kicking and punching. I wasn't afraid any more. I was in a rage. I would kill him.

"Stop!" He was panting. His hands were digging into me, holding me. I fought him. "The river," he panted. "The cliff. Christ! Jim the lights!"

But I saw it before the lights came on, dimly, over the slippery edge of the rotten railing. I saw the wet gleam of rain on the sloping black rock beneath us and below, emptiness. And I could hear it far below, the roar of the river. In the greenish electric light, we stood leaning on each other; holding to each other.

"Crazy!" he shouted. "You're crazy!" He pulled me back into the room and shoved me into the soiled pink chair. He wiped his face with his arms, one arm after the other. He was shaking when he sat down on the bed. "Okay," he said, "you win. Do you know what you might have done to us? You're crazy! I'm taking damn good care to get you back to that hospital, safe."

When we got in the car, and we started home, I vomited; projectile vomiting, all over that beautiful hearse.

They let us off at the corner. Carol pushed me through the basement window and I didn't wait to hear about her ruined evening. I took off, up the stairs, for the shower. And I didn't stop to undress. I turned the water on full blast and I soaped and washed and soaped and washed. I felt I would never be clean again.

16

In the gray dawn, hurrying, wrapped in our capes against the chill air, Loretta and I were coming off night-duty. The normal tour was four weeks, but I'd been on for three months and the past weeks had been hell. The hospital was short of nurses. Mrs. Graves had left the Office to take over the men's surgical ward and she had ordered me to go on day duty with her. I was flattered, but if I didn't get some rest I'd fall on my face. In the Nurses' Residence, I glanced at the mailbox and picked up a letter.

"Anything wrong?" Loretta put her chin on my shoulder and studied the loosely scrawled writing. "Who's it from?"

"Flora."

"Gee! By the look on your face, I thought someone dropped dead."

I had a sudden chill. Flora had never written to me. I shoved the letter in my pocket and headed for the stairs.

"Pill, your breakfast!"

I raced up the stairs to my room, kicked off my shoes, threw my soiled uniform into the laundry basket and grabbed a robe and towels. In the utilitarian, gray-walled nurses' bath, I turned on the faucets and sat on the edge of the tub. The hot water ran soothingly over my aching feet. I ripped open the letter.

"Dear Pill, I thought you would like to know I'm engaged ... "

Not Pa! I could breathe again. I dropped the letter on the floor and got into the tub. Flora engaged? I leaned over and picked up the letter.

"I don't know if it's a good idea or not, maybe it's a mistake, but I seem to be better off with him than without him."

Why the doubt? Didn't she love him? I could never think of Flora without hurt–her contempt for me! Now, confiding her most intimate feelings, did that mean she wanted to be friends? There were tears in my eyes.

"Sue is going to Acadia in September; Mrs. Lawson has been here for a month. She's made her some really lovely clothes."

I dropped the letter on the floor. Damn! I felt sick. Pa must know that it was my turn to go to college! They had shut me out again ... But how blame Pa? I had never told him I was sick of the hospital, that I had never

167

grown used to the endless nightmare of cheerfulness in the face of disease. I had never said these things, but I carried them in my heart, an unrelenting weight.

If only I could leave–go to college! But make a fuss? Upset Sue? I couldn't! Anyway, for the first time in my life I was of some use in the world.

"Hey!" Loretta was banging on the door. "Pill, let me in!"

I got out of the tub, dripping, and slid back the bolt.

"How's Flora? What did she say?"

"The most marvellous news," I said, brightly. "Flora's engaged! And Sue is going to Acadia."

I lay in bed twisting and turning my ankles. Since I'd gone on day duty, more than six weeks ago, we'd been short of help. This morning, I had taken my two hours off from six to eight and skipped breakfast, hoping my feet would feel better. Faint hope.

I got up and pulled up the blind. Two weeks, I mused, and I'd be on my way home. Time off, at last. I'd head for the woods! I glanced at my watch. Sixteen minutes to get dressed. I could get into uniform in one minute, flat, but I would need ten minutes for a bath.

Fifteen minutes later, I walked into the ward and stopped in shock. We were short of nurses and sometimes careless, but we didn't leave forty-eight post-operative patients alone. I crossed to the utility room and pulled open the door.

Mrs. Graves was vomiting into the sink. She wiped her mouth and looked up at me, tears in her eyes.

"Sit over here," I said. "I'll clean up." I pushed up a window and reached for a long-handled brush.

Mrs. Graves walked to the door and leaned on it. "I sent McDonald off ... "

"Your hair."

She started fumbling with her cap.

"You're pregnant," I said.

She stared at me. Then she attempted a laugh. "What makes you think ... "

I could have kicked myself. Mrs. Graves was a widow. In my confusion, my next brainless words didn't help. "I just know. How did it happen?"

At that, we both laughed. But tears were streaming down her face. "How do you think! Does it show?"

"Honestly," I said, "you can't. I just knew." I pulled my compact out of my pocket and handed it to her.

Mrs. Graves had always kept a good professional distance between us. Until now, we had been supervisor and student nurse. Now, she looked into my eyes. I don't know what she saw, but what I felt for her was compassion. And in her eyes, I saw relief replace fear.

I thought, gratefully, she trusts me.

She adjusted her cap and powdered her face. "Take over for me this morning," she said. "I'll be back after lunch. Tell McDonald ... a headache." She was gone.

I was alone on the ward for two hours until McDonald got back and it was a rat-race, making rounds with the doctors, doing dressings, handing out medications and drinks, rubbing backs, fixing beds, and even handing out bedpans and urinals. The male orderly was supposed to do that, but ... Then came lunch, and medications again, temperatures, visitors–the whole rigamarole a second time–and writing up charts in between.

It was almost five in the evening when Mrs. Graves came back. She sent McDonald to supper, sat down at her desk and pointed to the chair beside her.

I was glad to sit down.

She didn't look at me. She kept her eyes on the green blotter and she said softly and carefully, spacing her words to emphasize the underlying meaning, "The doctor tells me I should take a few days off. I'm driving to the country tomorrow. I wonder if you'd care to come?"

The words she didn't speak were so loud in my head that I jerked around to see if anyone else had heard them. Abortion! Illegal abortion! I hesitated.

"Perhaps you'd rather not?" she said under her breath.

"No," I said. "I want to. I mean, please let me come."

"Don't ... "

I knew what she was going to say. "I won't open my mouth. But how do I get time off?"

"I'll fix that. I kept you on night duty too long and since then you've been overworked here. I'll tell the Office you need a rest."

Strong white light flooded the kitchen. The small bulb above the kitchen table had been replaced by a large one. The table was covered with a pad and a sheet. On a small table near the stove, there were two or three kidney basins, gowns and gloves in sterile packages, sterile gauze, and wrapped sterile instruments. A big pot of water simmered on the stove.

I couldn't help the look on my face.

Mrs. Graves smiled at me. "Don't worry about operating-room procedure; it's impossible here."

"Yes?" I said. "I've been over-trained, I guess." No stirrups. What if her feet slipped?

"It's good enough," she said, nonchalantly. "Let's get out of here."

I followed her into the sitting room. This was crazy! I should insist ... but the doctor, whoever he was, surely wouldn't allow it. Her face was strangely without colour, her movements restless and jerky. She went wandering around the room, touching things. It was a beautiful room, large and light and handsomely furnished. She pulled at the curtains. Mild hysteria, I thought ... could hysteria be mild?

"Old-fashioned Abigail," she was saying. "Abbie, to you, Philippa. D'you like the room? I took it for the marble mantel over the fireplace. We had one just like it at home. When my parents died ... " She looked at her watch and her face grew a shade lighter. "My Catholic mother called this murder. I should never have allowed you to come. Go, if you want to. Leave!"

I wanted to run, mostly because of the set-up in the kitchen. "Mrs. Graves, why did you choose me?"

She crossed the room, stood in front of me and stared into my eyes. "I trust you." Then she went back to pulling the curtain. "Look at this. It never hangs straight. Besides, in an emergency, you never lose your head. I want you to call me Abbie."

Emergency! She was frightened. "But your doctor," I blurted, "surely he's competent? Mrs ... Abbie, do you trust him?"

"Of course I trust him," she said sharply. She crossed the room and sat down in front of the fireplace. "It's just that, actually ... " She gave a nervous little laugh. "Actually," she repeated, "you have as much O.R. experience as he has. He's had enough, of course," she added, quickly.

An intern, I thought. And she doesn't trust him an inch. Who the hell was he? And how could I take over if he made a mistake? The nearest I'd come to a curette was to slap it in the surgeon's palm when he needed it and see to it that the dirty nurse* picked it off the floor when he'd finished with it. And if he, in his inexperience, went through the uterine wall, what could I do? What could anyone do? Maybe one day, we'd learn to deal with peritonitis but in this year of grace ...

There was one resident, a surgeon I trusted implicitly, a Texan, who always wanted me on difficult cases. He'd come like a shot if I called him.

---

* The dirty nurse picks extraneous material, such as sponges, etc. off the floor.

170

But why this abortion anyway? My voice came out too loud, "Abbie, listen. Keep this baby and whoever he is, marry him!"

She turned to look at me. I had never seen her in anything but a uniform. Now she was wearing a soft, white silk robe. She stood, staring at nothing, and I was astonished all over again at her beauty. "I can't marry him. He's not established and he has no money. I'd be a burden. If I hadn't made one mistake–you know the hospital thinks I'm widowed but I'm divorced. That shocked my parents, but he was a brute. I entered training to get away ... If it wasn't for that I might insist. I don't believe in abortion. I want to marry him, but this time, when or if I marry, he must want me. You know, I sometimes wonder what secret other girls have. I don't seem to be able to ... " She broke off abruptly. "I'm talking too much."

I was embarrassed, thinking of all the things I couldn't say. "All I can say is, he must love you. He's risking his future. Does he know I'm here?"

She shook her head. "He said any old woman could do it, so he'd do it alone." She laughed. "But then, since you knew, I thought, just in case–and for his sake–it would be better if you were here. And then I wanted you, myself. I was wrong, though, to involve you in this."

It was my turn to stand up. I was too nervous to sit still. I said, "I'm here of my own free will. Come on, it's time to prep you. Where's your razor?"

Abbie went to the bathroom and I went to the kitchen to look at that table again. I hadn't been this frightened since my first months in training. Once she was full of morphine, would she maintain the position for a vaginal operation? Her feet should be held, solidly, in stirrups. Otherwise, if she dozed off, if her foot fell asleep and slipped while he had the curette inside her, if he pierced the uterine wall ... Did she want to die?

She would never have permitted this for a patient. Brainless, I thought, I'm brainless. After all I'd been taught and after all I'd read. I must do something about that table–find support for her feet.

Abbie, head drooping, was sitting on the edge of the bath tub. She had put on a hospital shirt, set out towels, green soap and a razor.

"Shave me here." She started to slide to the floor.

I was startled. "Wait! I'll get a blanket, a sheet ... "

She pulled herself up, opened a cupboard, took out a sheet and threw it on the floor. Then she lay down on it.

She was drugged. "Abbie! What did you take?"

She opened her eyes and looked at me. "Take? I took your life in my hands and ... " She began to giggle.

I put a towel under her. "I have to know. You must tell me. What did you take?"

"You dare talk to me like that? I'll give you a few demerits when we get back!" She was giggling again.

If we got back. I found the razor. I washed my hands carefully. I'd told Loretta and Carol that I was going to Boston to see Millie. If anything went wrong ...

"God," I prayed, "how can I brace her feet?"

I finished shaving her. "Abbie, get up. And now I must know. Is it time for your morphine or have you had it?"

"Don't be silly, Phil'pa."

Why was she so sleepy? "I'll wait for the doctor."

"No. Give it to me."

"Mrs. Graves, is it all right for me to give you morphine?"

"Yes! Now, or I'll do it for you!"

We went to the kitchen and I got the hypo ready and gave it to her. Then she got up on the table and lay down. I threw a blanket over her and put a small pillow under her head. She was quiet now. Too quiet? Morphine doesn't take effect that fast. I checked her pulse. Slow! I should never have given her the hypo! Her hands were cold and damp. Her eyes were shut and I didn't dare ask to look at her pupils. Somehow, I must brace her feet.

I looked around the kitchen. The little step-ladder she used to reach the top shelves was the right height. "Abbie, I want some rope or string."

She lifted her hand. "Uh, top draw ... "

I found a ball of heavy cord.

I put the step-ladder in place. It was all right; about eight inches above the kitchen table. I would fasten it to the table with the cord. I slipped my hands under her knees. Why was she so drowsy? "Abbie, lift your knees!"

Her knees came up, unevenly, so I helped her lift them. "I'm moving your feet into position against the top of the ladder. Hold them there and don't move. Don't push!"

"Uh ... per'fly still."

I got under the table and lashed the ladder to the legs of the table.

"Wha' you doin' under my bed?" She was giggling again.

"Don't move. I'll be right back. I'm going to put shoes on you." I ran to her bedroom, found a pair of walking shoes, came back and took off her slippers. The ladder moved.

"She giggled, "We goin' for a walk?"

I held on to the ladder, grabbed the cord and got down and tied it tighter.

"Phil ... Phil'pa. You sleepin' under there?"

"Shut up and hold still." I put the shoes on her feet and tied the cord around them and to both tops of the ladder. "Please, Abbie, don't move." I ran for a sheet, came back and dropped it over her legs. I stood there, panting. The whole thing was a horror.

I put the cord back in the drawer and took her hands in mine. "Abbie, talk to me. This is no joke. What did you take?"

She half-raised her head and squinted at me. "Time you started calling me Mrs. Graves." She was giggling.

A key turned in the lock. George Downer opened the door. Caught! No, safe! We hadn't started ... Unless? No! Surely not!

Dr. Downer stopped at the kitchen door. "Jerrold! Good. I'm glad you're here. Now I won't have to wash the dishes." He turned and threw his gloves, hat and coat on to the sofa and came into the kitchen.

Her eyes half open, Abbie lifted her arms. "George, dearest."

He kissed her.

I said, "Hello, Dr. Downer" to his back and walked into the sitting room. I leaned both elbows on the mantle above the fireplace and dropped my head in my hands. I was appalled.

I'd been in the operating room with him for a full month. He was on Gyniatrics and the Chief of that service hacked at the charity patients without mercy. He would ask some woman who weighed two hundred pounds if she would like to be thin. The innocent creature would sign a release, and he would slit her from sternum to pubic hair, cut out pounds of fat and sew her up. Perhaps she lived, or perhaps that long incision became infected ...

GYN was compulsory training for an intern but it was not compulsory to kowtow to the Chief. Downer hung on his every word. Like his Chief, he didn't worry if he bruised or injured tissue or chopped it away. And what was beyond pardon, I thought, was his sublime arrogance.

George Downer! I wouldn't let him operate on my cat.

"I can guess what you're thinking," Dr. Downer said, softly.

I turned my head. He was standing behind me, smiling.

My heart pounded in quick rage. "No. You couldn't possibly imagine." But I mustn't rattle him before an operation. "Abbie took some sort of drug before I gave her the morphine."

"Nonsense! She wouldn't do any such thing. You must ... "

I interrupted him. "What about that table? Do you think you should operate on that?"

"Thanks!" he said. "I believe I'm capable of a D and C! I see you braced her feet. Most ingenious. If Mrs. Graves is satisfied with the arrangement, I don't think you should worry."

"I don't like it. She's too drowsy. She ... "

"Oh, come, Jerrold, don't be hysterical. She won't be asleep, she'll cooperate. She's not a child. Did you prepare an extra hypo? If not, do it, stat. I'll scrub." He went to the bathroom.

I began to pray. These days, I never bothered to ask if God existed. He was present. I scrubbed up in the kitchen sink, shook lycopodium powder over my hands and pulled on sterile gloves. I pulled cap, mask and gown out of one sterile pack and slipped in to them. Then I opened another sterile pack.

Dr. Downer held out his dripping hands. "Ready?"

I handed him a sterile towel and shook out a gown. He dropped the towel on the floor and put his arms through the sleeves. I powdered his hands and held the gloves open till he got them on. And then, behind him, I adjusted his cap and mask and tied the strings of his gown.

And then, well, the whole thing went off all right. At least there was no apparent complication.

"Pack the evidence," Dr. Downer said. He skinned off his gloves and threw them into a kidney basin. "Make it a small, neat package and I'll dispose of it." And without looking at me, he added, "Thanks." He lifted Abbie off the table and carried her to her room.

I wiped the sweat off my face with a clean towel and sat down. I was weak. The more I thought of it, the madder I got. Downer was a fool. Abbie had had something other than what I'd given her. She was *out*. Was it just this once or was it a habit?

I cleaned up. When the place was a kitchen again, I started the coffee.

Dr. Downer came in and sat down at the table. "That coffee smells good, Jerrold. I'll have a cup."

I sat down opposite him and stared at his face until he lifted his head and looked at me. Then I said in my gentlest voice, "Miss Jerrold to you, you silly little man." Dr. Downer is over six feet tall. He knew I wasn't talking about his physical size.

"Oh, come on, you don't mean that."

"I mean it."

He sighed. "Yes, I guess you do. If you have scruples about abortion, why are you here?"

"No scruples," I said. "As far as I'm concerned, the embryo doesn't exist. But Abigail exists and so do I. You might have finished us. We may still be ... "

174

"Abbie and you!" he scoffed. "I took the same risk."

"I don't think you're worth worrying about," I said. "Did you take Abbie's pulse? Did you find it a little slow?"

"Of course I did! Yes, but she'll be all right."

"Abbie took some sort of drug before I gave her the morphine."

"Nonsense!"

"Dr. Downer, the next time you say 'nonsense' when I report a patient's condition, I'll report you."

"I believe you would!"

"You may count on it."

"All right, Jerrold, what if she did? Mrs. Graves knows a hell of a lot more about drugs than you do. I would trust her discretion and so should you. So why the fuss?"

"If she had admitted that she had taken a drug and told me what and how much, I wouldn't be concerned. But it's not credible that a professional nurse would try to conceal that she's taken a medication. It puts me at risk. That is totally out of character for Mrs. Graves. Is she taking drugs?"

"You're insulting!"

"I couldn't believe that set-up in the kitchen and by the time I prepped her, she was barely lucid. I gave her the morphine because she insisted. If it had been anyone else, I wouldn't have. Anyway, if she had been in her right mind, she'd have been in the hospital. You should never have allowed her to risk it!"

"Well, there's one thing, Jerrold, no one can doubt where they stand with you." He hesitated. "All right, you're right. I shouldn't have risked it, myself. I should have asked someone else. And now, perhaps you'll get me a cup of coffee."

"You bastard!" I said. "I won't."

He stood up. "Come on, Philippa." His voice was cajoling. "It's over, forget it." He brought two cups and the coffee pot and poured us each a cup of coffee. "Abbie's all right. Let's be friends. Do you think you could bring yourself to call me George?"

George! He could go straight to hell. I picked up my cup and we drank together, silently.

He pushed back his chair, stretched, yawned, and stood up. "Where's that package? Oh, fine. I must hie me to an incinerator. In the meantime ..." He pulled a prescription pad out of his pocket and scrawled a number on it. "You'll get me there. I'll be there in ten minutes, and then all night. I won't call here; I don't want to wake her. But keep calling, will you? If anything turns up, I'll come at once."

Turns up? Goes wrong, you mean. I said, "That's not the hospital number."

"My dear girl, you just talked me out of a good night's sleep in my own bed. If you ring the hospital, someone is sure to recognize that voice and it will be all over hell and gone," he grinned, "that you were pleading with me to come see you in the middle of the night. That's Mike's All-Nite Bar & Grill. Mike doesn't care how many ladies love me. Kiss and make up?" He bent and kissed me lightly on the cheek.

I knew he was selfish and vain, but when he kissed me, I felt that overwhelming male charm and I understood why Abbie had succumbed to him. For her sake, I would go along with it. "All right, George. That's considerate of you. Thank you. If I need you, I'll ring."

Dawn. I lifted the blind. My cheek flat against the cold window pane, I looked down into a narrow court. Abbie had slept heavily all night and didn't wake when I checked for bleeding. She'd be all right. Thank God it was over! I shivered. I pulled a blanket around me. My ankles. The pain never left them. If Loretta, if Edgeville ever found out! But how could they? There hadn't been even a hint of gossip about Abbie and Downer. The hell with Loretta! The hell with Edgeville! The pain in my feet. Would it ever stop?

17

The old train rumbled and shook, swaying from side to side on the uneven road-bed. I opened the window and settled back against the stale red plush seat. I was too tired to sit up and too tired—now that cinders and coal smoke kept blowing in—to get up and shut it. When I was finally told to take my two weeks vacation, I took one day to buy gifts for the family, but I had no time or money for myself. I was still wearing my shabby black suit and I had pulled my hair straight back under my equally shabby black, velvet tam. I looked a fright. I didn't care—with a new Supervisor on the ward who'd anchored herself to the desk—I'd been doing double duty and I was a wreck.

Abbie was back in the Office. I had feared some constraint between us, so I was overjoyed when, within the week, I was granted overnight leave plus half a day. She had arranged dinner at the Plaza, a musical on Broadway—*The Blackbirds*—and supper after the theatre at Sardies. I stayed at her apartment overnight and slept late the next morning, enjoying all of it. We talked about horses. She had a gift for me. Next year—and I couldn't talk her out of it—I could ride in the Park free of charge!

"Edgeville!" Mr. Judson slammed the door at the end of the car. He stopped at my seat and touched my shoulder. "Wake up, Philippa, we're home."

Home. The queasy stirring, premonition of trouble, began in my stomach. Abbie's abortion. It was history. No one had found out. Forget it. The train began to slow up.

Mr. Judson dropped my suitcase to the platform and put up a steadying hand.

I took it and jumped down.

Old George was leaning against the station house. He wore his usual sagging work pants, a collarless dirt-coloured shirt and, although it was June, heavy lumberman's rubbers. He might never have moved since the day I left.

"George!" I yelled.

He started towards me with a big grin.

I gave him a big hug.

"Hey! Cut it out!" He held me away from him. He said, severely, "Look at her, Judson. All growed up and no manners! Did she behave herself on the train? I hope you kept an eye on her!"

"Well, I tell you, George, she's some better behaved than she used to be." Mr. Judson sighed, mournfully. "You know, a little more sociable than when she was ridin' as a guest of the line. Can you get her home alone? Or should I come along?"

George and Mr. Judson had decided my destination when, aged six, I ran away. When I wouldn't go home, Mr. Judson put me off the train about four miles down the track. His sister picked me up and I stayed on the Judson farm for some days. My absence at home was not remarked except by Mrs. McCarthy who wanted to know what they gave me to eat.

George threw my suitcase on the back seat of his new Ford and I got in front with him.

He said, "Yore Pa and Ma is just fine. I guess they'll be glad to see you. Tell me, Pill, did you have a good time at that hospital?"

"Oh, sure. I learned a lot."

George kept his eyes on the road. "But I guess not too much to eat, huh?"

"Oh, well. You know, hospital food."

"You're too skinny, Pill. It ain't becomin'. Now, you just see to it that Mrs. McCarthy feeds you up!" George stopped at the store to let me out and went on to the house to deliver my suitcase.

Pa was waiting inside. He had aged. I felt sick. But I was well trained: I kept the happy smile on my face. "Pa, it's great to be back. You look wonderful!"

I ran all the way home. Mother was in the upstairs sitting room. She turned her head when I came in, hesitated, and stood up. "Philippa?"

But the look on her face! Forbearance? Dislike? "Are you all right?" She kissed me. For the second time in my life. "Do you have to wear black? You look ... " She turned away.

And then Flora arrived. She didn't speak, There was a defensive, secret look on her face. Now what? I heard Sue downstairs. I ran down to the kitchen.

"Eee!" Mrs. McCarthy shouted. "You frightened me! Creepin' around." She was getting deaf. She stared at me. "You look like the wrath of God."

I kissed her old soft cheek.

Sue was hanging around my neck. "Hello Dummy, you look awful."

"Thanks. Where's Martha?"

"Martha!" Mrs. McCarthy grumbled. "Pickin' strawberries for your supper and no need! They been starvin' you in that place?"

I opened my suitcase and handed Sue the manicure set I'd bought her.

"What's in the tissue paper?"

"Little silver candlesticks. Flora's engagement present. Will you take them up to her?"

Martha came in, grinning all over her face. She winked at me and handed me a heaping bowl of strawberries.

I had a navy blue, silk blouse for Mrs. McCarthy and a red scarf for Martha. On Abbie's advice I had an ounce of French perfume, Worth's Je Revien, for Mother. I hesitated about giving it to her. I stayed in the kitchen and sat over a cup of tea while Mrs. McCarthy, in better humour, informed me that I'd be dead in a week if I didn't get "some decent food."

I went upstairs and gave Mother her present. Flora's candlesticks, unwrapped, were on the window seat. Tossed aside?

"Flora, don't you like them?"

She glanced at me without expression. "I'm sure I'll use them a lot."

It was after ten when Pa came home. He sat down beside Mother and took her hand. He stared at me, frowning, but he didn't speak.

"Pa, is something wrong?"

"I don't know."

I hesitated. It unnerved me to see him with a clinical eye. I said, gently. "Pa, are you ill?"

"I'm fine."

Mother said, "How are you getting along in your work?"

"My work? Why, well enough, I suppose."

"Does Miss Carver like you?"

They couldn't possibly know about Abbie's abortion! I sometimes wondered about Mother's ancestors–did they initiate the Inquisition? Did she think the Director of Nurses got in a corner with students to talk girl-talk? She asked because Flora kept telling cosy little stories about Miss Carver's approval of her. "Uh, well ... " I said, at last, "Regrettably, Miss Carver never speaks to me unless she wants to bawl me out."

"Don't tell me you're in trouble!" Mother's beautiful voice, even without the "again" accused me of every one of my lifelong faults.

Why did she do this to me? "Well, Mother ... Uh, it's ... "

"It's what?!"

"It's conceivable that I'll graduate with everyone else, if that's what you're talking about!" Damn! I sounded sarcastic. I'd better stop talking. "Good night. I'm going to bed."

"You're in an awful rush to get to bed all of a sudden. Are you telling the truth? Are you in some kind of trouble?"

"As far as I know," shades of Abbie's abortion! "I'm not in any sort of trouble."

"'As far as I know!'" Mother mimicked me. "The way you talk, I never know what to believe. Try to tell the truth. Why doesn't Miss Carver like you?"

"The truth?" Why did I always get her so upset? And why did she always upset me? "W-well," I stuttered, "off-hand, I should say ... "

"What's wrong? Are you frightened to talk to me?"

"No, but do you really want the truth? You won't understand why, but here it is: I break rules, I don't observe seniority, I say what I please and if it weren't for the doctors and supervisors, Miss Carver would kick me out. She has told me more than once that I am not suited to the nursing profession."

"Oh, go to bed," Mother said, bitterly.

Home sweet home. I went to my room and fell on my bed. The room was stifling. I wanted to get out. I could die of exhaustion. I stood up, slid out of my clothes, dropped them where I stood and crawled into bed. I had a restless night.

Martha woke me with a cup of coffee. She sat down on my bed. "I heard them last night. They still pickin' on you."

"What can't be cured must be endured. It requires fortitude."

"Forta who?"

"Backbone and a hell of a lot of patience. One day they'll change."

"Huh! Your ma and Flora? Not likely. When are we goin' to get to go back in the woods? Before you go, Pill, huh?"

"Martha, my feet are killin' me. You'll have to haul me there."

"Oh sure. Gimme your cup."

I threw on an old bathrobe and went to sit by the window in the sitting room. Flora was buffing her nails using Sue's new manicure set.

"Flora, did you get my letter? I mean, I did write to tell you how glad I was that you wrote me about your engagement."

"Oh, that. I guess I did."

"Is Edward here? I'd love to meet him."

"No, he's not. And you can't."

"Don't tell me it's over!"

"What makes you think it's over? He's in Cape Breton. I'm going back tomorrow."

"Presumable, I'll meet him eventually."

"Not now, I don't want you to. I've asked Sue to spend a week with me."

Geoffrey came in. "Jesus, Pill! Are you still running around in your night dress? What a mess! I bet you're some nurse! I pity the patients."

There was nothing to do in the house. I slapped cold water on my face, pulled my hair back in a tight bun, put on my cheap black suit and went down to the store to talk to Pa. He was weighing out pounds of sugar and tea. I took over for him. This was the first time we had been alone and I wanted to talk to him. But ever since I'd laid eyes on him, I'd known something was troubling him. "Pa, what's wrong?"

He glared at me, so that I stepped back in shock.

"It's you! I can tell by the look of you what kind of life you've been leading: you look dissipated! No young girl, no virgin has that look in her eyes."

I had a sudden loss of sensation. I put both hands on the counter and held on. I opened my mouth but I couldn't speak. For what it was worth, I was still a virgin but certainly I had lost my innocence. But why try to defend myself? If I had lost his respect, there was nothing more at home for me.

I finished weighing out the hundred pound sack of sugar.

I wanted to leave Edgeville, but except for my fare to New York, I had no money. And I must have rest. I would stay. But this time, when I left, I would not come back.

I spent my first week at home in bed or in the woods; often, in the afternoon, Martha and I shared a picnic. I took tea with Mrs. West and, as always, I was happy and at ease with her.

"Dear child! Black circles under your eyes? You're not sleeping."

I had to laugh. "No, I get enough sleep. It's the hospital. A thousand patients and we're short staffed. When I'm on duty, I never sit down. But I'm fine, now."

Dr. West joined us. He took my hands in his. "Clever girl," he said, "you took my advice. You've stopped eating." He kissed my forehead.

I choked and put my handkerchief to my face. And then I laughed. "Really, Dr. West, I've had too much to eat. I'm just degenerating."

Gladys went swimming with me a couple of afternoons and I stayed at her house for supper. She was plump and pretty and I looked like a skeleton, or so she informed me. I stayed at home as little as possible and I kept out of the store.

But I took Pa's books to bed at night and re-read them.

"It belongs to human nature," Tacitus said—how many centuries ago?—"to hate those you have injured."

I thought of Flora, popular Flora, of her lifelong and never ending hostility and her determination to make me the whipping boy. She must hate my guts.

And then it was my last evening at home and I could not delay it: "When I finish training," I said, "I'm going directly to Russia."

"Charles! She's out of her mind! The Bolsheviks will kill her!" My beautiful mother was flushed with anger. "This is some of *your* nonsense!"

But Pa was pleased. "Liza, don't be a fool."

Perhaps he'd decided to ignore my "dissipated and degenerate" life. Perhaps my interest in "serious matters" justified it. I didn't know.

He said, "It's a good idea for you to see Russia, to be part of that great experiment." He was glad I had "the courage and energy to do it."

I didn't tell him it took less courage and less energy for me to go to Russia than it did to come home.

The morning train left at six. I got up at five. The house was silent. Martha was waiting in the kitchen with toast and coffee. She said, "Never mind, Pill, let them buggers sleep!" and hugged me. "Is it true you're not comin' home again?"

"You were listening."

"What else is there to do around here? But can you tell me somethin'? With all the pretty clothes for Flora an' Sue, how come you ain't got any?"

"I'm scared of Mrs. Lawson."

"Mrs. McCarthy says you don't fit in. Why?"

"I have a nasty tongue."

"How do I know you're not going for good?" She was crying.

"Look, Martha, I promise, I'm coming back. Cheer up, the next time you see me, I'll be wearing diamonds."

"Oh, Pill, you really are crazy!"

18

I hadn't been back in the hospital two days before I felt I had never been anywhere else. But despite ten-hour duty and my aching feet, I wanted to find out more about Russia. When I read the New York communist newspaper, *The Daily Worker*, I saw the promised land, enticing and in full view, but when I talked to the nurses and interns they thought it a joke: did I want to go, they asked, because sex was communal in Russia? But whatever Russia was or was not, I intended to go there because it was as far away from home as I could get.

I hadn't said much to Millie, in my letters, but she knew I would not leave before I saw her and Henry again. Millie was no longer in the chorus, she was getting small parts. "They're beginning to look at me," she wrote.

Abbie kept hounding me to go riding and finally persuaded me to let her lend me money for riding clothes and I began to ride in Central Park almost every week. We often rode together and sometimes on Sunday, if we were both free, I went to her apartment for lunch. If she was taking drugs she concealed it well, but knowing that in an emotional crisis she had used them recklessly, a sixth sense kept me watchful. There was still no gossip in the hospital about her and Downer, but his clothes were still in her apartment.

I looked at the calendar. I'd been on night-duty for almost three months! I pulled my cape around me and started softly on my rounds. Snores and groans. I tucked in a patient, touched the groaners and spoke to them soothingly. I listened to a heart patient's breathing. The phone rang. I walked swiftly to my desk. "Ward Seven, Jerrold here."

"Saunders. You got a bed?"

"Yes. What is it?"

"Nothing much. Sprained wrist, possible concussion, I'm sending her up. Keep her flat."

I hung up and pulled a new chart out of my desk drawer. I was glad it was Saunders. Of all the interns, he had the best relations with the patients; was the easiest to work with. He was very good looking; crisp brown hair over straight black brows, clear hazel eyes, a gentle mouth and a slim, powerful body. Along with a dozen other nurses, I had a crush on him.

An orderly wheeled the patient into the ward.

Saunders said, "Put her in the first bed where I can keep an eye on her."

Together, we slipped the patient off the stretcher and on to the bed. Her teeth were chattering. I removed the pillow, folded a blanket around her shoulders and put a hot-water bottle at her feet. Her pulse was all right. I clasped her good hand firmly in mine. "Go to sleep. I'll stay with you till you get warm."

Dr. Saunders was sitting at my desk, writing up her chart. He was not long out of medical school. Intensely interested in his work, he put in far more time than required. All the interns worked overtime but Saunders was exceptional. My patient was quiet. I went back to my desk and he blinked up at me, half asleep. "Good morning. And how is the Soviet Union this fine a.m.?"

"What happened to her?"

"Sprained her wrist socking her old man, or he sprained it for her. Possible concussion. No orders, we fixed her up downstairs."

"And she's slightly drunk."

"Slightly. But she won't vomit. I arranged for her to do that before I sent her up–for you."

"How kind."

"Not at all. Nothing but the best delivered to you. My standing orders."

"Yours!"

"Mine!" He leered up at me. "Tell me, my little communist, is there any coffee for a weary comrade?"

"I want some, too."

He followed me into the utility room and when I reached for the coffee pot, he pinched my bottom.

I dropped the pot. "Saunders!"

He was grinning. "Sorry."

"Dammit! You'll wake the ward. One of these days."

"What?"

"I'll line the bloody interns up in rows and shoot them!"

"Who else has been pinching you? I'll shoot them myself. Who!"

"No one who has the right. Sit down and shut up."

Saunders sat down on the aluminum covered table. "You know you're beautiful? If I'm not careful, you'll be my undoing."

184

"I know." I put the coffee on the gas ring and started washing the clean cups–I didn't trust the probationers. "Get off the table."

"Do you know you're breaking my heart?"

"I do it deliberately. Get off the table for God's sake."

"Very well, I'll get off. Your command is my wish." He stepped down to the floor. "It's your face."

"Saunders, it's getting on for ... Did you hear something? Just a minute." I stepped to the door, listened. The ward was quiet.

Saunders said, "Don't you care about your face? It worries me. It wakes me up and stares at me when I'm trying to sleep."

"My face? No other face? What about your little wife's face?"

"Oh, my wife. No wife, so no family. You know, Philippa, there is something wrong with families; they shouldn't be allowed in the same house. There were three children in ours and ... " He sat down, put his elbows on the table and his head in his hands.

"And you were the middle child."

"My God, what made you say that?" He was laughing. "I know. You were, too. Well, that's what's wrong with both of us. I knew we had something in common!"

"Look," I said. "Stop babbling. You're asleep! Here's your coffee. Drink it and go to bed."

"I'm sick of going to bed alone."

"I suppose so."

"You suppose so-what?"

"Oh, shut up! I'm tired. What do you suppose I suppose? By the way you keep pinching me, I suppose you're sex-starved."

"Would you consider sleeping with me?"

"I have considered it."

"You haven't! Have you? I thought so. All the time you were preaching communism, I could see it in your eyes."

"Oh, Lord! It's almost five! I still have the charts ... I'll tell you what, I'll consider it some more and have Miss Carver wire you my decision."

He put his empty cup on the table, stood up and took my hand. We searched each other's eyes. He put his arms around me and because I had so often wanted to, I put my head on his shoulder. "Philippa, spend a weekend with me when you get off nights."

"Do you really want me, William?"

"Yes."

"All right."

It took me two weeks to get off night duty. Because of a feeling I had, every time I started for the Office, that rather than an A for adulteress stamped on my chest, there was a large F for fornication stamped on my face.

When I could no longer hold out, physically, I dragged myself to Miss Carver and told her I refused to be responsible for my patients if I didn't get some rest. And I realized I had established my professional integrity with that formal block of ice when, without hesitation, she relieved me of duty on the spot. I reeled out of the Office a free woman for the next thirty-six hours.

Then, I was so jittery, I walked all the way to the end of the hospital grounds before I could make myself enter a telephone booth. But when I got Saunders on the other end of the line, my embarrassment, abruptly, disappeared. "William?"

"Yes, who is it?"

It was strange how, at the sound of his voice, I was restored emotionally. "Dear boy," I drawled, "this is your Aunt Mary, come to town." Would the switchboard operator know my voice?

Saunders said, "Do my ears deceive me? Is that you, Philippa?"

"It's me. I mean, Aunt Mary. Perhaps you could suggest a nice hotel. I'll be here for a day or so."

"No fooling!"

"No fooling. And hurry up, my feet hurt."

"My God, where are you?"

"What in hell difference does it make? I'm in a phone booth, so make up your mind. And, must I repeat? Hurry up!"

"Philippa, I'll get tickets for a play or a musical. The Blackbirds? Green Pastures? Anywhere you like to eat? What would you like? Tell me what you want."

"I want to go to bed."

"You do? What a woman! Hold on, I'll make it as fast as I can. Don't move! Stay right there!"

"It's not love," he said. "How could I love a Bolshevik beast?" Saunders was sitting on the bottom of my bed, holding my feet. He tickled my feet. "It hurts."

I was propped up in bed with six pillows behind me, eating bacon and eggs. "What hurts? Your ego?"

"That, too. What about your biological urge, don't you have any?"

I yawned.

"My God! I've been sitting up all night waiting for you to wake up. I haven't slept a wink!"

"What a lie! How was the play last night? Did you go?"

"Oh, sure, I went. You were snoring so I thought I might as well. I couldn't believe you were still snoring at midnight when I got back."

"What was it about?"

"Why should I tell you? All right; a crisis in heaven, God's angels were having a fish-fry and Gabriel was moulting out of season."

I looked at him and laughed. He was the most comfortable and the most likeable man I'd ever met. I adored him and to my surprise I had about as much sexual feeling for him as I had for my hat. "I didn't know angels had problems. It makes me feel closer to heaven. I like that."

"I knew you'd like it, so last evening I turned to pinch you and you weren't there. You can't pinch an empty seat! Philippa, for the love of God, if you're not getting out of that bed, I'd like ... "

"You mean you wasted my ticket? Why didn't you give it to someone?"

"I thought of calling that girl who's always hanging around with you. Whatsername?"

"Loretta? We grew up together."

"That's her. A pretty little thing, but I wasn't sure you'd let us get into bed with you. Look, what kind of hormones d'you think I'm turning out? Maternal? I'm going to a good reliable M.D. and have my glands checked. And you're going with me."

"William," I hesitated. "It's only fair ... I have to tell you. Here, take my plate."

Saunders put my plate on the service wagon and poured a fresh cup of coffee. He handed it to me. "Perhaps, after you drink that, you'll invite me back to bed."

"My God, William, I'm dying for sleep and my feet hurt."

"Still?" He groaned. "I don't believe it!"

"But, I said you could sleep with me. If you wanted sex, you should have helped yourself. I was right here."

"Oh, sure! Well, it's against my religion to rape a hot corpse!"

"Oh ... Have I ruined your day?"

"You've ruined my life. What's wrong with you?"

"But I haven't slept for three months, night or day. I haven't been able to sleep. I guess the only reason I sleep so well here is because of you. You're just what I need. You're wonderful! Cosy."

"Cosy! I didn't intend being that cosy! What about sex? Have you ever tried sex? Why do I ask? Obviously, not! But you ought to try it. It's supposed to make you sleep like nothing on earth!"

"William, I really need more sleep."

"My virgin bride!" He collapsed across my feet. "I would never have believed it. You slept all evening and all night and half the day and now you want more sleep!"

I said, "I love you, William, or I wouldn't be here. Can you forgive me? Please forgive me and please believe me. It's not that I'm insensible. Look, I was longing to be with you. When you came in from the theatre last night, I was awake. I loved the way you held me and I loved your kisses, but at the last minute I couldn't."

He took my coffee cup from my hand and took both my hands in his. "Do you know how beautiful you are? I've loved you from the first day."

I was embarrassed. He was serious. I took my hands from his and then took his hands in mine ... I had read and re-read it when I lost Bill ...

"When I behold, upon the night starred face,
Huge cloudy symbols of a high romance,
And think that I may never live to trace
Their shadows, with the magic hand of chance;
And when I feel, fair creature of an hour,
That I shall never look upon thee more–..."

"William, it makes me sad to quote Keats at this moment, but I can think of no other way of telling you that I love you. Perhaps if every bone in my body would stop aching, I might prove it in another way. Or does that make sense?"

He was laughing. "Oh, Philippa! I'll die of you!" He put his arms around me and held me close. "I love you, too. And I understand. But enough! So now, will you get out of that bed?"

"Must I? What for? Where are you going?"

"You mean, where are we going. I'm taking you to Forest Hills."

"You expect me to climb a hill? In my condition?"

"Tennis, my sweet, you've heard of the game?"

"Never. And I'd love to be with you but I need sleep."

"But it's our last day! You have to go back ... "

"I know. I have to sign in at ten and I'm on emergency tomorrow so I'll be running my feet off." I threw three or four pillows on the floor and started to lie down.

He stood up, took the blanket out of my hand and tucked it around me. "Go to sleep. I'll be back in time to give you dinner before I take you to the hospital." He went into the bathroom to get dressed.

I've been told all my life that my resemblance to my mother is uncanny. Yet she is one of the most beautiful women I have ever seen, and my looks ... My face is skin and bone. With graduation a few weeks off, I was thinking of buying a dress. I had saved enough to buy a decent dress for when Saunders took me out. He took me to dinner fairly often, and now and then the movies, but he hadn't invited me back to bed. He kept urging me to get some rest and that was impossible because Miss Carver had decided, I thought, to kill me. Her first thought in an emergency or a difficult case— no matter if I was off-duty—was me. She had kept me jumping all year.

Loretta slammed open the door and came in. "I got your mail." She held out a letter.

"Thanks. It's from Martha." I ripped it open.

"Dear Pill, good luck on your graduation. Flora says you're going away and not comin' back so you broke your promise to me. I was expectin' you here with diamonds all over you so I'm disappointed ... "

I sat down. "Bloody hell!"

Loretta asked, "What's in the letter? What's wrong?"

"I'm homesick."

"Now? After three years? That's new."

I counted my money. I had enough for a return ticket to Edgeville. I knew Pa wouldn't move, but maybe ... I went down to the telephone booth and called Mother. She sounded surprised and pleased when she said she "would be happy to come to my graduation." I went out and bought a ticket for her.

I was in Grand Central Station, an hour early, waiting for her. When I caught sight of her, it was because my attention was taken by the turning heads. Slender, glowing, elegant in her own unique style, she was sailing through the station as though she owned it. She saw me and smiled. And, somewhat awkwardly, I put an arm around her and kissed her. Pa had wired for a reservation at the Park Lane. Even in that smart hotel, heads turned.

For the next two days, ignoring my feet, I escorted her on endless shopping and sightseeing tours. I was willing to forgo the graduation exercises but she insisted that we get to the auditorium in time and I was glad to sit down.

I woke when the Mayor began to eulogize a nursing paragon. Who the devil could it be? One of us had broken all records these past three years for nursing excellence, both practical and academic. There was a purse from him for the girl. "Would Miss Philippa Jerrold please stand up?"

I didn't believe it.

"Would Miss Philippa Jerrold please stand up?"

Mother dug her elbow into my ribs. "He called your name three times. Stand up!"

I sat tight. How many times had Miss Carver had me on the mat for everything from insolence to insubordination? I said, "He's reading from the bottom of the list."

Saunders was waiting at the door with roses; he kissed me and put them in my hand. "Can't stay. Playing hooky, must get back to the salt mine."

Someone touched my arm and I turned. George Downer. He took my arm, leaned down and kissed me. "Congratulations, Philippa. Why didn't you stand up when Hizzoner called your name? Were you thinking of me?"

"Oh, hello, George, I ... Well ... I thought it was a joke. Mother, may I present Dr. Downer?"

George nodded in her direction, then turned to look. "Uh ... " He stopped, his eyes glued to her face. "Mrs. Jerrold?"

There was a hint of smile on Mother's face. "How do you do?"

He stared from one of us to the other. "You're twins!"

I said, "Yes, and I'm the elder. Don't be a damn fool! We have to go."

"No, wait!" And then to Mother, "Will you be staying?"

"I leave in an hour or so."

"I'm so sorry!" And then to me, "Abbie's apartment, dinner at eight. I have a date for you, a friend from medical school."

Mother looked after him. "Now, he's a good looking man. I wish you had someone like him."

"He's my best friend's beau and he's a skunk."

"You can't get him for yourself? Is that it?"

I laughed. For some reason, the usual put-down struck me as funny.

At the Residence, Miss Carver, all smiles, presented me with the Mayor's cheque for a hundred dollars. She was cordial to Mother and I left them talking while I went upstairs to change out of uniform. They were still talking when I came downstairs and as I entered the room I heard Miss Carver, my three year adversary, singing my praises. Mother's visit had been

190

a success! And, now, I thought, since I hadn't disgraced myself, I'd be granted amnesty.

I took her to her hotel to pick up her luggage and for a cup of tea before I took her to the train, and we had barely arrived when she turned on me: "I have something to say to you!"

She hadn't mentioned Russia and she hadn't asked me to come home. She was angry. I knew that glacial look. Trouble. I followed her to her room.

She shut the door. "Sit down!"

I sat down.

"Why did you make us believe there was something wrong at the hospital?"

"What?"

"Last summer. Why did you deceive your father and me?"

"Mother, I ... "

"Don't you care if your father worries?"

"But he ... you assumed ... " I stopped. No matter what I said, she would not excuse me. I might as well save my breath. I loved her and I wanted to make her happy. But I was sick and sorry and relieved when, late that afternoon, I put my mother on the train and kissed her goodbye.

The door was unlocked when I got to Abbie's apartment. I walked in and George's friend took my hand, kissed it and held me at arm's length. "My dear, let me look at you. How lovely! We've been talking about you. Do you know George is concerned for your future?"

They'd been drinking.

Abbie said, "Philippa, I want you to meet Warren Dalney, he's a Virginian, like me. We grew up together, he's ... "

"Over-endowed with regional charm. He's still got my hand."

"Oh, Warren, behave yourself!"

Warren dropped my hand and took my arm. "That's because I'm concerned for your future, too. George thinks he has a gift for you—lots of money—but if I were you, I'd look George's gift-horse firmly in the mouth."

Abbie said, "Warren's right. They sound like horrible people."

"Suppose you both shut up," George said, genially, "and let Philippa catch up. What do you want, Phil? Scotch? I can guarantee my bootlegger. This is just in from Canada. Then I have a little business to discuss with you. Would you take a case for me?"

"Yes. But not for a few days. I leave for New Haven tomorrow."

"You see," George said, triumphantly. "I told you. She doesn't even ask who! Okay, here's the address." He handed me a folded piece of paper. "This is a very private case. No talking to anyone. I'll fill you in, later."

"George! No!" Abbie was upset. "Don't be a fool, Philippa, you can have anything you want. Including your State Boards–I made out your report–your average was ninety-eight and every service in the hospital, every doctor, put you top in your class. Don't take this!"

"Oh, for ... Abbie!" George said, impatiently. "Abbie! Please don't interfere. He's a poor, sick old man and I promised. They need someone who's got good sense. He's my bootlegger's father, Philippa. Now, what's wrong with that?"

"It's all right, Abbie. After the last three years, what's different about bootleggers? I didn't expect to be sent to the Governor's mansion, not by George, but I'm sure he wouldn't put me in danger." I sat down on the couch. I had to get off my feet.

Warren Dalney crossed the room to sit beside me. Blond, big blue eyes, sure of himself, smiling at me, trying to ingratiate himself with me. I was too tired to care. I opened the slip of paper, read the address. My patient lived somewhere near Atlantic City on the Jersey Coast. George and Abbie were quarrelling!

Dalney said, glancing at them, "It's because Abbie is upset about your case. Perhaps you should think it over."

"I'll talk to her. If there's something wrong I won't take it."

"George is not always on the up and up."

I asked coldly, "He's your friend?"

"Which is no guarantee of his morals. Look, you were more than two hours late. There's still food. Can I get you something from the buffet?"

George and Abbie had stopped arguing and wandered off. After a few conventional words to Dalney, I said good night. I had the guest-room at the end of the hall. If George was staying overnight I wouldn't know about it. Abbie's room was in front. In anticipation of seeing Millie again and Henry, nothing else mattered.

As usual, I woke on the dot at 5 a.m., starving. I'd had nothing to eat since that wretched tea at the Park Lane with Mother. I didn't want to be late getting off. Millie and Henry were meeting me. I started the coffee and went to find out if Abbie was awake. Her door was open. She was being sick. Her teeth were chattering and she was in a cold sweat. I got her to the bathroom and she turned around, pushed me out and slammed the door in my face.

I cleaned the vomit off her bedroom floor and went to the kitchen to wash. I wondered, alcoholic hangover or withdrawal symptoms? Morphine or diacetyl-morphine: heroin?

When she came out of the bathroom, she was miraculously recovered. We sat down for coffee and I watched her eyes under that bright kitchen light. Every nurse knows why enlarged pupils don't contract under light: drugs or disease, generally syphilis. Abbie's large, dark pupils didn't react to light and Abbie didn't have syphilis.

She noticed. She knew that I knew. And, deliberately, she stared back at me, her eyes cold and remote. Without touching her coffee, she stood up, went to her room and shut the door.

I followed her. "Abbie," I knocked. "Abbie, talk to me." Footsteps. The key turned in the lock. She had shut me out.

I picked up her phone and rang George Downer. I wanted, urgently, to know what he was going to do about her–and if I could help–but he was on a hospital line and I couldn't mention her name. I said, "The condition as before, George, when you kept saying nonsense. Do you understand? Please take care of her."

At the Residence, Loretta and Carol were lounging around half dressed. They were staying on at the hospital as supervisors. A few of us had that option. "You're nuttsy-gaga," Carol informed me, "to go on private duty. Sure, you get more money but who knows if you'll ever get another case? You'll be sitting on your ass in a dither wondering how to pay the rent."

I picked up my suitcase, said goodbye and was half-way down the stairs when Carol yelled after me. "Oh, Jerrold, some guy named Dalney called while you were out. Some sexy voice! Was he the one you were out with all night? Did you get him in the hay?"

I stopped at the telephone booth downstairs and tried again to get Downer. He was off duty. I breathed a sigh of relief. He must have gone to her at once.

On the train to New Haven, I kept warning myself not to be disappointed. People changed. The train drew into the station and I stepped down to the platform. There was Henry! ... and the girl, running to me ... Millie! I dropped my bag. I wanted to get away and cry, in secret, but I couldn't move, so I stood and cried all over them. Millie! How she had changed! Her voice was soft and melodic and with Henry's accent. But it had an odd, new quality. Timing? The stage? Or was it different because she had acquired cultivated speech as one acquires a new language? Words fell, like jewels, from Millie's no longer over-painted mouth. The heavy make-up was gone, the over-curled, bleached hair. Clean and shining, Millie's handsome black hair emphasized the gentle contours of her face. Millie's clothes were as changed as everything else.

Millie had a small part in a new play–trying out in New Haven–hoping to open on Broadway. She was the maid, involved humourously with the scapegrace son.

That evening, in the theatre, Henry and I in the audience–holding hands–had stage fright. How could Millie do it? We watched the other actors come on. And then, strolling across the stage, confident, magnetic, Millie stopped, looked past the footlights, found us and winked!

Afterwards, we had too much champagne, too fast. We were convulsed with laughter and drunk, as much with happiness as with wine. We were family, one in Millie's success. I don't know what time Millie and I got to bed, but I had hardly got to sleep before she was shaking me.

"Philippa, wake up!"

"No! No! I can't ... Millie?" I sat up in bed. "Christ! What's wrong?"

"Wake up! I thought you told me never to say Christ."

"No. Don't. It sounds awful. My head! What's wrong? What time is it?"

Millie opened the door and someone handed her a bunch of newspapers. She threw them at me. "Look under 'Arts.' Hurry up! Read."

I checked the contents on page one and turned a few pages. I scanned a paragraph and then started reading it out loud. "Where has Millicent Davis been hiding? She was on stage, briefly, but we predict a future star."

I dropped the paper, stood up and put my arms around Millie. We were both crying.

She went back to bed with the papers and I called room service. I had a splitting headache.

The waiter knocked and wheeled in the wagon and I got up and poured the coffee.

Millie was reading the reviews. She threw the papers on the floor. "Can you believe it? They're all good."

I handed her a cup of coffee and went back to my own bed. "I believe it because I saw it. What I don't believe is that you never told me that Henry dotes on you. Will you marry him?"

Millie put her cup down, got out of bed and started swiftly across the room. She stopped in front of the dressing table, picked up a powder puff and flicked it across her face. She leaned forward and stared at herself in the glass. "I've changed, haven't I?"

"Unbelievably. You're stunning. So, tell me, will you marry Henry?"

"He asked me to marry him and I said, no."

"What! But you were madly in love."

"Oh, I love him. I mean ... but there's too much at the moment. How can I make you understand? There's the stage. I love it and I hate it. It frightens me. Last night was good but the next time I go on, they may throw things. With that and with all the rest, I'm walking on thin ice."

"What rest?"

"I lied to Henry about my mother. I told him she was dead. How could I tell him she was a whore?" She paused. "And that first night, when he took us to dinner, he was interested in you. After you left, why did he keep calling me? I know now, what I looked like to him."

I remembered the day on the Boston Common. Henry had disapproved of Millie. "Some of us know each other on sight. However much he didn't like the make-up, he recognized the true Millie. How could he not?"

"When I went to live with him, he got one hell of a shock when he found out I was still a virgin." She laughed. "Thanks to Mama, I was terrified of 'the life.' I knew all the words, but I knew nothing about sex. I was sure I'd lose him. I went crawling to Mama, begging her to tell me her whore's tricks. I paid her!

"'Tease the bastard,' she said. 'Rouse him and feed him and flatter and starve him—in bed.'

"Well, I learned and I hated myself. All that play-acting! When all I wanted was to be my rotten, vulgar self. But living with Henry was a step up for a street-walker's daughter. I loved him and I was frightened into fits at the thought of losing him. The more I learned, the more cultivated I became, the more I felt false. Yet I knew it was the only way to hold him. And then all the work! I didn't write you half. The chorus every night and lessons half the day. Voice, speech, dress, make-up; they even told me how to hold a fork!" She laughed. "I noticed, last night, that you know how. Why didn't you tell me?"

"I didn't know I knew. Anyway, I was too busy trying to teach you not to say, Christ. But now ... "

"Yes, now." She stood up and started pacing again. "Four days ago my dead mother walked in on us, drunk and sick. Syphilis! But they're tough, these gentlemen. Henry put her in a hospital and turned around and proposed marriage to me. He realized now, he said, what a hideous life I'd had."

"Well, what's wrong? You understand each other."

Millie laughed. "Understand each other. Lies! Nothing but respectable lies–on my part. Why Henry isn't sick of everything and me, too, I can't imagine. The funny thing is that since Mama showed up, he's more loving. But I'm not going to spend the rest of my life learning new acts for him. And then there's his family."

She's so lovely, I thought, staring at her. And suddenly she changed. I was looking at the old Millie–face, figure, voice. "Cha' unnerstan' kid? Too fuckin' much trouble!"

In the midst of our hilarious laughter, the phone rang. Millie picked it up. "Hello, darling. Yes. Yes, I am pleased. We're having coffee. Oh, not too soon." She hung up. "Henry sends his love. He'll be here in an hour. Tell me about Bill."

"I loved Bill. I loved him on sight, but I never really knew him. I only saw him three times in my life. But when I lost him I lost everything."

"You need someone," Millie said. "That's why you hang onto him."

"What I need is someone who's right for me. I knew that with Bill, and he knew it. It's never been right with anyone since."

Millie said, gently. "You must take care of yourself. You look ill. Are you all right?"

"Oh, Millie! I can't tell you how well I feel, seeing you and Henry again. But I'm tired. Every nurse in the hospital is over-worked. But, forget it! This is absolute heaven, lying here in bed and talking to you. I've finished training now and I have a job so I'll be able to get some time off."

"Surely," Millie said, "surely there's been someone in your life since Bill! What about the young doctors? Isn't there anyone you like?"

"Another Bill," I said. "I call him William. Dr. Saunders. He's wonderful with the patients and he's a friend. When he comes to the ward I want to put my arms around him but it has nothing to do with sex, it's pure unadulterated love."

There was a knock at the door.

Millie opened it and came back with a handful of telegrams.

After breakfast, Millie had to sleep and Henry drove me back to New York. He had no intention of losing Millie. "She's the only real thing in my life. My luckiest day was the day I asked these two odd-looking girls in for a drink."

"Odd?"

"Well, both beautiful: but strangely matched. One with a quiet, cultured voice and dressed like a nun; the other with a voice from the streets and dressed like a chorus girl on stage. I couldn't imagine where you'd run into each other. I was fascinated then and I still am." He turned to smile at me. "No matter how many times she says 'no' I intend to marry her. You love her, too."

"Yes. Very much."

He took one hand off the wheel and held my hand.

19

The sprawling, ramshackle house was painted a harsh red. It was situated on an isolated beach in a tangle of weeds and surrounded by a high barbed wire fence. When my taxi stopped, the woman who was standing outside the gate on the narrow, sandy road pulled open the door. "Are you the nurse?"

"Yes."

"Tell him to wait."

I paid the driver, picked up my suitcase and started up the cracked cement path to the house. I said, "I'm Philippa Jerrold."

"I'm Miss Smith. Don't talk here." She glanced around, nervously. "Let's walk back to the road."

"What's the patient's condition?"

"He's all right now but they keep giving him things to eat. He's diabetic."

"Yes. I talked to his doctor. What's wrong with the family? Are they trying to kill him?"

"If he goes into shock they blame me. You'd better keep him alive! Didn't the doctor tell you about them?" She dropped her voice. "They're bootleggers!"

"That doesn't concern me."

"What! Well, you'll find out!"

"Is there anything else I should know?"

"Nothing you won't find out fast! All I hope is you got good nerves."

"I mean about the patient."

"The orders are on the chart in the kitchen." Miss Smith ran back to the house, picked up her suitcase and ran to the taxi. She half-fell, half-scrambled on to the seat. "Good luck, Jerrold!"

The taxi sped off and I turned to look at the house.

The screen door opened a crack, then full out. A slatternly old woman with a wrinkled brown face and grizzled hair lifted a thumb to her mouth and spat it out in the direction of the receding cab. "Good riddance," she said, contemptuously. "Pop don't like that one. She's no good. Come. Change your clothes."

198

I followed her up the uncarpeted, wooden stairs to a small back bedroom. The narrow cot supported a sagging mattress, a blanket and a pillow. A Woolworth looking-glass, decorated with a blue ship and three white gulls, hung above a rickety table. There were no curtains but a green blind hung half-way down the small window. A wash basin and jug stood on a kitchen chair.

The old woman said, "I'm gonna fix it up for you. I just took out her bed clothes. The bathroom's in front."

"It's fine," I said. "I'll be down in a few minutes. Where's my patient?"

"In the front room. Downstairs. The parlour."

I went downstairs to the parlour. The patient, a slender, gray-haired, kindly-looking old man, with dull black eyes, was lying in bed, waiting for me.

"Hello, noice." He took my hand in both of his and held it, staring into my eyes. His old hands were soft and dry. "The hands speak," he said. "Good! You can call me, Pop."

I put my free hand on top of his. "I'd like to call you Pop. Dr. Downer sent me, specially, to see that you get well. We'll talk about it together, see if we can get you out of this bed. Would you like that?"

He said, "Your voice is different. Soft. I'll be good. We'll talk. Could you do that? Get me out of bed?"

"If we both do what the doctor says."

At the dinner table that evening, I met the family. The old man had seven children. The eldest son, the bootlegger, "Boss," must have been in his middle forties. The youngest child, "Babe," a sulky girl, might still be in her teens.

We sat at a long table covered with a worn and faded oil cloth in a dining room painted the same eye-wrenching red as the outside of the house. There were steaming platters of spaghetti, loaves of Italian bread, fried peppers and red wine. As we ate, the table was progressively spattered with grease and covered with broken bits of bread.

The conversation and the consumption of food were both uninhibited. The conversation began, easily and spontaneously, when I entered the room. It concerned itself, mainly, with the innumerable faults of my predecessor. If Miss Smith had a single virtue, no one had noticed it.

I waited for a pause in the talk, but when it went on and on, I finally created one by banging on the table with my fork. I said, loudly and coldly, "Listen! Miss Smith took good care of Pop. He looks fine. But, Miss Smith told me some of you fed Pop behind her back." I scowled around the table, and waited a second for that to sink in. "If anyone feeds Pop while I'm here," I proclaimed, portentously, "I'll turn him, or her, over to the police for attempted murder. Is that clear?"

The family absorbed this information with open mouths and raised forks and hands. They considered it for a second or two and then they began to shout at me.

I stood up. "Wait!" I yelled. "Shut up!"

The clamour subsided. Boss pointed his fork at me. "That's big talk from a small doll," he said. "And you can get it through your head right dis minute! You ain't sendin' no one from dis place to no police." He grinned. "But I guess Downer knows what he's doin'—wit you on duh job, nobody's gonna touch Pop neider! So, I'll let you stay."

They all began to shout again and I banged on the table again. "Listen! The food you give Pop behind my back might send him into shock and before I got to him, he might die. Do you understand that? That's why Miss Smith left. She was afraid you might kill him and blame her. Miss Smith had a bad time with you, but I won't put up with any nonsense." I looked at Boss.

He was sitting there, grinning at me. He said, severely, "Okay. Everybody hoid her! And now you, Doll, you siddown an' shuddup. Tha's enough."

I sat down and started eating. The food was sheer heaven.

Babe said, tentatively, "Pop didn' like 'er."

I gave her a dirty look.

Mama said, "Call me, Mama."

"Thank you, Mama. This is the best food I've had since I left home." I held out my plate. "May I have some more?"

The family attention now centered on me. I was asked to tell how old I was. Where I was born. Why I didn't speak like everyone else. What my father did for a living. Where I bought the suit I had on when I came. How much I paid for it. What I thought of Dr. Downer. How many sisters and brothers I had. Their names. Whether I was engaged? If I didn't think nurses shoes were ugly, and more, much more. I was glad to get up to bed.

I woke in the middle of the night to the sound of loud, rough voices, boots thumping, chairs scraping. There must have been a dozen men in the kitchen just under my room. The back door slammed, a motor started up and a car rolled along the gravel drive below my window. It turned into the sandy road, gathering speed. There were fewer men in the kitchen but they weren't any quieter. I lay awake, listening.

At six that morning, when I came downstairs to prepare Pop's breakfast, the men were still there and the kitchen door was locked. I knocked. "I'm the nurse. Let me in."

A middle-aged fat man, with reddened eyes and thinning black hair on a bullet head, opened the door and stood foolishly grinning at me. His teeth were yellow-stained. He was drunk. "Hello, noice. Shake hands."

I made an absent gesture towards him with my hand but drew it away before he could get hold of it. "Good Morning," I said. "Sorry, I can't talk. I have to prepare Pop's food."

He walked back to the table and sat down. He said, "Noice, I'm Louie."

I turned to look at him. There were four others at the big square kitchen table. There were a couple of bottles on it, a dozen half-filled glasses and, beside each man, a gun. The room stank of tobacco, alcohol and sweat. I said, "How d'you do, Louie."

My scale was on a small table at the opposite end of the room. I started towards it, pulled the cover off and went to the pantry for food.

Louie said, "Noice, look, dis is Jimmy, an' dis is Marty, an' dis guy is Maxie, an' dat mug ... "

I glanced at them over my shoulder. "How do you do."

"Aintcha pleased to meet us?"

"Yes indeed. Very pleased."

"She don't look pleased!" They laughed. They stared at me. The voices got louder; they were showing off.

"You ever go out nights, noice?"

"Noicie, dear, you ever go out nights?"

I had learned a lot in a city hospital in three years. I would have to stop them and do it fast. Conversationally, I issued an order. "Put up the window, Louie."

No one moved. I turned and looked at them. I stared steadily, coldly, from one face to another. My gaze stopped at Louie. He stared back. Then his eyes shifted.

"Put up the window, Louie." It was a command.

No one moved.

I walked softly toward him. "The window, please."

He understood me, now. I wasn't playing and I wasn't scared, but Louie wasn't taking orders from a woman; he was a man.

"You poor son of a bitch," I said, quietly, contemptuously, "Put up that window."

Louie half fell out of his chair, knocked it over, scrambled to the back door, opened it, ran out and slammed it behind him. I stood staring at them. Maxie got up and opened the window. He picked up a gun, twirled it in his hand, grinned, and made an effort to pass the whole thing off as a joke. "No need to be mean, is there?"

I stared at him without speaking.

"Come on, boys, we was finished anyways." They got up and filed out into the back yard.

Guns! Did Downer know? Bootleggers? They were gangsters! Of course he knew. But Boss would see to it ... Only this was no place to have an enemy. I'd slapped Louie down. I must pick him up–soothe him a bit and make friends–but on my terms.

That afternoon, I took an hour off to scrub my room. When I came downstairs, Pop was worried. He reached for my hand. "Noice?"

"Yes, Pop?"

"Noicie, you was bad."

"Was I, Pop? When was I bad?"

"This morning. You hurt the boy's feelings."

"What boy's? Oh, you mean Louie?"

"Louie's a good boy."

"Oh?"

"It wasn't him he minded. You made him cry for something else."

"But I don't understand. Why did Louie cry?"

"Well, you see ... " Obviously, it was a delicate subject, and he didn't want to hurt my feelings.

"Don't worry, Pop," I said. "Just tell me. I won't mind what you say."

"Well, you see, you called him a son of a bitch."

"Oh? Yes ... Well, something like that. Yes, I did."

"Well, you can't call a man a name like that, noicie! Don't you see? You insulted his mother."

"Good Lord, Pop! I didn't mean to say anything about Louie's mother. Where is he? I'll apologize."

"They're out back with the sick goat. Here, ring my bell."

I stepped into the hall and rang Pop's bell and five thugs came pounding along the wooden hall. "Louie!" I commanded. They all stopped. Louie looked suspicious and sullen. He brushed past me, came to Pop's door and leaned on it. "What's wrong, Pop?" He didn't look at me.

I said, "Let's get it straight, Louie, in front of Pop and everybody. I'm not mad at your mother. Right here and now, I apologize to Louie's mother. Do you all hear? I'm sure Louie's mother is a lovely lady. I'm mad at Louie."

"Tanks." Louie said. "Tanks for nuttin'." But he looked at me and grinned, nervously. The men turned and went back out to the sick goat.

They were slapping each other on the back and howling with laughter.

I didn't laugh. I'd performed my little act but I wasn't happy. Tears and guns. A shaky combination. I said, "Pop, where's Boss?"

"He's gone home. He don't live here. Boss got a family of his own. Sometimes he stays overnight. He's a good boy, Boss, he likes his Pop."

When Boss came to the house, he was full of arrogance and swagger. He had only to snap his fingers to be obeyed. And Louie was his personal bodyguard.

I told him I didn't trust Louie.

He knew about the window episode. "You're safe," he told me, "if yuh keep outa tings an' keep your mout' shut. Louie won't touch yuh–not unless I say so."

The thugs in the kitchen were hired to guard the consignments of bootleg liquor, which I soon discovered were hidden in the goat sheds behind the house. But they had other jobs, as well. I was one of the jobs and so was Babe. Both of us were under constant surveillance. I soon found out that it was Maxie who had orders to watch me, and I didn't like it.

I hadn't seen Downer and I hadn't been able to ask him about Abbie. The telephone was in Boss's office and the door was locked. I couldn't get in unless Maxie opened the door. Personal calls were out, but I persuaded him that I had to talk to the doctor.

When I finally got Downer, I said, "I'd like a private chat but I have a friend who's glued to my side. Would you speak to Maxie?"

"He's there to take care of you," George informed me.

"Ask Maxie to leave."

"Certainly not! It's not your place to interfere. You're there to take care of ... "

I cut the lecture short. "Fine. Don't go on. I have to talk to you. Ring me from an outside line."

"You can talk on this line."

"You're always in that damned hospital! How can I talk? Is she all right? I'm terribly worried. She was sick the morning after that party, locked in her room. You know what I'm talking about?"

There was a long silence. "I didn't know you knew."

"Of course, I knew! I told you ... Have you seen her?"

"Philippa, for God's sake! You're making too much of this, uh, temporary depression. There's no need to see her. She'll snap out of it."

"Have you seen her?"

"Look, what do you expect? I've been on duty and then on call. I haven't had five min ... "

"You haven't seen her!" I could kill him!

"Hey!" Maxie took the receiver from my hand. "Noice! You wanna say somethin' about Pop? or I put down the phone!"

"Give it to me, you ... " I grabbed the receiver from Maxie. "Listen, George, you had better check up on Pop, stat! I'll tell Boss you're coming."

He said, "No, I ... "

I banged down the receiver. The Bastard! He wasn't seeing Abbie. She needed help and there was no one I could call. Damn George Downer! There was no way to send a message. I was friendly with Babe, but Babe was under guard as well. Whether high-jacked, or for money, her husband had turned over a load of scotch to a rival gang and had gone to them, with it. Babe had come to my room, weeping, "Boss is out to get him."

I tried to comfort her. "I'm sure your brother wouldn't hurt your husband."

"He'll murder him! Louie will do it."

Pop showed me a letter. "Noice, look it's from Babe to her husband. Can you mail it? Look, it don't do no harm, read it. It's just to say be careful, stay away."

I took it, but under Maxie's watchful eye, I couldn't post it. When I went to the pharmacist for needles or insulin, he leaned on the counter between us, investigating every order, listening to every word, and inspecting the wrapped package when I opened it at home.

Warren Dalney had telephoned several times and I needed a day off. After promising to keep my "mout" shut, I persuaded Boss to allow me that. And one Sunday, two weeks after I had taken up residence with my patient's family, he came to the house to pick me up. When we went out that day, I posted Babe's letter.

I hadn't seen Warren since the night I'd spent in Abbie's apartment, and I was relieved to find him more attractive than I remembered. He was of medium height and slender: everything about him, physically, was understated. His voice was attractive, slow, drawling and quiet. That Sunday the contrast between his civilized restraint and courtesy, and what I'd been living with, would have been enough to drive me into his arms in sheer relief–that is, if he'd held them out to me.

We had a pleasant afternoon and a good dinner. He had finished interning and was establishing a private practice. We talked shop, and laughed at nothing. I asked, casually, if he had seen Abbie.

"She's in great shape," he said, "on vacation in Virginia at the moment."

It was after ten o'clock that night when I let myself in. Pop's light was off but he was awake when I opened his door. I turned it on. I wanted to check on him. "Hello, Pop. Were you good while I was out?" Our hands met. Our hands always met.

He blinked in the light. "I miss you. I missed you all day. They don't know how to fix me. I only had what you left—Babe won't give me no more to eat. She's a good girl, Babe; she don't want me to die. You're a good girl, too, noicie." He paused. "You look good in that dress but Mama says ... "

"I'm going to fix you now; rub your back and then you're going to sleep."

"I have to talk to you." He clung to my hand. He lifted his sallow old face to me and his forehead was creased and wrinkled. His white hair was tousled and no one had turned his pillows. There was the sick odour of the diabetic who's had a little more sugar than his body can assimilate. It might be just as well, I thought, to give him a hypo of insulin and a small meal. It would soothe him.

"All right, Pop, tell me what Mama said, and after that, because you're good, I'll give you something to eat. How's that?"

"Good," he said. "You eat, too! Mama looked at your man. She said I should speak to you. You said he's a doctor?"

"He is, Pop. He's a friend of Doctor Downer. They went to school together."

"Mama don't like him. Where's he brought up? She said he don't look like no doctor."

"No?" I was mystified. What was a doctor supposed to look like? "He's from the South, a very respectable man."

"Mama says you shouldn't go out with him. She says he don't show no respect for you."

"Was there something wrong?" I asked. "I didn't notice anything."

"It's Sunday, ain't it? Mama says he ain't dressed—no coat, and his sleeves rolled up. What kinda man is that for a doctor? You watch out, noicie. He's no gentleman. Mama can tell."

Gentleman or not, I was glad Warren kept calling. I could hardly wait to go out with him on Sundays. The house and its inmates got on my nerves to an extent that was, to quote Miss Carver, who used the word to describe everything from debased to deranged, "deplorable." As the weeks went by, I began to think, like Miss Smith, that I couldn't go on. I ran between the kitchen, in back, and the front parlour, Pop's room, all day long. With the perpetual commotion of men smoking, drinking and banging doors, it was almost impossible to establish the necessary routine, to prepare Pop's food, sterilize needles for his insulin, make sure he had rest periods, check his urine.

The house was like a barn; enormous rooms separated by partitions of wood an inch thick. The bootleg traffic went on in the kitchen, under my head, until dawn. Footsteps on bare floors echoed and re-echoed–it seemed to me like thunder–all day long. I felt that I had been caught up in a brutal and crushing machine and forced to become part of it. And I couldn't stop. Leaving Pop would be desertion, for who else would stay?

On duty I wore the assured, the authoritative façade of the trained nurse. Strangely, I had no fear of them. I matched the noisy, brutal aggressiveness with cold indifference. And they changed. They were, they tried to tell me, good fellows at heart. They fawned on me. They did me small favours, brought me gifts of fruit and flowers. But they did not relax their watch. Boss was on my side. But if I made a wrong move they would "rub me out." I had no illusions about that.

With Boss's consent I had written home and to Mrs. West.

Mrs. West answered at once to tell me, among other things, that my father was proud of me because I was going to Russia.

And then I received a Victorian postcard of a gentleman tickling a sleeping lady with a rose, and a message: "Should you awaken my sleeping beauty, I have the same telephone number. Why wasn't I told yours?"

Saunders! For the first time in months I laughed.

Warren was getting possessive. He thought me unreasonable because I wouldn't leave Pop. "I did my best to persuade George to take you off this case! He won't listen. His damned scotch means too much to him. Don't go back! It's not your responsibility! I'll call the Registry and send another nurse."

But my release was now in sight. Pop was getting better. The moment Pop was on his feet, he and Mama would go back to their own house where Pop could have a visiting nurse.

And then Boss agreed to allow Maxie to take Pop for regular drives.

Each time we left the house, we had to wait until Maxie broke open his revolver and examined it. Reassured and prepared for battle, Maxie put dull care aside. Louie carried Pop to the car and we were off.

We rode in state in a long, powerful, open car, a delicate light gray with chromium fittings. I imagined it had been designed for a woman of fashion with slender, white hands and ropes of glistening pearls.

Maxie, his greasy, half-bald head and ugly, unwashed ears uncovered and shining in the afternoon sun, sat pompously alone in front. Pop and I sat in the back seat, holding hands.

One afternoon we had just returned from our drive and I had put

Pop to bed when the telephone rang.

Maxie called me. "Noice! It's Doc, he wants you."

I was vaguely alarmed. George didn't call me. If I needed something, I called him.

Maxie was sitting beside Boss's desk holding the receiver to his ear. "Ssst!" he whispered. "Listen!" He handed it to me.

I could hear George, gasping, sobbing. I couldn't believe my ears. "George," I said, "What's wrong?"

"Philippa!" He stopped.

"George, what is it?"

"Abbie. She ... "

"Abbie?" I interrupted him. "She's ill. I might have known. I'll come at once. Call the Registry. Get someone for Pop."

"Stop! Wait! She ... "

"What happened? Tell me!"

"Stop," he said again, "she's gone."

"Gone? Gone where? "

"You don't understand. She ..."

"George! Try to make sense. What's wrong with Abbie? Where is she?"

"She's dead."

"Of course she's not dead!"

"She's dead. She sent me her will. She left you things. I have to see you."

"She what! ... No!"

"Please!"

"George! What happened?"

"I don't know. Suicide. I have to see you. She's dead."

I handed the receiver to Maxie and I walked up the wooden stairs to my room and sat down on my cot. I was deaf, my head under a roaring falls. My fault. I should have gone to Miss Carver. But it would have ruined her! Why didn't she come to me? Why hadn't I ...

Then the screams came up in my throat; I jammed my teeth together. If I once let go, I would go completely out of control. So, I sat there, hands clenched, and held on, screaming. Silently.

Babe yelled. "Yoo-hoo!" She came upstairs and opened my door. "Pop says it's time for dinner, he's hungry. Is something wrong? Maxie said someone died."

"Died?" I stood up. "Just a minute," I said. "I'll wash my hands. Tell Pop I'll be right down." I remembered that I had intended asking the pharmacist to send some new insulin needles. I was using the last new one and the others were dull ...

"You know," Warren said to me on Sunday–it was late in the evening, we were in a country lane sitting in his parked car–"I didn't know Abbie had died. I went to George's apartment to give him a blast: I intended to get you off this case if I had to strangle him. The door was open and I walked in. The place was indescribable! He was lying in his own filth, drunk and half conscious. I ... I finally knocked some sense into him."

Warren stopped, tears in his eyes. He turned away and hit the wheel with his fist. "George is nothing, Philippa, an irresponsible, incompetent fool. He started babbling about how he loved Abbie. He wasn't fit to touch her boots. He got her pregnant and aborted her. He said you knew about that–and the drugs." Warren turned to me and took my hand. "Is that true?"

"I assisted at that operation."

"My God! That's a jail sentence. And George allowed it? I'll kill him!"

"Not George, it was Abbie who wanted me there. At the last minute she took some sort of drug. I was terrified! I realize now she must have been on drugs a long time before that. Anyway, George refused to believe me when I told him she had taken drugs. He ... " I couldn't stop trembling.

Warren put his arms around me. "It's all right, Darling."

"No!" I pulled away from him. "It's my fault! I knew she needed help! I knew I couldn't trust George! I should have called Miss Carver!"

"Miss Carver knew."

"What! She knew? How?"

"She's no fool. She persuaded Abbie to take a cure–there's a private clinic in Philadelphia. A week ago Abbie discovered she was pregnant again and called George. He promised to marry her. She wanted a new dress for her wedding. The next day the clinic released her to go to New York, shopping, on condition that she check in with Miss Carver as soon as she arrived. Late that night when Miss Carver hadn't heard from her and couldn't get her on the phone, she went to Abbie's apartment–had the superintendent open the door."

"My God! She had drugs in her apartment! An overdose!"

"No overdose. She left letters, her will. Suicide. She slit her wrists."

"God! Why? She loved George. She wanted to marry him."

"George thought she was in Philadelphia. He'd been living in her apartment with some floozie, sleeping in her bed. She walked in on them." His words blurred, "She was the most loved ... loving. The most popular ... the nurses ... everyone. Her grave was covered with white flowers."

"Warren, no more! Please! I can't ... "

"George has to see you."

"No! I won't see George."

"Philippa, listen. Abbie left you her apartment. The key is there for you, but George ... "

"No!"

He took my hand and kissed it, dropped it and got out of the car. It was almost dark. I watched him walking, turning, coming back. He got back in the car. "The three of us have been friends since ... but no more." And then without pausing or turning to me he said, "What I need to know now is that you care for me, as I do for you. I want to marry you."

He drew me close and kissed my lips.

I felt nothing. I didn't move. He withdrew his arm.

"There are certain things I should like to know about you. I hope you won't be offended if I ask. Back home I'd know if a girl is a virgin, so if you're not–if you'll tell me about it, I'll understand."

I couldn't believe it. "W-why do you t-think ... " I stuttered. "What if I'm not? What difference would it make?"

"None at all. I trust your judgement as to the kind of man you'd choose. You're an exciting and beautiful woman, I can't believe I'm the only one who ... but *I* never get close to you. Still, I can't believe there's never been anyone else in your life!"

It was my turn to get out of the car. I stumbled along in the deep grass. What a cold-blooded, insulting proposal! Furious, I got back in the car. "Warren, virginity has nothing to do with innocence. I am no longer innocent. Whether or not I'm a virgin is none of your damn business!"

"You're putting me off?"

"You haven't asked if I'd be willing to marry you."

"I've been serious about you since the moment I set eyes on you. Don't think I'm stupid for saying this, I feel we were made for each other. But I'm not a complete fool. I must know about you. Please tell me. Are you a virgin?"

"All right, for what it's worth, by accident, I'm *virgo intacto:* virginal as hell."

"By accident? What ... " He started kissing me, again. He moved his hand.

The light struck suddenly into my eyes, blinding me.

I jerked away, shocked! "Do they react?"

"Yes."

"So I haven't got syphilis."

"No. Forgive me. Please ... But you kept avoiding ... "

"For God's sake, Warren, take me home."

If George asked the gangsters to release me, I didn't hear about it, but Pop was getting better. Every afternoon we went for a drive. One day, driving along the ocean front, a nondescript Ford pulled out of a side street and followed us. A police car turned sharply across the road and joined the procession. The three cars drove slowly, one behind the other.

Sweat broke out on Maxie's neck and turned his pink shirt collar a deeper shade of pink. The sweat spread down his back.

Pop clung to my hand. "This is no good."

After a few blocks, the car behind us turned into a side street and the police car followed it.

Maxie raced for home.

Boss was standing at the gate. "Get in fast! Get Pop to the cellar."

"How'd you know?" Maxie was still sweating.

"They rung us, said they'd get the three of you."

Maxie lifted Pop and carried him into the house and down the hall towards the cellar steps.

Boss locked and bolted the door.

I snatched up a couple of pillows and a blanket and was halfway down the hall when Boss grabbed me, painfully, by the arm. "Not you, Doll. You get back here. Pop's all right. I called an ambulance. You're gettin' outa here!"

"No! Let go! You're hurting me!"

He jerked me, stumbling, resisting, along the uncarpeted hall to the locked room where he kept the telephone. He shoved me inside, stepped in behind me, locked the door and picked up the phone. He gave the operator a number. "Taxi? Where the hell is that taxi? Get it here! Fast!"

"Let me out! Don't be a fool! I can't leave Pop!"

"Yeah? Look, Doll, can it! We have trouble here! It's for your own good." He unlocked a drawer and pulled out an enormous roll of money. "Here, take this."

"No! What hospital did you call? Did you call a hospital? He can't leave without his chart. He'll be hungry soon. I'm staying!"

"Not you, Doll! I want you out of here! Dis will cover tings for you, take it!"

"No! I can't leave him. He should have insulin. He must be fed."

"You're gettin' out. Now! Here ... " He shoved the roll of bills at me. "Dough. Take it."

"No! I'm not going to take it, and I'm staying. What happened? Why?"

He grinned. "I don't mind tellin' you. Babe's old man an' some of his pals got bumped off. Dey tink we done it. I want you the hell outta this house and fast, for me, not you. You understand? You want to get mixed up in a gun fight? You crazy?"

Babe's husband! They'd murdered him! There was not a sound in the house. Where was everyone? Babe? The letter had done no good! "Does Babe know? Where is she?"

He was suddenly impatient. "Listen, who's runnin' tings, you or me? D'you want your clothes?"

"Pop's chart. It must go with him. What hospital? I'll meet him there. He's used to me, he shouldn't be ... "

"Now listen! An' listen good. You get mixed up in this and we're in real trouble! You want your tings? Your suitcase?"

There was nothing upstairs but my uniforms, a few underclothes and my comb and brush. I had my purse in my hand and I was wearing my one good suit. In that split second I made up my mind. After more than three desperately hard years, I'd had enough. "Give my uniforms to Babe, or throw them out. Give her my love and to Pop and Mama."

He shoved that enormous roll of bills into my hands.

I stood looking at it. "Wait!" I started to count. "You don't owe me ... "

"Aw, listen, you was good to Pop. He liked you, keep it."

Blood money, I thought ... But he gave it to me because I took care of Pop. It was love money, too. I tried to stuff it in my purse.

He laughed. "Here." He handed me a paper bag.

"All right," I said. "Thank you. Be sure to tell Pop you gave it to me."

We sat, silently, locked in. He played with the gun in his hand, twisting it. When we heard the taxi horn in front of the house, he pulled me to my feet, hustled me to the front door, unbolted it and pushed me outside. "You're a good kid," he said. "Tanks for Pop. Now beat it! Get lost! Fast!" The door slammed behind me.

I ran for the taxi. Where could I go? Abbie's apartment. It was mine. I said, breathlessly, "New York City, driver, Park Avenue. Uh ... I'm not sure of the number, I'll tell you when we get there."

I sat there, worrying about Pop, clutching that enormous bag full of money.

20

New York City, 1931

I sat on her bed and wept. Her letter, crumpled in my hand, was wet with my tears. She had died in an agony of pain and remorse for her "betrayal of every moral value." She had forced me into a "criminal act." She had "murdered her child." The tiny gold locket with her picture inside was for me. She knew I cared for her. She had sent the family jewelry to a niece. The apartment and contents were mine.

I was so emotionally bruised that any social contact would finish me. I took the receiver off the hook. Abbie! My face was stiff, swollen with tears. I couldn't think. I shoved my purse and Boss's roll of bills under the bed, locked and barred the door, pulled off my clothes and let them drop where I stood. And then I fell into bed.

And for the next few days, helpless, I stayed there. Then one morning I woke, reached under the bed for Boss's money and started to count. One thousand, two ... I stopped counting. I had enough.

I made a pot of coffee and went back to bed. What now? I needed a passport, ticket and clothes. I had no idea where to start. Abbie ... always so elegant. Over lunch one afternoon, I'd admired her clothes. She took a card from the desk, wrote something on it and handed it to me. "You must let me take you to Madame Eugenia. She has a shop on Fifth and she's a genius."

I still had the card in my purse.

Going down town, I picked up a newspaper to see the date, I had lost track of time. The headlines were screaming about a gang war. Shocked, I folded it, took a taxi and left it on the seat–unread.

"Madame Eugenia?"

"Yes." She took me in from my head to my feet. Cold as ice. "You wish?"

So much for my fifty-dollar suit. I hesitated, then I handed her Abbie's card. "Mrs. Graves suggested that I come to you."

She glanced at the card. "Mrs. Graves. Well! Your name?"

"Philippa Jerrold."

"Ah! You ride in the park? Yes! She spoke of you. How can I help?"

I said, "I'm going to Russia. I have nothing to wear."

"Russia! At this time of year? All right. Come."

In a pink, satin-lined room she seated herself on a pink satin bench and stared at me. "Take off your suit. Five-seven? Five-eight?"

"I'm five-eight."

"Do you know you are the same height as the French models and the same size? No need for fittings." She left the room and came back with a soft tan wool dress over her arm and, without bothering to show it to me, slipped it over my head. "Look at yourself."

I was so accustomed to thinking of myself as plain, I could hardly believe what I saw. I said, "Good God! I'm handsome! How much is it? Never mind. I'll take it."

It was the last week in September. I had my passport and tickets and my two suitcases were packed. With my salary from Pop and Boss's roll of bills, I'd had more than enough to pay for my return trip but when I went to Eugenia for clothes, I forgot to count. Now I looked like a fashion plate, and I had a ticket all the way to Moscow and enough money to keep me a month or so, until I found a job, but only my steamship ticket from Southampton to New York. I'd have a long walk from Moscow to Southampton if I wanted to come back to North America. But I had no intention of coming back. I intended to stay in Russia and work with the Russians, who were creating a better world for the working man. In Russia, where everyone was equal and where all worked for the common good, I would find my niche.

The third-class deck of the White Star Liner was crowded with working people and in an uproar of confusion when I came on board that sweltering day in September. Men and women were kissing and laughing, crying and fussing over children. I stood with them, but alone. I'd had a brief note from Pa and a basket of fruit from Millie and Henry. I had written a belated note to Saunders but I hadn't heard from him. There was, however, a telegram for me. Abbie's niece, to whom I'd given her apartment and contents–everything except Abbie's white silk robe and her locket, wished me bon voyage.

The "all ashore" had sounded. I leaned over the rail and stared down at the swarming dock. Then I saw a hurrying familiar figure. Saunders, bareheaded, his white shirt open at the throat, looked up and waved. He ran up the gang plank, panting with heat and hurry.

"The landlady just brought your note! I didn't have time ... " He was waving a sheet of paper. "I grabbed this. Wait!" He unscrewed the top of his fountain pen and wrote hastily on the back of his own portrait: "A defense against communist competition. Let them kiss your hand and then stop." He took a deep breath and reached for my hand. "All alone. Aren't you frightened, Philippa?"

There was such solemn apprehension in his eyes that I had to laugh. "Of what?"

He pulled me into his arms. "Write! If you need anything, write to me. I'm frightened for you."

I held on to him. "William, darling William. I'm not frightened." I began to tremble. "I fear the known. I think the unknown must be safer."

The dining-room steward had placed me at a table with a group of medical students bound for the University at Graz. They were light-hearted and congenial and they drank too much. I drank too much, too. We paced the decks, danced and stayed up all night. And though meanwhile, and irrepressibly, I preached communism, not one of them succumbed to the true faith.

Then Marta Antwicz, a stringy red-head of thirty-five, attached herself to me when I took her six-month-old daughter, Hanitchka, out of her arms to let her rest. When she discovered I was going to Russia, with iron determination she dictated my enrollment in her circle. Marta and her husband were part of a group of Czech and Polish miners who were on their way to Russia. Many of them had come to America a decade or so earlier, looking for a better life. They had not found it. Now, believing they were going to a new and glorious world of their own, they had given up citizenship in the United States and were on their way to work in the mines in Siberia.

I was on my way to a new and wonderful world, too, so their interests were mine. Yet, listening to the parroted party line, I became bored. And I ran from them–my comrades–to the company of my pleasure-loving capitalistic medical friends.

At Southampton, reluctantly, I parted company with the medical students and because Intourist had booked us at the same hotel in London, I rejoined Marta, her husband and child and the group of workers.

But now, as our train approached London, my thoughts were with my oldest and dearest friends, the great and near-great in English literature. They, rather than Edgeville, had set a standard of behaviour for me: it was their culture I wished to emulate. They had taught me to read. I had laughed and cried with them and now I was about to set foot in the great urban center of their civilization. I thought, particularly, of John Keats, and of how from adolescence I had solaced anguish and forgot self in the colour and beauty of his words, and while growing up, had re-lived his life with him.

London, cold, gray and remote, did not welcome me. The people in our shabby hotel–cockneys, I supposed–spoke a language I'd never heard before. I didn't understand them. And when I ventured to open my mouth, the British native, equally puzzled, regarded me with a blank stare. It was just as well that we were scheduled to sail the following day on the Russian steamship, *Vladivostock*.

That night in a cold, sordid attic room on a narrow cot, I hardly slept. The next day I wandered about the streets. A thick fog had changed to an icy drizzle when, late in the afternoon, I boarded the *Vladivostock*. Since I thought I had paid the cheapest fare–tourist–I was grateful when the Russian sailor-steward showed me to a comfortable cabin. My luxury ticket, he told me, entitled me to sleep inside. "The miners and their families," he went on, "who are under contract to the Russian Government, will sleep on deck."

Hanitchka outside! "In this weather?" I asked, incredulously. "Show me." I followed him on deck.

One side of the ship had been reserved for men, and the other for women and children. The allotted deck space was only partly sheltered, top and sides, by strips of canvas. Between the narrow strips there were long and airy cracks. The "beds" were planks nailed on wooden supports a foot or so above the deck.

"P-perhaps," I stuttered in dismay, "s-since I have four bunks and a divan, the women with small babies might like to be inside. Find Mrs. Antwicz, please–the lady with red hair. She will know whom to invite."

"You think?" The Russian looked at me, doubtfully. Then he added, graciously, "Perhaps."

"So!" Marta shouted, when I opened the door to her. "So! Some day–maybe–you make a communist! Here, take my Hanitchka. I go get luggage."

I took Hanitchka and the diaper bag. Hanitchka, adorably without politics, gurgled up at me. Her pants were wet. I took her to the bathroom, pulled a flannel blanket out of the diaper bag and a louse–too cold to run–staggered across the back of my hand. I was shocked. The capitalistic poor were lousy–they brought a lot of lice to the hospital–but it shocked me to find the communists lousy too. I changed Hanitchka and took her back. A half-hour later, my cabin heaved with bodies; it housed four women and five babies and they were not clean.

I threw my two suitcases on an upper bunk and climbed up to wait for things to settle down. My guests, ignoring me, disputed noisily for the remaining sleeping space. When there was some semblance of order and when I was on the point of suffocation, I climbed down to open a porthole.

The mothers opposed me, unanimously. "No!" they shouted. "No! No! No!"

The majority won. I went out to get some air.

A man in a black leather coat and a black astrakhan hat was leaning against the rail and he turned when I stepped out on deck and yelled at me. "Careful! Watch it!"

I let go of the door and two inches of iron on the bottom slammed against the raised iron sill.

He moved his head, reprovingly, from side to side, "Come here!" He put out a hand as I approached, took mine and held it warmly. His eyes were gray, brilliant and penetrating; his face, thin, hard and clean. "They're still building this ship! We're underway and there are no airbrakes on the doors. If you're not careful, you'll lose an arm or break a leg." He stopped and stared at me. "What on earth are you doing here?"

I said, coldly, "May I have my hand?"

He released my hand and I ... felt lost!

"Do you know where you are? What ship? We're bound for Russia. Why would you want to go to Russia?"

"I'm a communist."

"Really? I'm fascinated. Perhaps you'd tell me why?"

I was sick of being questioned–forced to defend my beliefs. I drawled, "The measure of a bore is the number of personal questions he asks, per second." I started to turn away.

He caught my arm. "Wait!" He threw back his head and laughed, so spontaneously that I couldn't help laughing too.

"My dear, if you don't like questions you'd better keep your distance. I'm paid to ask questions." He didn't release my arm.

While I was saying it, I knew it was stupid. "Are you OGPU?"

He groaned. "You think I'm Russian secret service?"

"I'm sure of it, let go."

He dropped my arm and, as I turned away, the ship lurched and dropped. I was tipped off balance and he caught me by the elbow again, to steady me. "It begins," he said, gaily, "and I love it! Are you a good sailor?"

"I'm fine–between Yarmouth and New York."

"Brace yourself." He let go of me. "Are you all right? Be careful. The

North Sea is one of the roughest seas in the world; it's shallow." He looked at my legs. "Silk stockings! You'll freeze! Go below."

"I have a choice. I can either freeze or suffocate, so I think I'll freeze, thank you."

"Your cabin is too hot? That's a break–for the moment–but don't count on it to last."

"Not that. We're ten in my cabin."

"Ten! Let me talk to the Captain."

"No, don't! I invited them."

"Good God! What other disposition have you made for your comfort?" He looked me up and down. "Your clothes, for instance, what do you intend wearing?"

"Why–what I have on."

"On this ship? My dear girl, where do you think you are, the Rue de la Paix? You ... I suppose you have a name?"

"Philippa Jerrold."

"Well, Philippa, you'll need trousers. I'll lend you a pair."

"To begin with," I protested, "they wouldn't fit. And to end with, I don't know you. I won't take them." But, standing beside him, I felt I'd known him all my life. I was happy.

"I do dislike silly girls who prefer to ... "

A wave of icy spray swept over the rail and slapped into my face. I shrieked and jumped back, dripping. "Damn! All right, get your pants. I'll put them on. No! Wait! I have riding breeches."

He said, "You'll be soaked to the skin and you'll ruin them. Hang on and I'll get you something suitable–waterproof–so you can get out on deck."

"What's your name?"

"Philip Holmes. You see, we have something in common." He went away, laughing, and came back with a pair of his trousers and a necktie to string through the loops on the waistband, to hold them up. The legs were too long and my riding boots too well fitted to tuck them inside, so I turned them up and borrowed safety pins from Hanitchka's diaper bag to hold them.

That night the sea went mad, my guests were prostrate and, perforce, I resumed the occupation I had given up: I took up nursing again. The women lay in their bunks with feet braced, hanging on to their babies with one hand, clutching the bunk with the other, trying to keep from being thrown to the floor.

Encased in Holmes' trousers, I ran all day long and half the night. I washed, dressed, changed and fed babies, and washed their mothers' hands and faces. I made beds. I carried slopping mugs of tea, bread, apples and sandwiches, fed my charges what they'd eat and then washed up the vomit.

As Holmes had informed me, the *Vladivostock*, although obviously seaworthy, had not been finished before sailing. The crockery, loose on shelves and tables, was flung to the floor, and much of it smashed. It wasn't possible to keep a pot on the stove but the engineer provided hot water from the ship's pipes and the cook made sandwiches.

Holmes was on his way to the interior of Russia as correspondent for one of the big news services. He refused to admire or applaud my all-out effort to care for my guests. "These people can take care of themselves!" Insisting that I have some rest, he would come to the cabin, put his greatcoat around me, take me on deck, allow me a swallow of brandy from his flask, support me against the rolling bumps and then put me through the third degree. "Do your parents know where you are?"

"Of course."

"I don't believe it. Are you a member of the Communist party?"

"Well, not exactly."

"Just why are you on your way to Russia?"

"I'm a working woman."

"You aren't working class. Who paid for those clothes? Not you!"

"You're rude, but I don't mind telling you, a bootlegger."

That amused him. "Liar! Come clean."

"I swear! I give you my word. A friend of mine. A bootlegger."

"Well, if you can get away with that, you'll do all right in Russia!"

He didn't believe me but, he took care of me, with great affection and great respect. I thought he was quite old, probably close to forty.

The storm grew worse. The women wouldn't–or couldn't–care for themselves. They lay and groaned. They were dreadfully seasick and there was no one to care for them or the babies but me.

I was bruised all over from banging against walls and doors. My arms and legs ached from carrying things, from bracing myself while running, and again in my bunk while I was trying to get some rest. After five days of violent jerking, filth, stench and groaning, I was conscious that my head itched. It seemed to me it crawled.

Marta was asleep. I dug Hanitchka's fine-tooth comb out of the diaper bag, took it to the bathroom and washed it, carefully. Then I went back to the cabin. Marta was still asleep. I shook her awake. "Marta!" I held the comb in front of her face. "Is it all right if I use this?"

"Uh? What for?" She was half asleep.

"For lice."

"Whose lice? Oh, my stomach!"

"Mine. Poor Marta, I'll get you ... "

"No!" Marta rose from her bed of nausea and snatched the comb. "No! No one use it but me!"

"But ... I'll be careful. I'll give it right back."

"No but! Is mine. Don't touch." She stuffed the comb back in the diaper bag.

I went out on deck. As usual, Holmes was leaning on a rail looking at the sea. I put my hand on his arm. Then I remembered that lice can travel so I took it off and moved away. I yelled above the wind, "I have a secret to tell you."

"You don't like me any more?" he yelled back. "That's all right; I still like you." He moved over and took my arm.

"Touch me at your own risk," I shouted. "I'm lousy."

"Oh? So that's where I got them!"

"You, too? Good! Now we can put our heads together and you can tell me what to do. What infuriates me," I complained, "after taking care of her, Marta won't let me borrow her fine-tooth comb."

"Won't let you?"

"I took it, but she took it back."

Holmes said, "You're not of this world!" He grabbed my shoulders and shook me. "Listen, go get that comb, steal it! These people are used to being lousy; it's a tradition with them: it keeps them fertile."

"Fertile!"

"Certainly," he shouted. "Any Russian peasant knows she can't get pregnant if she isn't lousy."

"Let go! If we get any closer ... " He didn't let go and I leaned on him, laughing my head off.

"You damn fool! The things you make up!" When I caught my breath, I shook loose of him.

"I'm not making it up. During the famine, because the woman were in such wretched condition, we took a string of box cars, bathed them in the first car, deloused their clothing and laundered it in the next cars, dressed them and sent them out clean. When they stepped off the train, there was a comrade selling them lice at a rouble a head, to make sure they'd be able to get pregnant again."

"Really? ... But not Marta; she's emancipated. She ..."

"Never mind that ingrate, think of me; think of yourself for a change. Do you want to get pregnant?"

"Not in these trousers!"

"Then, get rid of those lice! Get that comb!"

I stopped by the galley to get an apple for Marta's stomach. When I got back to the cabin the diaper bag was on the bed and she was asleep. Apparently full of concern, I put the apple on the bed, tucked the blanket around her and removed the comb.

Perhaps because of their limited English, my guests had not paid me much attention, but in the last few days the atmosphere had grown noticeably colder. Marta sat up in her bunk and put Hanitchka on my left arm. I handed her a steaming mug of tea and she drank it slowly and loudly.

"Good?" I asked, brightly. I waited.

She gave back the empty mug and put her arms out for her baby.

"I'm going to get you all something to eat," I announced.

"We can eat something," Marta deigned, coldly. The others neither spoke nor smiled; they merely lay and looked–anywhere but at me.

I went out and brought back sandwiches. Then I went out and brought back wet towels. While the women ate, I cleaned babies.

"While you was out," Marta said, her mouth full of sandwich, "we look again. It ain't here." She stared into my eyes, a hard and suspicious stare.

"Did you lose something?" I shook my head. "No wonder. Your bunk is a mess." I turned away. "It's hot! I really must open a porthole."

"Never mind porthole! You should hide your face!"

"That's ridiculous! Why should I ... "

"What kinda communist go in ship taking what don't belong to her?"

"What? What are you talking about? The sandwiches are free."

"Never mind sandwiches. What happen Hanitchka's comb?"

I opened my eyes wide in an attempt at innocence. "Oh? You mean you think I took it? How could you? If you'd get out of that bunk and really look, I'm sure you'd find it."

The lady in the top bunk opposite mine, infuriated by my hypocrisy, leaned down to examine my face. "Two days now, it gone," she reminded me. "Everybody look."

"Then it must be under the bunk. You all ought to get up this afternoon and go on deck. I'll clean up and make the beds and I'll look for it."

"*You* look for it!"

"Ha!" said the lady on the top bunk. "Ha! Ha!" said the others. But they weren't laughing.

I said, reproachfully, "If you'd have let me have it, you'd still have that comb. I take good care of things."

"It belong Hanitchka. I ain't lend it nobody."

I sighed. "Marta," I said, "you hid it from me. That's what happened. And now you forget where you put it, or dropped it." I added, sadly, "I'm afraid you were selfish."

She glared at me. No one spoke. The atmosphere was rarefied hostility.

I took off for Holmes' cabin and banged on his door. "Let me in."

"If you're up," he yelled through the closed door, "bring me some tea."

"D'you think I'm my ghost? All right." I ran to the engine room and the engineer drew hot water from the pipe for the tea. The sea was calmer but they still weren't using the stoves.

Holmes opened the door–in his dressing gown. "I see you spilled quite a bit. Is it hot?" He took the mug.

"You're welcome. Any time. Look, give me the comb. I have to give it back. Marta really needs it: they're crawling. Where is it?"

"If they're crawling, you'll be crawling, and if you're crawling, I'll be crawling, so I guess I'll keep it."

"You can't. They really need it. I have to ... "

"Tell you what," he said sucking up the steaming tea, "as soon as I'm up, meet me at the end of the corridor near the dining-room and I'll give it to you. Nice seeing you. Goodbye." He shut the door in my face.

"You ingrate! When?"

"Twenty minutes."

I went to the end of the corridor to wait. The sea must have come up again; we were rocking ...

Holmes appeared finally. He said, "Look, I've considered it, and our need, and I've changed my ... "

He had probably slipped the comb in his right hand overcoat pocket. I said, "Look out! There's the Captain!" I grabbed him and he staggered around the corner after me, looking both ways.

"Where? What do I care!"

"Okay," I said. "I've got it. I had a pickpocket once as a patient."

Holmes reached in his pocket. "Good God," he said, "so you have! Give it back!"

I ran. I turned the corner again and bumped into the engineer. I hung on to him. The sea was going crazy. The engineer had been trying to talk to me for a week. He had a Russian-German dictionary, very dirty. He was very dirty, too. Every time I'd gone near him–and since he was our hot water supply, I saw him about fifty times a day–he tried to make me stop and talk.

He shoved the dictionary under my nose. I didn't speak German but I recognized the word he had underlined. "*Frau?*" I said. "In English that means woman. All right?" I started off.

"*Pajolista!*"

Please? I stopped. "Yes?"

He turned his grimy thumb towards his chest and looked at me–beseechingly.

I shook my head. "No. You're a man, *nicht frau.*"

"*Frau? Da. Da. Da.*"

Yes, yes, yes? What on earth ... I turned my head. Holmes was standing there grinning at me. He hesitated, stared for a moment and then went briskly on his way.

The engineer motioned with his head for me to follow him. He opened a door.

His cabin! I backed off. "*Nyet!*" I said. "*Nyet! Dasvdania!*" I hoped that meant goodbye! No matter how stupid he is, I thought, he must know that *frau* means woman!

He watched me go with tragic eyes.

As I looked back, through the open door, I saw two oranges lying on a shelf.

A short time later Holmes came to take me on deck. "I've some interesting news for you."

"Now what? Did the Captain find out I stole Hanitchka's comb?"

"Never mind the Captain, the engineer wants to marry you."

"He does? Does he, really? How nice." Then light broke through the mysterious gloom. *Frau!* Wife as well as woman! "Is that what it was all about?"

"Don't be stupid," said Holmes, it's not you he wants. He's trying to get out of Russia. He didn't say so, of course, but they all want to get out of Russia. Marrying is the way to do it."

"How revolting!"

"You're the one to talk! Hanging on to his arm this morning. No wonder the fool thinks ... "

"I bumped into him! I grabbed him to keep from falling! You think he thinks I encouraged him? Oh, really, Holmes! I was just ... "

"I know, trying to get away with the comb. Have you still got it?"

"I gave it back."

"Hmm," said Holmes, "Then please get it again. Well anyway, about the engineer, he wishes to declare his love for you, so you'll have to listen."

"Oh, I couldn't. I don't want to."

"I promised," said Holmes. "In about ten minutes, in my cabin. Come along."

I followed Holmes to his cabin and the engineer was standing by the door waiting for us. He had washed his face but it was still dirty, in spots, around his ears. I stood near the porthole as far from the door as I could get.

Holmes, gazing fixedly at a spot on the door, a little above the engineer's head, translated gravely. "He says he loves you and wants to marry you."

"Tell him," I said, examining my boots, "that I don't love him, so I won't."

Upon hearing this statement translated, the engineer got down on his knees.

"For God's sake stop him!"

Holmes said something in Russian. His voice was severe. The engineer stood up, turned and took hold of the doorknob. His head was bowed.

"Wait a minute," I said. "Even if he can't have me, he might like to do something for me."

"What!" said Holmes. "Let him go!"

"No, he's got something I want."

"Something you want! I'm damned!"

"Ask him if he'll do something for me."

Holmes looked at me and I looked right back at him, boldly. "Go on, ask him."

He translated and the engineer answered him fervidly.

"He says," Holmes looked at me, crushingly, "that there is nothing in the world he wouldn't do for you."

"Great. Tell him I want two oranges."

"What! I won't!"

"Tell him."

Holmes hesitated and then, gravely, translated.

The engineer looked stunned. He pulled open the door and rushed into the passage.

"It takes a lot to shock me," said Holmes, disgustedly.

"Please wait."

In a few minutes the engineer opened the door a crack, threw the oranges at me and slammed it shut.

I stooped to pick them up. "For my babies. They've had little but bread and tea. Do you realize? They're on their way to Siberia! If those women aren't careful they'll end up with scurvy! I don't know how much good this will do, but ... "

The oranges were ripe and good but as usual there was opposition. Two women insisted that "Sour things upset babies' stomachs." They wanted me to throw them overboard. Marta, an unexpected ally, persuaded them to try them.

And the atmosphere in the cabin had changed somewhat for the better since the fine-tooth comb had been discovered, rolled up in a pair of Marta's corsets. And on the last day out–when we were in sight of land–the mothers forgave me. I came in to change my clothes and found them smiling at me!

As usual, it was Marta who spoke for them. She had piled her red hair high on her head and was preparing–still without washing–to get into a dress. "Philippa!"

"Yes?" Whatever she wanted now, I thought, she could get for herself. The sea was flat as a board.

"We forget about the comb."

"Don't tell me it's lost again!"

"Oh, no, not. I have ... Never mind. Something else we talk over."

"Yes? What?" I couldn't believe they were going to thank me! Were they? At last! The whole atmosphere in the cabin had changed. Not the air–unhappily, that was the same–the porthole had remained shut for eight days. But the mothers were quivering with good will.

"We think you not bad."

"Bad!" I said, astounded.

"Now don't worry. We think you not bad."

"Well, that's good," I said slowly and gently. "And just why ... " I wondered if I would find out, at last, what was wrong with me. "Please tell me. Why did you think I was bad?"

"Look at you!" Marta shouted, indignantly. "How we not think something!"

224

I looked at myself. I was still in Holmes' pants and the sweater I had put on eight days ago. They were certainly dirty, but dirt didn't seem to bother my guests. "I'm not sure what you mean," I said.

"We think," said Marta, "for your own good, we tell you something that help you. You young woman, you should know something of the world, so we tell you." She took a breath. "First, we think you lady, then ... Well!" She sighed, shrugged. "You act like bad woman."

I knew what she meant. Bad: immoral, a whore. I searched my past. Here I was–after God knows how many encounters with all sorts of men– still a virgin! Why in God's name did people always think I was bad? I said, "I don't understand. You'll have to tell me."

Marta looked at me without coldness now, and without contempt. Then she modestly dropped her eyes. The others dropped their eyes, too, but they were nodding in agreement. "Yes," they said. "Yes, yes."

"What you think the men think of you?" screamed Marta, looking up–to heaven–for help.

"The men?"

"You go in all the ship! You have disgrace yourself!"

"How dare you."

"Philippa," wailed Marta. "Please. We talk. Is for your own good."

"Disgrace myself!" I was furious. "You'd better explain!"

She explained: "Philippa! How you think we think when we looking at you? Look! Look at you!" She paused, she wailed, "How you feel no shame?"

"What? For what?"

"You go in all ship. Every day in front of men. You nice woman. How you feel no shame wearing pants?"

21

The Russians had more than fulfilled their contract on my excursion ticket: along with the privilege of sleeping inside, Intourist had provided a group guide. But since I comprised the group, the Russian girl, Olga, and her attendant dockhand–"This comrade-worker will carry your luggage"–who collared me as I emerged from my cabin, had come aboard solely for me.

Olga, twenty-five years old, five feet high and wrapped in a rusty green coat, was as broad as she was tall. Her black hair, under a hideous pink hat of crocheted wool, framed a pasty sick-white face, but her flashing black eyes and flashing smile were extremely attractive. I was happy, indeed, to meet two genuine native communists, although her exorbitant delight in meeting me, a capitalist, surprised me.

"Olga." I put out my hand to the comrade-worker. "Would he take these and have them cleaned?" I handed him Holmes' pants and sweater.

Olga took them from him. "My mother will clean. *Tovarish!*" Olga gave the comrade-worker a hard look and he stopped gaping at me and picked up my suitcases.

"You are so charming," Olga exclaimed, gazing admiringly at my head. "So intelligent. So good. I can see it, at once, in your face." She took my arm. "We say in Russia, *orchen sympateeshnia*, in English, sympathetic, the same–no? It is such pleasure." She was pulling me.

"Oh ... " I said, pulling back. "Thanks! That is, how kind of you to say all those nice ... But look, wait a minute, I can't leave just yet. I must see Mr. Holmes."

Coming into Leningrad Harbour while reluctantly removing Holmes' horrifying pants–jumping up and down in my icy cabin and trying to bathe all over with a small washcloth and four ounces of cologne–I had caught glimpses, through the still-closed porthole, of a flat, long, low shoreline with a church and spire, gleaming in the distance. I hoped Holmes would get a sleigh and take me for a drive.

"And then I have a little scarf for a baby, Hanitchka, and I want to say goodbye to her mother, so ... "

"Of course!" Olga shut me up with a peremptory, raised hand. "Of course! *Seechas!* It is arranged. *Seechas!* "

"*Seechas?* " I echoed.

"*Seechas,*" Olga repeated and she flashed her sun-lit smile once more. "*Seechas.* It means in English, immediately. Come! You will see Mr. Holmes and you will say goodbye to Hanitchka and the comrade mine workers. At once. *Seechas.*" She steered me across the deserted deck and up the gangplank to the shore.

"Here!" I protested. "Wait! I think they must still be on board. Where's Mr. Holmes?

"Mr. Holmes? *Da!* Yes! *Da. Da. Da.*" Olga's eyes and teeth flashed behind a cloud of frozen breath. "Mr. Holmes. *Seechas!* Come, we walk."

I pulled back stubbornly. I meant to wait. Holmes would not have left the ship without seeing me. "Then you know Mr. Holmes and where to find him?"

"I know all passenger on the ship. Is all right. You see him."

I might as well go on. Holmes would find me. If I didn't move I'd freeze to death. I was wearing clothes Madame Eugenia had considered adequate for a Russian winter: long woollen underwear, woollen stockings, galoshes, a woollen dress and a sweater under my heavy tweed coat but, surrounded by vastnesses of snow and ice, even my teeth were cold. I began to shiver and shake and hold myself.

There was room for two abreast on the path and I started off, dizzily, beside Olga. After eight days at sea I had lost terrestrial equilibrium and the brilliant white earth was rolling. We followed the bank for a few hundred yards to the customs shed, a single room of rough, unpainted wood with a high bench along one side. My suitcases were lying open on it and two customs officials, heavy-set men wearing peaked caps, were sitting behind it on wooden chairs. They didn't stand up. One addressed me, solemnly, in Russian.

"There is no suspicion about your possessions," Olga translated, "except for the sealed, blue cardboard package." She handed it to me. "Open, please."

I shook my head in embarrassment. "Olga ... I ... That is if you don't mind, I won't."

"Won't!" Olga popped her eyes at me. "What? You refuse to open? But we do mind! Please! Open, at once!"

"For heaven's sake!" I said, under my breath. "Don't be ridiculous. There's nothing subversive ... That's a box of sanitary napkins!"

"Sanitary?" Olga smiled. She had great charm. "Then is no need to hide. Open, please. It is the law."

"No. No, I won't."

One of the men rose from his chair and walked carefully across the floor to stand guard beside me while the other ripped the top off the box of Kotex and, delicately, inch by inch, removed and explored each separate napkin.

When he had finished bending, shaking and probing with his filthy hands, I took them from him, stuffed them back in the box and dropped the whole thing in the coal scuttle.

"What they cannot understand," Olga explained, kindly, after they let me go, "is why, at first you won't open and then why, if you carry this sanitary business all the way to Russia, you throw it away? I, naturally, do not think, but what they think is crazy capitalists!"

We descended steps, cut in the snow, to a great, wide street and stood for a few seconds on the half-cleared sidewalk at the foot of a sloping hill. The dockhand trudged ahead of us, on his way to the hotel with my luggage. The sky was woolly-white and it seemed to rest on the snowy roofs of the low, worn buildings. A streetcar came clanging downhill towards us through the blackened snow. It slowed and stopped and a woman conductor in a round man's cap, with a coinbox attached to a leather strap across her chest, jumped off and ran around in front of it.

"Russia!" Olga blew clouds of visible words at me. "You like Russia? Yes, I see you do! It is the most beautiful country in the whole world! *Nyet?*"

I nodded and turned away from her demanding stare. Lot's wife, I thought, had nothing on me. It was madness to stand still. I would soon be a solid pillar, though not of salt.

"Olga," I muttered with my mouth shut, "for God's sake let's move!" And I stepped along, stiff as a board, after my suitcases.

The Sovtorgflot was a great barn-like hotel facing the waterfront, and in 1931 the only decorations in the empty public rooms were blown-up photographs of Lenin and Stalin draped with red bunting and decorated with hammers and sickles. The largest one, five feet high, of Stalin, was set up in the centre of the room on an easel.

There was no evidence in the hotel of any kind of heating in this sub-zero weather. The windows were uncurtained and the wooden floors and staircases, scrubbed spotless, were uncarpeted.

Olga, walking sidewise, a step ahead of me, led me across the floor and up the stairs. She opened the door to my room. Except for a clean, white, narrow bed, a wooden chair and my suitcases, it was completely bare, walls and all. "You'll be comfortable here," she said, enviously.

"Thank you," I replied.

Since the moment we'd met on board ship, she had never taken her eyes off my face. "Tomorrow," she said now, "I shall call for you and take you to see the things of interest."

"Thank you," I said again. The only thing that interested me was getting warm, but I had been received with such cordiality that I hesitated to mention it. The Russians, apparently, ignored the weather. I thought I was obliged to ignore it, too.

Olga stood at the door, still staring, seemingly hypnotized, a truly incandescent light in her eye.

"What is there to see?" I asked, to relieve the pressure.

"The Winter Palace, of course," she said, quickly, as though reciting in her sleep. "We have the finest collection of pictures in the world." And then what had been on her mind since we met came to the surface. "I ... I must tell you," she gulped, "that in Russia, I have not seen such a fashionable thing for the head."

"Oh!" My hat! At the risk of freezing my brain, I pulled it off my head. "Here. Try it on."

We were alone but she jumped and looked over her shoulder. I pulled out my compact, rubbed the frost off it, opened it, handed it to her and took her sad crocheted, pink woollen hat from her out-stretched hand. Then I remembered my lice. Were they still with me?

But watching her trying to see herself in that tiny looking-glass, adjusting the brim over her eyes, tilting her head, I realized she was too charmed to care.

Tentatively and with longing, she said, "There is a man ... I should so much like if he should see it on me."

I remembered the awful need I used to have, in Edgeville, for something pretty. It would be contemptible to snatch that dazzled look from her face. "Well," I said, bidding my headgear a fond farewell, "let's trade. I'll take your hat and you take mine." And then, seeing the astonishment in her eyes, I added, "In America, we prefer things that are made by hand."

But it was not a bad exchange, really. When she left, which she did at once, I discovered that if I pulled her hat straight down over my frigid face, which I did at once, that I could wear it like that. It was warm and I could see through the stretched holes. And then there was something about that hat, with its attached, crocheted roses that reminded me, nostalgically, of my childhood "ideal lady," Miss Annie O'Reilly, whom, when I grew up, I found out was Edgeville's "Anytime Annie." So-called because, reputedly, the only time she said "no" was when she didn't hear the question.

I stripped the bed of its woollen blankets and wrapped them around me, hat, coat and all, and went to the window. It was late afternoon and the brilliant sun was reflected on the snowy street below me. Where was Holmes? In some swank hotel–heated of course. Or was there any such thing in Leningrad? But wherever he was, there was no need for me to look for him because he would find me.

I opened the window and leaned out. It was slightly warmer outside. I pulled the chair to the window and sat down to look.

A man and a woman, carrying an oblong wooden box held above their heads, walked slowly past the window. They came to the end of the street, turned right and disappeared. The street was empty. A few minutes later, three people appeared carrying a slightly larger oblong box. They took the same route. Then another group appeared. This was the only traffic past the hotel, these small groups of people carrying boxes. Boxes? Coffins! I started to count. When I had counted eleven more, I left the window. I was freezing. I lay down on the bed. I felt sick.

I woke to sunshine and the residue of melancholy reflections. The coffins had almost all been small–children's. Was it disease, starvation or exposure? Perhaps I would die of the cold myself! I heard footsteps in the corridor.

Olga called out, "*Mozhna*–may I?" and burst into the room. She looked radiant! She was wearing my hat. What a dope I was to give it away. I said, sourly, "Well, did your man approve?"

"Ah, yes, yes, yes! He has never seen me so beautiful." Quick tears brimmed in her eyes. "God will bless you!" She held out an envelope. "Mr. Holmes has paid for your meal tickets. He is looking for you last night but you are asleep. This evening, also, he will take you to dinner." She hesitated. "Your hat," she exclaimed, and the light went out of her face. "You wish to wear it perhaps?" She looked defeated.

"No! No, of course not. It's yours." I ripped open Holmes' letter. He wouldn't care if I appeared in a gunny sack. The meal tickets were enclosed; he would call for me at five. It was signed "with love." I thought, joyfully, it's not really cold, and leapt out of bed.

Downstairs the great dining room was empty, except for Lenin, Stalin, forty or fifty yards of red bunting and a ten-foot long, bare, wooden table. A man-servant in an ankle-length, mattress-striped, cotton apron brought us buttered sour black bread and steaming glasses of sugared tea.

"Ah," Olga sighed. "It is good–no–to have butter and sugar? Listen, since you do not use your ticket tonight for dinner, I should be glad to buy it. You have still two tickets for tomorrow. Then you take the train at twelve in the night and the next meal tickets you will get from Intourist in Moscow."

Must one always arrange for a meal? I thought about those coffins and lost my appetite. Starvation? "If you had two tickets," I suggested, "both lunch and dinner, could you dine with your man tonight? Because, truthfully, I'm not hungry and since Mr. Holmes has already paid for me, please take them." I pulled the envelope out of my purse and handed it to her.

Olga turned her head away. "You are my sister," she said, "my sister."

Outside I had that strange sensation the French call déjà vu, as though I had returned, after a long absence, to a country I had once known well. A troika came racing down the street, its three black horses emaciated and the driver bundled in rags. I had never seen one before, but it was as familiar as a sleigh in Canada. The day was clear, cold and exhilarating and I thought, happily, I shall soon be used to the cold.

Olga was taking me to the Winter Palace to see the treasures of the Hermitage. I had never been in a palace or a museum, but now I would see the elegance I had dreamed of, the pictures the world called great. In my mind I had a confused image of great halls, brilliant lights, and colour.

"It is right here," Olga said, pointing, "in front of the Palace, that the Czar's Cossacks slaughtered the starving peasants in nineteen-five. Nicholas was frightened ... "

The starving peasants. Where had I heard it? Nicholas wasn't in the palace that day. And after three years in a city hospital I didn't want to hear about starvation and slaughter.

Brown. Solid, dull, plain brown. What a drab colour for a palace. What did I expect? I didn't know. The starving peasants! I felt sick and frozen.

We crossed the snowy square and opened the door to a dim, echoing space. There was an occasional table, an occasional piece of furniture, roped off. Was this a palace? We went up a broad staircase and came to a high-ceilinged room.

Olga pointed to a round, brown table. She said, "Once upon a time, in Catherine's day, that table can descend through the floor to the kitchen. There, it was loaded with provisions: caviar, fruits, sweets and wine and sent up again. No one entered this room to serve the masters."

Once, but not now. Perhaps houses live when men live in them. This palace was dead. I caught my breath. All my life, I had criticized the houses I knew, and now I was dissatisfied with the palace of the Russian Czars. Of all men, Kings and Emperors must live in beauty, yet, to me, this palace ...

We started through the galleries and Olga began her professional patter. It interfered with my concentration. I had to look at the pictures alone; judge for myself; find out if my own feeling for beauty conformed to what the world called great. I confronted Olga. "Would you think me rude if ... Olga, I must look at the pictures without you."

"But it is my work!"

"If you talk, I can't see or think. It distracts me."

"Ah." She gazed at me, admiringly. "Of course. You are a true communist. Sensitive. Well, now we shall arrange. There is no attendant at this time of year. You must ring when you have finished and I shall meet you. I shall take a glass of tea with the concierge; he is a friend. Tell me, when do you think to finish?"

There was nothing to go "home" for. "Three hours? Or four, or five? You see, Olga, I've waited a lifetime."

A light dawned in Olga's expressive eyes. "You spend the day. Good. And I... I go see the concierge and tell him to let you out. And my dear sister, I shall take this day for me. Goodbye, goodbye, goodbye! Tomorrow, at ten, I meet you at the Sovtorgflot. We shall take the train and go to the Summer Palace. Ah, how I shall enjoy, after this little holiday, showing you the summer home of the Czars. Come quick, I show you the bell." She clattered down the stairs.

I went back to the galleries. I walked from picture to picture and I did not look at the names. I waited to be overwhelmed by beauty, but nothing happened.

I stopped looking at the pictures and sat down on a bench. I tried to remember the names of the great painters. I must have read about them some time, somewhere, but in my confusion I could remember one name only: Rembrandt.

I got up again and started looking at the bronze plaques. No Rembrandts. And then I walked into an adjoining gallery and came face to face with a bearded old man in a turban. We stared at each other. His eyes were powerfully alive: dominant: the longer he looked the more he dominated me–the cipher posed in front of him. I read the name plate: "Rembrandt. *An Oriental.*"

I walked from one Rembrandt to another. *The Man in The Fur Hat, Abraham's Sacrifice, Joseph's Robe, A Little Girl with a Broom–La Balayeuse,*

Adrien: Le Frère de Rembrandt. I began to wish, with all my heart, for Pa. I wanted him to see these pictures–perhaps he had–but I wanted to look at them with someone who could share their magnificence.

I paused in front of a little boy playing with cards, *Le Chateau de Cartes* by Chardin. Here was restraint, elegance. And now I was overcome with a feeling of desolation. I had caught a glimpse of a world that was exhilarating and inspiring, but it was a world closed to me. And I wanted more than anything I had ever wanted in my life to be part of that world. I wanted ... What utter nonsense! I, much too old to begin all over again, I wanted to paint!

I found another room and more pictures.

I stood, marvelling at the Van Dykes, at the Gainsboroughs, at satins and velvets and taffetas, painted more truly than life. I stood before Rubens' *Bacchus* and laughed. I found the primitives–the early church pictures– small, pale blue, red and gold. They were lovely in their cramped form, but too static for my soaring mood.

It was late afternoon when I left the galleries. I was tired and shivering and bursting with excitement–and I was cold. I started towards the hotel. There would be no hot bath at the Sovtorgflot, and Holmes would not be there for another hour.

On a wide, empty street, the Nevsky Prospekt, I turned left and began to run, full out. When I came on a group of sculptured, rearing horses, black and powerful against the brilliant snow and the graying sky, I stopped, pulled off Olga's hat and held my breath, choking. They were so magnificent I couldn't breathe!

When I finally got back there was a message for me: Holmes was sending a troika! I felt like Cinderella–but how did I look? Except in two-inch sections, looking in my compact, I had no way of finding out, but I decided, shivering, to wash my face. And Olga's hat was so stretched from pulling it down to my chin that it wouldn't stay anywhere else. I must fix that.

It was almost dark when the troika arrived and I was impatient to see Holmes. When we slid, jingling, up to his hotel and I caught sight of him waiting on the sidewalk, a verse from the Psalms of David flashed into my mind. "He that hath clean hands, and a pure heart; who hath not lifted up his soul unto vanity, nor sworn deceitfully." I felt such an intensity of emotion that my heart stood still.

"Philippa," he called out. "At last!"

"Catch!" I stood up in the troika and threw his sweater and trousers at him.

233

He reached for my hand and I stepped down. "I called that place twice today," he said. He spoke to the driver in Russian, dismissing him.

I held on to his hand. "Holmes," I said, "Holmes, there's been something missing ever since I got off the boat–you! I can't do without you! And thanks for the meal tickets, and the troika. It's like sliding on silk; I loved it."

"Here, here," he said, "catch your breath."

We ran up the steps to the lighted lobby. Holmes said, "What on earth have you got on your head? Let me look at you."

Deliberately awkward, I pivoted on one heel.

Holmes shut his eyes and shook his head. "What happened to your hat? Do I have to take you into the dining room in that?"

"I traded it."

"For that! You couldn't have ... No normal woman. Christ! Turn around again."

I turned around. I had removed the roses, pulled the hat tight and low on my forehead and eyebrows, and pinned the overlap behind with two large safety pins. What difference did it make in Russia?

"A couple of oranges to hide the pins might help. God Almighty, are you going native?"

"If you think I'm going to freeze my face to indulge your fatuous conceit," I said, and paused. "Look, is it a degree warmer here? How is it you're not cold? Why even the Russians ... " Holmes wasn't wearing his hat or overcoat. He looked like a tailor's dummy.

Holmes looked at me speculatively. "If this worries you, what will you do in December?"

"You cold-blooded fish! Perhaps you're drunk."

"That's right," he agreed, laughing. "I'm drunk, and hot on the trail of another drink. Now, pull that atrocity off your head and we'll go in."

"Give up my hat? I won't!"

"Oh, come on. Off with it!"

"But, my face, Holmes! When the horses started, when the wind hit it, I thought it would fall off. It aches. All right, don't frown, I'll give you an inch." I pulled Olga's hat just above my eyebrows. "There, how's that–smart?"

"Smart? Yes, indeed. You look like the Russian bulwark against the inroads of the degenerate capitalistic world. How long have you been here? Twenty-four hours? At the rate you're going, you'll find your face on a Russian poster."

"I'm hungry," I said, coldly. "And I know now what they mean by the bourgeois mind."

"Dear God," Holmes muttered, gazing with distaste at my head. "It's barbarous, but I don't want you to be unhappy. Pull it over your eyes again. Do you intend to eat through it? Quick! Let's get into the dining room. I need that drink."

The dining room was covered throughout with a worn, crimson carpet. Shining, white damask cloths covered the dozens of square tables, but only a few were occupied. The wide, damask napkins bore royal crests, woven into the material. Holmes and I sat under a magnificent crystal chandelier and the electric light dimmed and wavered over our heads.

A waiter in a heavy black jacket served us, formally, thin slices of some lugubrious, overdone, coarse-grained meat. Holmes tested his with his fork.

"Mountain goat," I said, with my mouth full. "I'd know it anywhere. They serve it all the time in the hospital."

"You feel at home, then?" he said. "I envy you."

Half-way across the room, and almost invisible in the dim light, a young man, with a book propped up against a wine bottle, was eating his dinner. Reading at dinner! Just like Pa.

"He's not Russian. All foreigners here," Holmes said, following my eyes. "This place is maintained for one purpose: *valuta*–American, English, French, German–any outside money. They need it to buy equipment and men, technicians for their five-year plan. No foreigner will take the rouble. You're dining," he added drily and softly, "in a restaurant run by murderers, reserved for capitalist parasites, and equipped with stolen silver and linen."

"The linen is handsome," I said, "and the silver. According to Russian report, both are now owned by the people who have a right to them."

"Uh-huh," Holmes sighed. "No need to dispute the ownership. It's owned by communists. And, comparatively, the food is not bad. The people have much worse and much less–except the communists."

"The communists? Isn't everyone here a communist?"

"My dear, how naïve! Hardly anyone is a party member. Don't you know that there is more than one political party in Russia?"

"No."

"Yes, of course," said Holmes. "Just like at home, with one slight difference. Here, one party is in power and–when they talk out loud–the other parties are in jail."

"Is there any place in the world," I murmured, "where men are happy?"

He put his hand gently over mine. "Philippa, has no one taught you to take care of yourself? You suffer too much."

I looked up, astonished. "Suffer?" I said. "I hate that word. It's mawkish! But, yes. I can't help it. I do. Don't you?"

"I? My dear girl, get this straight in that kind, that generous … "

He rolled his eyes to the ceiling. "That chic little woolly head. I see it, I write it, I forget it; and that's what you must do if you are to survive. My dear, I hesitated to interfere, but I was shocked. Running your feet off on the boat night and day, exhausting yourself for that pin-headed clutter."

"The women? They were sick."

Holmes lifted his hand from mine and I wanted to reach out and take it back. I didn't, of course.

"And if you hadn't been there?" he asked, adding cynically, "you must feel yourself indispensable, is that it?"

"Self-important? V-vanity? W-well … " He was right, half-right anyway. "D-d'you know," I stuttered, "now that I think of it, it could be vanity. Only, is that sort of vanity a fault? Holmes, I'm full of faults. All my life I've tried to discover and rid myself of them, and all my life, I've been called … Do you think I'm crazy?"

"Crazy? You innocent. If you're crazy, love is crazy for it's in your every gesture, it shines out of your eyes. No, you're not crazy but you're living in a crazy and merciless world. Unless you understand that and learn to protect yourself from it, it will drive you crazy."

"Then, you suffer, too," I said.

"I? Oh no. No, thank you. I don't like what I see, but I refuse suffering. How can I make you understand?"

Holmes' gray eyes were so concerned, so tender, that I knew he wanted very much to teach me how to prevent getting hurt.

"Philippa," he went on, "it's important that you do understand. I shall survive because, of necessity, I have cultivated detachment. Or, put it another way, like a running stream, I go over and around the savage rocks, and remain as you see me, placid and whole. Philippa, perhaps I shouldn't say it, but I think I know you. I love you. I'm not trying to … I have no intention of shoving you into bed. You love me, too?"

A rush of affection for him swept through me, of love. There were tears in my eyes and a lump in my throat. When I could speak, I said, "Yes, I love what you are. I trust you. With you, I'm at peace. Tell me, how did you get so detached?"

"That's a long story. I'll tell you some time, but not now. I've things to do tonight and I'm leaving very early in the morning. We mustn't lose touch, though. I must know how things work out for you."

He took his wallet from his pocket and handed me a card. "This is a permanent address. Use it. Write me everything. And look, I'll phone you in Moscow; I should be there within a week or so. Where are you staying?"

The Grand Hotel. I put the card in my bag. "No advice?"

"I can think of a dozen 'don'ts' for you. One, don't give away everything you own the first week you're here."

"And?"

"Later. Let the rest go till later." He lifted his glass. "Your eyes–the eyes of a saint." He drank. "But the hat?" He put the glass solidly on the table. "The hat, no!"

The coffee was good and hot.

"No tipping here," said Holmes. "But he'll take this." He placed an unopened package of American cigarettes on the table.

We rose to leave and I looked across the room. The young man with the book was looking at us and questioning the waiter. No need to be clairvoyant to guess that he was asking about my distinguished companion, Holmes.

When Holmes took me back to the Sovtorgflot, he didn't kiss me goodbye. He put his arms around me and held me for what seemed like no time–or eternity.

I thought, I'm at home in his arms; I sighed and leaned all my weight on him. Then I went upstairs, drowsy with happiness and fell asleep at once.

I woke at dawn, terrified and trembling. Holmes was gone. I would never see him again. I knew.

When Olga came to take me to see the Summer Palace, I could barely lift my head. I waved her away. Idiotically, I had imagined myself into a fever.

The whole thing is ridiculous, I told myself. What could happen to Holmes? Nothing. I'm ill from the cold. I'll get up in a minute.

But when Olga came to my room at ten-thirty that night I was still in bed. I got up and dressed and we went downstairs for hot tea.

She shoved me aboard the train for Moscow five minutes before it was due to leave, at midnight. I felt, guilty, quite unable to respond to her spontaneous outpouring of love for her sister.

"I'll write you," I promised, "when I feel better."

I had no idea what to expect on a Russian train, but when I saw the two rows of bare planks along each side of the empty, icy car, I knew that the meagre bed in the Sovtorgflot had been luxury, indeed. Halfway to Moscow, I remembered I didn't know Olga's last name.

22

My respect for the stamina of the Russian people grew daily. There were more than three million people living in Moscow, a city that had been built, years before the Revolution, to accommodate a million inhabitants. If they were uncomfortable–I was never sure they were–they shrugged and said, *nitchevo*. Translated, this means "no matter" or "think nothing of it."

I hadn't had a bath in a week–*nitchevo*. My underclothes had taken on a general Russian grayness–*nitchevo*. The smell–*nitchevo*–was frozen in. What if they thawed?

I had left the United States confident that I could be of some use to the Russians but so far I had only frozen with them. And then, too, I had anticipated a clear, bright light, shining on everything in Russia, but my questions–Were social distinctions abolished? Was the worker happy? Were things going well in Russia?–all hung in abeyance. Without the language, it was impossible to know what was going on. I began to study Russian.

But if I would not allow myself a political decision, I must make a personal one. The three weeks allowed me on my excursion ticket would soon be up and no one knew, or would tell me, how to find a job. Every day at Intourist when I picked up my meal tickets, I asked to see someone in authority. If necessary, I would go back to nursing–in any case I wanted to see a Russian hospital–and every day the frosty female, who pulled her black hair back, skin-tight, off her broad, intellectual brow, stared me down through her pince-nez and brushed me off with *seechas*.

A wonderful country, Russia. No one ever said no. Waiting for *seechas:* at once: immediately, I spent days wandering around the streets. There was no writing paper in the hotel and none in the dreary holes in the walls the Russians called shops. At night, rubbing the ice out of my fingers, I wrote to Pa on toilet paper.

Dear Pa,
I am living just across from the walled Kremlin and that great block of green marble–malachite?– in Red Square: Lenin's tomb. Today I joined the queue

of peasants in their drab garments and high felt boots and went in to see him. He lay, embalmed, a slender man in a khaki uniform, a khaki blanket drawn up to his chest. An idol to be worshipped and a monument to himself.

I told Pa about Saint Basil's Cathedral and how, after it was built, the Czar burned out the architect's eyes with a red-hot poker so that it might never be reproduced. I told him about the breast-shaped, onion-domed spires of Moscow's hundreds of churches, which were dull and tarnished. I told him about the sculpture: the horses in Leningrad and atop the Bolshoi Theatre. I told him about the museums: the new murals of workers and industries, in harsh black and white. I told him of a thirteenth-century head of Christ–brought out from the archives and shown me as a special favour. I told him I was haunted by the pictures in the Hermitage and that if I ever had a chance I would paint. I told him many things, but I didn't tell him Moscow was overcrowded and that I had been searching frantically for a room, and that unless something turned up very soon, I would have no money and nowhere to stay.

Then one morning, the desk clerk, who had been trying to help me find a room, handed me a slip of paper. He had heard of a woman who was willing to take me in.

Starting out with my limited Russian–*gydyeh eta:* where this?–I almost wore out the transparent slip of paper, but I found the building. It was an impressive edifice of gray stone, which might once have been an institution of some kind, perhaps a hospital. Wide stone steps led up to a rusty, iron grille, massive, carved doors, half-open behind it.

A woman carrying a pickaxe over her shoulder came down the steps. She wore the usual nondescript dirt-brown canvas coat, bulging around the rag tied around her middle. Her feet and legs were encased in knee-high, felt boots. The peasants made the felt by chewing wool until it was a pulpy mass, then shaping and drying it. She was one of the women–I had seen them all over Moscow–engaged in keeping the streets and the streetcar lines clean and in repair.

"*Pazholista,*" I asked, in my best Russian. "*Gydyeh, komnata tovarish Popow?*–Please, where is the room of comrade Popow?"

The woman turned and pointed behind her. "*Piat.*" She grinned and put out a hand to feel my coat. I grinned back and waited to be examined.

Piat: five. I climbed the steps and entered the building. There were two rows of doors running along each side of a long corridor. Light shone dimly from a window at the far end. Outside of every door burned a smoky little primus. It was high noon and a pot of soup boiled on each. The air was clogged with smells of oil and food and soot. If I threw a handful of this air out of the window, I thought, I'd hear it thump when it hit the ground. I breathed shallowly. I walked along the stone corridor and knocked on the door marked "5." The voice inside was high and piercing. " *Mozhnuh!* "

I turned the heavy knob and pushed open the door.

A woman with great, blurred-black eyes and a tangle of coarse black hair hanging half-way down her back, was squatting on the floor under a window, peeling onions. She was clothed in heavy, rusty-black wool. Her undershirt–had it once been white?–was pulled through the neck of her dress and pinned tight about her throat. She lifted the hand that held the knife and wiped onion tears from her eyes.

"Please," I said in my best Russian, "have you a room to rent?"

Her face became suddenly animated. "English!" She dropped the knife, jumped up, ran to me and clutched my sleeve. "Yes! Oh, yes. This is it. We stay–both–here."

I looked around. The walls were of gray stone and caked with dirt. The solitary window, shut tight, was packed with rags around the sides, top and bottom. It was bright daylight outside, but the glass was so encrusted with filth that the room was dark. The furniture consisted of a heavy armchair and a bare table. There was black bread and a piece of salt herring spread on a newspaper on top of it. Two ragged blankets lay in a heap on the floor in a corner.

"But this is enchanting," she exclaimed. "We speak English together. Good! I like you very much." She scratched her head enthusiastically and beamed on me.

"Uh ... W-well," I stuttered, probing my suddenly blank mind for an excuse that would not offend. "No ... T-that is, you see ... " I reached for the doorknob.

"I speak many languages. You will be at home. We shall be so, so happy!" She yanked me away from the door.

"No," I objected, "I can't! T-there's no bed!"

"Bed? Oh?" She shrugged. " *Nitchevo*–bed is nothing!" But her face grew bright, with expectation. "Ah! A-hah! You bring a bed?"

"Well, no. I mean ... I have no bed."

"You have no bed, too? *Nitchevo*, we do not need a bed." She shrugged again. "Is enough here."

"But I can't sleep with anyone," I protested, desperately, "and you have only two blankets."

240

"So?—you think? But is more warmer with two. And, naturally, you bring also your blanket."

"I'm sorry. I haven't got a blanket."

She stared. "You make joke?" The uncertainty in her eyes changed to suspicion. "Since when in your country you travel without blanket?"

"Not," I said feebly, "not since the day of the American Indian. I can't stay" I said, decidedly, "I really can't." I slid one foot behind the other. I took two good steps backward, bumped into the door, got it open and ran. "Goodbye," I gasped out, "goodbye."

Out on the sidewalk, I collapsed against a lamp post. I couldn't take another step. In the past three years my feet ...

Every morning in bed, I stretched my aching ankles and wondered if the day would come when I could do it without pain. My feet were killing me! I had to get back to the hotel. The streetcars here were much worse than the New York subway in the rush hour. There were as many passengers hanging from every handhold on the outside of the cars as there were inside. But now, summoning courage, I waited for a tram and when it stopped—prepared for combat—I gritted my teeth and shoved and pushed and butted my way into it.

Then, I thought, I'm hallucinating. I had caught a glimpse of an empty seat at the far end of the car. At the risk of having my clothes ripped off, I wriggled and squeezed through the jammed bodies. Two empty seats—one on each side. I dropped down, gratefully, on one of them.

But I had hardly done so when there arose from my fellow passengers a concerted roar. Men and women pointed, screamed and shouted at me. The conductor turned and, seeing me, jerked the car to a halt, leapt from his seat and rushed at me, waving his arms. He yelled, " *Rouble! Rouble!*"

What have I done? I wondered, confused by the screaming and shouting and the conductor's excited harangue. Perhaps one had to pay extra. Yes, he was asking for a rouble. I gave him a rouble. He snatched the money, but it didn't help. It seemed to drive both him and the passengers into a further frenzy. I sat there stunned.

Our car blocked the track. Another car stopped behind us. Bells began to ring, pedestrians; a horde of angry people, howled, chattered and pointed at me. The conductor pointed peremptorily to the door. Vanquished, but clutching solemnly at dignity, I stood up, stepped down into the street and escaped through the jeering crowd.

What was wrong? I wondered. If only I could understand Russians! I pushed my aching feet in the direction of Intourist. No one wanted to talk to me, but I would make this woman explain. "Uh, Miss ... " I coughed to attract her attention as I approached the barred window of her cubicle. She looked up. "Miss, would you be kind enough to explain ... I got on a street car and sat down in an empty seat and ... " I stopped. Her piercing look went straight through me.

"You!" she said, contemptuously, and she looked me up and down. "And what fiction did you invent as an excuse to take that empty seat?"

"Fiction? My feet hurt."

She stopped me with an out-thrust hand. "Hah!" She denounced me. "Hah!" Under her breath she said, scornfully, "What lack of understanding! The rouble was a fine. And why should I explain what every schoolchild understands? The two seats are inviolable: sacred to the future of Russia."

"Please be explicit. What future?"

She made an expressive gesture with both hands, of roundness, of fullness. "To explain the obvious is ridiculous," she snorted, dismissing me.

I waited, stubbornly.

She sighed and weariness softened the hard outline of her jaw. "The seats," she explained, shaking her head in despair, "are, naturally, in the shape of the pregnant woman to preserve the coming child."

"You mean the seats are reserved for pregnant women?"

"Haven't I said so? Is it not so in every civilized country? Or are capitalists ignorant of pregnant women's needs? Yes, the seats are only for the pregnant woman. How you don't know, I don't understand."

I was properly abashed. I apologized for my capitalistic ignorance.

Back at the hotel, I stopped at the desk. "Look," I said to the clerk, "I'm used to a bed and Madame ... uh, Comrade ... I mean, do you think you could find me a room with a bed? I'd like to be alone. I ... " I stopped. My voice had gone out of control. I knew very well the Russians needed all the beds and all the rooms they had for themselves and I was embarrassed.

The clerk kept shaking his head. "Ah," he said. "Ah-hah. That is difficult."

"Have you ... " I hated to ask because he always said no, but I was longing for a kind word. "Have you a letter for me today?"

He shook his head again. "But, no. No letter."

Where was Holmes? I felt sick. I still had eighty-five dollars. Was it enough to pay my way to Southampton? I stood, staring at the clerk. I said, desperately, "Please, I must get a room. I must!"

He turned his head away. He looked thin and worn and cold. His hair

was gray and he was old. He said, soberly, "You want it very much. Yes."
He pulled a slip of paper out of a pigeon-hole on the wall behind him,
considered it, and cleared his throat. "I have a friend whose father die. No
one wishes to sleep in this room."

"What did he die of?"

He shrugged. "You need the room?"

"Has it a bed? Could I have it alone?"

"A bed, yes. A very good bed. You may have it alone."

"What did he die of?"

"Nothing, nothing. A few red spots."

Red spots: measles, typhoid, syphilis, small-pox? *Nitchevo.* "Thanks,"
I said. "That sounds wonderful. I'll take it. I'll go right now."

"Wait!" he said. "You must wait until the family is prepared to receive
you. They will tell me. I shall let you know."

They were quarantined!

There was someone behind me, breathing down my neck. I turned
and bumped into a young man I'd seen now and then at Intourist.

He held out his hand. "I bin watchin' you. You English?"

"Canadian. How do you do?"

"Geez! That's great. Look, my old man is here for an engineer and
I'm goin' nuts. Nothin' to do. Say would you have a drink with me? I'm
American."

"How kind of you. Another time, perhaps."

"Aw, geez, no. When?"

"I may be leaving and I have things ... I'm waiting for a long-distance
call."

"Look, if it comes will you meet me at the bar? I'll give you a drink.
My name is Teddy."

"I have no idea when I'll be free. I must pack."

"Okay, I'll call you. If you're free, will you come? Please!"

"All right." He didn't know my name so I was off the hook. Waiting
for a call I would never get. I wouldn't believe what I knew. Holmes was
gone.

The following evening when my phone rang I thought, Holmes!

"Hey, it's me."

Damn! "Teddy."

"Say, c'mon over to the Savoy with me."

"Sorry, I can't."

"Hey, Don't hang up! C'mon, please, I'm lonely."

I'd had a miserable day. I was cold and hungry and I was going to bed. I was so disappointed I could hardly speak. "I'm sorry. I don't mean to cut you off, but ... "

"Aw, geez, look, I got to go over there. I left my galoshes in this guy's room an' I got to pick them up. Besides, if we go over now, it's cocktail time, he'll give us a drink."

"I don't want a drink!" But ... I was dying for a drink. I was dying to get out of my room. I was dying of my own dreary company. The hell with it! "Teddy, who is this guy? Is he ... I mean, I don't want to go to some strange man's room if he ... "

"Aw, geez!" Teddy said, contemptuously. "He won't hurt you. He's one of these guys that don't know from nothin', college boy. He's okay, American. And he's got some wonderful stuff over there. Tokay. The emperor's stock."

"Teddy, are you absolutely sure about that drink?"

"Sure I'm sure!"

I met Teddy in the lobby and we walked to the Savoy, climbed the stairs and Teddy knocked on the door. Then he gave me a playful push, turned, ran down the corridor and disappeared around the corner.

A young man opened the door. It was the young man I'd seen in the dining room in Leningrad the night I dined with Holmes. Embarrassed, I said, "I came with Teddy. He left his galoshes here. He's hiding."

The young man smiled. He said, "Oh, hello. You're just in time for a drink. I'm Dick Bentham. Please come in. You know, I've seen you before–in Leningrad. You were with that newspaper man, Holmes. Shall I leave the door open for Teddy?"

"Please do." My heart started racing. "Do you know Mr. Holmes?"

"Only by sight. The waiter didn't know you but he knew him. Let me take your coat."

My coat! Where did he think we were, the tropics? But there was heat in the room! He must belong to the OGPU.

He hung my coat carefully on a coathanger. I noticed his hands. They were immaculate and obviously innocent of any sort of hard labour.

"Too bad about him," Bentham said.

"About who?"

"Why, Holmes. Don't you know?"

Holmes! Too bad? I couldn't breathe. "What do you mean? What happened?"

Bentham had big blue eyes and long lashes. He stared at me. "Did you know him well?"

244

I turned away and took a breath. I said, lightly, "Oh, a week or so. He was on the boat coming over."

Bentham's quiet voice hit the back of my head like a padded sledge hammer. "They crashed."

"He's dead. When?"

"The day after I saw you. They left before dawn and the plane hardly got off the ground. They were all killed. Look, I've got some Tokay. Would you care to try it?"

The room was long and narrow and clean and bare, except for the piles of books and papers on the desk. It was empty. Russia was empty. The whole gray world was full of emptiness.

Teddy banged into the room, giggling, and slammed the door behind him. "Geez! Philippa! What you doin' in this guy's room? Anybody introduce you two? Where's my drink?" He grabbed the bottle and poured himself a long one.

Bentham sat behind a desk near the window and talked. He had just got his B.A. from Yale and he wanted to write plays. He knew a group of young actors in New York who were extremely talented, Katharine Hepburn, Franchot Tone ... He had come to Russia with a letter of introduction to Stanislavski and he went to the Moscow Art Theatre every day. He ...

There was a dreadful, resounding hollow in my head. Was I going to faint? There was a horrible sucking vacuum in this room. It took my breath. I wanted to slam my glass on the floor and smash it to bits but it was an effort to lift it to my lips. I had to get out. I stood up. "I must go."

"But you just came!"

I took my coat from the wardrobe and Bentham got up, hastily, and held it for me. Then, "Wait a minute." He opened his wallet and took out his card. He wrote his room and telephone number on it. His hands were trembling! "Call me in the morning and I'll take you to see a Russian movie."

I had never fainted in my life but now I kept going in and out of shadowy blackness. God, I prayed, in shock, Holmes. Abbie! I cried to an empty world, Holmes!

For the short time I had known Holmes, I had felt happy and secure. At times, I had thought him hard, perhaps cruel, in his detachment from the suffering around him; but later I realized, as he had insisted, that his strength lay in detachment. Holmes had been strong, not through lack of sensitivity, but because of emotional and mental discipline. It was the same discipline I had learned in the hospital. Yes, I understood him. And I loved him. I loved both of them.

A little past five the next evening, when I had three days left at the Grand Hotel on my excursion ticket and when, fully dressed except for my galoshes, I was lying in bed considering, in dismay, the sad political situation in Russia, and my singularly unattractive personal situation, my telephone rang.

It might be the desk clerk, I thought, to tell me when I could see the dead man's room. Or it might be Teddy. But because of the pain that lay heavily on my heart, I couldn't speak to them. I let it ring.

I was still in bed half an hour later and given over, hopelessly, to bitter thoughts when the telephone rang again. What if it was a letter? A telegram begging me to come home? I reached above my head to the wall telephone and pulled the receiver off the hook. "Yes?"

"Miss Jerrold? Bentham, here."

"Oh, hello."

"Are you doing anything this evening?"

"No."

"Good. How about having dinner with me?"

The thought of food made me sick. "No. I'm sorry. No."

"Oh. Are you eating with someone else?"

"No."

"You're not? Then why ... "

Why? I gave him the first excuse that came into my head. "I have to wash my underclothes."

"Your underclothes!"

"That's right. I've only two pairs. They're filthy." What was I saying? I sat up in bed in a panic. How had I got into this conversation, anyway?

"Oh, Gawd!" He was laughing. "Oh, Gawd," he said again, after he stopped laughing. "Do them tomorrow. Come on over and have a drink and I'll take you to dinner, or would you rather I called for you?"

When had I eaten last? I'd had nothing but tea: chi. Suddenly, I was starving! "I'll come to your hotel."

"I'll wait," Bentham said, "but hurry up." He was laughing again.

I'd told a lie: I did have a pair of long drawers I could wear. I'd washed them a week ago and hung them up to dry. Only they didn't dry. They froze solid. After that, for a week, I'd taken them to bed with me, to thaw out. They were only slightly damp now. But I would have to undress to change.

I left on Olga's pink hat (I went to bed in that hat) but I had to remove the woollen stockings I wore on my hands. I turned on the tap and looked at the sad trickle of water that came from the ancient plumbing. Dick Bentham was the cleanest looking thing I had seen in weeks and I hadn't

246

had a full bath in weeks. I stripped naked and washed all over, jumping up and down in front of the tiny basin, gasping with shock. I turned bright red, but when I pulled on the clean long drawers, I began to feel warm.

When I arrived at Bentham's room, he was still drinking the emperor's stock. He handed me a drink. What was wrong with him? His hands were trembling. He went back to his desk, sat down and raised his glass. "To your beautiful eyes," he said. "You ought to do something about them. They've been haunting me."

Haunting him. That was Saunder's line. I had a moment of panic. The room was stifling, the heat was unbearable. I said, "I know this sounds insane but can you cut off the heat?"

"I can open a window."

"Please do."

Bentham pushed up the window and took a brown paper package from the outside sill. He handed it to me. "Butter," he said, smugly, "four pounds."

"Butter!" I exclaimed, "Now I'm sure you belong to the OGPU! Is this our dinner?" I untied the string.

He laughed. "I can do better for you than that." He went to the wardrobe and brought out a package of rusks and a block of pressed caviar. He spread the rusks thick with butter and caviar. Except that it was fishy, the caviar was of the consistency, and had something of the taste, of boiling tar; I'd tasted it as a child, when they mended the road near the house by the tracks.

"It's delicious," I lied. "I've always wanted to taste caviar, I've only read about it."

"You don't mean it." Bentham was horrified. Then he remembered his manners and, hastily, began to talk. It seemed that the most important things in Bentham's life were things that had happened to his family–in the past. Each generation had produced it's big men: governors, legislators, a signer of the Declaration of Independence, pioneers of industry ... Was Bentham trying to tell me he was one of those big men?

He's handsome, I thought. I couldn't help but notice the regular features, the perfect teeth, the candid blue eyes and the long eyelashes. He was six feet tall and slender and he wore an impeccable, tailored suit.

"More caviar?" Bentham stood up and refilled my glass.

How could he eat this dreadful, fishy tar? "I still have some, thank you."

"I'm not really interested, you see."

What was he talking about? Wondering about tastes and ancestors,

I'd lost track of the conversation. The Tokay was too sweet.

"And I don't mind admitting to you," Dick laughed, "that I came to Russia to get away from the family. They know every damned thing I do when I'm there and, to say the least, it's limiting!"

His teeth were beautiful. So were his eyes.

"I'd like a little private life and I certainly can't have it at home. None of the girls I know ... I mean, I know their families and they know mine. They're as tied up as I am."

Hell! He was going to talk about sex. Why did every stupid man think he had to talk about sex? Now he was staring at me.

"You're worried about sex? Why don't you go to Paris. Isn't that the classical thing? Sex and Paris, they're synonymous, aren't they?"

"Oh Gawd! I've got family there too! Besides, the situation is better here in Russia. They're emancipated about sex."

"Did you really leave home because of what people think? Who cares?" Then I remembered Edgeville where everyone's business was a village affair–and my own family. I had to run from them, too. "Of course," I exclaimed, "It's not possible to be free at home!"

"Philippa ... "

It touched me when he called me by my first name for the first time. "Yes?"

"Do you know what I thought the other evening when you walked in this room? I thought, I've found what I've been looking for."

"You didn't." I was astonished. It hadn't occurred to me that Bentham was interested in me.

He came to me and took my hand. "I still think so."

"Oh, please." I was embarrassed. "Please don't."

He dropped my hand and went back to the desk and sat down.

But I hadn't meant to hurt him so I crossed the room and, tentatively, touched his sleeve. "I do understand, Dick, but we don't even know each other."

He seized my hand and clung to it. "Philippa, how long are you staying here?"

"I'm not sure. Perhaps a few days. I may not be able to stay."

"Would you stay with me?"

"With you! What do you mean?" But I knew very well what he meant. I pulled my hand from his and turned my back on him. Why did everyone take it for granted I was a bad woman? I was sick of it. I started across the room. "I must go. Where's my coat?"

248

"Don't say no. Let's talk about it."

I yanked the wardrobe door open. "There's nothing to talk about. I'm going back to my hotel."

"Oh, no, you can't!" He jumped up and stood in front of the door. "You promised you'd have dinner."

He looked so absurdly disappointed that I had to laugh. And my sombre mood was suddenly reversed. It was terrific for my ego to have someone plead for my company. Was it Eugenia's clothes? "All right, I'll have dinner, but that's it!"

The main dining room of the Savoy Hotel was almost empty–a few couples scattered around the very large room. I looked at Dick across the square of shining, white damask. Except for Holmes, he was the handsomest, the most elegant man I'd ever met.

"The wine cellars," Dick was saying, "are pre-Revolution. I can't say I'm a true connoisseur but I do know the vintages. One can have a really superior wine here." He turned to the waiter. "We'll have a Nuit St. George, with our steak. Let's see, the year ... "

We were easy together.

For desert, Dick ordered fresh pears.

"Ripe pears!" I exclaimed. "In the Russian winter?"

"There's everything in Russia," Dick said, "for the foreigner who can pay with *valuta*." He held his pear with a fork and cut it into quarters, then he peeled it carefully and ate it with a knife and fork.

I picked mine up whole, peel and all and ate it bent over my plate, the juice dripping down my chin.

Dick glanced at me and abruptly turned away.

I felt like a cannibal. I said, "I can't thank you enough! That was delicious."

"Glad you enjoyed it."

We walked through the snowy, starry night to the Grand Hotel.

I was still in bed the next morning at eight when Dick telephoned. "I'm downstairs in the lobby," he informed me. "May I come up?"

"Oh, all right, but would you please have them send up coffee?"

I slipped the woollen socks off my hands, removed Olga's hat, ran a powder puff over my frozen face, combed my hair and put on Abbie's white silk robe. At the knock, I said, *mozhna*.

He opened the door. The waiter was behind him with coffee and two cups and a folded note on a silver tray. He put the tray on the narrow bedside table and handed me the note. "From the desk clerk, Mademoiselle."

I opened it. It was permission to see the dead man's room.

Dick said, "I hope that's not from a rival."

"It's nothing." I was freezing again. I poured the coffee, handed a cup to Dick, sat down and put both my icy hands around my own hot cup. "Forgive me if I don't ask you to take off your coat. We have no heat. But do sit down."

Dick said, "Have you ever looked at your eyes?"

"What!" I was shocked. How could I forget Pa's "No virgin has eyes like that."

"They're startling! They blaze out of that white face. You don't look like any nurse I've ever seen. I mean, I've never looked at a nurse in my life. I was thinking ... "

"That nurses belong to the lower orders?"

"Gawd, no! Anyway, not you. I mean, you just don't look like ... You're stunning. And I think the loveliest voice I've ever heard. I was thinking last night on my way back to the Savoy that you have to stay. Please, Philippa, I want you. Won't you please stay with me?"

I shrugged and stared into my coffee cup. What in hell did I look like? Pa said ... But Holmes said, "the eyes of a saint." Dammit I was neither bad nor a saint. And I had no intention of falling into his bed. I said, "No. And please don't ask me again."

"Look," Dick pleaded, "Why are you in such a hurry to leave? If you'd stay a week or two we could ... You can do as you please, can't you? Or is it something to do with your passport? If that's all, I know people at the British Embassy."

"You've told me your life history," I interrupted, "now I'll tell you mine. I have eighty dollars, no job, and no prospect of getting one. And I may have to leave this hotel tomorrow or the day after."

Dick said, "You're joking! No one would come abroad without money. You must be ... "

"That's right," I interrupted again, "go ahead, say it. I must be crazy."

"Well, imprudent. How did you expect to live?"

"Why imprudent?" I asked. "I'm a working woman. I expected to get a job and work for my living."

"Work! Gawd! Well never mind. Look ... Look, this may surprise you. I made up my mind last night that if I couldn't get you any other way ... Philippa, marry me."

"Marry you!" I repeated, startled out of my wits. Then I thought, this is the classic moment to say "this is so sudden" and I began to laugh.

"I mean, according to Russian law," Dick added, hastily. "We'd have to stay here."

"Russian law? What on earth are you talking about?"

"It's simple," Dick explained. "In Russia, you just register your marriage and you're married. And if you want a divorce, you register that, pay a few roubles–fifty, I think–and you're divorced. There's no legal rigamarole. All you do is send your wife a postcard–or she sends you one–announcing that you're no longer man and wife. Actually, I believe the bureau of statistics does it for you."

"Good God! How awful! What happens to the children?"

"What children?"

"Who takes care of them? The bureau of statistics?"

"Oh, the State does. Whether you stay married or not. They don't believe in family life in Russia. Everyone works. In any case, I don't want any children."

"No?"

"No, I want you."

"And to hell with me if or when you decided to send me a postcard? What a charming proposal!" I was so angry I forgot to feel cold. I was hot.

"But Philippa! Why would I? How do you know it wouldn't work out? We could make it permanent. Please, Philippa, I do want you."

I thought of our dinner the evening before, and I had to laugh. I said, "Are you sure? I saw your face last night when I was eating that pear."

"Yes," he admitted and laughed. "But if you don't know how to eat a pear, I can always teach you. You know, I've never felt like this in my life. I couldn't sleep last night. I even thought of writing home to the family about you."

Teach me? Yes. Brought up in the backwoods, of course I was gauche. Would I ever rid myself of my shortcomings? "Anyway, what about your family?" I asked. "From what you've told me, I take it they wouldn't approve of your marrying a nurse."

"No," he said, soberly, "they wouldn't. But I don't intend to tell them. At least not now. Let's get married and see what happens. If it works out. Fine. If not ... Well, but why anticipate? We can keep it secret. Tell them later."

"And this postcard business?" I asked. "If we went back to the United States with a postcard divorce, would the United States recognize a Russian divorce?"

"I'm not sure," Dick said, "that the United States would recognize a Russian marriage. We don't recognize the Bolsheviks; we have no

251

diplomatic relations with them, so perhaps we don't recognize their law."

There was a directness and candour about him that I had to admire. He was truthful and therefore honourable. I liked him. He crossed the room and took the cup from my hands. He pulled me to my feet. "Philippa, marry me." He pulled me against him, awkwardly. He kissed me, his mouth hard and dry against mine. I didn't object to his kiss but it didn't move me either.

I pushed him away. I said, "I must get dressed, I have an appointment to look at a room."

"Don't look for a room. Marry me this morning and move to my room."

"Don't be silly," I protested. "You must go, I have to dress."

"I'll wait for you in the lobby," Dick said. He went out and shut the door.

I started pulling clothes out of the wardrobe. I was flattered–and revolted. I had the choice of going on alone–and I was miserable alone–or going to live, experimentally, with a man who didn't love me. Marriage would be an escapade for him; something to be enjoyed and, at his convenience, abandoned. And my position, if he wrote that postcard? I could never go home. But, I could never go home anyway. I didn't want to go to bed with a man I didn't know. I wanted to have someone to love–as I had loved Bill. But love, it seemed, was not for me.

Dick and I walked briskly, arm and arm, matching strides, through the frozen, snowy streets, to find the room where the man with "a few red spots" had died. We stopped to ask directions, got lost and ran around in circles. The sun and the icy air were exhilarating. We laughed at the Russians and they laughed at us; a group of young people surrounded us, joined hands and wouldn't let us free. We were amused and happy. It was a magnificent morning.

The streets became more and more shabby, and we came at last to the right address. It was a dilapidated wooden house. A few of the windows were intact, the rest were broken and boarded up or stuffed with rags.

Dick stopped, stared at it, and laughed. "You're going to love it here! Seriously, you're not going in."

"Of course I'm going in." I knocked on the door.

A bent old woman wrapped in a black shawl opened the door. She took my hand, drew me inside and I followed her along a narrow, dark corridor. After the blinding sun on snow, I could barely see.

Dick came with us, laughing.

There was light in the room. The one window had no glass, but a piece of sacking was nailed along the top. The bottom part hung free. The wind was blowing in. The room was newly scrubbed. There was a narrow iron cot, a soiled mattress, a rickety chair and a broken cup.

"Now that you've seen it," Dick said, "let's go."

"But I'm going to take it. It's not bad. Besides, I have no choice. I have to take it."

He put an arm over my shoulder and urged me back along the dark hall. "That settles it," he said, "we'll get married today." He opened the door and shut it behind us. When we were alone, standing in the sun and the snow, he said again, "Philippa, we'll get married today."

I looked at him steadily. "I can't get married," I said. "That's impossible."

"Can't? What's stopping you?" He was laughing again.

What beautiful teeth! What was stopping me? Nothing. I suddenly felt light ... Free! I said, "Because ... " and I began to laugh, too.

"Because?"

"I have nothing to wear."

Someone tapped, opened my door and turned on the light. Elsie with my early morning coffee–and a cable. I glanced at the clock and sat up in bed. Six o'clock. "Good morning." I motioned her away. "I'll brush my teeth first."

Elsie put the tray on the table, drew the heavy draperies and took Fish off the bottom of my bed. She smiled at me. "Good morning, Philippa, you were up late last night, are you getting enough rest?"

I was the future Mrs. Milford. They were taking care of me, all of them. I loved it and them–no matter my uneasy feeling that the whole thing would blow up in my face. I said, "Too much, I imagine."

"Lottie said to tell you eight o'clock."

"Tell her I'll be ready and tell Cook, no breakfast." Lottie and I were riding to the village. She had letters to post and I needed more paper. The weather had been marvellous, the horses needed exercise, we got out as often as possible. I was getting back in condition.

Elsie closed the door gently behind her.

The cable was out of my reach and I didn't want to get out of bed. I was afraid Johnathan was on his way home. I had been writing steadily, trying to finish this opus before he got here. I had worked late last night and I was awake at five, thinking of Dick and that, strangely, with the men in my life one or both of us had recognized the affinity between us at once.

That Dick asked me to marry him the second day we met–no matter that it was à la russe–was not, he told me later, "an act of folly." Not only had he loved me on sight, but he had recognized in me "a basic morality."

Dick was tall, handsome and literate; interested in global affairs and willing to accept the Revolution as progress in Russia. Further, he had been honest with me. Without consciously thinking about it, I trusted him: he was the kind of man I ought to marry. Moreover, in his presence, I had begun to feel restored.

At that time I was both physically and emotionally depleted and in an acute state of depression. Except for that one brief week with Holmes, I had not laughed for a long time. I had just come away from three years of heavy-duty work in a city hospital. Added to that was my stressful, criminal involvement in Abbie's abortion; months of living with the brutal gangster-bootleggers; Abbie's shocking suicide followed by the air crash that had killed Holmes; and the fact that, of my family, only Pa and only because he was "proud" of me, had bothered to write. Abandoned by my family, it was easy to go to someone who wanted me. I went to Dick carelessly, without emotion...

It was time to get up. I got out of bed and ripped open Johnathan's cable: "My love, be prepared." I stood there smiling. To accept my destiny and marry him? He would be home soon. I picked up my cold coffee and went to stand at the window. How different I feel this morning: full of a sense of burgeoning life. I am part of the earth, the sky and all living things, part of time and space. I have recaptured the experience of belonging that I knew years ago, briefly, when I first met Bill. I am incredibly happy. At peace.

23

F rankly," Dick said, "I'm disappointed."

"Yes?"

"There's nothing much to it, after all."

"No," I said.

"Why do you suppose everyone makes such a fuss?"

"I can't imagine. Hand me the sugar, Dick. You know I never could drink coffee with sugar and now that there's no sugar, I can't drink it unless it's over-sweet. Do you think it's the cold?"

We were having breakfast and discussing our first night of sex. It had been quite a struggle, but neither of us was a virgin now.

"Look, tell me, was it all right for you?"

"Uh," I said. "Perhaps if I could get my mind off the weather–how can I tell if it's me or the climate that's frigid? The blankets kept sliding; all I could think of was the draft. I do feel comfortable with you, but I rather expected that sort of thing would bind you–us–together. I mean, I don't feel bound."

"You're ridiculous! If the heat's on, you're too hot. When they turn it off, you're too cold." He looked sulky.

"Well," I said, unexpectedly amused, "there didn't seem to be much heat last night. Maybe we're not suited to each other. We needn't go on; we're not married."

The Russians had refused to allow us to marry. Our passports, they said, were not in order. But Dick had already moved my suitcases to his room in the Savoy and I had agreed, finally, that it would be foolish to move them back to the Grand Hotel for a formality.

"No," Dick said, "I want to marry you, Kitten."

Kitten? In my entire life no one had used pet words to me. This one struck me as inappropriate to the point of foolishness. I looked at Dick across the narrow table. The sulkiness had disappeared. His face was glowing with affection. "But if it's no good," I protested, "it's stupid. I can still get that room. I'd better leave this morning before someone else gets it."

"You mean you'd really live in that room? I won't let you!"

"How kind. But all this luxury, heat, breakfast, sex, hasn't seduced me from my noble purpose. If the Russians can live with the climate, so can I. Besides, now I have a chance to get a job." Just before I'd signed out of the Grand Hotel, the desk clerk had given me a letter to the director of Moscow's schools.

"No," Dick said. "I won't let you. It's fun eating breakfast with you. It feels natural. I feel ... I don't know ... lazy. I'll go to the passport office this morning and talk to them." He was laughing again. "I can't have my future wife living in sin!"

When Dick left, I lit a cigarette and sat down to think. I wasn't going to stay. From the moment we'd waked–until the waiter brought breakfast–he'd been sulky. Not cordial. He didn't want me. Not really. I'd pack and get out.

But before I left, there was one thing I must do. Dick had told me the night before that in this hotel one could buy a bath, and considering Russia it was not expensive. For one American dollar, one could have a steaming hot tub of water. I rang the hotel desk and ordered it, opened my suitcases and collected my dirty clothes. But I had no soap. I hesitated, then I went to Dick's wardrobe and took a bar of his precious soap.

I soaked for a magnificent length of time, washed my hair, then washed my soiled clothes in the dirty bath water. I was dressed and considering the problem of how to pack wet clothes in my suitcases–should I hang them out to freeze first–when Dick opened the door.

He came in full of good spirits and devotion. "Tomorrow," he said, kissing me, "for sure, Kitten. They'll let us get married tomorrow. Aren't you glad? I am."

"No." I pushed him away. "That is, I'm not at all sure. I think we'd better wait. Dick, I hope you don't mind, I took a bath and stole a piece of your soap. Now I have to get back to my hotel." I pointed to the bed. I'd thrown the sheet-sized bath towel on it and my wet clothes were strewn across it. "How in hell am I going to get these wet clothes across town? Have you anything to wrap them in?"

He stared at the bed. "Gawd!" he said. "What a mess! You can't hang them in here. Look, don't ever do that again! The hotel will have a fit if they catch you washing in your room, Kitten." His laughter sounded a trifle strained. He picked up the phone. "I'll send them to the laundry."

He hadn't heard a word I said about leaving!

Perhaps my bath had weakened me. All of a sudden I lost my urgent need to rush across Moscow and grab that frigid room. It was absolute heaven being clean and I felt comfortable for the first time since I'd left New

York. I sat down. "All right, I'll stay, but only till they send my clothes back."

"You'd better think about that," Dick said, solemnly. "You may be committing yourself to a full year."

"*J'y suis, j'y reste,*" I quoted, "until my clothes come back."

And we howled with laughter.

We sat around lazily, talking. Dick didn't go to the theatre. About one o'clock–with no word from the laundry–we had a leisurely lunch in the hotel dining room. Back in Dick's room, I said, somewhat reluctantly, "I really should run over to the Grand Hotel and make sure I can still get that room."

Dick said, "But I told your hotel that you were moving out permanently. I doubt they're holding it. Anyway, it's foolish to leave when we'll be married tomorrow."

I thought, I can't marry him. Still, if not love, there was very real happiness in just being with him. At four, we had tea and rusks in our room. At six, we changed for the evening. Thanks to Eugenia, my clothes were restrained, but stunning. We went to the Hotel Metropolitan for cocktails and then back to the Savoy for dinner. What a dinner. Soft lights, good food–they certainly turned it on for Dick–a bottle of burgundy, coffee, liqueurs ...

We came back happily to bed and another night of struggle. I had no idea it took so much energy to get deflowered! Sex! In novels I'd read about the burning passion, to say nothing of the fiery and impetuous lover. Dick consoled me for my lack of real interest, by referring to how-to books on sex. "A woman," he said, "is normally frigid. She has to be aroused. There are certain, obligatory preliminaries to accomplish this." Dick had read a lot of books.

By the time he had led me through the regulation preliminaries, I was in a nervous tizzy. My spontaneous affection for him had drained away. I felt like an icicle. As far as I was concerned, love-making by the book required a considerable expenditure of effort with no particular reward.

That night while Dick slept, I lay awake worrying. Added to my other ineradicable faults, was it possible I was going to be lousy in bed?

Half awake the next morning, I found myself wondering how fast I could leave. If I rang the laundry would someone say *seechas*, or would I spend the next few weeks waiting for my clothes? I ought to get up and go straight to the laundry and pick them up. I'd better make sure I could still get that room.

And there was something else. The waiter and the man-servant who cleaned our room obviously knew we weren't married and, obviously, they disapproved. They kept looking at me–reproachfully. They worried me. Russia–the government–was emancipated, but how bring the people to enjoy their freedom? Their brains and emotions were still riddled with an outmoded morality. It was time I pulled myself together and got out. I glanced at my watch. Nine o'clock. Good God! I jumped out of bed. Today was the day I had a ten a.m. appointment with the director of Moscow's schools–half-way across town.

The director of Moscow's schools, Borodina (the Russians add an "a" to the husband's name for the wife) was a middle-aged woman who had lived and worked in the garment industry in New York before her marriage to Michael Borodin, the editor of the English newspaper in Moscow.

Borodin had been Russia's ambassador to China when Moscow supported Sun Yat-sen as head of the Nationalist party or Kuomintang. When Sun died in 1925, Chiang Kai-shek became prominent in the party. In 1928 Chiang broke with the communists and Borodin was forced to flee. He escaped across the Gobi Desert, to Russia.

Borodina was interested to know that I was a nurse. Her back was killing her. Perhaps we might make an appointment for me to give her a massage?

I said I'd be delighted to do that.

As for the job, since I spoke no Russian, as far as she knew, there was nothing for me in the Russian schools. But while she was talking–perhaps she saw my desperate disappointment–she changed her mind. She looked at me, speculatively. "It might be an advantage, your not speaking Russian, you might talk English to the workers who have begun to speak it. You could tell them about conditions in America. I'll discuss it with the committee. Where are you living? Give me your address and I'll let you know. If they agree, you can start next week."

My address! Well, no need to explain. I said, "I'm at the Hotel Savoy." I gave her the number of Dick's room, thanked her and left.

I ran all the way back to the Savoy. I was freezing again. I'd chosen to wear gloves instead of woollen stockings on my hands and they were frozen stiff. But I was happy. I liked her and she liked me. I was sure I'd get the job. And whatever money they paid me would be enough for that room.

Dick was waiting to have lunch with me. He said, reproachfully, "You weren't here for breakfast."

"Sorry. I was late, I had to run." I shook the contents of my purse on to the bed. "I think I'll get the job. I had to give her this room number. She'll call me here. Have you any idea what we did with that slip of paper?

Did I give it to you when we were looking for that room? I ought to go there right away and take it."

"But I stayed home on purpose to be with you! You can't rush off and leave me now. Besides, I threw the address away. And I have news. We can't be married today. I have to go back again tomorrow. Anyway, you can't leave if that woman is going to call you here. D'you have to make that mess on the bed? Gawd! Come on, let's have lunch."

"True." If I wanted the job, I couldn't leave. And I was really hungry. It would do no harm to have lunch. I loved looking at Dick across the table: everything about him the antithesis of Edgeville.

Was my brain, I wondered, frozen? After lunch the only thing I felt like doing was returning with Dick to his room to enjoy that delicious heat. I was always cold and hungry. I was barely upstairs after lunch when I started looking forward to cocktails and dinner. And as long as my reputation was ruined anyway, I might as well stay another night.

Otiose, I couldn't bring myself to leave. But every morning–just in case the school turned me down–I looked for a job while, ignoring my protestations, Dick haunted the passport office. In the end, the school decided to hire me and the Russians relented. Dick got permission for us to marry.

He was determined to marry me. Perhaps he knew that if he didn't, he'd get home one day and find me gone.

I'd been living with him for a week–but, awkward, frigid, really I was not cut out for sex!–when one afternoon he returned in triumph. "It's fixed, Kitten. For sure. You have to go down with me to sign some papers. Then we've got to be at Zags, the marriage bureau, about eleven tomorrow morning."

I was still wavering. I still hadn't decided to marry him, à la russe or any other way. Was it possible, I asked myself, that I had been seduced by the heat and food? But the servants still looked at me with the same suspicious contempt with which my guests had regarded me on board ship. This time for *not* wearing pants. Perhaps my reputation could be retrieved with a marriage license.

Dick kept insisting that he loved me, although I didn't feel that he did. Disconcertingly, he talked baby talk: kitten, angel-puss, yabbit. He always woke up sulky and didn't recover his good humour until he'd had food. Out of bed, when he wasn't sulking, we had enormous fun together, talking, walking, dining. I had only to look into those candid eyes to know that he was essentially fine and honourable.

He had bought himself a very handsome mink-lined leather coat and

I had taken to wearing his old sheepskin coat. It was far too large for me and the tight belt around my middle bulged the top and bottom. Holmes, my beloved Holmes, I'm going native.

"Hurry up!"

"Wait!"

"What's wrong?"

"My hat."

Dick said, impatiently, "I like that hat."

The strange thing was that he did. I'd stretched Olga's hat to fit close to my head but it wasn't exactly bridal headgear. Eugenia would have a fit! But I had a plain gray cloche in my suitcase. "Go ahead. I'll be with you in a minute."

When Dick was impatient it was Edgeville again; I couldn't hear or see or think. And this morning everything had gone wrong.

"Well, hurry. Yuri is waiting." He went out and slammed the door.

I found my hat folded in my suitcase, slapped it open and put it on. Then I stood for a moment in front of the full-length looking-glass, pulling at it and staring at my face. "Holmes, Holmes!" I said out loud, "Stay with me, Holmes."

Dick was standing at the main entrance of the Savoy, waiting for me. He had hired one of the few government-owned taxis. It was the first car I'd been in since I'd arrived. The cars in the city belonged to the Kremlin or to foreign diplomats.

There was no traffic. We drove through shabby, empty streets to the marriage bureau.

Yuri, Dick's guide and interpreter, came with us; he was determined, it seemed, both to practise his English and to show his understanding heart. He sat opposite me, knee-to-knee, and stared into my eyes. He, too, he said, was in love–with a very famous woman, a dancer. They'd been living together for some weeks. And to use Yuri's words, they'd been "plumbing life to its depths."

Zags! The bare room reminded me of the waiting-room in the railway station in Edgeville. There were a few couples sitting on the wooden benches that ran around three sides of the room. Every public room I had seen in Russia was over-decorated with pictures of Lenin or Stalin, but these walls were nude. It occurred to me that this was the perfect place for the slogan chalked up on buildings all over Moscow: "Workers of the world unite!"

I touched Dick's arm. I wanted to tell him to look. Then I lost my breath. I began to shake and my eyes filled with tears. Dick looked at me, took my hand and pressed it, hard. But the expression on his face— patronizing, indulgent of my nervousness, angered me. My tears dried. I stopped shaking and breathed again. Would he understand if I told him it wasn't marriage that frightened me, that I wept because I had realized the end of hope, my failure in work and love?

Yuri said, "Now, you."

We followed him to a secluded alcove where a middle-aged woman sat at a desk. She gave us an official smile, then took a gray oblong of paper from a stack at her left hand, lifted her pen and glanced at Yuri.

Yuri opened a small exercise book. Apparently Dick had briefed him. He read, in Russian, from prepared notes.

The woman copied.

Now he turned to Dick and now to me to say, "Yes." In a few minutes, the ceremony was completed. Neither Dick nor I had understood a word.

The woman blotted the paper and handed it to me. Yuri took both my hands in his and announced, solemnly, "You are married."

I looked up to find Dick gazing down at me with a truly beautiful expression on his face. And I thought suddenly, he's my husband. At that moment, overwhelmed, I loved him. Except for Pa, no one cared enough ... I tried to hold his eyes with mine, to let him know. But he had turned to Yuri and was handing him a camera.

The marriage ceremony was a reproach to me for my doubts. I knew now Dick loved me. I was impatient to be rid of Yuri, to be alone with Dick, to tell him at once I would be a good and faithful wife. There was nothing, I thought, I would not do for Dick at that moment and for the rest of my life.

Outside the office under the swinging sign "Zags," Yuri took our wedding pictures. Our taxi was waiting and Yuri held the door for me. I stepped in. Dick was still standing on the sidewalk. "Yuri," he said, "will you tell the driver to drop me off at the theatre?" He got in and sat beside me. "It's Thursday," he explained, "and they always have a special lunch on Thursdays, little game birds, like snipe. You don't mind, do you, Philippa? I'll be back soon."

I opened my mouth but no words came out. So I shut it. After a second or two I could speak. "Of course not. Enjoy your lunch."

We drove through the empty city streets silently. At the theatre, Yuri got out with Dick. I was glad to be alone. The happy smile I'd been holding on my face had begun to slip.

Back in our room, I yanked off my hat and coat and threw them on the floor. "Holmes!" I said, "Holmes, I almost fell in love." I found a cigarette in my purse, lit it and sat down. I was alone. I had always been alone. The day stretched ahead of me, a thousand years long. "Holmes," I said again. And then, in shock, I felt him. Close. I was enveloped in his love.

Abruptly, I was back in Edgeville with Mrs. West–and remembering the curious incident in the classroom when I had asked help of my ancestors and received it. How incredulous I had been, of her belief that the body was simply the vehicle that carried life: that being or spirit left when the body was destroyed but was not itself destroyed.

Holmes' body was dust, but Holmes' spirit was not. At this moment, Holmes was with me in this room and in response to that beloved presence, I was no longer lonely. Holmes. In my mind's eye, I saw him solid, unsmiling, and just.

Just. Be just, I demanded of myself. Dick had not deceived me. He had gone through a ceremony to protect me. I couldn't expect him to love me. It was my vanity that had suffered. I must commend his honourable act. Only, believing in his love for me, I had been ready to offer him my life, had offered it to him with my eyes.

And then Holmes' voice was clear in my head: "If he bothered about your life, he might miss lunch."

I was startled. Trust Holmes' cynicism. But he was wrong. Dick had protected me. It was all right. I jumped up, snatched my hat and coat off the floor, and began to tidy up the room.

I was starving. I'd had nothing but coffee. I didn't want to go down to that big empty dining room and Dick might think me presumptuous if I ordered food. There were rusks, caviar, jam and part of a loaf of black bread in the wardrobe and butter on the window sill. I wanted toast, but there was no way to make toast–unless a hot iron would do it?

I sliced the bread, connected my iron to the overhead light, and waited until it was sizzling. Then I ironed the bread. I turned out hot, black squares of pressed bread, buttered them and had my wedding breakfast.

Around four that afternoon, Dick came back. He opened the door, walked in, took off his hat and coat and put them in the wardrobe. He was unhappy. Sulking. He barely looked at me. He crossed the room and sat down at his desk.

I waited for him to speak. When he didn't, I said, "Is something wrong?"

"Frankly," he said, "now that it's done, I'm sure we shouldn't have. I must say, you looked wonderful when you got that slip of paper in your hand. That was great for you, but I'm the one who has the responsibility. I took one look at your face. Really, Kitten, sometimes you are very pretty. Your face was transfigured. And then I realized, I'm married. What if the family ever finds out? The newspapers! I'll have to see the journalists right away, ask them to keep it quiet. Russian marriage or not, it's a marriage just the same. Well, I did it: we're in it now, and I'm not going to complain, but I want to make it very clear to you that this marriage is temporary. So don't start getting ideas. Tell me, what does a woman think when she hooks a man? Relieved as hell to have a meal ticket and someone to think for her and pay her way. Is that what you think, you women?"

For a second or two I was in such a rage I couldn't speak. I'd been a fool! The marriage was a farce!

What hadn't been farcical was my momentary transformation following that travesty of a ceremony. I loved him then with all my heart. Now he distrusted me, degraded me–degraded all women–by attributing to women the lowest and meanest motives for marrying. I said, "When Yuri told me we were married, I loved you. But not now." I went to the wardrobe and took out my coat and hat.

"Where are you going?"

"The Grand Hotel. I'll divorce you tomorrow and I'll pay back every cent you spent on me."

"Oh, no! Oh, my darling, you don't understand. I love you. It's just that when I'm away from you everything is wrong. But the minute I see you, I know everything is right. Please don't leave me. I've been a fool–frightened–marriage is a big step. I can't imagine ever not loving you." He came to me and took my coat from my hands.

He wasn't really malicious. I began to understand that in accepting responsibility for me, he'd been frightened. I sat down.

"Did you have lunch?" He glanced at his desk. "What are those things?" He began to devour what was left of my wedding breakfast. Then he threw caution to the winds. "How would you like," he said, "to be on the Social Register when we get back to New York?"

"And what," I asked, "is the Social Register? I never heard of it."

"Gawd, Bentham!" Dick addressed himself. "Be reasonable, Bentham. I suppose the New York Social Register doesn't mean much compared to world affairs. But is it possible there are people who never heard of it? Be calm, Bentham. She's ignorant. You'll have to teach her a few things if you take her back to New York."

I knew he meant to be funny. What in hell should I do? I waited to hear Holmes' decision in my head, but there were no words. I said, "Fair is fair. I'll take you to Edgeville and introduce you to the Ladies' Sewing Circle. Have you heard of it?" I wasn't happy.

He laughed. "Let's have a drink."

24

The morning after our wedding, Dick was in a hurry to go out. "I'm sorry to leave you, Darling," he said, "But I don't want news of this wedding in the New York newspapers."

I was astonished. "Why would the New York newspapers be interested?"

"Oh, family."

"Fame or money?"

Dick hesitated. "They're fairly well known."

"Yesterday wasn't doomsday," I reassured him, "but you're right. It's best to keep it quiet. When the time comes to end this, you won't make a fuss and neither will I, no matter whose decision."

"Oh, Kitten, it won't be mine. I adore you, but at the moment ... "

Dick was perpetually hinting at the importance of his family, yet if I asked about them he was evasive. I had begun to wonder if he was telling the exact truth but, after much talk the night before, I was committed to this marriage. I was more and more fond of him and listening to him talk, I admired him tremendously.

With the journalists' promise not to tell, Dick was at ease. The world shut out, we talked, laughed, ran around Moscow filling our eyes and ears. We visited the Stanislavski and the Bolshoi theatres, the galleries, and a once famous monastery just outside Moscow. The days were full of fun.

Dining each evening, gazing at my handsome husband across the table, I loved him. I also loved the soft lights, the food and wine, the efficient service, the damask table linen, and the crystal and silver. I tried to put away the thought of the Russian people. But like an incubus weighing on me, intermittently, I was aware that outside our door Russia was hungry. I shut that out and succumbed to luxury.

I was enchanted–what didn't enchant me was Dick's love-making. Was it his incongruous baby-talk that inhibited me, or an instinctive feeling that he didn't love me? Or was the lack in me?

We speculated endlessly about Russia. I had discarded my original euphoric opinions. Dick refused to decry the fear, the misery and the suspicion around us. "You should listen to the experts," he insisted. When I suggested secondhand opinions were not to be trusted, he was indignant. But my "inane" remarks made him laugh.

One evening after cocktails in the Hotel Metropole bar, we had barely sat down to dinner when I glanced up from the menu to see him sulkily frowning at me.

We had been married two months and lately he'd been restless. He sulked and complained about nothing. I suspected he wasn't accomplishing much at the theatre and was discouraged. How could he master the technique of the Russian stage when he didn't speak the language? He'd stopped taking lessons but now and then he sat, listlessly, with the book open in front of him and practised sounds. He had all sorts of off moods during the day but he was never anything but carefree and charming while dining out. Now I saw he was miserably unhappy. "Dick," I said, gently, "what's wrong?"

"Darling, why do people always stare at you?"

"Do they?" I asked. "I hadn't noticed." He was angry with me.

"You must have noticed. It's been going on for weeks. Every time we walk into a room every head turns in your direction. Frankly, I don't like it. A lady is unobtrusive."

I was suddenly and immeasurably hurt. "A lady." Meaning I wasn't one! I kept my voice light and controlled. "People look at everyone, Dick," I said. "I do; I love watching people." And what "lady" I thought—except the old girl the nurses called Flossie Nightingale—had ever voluntarily been up to her elbows in everything from gangrene to VD in a city hospital? Now I was angry. In a sudden change of mood, I wanted to kick him in the face and leave the table. I sat still.

"No one," he said and his voice was accusing and vindictive, "looks at anyone the way they do at you!"

Was he jealous? Of course not. Dick was a reasonable man. I said, slowly, "Dick, why did *you* look at me? Did you see anything wrong?"

"Oh that. No. That's different. I love you. These people have nothing to do with us. Anyway, I'm not accustomed to ... "

I finished the sentence for him, "being seen with anyone but ladies?"

"Well ... Yes. If you insist on putting it so crudely."

"I see." A lady. Ye Gods, it was years since I'd given up trying to be a lady! I'd been too busy. Perhaps I ought to start all over again. Abruptly I remembered that when I first left Edgeville, I'd started out to be both a Bolshevik and a lady. It seems I hadn't made either one. It struck me funny. I laughed.

266

"It's no laughing matter!" Dick said, furiously.

"N-no ... Quite ... S-s-sorry ... Really ... Dick, I ... "

"Control yourself! The whole place will be staring at you! Now I ask you, when you first saw me, did you sit and stare?"

I had a vivid sensation of being back in that dining room in Leningrad with Holmes and I was suddenly sober. "Look, Dick, I ... " No need to tell him that with Holmes, I wouldn't have looked twice if he'd had two heads. "I ... of course saw you. I recognized you when we met."

"But you didn't keep on staring, did you?"

"No."

"Then why does everyone keep staring at you?"

"Are you sure they do?"

"Yes. I am sure. I've been watching. It happens all the time. You come sailing in as if you own the place and every head turns. Why?"

"Oh, my God! Mother!"

"What!"

"She ... " I remembered her walking through the crowd in Grand Central Station in New York, turning heads. But that was ridiculous. "Nothing."

"What do you mean?"

Was he tired of me? Trying to pick a fight in order to end our marriage? Perhaps. If it was that, I had to know. "Perhaps you can tell me what else you don't like? Look, if there are things about me that upset you, you'd better tell me now. What is it?"

"I don't know. Maybe it's your clothes."

"My clothes!" I was wearing Madame Eugenia's straight, tan wool dress, it had long sleeves and covered me to my chin. Everything I owned had one characteristic: simplicity. I said, "Oh? Well, it's difficult to be objective about oneself so perhaps you can help me. Are my clothes loud? Garish? Too tight? Fussy?"

"It's ... You just don't look like anyone else in them. You ought to do something about it."

He was out of his mind! There was nothing wrong with my clothes. Aside from being absolutely plain, they were comfortable. "Shall I," I said facetiously, "replace them at once?" I might have added, "here–in Russia with no money?"

Money! Was Dick short of money and trying to get rid of me because of that? I was worried about money. I couldn't get used to having him support me. I had tried to find out if he could afford it but except for "I have enough for us both at the moment," he left me guessing. He was uncom-

267

fortable when I talked about money. And then I had been extravagant; I was always running upstairs to that magnificent, hot, one-dollar, pre-Revolution-Imperialistic bath tub and putting it on his bill.

"You're not being sensible! But something's wrong and it's either your clothes or ... "

"All right, Dick," I interrupted, sarcastically, "if you don't like my clothes, I'll take them off. Shall I do it here? Now?"

"You! You're indecent!"

"What!" I could feel my face burning. "Perhaps you mean despicable?" I said.

"Look, don't put words in my mouth. I didn't say that."

"Dick," I interrupted again, "I would hate to embarrass you so let's clarify the issue. Tell me what else is objectionable about me?"

"I'm a man. How do I know what's wrong with a woman's clothes? But there must be some reason why everyone looks at you. Something's wrong. Perhaps if you didn't wear lip rouge?"

Lip rouge, for the love of God. I laughed again. "Well, that's easy. I can remedy that." I reached in my bag for a handkerchief and carefully wiped off my lipstick. "Is that better?"

"Yes ... No ... I don't know! Look, forget it. Let's have dinner. Would you like a steak?"

Just like that! Forget it! "No thanks! I've lost my appetite."

"Don't be ridiculous. You had no lunch. Now tell me, what do you want?"

I was in a rage. "Nothing!"

"Kitten, must you be so childish? Sitting there, scowling. Just because I made a few suggestions. Please have a steak."

"No."

"Are you going to make a scene? Here!"

"Oh, order something, anything." Was it me? This assault on my clothes was, plainly, an excuse. For what? Whatever it was, I wasn't having any. I'd find a room. But my job? How long would I have that? I would have to think.

I had been teaching for almost a month. Carrying on conversations with a group of factory workers, middle-aged men and women who were fairly proficient in English. My class preceded their work day and in spite of getting up at four every morning to meet them at five, it had been fun. I talked about anything and everything.

Now, the Committee had questioned my subject matter; it didn't conform to the prescribed aim of the Party. I had to be "instructed." But what those didactic, cut and dried briefings amounted to, in sum, was that everything in imperialistic Canada and the USA was bad, and everything in communist Russia was good! And they gave me no leeway: I was not to deviate from the party line.

In all conscience I couldn't accept the party line. True, our Midwest was a dust-bowl, the trees had been ruthlessly cut down and the good top soil was blowing away. True, the banks were foreclosing because the farmers could no longer keep up the mortgage payments. True, we had labour problems, violence on the picket lines, strikebreakers brought in by the bosses to protect the scabs. True, the police were on the side of the property-owners.

But did any of these things compare to the omniscient, omnipresent terror of the OGPU? Or the daily hardships the Russian people were forced to endure?

Although I had never joined the party, I had been given a bankbook and some roubles and I could buy in the special stores reserved for communists. But, it amounted to nothing. I was practically penniless. Finally, I would have to wire for money. I felt sick. I pushed back my chair. "Dick, I'm not hungry. I ... "

"Where are you going?"

"I'll meet you at the Savoy."

"And leave me to eat all alone?"

"Sorry, but ... "

"Please don't go, Kitten. Oh here's ... "

The waiter wheeled a serving cart to our table and placed a plate in front of me. He smiled at me. "Steak for Madame?"

I couldn't jump up and storm out of the room. I would have to eat this damn dinner. I smiled up at our waiter. "Please."

That caressing voice. He was smiling at me. That quasi-amiability, when he was boiling inside! "What?"

"Your steak. You haven't touched your steak. Is there anything wrong with it? I can send it back. Or would you prefer something else?"

I had an irrational impulse to pick up my plate and throw it at him. I said, "It's just what I need."

"Then stop wool-gathering, Darling, and eat it. And try the wine. I think you'll find it excellent." He lifted his glass, "To your beautiful eyes."

He was his own charming self all through dinner and I managed not to disturb the peace. Going up to our room in the little self-service elevator, he tried to put his arms around me. I pushed him away.

"I hope you're not going to hold it against me when I say what I think."

"Not if you grant me the same privilege."

"Darling," jokingly, "you're ruining my digestion."

I was ruining *his* digestion?

Once in our room, I avoided his arms again. "Wait!"

"Oh, Kitten, don't be like that."

"I'd like to say what I think now."

"Oh, look, just because I'm frank with you, I hope you're not going to resent it. If you don't agree with me, you might at least ... "

"Am I allowed to speak?"

"Of course. Go ahead."

"I'll make it fast and plain. It's time to send that postcard. Will you send it or shall I?"

"Postcard? What are you talking about? What postcard? Where?"

"The one that gives us a divorce. To the bureau of statistics."

"What! You don't mean that!"

"I do mean it."

"But why? Just because I suggested you might do something about your clothes? You're absurd! You ... "

"Oh, for God's sake, Dick, shut up. It's not just that. You're dissatisfied with me. You're always worrying about your family. Well, now I'm worried about mine. How can I explain what I've been doing here? I've had to lie to them. If they ever found out ... And I'm sure I'll lose my job. If that happens, I'll never get another one in Russia. God knows what I owe you but whatever it is, I'll pay it back. I have to go home. Now, either I see Yuri in the morning and find out how to get that divorce, or you do."

"No! You can't! I won't let you!"

"You won't let me?"

"No!"

"Of all the bloody nerve! How do you intend stopping me?"

"Kitten, wait! Let's talk about this."

"There's nothing to talk about. I'll see Yuri in the morning."

"No! Wait! You can't! Look, I hadn't intended saying this, not so soon, but I've been thinking we'd make it permanent. I want to stay married."

"You what! No! The whole thing is impossible. We can't go on like this. You're not happy and it's because of me. Or is it money? You never tell me. How do I know if you can afford to keep me?"

"Money! What makes you think ... Haven't I taken care of you? Just because I don't tell you every detail of my personal affairs."

"Is it money?"

"Forget the money. If you must know, I have quite a bit of money." He was trembling.

I hesitated. "Then what's wrong?" I demanded. "If there's no good reason, why are you so keyed-up over trifles?"

"Look, I married you, didn't I? Can I help it if that's the way I'm made? Kitten, please! Don't you love me at all? I said I want to make this marriage permanent and I do. The least you can do is not jump into things with both feet just because I say something you don't like. Besides, what about your fare to Southampton? You haven't got it."

"If I wire Boston, I'll have it overnight." Money! Did he think that would stop me? "Or perhaps," I added, "you'd prefer to lend it to me?"

"Now who's keyed-up! Oh, Kitten, what's wrong? Why this sudden decision to ruin everything? Of course I'd give you your fare if I thought you needed it, but do you really want it to come to that? Why break up everything on a whim? Look, if it's only your family, you needn't worry. I'll write them myself and tell them we're married."

What a relief it would be to stop lying to Pa. Had I been making a big fuss over nothing? If he'd give me half a chance, I'd adore him. When he wasn't out of humour and complaining, I felt we were made for each other. I said, "Will you write to my father?"

"Yes."

"Dick, are you sure?"

He put both arms around me and held me close.

It was comforting and, yielding to my body's unexpected response, I threw my arms around him.

"I'll never let you go. I need my bed-yabbit."

Bed-yabbit! I jerked away from him. Baby-talk! He had a singular talent for reducing passion to a cuddle. It irritated and offended me. I felt frustrated.

"Kitten! Now what's wrong?"

I'd like to tell him, dammit!

"Don't you love me at all?"

"Dick, of course I ... "

"Well then, you silly little thing, I love you, too. Now, Darling, stop mooning. Start your letter. You'll feel better when it's gone. You write it and I'll add a few words at the bottom."

We wrote the letter and posted it that night.

For the next week or so I heard nothing from "the Committee" about my job. In the meantime, it had been suspended. But the communists–or at least Borodina–trusted me. She asked me "alone, without your charming husband" to come to a small evening meeting to meet some "very important people."

When I hesitated about accepting an invitation that did not include him, Dick, amused, insisted that I go, so I was at a loss to understand his behaviour when I got home.

"I hope you enjoyed yourself while I sat here alone all evening!"

Another mood. "Never mind. I'm here now."

"Who was there?"

"Just four of us besides the Borodins."

"Very important people, I suppose. Who were they?"

"Actually, they were. Madame Sun from China, Anna Louise Strong from the USA and a German woman–communist–I didn't recognize her name. They were fascinating! I sat and ... "

"Madame Sun Yat-sen?!"

"Yes. They called her Madame Soong."

"You mean the widow of Sun Yat-sen?"

"Yes, and what a beautiful woman. Madame Chiang Kai-shek is her sister, but apparently they are totally different in character. They were talking about the break in the Communist party in China and the Borodins' escape across the Gobi desert. Anna Louise Strong was with them all the way. The German woman spoke English but didn't want to so I missed quite a bit, but the others were quite open. You really should see Borodin* in his Chinese robes! What a stunning man! They have one enormous room and a communal kitchen, no better than ... "

"And you were the only other guest?"

"Yes. Why shouldn't I be? Dick, what's wrong? Borodina's been very good to me, we liked each other on sight."

"But the communists don't do that!" Dick protested, "Not at that level. You're not even a party member and she knows it. I've met dozens of commies since I've been in Russia but no one has asked me to that sort of party. Whom have you been seeing that you haven't told me about–some man?"

"Dick!" I was flabbergasted. "I haven't spent two minutes out of your sight. You're insulting. Perhaps it's as difficult for the upper class to get an invitation from a communist as it is for the lower class to get on the

---

* Borodin: Russia's ambassador to China. In the 1930s, Editor of *Pravda,* the official organ of the Communist party in Moscow.

272

New York Social Register. Hell and damnation! If that's what you think, you can sleep alone."

"Oh, Kitten, I'm sorry. It's just that I miss you when you're not here. I want to be with you all the time. Please don't be cross, it's not like you. I know you don't look at anyone but me. I'm sorry, really."

Hell, I was freezing! They must have turned off the heat in the next room. I was dying to get to bed and warm up. What a reason to make up. "All right, Dick. And by the way–if it makes you feel any better–I did wear the wrong clothes this evening. The minute I stepped inside the door, Borodina took one look at my long black dinner dress, tied a string around my middle, pulled the skirt up to my calves and handed me an old red sweater to cover my top. After that, she ushered me into the room. Maybe you're right, maybe, in Russia, I do stick out like a sore thumb."

"Oh, Kitten," Dick said, "how funny. I'm sorry. I do love you. I can't help it. Come on, let's go to bed."

We had been married a little more than three months when Dick woke up one morning feeling, he said, dreadful.

I put my hand on his head.

"A slight fever, perhaps."

"Slight! I feel terrible."

"Too much to eat and drink last night, and the cold probably, but the hand is not accurate. I'll take your temperature."

"How can you be so callous?"

"Would you like to have the flu?"

"I think I've got pneumonia."

"You can have whatever you like." I found my thermometer and handed it to him. "Keep your mouth shut, my love." I put a finger on his wrist. His pulse was full, round, strong and 68: normal.

I knew no more about Dick now than when I first met him. It was impossible to know if he was telling the truth or lying his head off. I was no nearer to understanding him than I had ever been. If I treated him kindly, as was my instinct, he spoke contemptuously to me but when, my patience exhausted, I disdained his criticisms, he was on his knees.

I took the thermometer from Dick's mouth. His temperature was normal. I said, "Stay in bed this morning. You may be catching cold. I'll go out and see if I can find some oranges or lemons at Torgsin."*

"Must you go? Well, I would like an orange all right. Don't be long, Yabbit."

---

* The shop where one paid with 'valuta': foreign money.

I ran all over Moscow, and finally found a solitary lemon. I came home, triumphant, to find Dick sitting up in bed, paring his finger nails.

"Kitten?"

"What?"

"We're leaving. I've been on the phone to Intourist. We're taking the train tomorrow."

"But we can't!"

"Why not? There's nothing to stop us."

"But what about our divorce? You know we can't go on. You're forever vacillating. You can leave if you want to but I'll stay here until I get that divorce." Why had we written that stupid letter to Pa?

"You mean you'd divorce me now? Just when I need you? Kitten, don't you care what happens to me?"

"Well, yes, but ... where are you going?"

"I won't go alone and I'm ill. You'll have to come with me. We'll go to Paris."

"Oh, Dick, Paris! How wonderful! Borodina will want to know."

"Why? You haven't heard from her since that party, or at least that's what you tell me. I don't know who you see when you go out."

"I don't see anyone. I want to say goodbye to the Borodins. They've been kind." I picked up the phone. "I'll call them now."

"Gawd, Darling, they couldn't care less. You *are* crazy!"

"Quite!"

We spent the day packing. The next morning–our luggage stowed away–we had just got in the troika when the desk clerk came out waving. He smiled at me, bowed, and handed me a sealed envelope. I ripped it open.

Three identical notices, official notices headed TO WHOM IT MAY CONCERN, which stated in Russian and in English that Philippa Jerrold Bentham was a friend of the Soviet Government and was to be shown every consideration while she was in the country, and was to be allowed back whenever she wished to return.

Tears in my eyes. Tears streaming down my face.

Dick took the slips of cheap paper from my hand. He read the notices. "Whom have you been sleeping with?"

"Oh no!" I stopped crying. You bloody coward, I told myself, leave him! Now! I felt stunned.

The driver whipped up his horses.

Jump! I told myself, jump! Paralysed, I sat still.

There were no wooden benches for me on the train leaving Moscow.

274

We travelled first class. The old-fashioned red plush seats were high, wide and well-upholstered, and the car was warm. But I was not comfortable. Was Dick really ill? He was sulky, abrupt; everything was wrong. The car smelled, the train rattled, the food was impossible, the coffee cold.

Mile after mile of level country, mile after mile of birch forest. We crossed the border into Poland. Warsaw!

Dick said, "Let's get a decent cup of coffee."

We stepped out of the train and walked into the station restaurant and I stopped in shock. The narrow counter was loaded with food: meat, sausages, cheese, bread, cakes, chocolates and oranges. I couldn't take my eyes from that great, heaped, glowing bowl of oranges. In the cold light of Russia, remembered, that pile of rich, ripe fruit was a fabulous unreality.

The Russian bear, I thought, lying on it's hunger-cramped belly. And I felt Russia, as I had not consciously known it while I was there, as mysterious, ponderous and threatening.

A group of Polish officers in smart uniforms and polished riding boots were sitting in a corner laughing and drinking coffee. Was it possible they thought the miles of birch forest adequate protection?

Mikhail Borodin had talked to me. "It may not come for a hundred years," he said, "but we shall conquer the world. Communism cannot exist in one country. Communism must be universal."

In Berlin we stopped at a comfortable commercial hotel. I put Dick to bed and asked the clerk to send for a doctor.

He came at once, looked Dick over, smiled and said, "Perhaps Mr. Bentham would like to spend a day in bed?"

Reassured, when the doctor left, Dick had a few words for me. "About this marriage of ours," he said, "just because I brought you out of Russia, I don't want you to start getting ideas. I don't want you to think that it's permanent."

Had the whole thing been put on? Why? "Good," I said. "I'll take the next train back to Moscow and send you that postcard." Just married and now divorced. How Flora would gloat. But I couldn't bear to hurt Pa ...

"No you won't. I won't let you. Not now, anyway. When we decide ... I mean, one of these days one of us, I guess you'd better do it, but not now. It's just that, well, look, Yabbit, let's stay married as long as it's convenient."

"Convenient! Are you thinking of my convenience, Dick? Or yours! Look, I'll give you your divorce the moment you want it but, as long as we're married, won't you try to think of me as your wife?"

"Oh, I do!"

"You don't! But do try. Please let it be a real marriage. It's not pleasant this way."

"Kitten, you know I love you."

"*Pro tempore*," I said, "for the time being," remembering Dr. West's Latin lessons.

He began to laugh. "You silly child." Had I taken the words right out of his head? "Look, I'm stuck here in bed, but you don't have to stay. Why don't you go out and look around? Go to a café–any café–and ask for a glass of Rhine wine."

I washed my face and hands, brushed my hair, put on Olga's hat and looked at myself in the glass. I took off the hat, found my scissors and started hacking it to bits.

"Kitten! Don't! You can't go out on the street without your hat. Besides, it's freezing out."

I threw the mangled remains of the hat in the wastebasket.

"Where's your wedding hat?"

"I gave it to the laundry woman. She wanted it. I may never wear a hat again. And don't tell me it's freezing. I've been dying of the heat ever since we left Russia."

"Oh, Gawd!" Dick began to laugh. "Oh, Kitten, you should see your face. You know, sometimes, I really can't help it, I love you. Here." He handed me a slip of paper, "Just read it to the waiter, and say *bitte!* Throw me my wallet."

I handed it to him.

"Here's a few marks to pay for the wine."

I hesitated. We had been married almost four months, and this was the first time he had given me money. I couldn't take it. "No. I'll change a few dollars at the desk."

"Nonsense, Kitten, I want to pay for your first glass of Rhine wine."

"It's not my first." I thought of Henry and Millie. "I've had it before in Boston."

"It's never the same when it's exported. You'll see." He looked at me anxiously, "What's wrong?"

Well, I was the one who insisted that this be a real marriage. "All right. Thank you, Dick."

He put the money in my hand, patted it. "Run along and enjoy yourself."

Run along? I didn't know whether to laugh or cry.

The precious, pale-gold wine had a delicate fragrance. I lifted the long-stemmed glass in my hand and sipped. Dick was right. It was different here. Delicious. It should be shared. I raised the glass. "Holmes! To you. Are you enjoying this, Holmes?" I said it in my head. You can't talk out loud if you're alone–unless you're crazy. I could see the expression on Holmes' face. Was that contempt for me?

"If you're going to turn into an extra conscience, Holmes," I said, "then go away and leave me in peace."

Peace. It was obvious what I must do. Get a job. Be independent of Dick. This marriage was degrading.

I returned, reluctantly, to the hotel to find Dick bored with bed.

"Let's go out for dinner, Kitten, to Hoschers. It's one of the best restaurants in Europe, and I haven't been there in ages."

We dined at Hoschers. Food: exquisite food. Wine: exquisite wine.

Waiting for Dick to feel well enough to travel, we stayed in Berlin for a week–eating and drinking–and to please him, I bought a hat. I also remembered to send Borodina what she couldn't find in Moscow, a nail file.

The afternoon before we left, Dick went out alone. He came back in high good humour. He had, he said, decided to stay married to me. To prove it, he'd bought me a wedding ring. I hadn't had one in Russia. I hadn't even thought about it. For all I knew, the Russians didn't wear them. At any rate, perhaps not the communists. I opened the little box. It was a circle of ... "Diamonds!" I said, astonished. I was incredibly happy.

Dick beamed with satisfaction. "No," he said, "paste, but isn't it pretty?"

25

At dawn, as we stepped off the train in Paris, the world was luminous gray: haunting, sombre. Two blue-bloused porters scrambled for our luggage, piled it perilously on a high-wheeled rack and hastened us along the platform past those steaming, squealing small black monsters, hurriedly puffing smoke.

The antiquated taxi jerked us across cobbles, and through one narrow winding street after another. Except for a few workmen and a boy carrying three-foot loaves of bread in a narrow two-sided basket, the streets lay deserted.

The night porter in the elegant hotel showed us to our room. Red and yellow and orange flowered wallpaper. Heavy brass bedsteads. A thick red carpet. Red draperies drawn tight over tightly-closed, lace-curtained french windows. A double armoire, solid and ornate with four full-length looking-glasses. A luxurious double bathroom. It was unbelievably warm.

While we waited for hot chocolate and croissants, I ran water in the huge white tub. As it filled, the water turned a crisp aquamarine blue. There were big cubes of scented soap and two thick white towels the size of bed sheets. I threw off my clothes and slipped into the shining bath. I was exhausted. Lying, half floating, in the heavenly water, I couldn't stop the tears. Dick ... However much he vacillated about our marriage, no one had ever been as protective of me. I was beginning to care for him deeply. I said, "Dick."

"What do you want? I'm unpacking."

He would be lifting each meticulously-folded article of clothing and placing it, exactly, in a drawer or on a hanger. I said, "Never mind."

"Well don't start something and then stop. Get out of that tub. I hear the elevator. Breakfast is here."

In bed, propped up on down pillows and covered by the silk-textured linen sheet, I drank the thick hot chocolate slowly.

"You're my kitten," Dick said, tenderly. He pulled up the down quilt and tucked it around me.

I was too warm but the gesture touched me. "Thank you, Darling."

278

He took a small address book out of his pocket. "I must phone my aunt."

"At this hour? You'll wake her."

"I'll leave a message, her maid must be up. Why don't you unpack? Well, perhaps I'd better wait." He went to the bathroom. "Darling! Your clothes are all over the floor!"

"Yes."

"Get up and hang them up!"

"Throw them somewhere, Dick."

"Where?"

"Out of the window." The hell with my clothes, they could stay there. He had slept on the train but I hadn't. He could sleep anywhere. Baring fits of total exhaustion, such as when I went home at the end of a year of training, I hadn't slept adequately for years and it had been awful in Moscow in that narrow, single bed, with Dick snoring.

He was standing at the foot of my bed holding my clothes. "What makes you so sluttish?"

I sat up, shocked. "Put them on a chair." I reached for the dictionary, opened it. Slut ...

He threw my clothes on the bed and snatched the book from my hand. "My English-Russian dictionary! Pick up your clothes! You haven't unpacked yet!"

I put out my cigarette and reached for another. He pushed the package away. "Oh no you don't. Come on, get up."

I held out a hand for the dictionary. I said, "Let me have it for a second, I was looking up a word."

"I'll do that for you. What word?"

"I won't remember the Russian unless I see it."

"That's nonsense. Tell me what it is and I'll look. What word?"

"I don't remember."

"Of course you do." One eyebrow lifted, a half-smile. With condescension, he said, "You don't want to tell me."

"Yes."

"I thought so. Tell me!"

"No."

Now he was playful. "Oh! So It's got a secret, has It?" He got off the bed, yanked the bedclothes off me, and threw them out of reach across a chair. "Now you'll have to get up!"

I got out of bed and picked up my soiled clothes. I was thoroughly awake now and tense. I went to the bathroom. I might just as well wash my hair. I could hear Dick talking on the phone, in French.

I had never seen him in evening clothes and I was jealous of his high spirits and his good looks. I didn't want to spend my first night in Paris in a hotel room ... but it was his aunt.

He kissed me, tenderly. "You're my wonderful Kitten. I shouldn't leave It alone tonight but I confess I'm looking forward to a civilized dinner."

It! Damn the baby-talk!

"If you don't want to eat in the dining room, I'll have them send up your dinner."

I had nothing to read. I could write home another charming letter about my wonderful husband, soon to be my ex-wonderful. I could write to Millie or to Saunders but I didn't want them to know I was a fool. I knew the Russian for fool. *Durak!* Me: *durak.* If only I could sleep.

It seemed an eternity until I heard the lift and Dick's key in the lock. I had got out of the habit of being alone. I said, "Dick? I missed you!"

He turned on all the lights and put his hat and gloves carefully on the armoire. He was sulky.

"You still awake?"

I was still awake. "What time is it?"

"Late. She had guests, a dinner party." He came over and sat down on my bed. "I think we ought to talk about our divorce."

"Now?"

"Well, I've been thinking. Now that we've left Russia, it's not as simple as it might have been."

"But you knew that!"

"I know. But seeing my family made me think ... I'm sure they'd be upset, I mean if they found out. You'll have to go back to Russia."

"Dammit Dick! What about my family? Why did you insist on telling my father we were married? Do you realize how awkward this is for me?"

"I know, I know. It's my fault, don't rub it in!"

I was shaking. "How many times do I have to tell you, you're free."

"Oh, Kitten, I love you."

I laughed. And then I couldn't stop laughing.

"What's so amusing? Control yourself!"

"N'nothing. I'm sorry." If I didn't stop laughing I'd burst into tears. "J-just a m-minute ... Dick, tell me, why now? I offered to go back while we were still in Berlin."

"Oh, it's for you, really. I don't want them to think you're after my money."

His money! Did he have any or was this more poppycock? I looked at his sullen face. My hysterics evaporated. "Do you?"

"Kitten, no. But it's not what I think, it's what others will think."

I closed my eyes. Except for money for the glass of wine, Dick had never given me any money and I'd spent most of mine. I had twenty dollars left. "I can't go back to Russia. I told my father we were leaving. I don't care what people think."

"Well, you haven't said what you are going to do."

"I'm tired," I said. "Aren't you?"

"No. Let's have this out."

"But there's nothing to have out."

"I think we ought to start getting our divorce."

I was so choked with fury that I didn't trust myself to answer.

He put both hands on my bare arms and shook me. "Philippa!"

I bit back my rage, tried to keep my voice quiet. "There's nothing for you to worry about. You can start divorcing me tomorrow, or I'll divorce you. I don't care which."

He was relieved, but there was more. "If we don't want everyone to hear about this, one of us will have to go back to Russia."

"Yes. Well, who's going back?"

"Well I can't go. You know I can't. How could I explain that to the family?"

"I see. All right. I'll go back. When do you want me to leave? Right now? Or can we wait till tomorrow?" How would I tell Pa?

"Oh Kitten!" He leaned over and pulled me into his arms. He was happy. "Kitten, you know I love you."

Love. I was developing a certain distaste for the word. All the tenderness with which I'd awaited his return! But I was barren of feeling now, even my anger dissolved. I was unbelievably tired.

"Let me come to your bed," he said huskily. He got up and turned off the lights and began to undress in the dark.

"No, I don't want you in my bed."

Perhaps there is nothing more disagreeable than lying sleepless at night listening to someone snore. I was still awake at five in the morning when Dick got up and stumbled to the bathroom. He stumbled back a few minutes later and got into my bed. I disengaged his arms from about me, got up and pulled back the heavy red draperies. I watched the morning light come through the lace curtains.

At breakfast, Dick decided there was no hurry about my going back.

"I can't think," he said, "why I was so upset last night. Why do we have to get divorced right away? I like having you around. You know, I ought to go home, but if I stay here a couple of weeks, we can run around and see things, have some fun. I'll hire a car. How would you like that? What do you say, Yabbit?"

He could go to hell! But I was reprieved. I'd been trying to invent some noble lie the family would swallow about my going back, immediately, to Russia. Nothing I could think of sounded plausible. But he was using me! "I think not."

"Don't you want to stay with me?" Aggrieved.

He was incredible! I had to laugh. "Oh, of course. But do you mean it?"

"Of course I mean it!"

At home, Martha had a response to a tall tale and I thought it appropriate now. I said, "In a pig's eye!"

"Oh, Yabbit! Vulgar, but funny!"

Dick hired a car and we drove through France. His two weeks stretched into five. "You know, I've got no real reason for going home, and I've been thinking, Kitten, why is it that I can talk to you as I've never been able to talk to anyone else in my life? I've really begun to discover myself: my serious self. I confess it didn't please me when you asked if I intended frittering away my life, but to give you your due, you're right. One can't.

"I'm still interested in the theatre, but in another way. I want to write. I think I'll write a play. I've thought of a plot. And I've been thinking an awful lot about you, too. You're at loose ends, so why not ... I mean you have so many ideas, there's so much you say that's amusing. All those stories about Edgeville. I mean, I think you ought to write. I've been thinking of buying you a second hand typewriter. If I get it for you, you could do short stories. Would you like to try?"

"I've wanted to write but I can't, besides, what about our divorce?"

"Well, what's the hurry? I can't stay in France for the rest of my life, that's true. I have to go home, but I'll be back, and if you'd be modest about it–don't expect to live like we're living now, I'm not Morgan's bank–I might be able to keep you here till I get back. You could learn the language, write, and next year when I come back, we'd still be together."

"Yabbit, listen to this. You know I told you about Harvey Wilson? He's my best friend. Wait till he hears this!" We had come up to our room after dinner and were writing letters.

I held out my hand. "Let me read it."

Le Man, France

Dear Harvey,

You may be amused to learn I'm taking a tour of the Chateau country with "my wife" (pro tem). I hate to announce this so abruptly, as I wouldn't want you to be so shocked you'd fall flat on your ...

I dropped the letter, walked to the door, opened it and ran: I ran down the corridor, down the stairs, across the lobby and blindly into the night. I ran bent, cramped, hurting. He was branding me a whore. I stopped, shivering.

I was standing near a pale column of cement. I had seen it in daylight. There was a man on top of that column, naked, reaching to the sky. Wright. The man who wanted to fly and who had learned to fly. I should take courage from it, but it dwarfed me. In a rage with myself, I pulled the circle of paste from my left hand–the false wedding ring–and hurled it into the dark. Dick was standing outside the hotel waiting for me when I got back. "What's wrong? Why did you run away? You frightened me!" His voice softened. "You'se a bad cat. Did I do something to upset It?"

"I wish you wouldn't send that letter."

"Is *that* what all the fuss was about. The trouble with you, Yabbit, you've not got even one snitch of a sense of humour."

The day after we arrived back in Paris, I went to find a job. Foreigners in France were obliged to have a worker's permit. For two weeks, I ran from office to office trying to get that permit but French bureaucracy baffled me. I stumbled over my high-school French, mispronounced or misused words and gave the wrong answers. The permit was refused. Other foreigners worked in France. How they obtained permission remained a mystery.

I had my steamship ticket to New York. I'd find a job there fast enough. All I had to do was get to the boat. That, however, meant admitting everything. Aside from his hurt and disappointment, Pa would never forgive me.

Dick had begun to look up his friends. "The Stevens want me for dinner tonight."

"Just you?"

"Well they don't know about you, Kitten, and I don't want to spring you on them."

"You're contemptible!"

"Darling you don't mean that. Look, Ed Lawrence is in town. He was in Russia last year, so you'll have lots to talk about. I'll ask him to take you to dinner."

"But I don't know him," I protested. I was in a rage. "I don't want to! No!"

"Don't be silly, he's a friend. And I'm not going to leave my Woof all alone."

"Please don't do it."

But Dick was looking up the number in his little book.

Ed Lawrence was a good-looking young man, well dressed, quiet, reserved. I faced him across the tiny table at Le Boeuf à la Toit. Angry with Dick, I was ready to cut Ed's throat. I stared at the menu. "I suppose it's beef stew."

"That sounds good. I'll have it, too."

The indifferent overcooked food was served on small hard plates, once white, now brown from much heating and use, hospital plates.

After dinner, we wandered around the streets. I was bored and ill at ease. At midnight, we met Dick at a café and Ed faded away.

"Kitten," Dick said, "you know the Stevens are really horrified about this whole thing."

"But they don't know me!"

"I know. That's why I want them to meet you, so they'll change their minds."

Had Dick influenced them against me? I said, acidly, "I'm riddled with guilt at having roped you into matrimony against your will."

"That's not funny."

"I guess not. But Dick, why be horrified if people marry? You must have said something ..."

"What gives you such mean ideas about people?" Dick demanded. "They're thinking of me. They think you're after my money. They think you're some little ... Oh, Piglet, don't be like that!"

Money again? "There's not much point in my meeting them if they've made up their minds. I'd rather not."

"But you have to meet them. They're friends of mine. I've asked them for lunch tomorrow."

Perhaps if I met them, they'd realize I wasn't after his money. They were fond of Dick and concerned for him so it wasn't fair to judge them unseen. But my clothes. "Dick, you always complain about my clothes. What shall I wear?"

"Are you trying to tell me you want me to buy you something? Well, I can't. I haven't the money. Who cares what you wear?"

"I thought you didn't like my clothes."

"Of course I like them! What gave you that idea?"

Dick drew lines on the white tablecloth with his fork, twisted his glass, fidgeted. He was nervous. The Stevens were late. I had been nervous, too, at first; but Dick's concern for their opinion annoyed me. My nervousness vanished. I was angry!

"Oh, there they are." Dick stood up hastily and went to the restaurant door to greet them. They were his guests so I remained in my seat.

They were middle aged. Mrs. Stevens was tall and beautifully dressed. She had a heavy, sallow, rather unattractive face. Mr. Stevens was a handsome, blond, clean shaven, somewhat effeminate looking man. He was younger than his wife, much younger. He grasped Dick's hand, held on to it, looked towards me and then looked away. Dick led them to our table. "I want you to meet Philippa."

The two made polite noises.

I didn't offer my hand. "How do you do," I said. But I was tense again. I gestured towards the empty chairs. "Won't you sit down?"

Mrs. Stevens turned her back on me and facing her husband said something in a low voice. Her husband turned to Dick. The three of them, a closed circle, stood murmuring together. I felt my face go white. After a minute or two, Mrs. Stevens raised her voice. "Shall we eat?" She had assumed the prerogative of hostess. They sat down.

"What will you drink?"

"Sherry for us," said Mrs. Stevens.

"Kitten?" His attention concentrated on his guests, he didn't look at me.

"What do you suggest, Dick, sulphuric acid?"

"Fine," Dick said, "four sherries." He looked at me. "You did say Sherry? A dry sack?"

"Thank you." As long as we were still married, they were my guests, too. I signalled to an approaching waiter and he handed me a menu. I turned to Mrs. Stevens and courteously, inclining my head, passed it to her.

She stared at me for a moment, took it and looked away. Whatever my crime, she was not about to forgive it.

The gossip started with the drinks. It was amazing to see how the general was dominated by his tiny wife; Cornelia had got herself engaged to Ronnie, but he was still seeing the Comtesse; Did Dick know that Jeremy was in Paris? There was a little Russian woman who made the most divine lingerie. The conversation flowed–over my head.

Towards the end of the meal, Mrs. Stevens noticed that I was at the table.

"Dick tells me that you have been in Russia. Are you a communist?"

They'd had their fun, now I'd have mine. "Of course, dedicated, down with capitalism."

Mrs. Stevens turned her head away and laughed, lightly. "Imagine!"

Dick glared at me. "She's not!"

I opened my eyes in wide surprise. "Why Dick, you know I am and you are too."

But Mrs. Stevens wasn't listening. Mrs. Stevens was shaking her wrist watch. "What time is it, Dick? I must get this thing fixed."

Mr. Stevens bent towards me and put his hand over mine. His voice held a special kindness, a special softness. "It must be good to get to Paris after Moscow. Dick tells us it's been very cold there."

I pulled my hand away. His voice–the gesture–implied we were partners in condoning illicit sex. As Mother would say–and how aptly–it made my blood curl. I couldn't control my angry voice. "Yes," I said. "Cold but clean."

Mr. Stevens turned to Dick. "Bring Philippa with you this evening." He turned back to me. "We're having a few friends for cocktails. You must come."

So that's what they'd been arranging in that private conversation before lunch. "Thank you," I said. "I'm afraid not."

"Oh, but you must!" Mr. Stevens looked at his wife. "We'd love to have her, wouldn't we, dear?"

Mrs. Stevens glanced at me, then looked hard at Dick. She raised her eyebrows. "My dear Dick, we'd love to have you, of course! Arthur," her voice warned him, "we must fly!" She stood up and Dick stood up with her. She smiled at him, ignoring me. "A lovely lunch. Thank you. We do enjoy seeing you."

Mr. Stevens, still sitting at the table, put his hand over mine again. "This evening, then."

I pulled my hand away. "No. Sorry."

"Come along, dear."

Dick walked to the door with them. He came back all smiles. "They liked you, Kitten. I saw the way Steve kept looking at you."

"Dick, you must have noticed the atmosphere."

"What atmosphere? The lunch was perfect. I had a wonderful time. And Steve likes you. I saw him. He wanted to hold your hand. Look, crazy coot, don't begin imagining slights. Do you think he'd have asked you for tonight if he didn't want you? Please give me credit for knowing a little more than you do about my friends. Steve likes you, so you're going."

He likes me, I thought, helplessly. And what in the name of God would I wear? I hadn't had a dress cleaned in months. I felt soiled.

26

The high-ceilinged drawing-room was lit by a crystal chandelier. Crystal wall lights, shaded in ivory silk, glowed on panels of brocaded satin. Here was the elegance I had once dreamed of but, because Dick had coerced me into coming, I was ill at ease.

Mrs. Stevens greeted me pleasantly and introduced me to several people–as Miss Jerrold–but so quickly that I didn't catch a name. However, I smiled and was smiled at. Dick was greeting friends and I found myself on the outer edge of that chattering circle still smiling, somewhat painfully, at no one.

"Would you like a drink?" A young man, his hand on the back of an empty chair, nodded for me to sit down.

"Thank you. A martini."

He brought my drink and sat down on the ottoman at my feet. He smiled up at me and began to talk. "I'm Clayton Hammond."

I watched his upturned face, the delicate features and the translucent gray eyes. Black brows and black hair made his face look very white. He'd just had an extraordinary experience, he'd seen Argentina. "Have you seen her?"

Argentina, South America? "Her?"

"You really must."

Must? Rush off to South America? Her? Not only a new environment but I didn't speak the language. "And you," I said, must go at once and see Edgeville."

"Edgeville?"

"A village in Nova Scotia."

"What are you talking about?"

"What are *you* talking about!"

We began to laugh.

"Argentina," he said. "She's a dancer."

"Sorry, I never heard of her. I just came out of Russia and before that ... "

"Russia? How interesting. Look, it's impossible to talk here and I'm tied up tonight but why don't we go out one evening? I'd love to talk to you. Where are you staying?"

I hesitated. Dick wouldn't like this. I said, "The Meurice."

"Oh! I believe Bentham's staying there. He's just come out of Russia, too. Of course, you came in with him. Did you meet him there?"

"We came out together." Apparently it didn't occur to him that my acquaintance with Dick was more than casual.

"Bentham," he mused. "He's an odd chap. Too much money and too much ... " He stopped.

I was looking at him with too much interest. "And too much what?" I asked. But I'd warned him.

"And too much money," he repeated, smiling.

I liked this man.

Dick put his hand on my shoulder. "I see you two have met."

"Oh, hello, Bentham." Clayton stood up. They shook hands. "Have a good trip?"

"So' so'." Dick looked at me and then away. "How long are you staying in town, Clay?"

"Indefinitely."

"Have lunch with us tomorrow. I'm taking Philippa to lunch."

They arranged to meet at Fouquet's. Dick went off and sat down beside a very pretty young woman.

I nodded towards them. "Who is she?"

"White Russian. Princess. A genuine one. Her mother and Bentham's aunt were friends before the Revolution. She was telling us all about it just before you arrived." Clay took my empty glass and brought me another drink.

Whether or not Dick had money, he was obviously of the elite. I said, "Have you met Dick's family?"

"No, have you?"

I looked up to see Dick watching me. "No, I met Dick by chance in Russia." I glanced at my watch and stood up. "I think we're leaving, we have a dinner date."

Clay stood up with me. He took my hand. "You're Philippa Jerrold. I know. I asked. I'll call you."

I hesitated. The hotel knew we were married and that our passports had not been changed, but this was not the time for explanations. "If you like."

He held on to my hand. "I do want to see you again."

Impulsively, I leaned forward and kissed him on the cheek. Dick put his hand on my arm. "Let's not keep Alex waiting."

The telephone woke us. Dick said, "I can't imagine who'd call me at this hour! There's something wrong–unless it's my aunt."

"What time is it?"

"Ten o'clock!" He got out of bed and picked up the receiver. His playfully teasing voice didn't conceal his annoyance. "Dear, it's for you. I didn't know you knew anyone in Paris."

The voice on the phone sounded a little strained. "Are you Philippa Jerrold?"

"Yes."

"And are you Mrs. Bentham, too?"

"Yes."

"You forgot to mention it last night."

"It's a delicate subject."

"I wanted to take you to see Argentina but, well ... "

"Yes."

"I'll see you at lunch."

"Yes."

He hung up.

"What was that all about?"

"Your friend, Clay, wanted to take me to the Opera but he knows now that we are married."

"Oh, Clay's all right. He's a lawyer. He might have some ideas about our divorce. We'll tell him about it at lunch. In any case he'll keep his mouth shut. By the way, it was discreet of you not to wear your wedding ring last night, but you don't have to do that. Put it on."

"No."

"No. Why not?"

"I threw it away."

"What! You didn't! When?"

"Ages ago."

"Kitten! Why would you do a thing like that?"

"I was sick of this so-called marriage!"

"Well, of all the ... Just don't expect me to buy you another one!"

Our nights grew longer and our days just about disappeared. We went endlessly to the French *boîtes* and the Russian night-clubs. There were no reds here. White Russians–aristocrats, former land-owners, former officers– were now poor Russians. Were they sad? It didn't seem so. What vitality! We sat till morning listening to the gypsy singers and joining in. We drank champagne, brandy and liqueurs. We ate every delicacy known to the French and Russian cuisines. And everywhere we went, we went with Clay Hammond. He had attached himself to us from the first day.

I asked Dick about him.

Dick said, "I really don't know much, except he's a lawyer. Harvard. Steve says he's charming but has no money."

"And obviously," I added, caustically, "Steve thinks he's immoral since he's never protested my unsuitability for you!"

"Steve doesn't think that! Steve thinks you're one of the most beautiful women in Paris. In fact, Hilda insists I married you for your looks but, Kitten, I didn't, it's you."

"Really? Well, you might remind Hilda Stevens that we're married. She's still calling me Jerrold."

We had been living in Paris for more than six months when I woke one late afternoon to discover in myself the first symptom of a drunkard: I didn't want breakfast until I had a drink. I had no trouble getting one, Dick wanted one, too. Our breakfasts were preceded by good strong martinis.

Now and then, for Dick had friends who slept at night, we pulled ourselves out of bed in time to go to lunch. We were popular. I was running around without a wedding ring but everyone knew about our Russian marriage. Oddly, it was the French, the English and the Russians who were cordial to me and who called me Mrs. Bentham. Thanks to Hilda Stevens, who seemed to have considerable clout in the colony, the Americans called me Miss Jerrold.

It was Mrs. Stevens who sent us to the Volkhovs: "My dear Dick, you must buy a few gifts to take home from this little Russian woman. She has the most divine lingerie, handmade and inexpensive."

Baroness Volkhov had enlisted a group of Russian refugees, women who could find no other employment, to make the delicate silk and lace underwear which she sold to tourists and to the wealthy French.

I was astonished when Dick put that address in his little book. Sometimes when I saw the francs he was handing over for an evening's entertainment, I wondered if I dared tell him I'd stay home a few nights if he'd give me money for stockings. I had very few dollars left.

I smiled at Dick over the extravagant silk and lace underwear.

"What do I need, Kitten?"

I said, tentatively, "A slip and if it's not too much, a nightgown?"

"No. That's not nearly enough." Dick took his little book from his pocket and started turning the pages. He began to make a list. "Let's see, my sister and my two cousins and ... " He stopped, his pencil poised in mid-air. "Do you need anything, Kitten?"

"I'd like ... "

"Not what you'd like!" Dick interrupted me, "I said do you need anything! Now don't be silly and don't be shy, Darling, tell me frankly, do you need anything?"

I could feel my face burning. "Not a thing." Where was Dick's vaunted money? He hadn't spent it on me.

"Are you sure?"

"Quite sure, thank you."

Dick ordered his gifts and Baroness Volkhov asked us for tea.

"We'd love to stay, wouldn't we, Darling?" Dick said, hugging me.

After tea, Baron Volkhov arrived with a bottle of Pernod. The four of us sat on talking, laughing and drinking Pernod. It was late when we left. I was drunk. Running across the open court I held on to Dick's arm. "Did you hear?" I asked him, "Tasha is going to give me Russian lessons."

We were having breakfast, sitting in a café–at a little past three in the afternoon.

The traffic, slightly fuzzy, oozed by, jerkity-stop-start-roll. I shook my head. Don't look, I said to myself. You idiot! Dizzy ...

Dick was reading a letter and laughing.

"What's the joke? Don't tell me. I've got the world's worst hangover. What did the Volkhov's give us to drink last night? It's lethal. And why did we have to go out after that?"

"Well, Kitten, this settles it. I have to go home. I've been trying to think of some way to tell you without ... "

"Breaking my heart?" That struck me funny and I began to laugh. "D-don't w-worry! I've been w-warned. When are you l-leaving?" I couldn't control my tongue.

"Actually, I've picked up my tickets. I leave on Wednesday, next week. But you have nothing to worry about. I'll make sure you don't starve."

"What!" I laughed so hard tears came to my eyes.

"Oh, Kitten! I had no idea you'd take it like this! You're hysterical! You're crying!"

"W-what?" It wasn't only that my head was foggy; lately, I had to concentrate on what Dick was saying. His words didn't penetrate my thick skull.

"Oh, Sweetheart, you musn't!"

292

"Did you say you bought your tickets and arranged to go home, without mentioning it to m-me?"

"Philippa!" Impatiently, "I just told you."

I turned my head away. I couldn't catch my breath. The couple at the next table were staring at us. The hell with them. I picked up my glass. I said, facetiously, "I must be upset, Dear." I couldn't stop laughing. "Uh ... uh ... at losing you. Forgive me. Tell me again. What day?"

"Kitten! For the love of heaven! What's so funny? Control yourself! Here." He handed me his handkerchief.

In a minute, I'd start sobbing. I couldn't. I was suddenly sober. My head hurt. I wiped tears from my face.

Mollified–flattered, Dick said, "Oh, Yabbit, I can't think what you'll do without me. You're so impractical. You need me to take care of you."

Impractical? I was choking. Me? The best nurse in my class?

"I hate to leave you but you'll be a grass widow next week."

"Next week?"

He raised an eyebrow. "Do you want me to show you the tickets? Gawd! What I'm trying to get through your head, you silly child, is that you'll have to wait here alone until I get back. I must look over my accounts. Too bad you didn't get working papers. I'm afraid I've spent quite a bit of money, so I won't be able to leave you too much."

I said, "Dick, I must go to Russia. Now! I have to ... "

He took both my hands in his. "Kitten, we've settled that. You're going to stay right here. You're going to learn French and Russian and you're going to write. I'm sure you can write. All you need is the technique. And I'm going to take care of you. Will It please be a good cat? Angel, please! Don't start again!"

Dick had found a boarding house, a *pension*, for me to live in while he was in New York. After looking over his accounts, he had discovered that he could barely afford it. It was a working-class neighbourhood, a long way from our fashionable haunts. But I'd be writing or studying, with no time for running around, so it would do.

"You'll need a few francs for extras," Dick said, "I'll pay your board and lessons. Aside from that, can you manage on ten dollars a month?"

Ten dollars a month? Living with him has spoiled me! Stockings, tips, cigarettes, the metro, bus fares, museum fees, books ... I shut my mind to the things I thought I needed; it wasn't my money.

Perhaps he saw the consternation in my face. He was playful, "It mustn't learn to be extravagant."

It was one o'clock. We'd got up early that day.

"Shall we eat at the *pension?*" I suggested. "Try it?"

"Oh, Gawd!" Dick shoved me out the door. "Let's go somewhere decent for lunch."

Crossing the Place Vendôme, wc ran into Clay Hammond.

"Have lunch with us," Dick said, gaily, "and we'll tell you our news." We had a couple of cocktails, a good meal, vintage wine, coffee, brandy. I was still awake when Dick paid the bill. Heavens! My income for the next three months! Perhaps I should take a final look at the Ritz.

We were standing on the Station platform.

"Take care of yourself."

"Yes."

"Write to me."

"Yes."

"You'll work hard, won't you?"

"Yes."

"Kitten, I hate leaving you. I'll write from the boat."

"Dick ... "

"I know, Darling, it's as bad with me."

The train was moving, he jumped on. "Goodbye, Kitten.

"Au revoir."

In the empty hotel room, I remembered what I had come back for. I must pack my two suitcases, leave the hotel and get settled in the *pension.* Dizzy, I lay down on the bed. There was plenty of time, time didn't matter.

The telephone rang.

He must have been near because it seemed I had just put down the receiver when he phoned again from the hotel lobby.

We walked around the corner to a small café. Clay said, "What will you do?"

I picked up my glass and drank. I couldn't admit to him that I felt lost. I said, "I've been drinking far too much. It will be good for me to be alone. Dick bought me a typewriter. He made me promise to try to write. What about you?"

"I may go to London for a time."

I felt my face go white. Clay, leaving? I bit back the words I was about to blurt out: "You can't! I love you." I sat there, tongue-tied, staring at him.

"Philippa! Are you all right? You look as though you'd seen a ghost!"

I finished my drink in one gulp and jumped up. "I must go! I have to pack, get out of the hotel. Goodbye."

"Wait! Where can I reach you? Philippa!"

I rushed out of the café.

The ancient wall paper breathed obscenities. Above and alongside the bed, it was darkened and streaked with grease, cheap hair oil, soiled hands. Age had not mitigated its crudities of colour. The rotting baseboards had absorbed the dust of a hundred scuffing slattern's mops. The rickety armoire smelled of unwashed clothes–other people's clothes.

"The trouble with me is," I said, aloud, "Dick spoiled me." The long window looked as though it had never been opened. I pushed at it, beat at it with my hands. Someone knocked at the door. Without turning I said, "*Entrez.*"

The door opened. I kept shoving at the window, trying to force it open. The silence behind me made me turn my head. "Clay! No!" But it was too late. He'd seen the room. I walked, spinelessly, to the bed and sat down.

He didn't sit down. Hat in hand, he stalked back and forth across the narrow floor, flipping his gloves against his hand. He stopped at the small wooden table and picked up the books, the cheap editions I had collected to read in French: Daudet, Flaubert, Balzac, Zola, Hugo.

"Who's teaching you?"

"How did you get my address?"

"Your hotel. Are you taking lessons?"

The hotel had insisted that I leave a forwarding address: it's the law in France. The police must know the movements of aliens. "Not yet. Perhaps later." I couldn't tell Clay I was worried about *bus fare*.

Clay slammed my French grammar on the table, took my hand and pulled me off the bed. "Let's get out of here. We both need a drink."

We had a couple of drinks but we didn't seem to have much to say to each other.

I came back to my room. I was in love with him.

I threw the contents of my purse on the bed and picked up the engraved card. The Duchesse de L ... was receiving on Thursday at 10 p.m.

Damn! I couldn't go. After almost a year of living out of two suitcases, my clothes ... But I still felt good in them. How, though, accept hospitality I could not repay? I wanted to go! I loved the elegance, the luxury and the inimitable wit of the French. I loved their literature and, in particular, I loved Beatrice, the Duchesse de L ... As Olga, my ex-Russian guide would say, we had been *orchen sympateeshnia*, on sight. I had suffered years of

Edgeville, I had suffered through three years of nursing and I had been frustrated in Russia. Now, alienated as I had been from my former worlds, how foretell that in this sophisticated, international society I would feel as though I had been born into it? For the first time in my life I was home.

Arriving in Paris, Dick had been over-anxious about my reception by his friends and although always courteous in public, he had dissociated himself from me. But these past months he had never left my side. Was he jealous? Was that why he'd put me in this rat-hole, cut me off from everyone I knew? I'd been a fool to agree to stay. The moment he came back I would leave him.

At ten o'clock that evening, rattling along in the half-empty *metro*, I knew it was stupid to go to a party alone. I had half a mind to go back but I couldn't face my squalid *pension*.

There were twenty or thirty people in the room when I arrived. Clay was standing in a corner talking to a tall man in a long white woollen robe with sandals on his bare feet.

The slender young man talking to the Duchesse, my hostess, was Alex, Comte de S ... He'd dined and wined us many times. I liked him. They turned to greet me. The Duchesse said, "Philippa, I'm delighted to see you. May I present Comte de S ... ?"

"Thank you. I'm happy to be here," I said. "Hello Alex."

"Oh, you know each other. And how is my dear Dick? Have you heard from him?"

"Philippa," Alex bowed over my hand, kissed it and held on to it. He glanced behind me. "You are alone?"

"Yes. Beatrice, I haven't heard from Dick, there's not been enough time."

"Isn't it true, Beatrice," Alex said, holding on to my hand, "Philippa– she's not like the others, the Americans?"

My hostess laughed. "I hope *you're* not leaving us, Philippa, my aunt would miss you. She has become quite miserly about you–wants you as often as possible–and to herself."

"I shall be here for some time. I love spending time with her."

"Alex get Philippa a drink, I must speak to le Duc."

Alex tucked my hand under his arm and led me to a divan. "Let us sit down and chat."

A man-servant brought a tray: coffee and cognac.

I said, "Coffee," to Alex.

"But, no!" Alex spoke to the servant. "Please, for Madame, bring champagne."

I nodded towards the corner. "Who's the bed sheet with Clay?"

"What bad manners!" said Alex. "With me, how can you look at another man?"

"Is it a man?"

"Duncan, the brother of Isadora and a man. Don't look. He has a whole colony of wives."

"Oh? Tell me."

"I have told you," said Alex. "Nothing else. To tell the truth, I know nothing about him, just the gossip." He dismissed Duncan and his affairs with a shrug. "Philippa, I thought you had left Paris. I haven't seen you in ages! Do you leave soon?"

"I shall be here for months."

"And Bentham?"

"He's on his way to New York."

"What a pity," said Alex, happily. "Do remember me, to him." He paused. "And you? You are free?"

"Free as the air," I said. "I'm getting a divorce."

"A divorce! No! And you are not sad? No?"

I shook my head. "Not at all."

"Not sad!" His eyes sparkled. "I'm horrified! Philippa, do you believe in dreams?"

I said, laughing, "Don't be stupid. I never have dreams. I have nightmares."

"Nightmares?"

"*Cauchemar*," I translated.

"Aha!" said Alex. "*Cauchemar*. You know, my darling, it's what I have when I see you with Bentham."

We began to laugh. After a long, frivolous conversation, we arranged to spend Sunday together–to go to the Louvre, to have tea, and later to dine and dance. Clay came over in time to hear us arranging the hour. Alex bowed, kissed my hand and left.

"And where," Clay wanted to know, "do you think you're going with him?"

"Didn't you hear?" I said, "The Louvre."

"The Louvre! You'll end up somewhere else if you run around with him."

"Oh, nonsense, Clay. Alex!"

"All right. Have it your way." He sat down beside me.

I was embarrassed in his presence. I felt exposed, as though he could read my mind. I stood up. "I must leave. I have to go all the way across town."

Clay said, "I'll take you home."

We said good night to Beatrice and had started towards the door when we met Alex, hat in hand, coming back in. "Philippa!" He took my hand. "It just occurred to me. Did you come alone? I'll ... "

Clay said, "It's all right. I'll see her home."

"It's such a pleasant night," Alex sighed. "Why don't we walk a little?"

The three of us left the house together. I was sick with disappointment; I wanted to be alone with Clay.

We strolled along. Alex began to sing.

"Damn this city," I said, "I'm tired of it!"

"What?" said Alex, "Paris?"

"Paris bores me to death!"

"What?" said Alex, again. "Paris bores you to death?" He laughed all the way down the street.

I stopped. I was in a rage with him. Why did he have to tag along? Neither would leave. The hell with them both. I saw a taxi, waved at it. It stopped. Too bad about my vanishing francs. I jumped in and closed the door. "*Allez!* "

I left them standing there, staring after me. That'll hold them! I went back alone to my miserable room.

27

I was awake but I hated to open my eyes. When I looked around my room, my faith in Dick's love for me seemed idiotic. I had promised to stay till he got back from New York ... The alternative? Write home: confess my failed marriage? Go back to New York? Embarrass Dick? I felt sick.

Clay ... I'd been awake half the night thinking about him. As for Alex, what a flirt! He was the handsomest man I'd ever met: slim, black hair, black eyes and a narrow black moustache. He looked like a film actor and in fact was connected in some way with the French motion picture industry.

It must have been Alex who told the Duchesse, some weeks ago, that Dick was going to New York, leaving me here alone. She had asked me to lunch, wanted the latest news of "dear Dick" and, intimating that I would do her a great favour, arranged for me to take French lessons from her old aunt, the Comtesse de B ... , who is something of a recluse. I go to her almost every other day. She talks about France and I talk about Nova Scotia. I've acquired a fashionable accent. Every time I mispronounce a word, I'm drilled on it. As for grammar, we don't mention it! I'm not allowed to pay for my lessons. Today I'm staying for lunch. I'm looking forward to the talk and the food and wine. Paris has been kind to me–Beatrice, the Volkovs, my old Comtesse–if it hadn't been for them ... But my situation is intolerable! In a fury of frustration, I leapt out of bed.

At the banker's Trust there was a letter from Millie and one from Dick from the boat train. I sat down in one of the comfortable customer's armchairs and opened Millie's letter.

Darling Philippa,

We haven't set a date, but soon. Henry took me back to that gorgeous mansion where we first met to meet his grandmother–a regal old dame with, believe it or not–a sparkle in her eye for me. After all my worry, all the secrets are out in the open. She said and I quote, 'I would hate to have you investigate the morals, either female or male, of our progenitors. (!) Henry knows about Dick's family, very rich and all the rest.

Millie to marry Henry! There was such a glow in my heart. I glanced at the clock. I didn't want to be late. I stood up hastily and bumped into an old man. He said, "That's a lovely smile! Good news?"

"Oh, yes! Very! Thank you!"

I'm home, comatose, but still laughing. Our luncheon lasted until almost five o'clock. After three wines with three courses, the Comtesse decided I was in such a good mood we needed champagne. I started talking about nursing, the bootleggers and communism and she wouldn't let me stop. We were both unmistakably soused and it was hilarious! She cannot understand how I "so delicately reared, had the courage ... " I tried to explain that in the backwoods of Canada, no one was delicately reared, but I'm not sure I got through to her. Anyway she is going to help me save the world, as I am too delicate. We haven't decided how. Oh, Dick's letter! I took it out of my purse.

Kitten,

I wish It was here now to give It a big kiss to make It cheer up. When I think of It, alone, it makes me feel nasty for having left It. I do hope It will forgive.

Did you finish Man and Superman? *I didn't think when I stole it so peremptorily. Please forgive! And if It wants to finish it, buy another copy.*

I do hope it isn't as bad for you as I'm afraid it will be. It gives me a very hollow feeling to think ...

I couldn't keep my eyes open. I dropped Dick's letter, ripped my clothes off and fell into bed. I thought of the Comtesse's concern for me and began to laugh. Buy another copy of *Man and Superman*? Where in hell would I get the cash?

I have been spending more and more time with the Volkhovs. Tasha started giving me Russian lessons and the Baron joined us, since then the visits have become social hours and they, too, refuse payment. They are incredibly kind. Their elegant, small apartment is home to me. I am more cared for here than I ever was at home. The rapport between us is something I have never experienced with anyone else–except with the Comtesse de B ...

More letters from Dick:

Cherbourg

Dear Kitten,

Did you remember you were asked to the Bishop's party on Wednesday evening? I hope you went and met some interesting people.

I'm living the life of a hermit. I can't see that there's anyone on board worth knowing. There's one tall, slim, golden blonde who has been walking off with all the men, but she doesn't attract me enough to look twice. She's never worn the same dress more than ten minutes in the hour. I do wish you were here.

They passed around declaration slips today which makes me foresee much expense at customs. All Tasha's expensive nothings! I'm going to take Ulysses through if I have to disguise it as an antique persian vase!

I'm reading Babbitt *and am most impressed. Finished a bottle of wine along with it. I'm up in the bar. The aeroplane doesn't fly in winter, hence will mail this on landing. Little by little we're getting closer to ye old oasis. Should just about heave to about 3 p.m. The old cardiac organ does pop a bit at the thought of getting home, but I'm pretty sober, just the same. The bartender just reminded me, with a glint in his eye, that I could have a glass any time I want before getting off! I hate to finish this. Goodbye, my angel, we're almost there.*

Love, Dick

270 Park Avenue
New York City

Darling,

Here I am writing from New York! I'm sitting at a comfortable desk drinking beer—I'd forgotten how good beer can be. I've loads of things to do and haven't accomplished anything except order a couple of suits today and then my tailor told me how bad business is. He should worry. I pay him a small fortune.

I took your picture out and sat over it in a trance for ten minutes, then had to hide it away so I could get things done. Really, ducky, if you get sick of things over there. Well, never mind. Please don't put return address on letters, Mrs. Philippa Jerrold Bentham! What a jolly explosion would occur if such a letter should come for me. I'm quite sure my fears have no cause for existence, but please remember. Must run, angel. More love than you really deserve!

Dick

Preposterous! He claims to love me in one sentence and removes himself from me in the next. If it wasn't so infuriating I would laugh. Well, as Martha says, "I should worry, get a wrinkle on my hip and ruin my figger!" I can't believe Dick will read *Ulysses.* As for *Babbitt,* I took a look

301

and gave up. One thing Dick and I don't have in common is our taste in fiction. I am more than ever determined to get out of this stupid marriage.

Another letter. At least he's still writing.

270 Park Avenue
New York City

Dear Woof,
Curses, tragedy, horrors and much dismay. In other words, I think I have lost my little notebook with all the notes in it about everything ... including your insurance. Now just what in all hang can I do? My God, I know where I left it. On the train from Paris to Cherbourg. Gripes me horribly. Will you please send me your insurance company's address?

I love you so much. I am in hopes a letter came on the Europa. *Was welcomed at a tea I went to yesterday by Cheryl's younger sister, who remarked, "Oh, how are you? Is it true you were engaged in Moscow?" I carefully denied everything, and now I'm in a quandary to know what I shall say about it when I see her mother who heard it directly from Stanislavski! I've got to phenoogle around and smooth out rumours.*

Have phoned and find I can't get the reduction I'd hoped for on a new typewriter, but I guess I'll get one anyway. Oh enfant, I wish I knew what I shall be doing. If, for example, I go to New Haven next year, what can we do about it? I am desperate. This feeling of having done nothing for so long is getting my goat. I can't go on without something definite to work for. I think more than ever that the theatre is the thing. At least, the family are all back of me on that because they agree with me now that it would be unfair for me to up and get a job, even unpaid, which might cut someone out who needs it.

Well, this goes on rather dismally, doesn't it? Right at this moment I would give anything ...
Love, Dick

It's been six or seven weeks since Dick left. He writes almost every week, but nothing has changed. I get half-way through his letters and rip them up. I've sent him two badly written, badly composed short stories. I can't study and write and I can't think.

270 Park Avenue
New York City

Dear Weeso-woof,
You have no idea how your proximity would be appreciated at this

moment. Somehow, even with some of the best people I know, I find myself coming home after an evening out with the feeling that jaws have been wagging all evening over nothing. Now this is a great slam at the noble friends, but none the less I have that waw-waw-waw-of-the-lower-jaw-flapping-around-in-the-breeze feeling. You know what I mean?

I may be going to Bermuda this week. Have never been there and I think it will give me a chance to try some writing because I now feel desperate and sitting around here is no way to get things accomplished. Will be gone only a week at the longest.

All I have to do to get a divorce is to send a postcard to Zags, the marriage bureau in Moscow. At least that's what Dick told me. Is it a special government postcard? If I sent it from here would they acknowledge it and inform Dick in New York? I must get out of this marriage legally! I can't take a chance on a Russian postcard divorce!

I'm obsessed with Clay, I'm madly, desperately in love with him. I can't get him out of my mind. He's been in London this past month. He keeps in touch, a postcard or a short note, but I have no idea how he feels about me. Dick told me he's Catholic. Would he marry a divorced woman? What a mess I've made of my life!

I've been seeing a lot of Alex. He appeared at my door, unannounced, one morning and I almost died of shame. My bed was unmade, I was wearing Abbie's, not too fresh, white silk robe and I hadn't washed my face. I thought, "he'll never come back."

The next day, he sent masses of yellow roses and an invitation to dinner. He sits in my sordid room as much at ease as if it were the most elegant drawing-room. He is light-hearted and amusing. He knows I am penniless and alone and that my marriage is a farce, but he has never asked anything of me but friendship. He does insist, though, that I take a loan from him—just enough to get me into a decent apartment. Of course I refuse.

At dinner one evening he said he had written his mother about me, and that I should go to her in Italy. She would take care of me. I would have a letter from her. Much as I would love to get out of here, how can I rush off to Italy? To a stranger. Besides, if I go away I won't see Clay.

I have had a letter from Alex's mother, from Monselice, Padova, very impressive, addressed from a castle. She's expecting me. I wrote to her today—to thank her. It's raining and I can't stand this room! I'm off!

I've just got in and I'm soaked to the skin and I haven't done my daily quota of work. I've sent Dick outlines for two more stories and now my brain is a blank. I must get out of my clothes and get to work. I sit in front of the desk and nothing ... I might write about my day. What shall I call it? "Mrs. Bentham's Day!" No; just the date.

Paris, March 30th

All night the rain fell heavily and the cold dampness that hung over Paris held no hint of the awakening of Spring. I woke feeling ill–alienated from the human race. A door banged in the next room. The art student on his way to class? His amoureuse leaving for Mass? I reached for my French grammar, then let it drop. I have parrot-like repeated so much French with the old Comtesse that the French idiom is fixed in my brain for life!

With a superhuman effort, I launched myself out of bed and reached for my oldest clothes–or at least the dirtiest–they're all the same age. I had to go out and run: fly through the rain! As an unhappy, misfit child, taut with nervous tension, running in the rain restored me. Today, in Paris, where I am no longer a misfit; the rain will restore me again.

How strange that in Paris, the most cultured and sophisticated city in the world, I'm at home. I belong here. How strange to hear from these people that I have charm and beauty, and from the old Comtesse, that I have one of the loveliest voices she has ever heard. Question: Would my family believe it? I know the answer, "That's a lie."

With every intention of buying something different to read, I started for the Left Bank and the book stalls and while sheltering under the meagre canvas to pore over old books, it occurred to me to look in my purse. If I bought a book, I couldn't eat–or at least no dinner with the Volkhovs. I found a café and stopped for coffee and then, greedily, ordered an omelet. Then I rushed through the rain to the Louvre where I spent the afternoon. I have decided to become a famous painter as soon as I move to the classic Paris attic.

I was wet but I didn't want to take the *Métro* back to my *pension,* not because of the stale air, but because this world depression has made the underground a place of shelter for people, who are so destitute that I cannot bear to look at them. These hungry derelicts in their shabby caps and rags, leaning against life-sized posters depicting steaming plates of spaghetti, make me feel guilty. I am wasting my life! But with wet shoes, exhausted and hungry, I took the *Métro*.

Paris is plastered with posters, from the ones warning of the danger of disarmament, to the horrible pictures showing the horrors of war, to those begging for money for veterans of former wars. I stop, look and wonder at man's insanity. There is one poster that is innocent of war: it depicts a huge rosy-cheeked infant using the right kind of soap.

When I arrived at my station late this afternoon there was some sort of commotion going on under the baby picture. Two gendarmes were trying to hold a young woman who was screaming and beating at the baby's face with her umbrella. Someone behind me took my arm. "What happened?"

The crowd had the answer. "Watch out! She's crazy! She lost her baby! Watch yourself!"

I ran. I lost my appetite. I rushed past the dining room and upstairs to my room. I'm sick. I'm sick of myself and I'm sick of Dick. I must get out of this miserable *pension,* this intolerable situation. I want a divorce. Now! There would be no looking back, this time. I would settle this. I picked up my pen.

I finished the letter, checked the sailings and ran out to post it; it would go on the *Europa.* If Dick answered at once, as I had demanded, I would have approximately two weeks to get ready to leave for Russia. If? On my way back to my room, I began to wonder if I had been definite enough, if he would understand finally that I would not go on? I began to run. I reached my room, breathless, and wrote again, ran out again and posted it. He would get both letters at the same time.

I breathed in relief for the first time in months. I had done the right thing. I was free. Free!

Park Ave., New York City
April 8th

Damn it all you infant!

I have exactly 15 minutes to get entirely changed into full dress and get off to dinner, but just got your two letters on the Europa *and must send this back with it if I can. God knows, I wish I were sitting on your neck at this moment so I could give it an extra squeeze. Well never mind, there is no time to write it all now.*

Angel, it's just as I thought, this long wait is getting under your skin.

Well, it's under mine too. So don't feel hurt. I am coming over as soon as I can but don't know yet. Yale, writing, you ... My God, I ... Perhaps I should kill myself!

Well, never mind. I'll be jittering in a minute and that won't do. My God, if I make you riled, you have no idea what a mess you stir up in my mind when you speak of doing something foolish like going back to Russia!

There is no more time. I can't be late and I must get this down to the boat before the mails close. Please don't go off and do something rash until the next boat arrives and you get my letter. And, my God, how I'd like to wring your neck! Oh, of course I understand, but darling please wait till I come over.

I'll come as soon as I can, you foolish angel.

Love, Dick

He hasn't sent the money. How can I do anything rash? I made it very clear that I need money, that I want a divorce. He can't stop me! I'll write again and this time he'll get the message!

Park Ave., New York City
April 15th

Dearest,

If you take the situation into your own hands and tear off to Russia, aside from how it will make you feel, I'm sure you'll never forgive yourself.

Oh God, angel. Your last letter is about the most depressing thing I have ever read. If things keep up over here much longer, I may soon be in a position to apply for charity ... not that I have been affected seriously myself, but business is just creeping along, things are going under all the time. I would not be the slightest bit surprised to wake up and find myself heir to and in possession of $00000.00.

Oh dearest, I know your life has not been easy in Paris; I know that my leaving you must have hurt you terribly, but well over three-quarters of the time has passed! Don't you know, angel, how I do feel towards you? I have told you it is Love. It is something profoundly deep; it is a feeling of kinship, a feeling of fundamental sympathy. I have looked for it for a long time and found very little trace of it till I met you and accidentally stumbled upon it. Then I found just that thing I was looking for, but in such a large degree, and combined with such strong features of other sorts, that the result was my whole development was checked and piled up on itself till we were no longer together. It has taken these weeks of sort of phenoogling around here to sort that piled up conglomeration out. Now I feel better fitted to go back to you and cope with you more

306

appropriately. Please don't think I am out of my head, I'm only trying to tell
you something, and it is extremely difficult.

And so goodbye darling; do write and tell me what you decide.

Dick

P.S. *I have been told that recently certain foreigners have been ejected from
Moscow because of teaching and making money. If you are thinking of staying
there, I should certainly try to find out if it means foreigners will be prohibited
entirely from teaching. Of course, the official letters you have from the Russians
should be of much help.*

If only I dared take Alex's money! He appeared at my door again this
morning. Thank God, I was dressed! It seems the Duchesse has talked to
the Comtesse. She's concerned for me and will call me for lunch. In the
mean time, Alex is "ready to do anything in the world" for me and has again
offered me money. I put him off, asked him to leave, but promised to have
dinner with him tonight. At the door, he took both my hands in his.
"Philippa, you must come to me. I love you."

I couldn't stop the tears.

He held me. Then he left.

I'll make very sure this time that Dick knows what I want. If I have
to, I'll borrow money. Where? If only the Volkhovs had money. If only
Abbie were alive. If only I'd sold her apartment instead of giving it away.
If only Clay were here. I haven't heard from him. I don't know where
he is.

Park Ave., New York City

You crazy little angel,

*I am, though not drunk, in a condition which, if it had been good liquor,
would be called drunk. Kitten, at this moment, I could wring your damned
little neck and enjoy the very wringing of it. Why? None other than your latest
epistle which came to smack me in the teeth tonight. Can't you wait, darling,
until I come back, before you tear off? Must it be immediately? You say it is "for
your very preservation." Why? I cannot understand. I only wish, and oh how
much, that I were with you right now, in bed with you, holding you to me.
Kitten ...*

Dearest, I do love you as I have tried to tell you. What more can I say?

I threw his letter in the waste-basket. I'm in such a state of frustration, I can't think! I'd better finish reading it.

Now, for once and all, Darling, will you wait for me? I cannot go through the whole thing again of explaining my feelings, opinions, wishes to you. You know them as well as I do. There will be no time to exchange letters now before the earliest possible date of my departure. Dearest, I'll try to write another letter to you on the Ile de France. *Oh angel, please stay. I do so want you.*

If you will join me in Plymouth on the 10th of May, we could have five weeks together, or more. Then you could go by boat to Leningrad or come to Paris and go by train, depending on which way is best. Having carefully read over your last three letters, I end up with the feeling that life is hell.

Dick

We could have five weeks together and then I'd go to Moscow? He's using me! I should have known he wouldn't send me money! I should have written Pa. No matter what I said or did, Pa would send me money. But I can't hurt Pa. I'm stuck now, with my lies to the family. I'll have to sit it out till he gets here. Why bother to answer? I can't afford the stamps.

It's ridiculous, but I can't force myself to do things any more. My room nauseates me. Morning after morning, listlessly, I lie in bed with neither the will nor the energy to get up. Sometimes, except for the chocolate and the stale roll with its minuscule pat of butter and the weary, sticky dab of marmalade brought to me by the slovenly maid, I don't eat. Sometimes I don't dress during the day. I have no reason to get up, no place to go and no money. All my stockings have runs.

At night, if I remember in time, I throw on a dress and go down to the dim, soiled dining-room to eat the wretched food. I smoke endlessly, the cheapest French cigarettes. I wanted to go again to the galleries to look at pictures, but each day by the time I make up my mind, it is too late.

I scarcely bother to look at myself these days. My face, if I see it by chance in the stained looking-glass, frightens me. Perhaps it's the glass. I have always been thin. Now I've begun to cough–too many cigarettes, but I can't be without them. But I have lost my craving for alcohol. I've had no money for drink.

What did Alexander Pope say in his *Moral Essays*? "Most women have no character at all." When I read that, long ago in Edgeville, I scoffed at it. Now, remembering, I could weep. Abbie killed herself because she had betrayed her integrity. She was too weak to uphold principles necessary to her. I know, now, the abysmal pain and disgust she felt for herself.

28

Western Union
Cable
To: *Philippa Jerrold Bentham*
      Banktrust Paris, NLT
TAKING BREMEM. MEET YOU LONDON MAY 9TH. FINAL LETTER ILE-
DE-FRANCE. IGNORE EUROPA LETTER. DICK

I stood in the ticket office and counted my money. I had the fare for the Channel and a little over. If I went directly to Moscow from London, I might never come back to France. I couldn't leave without saying goodbye. A cable would cost too much. A postcard to Dick's hotel in London would have to do; he could meet the ferry in Southampton.

I found a public telephone and rang Tasha. "I'm taking you and Serge to dinner tonight," I told her. "I'll be there around seven."

"You are rich? Yes? Dick has sent money?"

"That's it," I replied, "I'm rich. We can eat."

When I got off the ferry, I saw Dick before he saw me. He was running; he looked as though he hadn't slept. And even though I'd hardened my heart against him, I had the urge to run, too, to console him. I'd gone back to my wretched *pension* the night before with such an overwhelming sense of frustration that I couldn't sleep. After I'd paid for dinner, I had nothing left but my ticket and a few ragged francs.

He saw me, stopped, then came towards me. His eyes were red.

I stood stubbornly rigid. "Hello, Dick."

He stared at the roses I was carrying. He said, resentfully, "You didn't have to bring me flowers."

"Alex ... He saw me off."

"With roses."

"Yes."

"That rat! And what did you give him?"

I could feel the angry blood in my face. "I'm extremely fond of Alex."

"And?"

309

"If you must know, I kissed him."

"I'd like to kiss him, too, with a brick. Never mind. The hell with Alex. You're here now, you're mine. Come on." He seized one of my suitcases, ran ahead of me to a small car, flung the boot open, threw the case inside and stood there with his face averted and sullen.

His rage was incomprehensible. I walked over and stood beside him. "Just what is wrong?"

"You didn't cable me in New York," Dick exploded. He was shaking. "Not very thoughtful of you, was it? You couldn't spend a little money on me for a change, could you? I give you enough." There were tears in his eyes. "I thought you'd walked out on me. I've been through hell."

"Oh? But I wrote you I'd wait." So that was it. I'd neglected him.

"But I expected a cable and when it didn't come, I thought you'd changed your mind. You should have realized how I'd feel after those awful letters. I was so miserable on the boat I couldn't eat. I was sick," and, he added, aggrieved, "it's all your fault. I thought you'd left for Russia."

"I see. Well, I'm sick, too: sick of your shilly-shallying! Let's not deceive each other. I need money. I want to leave for Moscow. Now."

"You can't! I told you we'd talk it over!" He snatched at my hand. "Damn those flowers! Throw them away! How do you know how I feel? I won't let you go. I absolutely refuse to go through that again!"

My knees began to tremble. What a relief it would be to fall on his neck. For despite all of it, seeing Dick was like coming home. I said, uncertainly, "Dick, judging by your past behaviour, I find it difficult to believe ... "

He put both hands on my shoulders, "You'll have to trust me," he said, earnestly. His pleading eyes, still wet with tears, held mine. "All I know is, you're my wife and I want you. I won't let you go."

"Are you trying to tell me, after all the vacillating, that you want to stay married?"

"Yes!"

He wanted me. I turned my head and put up a hand to hide my face for my eyes, too, were full of tears. He wanted me. I could forget my anxieties, the humiliations. This long, unhappy separation had ripped up the weeds of doubt and laid bare the truth: he loved me.

He pulled me to him and put both arms around me. I dropped my head on his shoulder, leaned on him, limp with relief.

All at once, we were at ease with each other. We drove to London in an atmosphere of gay tranquillity.

A porter carried my luggage into the hotel. Dick said in my ear, "Do you want to eat before you go to bed?"

"Yes. I'm starving, I haven't had anything since ... "

"You don't?" Dick grinned. He grabbed my hand and pulled me across the lobby. "There's the elevator, run!"

That afternoon, I forgot the wretched months in Paris. I was no longer alone. I gave myself to Dick in love and tenderness and for the first time since our marriage, sex, for me, had meaning.

We dined late that evening. Dick said, "I'm hungry. Let's get dressed. Cheryl gave me the name of a good French restaurant; I'd like to try it."

Cheryl was right. The restaurant was good. And Dick—how handsome. What a shock Pa, Mother, Edgeville would get when the ugly duckling came home with her charming husband. Abruptly, and with a painful sense of loss, I thought of Clay. I hadn't heard from him. He'd never even held my hand and yet.

"Stop staring into space. You're not listening."

"What? Of course I'm listening." My mind played back the sounds I'd just heard. "You were talking about O'Neill's *Mourning Becomes Electra*. I saw that before I left New York."

"Yes, well, the man is morose to the nth degree. He didn't fully develop the possibility of incest that he hinted at, he killed off the brother and saved himself from the censors. Doris said ... "

Doris, Cheryl, Alice—the girls he knew were attractive and clever, wore lovely clothes. And me: the rustic in elegant company. I'd been wearing the same suit almost daily for two years. I interrupted him, sharply, "Dick, don't you object to my clothes? They're getting ... "

He raised one eyebrow. "You silly cat, who mentioned clothes? Aren't you interested in what I'm telling you?"

"But I saw the play. And I can't help thinking, after all your beautiful girls, you must be tired of seeing me in ... "

"Really, Kitten! What makes you think I care about your clothes? I married you in a sheepskin. Anyway, what's wrong with the suit you wore in Russia? We'll be travelling, that's all you'll need. And by the way you haven't even mentioned the itinerary I sent you."

"I thought I was leaving for Moscow," I reminded him, "so I didn't look at it." I had ripped his precious itinerary to shreds and flung it in the wastebasket.

Dick pulled a map out of his pocket and unfolded it on the table between us. "Pay attention now and I'll go over this with you. We leave London ... " He began to trace a line on the map.

The pencil in his hand was from Tiffany. Heavy and shining: gold.

He looked at me. "Is there anything in particular you'd like to see?"

Keats. I hadn't thought of him in ages. The Swan and Hoop livery stables in Finsbury. London, where his father worked when he was born. Was it still there? I said, enthusiastically, "Yes, a livery stable!"

"A stable? Oh, nuts Kitten, will you be serious?" Dick sighed. "Look, if you want to ride, when we get to the country, I'll take you. But, if that's all you can think of to see in this country, it's just as well I've done the planning." He glanced at his watch. "It's getting late. We should get back to the hotel. We'll have to get up early if you're to see all the things I've arranged for you to see."

What price marriage? Must one settle for being a fifth wheel? We'd been in England more than two weeks and all I'd done was sit in the car. Dick drove steadily all day long. I was sick of sitting, sick of leaping out of the car to stare at monuments. The architecture–all of it–was magnificent. I could see that. But I was sick to death of being led around by the nose.

I was bored. Bored with Dick's determination to control me. Bored with his preoccupation with every practical detail of everyday living, and his insistence that I share that interest. I was bored with his eternal little notebook.

"How many miles, Kitten, since we stopped for gas?"

"I didn't notice the mileage."

"Damn! Now I've lost track. I'll have to look it up on the map again. I thought you were interested."

I yawned. "I think you worked it all out in your little book last night."

"That's right. I forgot. Where's my book?"

"In your pocket?"

"Well, I won't stop now. Don't forget to remind me when we get there. I thought I gave you the book. Didn't you write down what I paid for gas?"

"No, you did. Oh, now I remember, you had the book in your hand while he was filling the tank. What difference does it make?"

"Well, of course," sulkily, "if you don't care. I thought you'd be interested to know how this car goes in comparison with an American car."

"Let's see. That gives us an hour for lunch and then you have at least half an hour for the cathedral because we have to be in ... Where's my map, Cat?"

312

Where the hell was his map? "I don't know."

"Well, look!"

"Dammit, Dick, you probably left it in the car."

"No, I didn't. I brought it in, and the last time I lost it," Dick said, suspiciously, "you were sitting on it. Will you please get off that bed a minute? I thought so. Gawd, my love, will you please try to look the next time and see what's under you before you sit down?"

"Sorry, I'm exhausted. Perhaps you shouldn't throw it on the bed."

"I think you threw it there. Gawd! You haven't improved it much by rolling around on it. I could cheerfully wring your neck. Hell! Where was I? Oh, yes, a half hour for the cathedral. I could stretch that a bit if you're interested. How about it, Kitten?"

"Why do you ask?"

"Why? What do you mean, why do I ask? This trip is as much, or more, for your benefit than for mine!"

"Uh-huh. Well, look, Dick couldn't we sort of just go along till we feel like stopping, and then stay as long as we please? And to hell with the cathedral. I'm sick of cathedrals!"

"What? What are you talking about? Don't you ... "

"I said I'd like to stop some place and rest."

"But you won't see anything. We haven't got the rest of our lives, you know. We have to get back some time. Don't tell me you don't want to see the cathedral!"

"Well, I ... " If I saw one more cathedral, I'd have kittens! But the look on his face. "Well, of course I do, Dear."

There were days when I thought I'd starve to death. There was no such thing as stopping any old time for a bite to eat; we had to find the right place.

"Baked apple! You can't order a baked apple in this place. It's famous for its English puddings."

"It's on the menu."

"You'd better have the suet pudding. You can have baked apple at home."

"What home? I don't feel like suet pudding."

"Oh, come on now, don't be silly, please. Shall I order the pudding?"

"Does it matter so much to you?"

"Of course it does. Why do you think I brought you here? You should eat the cooking of the region. Will you have the pudding?"

"I'd prefer ... "

"Oh, stop it, Cat! Waiter! Two suet puddings."

We were racing through England and Scotland, seeing it all in one quick look. Including a Roman villa and a Pictish tower that I discovered were, respectively, a few old tiles, a few yards of earth-bound aqueduct, and a few stones in a hole in the ground.

As for my sex-life, after that first happy encounter, my enthusiasm for it had dwindled. But my fear of being lousy in bed had fizzled out a long time ago. Dick had enough enthusiasm for both of us.

"If only you and Doris could combine," he yearned one day, "my bachelor days would be over."

"I thought they were over."

"Oh! Yes. Well, I didn't mean ... "

"Forget it, I'm not sure I feel married, either. What's she like?"

"Well, you're both strongest on the other's weakest points. You have the sex-appeal and the figure. You disagree, rather than agree with me. Doris knows the theatre, and she's stimulating. She has a genius for dealing with people."

I thought about that. I could deal with the sick: it was routine on the wards for the doctors to put me in charge of difficult cases. But outside the hospital the whole world knew more about people than I did. As for stimulating, perhaps enforced sitting engendered apathy, for on this trip I was a drag. "I'm not too good with people," I admitted.

"No," Dick agreed, "you're not. Actually, you've got a rather warped viewpoint. You know," he went on, "you were right. Mrs. Stevens doesn't like you."

"Oh, her! That woman took an instant dislike to me before she set eyes on me." Just what was wrong with my thinking? I braced myself to find out. "Do you really mean 'warped'? How?"

"Yes, I do. You always view things with pessimism and I view them with optimism: I'm happy and you're sour. I wonder if you know what I mean? You're cruel at times, you ... "

Cruel! I sat there stricken. Cruel!

"What I mean is it's the sort of coloured glasses you look through at life," Dick stated. "I mean, when you come down to it, Angel, you've somehow acquired a pair of solid black ones, with some streaks of red, not for communism, but for the kind of gory and sordid features you always pick out. Perfection is having a little of everything in your glasses from black to golden yellow. Does that help you see what I mean?"

Cruel! I was appalled. "Be specific, Dick when was I cruel?"

"Oh, there you go! Trying to pin me down! How can I remember? It's little things, like always mentioning your clothes when there's nothing wrong with them. It ought to make you feel very sheepish."

"Always? You mean once at dinner before we left London!" If either of us had been cruel, it was Dick, keeping me on pennies, and on tenterhooks, for months. I said acidly, "Shall I change? Perhaps you prefer the sheep's character—timidity, stupidity, blind acceptance of the dog's control or the master's whip—to my pessimistic, sour and cruel character?"

"Come now, I didn't say that!"

"No? What did you say? Never mind, go on, what else is wrong with me?"

"Well, if you won't deliberately misunderstand, I'll tell you. For one thing, you've denied the rightness of those you grew up with. Your foundations are weak and away from home you've just floated around. And now you want to rely on me. But I won't let you. You have to rely on yourself. You know, Angel, I want the best for you. If I didn't, I wouldn't be saying this."

"That's ridiculous! Do you think I was 'floating around' for three years in a city hospital—or looking for work in Russia? It's since I married you; it's you who persuaded me to hang around in Paris. I couldn't get working papers." But was Dick right? His character analysis unnerved me. Should I have ignored his wishes? Was I irresolute? Weak? But, suddenly furious at his presumption, I said, coldly, "You're wrong, Dick. I have a most stable, lasting and solid foundation at home: my father. There's no circumstance in which he would not support me. And get this straight, whatever our differences, I respect and love my family." Yet even while I was saying it, I had a bitter feeling that Mother and Geoffrey and Flora would never support me in anything.

"Are you sure? Then why didn't you tell them this marriage was temporary?"

"You know why! I'd have lost my reputation and disgraced them as well. I would not impose that unhappy condition on my family!"

"So, you lied to them. You're still lying to them."

Still? "I just didn't tell them. But if I'm lying to my family, you're lying to yours, too."

Dick said, contemptuously, "I'm not lying. This is my business, not theirs. And I haven't disgraced them. It's different for a man. They probably expect me to keep a mistress."

His mistress! That pompous ass! Patronizing me because ... He kept me all right. Hanging around that cheap, miserable *pension* while he bleated about his concern for me. "T-tell me," I stuttered, choking with rage, "At what date do you intend leaving me?"

"Oh, Kitten, please. Ever since you got up this morning you've been trying to make me miserable. Are you trying to spoil the trip?"

I was in such a rage, my ears were buzzing. "Just answer me. Are we going to stay married? Yes or no?"

Dick sighed. "You always manage to take the joy out of life, don't you. I told you we'd talk it over, so why start on it now when there's plenty of ..."

"Plenty of time?" I interrupted. "Do you expect me to believe you? You have no intention of staying married! Do you love me?"

"Well ... If you must know, I guess it's not love. No, I'm sure I don't love you. It's infatuation: I'm infatuated with you."

I sat quite still. I was frightened. He loved and respected me in the beginning and now he considered his attachment to me folly. Why? Why had he lost respect for me? But I would never have agreed to be his mistress. Suddenly, I was boiling, my face red hot. "Y-you think our marriage ... this s-situation, is all right for you but w-wrong for me?"

"Well, yes. Look, I don't make the rules! It's just that it's different for a woman. Your position ... "

"Different!" I shouted. "You bastard! You're infatuated, are you? Get this damned car moving back to the hotel! I'll have to cable Pa. You self-righteous, sanctimonious, hypocritical ass! Turn around! Get me back to the hotel!"

"Look, will you calm down? Kitten! Please! I've been looking forward to this trip for months and now you ... "

"Shut up!" I must get out. Where? Back to Paris and that stinking *pension?* No, not Paris, Moscow–the divorce. I must cable Pa for money. At once. I'd never take another cent from Dick as long as I lived.

"And how do you know it won't be you who wants to end it?" Dick was shouting. "Answer me!"

"I'm ending it now! Take me to the hotel!"

"I'll do no such thing!"

"Then I'll walk." I opened the car door. "If you don't stop, I'll jump."

"Kitten!" Dick slammed on the brakes and pulled up to the side of the road. "Kitten! Stop!" He grabbed my arm and held on.

"You're hurting me!"

We had stopped in front of a high wall. A woman with two Scotties on a lead was standing beside the gate. She came towards us and called out, "Did you want to see the puppies?"

"Yes," Dick said, "we do." He lowered his voice, spoke in my ear.

"Cat! Try not to make a spectacle of yourself. Look, I'll never forgive you if you make a scene." He dropped my arm. "Get out of the car."

I got out and Dick followed me.

The woman said, "Come inside. They're beautiful puppies and old enough, now, to leave the mother." She held the gate open for us.

We stood outside the wire watching them. They were enchanting. Little black locomotives! Puffing, playing, scratching, climbing the wire ...

Dick said to me, tenderly, "Pick out the one you want, Darling."

"Yes, do," the woman beamed at me, "and I'll bring it out to you. Which one would you like to see?"

"None of them. Really. I'm sorry. They're lovely, but we're travelling. It would be impossible."

"Nonsense," Dick interrupted, "Say which one you like." He took my arm, held me. "Please, Darling, choose one."

"It's no trouble at all for me to bring one out. Or several, if you'd care to look at them."

"No." I tried to smile at her. "I couldn't possibly take it. I'm leaving for Russia within days."

"Now, Darling, we haven't really decided on that trip, have we? In fact, although I haven't told you, I've just about decided we're not going."

I was speechless. That stupid ...

His long-lashed, innocent eyes pleaded with mine. "What do you think, Dear?" He turned back to the wire where one little black thing was clinging. "Wouldn't you like that one?"

"No!"

Dick said, "I think my wife would love it. Could we see it?"

"I'll get it for you." The woman brought the pup and put it in my hands. "Can you resist that?"

I wanted to knock his damned head off. I said, with a saccharine smile, "It's all yours, Darling," and handed the pup to Dick. Dick said, "How much are they?"

"We're letting them go for almost nothing. They're very well bred. Champions." She looked at me, paused. "The important thing is to get them in good homes. I'll let you have that one for ten guineas."

Ten guineas! Fifty dollars!

"Fine, we'll take it."

"They've been wormed. Come along to the office and I'll give you the pedigree. If you ever want to show it, you'll need that."

Ten guineas!

"I don't know what you think I said," Dick informed me when we got back in the car, "but whatever you thought, you were wrong. I love you. When you said you were leaving, Piglet, I just ... I can't be without you. Now listen carefully, I'm going to marry you, legally. It can't be this summer because I really must arrange things at home, but I mean it. I won't let you go."

I knew very well what he'd said. Infatuated! Should I stay or leave? The same old dilemma. I was confused. If I divorced Dick, the family wouldn't blame him, they'd accuse me.

There was mail for us in Edinburgh. Dick had wired the bank to forward it. Doris was expecting to see him in Paris.

I found a packet of letters from Alex. I sorted them according to dates with some trepidation. I hadn't really taken Alex seriously. And I forgot I'd told him I was on my way to Moscow to divorce Dick.

The first one was written on both sides of his visiting card. I was trying to read it when Dick snatched it out of my hand.

"What is it?" he said, "The Ducal Coronet? He must come from a good family. What does he want?"

"Give it back."

"Are you keeping secrets from me? What about Alex?"

"Don't be silly, he's a friend. Let me have it."

"If he's just a friend, I'm sure you won't object to my reading his letters."

"Look, Dick, there's absolutely nothing between Alex and me. All right, read it. I don't care. Here, read them all! But would you mind if I read them, too?"

Paris, Mai II

Philippa!
You will not believe, but when you left me my eyes were full of tears. The first time in my life. You have taken my heart and mon sentiment and I am content that it is you.
A kiss, an embrace. I love.
Alex

Paris, Wednesday

Dear Philippa,
I have written to you three times. It is a necessity that you reply to me at once—for me it will never be possible to forget you. You are always in my heart.

318

You cannot imagine. I wait for you. Always.

Everything here, all of Paris, in flower. I am—dispose of me as you will—
I am your slave. I cannot forget you. I wait.
Alex

Paris, Monday

Philippa,
Why have you not written to me? It is a month! 'One must always be gay!'
you used to say to me. I try, but I tell you one must be strong to wait for you. I
love.
Alex

Paris, Friday

Dear Philippa,
Is it that you are ill? I would be at your side to say many tender things.
For to tell you that you are the finest woman I know. To tell you that I love
because you have a character of gold. To tell you, if you desire it, that I shall be
yours for always.
Philippa, listen to me. I speak sincerely, if you cannot stay with him, never
forget that in Paris you will find Alex, who waits for you. Who loves you. Believe
me, it is true. Never in my life have I found a woman like you. You have
something ... Who can explain? Write me. Always for you,
Alex

I was touched, but embarrassed. He was the dearest friend. I loved being with him, but the idea of his being in love with me seemed impossible.

Dick gave back my letters. "So you told him you were getting a divorce."

I said, "You have a short memory, Dick. Following your instructions, I told all of Paris." And then, although I had no intention of doing it—because it wouldn't hurt to let Dick know he wasn't the only pebble on the beach—I said, "Perhaps I'll marry Alex."

"You're married to me."

"Not exactly—since you were about to marry Doris, in New York."

"Kitten, you know I can't do anything about it this year, but it's settled. It won't be bad waiting in Paris now that you've got our snuzzle-dog with you. When we get back to London—I've never given you one—I'm going to buy you a ring. I want you to wear it, look at it and know you belong to me."

"I'll have to write Alex. What shall I say?"

"Tell him your husband loves you and you're going to stay married to him for the rest of your life."

In London, we went to a jewelers to look at rings. Dick was in a proud and benevolent mood. "Take what you please, Kitten, it's for always."

I chose a diamond wedding band and a square emerald. I had never had anything so beautiful in my life.

Paris! How wonderful it looked, now my marriage was secure. I could hardly wait to get to the hotel, hardly wait while Dick signed us in, hardly wait for the porters to bring up our luggage.

"Aren't you going to change?"

"No. I'm going straight over to see Tasha."

"You can phone her."

"No, Dick. Do you want to come?"

"I'll wait here for you. Don't be long."

"I know you don't want me to tell people yet, but I want to tell the Volkhovs. They'll be so happy."

"Say what you please to them. They're all right."

"Dick, I'm very happy."

"I know, Kitten."

He held me against him for a second. "Silly cat." He reached for his wallet. "Here's some money. Take a taxi."

"Take care of the Scotch dog."

"Yes, but hurry back. He'll soon have to go out!"

I ran across the narrow court, up the dark staircase, knocked at their door, flung it open and threw myself at them. "Tasha! Serge!"

"Little one! Our little one!"

"It's all right, we're going to stay married!"

They bought out the cognac. "To our little one. Many happy years."

I was terribly happy. A little drunk. Dick was impatiently waiting. I rushed back to the hotel. The dog had to be walked.

Lunching at Fouquet's next day, we ran into Clay Hammond. My heart skipped a beat. He came towards us. I said, "Clay!" I stood up, leaned towards him and kissed his cheek. Just having him near made me happy. I loved his eyes, I loved his quiet voice. I loved the way he smoked a cigarette.

Dick said, "If you're free this evening, have dinner with us."

320

"As far as I know, that's all right. I have a pow-wow scheduled for late afternoon, but I should be able to get away. I'll call you." He went back to his table.

"I'm so glad he's in town," I said to Dick. "It's such fun being with him."

"Yes," Dick agreed, "he's a nice chap."

"Dick, I need clothes. Now that we are to stay married, I thought I might ask."

"You're always thinking about your clothes! Have you any idea what I've spent?"

"A lot, I suppose. If I can't have them, it's all right. But, almost everything I own, to quote Edgeville, is 'rump-sprung.'"

"Oh, Gawd!" Dick laughed. "What do you need?"

"My suit is ruined and my coat is too heavy for Paris."

"Is that all?"

"I could use a summer dress."

"Well, don't break the bank. Be reasonable."

"Then, I can have them? All of them?"

"I don't want my wife looking like a ragamuffin. Have you any idea what they will cost?"

"Tasha works with the big couturiers. She says one of them will do it for her as a favour—for very little."

"Oh, so that's it, you had it all hatched up!"

"No, of course not!" No need to tell Dick I'd hardly announced my marriage, before Tasha said, "Good! The first thing you have to do is get some clothes. I'll take you to ... "

"What would you like to do this weekend, Kitten?"

"Let's get out of Paris." I had an unbearable need to stop running around. I wanted to sit in the sun and not move. "Can we drive to the country quietly, and just stay there, not look at anything?"

"There's nothing I'd like better. I'll hire a car."

When the phone rang Friday morning, we were dressed and ready to leave. I was sitting on the floor putting a few things in a suitcase when Dick picked up the receiver. He said, "Now? Yes. Yes, of course I understand. I'll take care of it. Fine. Let's see, I can leave here in about half an hour. Yes. All right. Fine." He hung up.

I said, idly, "Now what? Do we have to stop somewhere?"

"Look, Kitten, that was Mrs. Stevens. She wants me for the weekend."

"Oh, dammit, Dick, no! It's bad enough eating with them, I don't want to spend an entire weekend with them!"

"Well, she didn't ... I mean ... Well, look, she made a point of asking me to come alone."

"Without me? But surely ... Are you going?"

"I told her I'd come. I knew you wouldn't mind. I knew you'd understand."

"You're going? Alone? But you promised me this weekend! Well I do understand. You prefer to slight me rather than put off seeing Mrs. Stevens! Don't you think you should have asked me first?"

He said, "But Philippa! You never object ... You never mind what I do!"

"No, I don't do I? Or rather, I have never said so. But now, we're committed to this marriage. She knows better, and so do you. Call her back, Dick, and tell her you promised me the weekend."

He looked frightened. "No. I won't."

"Don't you think you should have asked me first if I would mind?"

He wouldn't look at me. "I didn't think ... I don't think it matters."

"You don't think it matters what I think or how I feel?" I was still sitting on the floor.

"No."

"Dick, I'm now going to do something I've wanted to do for a long time." I stood up, doubled up my fist, and struck him on the face with all my strength.

He didn't move. One corner of his mouth puffed, a dribble of blood came out of his closed lips.

"Have a nice weekend," I said. I picked up my bag, went to the door, opened it and shut it quietly behind me.

29

When I left Dick on Friday morning, I was in a cold rage and, except for a brief meeting with Tasha, I spent the weekend in that hard, icy temper.

For the first time I understood what had been an inexplicable trait of my father's character. Aware of betrayal, he would go on and on, refusing a final judgement that would condemn another, until the accumulated deceptions and prevarications threw him in to an uncompromising rage. Then, no matter the consequences, he would make a decision and stay with it. It seems we had something in common. When Dick left to go to the Stevens, my marriage had ended. Nothing, now, would prevent my getting a divorce.

When Dick came back to the hotel Monday morning, I was on my way out for a fitting. He opened the door, shut it behind him and stood there looking at me. His lip was still swollen. He looked sullen. Shamed? He said, tentatively, "Hello."

"So you're back. Did you enjoy your weekend? Was Mrs. Stevens upset about her darling boy's face?"

"I didn't tell her. I said my taxi had an accident."

"Too bad. I'd like her to know what I think of you."

"Kitten, I ... "

"I have an appointment in twenty minutes, then I'm meeting Tasha. I should be back around three. Take the dog out at twelve o'clock."

"Look, wait! I'm lunching with the Stevens, I want you there to ... "

"What! The bloody nerve! Sorry, they're off my list. I'll be here at three—or four—we'll settle things then." I pushed past him and opened the door. He didn't try to stop me. If I hurried, I could walk to the dressmaker and, by the time we met for lunch, Tasha would have found me some sort of room. There would be no need, now, to depend on Dick for my trip to Moscow; she would have exchanged my emerald and my diamond wedding ring for cash.

When I finally got away from my fitting, it was late. Tasha was waiting at the entrance to the *Métro*, clutching her bag and looking very worried.

I took her arm. "Come, let's have something to eat." We headed for her usual café.

We sat down and I ordered two pernods.

Tasha hid her handbag below the table, opened it and pulled out a huge roll of francs. "There!" She handed it to me, looked again in her bag and pulled out a key. "I've done everything you asked, but ... " She shook her head. "The money's not half what the rings were worth, but what can I do? He's the best in Paris for us, the Russians."

"Thank you. I'd have had no idea ... "

"Your beautiful rings!"

"*Nitchevo*. And the room?"

"At least it's clean. It's on the rue Lamarck, a small apartment. But the concierge demanded ... I was forced to pay a full month."

I took the key from her hand and stuffed the money and key in my handbag. "You did well, thank you very much. Now, what would you like to eat?"

She swallowed her pernod in two gulps. She said, "Another, please."

I got back to the hotel at a little past three. Dick was waiting for me. "Did you take Fish out?"

Dick was sulking. He wouldn't look at me. "The porter took him. I went out to lunch. I have to talk to you. Please sit down."

"I'll talk to you later."

"Kitten, now!"

"Well, make it snappy. I have to get out of here." I wasn't in the mood for one of his specious monologues.

"Will you please sit down?"

"I'm in a hurry."

"Sit down!"

"What is it that can't wait?"

"Look, I've been talking things over with the Stevens ... about us."

"What business have the Stevens with our affairs?"

"They're friends of mine, even if you don't like them."

"I detest them."

"How can you say that? You hardly know them. How would you like it if I said things like that about your friends!"

"So you talked to them about us. What did they tell you to do?"

"If you're going to be like that."

"Dick, I'm in a hurry! What did they say?"

"Well frankly, they're horrified. They didn't expect this thing to drag on like this."

"Isn't it time they got used to it? They were horrified last year."

"Don't be funny. It's not funny. They are horrified."

"But why, for God's sake? We're married."

"Well, they think you're out for what you can get."

"You mean they think you so unattractive that I only want you for your money?"

"Now don't say anything you'll regret. They think my family ... "

"Do they know your family?"

"Well, no, but they know who they are. They think my family will say I'm too young to be married."

"They're right, for once."

"You're insulting. We are the same age! Still, I do think it wouldn't hurt to wait awhile. Anyway, I've got to ask you ... "

"To go to Russia? What a coincidence; my suitcases are packed. I'm about to leave."

"For Russia? No! That's what we have to talk about. They think a Russian divorce might not be legal here. They think we should get divorced in Paris. I mean, if I ever wanted to get married I might run into complications. It's not just for me, you might, too. But I've got to ask you: what do you want out of this?"

"What do you mean?"

"I mean money. They say you'll get a shyster lawyer after me. What do you want as a settlement?"

I couldn't move. Something like this had happened before. My wedding day, in Russia! Holmes! Imagine, I'd forgot all about Holmes. The sudden pain for him in my heart.

"Well?"

My body felt light: if I took my hands off the arms of the chair, I might float.

"Well, answer me!"

Suddenly, it burst from me, "Dick, for the love of God! After all we ... Do you really believe I'm after your money?"

"Oh, Kitten." He stood up, turned away from me. "Don't be like that. Answer me. Do you want a lawyer?"

"No! Get a lawyer for yourself! I'll sign anything you want me to sign."

"But what will you do?"

"Do? What do you expect me to do?"

"Don't be stupid. I mean for money."

"Money! Stop worrying about your money, Dick. Your money is safe from me. I have my steamship ticket to New York. I'll have no trouble getting a job." Holmes. How I'd love to see Holmes. He was dead. I didn't feel light anymore. I felt like a ton of lead. I was so tired I thought I could never get out of that chair. But I had to go. I stood up.

"Wait! Sit down! There's something else."

"I can't imagine what more you have to say."

"Well, you know how news travels."

"News? Yes, well?"

"I expect to be here a couple of weeks, maybe more, and there are a lot of people here from home." He hesitated.

"I'm waiting."

"I mean we don't want people falling all over us. It might be embarrassing for you. The Stevens think it would be better if you had a place of your own."

"Embarrassing for me? How thoughtful of them."

"I mean I'll get you something. I haven't had time yet but ... "

I said, "Why don't I just stay here and you get something for yourself?"

"What? But everyone knows my address."

"You mean I'm the one who has to stay in Paris–out of sight–until we get the divorce?"

"But, Kitten, it's easier for you."

It was strange that I felt no rancour. It was crazy, I was sorry for him! I said, "Is that all? Now if you'll ring the desk and ask for a porter and a taxi, I'll be on my way."

"But we haven't decided yet. Where are you going?"

I opened the wardrobe door. "Look, pull these cases out for me and ring the desk. By the way, where's Fish?"

"I shut him in the bathroom."

"How long has he been ... Just what do you intend to do with him?"

"Me? He's yours! You don't think I'd take him away from you, do you?"

What in hell would I do with a dog! But I couldn't leave him; Dick was hopeless about feeding him. "Mine. I see. Well thanks very much ... I think you'd better come along with me, my place is on the third floor. I'm not sure I can manage three flights of stairs with the luggage and the dog."

"Kitten, you must know this doesn't change what I feel for you. I hope you'll go on seeing me. I ... "

"For the love of God, Dick! Call the porter! Where did you put the leash?"

"I guess it's still on him." Dick looked at his watch. "Well, all right, I'll go with you if you want me to, but I hope you don't expect me to stay. I have to get back and get dressed. I have a dinner engagement."

At twelve noon the next day, I woke suddenly, in fright: someone was trying to knock down my door! I'd been up half the night and I was still half asleep. I threw on a robe. "Who is it?"

"Me. Let me in."

Fish was scratching at the door, jumping, trying to get out. I opened it and he leapt on Dick. I said, "You're up early."

"I brought your mail. Listen, what about coming out for brunch? Do you mind if I come in?"

"What for?"

"Kitten, go get dressed! I'm starving. I've only had a croissant and coffee. Hurry up."

I stood aside and he came in. "There's a letter from your father, one from ... "

"If you don't mind," I said, and took them out of his hand. "Oh, Alex. He's still in Paris!"

"I know, I recognized the writing. What does he want?"

"Perhaps I'll find out when I read it."

"Well, read it now. I'd like to know. I suppose the minute I move out the vultures will move in. Are you going to see him?"

"Oh, shut up, Dick!"

"Look, get dressed. I'd like something to eat."

"Well, run along. I'm not hungry. Fish and I had breakfast around four a.m."

"But we have to talk. I should think you'd be as anxious to get this settled as I am."

"All right." I put the leash on Fish. "There's a café a few blocks down the hill. Take Fish out for a walk and I'll meet you there in about ten minutes." I shut the door, ripped open my letters and glanced through them. How news travels! Alex had run into the Stevens and discovered my divorce was imminent. He had friends from Italy staying with him. He wanted me to meet them. Could I dine, at the Lido, tomorrow?

I threw on my clothes and went to meet Dick. He had our situation well in hand. The courts, he informed me, were slow. Our case might not be heard for months. I would have to wait in Paris. He would go back to New York. He had talked to my concierge after he saw me; and he would pay for my apartment until he left, but I must have something cheaper, a room. And, as long as I was in Paris, why not go to the Sorbonne? Enroll in the school of journalism? He had no intention of abandoning me: he expected that he would see me as usual. "And that," he said, "is about all for the moment. I'll pick you up at seven for dinner."

What a dazzling prospect for my winter. Sitting in a cheap room, counting my francs. I didn't know whether to laugh or cry. Did he think me a robot–to obey on command? I said, "I hardly know how to tell you, Dick, but I'm busy this evening. The Duchesse–didn't she ask you?"

"Oh, hell! I've nothing else lined up. I was counting on you. What about tomorrow?"

I frowned. "Dammit, I forgot my little book. Oh, now I remember, I've got a date tomorrow, too."

"Are you trying to tell me you're going to blame me for this divorce? That you won't see me? Just what was in that letter from Alex? Are you going to see him?"

"Yes."

"No! I won't let you."

"You won't let me!" I swallowed my coffee, picked up my dog and left him sitting there. I walked out quickly. For some stupid reason, I was shaking!

I didn't want to see Alex, but I didn't want to be alone. The concierge had a telephone. I stopped and telephoned Alex. I would love to dine with him and his friends the following day. Then I went upstairs to try to get some sleep.

At the Lido with Alex and his friends on Thursday evening, surrounded by people, by gaiety, I did my best to be part of it. I felt slow, unattractive, only half alive. We were in the middle of dinner when ... There was someone behind me. Staring at me. I sat frozen; I couldn't turn my head. Alex was smiling at me across the table. I said, "Alex, there's someone behind me!"

Alex said, "Yes. I've been watching him. He wants to sketch you. If you'd allow it, I'd like very much to have it." He nodded and the man behind me moved to my side. He was carrying a large sketch pad. He stared at my face.

328

Why was I frightened all the time? I spoke to him, sharply, "Thank you. No!"

"Philippa, I would love to have it."

"Please! No!"

"But, why, Philippa? Why not?"

"Alex, I'm frightened."

"Of what? What's wrong?"

"Nothing ... I don't know." I stood up. "I must leave!"

He glanced at the other couple, said something to them in Italian, came to me and offered his arm. "Let us go."

In the taxi, he held both my hands in his. "Tell me, Philippa, what is wrong?"

"I don't know."

When the taxi stopped, "I can't leave you like this. I'll come up with you."

"Please! No!"

"I can't part from you like this."

"Please, Alex, I must be alone."

"Philippa, forgive me, are you frightened of Bentham?"

I hesitated ... Was I? "No! Certainly not!"

We stepped out of the taxi. Alex lifted my hands, kissed them. "Perhaps tomorrow you'll allow me, if you're feeling better, to take you to lunch?"

"I can't ... I'll let you know. How can I thank you? Your friends will be waiting, you must go."

I climbed the stairs and put the leash on Fish. Then I sat down. I was afraid to go out. I should have asked Alex to stay, to walk Fish with me. But there was no danger. The street was deserted. I took Fish out. It was a lovely night. We walked slowly and it was close to midnight when Fish scampered up the stairs ahead of me. I gave him his biscuit and threw off my clothes. Perhaps I would sleep. But, there was someone at the door!

I stood in terror, unable to move. Fish was wagging his tail, scratching at the door. It was Dick!

I threw open the door. "Dick! Thank God it's you!"

He was dreadfully, dreadfully drunk. I'd never seen him drunk. Not like that.

"I thought you'd like me to greet your boy friend. Where is he? Didn't he come up?"

"No."

"Are you sure? Did you go out?"

"Yes."

"With Alex?"

"Yes, I went out with Alex. What business ... "

"He brought you home, I suppose. Kissed you." He pushed me roughly away then caught me to him, lifted me and threw me on the bed.

I fought him, panting, scratching, kicking. "No! Dick! No! God in heaven ... "

But he was stronger than I was.

Rue Lamarck was some distance from the Volkhov's. Too far to walk with Fish, too expensive to take taxis every day. Fish wasn't allowed on the *Métro* or the buses, and Fish didn't like to be left too long. Fish liked to amble, sniffing along the streets, for hours at a time. Ambling with him, I thought I'd fall down and never get up. I kept on ambling. I couldn't work, I couldn't write, I couldn't concentrate. Another winter like the last? I couldn't face it. Yet I couldn't think how to avoid it. I was frightened of being alone.

I locked my door against Dick. When he phoned I didn't answer. Then he wrote. How could I call it rape? If I wanted it that way, he would never touch me again. He'd be going soon. There were papers to sign. He had to see me. If I came to the hotel dining room to lunch I'd be safe.

Tasha insisted that I see him. She was hoping we'd make it up. Dick had come to her explaining how much he loved me!

I went to the hotel. Dick was sober. He said, "I won't insist, but since we must talk, please let's have lunch in my room. I give you my word ... Please!"

We were sitting over a bottle of champagne in Dick's room when the phone rang.

He said, "Yes? Send it up." He turned to me. "It's a cable."

"From your family?"

"I don't know."

I watched him while he tipped the porter, watched him carefully slit the envelope with his pen knife. I watched his eyes slipping from word to word. He always read with deliberation. He folded the form, put it in his pocket, ran his hand, caressingly, over his hair. "Kitten ... "

"Yes."

"It's definite. I'm going home."

"Yes?"

He picked up the phone, spoke into it, waited. "Steve? You told me

330

you'd give me the name of your lawyer. Yes. Just a second." He turned to me, "Take this down, Kitten." He handed me his pen. Then he carefully spelled out a name and an address. "Thanks. Good. I'll call him now."

He rested the receiver in its cradle, waited a few seconds, then lifted it. "Yes, it is important. Yes, I'll be there. Twenty minutes." He picked up his hat, kissed me lightly. "Wait for me here. We'll have some lunch later." He went out, jaunty, smiling.

Though I had agreed to it all beforehand, I was shocked to read it in black and white, and in the presence of an indifferent lawyer and his attendant clerk. I had thought that Dick would allocate a definite sum to me so that I would know how I could live, while waiting in Paris for the decree to become final, but there was no mention of that. The agreement was coldly formal and exact: Richard Bentham and Philippa Jerrold Bentham had registered their marriage at Zags, in Moscow. Philippa Jerrold Bentham hereby declared her intention of obtaining a divorce. She was fully capable of supporting herself, and she agreed to make no claim on any monies or properties belonging to Richard Bentham or on his name. She agreed, unqualifiedly, to leave him as free as though their marriage had never taken place.

We both signed this paper in the presence of witnesses. There would be some delay, the lawyer said, if the case went to court, but it was possible that it could be settled out of court. He would let us know.

We stopped at a café for a drink.

"You didn't tell me, Dick. What made you decide to go home right away?"

He pulled the cable out of his pocket and handed it to me. "Don't be jealous, now."

WILL YOU ESCORT ME TO CORNELIA'S ENGAGEMENT PARTY AUGUST 8TH. LOVE DORIS.

30

I n that uneasy atmosphere of constraint that precedes a departure, Dick, Clay and I stood on the station platform waiting for the boat train to leave.

"Kitten ... "

"Yes?"

"Don't forget to write."

"I'll remember." I tried to pull my hand away but Dick held on to it. "Have a good trip. Clay, take care of her while I'm gone."

"Yes, of course."

"Don't let her be lonely. Take her out."

"I'll do that."

I caught sight of a neat, dark man strolling along the platform towards us and I began to shake. "Dick! What's your lawyer doing here?"

Dick hastily dropped my hand. "I must have forgotten something. Kitten would you ... "

"Forgive me if I don't wait to hear it." I took two steps backwards and waved awkwardly. "*A bientôt.*" I turned away. I walked carefully, stiffly upright; it was an exercise I must perform well. I concentrated on it.

Clay caught up to me in the booking-hall. "Wait! You look a bit rocky."

"I need a drink."

He steered me across the street to a sidewalk café and I collapsed on a chair.

"What do you want?"

"Pernod."

The waiter flicked a towel over the table and went for our drinks.

"Philippa ... " He hesitated. "I don't want to pry; it's none of my business, but perhaps you'd like to talk to me. What was in that paper you signed with Dick?"

I kept my voice even. "I thought he told you last night." The three of us had been out until dawn. "Mutual agreement–announcement of our intention to divorce."

Clay said impatiently, "I know that, but the terms? Did Dick make some sort of settlement? You're his wife; he has to support you."

"Money? No."

"There was no mention of money?"

"Just that I made no claim on his. Why should I? He is supporting me."

"Yes, I've noticed," dryly. "A good hotel for him, while you ... Bentham wouldn't be caught dead in that cheap ... Who's your lawyer?"

"You just met him. Mr. Simmons."

"Simmons is Bentham's lawyer. Didn't you have a lawyer of your own?"

"I don't need a lawyer."

"You need your head examined."

"Clay, I haven't had breakfast. We've been out all night. I'm dizzy. Dick and I agreed in Russia ... Look, I don't need a lawyer to tell me what's right."

The waiter put two glasses in front of us. Clay poured water into mine and I drank the cloudy, yellow fluid greedily.

"Did Dick leave you any money?"

The morning sun hit my head, shone directly into my eyes. The heat was unbearable. I began to sweat. I was shaking again. "Some."

"How much?"

How much? I had no idea. What was left after last night's party, the rest of his francs, and some odd sum in dollars–sixty-nine? I was ashamed to admit to Clay what he already knew: Dick thought so little of me that he kept me like a pauper. I said, shortly, "As you say, it's none of your business."

"Sorry."

I got to my feet. "I must go."

"What about breakfast?"

"Fish." I made a face. "He's alone." I backed into my chair, knocked it over, picked it up and set it straight. I didn't look at Clay. "Thanks for the drink. Goodbye." I ran. I came to an intersection, stopped. I was going the wrong way. I didn't want to go back–pass Clay again. I darted into the street and beckoned to a taxi. I jumped in, gave the driver my address and settled back on the shabby seat. Shaken, I found a cigarette.

Foolish to take a taxi. What did I have to live on? I had to feed Fish. I had to ... I had to leave the apartment tomorrow and hunt for a place to live. I had no idea ... Perhaps Tasha would tell me where to look. The taxi ground up the hill, the narrow, cobbled street, stopped in front of my door. Money ... I opened my purse.

I ran up the three flights of stairs, unlocked the door, flung it open and leaned against it trying to catch my breath.

Front feet braced in a corner of the stuffed armchair, Fish looked up from his digging. He was breathless, too. Scraps of white on his eyebrows, his black face. His red tongue hung out of his mouth; it had bits of white cotton clinging to it. He looked at me for a second, dropped his head and began to dig again. I crossed the room and snatched him up. I saw the ragged hole.

"Fish!" I heard my voice loud in my ears, the words strangled, scattered, screaming. I struck him. "Fish! I'll kill you!" He slipped, wriggled, jumped, ran cowering under the bed. I threw myself on the floor, reached for him, clawing, beating.

How long had it being going on? Seconds? Minutes? How long had I been hearing it when I realized the screaming wasn't mine? It was Fish's!

I couldn't control my voice, my rasping breath. I crawled across the room, raised myself, grasped the doorknob and pulled the door shut. I slumped to the floor. I lay there, shaking.

Tail between his legs, belly pressed to the floor, wary, Fish approached me. He reached out and licked my hand. Then he pressed his trembling body against mine. I moved my head till it touched his. Gently, I lifted an arm and held him close. Frantic still, he kept licking me. We lay huddled together on the floor.

The large roll of francs from the sale of my rings began to get smaller: shoes, stockings, taxis, cigarettes, meat for Fish ... I found a clean room in a cheap hotel. It was too small. There was no place for my typewriter, my books, my clothes.

Paris was hot. The city stifled me; I couldn't breathe. I couldn't stay in the room. I couldn't bear to sit through French movies. I tried to stay away from the Volkhovs. This was their busy time, but one evening Tasha came to my room and insisted that I have dinner with them.

My misery came out with the wine–I had too much. "I understand the criminal mind," I said. Once I killed an innocent hen for, really, nothing! I mean, take the chair for example, for the cost of a cheap chair ... I mean for a few francs, can you believe it? Savage, unmerciful I ... " but I couldn't say that I had hurt Fish. I choked on it.

"Serge, she's had too much."

"Let her drink, it won't hurt her. Garçon, three more."

"This stupid divorce. She's upset." Tasha put her hand on my forehead. "Feverish. I knew it. She's delirious. Serge, she should be in bed. She's not strong."

I bent down and lifted Fish carefully off the floor. He licked my face. I wanted to weep in anguish, in shame, but my eyes remained dry: I had renounced tears a long time ago. I said, "Come on, Fish, tell everyone how good I am to you."

"Good little dog." Tasha reached to pat him.

"Watch it, he's ferocious!" I giggled.

"This chair. What about it?"

That ghastly chair! "Oh, that." I giggled. I couldn't stop. "R-red w- with orange s-spots, what you might call French-hideous. Where's my drink?"

"Enough! No more to drink. Serge, look at her, she's feverish, I tell you. She's sick."

I was sick all right. If the Volkhovs ever found out what I'd done to Fish, I could never face them again.

"It's because of that foul paper!" Serge made a grimace of disgust. "You've had a shock but, believe me, Philippa, Dick didn't mean it. Seriously, Philippa, you must wait. If you write him as usual, he'll change his mind."

I put my head on the table.

"Philippa!"

"We'll sleep here. Fish, say goodbye to Tasha and Serge."

"Serge, talk to her."

Serge said, sharply, "Philippa, Fish has to go out!"

I jerked to my feet. "Oh! Sorry! Sorry ... "

Boat train to Cherbourg
July 2nd

Dear Fish,

Be a good pooch now, and take care of your mistress. I realize that I have been very inconsiderate to leave her but then she has you take care of her. Make her talk to Tasha and Serge, who will console her by telling her how worthless I am. And be a good pootch and give my worthless love to my very sweet Kitten and a bit for yourself.

We just had lunch. What is more, Steve and I have been talking and we have both come to the conclusion that you are a very good egg, to wit, too good for me.

The crowd on the train is just lousy. I foresee a peaceful trip ahead, which

I really don't mind as long as we can get some exercise, play deck tennis, etc. So it will be like last time only better with Steve along. Wish us a bon voyage.

Goodbye, Darling, I must write a note to the Volkhovs. Sorry I didn't have time to call on them. See to it that you don't go all to pot. And look after my weezle-woof, Fish.

Love, Dick

Fish woke me late in the morning. I felt dull and lethargic. I knew I had to make some sense of my life. I must put the rest of my ring money aside. I had to make sure that when the time came to go home, I'd have enough money to get Fish and me to the boat and to pay for a place to stay in New York until I could find a job. And this was my lesson day with the Old Comtesse. There was someone at my door. I pulled myself out of bed. "Tasha! Fish, stop! Do come in."

Tasha sat down and put Fish in her lap and I got back into bed. I said, "I'd offer you coffee, but ... "

"*Nitchevo.* Little one, the Comtesse de B ... telephoned."

I had a sudden fright. My old Comtesse! "What's wrong?"

"She's worried." Tasha kept her eyes on my face. Her searching eyes probed mine. "She says if you will not go to your family or see a doctor she must talk to you."

"A doctor. But there's nothing wrong with me. What on earth is she talking about?"

"Little one, you must tell me the truth. The Comtesse says you are taking drugs. She is sure of it."

I was wide awake now. I said, "Drugs! Really! She must be out of her mind!"

"She says she can tell by your eyes. You come to her in a stupor. You sit and stare into space. If she speaks, you look at her but you hear nothing. Is that true? Are you taking drugs?"

"No! Of course not! Tasha, I'm a nurse. I've seen drug addicts. Once they start, they're ruined! I'm not such a fool! You must believe me. Besides, where would I get the money? Drugs are expensive."

"You wouldn't lie to me?"

I shook my head. "I do not now, nor have I ever taken drugs. I'll see the Comtesse today and tell her so!"

I was trapped. I had no place to go and nothing to do. I had to sit in this sad hotel room and wait. How long? For what? I should go home, get a job, forget all this. My head ...

336

The Comtesse wouldn't be put off. If it wasn't drugs, what was it? She summoned Tasha and her niece, the Duchesse, to investigate my recently abnormal behaviour.

Tasha came to see me afterwards. She was smiling.

I held my breath. "Well?"

"*Eh bien*! The Comtesse knows you're not on drugs. I had a long talk with the Duchesse before we saw her. I told her what had transpired between you and Dick and we agreed; your condition is not due to drugs but to shock. It was the Duchesse who defended you. She is your very good friend."

"But I barely know her! How could she defend me? What did she say?"

"You want it verbatim?" Tasha laughed. "It seems you are better known than you suppose. Gossip!"

"Oh. What did she say? Please!"

"She said, and I quote, 'all of Paris knows that Dick is insanely jealous. He wouldn't allow Philippa out of his sight. And both times when he sailed for New York, he hid her in a slum. It was only by chance that we discovered where she was living. Now this *Americaine*, the joke of Paris, out of some sick passion for him, has persuaded Dick that Philippa is after his money.'"

"'This female,' the Comtesse asked, 'Who is she?'"

"'*Quelle chienne!*' What a bitch, the Duchesse said. 'She's not important. You wouldn't know her.'"

"So much for Madame Stevens," Tasha laughed. "The Comtesse was angry; she has a high opinion of you. She turned to me. 'And you, Natasha, what do you know of this affair?'

"I told her you gave up Dick's name and his money and that as a reward for your generosity he has left you living in one room in the rue des Entrepreneurs."

I couldn't speak. I stood up and put my arms around her.

"Ah, little one, *pas de quoi*. It's nothing."

The following day, the Comtesse sent her chauffeur to summon me to tea and a private conference. She asked me to bring our divorce contract.

When I entered her drawing-room, she took a long look at me. She didn't greet me and she changed her mind about tea. "Well, Madame, it seems to me what you need today is a pick-me-up! An American cocktail would please you?"

I laughed. There was a bedrock understanding and liking between us. "Yes, thank you."

She nodded to her maid, who left the room. "This document, you have it with you?"

I handed her my copy of our divorce agreement and took my usual chair opposite her.

The butler brought manhattans–or something resembling them made with brandy.

I sipped.

The Comtesse drank her drink in two gulps while the butler waited. He took the glass from her, handed her another drink and left. She began to read. She took her time. She finished her second drink and turned to me. "The audacity!" Then she said, "We shall speak English so there will be no mistake. You were alone when you made this idiocy? No advice? No one?"

"Yes. I was alone but I have no intention of changing ... "

She stopped me with a raised hand. "Enough! How long have you been married?"

"It will be two years in November."

She was silent for a moment. "You know Bentham's family? He has an aunt in Paris."

"No."

"No! An old family, distinguished, very rich. I know the mother, Elizabeth. Betty is a pretty woman with a good heart; patrician. She will recognize you. Breeding cannot be disguised."

"Comtesse, please! I beg of you! I don't care. I shall be divorced. I want that."

"Hush! Marriage is important." The Comtesse rarely smiled. Now she gave me a sort of half-grimace. "Marriage. It is necessary, a place to hang your hat. No? We shall talk. *Attendez!*" She reached for her cane, stood up, limped across the room to the fireplace, and threw my divorce agreement into the fire. It went up in smoke.

I had no intention of trying to stay married to Dick but since I couldn't stop her, I might just as well hold my tongue. This regal old woman was my friend and I felt a sudden rush of affection for her.

"*Alors,* I have consulted with my secretary to know the amount of monies we shall elicit from Bentham in order to provide accommodation suitable for Bentham's wife. It is not our intention to alienate him. If you will be so kind as to read this prepared cable," she held out a slip of paper. "Which needs only his address and your signature and it shall be sent at once."

I stood up and took the cable from her. The "reasonable sum" was five times the amount of money I was living on. The cable asked for five hundred dollars a month, suggesting that if I'd had legal advice, it would have been mine automatically. I stood for a moment. Then I said, "May I have a pen?"

338

The Comtesse touched a bell. Her secretary arrived. The cable was on its way to New York.

Then she got down to brass tacks concerning men. The essential was a good marriage. How I accomplished that–while having *affaires de coeur* of my own–was to be practical with regard to the over-developed ego of the male. However brutal, that ego must be treated with delicacy, etc. The Comtesse ordered a light supper and continued with her information about the necessity, and the way, of controlling men. I had heard it before. In essence, it was the advice which Millie's mother, the whore, had given Millie.

Clay said, "I've phoned this place a couple of times but you're never in." He sat down on the narrow bed. He looked around the cluttered room: dog's dish, suitcases, papers ... "Hello, Fish," he said. "How are you? How's your French?"

"His French is fine," I said. "His accent perfect. Would you like to hear him?"

He looked at me. "Little Nell."

"The beggar? The match girl?"

"The orphan."

"Well, I'm not exactly ... "

"Would you like a day out of Paris, Nell?"

"The country? Where?"

"Well now, there's a magnificent cathedral in Rheims. I know how interested you are in seeing the sights. And there's a widow, name of Cliquot, who makes wine. We might go and let you look at the cathedral and drink the widow's wine."

"What about Fish?"

"Does he like cathedrals? All right, we'll take him along."

Outside of Paris, Clay pulled the car to the side of the road and stopped. He put his arm across my shoulder, leaned over and kissed me lightly on the cheek.

I said, "I've wanted you to do that for a long time."

He said, "I've wanted to do it for a long time."

We drove on, in silence. Towards evening, we stopped at an old inn. We dined leisurely. The food was good, we drank the widow's wine. Clay glanced at his watch. "Nine o'clock. Are you happy? We don't have to go back tonight."

Happy? No one had ever asked or cared if I was happy. I was astonished and touched. I said, "I'm happy."

"Do you want to go back to Paris?"

"I want to be with you."

"Wait, I'll get you a room."

He came back with a large, ornate, iron key and handed it to me. We walked upstairs together, stopped in front of my door. He hesitated. "Nell..."

"Don't leave me."

We stayed in Rheims two days. I wanted to stay for the rest of my life. I could not have imagined the tenderness, the fire, the ecstasy of love. When we started back to Paris, I kept my feet jammed to the floor–imaginary brakes–I fought against every inch of the road.

There was a wire for me from Alex, from Italy. It had come the day we left for Rheims. He was in Paris. I rushed to get a note off to his apartment to tell him I was sorry to put him off and to ask that he see me at another time. I expected to hear from Clay at any moment.

For the next ten or twelve days, I barely left my room. More and more depressed, I must admit that Rheims, to Clay, was not love but a sordid affair. I hadn't heard from him. I couldn't face Alex.

> *Paris, 1st August*
>
> *Philippa,*
> *I have received your note. Allow me to agree that you are indeed "horrible." I came back to Paris only to see you and I have been waiting for days, and you are still trop ennui? You cannot see me? Are you bored with me? You do nothing but read? You cannot be a friend to anyone? I cannot believe ...*
> *Allow me, nevertheless, to force upon you my very best wishes.*
> *Alex*

> *Paris, 4th August*
> *13 heure*
>
> *Philippa,*
> *I have received your message. I am sorry indeed that you are still ennui. Why, Philippa? What is it? I am concerned only for you. For me, you are the finest woman I have ever know.*
> *I wait, always.*
> *Alex*

I had expected a cable from Dick but he sent a letter.

Park Ave. New York
August 20th,

Dear Kitten,

I must say I was amazed to receive your very curt message. It's all very well for you to sit over there and cable me for money. But I'm the one who has to dig it up. What happened to all the cash I left you? It should have lasted much longer than this. I'm sorry, but I'm not going to send it. If you're so short of cash, you'd better send me an accounting of how you've spent it, and then I'll think about it.

I really don't want to seem hard, but it does seem to me ... Of course I'll send enough for next month, but don't think ... Take care of my snip-widget, Fish.

Love, Dick

I was in such a rage I forgot about my disappearing francs. I went out and sent Dick another cable. "How did I spend it? I bought a hat."

And now I had an abrupt, impersonal note from Clay. Directly upon our return from Rheims, he had left Paris. He was in London.

I knew what I must do if I wanted to survive: work. But I was without working papers and in no condition to cope with French bureaucracy. I decided to enroll in the school of journalism at the Sorbonne.

I had a letter from Pa. He was disgusted with me for running around, having a good time. Was there nothing serious with which to occupy myself?

I longed to talk to the old Comtesse but she had left Paris for her estate in the country.

At the Sorbonne, my French wasn't as good as I had thought, neither was my attention span. Armed with notebook and pencil, I arrived early for my first class. I took a chair about ten rows back from the speaker's platform. I didn't want to be noticed; I knew so little.

The students arrived. The classroom filled up. The professor walked on to the platform and began to speak. Pins and needles in my hands. The hard chair. My restless knees. I yawned. I couldn't sit still. I tried to concentrate on the mellifluous voice. My ears were stuffed with cotton; I couldn't distinguish one word from another. I yawned again. I wanted a cigarette, a drink. I stood up carefully and slipped out of the room.

It was clear outside and sunny. A fresh and gentle morning. I sat down on an empty bench and lit a cigarette. I began to cough; tears came to my eyes. I pulled out my handkerchief; wiped my eyes; wiped the perspiration from my forehead. I had paid for the classes. A waste of money. Useless, I couldn't go back. I threw my cigarette on the ground, stepped on it, got up and went back to my room.

341

Dick sent me the usual cheque for October.

And then I heard from Clay.

I hastened to write to Dick:

rue des Entrepreneurs
Paris 10 October

Dear Dick,

Because you insist it will complicate matters if I come home and because I won't stay here without more money, I have accepted Clay's invitation to drive to Spain with him. We leave in about ten days.

Philippa

Our luggage was in the car. We were ready to leave. Clay drove to the Place Vendôme and stopped the car. He held out his hands for Fish. "Hurry, Nell, I can't park here too long."

"There may be a letter from my father. I'll just be a minute."

I ran across the street and into the Banker's Trust. There was a cable for me. I opened it, read it and walked downstairs to the teller. "My husband cabled me money. Is it here?"

"Good morning Madame Bentham. One moment, please."

I waited.

"Yes, Madame, I have it." The teller counted out $250.

I shoved the money in my purse. "Thank you."

"Don't frown, Nell," Clay smiled at me. "We're heading south. We'll soon see the sun. Cheer up. You didn't get your letter?"

"No." I handed him the cable. "I got this, from Dick."

"Do you want me to read it?"

"There's no reason why you shouldn't."

HAVE CABLED MONEY BANKTRUST. DON'T LEAVE PARIS ANY CIRCUMSTANCES. LOVE DICK

Clay handed the slip of paper back to me. "I'm leaving for Spain in two minutes," he said. "Where do you want to go now? Home? I can put your things in a taxi."

"All this means is that I can pay my share. Half of everything. Hand me my dog."

He hesitated. "Are you sure?"

I said, "Let's go!"

31

It was November. The sky was gray and the air was heavy and cold. "It will be warm in Spain," Clay promised. "Sunny."

Our second day out of Paris, it began to rain. The canvas top of our Ford convertible flapped and shivered in the wind. The rain beat at the windshield, the transparent side panels, it leaked in and dripped on the floor.

Fish was restless, climbing over me, climbing over Clay. He smelled the damp earth, the trees, he wanted to be free. I fussed, petted him.

"You spoil him," Clay protested. "No one should dote on an animal the way you do."

When the rain stopped, we stopped. The road was empty so it was safe to let Fish off the leash. He tore into the woods, tore back, raced back and forth between Clay and me. We wiped the mud from his belly and paws and put him back in the car.

It rained. Shut away from the world, by this superb weather, I marvelled. We were miles from Paris, miles from Edgeville. Miles of straight road bordered by plane trees.

"Napoleon's military highway," Clay said.

Concentrate on the moment, I told myself. But thoughts I could not banish intruded. If Edgeville found out I'd run off with Clay, there'd be such a scandal I could never go home. Dick's shocking refusal to defend me against the Stevens' accusations. His monstrous assumption that I had married him for money. My monstrous behaviour to Fish. What had happened to me?

Clay, too, seemed to be having second thoughts. Beneath his amiable surface, I sensed a hidden disquiet. He was remote. Absorbed in unpleasant reflections or doubts? Could Dick name him as correspondent in our divorce? Had I prevented that by signing away my claim to Dick's property? Dick was unpredictable: jealous and brutally careless of my reputation. Clay had just finished law school; he had still to write his bar exams. A scandal at the beginning of his career would ruin him.

He talked about impersonal things. At times, apparently carefree, he sang or quoted verse. "Do you like poetry, Nell?"

John Keats, my love. Wary, I could not risk mockery of Keats. "Uh," I said, confused, "Why, I don't know," and at random, "Wordsworth, I guess."

"That bumbling old man!" Clay laughed. Then, disparagingly, "'A voice so thrilling ne'er was heard in Springtime from the cuckoo bird.'"

My talk, too, was facetious. I was tormented by my need to confide in him, but how impose my ill-timed, morbid, thoughts on this idyll? How confess my feeling of being trapped in a dubious situation?

At night we stopped at small inns, obscure hotels. If he was asked for our passports, Clay said, impatiently, "Yes, yes, in the morning." But in the morning, the passports were in the locked suitcases that had been sent out to the car. The French are lenient with lovers.

At night, our unacknowledged estrangement was vanquished by passion; we could not give enough, each to the other. At night, my fears, my doubts, the world, were all forgotten. Transmuted by his touch to rapture; in a delirium of joy, I loved him beyond consciousness. Yet our thoughts remained separate, harsh and private. Clay never said, "I love you." He never said, "Marry me."

At Biarritz, the rain stopped. We left the car at a big resort hotel and went down to the sea. Towering waves crashed over gray boulders. The beach was deserted; Fish went racing along the shore. "Fish!" I screamed against the wind. My feet were lead in nightmare terror of the rushing, foaming waves. "Clay! He'll be washed away!"

Clay ran, snatched Fish up and held him while I put him on the leash. "Nell, he's a dog, not a child. You're obsessed."

The summer guests had fled: the hotel was forsaken. We lunched in a splendid restaurant, empty except for a single waiter and ourselves.

Past Biarritz, except for an occasional trudging figure, the road was empty. "This is Basque country," Clay said. He began to talk about the people: the unknown origin of their unique language, their pride of race, their industry. "As emigrants," he told me, "they took their full part in the colonization of America. They were the first to establish the cod fishery off the coast of Newfoundland. Although provinces of Spain," he explained, "they are self-governing and independent." And then, laughing at his profession: "As a precaution against absolutism, no lawyer is allowed to be deputy to their Junta and all clergy are excluded as well."

We were going through a long, dark tunnel. Fish kept jumping from my shoulder to the back seat. I said, "Perhaps we should let him out."

"Yes." Out in the open, Clay pulled the car to the side of the road. I dropped Fish over the door and got out of the car. He sniffed, burrowed in the grass, flashed across the road, jumped up on a low stone wall and sat for a moment looking at me. Then he turned and disappeared.

I bounded across the road and glanced over wall. "Fish!" I screamed, but no sound came from my throat. Straight down. Precipitously deep, a roaring whirlpool of water. For one dreadful instant, that black head was thrust to the boiling surface. Then it was sucked under.

Clay was beside me–over the wall, hanging in space, searching for a non-existent footing. I caught his hands, braced my knees against the stone. "No!"

"Let go, Nell! Let go!" He swung back to the road. "I'll try further down."

High above it, searching, we followed the raging water. When the sheer rock was interrupted by vegetation, Clay crossed the wall again.

Helpless. Terrified for his safety, I stood on the road and watched him find his way down that precarious cliff to the water. He came back empty-handed. We never saw Fish again.

I wept: I wept on the road, in the car, in restaurants and hotels. My face was blotched and swollen. I couldn't stop. I wept tears of anguish. Shattered beyond control, I wept the lifetime of tears I had held back.

Clay made no attempt to stop me. And in dumb gratitude for his silence, I loved him more than anyone I had ever known.

At the foothills of the Pyrenees–in St. Jean de Luz–Clay asked a local policeman about our route.

The man stared at us in disbelief. "To cross the mountain at this season," he expostulated. "In an open car? Impossible." His shrug indicated his opinion of our sanity.

"How about it, Nell? Do you want to go back?"

"No."

"But the roads. Eh? There is snow on the mountain. Eh, *bien*. You won't get far!"

"If it gets too bad," Clay assured me, "we'll turn back."

We drove up and up the long ascent, through pools of water on muddy, rutted roads, in icy, pelting rain, in snow. We found shelter and food in impoverished inns. "I'm trying to remember," Clay said, "who said, 'Love is like a Spanish inn, the only thing you find in it is what you take to it.'"

We drove higher and higher. Far up the mountain the snow became dangerous. In a big resort hotel, closed for the winter, the caretaker prepared a bedroom, piled logs in the fireplace, set up a table in front of it and brought us food and wine.

We crawled, through snow and ice up along the face of the mountain. Near the peak, the road narrowed to a path just wide enough for the wheels of the car. Should we meet anyone, there was no room to pass. Rounding a long curve, suddenly, dead ahead, there was only sky. The road ended in space. Clay stopped the car. He sat for a moment, then opened the door and with extreme care, stepped out. He had barely room to stand. He said, "Wait here. I'd better take a look."

Far below lay endless, snow-covered wastes, ravines of jagged, jutting rock. An occasional scraggy tree lifted withered, snow-encrusted arms to the empty sky. On my right, rising straight up, the mountain. On my left, within icy inches, the edge of the cliff. Rigid with fear, I waited while Clay explored the road beyond my sight.

He came back slowly and got in the car. He didn't look at me. "It's a very sharp turn, slippery and narrow. Get out, Nell. Follow me on foot."

Get out? If the wheels slipped—even a fraction—we were lost. Get out? Watch Clay fall to his death? No! "If we're going over," I said, "let's go together."

He hesitated, turned to look at me, then turned to face the road. Under his breath, he said, "Yes." And slowly, cautiously, he put the car in gear and gently, inch by inch, eased the car around the curve ... And now we began the long descent.

After awhile, the ice and snow lay above and behind us. Around and below, as far as the eye could see, were the mountainous hills, great curving masses of bare, brown earth. Here and there, huddled in protective valleys, there were olive groves, vines, clusters of primitive buildings.

Late that night in a village—a single street of miserable rain-drenched huts—one hovel declared itself "Inn." Goats, chickens, a mule, wandered in and out of the kitchen that opened on the ankle-deep slime in the road.

On a rough table in the dim, candle-lit bar, we drank the harsh red wine, pushed aside inedible food. Forced to stay the night, Clay looked around our dingy, lime-damp room and, carefully enunciating the saccharine words, sang the current popular song: "In a little Spanish town 'twas on a night like this ... "

In the primitive bed, we forgot the world and everything in it. We were still in bed at daybreak when the proprietor, attended by half the village, opened our door and stood gawking at us. Did they think we were escaped felons? Who else would be coming from the mountain at this time of year? Clay sat up in bed. "My Spanish Beauty," he said, "I hope you're impressed. I arranged this just for you."

What impressed me was a man who laughed off embarrassment and difficulties, who didn't complain or blame or coerce me, who, even if it might mean death, did not question my right to my own decision. I said, "Please, ask them in."

At the foot of the mountains, we stopped overnight in a small town. Protected by the surrounding hills, the temperature and landscape had changed. The air was almost tropical and from the wide red-tiled balcony off our bedroom, we looked out on orange trees and palms.

But in Barcelona, the skies were still gray. Clay found a modest hotel in the city. He said, "Wait here. I'll be back soon."

Our room was poor, sparsely furnished. Cold light filtered through the high narrow windows. When he was away from me, it was as though part of me was torn away.

I took a bath and unpacked a bag. He had been gone almost an hour. What if he'd left me? One of these days he must leave. When that happened ... Perhaps he had gone to the bank. He had refused my money, but he must have spent a great deal. If I paid my share, I'd have nothing left when this was over. I'd be stranded.

That smug, patronizing look on Dick's face when he told me Clay had no money. Clay had no job and no income. This sojourn abroad was a gift from his family. Was he short of money, too?

Damn Dick and his penny-pinching! He made no bones about his opulent lifestyle–his many girl friends–while he kept me in penury. I had never lived in such squalor as he had forced on me when he left me in Paris. And all the talk from the Stevens about saving him from my mercenary clutches!

And what would Clay's Catholic family say if they knew he was running around Spain with another man's wife? The old Comtesse was right. Dick insisted that I stay in Europe so he must support me. I would insist that Clay allow me to pay my way. I had to wire Dick for money.

"Nell, let me in."

I ran to draw the bolt on the door.

"Were you asleep?"

"Thinking. How do I send a cable?"

"Do you want me to do it for you? There are forms downstairs in the office."

"Thank you. I'll manage. I'll be right back."

We were in Barcelona for a week. There were repairs to the car. Reluctantly, Clay accepted $150 from me. I knew it was not nearly enough. At the end of the week Dick wired me $100.

It had stopped raining when we arrived in Madrid. "Let's break the bank," Clay said. He drove to the best hotel in the city and parked the car. "I thought you might enjoy a slight change in your lifestyle. We'll get some rest, have a decent dinner and crack a bottle of champagne. All right?"

I sat still. My clothes were wrinkled, my gloves soiled, my shoes had been through a lot of mud and snow. I hardly dared face the desk clerk. And our passports–with different names. I said, "Get me a room alone."

"Yes. They'll insist on identification here. Come on, get out, I'll register for you."

I managed to climb what seemed like half an acre of steps while enduring the stares of a few hotel guests. Safe in my luxurious room, I took a bath and washed my hair. I pulled my beautiful black Balenciago cocktail dress out of the tissue paper and rang for the maid to press it. I found silk underwear, dug into my case for a pair of high-heeled pumps and one of my last pairs of silk stockings.

I sat at the dressing table and studied my face. It looked haggard. The lipstick? I put a film of powder over it. I looked ghastly! I wiped the lipstick off, put it on again. I sat there staring at my face. I hadn't seen myself for a long time. I looked … impossible!

"Nell," Clay opened the door and crossed the room to me. "Are you ready?"

At dinner, Clay frowned over his drink. "I'd thought of going on to Seville, but we were so long getting over the mountain, and the weather … Perhaps it's time we were starting back."

He was ending it. The thought of leaving him was unbearable.

"Did you give your room up before you left Paris?"

"Yes, but … " I must not let him see my dismay.

"Where will you be staying?"

"I … I can find a room. I know Paris." There was one thing worse than leaving him–staying if he didn't want me. "I mean, since it's just a case of waiting somewhere until my divorce, I can do that anywhere. I … I think I'll sit it out somewhere else."

"Do you want to do that?"

No protest? I said, slowly, controlling my voice, "There's all Europe. I … I mean, you've been around. Perhaps you could tell me where to go?"

"Do you ski?"

"No."

"Oh, you must learn! There's nothing in the world like it! Why don't you go to the Austrian Tyrol?"

On two cents a day? But what difference? I said, "Austria? That sounds interesting." I could go find mother's butchers, the Laubers, or perhaps her family. That would shake them. "What part of Austria do you recommend?"

"Any hotel will tell you where to go for good skiing. You know, Nell," he paused, "you've been looking ill, lately. I think perhaps a rest, away from everyone and everything, would do you good. And in the sun and snow you'll soon recover."

He wanted to be rid of me! I couldn't leave fast enough! I said, mildly, "I do feel a bit dull. Perhaps I can get a plane, or a train, from here, within the next day or so."

"From Madrid?" He hesitated. "Well, if that's what you want, but why not wait until we're on our way back? There'll be some place closer. I'll take a look at the map. Would that ... Oh, I forgot." He pulled a packet of letters from his pocket. "I picked up the mail. I have some letters for you."

"Thank you." I shoved them in my bag. "I'll read them later."

Back in my room alone, I was lost! Did Clay care for me the way I cared for him?

There were two letters from Tasha. There was also a letter from Dick. I opened the latter.

Park Ave.
Dec. 10th, 1932

Darling,

I've rather hoped for a letter from you these past few days. And now I feel very much disgruntled. So I sit down to write because I have had a bad conscience since last writing. I suppose I was very nasty.

Now, don't for a moment suppose I don't think you deserve to be spanked. I'd spank you just as hard now as I would have before. So abandon all delusions. You're an exceedingly naughty infant and probably need chastisement at the moment more than ever. So consider yourself soundly spanked!

Now, where are you? I don't know yet where to send this so will settle for Barcelona. Of course, I have given up all hope of a letter of information from you. Wherever I send this, it will probably hang around waiting for years.

Now I've said enough. The Europa leaves today. I'll try to get this on it and wait for the next boat and hope for a word from you. Incidentally angel, please let me know in advance in the future when you need cash. That little money cable to Spain cost me some six and a half dollars. No, not a fortune, but a little warning and it could be done as easily by letter.

Now listen, you woof in the bushes. I am getting on my tin ear. Just what do you mean by not writing? I know it costs you money to live, I'm not griping

about that. But I would like to have a vague idea of where it is going. Now don't get all mad. I don't mean to be nasty, but I do want to know what is going on.
Now, good night, be good and in spite of all,
Love, Dick

He was incredible! Not a word about Clay! But he had sent the money. It was strange that I couldn't stay angry with Dick. For some obscure reason, I felt, as he appeared to think of me, as though he belonged to me.

Leaving Madrid, we spent long days driving. Finally, the time had come. Clay stopped the car at a minuscule railway station. He looked up trains and bought me a ticket to Munich. I let him do that.

"Nell, you're alone, so go to the best hotel. It's out of season so you won't have trouble getting a room. The desk clerk will know where to send you for the best skiing. Nell! Are you listening? Go to the Vier Jahreszeiten. Promise me! Just tell the taxi. If you need anything you have my address in Paris. I'm not sure how long ... "

"I'll be fine."

"Just a minute." He reached for his wallet and handed me his card. "My address in New York."

"Thank you."

He said, "This time with you has been ... " He stopped.

"Yes."

"What about money? Have you enough?"

"Yes, really."

"Don't lose my address."

"No."

"Perhaps you should stay in Munich for a few days, get some rest, take a look at the museums."

The museums! The last thing I intended. "Perhaps I shall, but of course, I'm looking forward to skiing." I was wretched, torn apart at the thought of leaving him. I had no intention of going skiing.

"Well, good luck. Good skiing."

He was so terribly pale. I put out my hand and he took it. "Promise me you'll take care of yourself." He was so thin I'd begun calling him "Bones."

"Yes, and you ... "

I could no longer bear his touch: I'd fall apart and beg him to stay. I stepped back and he released my hand. I said, "Please drive carefully."

"I always do."

"Goodbye Clay."

He said, "I'll be seeing you."

"Yes." I turned away. I couldn't watch him leave. I started for the station platform. Without looking back, I lifted a hand in farewell.

I was calm on the train. In spite of the fog in my head, I had it all straight. I was to get off at Munich, go to the Vier Jahreszeiten, ask the clerk where to go skiing ... I had Clay's address in Paris, in New York. In Munich, with no hotel reservation, I must find a taxi.

But, strangely, there was no bother. The conductor handed down my two suitcases and I was standing on the platform thinking, I must find a porter, and fumbling in my purse for some kind of a tip, when a man approached me, hat in hand. "Milady, forgive. I have watched, but your car is not here? You wish a taxi?"

"Why, yes. Thank you." Where? Clay's hotel. The name eluded me.

He stooped to pick up my luggage. "You wish to go ... "

"The best hotel."

"Hotel? Not ... "

"Would you choose it, please? The best hotel."

"Yes, Milady, the best hotel."

When I signed the hotel register, the desk clerk turned it, glanced at my signature and turned pale. He looked at me. He was frightened! I said, "Is something wrong? Do you want to see my passport?"

"No! No, Milady, of course not! I send your baggage up at once. I hope you are satisfied. Right away!" He chose a key and, hastily, motioned to the bell hop to take me to my room.

I was tired and hungry. I barely looked at my magnificent room–God only knew what it would cost. I took a leisurely bath and changed to my second-best black dress, a Vionnet. When I entered the dining room, heads turned and the maître d'hôtel came rushing to me. What was wrong? Was something wrong? But he was smiling. He bowed. "Milady, one moment." He motioned to a very old waiter.

The old waiter bowed and smiled. "Milady is dining alone?"

"Yes."

"I take you to your table." And then, turning to me, he said, as though personally concerned, "Ach! Milady is alone. That is sad today."

I stared at him. He was a kindly old man, tall, a little stooped, but that odd expression on his face baffled me. He was too familiar. I said, coldly, "Sad? Why?"

"I only meant Milady ... " He dropped his eyes, turned his head away.

"It is better with the family ... "

The family! What could he possibly know about me or my family! The man was mad! Then it occurred to me. Perhaps it was some kind of local German holiday. I said, "What day is it?"

"The day?" He turned to look at me. He looked surprised.

"Yes. The day."

"Please!" He backed away and hastily pulled out a chair. He said, "Your table." He hesitated, bowed, his old voice quavered. "Milady, it is December twenty-fifth."

32

I couldn't sleep. Lying in that sumptuous bed–worried about the expense–I was awake half the night. A ski resort would cost a fortune. I had to get out of here, find a cheap hotel and get some rest. At half past seven I rang for coffee.

The clerk smiled as I approached the desk, then dropped his eyes. "Good morning, Milady."

"I wonder if you can help me? Do you know of a small, inexpensive lodge or hotel, in a village perhaps, where I could ski?"

He lifted his eyes. "Ach, yes. There's a small lodge in Obergurgl, above Innsbruck. Milady would find the kind of people she's accustomed to, but the route is difficult."

The kind of people? I hesitated. Was it because I was overtired that everyone in this hotel seemed a little strange? *Nitchevo*. "Please reserve a single room, no bath." His hands were trembling. "Are you ill?"

"No, no. It is just that I understand Milady's situation."

"You what!" Coldly. "What situation?"

He said, hastily, "Please, Milady. Forgive me. Please! I would not in any way embarrass Milady. We very much appreciate your patronage."

He was embarrassed because I couldn't afford a bath? What a kind man! "You may omit the title. I am plain ... "

"Of course," he interrupted. "It is on the register. You are Miss Philippa Jerrold from Canada. We know."

"I should like to leave Munich today."

He pulled a timetable from a rack. "Yes, good, there's a train. You must first go to Innsbruck. From Innsbruck you take a local train to the foot of the mountain and from there it is a nine kilometre climb to the village Obergurgl. Milady is sure?"

Nine kilometres up a mountain? It would kill me! And what about boots? But I had to get out of this costly hotel. I said, "I'd better think about it. In the meantime would you be kind enough to get me a room, without a bath, in a modest hotel in Innsbruck? If I decide to go, I'll reserve a room from there. And would you please prepare my bill?"

He was looking at me, his mouth half open. "You want to pay? But the suite is paid for."

"The suite! By ... by whom?" Then it dawned on me: Clay's insistence that I go to the best hotel. "What is the name of this hotel?"

"Milady? You don't ... It is the Vier Jahreszciten, Milady."

Clay had wired the money. "Oh! Thank you. I know who paid for it." How lucky that the taxi driver had brought me here!

He stood there beaming at me.

In Innsbruck late that afternoon a taxi was waiting to take me to my hotel. I had a room next to the bathroom in an elegant, small hotel and the service was swift, unobtrusive and quiet. The desk clerk in Munich had been as good as his word.

I stayed awake long enough to send my address to Clay and to Tasha and then I fell into bed and, except to get up and eat, I stayed in that room for more than a week. I could do nothing but sleep. I couldn't think; I didn't want to think. My life was a disaster.

Then one morning I opened my eyes and I was wide awake. The constant dull pain that had deadened my thoughts had gone. Perhaps subconsciously, my doubts had been removed. Clay could no more stay away from me than I from him. I would be divorced in April–in three months I'd be free–and then, his career no longer threatened by scandal, Clay would come to me.

I jumped out of bed, pulled on Abbie's robe, opened the french window and stepped out on the balcony. It was a magnificent day, the air sharp with ice and sun. I threw my arms over my head, stretched and took a deep breath. I must breathe, be alive again!

I stepped back into my room, closed the window and rang for coffee. A nine kilometre climb up the mountain? I would fly up! I was going skiing!

The waiter knocked and opened the door. "Your coffee, Milady, and the post."

En route
26th December

Nell dear,
Hope you made it all right. I've just stopped long enough to catch my breath. Still looking for the sun but there doesn't seem to be any in this country. If I can make it, I may follow you into the mountains.
Adios Senorita, keep your chin up.
Clay

Just rec'd your note. I've notified Tasha and your bank of your address.
C.

Dear Philippa,

Mrs. Stevens called to tell me you had been seen leaving Paris with Clay, so I could not deny it. She says you have ruined him and that you tried to do the same thing to Dick but, fortunately, Dick is getting rid of you. Please don't worry about this stupid gossip.

Clay came to see us. He is thin and sad. He said very little except ... Perhaps I should not tell you? "If she goes back to Dick, after this, it is over between us." It is very clear that he is in love with you. He spoke of nothing else.

Now, in winter, there are no tourists so our business goes badly, but nitchevo. You must not worry about that. We think of nothing but the day of your return, of the happiness of seeing you again.

The old Comtesse asks for you. She is not well this winter. Beatrice says she has feeling for you because you two are much alike. She's a great lady so you may feel flattered.

Let us know when you are coming back.
Love from us both,
Tasha

270 Park Avenue
New York

Dear Philippa,

Not a word from you as the Bremen got in this morning. I have waited in hope of a letter as I wanted to know your address in order to send you something for Christmas. As I haven't it, you will have to wait, but for the time being, I want you to invest in something nice for yourself, which would be foolish for me to send, owing to customs, etc.

I have sent Christmas cards to Beatrice, Tasha and Serge and, although he doesn't deserve it, to Alex. He wrote me a few weeks ago to ask for your address but since I don't know it ... Look, I know I owe Tasha a present, they've been good to you, but it's utterly foolish to send things from here, so when you get to Paris get something for them, take them out to dinner and the theatre or something of the sort. You will know what is best.

Now listen, will you come down to earth and tell me about yourself? All I can think of is, I don't know where she is, what she's doing, how she is or what she's thinking! So don't be upset if this letter is late for Christmas. I know that's not nice but it's your own fault.

It didn't occur to him to send me a cheque? I didn't bother to read the next page. I ripped it to shreds and threw it in the wastebasket.

Out in the town everything was fresh and sparkling in the icy air. The houses, the evergreens, the brilliant mountains ringing Innsbruck were all sharply alive under the shining sky. I ran towards the mountain into a park and stopped. A thousand swallows, gathering for their journey south, curved and darted over my head. I stared in wonder. A portent?

Running again and out of breath I stopped at a café to drink the Austrian-style coffee: hot with whipped and sugared cream floating on the charred surface. Today for me, I decided, was a new beginning: no more wishing and waiting, my life on hold, no more worry about love or love lost. I was going to an obscure village on the mountain to forget everyone, to learn to ski!

I wandered back to town to buy heavy woollen socks, ski boots, skis, poles, seal skins, wax, two cheap navy ski suits, two heavy white sweaters and a backpack large enough to hold it all, plus my few toilet articles. I would leave everything else in my suitcases at the hotel.

At three o'clock the next afternoon when I stepped on board that freezing, single-car train to the foot of the mountain, every seat was empty. I was balancing my skis at the end of the car when there was a rush of cold air from the door at the front and two people came in. I heard my mother say, "Don't be stupid. Shut the door."

I stood in shock. I was hallucinating! Then I turned and saw her. Mother! Wearing a sable coat, standing in the narrow aisle hanging on to the arm of an elegant, tall, blond man. Our eyes met and held for a moment. I couldn't imagine the expression on my face; I was stupefied! Her face was blank. She moved out of the aisle and sat down with her back to me and he followed her.

There were still some hours of daylight before we reached the foot of the mountain, and I couldn't keep my eyes off her back, but she didn't turn her head. When the train stopped it was dark and snowing and the two guides who met us were eager to start. One ahead and one behind–the three of us sandwiched between them–the guides set a fast pace up the snowy trail to the village.

At the end of the nine kilometres straight up, I was happy to glance up and see windows, luminous squares shining through a curtain of snow,

356

in a modest building. A door was flung open and our host stepped out to greet us. "Welcome! Welcome *Graf, Gräfin*, Milady."

She was a Countess. He ushered us into a large square room. The bare floors and walls of polished wood were warm from a glowing fire in the huge fireplace. A few people in ski clothes were sitting around the scattered bare tables. The proprietor smiled at me. "And you, Milady, will be taken care of at once." He beckoned and a maid came to show me to my room. It was good to be taken care of but ... was there no register in the Inn?

The maid drew a curtain over a high, minuscule, rectangular window and turned down my bed. "Milady, on this floor there is only one bath. You will please wait for your Lady-cousin? She is older."

My Lady-cousin! "Yes, of course."

"Good. I will come for you. Shall I send up a hot drink? Chocolate?"

"Please."

"Dinner at eight. You will hear the bell."

"Thank you."

My Lady-cousin. I sat down on the bed. It was a freak resemblance, an Austrian type? Except that from the moment I'd arrived in Munich every hotelier had treated me with the most unusual courtesy–believing I was part of her family? But she hadn't noticed me.

I drank my chocolate, had a long, hot bath, changed into my other ski suit and went downstairs. There were six or eight couples in the lounge. The women wore simple afternoon dresses. I was the only one in trousers. Ah, well, I hadn't come to compete. I ordered a martini. I might as well enjoy it. Whether or not I could pay for it was another matter. I knew Tasha would not have mentioned money, unless they were broke. Before leaving Innsbruck, thinking I would economize in this small village, I'd sent her half of my remaining cash. I ordered another martini.

The lounge had emptied before I went to the dining room. The waiter bowed to me, "A good table by the window, because Milady is alone."

My "Lady-cousin" and her companion were nowhere to be seen. There was no one at the table behind me. Was it theirs? Perhaps I could discover her name. I said, "Who will be sitting at the table behind me?"

"The Belgian Prince, Milady."

Money! I had a moment of panic. Judging by the clothes and the clientele, the rates here would be astronomical. Go back to Innsbruck tomorrow? And then I was in a rage! Was I supposed to run all over Europe looking for the cheapest hotel? I could hear my old Comtesse, "*Alors,*

Madame, with Bentham's money and his family's international banking connections, you have but to send him the bill." Until now, I'd been so reluctant to ask Dick for money that I'd accepted every indignity he'd imposed but, I'd had enough! He would pay this bill or I would refuse the divorce! No, not that! I'd think of something! The hell with him. I was starving!

"Milady?"

I ordered dinner.

The sun, slanting down from the narrow window woke me early the next day. I could hardly wait to put on my skis. I was alone on the beginner's slope and I was carried away. I couldn't believe it: keep my balance and keep my knees loose? That was all? At the end of the morning, I was going far too fast for the snow plough. Hans, the ski instructor, was teaching me the telemark.

I was at breakfast the second day when she came to my table. She stood–holding on to the back of a chair–staring at me. Face to face with that too familiar countenance, the shining black hair against the transparent, white skin, the curve of the eyebrow, the colour and shape of the eyes, I had a stab of pain. I knew her. This woman–her family–brutally careless if she lived or died, had disposed of my mother as though she were trash; kicked her out at seventeen.

She pulled the chair out and sat down. "I can't stand it any longer. Who are you?"

I couldn't take my eyes off her. "My name?"

"I know your name. Schreiber told me he'd been advised by Innsbruck, through our hotel in Munich, that you're ... " She stopped. "I rang Victor,the desk clerk at the Vier Jahreszeiten, he said he recognized you."

"The desk clerk? That's nonsense! I never saw him before in my life! You own the Vier Jahreszeiten? Who's Schreiber?"

"The proprietor here. We have a castle near Munich but we've kept a suite at that hotel for years. Victor's known us all since we were children. He knew you. That's why he put you in our suite."

"He what!"

"For God's sake! You told him you knew who paid your bill. Who are you?"

I hesitated, uncertain. I could hardly breathe. "Why would the desk clerk put me in your suite? I asked for a room." But the atmosphere in that hotel had been weird. The staff behaved as though they knew me. As though I ought to know them. And there was Victor's uneasy behaviour. Did he know about my mother–that she had been shipped off to Canada? How explain "*It's just that I understand Milady's situation!*"

She said, stubbornly, "Victor says he knows you."

"He's confused. That was the first time I ever set foot in Munich. When he told me my bill had been paid, I couldn't imagine who ... until it occurred to me that a friend had wired the money."

"Oh, would you mind? ... Perhaps I know her–or him."

"Really! That's none of your business!"

"I see. You must forgive me. But you really didn't know you were in my suite?"

No!" And then because, in bitterness and for years, my mother had mourned her "ruined" life, I lashed out at her. "But there may be some sort of rough justice in having someone in your family pay my bill." I stopped, acutely embarrassed. Why did I always blurt things out. "P-please ... I ... "

"Go on."

I caught my breath. I was trembling. "I ... I can't. I'm sorry. I'll pay for the room." I stood up. "Hans is waiting, I must go."

"Wait! Sit down. I don't want your money. We're related? Is that it? I believe it! When I saw you on the train I was stunned. I thought I'd seen a ghost–my late aunt–resurrected! But this has been happening for generations. I could show you ... "

"What? You mean your dead have been coming back from the grave?" My voice was going out of control. And then I sat down. I couldn't stand. That resemblance! I couldn't disassociate her from my mother. I said, slowly, trying to catch my breath, "Show me what?"

"The portraits. Ten generations back–or eleven–twins married twins, later cousins married. There's been much inbreeding in our family with the result that in almost every generation we have throwbacks. If you saw the portraits, I don't believe you'd deny your blood. I think Victor's instinct is valid." Then she said, gently, "He's concerned for you. He thought you were ill. You're very pale."

I didn't need the portraits. On the train, before I saw her, I had recognized the timbre of her voice. I said, "Did he know you'd be here?"

"Victor takes care of my mail. He always knows where to reach me."

He'd sent me to her! I was overcome by so many conflicting emotions that I thought I'd faint. I had to get away from her–compose myself. I stumbled to my feet and headed for my room and she followed me. I opened the door and fell on my bed in a passion of tears and sobs. Her soothing hand on me made it worse. When I finally stopped, she said, "Cousin, why are you here, alone?" I couldn't believe I had more tears.

She stood up. "Is it that bad? I hate tears."

"M-me. M-me, too!"

I turned my head. She was offering me a miniature, scented handkerchief. I sat up on the bed and looked at her. I couldn't stop the tears. I could feel my face twisting because I was laughing. "N-no s-s-sense of proportion."

"What? What's wrong? Take it!"

"What I need is a towel."

And then we were both laughing.

I got off the bed and washed my face.

"Perhaps I should go."

"No. I was rude. You look like my mother and I haven't seen her in more than two years. Besides I'm ... "

"Curious?"

"Very."

Isabeau–Gräfin von M–could not determine our exact relationship, but she threw a very different light on my mother's "ruined" life. "I can't think which of those old Viennese matriarchs threw your mother out, she must have been bedded but not wedded, otherwise there'd have been no problem. Not that I don't consider it a waste that a girl of her class was brought up by illiterates and then thrown to the wolves, but her breeding is such that she would survive in any society. In 1914-1918 your mother was safe in Canada with a husband and children and no one of an age to go to war. If she'd stayed in Austria, her life would have been ruined in a far more tragic fashion. But you don't want to hear about ... "

"About what happened in the war? What might have happened to my mother? Oh, I do! Please tell me."

"No. I want to know about you."

The last thing I intended was talking about my miserable situation. I said, stubbornly, "No, Isabeau. You first. I think my mother should know ... "

She began to laugh. She shook her head and I couldn't help it, I laughed, too. She said, "Good God, if I didn't know it before, I know it now. You're family, all right! Will you write to her?"

"That would upset her. I'll talk to her when I see her."

"What do you want to know?"

"Everything."

"Really? How much do you know about that war? Did it touch you at all?"

"But of course it did. Canada was at war. Three men from our village were killed and one came back without his right arm."

"But surely you must know what happened in Austria."

"In 1914, I was eight years old. I hadn't the perception to imagine what might happen in a war."

"And you mother's concern?"

"She was in tears, and that was strange because she has no tears. She thought Austria-Germany would win. Pa said they would not. He has little confidence in the German military mind."

"How perspicacious. And you were taught to hate us?"

"Not me. Pa said the tragedy of war is that it perpetuates hatred against the people, rather than those responsible for it. But ... what happened to you?"

"What shall I tell you? That I still have nightmares? That after all these years, there are times when I'm frightened to go to bed? If I tell you about starvation and death and being vilified by former friends, what does it mean to you except the usual horror stories that go in one ear and out the other because to dwell on them is to be sick. That's enough! Tell me about her. Tell me about your mother."

Absorbed in talk, we forgot lunch. When it began to get dark, we ordered tea. We had a late dinner in my room and at midnight, we went for a walk. Whatever our blood relationship, there was no denying a mutual feeling of familiarity and trust; the rapport between us was unlike anything I had ever experienced. When I left her to go to my room I was elated; aware of a mutual bond that could not be broken. But when I remembered–however much I wanted to stay in this rarefied atmosphere of aristocrat and royal skiers–that financially I was in over my head, I was crushed.

I had not written to Dick since I signed our divorce agreement; his persistently friendly letters had done nothing but anger me. He had wired a hundred dollars–complaining about the expense–when I cabled him from Barcelona. Arriving in Innsbruck, I cabled him again: FORWARD DOLLARS IMMEDIATELY BANK VEREIN INNSBRUCK. However much as that displeased him, Dick would send the money. Enough, perhaps, to allow me to stay a few more days. My mind at rest, I fell into bed.

I was asleep early the next morning when the maid woke me with his wire. It was short and shocking: NOT WITHOUT FULL WRITTEN EXPLANATION. DICK.

Enraged, I leapt out of bed. Explanation! Of what? I had my steamship ticket to New York. I found my purse. Did I have enough money for my fare to Southampton?

Isabeau knocked at my door and walked in carrying an arm-load of underwear. She had examined my wardrobe the evening before and declared it ridiculous! "We're climbing the glacier today and staying overnight at the..." She stopped. "I brought you ... "

"I have to go home."

"My God! Did someone die?"

"Not that, but I have to go today."

She threw the underwear on a chair and sat down on my bed. "You couldn't put it off till tomorrow?"

"I'd like to, but I have no choice."

"All right, out with it! What's going on?"

"My soon to be divorced husband has decided not to support me unless I ... "

"Money?" she said. "Forget it. I'll have Schreiber put your account on mine."

"Thanks, but no thanks."

"Is it because he has no money?"

"The greatest concern of his dearest friend is that I'll get my gold-digging hands on his fortune. His family ... "

"I see. Never mind. If he's not a complete fool, he'll pay your bills. If he doesn't, it doesn't matter. Money is the least of my worries."

"But I'm sick of being dependent. I have to get rid of him on my own terms!"

She said gently, "Is he important to you, cousin?"

I turned to look at her. In an inexplicable feeling of awe I felt the hairs rising on the back of my neck. I had never before experienced the solidity of family; Isabeau would protect me without question as though it were her right–or mine. I caught my breath. "No."

"Well, let's do the glacier and tomorrow we'll talk." She took the underwear off the chair and threw it on the bottom of my bed. "Don't drink too much coffee, be sure to pee pee before you leave, and I'll see to it that your clothes are warm enough."

Four of us climbed the glacier–the one Picard had landed on in his balloon a short time before. We stayed overnight at the top of it in a one-room hut. Isabeau insisted that we write Victor a note and at the risk of losing our hands, we did. It was so cold that, drinking straight from the bottle, brandy went down my throat without stinging, tasting like water!

"Americans are terrible snobs," Isabeau said. "Do you want this divorce? If not, come, stay at the castle and we'll ask him to visit. I'll give you a smashing wedding."

We were laughing.

I'd told her everything I could remember about myself, almost from the moment I was born–and because I knew it would not change things between us–even to my mother's distrust of me.

"She looks like us–like you and me?"

"Yes."

"That's the answer."

"What?"

"You are rivals for your father's affection. I'm willing to bet you're rather special to him."

"He's special to me, but that's nonsense. He can't bear her out of his sight. If she's away overnight, he walks the floor."

I told her about Millie, about Abbie's abortion and death, about the bootleggers, Holmes, Russia, my foolish marriage to Dick. I told her of my feelings of guilt about living with Clay on Dick's money.

"Be sensible! You're getting a divorce. Has he promised to remain faithful to you? Of course not! In effect, with this wire, he's trying to bring you to heel. He's left you penniless, or near it, and you know why? It's because you're alone, no family to protect you. With someone of an acknowledged position in society, he wouldn't dare. Don't go back to Canada. Live with us at the castle. My brother's children are there. They'd welcome you. We'll find you a good husband."

There were three in Isabeau's party and I made four. With so little practice on the easy slopes, I was not prepared to ski with them. Since they insisted, however, I went with them. There were long climbs up through virgin powder snow and swift schusses to the bottom. I followed recklessly and strangely, despite numerous falls, without serious mishap. Within a month, I felt nothing but exultation in the long swift runs.

Each brilliant sunny afternoon we lay nearly naked on deck-chairs in the snow, the torrid winter sun turning us to living bronze. When the sun dipped, the frozen air drove us indoors to a hot bath, an hour in bed with a book or, for Isabeau and me, long sessions of talk. In the evening we had cocktails, danced or sat idly talking. Perfect days, perfect evenings–except that I hadn't heard from Clay or Dick.

About the middle of February–despite the fact that I had not written to him–Dick sent me a thousand dollars. Towards the end of March, Mr. Roosevelt closed the banks and Isabeau insisted on paying my March bill in Austrian currency. And then, since I was to meet Dick in Paris on the 5th of April, and because I wanted to stop in Munich to see Victor before I left, it was my last evening in Obergurgl. There was a party for me with much champagne, much fun, much affectionate banter, and many promises to write and to meet again.

At midnight, Isabeau came to my room to urge me again to stay–to live with the family. I had become deeply attached to her, but however much I wanted to stay, it was essential that I get divorced. "If I ever get things straightened out," I promised, "I'll be back." I slipped off my shoes and sat down on the bed and she took the rocker opposite me. I said, "It's time."

"Time?"

"For the skeletons."

"What?"

"The skeletons in your closet. You promised to tell me about your war." I was pulling my stockings off, but at the silence I looked up. Her face was white.

"My dear that's an unfortunate choice of ... "

"Oh, I'm sorry! I didn't mean to upset you. Look, it's late, if you'd rather call it a day ... "

She hesitated. "No. Perhaps you're right. It may be time to throw out a lot of ... "

"All I meant was that I can't understand why you never married. What happened?"

"The war happened. In 1914 I had every intention of getting married. Since then ... I have never been sure with anyone else. With my brother's death shortly after the war, I felt it my personal responsibility to determine the future of the estate; I had little time or thought for marriage. But it *is* late, are you sure you ... "

"You think I'd rather go to bed than hear ... "

"All right, but for you to understand you must know what was going on before the war. Before 1914, although there were uneasy times, we had friends in every country, especially in England. In 1858 the Princess Royal of England married Prince Frederick William of Prussia. Their son, Emperor William, a frequent guest of Queen Victoria, attended her funeral in London in 1901. In 1913 the King and Queen of England came to Berlin to attend the wedding of Emperor William–the Kaiser's daughter, Viktoria Luise.

"I was twenty-five in 1914, thoroughly spoiled and selfish. My sister had married a Russian who had an appointment at Court and late that summer I went to Russia to stay with them. At one of the balls I fell in love. When we met it was immediate and it was certain, we knew we would marry. Since we both had connections in several countries and would have guests from England, Belgium, Italy and Russia, and because there was much to arrange before the wedding, we set the date for the eighteenth of September.

"I went directly to Paris with my sister, for clothes for my trousseau and for my wedding dress, and my fiancé went back to London. He was an Englishman. On the twenty-fifth of July, I went home to Munich and my sister rejoined her husband in Russia.

"On the first of August, Germany declared war on Czarist Russia. On the third, France entered the war against us, and on the fourth, England declared war on us."

"My God! Did you hate us?"

"I had cousins in England, Belgium and Italy, a sister in Russia. The feeling was horror at cousin killing cousin–even to Royalty. Queen Marie-Therese, in Munich, was considered by the Jacobites to be the rightful Queen of England. Each year on the date Charles the 1st was hanged they sent her white roses. Her son, Crown Prince Rupprecht, commanded the German Army Group.

"I had half a dozen letters and wires from my fiancé in England and then everything stopped, but news of him came through from neutral countries. He went immediately on active duty in the army. Incredibly, British officers led their troops out of the trenches, 'over the top', carrying a swagger stick and revolver! He was killed early in the second year of the war. My father died of pneumonia that year. And that year–the year of the Russian Revolution–we lost all hope of hearing from my sister. We never did hear of her or her husband again.

"The young and the able-bodied men were called up early for the army. My mother and I were alone, trying to manage the estate. From the beginning, I took care of the stables. They had one advantage: in the winter they were warmer than the castle. But shovelling manure makes you thirsty. I developed a passion for tea. To this day, if my cup isn't filled to the brim I feel cheated. In the third year of the war, with the British blockade, Germany was starving. In Berlin, the meat ration per person, per week was eight and a half ounces; it was eight ounces in the provinces.

"We had no one left on the farms but children and the aged, and working with those truncated families my loyalties changed. I was no longer devoted to myself. It is agony; against every instinct to put food in your mouth if children are hungry. And then it seemed that every nation in the world turned against us–even China." She stood up. "Does that convince you that your mother was lucky to be in Canada?"

In the morning Isabeau and a whole group skied down the mountain with me and waited to put me on the train. I picked up my suitcases in Innsbruck and went directly to Munich where Victor and his wife greeted me with a great deal of warmth. It was Victor's brother in Vienna who had put Mother on the ship that carried her to Canada. It was Victor's wife, at that time my grandmother's personal maid, who had dressed Mother and packed her clothes. They were fascinated to hear of Mother and wanted every detail of her life, as well as my own, but they did not tell me my grandmother's name. Victor said, "I leave that to your mother. She knows it." I left, feeling them unexpectedly close and dear to me.

Tasha and Serge met me in Paris and took me to their apartment where I stayed overnight. Dick had not yet arrived. In the morning, I telephoned his lawyer to find out when he was expected.

"But Madame! Mr. Bentham informed me there had been a reconciliation! He is not expected. Surely you ... "

I dropped the phone. Then I rang the steamship company and arranged my passage to New York. Tasha saw me off, weeping.

Just before I stepped on board, I wired Dick to meet me.

33

He was waiting for me as I came through customs. I had long since lost my anger against him but not my determination to be rid of him, but as always with Dick there was an inescapable feeling of family. Irrationally, I was glad to see him.

"I have a porter for you." He took my hand luggage. "You realize you've come at an inconvenient time? Who's the louse you were kissing on the ship? My God, Kitten, you're beautiful!"

He held my hand all the way to the hotel–the Plaza–registered me as his wife, sent my luggage up, followed me to my room and reached for me.

In a sudden rage, I shoved him out of my way. "You bastard! You left me stranded in Europe. You're contemptible!"

He stepped back, his face white. "Just a minute! You took off with Clay. What did you expect?"

"I didn't expect to be abandoned."

"But you put me through hell! You dropped me without a word! You're cruel! I couldn't believe the minute you signed that divorce agreement, you'd spoil everything."

"That divorce agreement left me dependent on your charity! If you thought I'd still be at your beck and call you were hallucinating! Enough! I want you to go."

"What! What are you talking about? I won't go! If it's that stupid paper, forget it. I had no intention of leaving you. I never dreamed you'd leave me! Half of Paris knew you'd gone off with Clay. How do you think I felt? Think how it looked! And then you vanished! I didn't want to hurt you, but what could I do? I thought if you were really short of money, you'd write."

"You had my cable didn't you?"

"Well, I'm sorry, it upset me. After everything we've been to each other, all you did was demand money. I think you owe me an explanation."

"I owe you nothing."

"But you dropped me without a word!"

"You're insane! You dropped *me*! And then to be ordered around and left without money the minute you got what you wanted? Do you think I'd submit to that?"

"Darling, please! I can't think why I started that nonsense in Paris. Look, I've something to tell you, important to both of us. I know it will make you happy, I ..."

"Enough! I don't want to hear it. You've imposed on me for the last time. You kept me in Europe at your convenience. Now I intend to divorce you at mine–the minute I get to Nova Scotia."

"That's ridiculous! You can't divorce me in Canada. I stopped proceedings in Paris–didn't it occur to you that I don't want a divorce?"

"It occurred to me that you're an arrogant, calculating bore! Determined to keep me under your thumb."

"That's insulting! I called it off, because of you! *You* didn't want a divorce! That's why I changed my mind!"

"Your convoluted, reversible mind? You'll change it again tomorrow. But I haven't changed mine. I'm divorcing you."

"Oh, Kitten, be reasonable. You're not divorcing me and you know it." He came to me and took my hand playfully–tried to raise it to his lips. "You're joking. I know my bed-yabbit, she's all mine."

I snatched my hand away. "No more."

"Kitten surely you forgive me–or you know you will. So, what's wrong?"

"Everything. Why don't you go? You said I'd come at an inconvenient time."

"I was miffed. Please don't punish me for that. I only said it because you didn't let me meet you in Paris."

"Dick, it's over. I'm in love with someone else."

"I don't believe you."

"You'd better, it's true! I want you to go."

"D'you think you can discard me like a used ... "

"The way you discarded me?"

"Darling, that was unconscionable. I won't forgive myself, but please don't try to put me off by pretending you love someone else. How can you!"

"It happens to be true. So go!"

"Will you stop it?"

"Shall I call the desk–have them throw you out?"

"Kitten, wait. Who is it? Alex? Is that buzzard still chasing you? I haven't seen Alex since ... "

"Clay! You were with him for weeks. He looked guilty as hell when he got home. Did you have an affair with Clay?"

"How dare you!"

"Oh, Kitten, I'm sorry. I know you wouldn't do that to me."

"I take it you never looked twice at anyone else."

"Oh, I looked. But did it ever occur to you that I might feel married to you?"

"I don't feel married to *you*! I'm in love with Clay and I have every intention of divorcing you as fast as I can ... "

"So it *is* Clay! Has he asked you to marry him?"

"No, but as long as I'm living around ..."

"That's shocking! You're my wife!"

"Pro tem! Does that sound familiar?"

He was angry. "That was a long time ago. In spite of everything, we're still married. Look, I won't live without you. D'you realize how I've suffered these past months, not knowing ... "

"How I was living in hotels without money?"

"Oh, God! Stop it! I made it up to you, didn't I? Do you need money now? Look, forget it. I have something ... I didn't intend telling you till later but ... " He took a small velvet box from his pocket. "I've been thinking, if you're worried about Russia—the legal thing—we can be married again right away, here in New York, tomorrow. Please, darling, this is for you."

I backed away. "No! I'm leaving tomorrow for Nova Scotia."

"But surely you don't intend to walk off and leave me. Darling, please! I want you to take this."

"No!"

"You mean you won't even take ... "

"No"

"Oh, Kitten, do you hate me that much?" He turned his head away, sat down on the bed and put his face in his hands.

"For God's sake, Dick, I don't hate you."

"I know. Uh ... just a minute." He reached for his handkerchief and I saw the tears. He wiped his eyes. "I'm sorry. I didn't mean that. I know you don't, but since you left ... I don't think I can ... "

Did he really love me? Too bad! I felt maliciously gratified. And then I was touched. "Dick, I don't want to hurt you, but ... "

"I know. I'm sorry. I haven't slept. I've been worried to death. I love you and no matter what I did, I believe you feel the same way. When I left Paris—realized what I had done—I was utterly wretched. Since then, no matter where I go, I can't be bothered with anyone or anything. If you leave me again, I know this sounds crazy, but I don't want to live. Kitten, listen to me, I have a question for you. Do you or don't you feel we belong together?"

I hesitated, suddenly sober. The feeling I had for him ... Was that what happened in marriage—that the stupidities and grievances could not destroy the bond? From the moment we met in Moscow, for the most part, I'd been happier with him than with anyone ... until Clay. "If you'll not misunderstand ... "

"I won't."

"I have some sort of feeling of affinity—of kinship for you—but as for love ... "

"That's it! I don't care what you call it. You know what I mean. It's happiness in just being together that makes everything else worthwhile. Oh, Kitten, I must have been out of my mind. When I think what might have happened to you. Please talk to me. Please don't be cruel. I'll go if you want me to, but please have dinner with me this evening."

"My knees were shaking. I couldn't take any more. I'd been in a constant state of anxiety for a long time. I felt faint. I should have had lunch on board ship but I'd been too nervous to eat. "Dick, I'm terribly tired. I have to get out of here—arrange for my trip, pick up tickets, so please leave."

"Are you ill? You're dreadfully pale!" He reached for the phone. "I'll have them send up tea. You get some rest. My car's here, I'll pick up your tickets. I'll have everything ready for you. I'll pick you up about seven-thirty for dinner."

I had dinner with him. I barely touched the food, watching Dick. Dick at his most charming. What a handsome man. I couldn't credit his love of me but what was constant between us—our ease in each other's presence—finally brought me to some kind of peace. But I was emotionally drained and physically exhausted. I wouldn't allow him back in my room.

He put me on the train in the morning, still protesting his love and insisting that we be married again. And then, just as the train was pulling out he said, "You know the one about 'All's fair in love and war,'" and handed me a packet of mail. When I'd left Paris with Clay, Dick had notified the Paris bank to send all my mail to him in New York. There were two letters from Clay.

Washington, D.C.
January 10th

Dear Nell,
Your note from Innsbruck was very gratifying. It's great to hear you're going skiing. I know you'll love the mountains.

370

What becomes of the divorce plans? Skating back to Russia? A Paris divorce? Or no divorce at all? I suppose you and Dick have reached some kind of a decision.

My Spanish beauty, I think of you often. I think of heaps of happy hours in happy places. I suppose I have no right to think. But at least I deserve a few lines about what you're doing and why. Everything of the best to you.
Clay

Washington, D.C.
February 15th

Dear Nell,
I wonder if you've had my letter? Since I didn't have an address after Innsbruck, I sent it to your Paris bank. Are you still in Austria? I do want to hear from you.

This, as you probably know, is the first time in many a long year that I haven't planned some foolish adventure that would put a few thousand miles behind me. I can be philosophical about it–argue that it's the best thing–but I'm feeling a bit lost and cheated. Anyway, I must stay put for awhile. I am now devoting my legal mind to being a cog in a big machine.

But anyway, I am single. The chances are I'll remain so for a long time. Beyond that there is little to say. Without an objective in view such as marriage, I duck any maudlin talk of love and kisses etc. It is far easier to keep things on a plane that is not too serious until the cards fall the right way. At any rate you will know as soon as anyone what happens, and you can let it ride until then.

I was interrupted and now I don't know where I was or what I've said. It makes no difference really since I'll have to quit in a minute. Be sure my regards get to Tasha and Serge, if you're still on that side of the world.
Take care,
Clay

I read them over and over. He intended to stay single for a long time? He refused to talk of love because he had no intention of marrying me? Dick's affairs were front page news. Was Clay too frightened to commit himself to me for fear of scandal? Clay could not afford a scandal at the beginning of his career. I knew that and yet I despised his caution. Unless he was a consummate actor, I knew he loved me. I felt a disappointment close to despair. I longed to be with him.

Leaving Boston–before boarding *S.S. Evangeline* for Yarmouth–I sent Clay a brief note: I was on my way to Nova Scotia but I should be in New

371

York within the next few weeks. A letter c/o the Nurses Residence would reach me eventually.

In Edgeville, I was standing on the step as the train pulled into the station, watching Flora and Sue who had come to meet me. And because it had meant so much to Isabeau, I really looked at them. There was a remarkable resemblance in all of us. As I stepped down to the platform I said, "You look exactly like me!"

Sue burst into tears and ran.

I stood, uncertain whether to kiss Flora or hold out my arms, but she made the decision for me.

She motioned to a boy to take my suitcases and turned away. "Come on, we have the car."

"Where's old George? Is he all right?"

"What do you care?" Flora kept her unsmiling face firmly fixed on the road.

Mother opened the door. That striking resemblance to Isabeau! She was pale and thin. "Hello, Mother."

"Hello, Philippa." She stood, looking at me for a moment, then she moved aside. "Take your cases to your room."

I took my luggage upstairs, opened my door and Martha leapt off the bed, grabbed me, and knocked us both to the floor. "You're home!" She was breathless. "I could hardly wait! But, Pill, you're in trouble!" Mrs. McCarthy was spending her day off with her daughters and Martha had to run and fix supper. She didn't have time to tell me about my trouble.

I looked out of the window and saw Pa coming along the sidewalk and I went downstairs and outside to greet him. "Hello, Pa."

"Ah, Philippa, you're home." He stopped for a moment. Then he passed me and went into the house.

"Ah, Edgeville," I muttered, "I'm home."

The unanimous, indifferent family welcome made me feel snubbed and threatened: an attack on me was imminent! I had intended telling Mother about Isabeau, asking Pa to help me with my divorce, but their inimical attitude made it impossible. How many times had I sworn I would never come home? I went to my room and somewhat irresolutely began to unpack. I hung up a few dresses and stopped. I had to get out of here.

At supper, bracing myself, my face a blank, I forced myself to eat. I expected a barrage of questions but no one spoke to me. Pa had a book, Mother was silent and Flora and Sue were talking about clothes. When the telephone rang and Martha told me Mrs. West wanted me to come for

372

breakfast the next day, I was glad of an excuse to leave the table.

Martha had a date with Lester. Flora and Sue had disappeared. I was the local pariah. I wished that somewhere along the line I had learned to really cry. I had to get out, get down to the woods. I'd wait until the house was quiet. I lay down on my bed.

I woke from my dream trying to break my fall, shaking, disoriented. Where was I? Paris? New York? I was still in my clothes. Then I remembered. Edgeville. I found a sweater and crept down the back stairs and out to the woods. The birds were waking, the woods hushed. It was getting light. I went back to the house.

Mrs. McCarthy, her teeth in a saucer, an old sweater over her night-dress, was sitting at the kitchen table dunking bread in her tea. She turned when I opened the door. "You're home! Well, now, you just set right down!" She put out a hand, patted me and poured me a cup of tea. "What divvlemint be yez up to now?"

"Hello, Mrs. McCarthy. I missed you yesterday. How are your girls? Tea! Just what I need." I sat down. The tea was hot and strong. I added milk and sugar. Mrs. McCarthy's India tea–not Pa's smoky szechuan with those "un'natrul" slices of lemon! It somehow restored me. And Mrs. McCarthy, my old sparring partner, was happy to see me.

"The girls is fine. I hear tell you took off from your husband." She leered at me. "I always said you got guts! You don't let no man get the better of you, huh? The same as I'd do meself. Let them worry. Don't forget to say hello to Miz Porter this mornin' She knows you're home."

I swallowed my tea. "I needed that, Mrs. McCarthy. Thank you. Now I must run. I'll see you later." I stood up, shaken. I had never told them that Dick and I were living apart, never hinted at Clay. How could she possibly know I'd left Dick?

It was a beautiful spring day–warm enough to have breakfast on the veranda. Dr. West had waited to see me. He gave me a hug, then took a look at me. "Lovely Philippa. Sit down and eat, you're too thin!"

Mrs. West said, "Dear child, the strain on your face! Do you want to tell us why?"

When the doctor left, I swore her to secrecy and told her.

I left her feeling relieved; almost happy. Mrs. West had persuaded me to talk to Pa; she knew he would understand. I was ready now to talk to him, and to stay for a time. At home I went upstairs to unpack. I opened the door to my room.

Flora was sitting on my bed. She had my passport in one hand and

Clay's letters in the other. The contents of my purse were scattered over the counterpane. I felt a sudden jolt–my heart–"You're reading my mail!" I ripped the passport and letters from her hands. I said, shocked, "Wait till I tell Pa!"

"Try it. You think he'll believe you? After all your lies?"

One suitcase had been opened, the contents strewn over the floor. I picked up Abbie's silk robe; it was soiled and limp with age and wear. I hadn't washed it since Obergurgl. I was in a rage. "You've been going through my things! Did you have to throw them on the floor? What are you doing here! Get out!"

You were in Spain with another man." Flora began to giggle but she got the word out. "Whore!"

"You unscrupulous fool! You have the audacity to sneak in here and read my mail? Wait till I tell Mother."

"Oh good." She tried to stop giggling. "She's on her way to Pa right now."

"What! What did you tell her? You had no business ... What did you tell her?"

"Nothing! I didn't have to. It was Mother! She went through that suitcase like a bat out of hell–picking things up and dropping them–you should have seen her. She kept saying, 'Look at these rags!'" Flora stopped giggling, her voice was clear now, in contempt. "I wouldn't be in your shoes if you paid me. She took a look at your passport. You name's not changed. Were you ever married? Where's your wedding ring? Mother knows you're a whore! How dare you come back here! You're crazy!"

"Get off that bed and get out."

"When I'm good and ready. Does Dick know you're here?"

"You despicable half-wit. Get the hell off my bed and get out! Dick's my husband. He always knows ... "

"Liar! He didn't know where you were a month ago. He phoned Pa, said he'd mislaid your last address. He wrote at Christmas, too, from New York, when you were writing from Spain. How come you never mentioned you were separated? You've got some nerve walking in here pretending innocence. You're a whore!"

I took a quick step towards her. "You want me to throw you out?"

She scrambled off the bed, backed away. "And don't try to get next to Sue, she's ..." Flora got out and slammed the door.

I started to pick things off the bed, slipped and collapsed to the floor. My knees felt like chilled water. I wanted to stay there and die. Flora had knocked me off balance, but before I left this house I would have a final showdown with Pa. I got to my feet, trembling. I had to pack and get out. There was someone calling from the foot of the stairs. I opened the door.

"Are you deaf up there? He says he's your husband."

I went downstairs and took the receiver from Mrs. McCarthy's hand. She stood at my shoulder. "Just a minute. I want you to know–like I told Miz Porter–you don't have to believe all you hear in this house. If you ask me some of them knows too much for their own good. They should leave you alone!"

"Thank you Mrs. McCarthy."

It was Dick. We settled it in minutes. He would expect me in a day or so. I was to go directly to the Plaza.

It was midnight before I finally found Pa alone. He was lying on the couch reading. "Pa ... "

He didn't take his eyes from his book. "Yes, Philippa."

"I've come to say goodbye."

"Yes?" He was still reading.

I said, loudly, "Pa, I'm leaving in the morning, for good–for the last time."

He looked up, startled, "You've just arrived."

"You noticed? I thought I must have been invisible, or disowned."

"Gad!" He took his spectacles off and sat up. "Don't talk nonsense. You're my daughter."

"Your immoral, licentious ... "

He slapped his book on the table and stood up, "Philippa!"

"Your daughter, the whore?"

He stared at me for a moment. "Flora?"

"Yes."

"Sit down." He touched me gently on the shoulder, indicated a chair and sat down opposite me. "How many times must I tell you ... "

"That Flora's a fool? Flora has destroyed my credibility in this house." And in a sudden and violent rage, "And so have you!" I stood up. "I won't wait till morning. I'll go now!"

"Sit down."

"I've had enough!"

"Philippa, sit down. If you walk out now, the breach with your mother will never be healed and I'll never have peace of mind."

I said, bitterly, "I've never had peace of mind in this family since I was born."

"You're right."

"What!"

"You're quite right. And in many ways, I'm at fault. There's been a senseless, primitive prejudice against you since you were born. Sit down."

I sat down, stunned, uncertain. "I don't understand."

He hesitated. I'm not sure I can make you understand." He was uneasy. He stood up, began to pace the floor. "It's bothered me for years. Now ... " He stopped to stare at me. "If I speak, I violate your mother's confidence. I must trust to your good judgement that what I say remains between us. Do I have your word?"

I said, bitterly, "You astonish me! You'd trust it?"

"I trust it–and you."

"Well, you have it, but if you're about to tell me my mother hates me, you're not violating her confidence. I'm well aware of it."

"Your mother loves you. At the same time, she distrusts you."

I said, desperately, "But why? What have I done?"

"Nothing. You are not to blame. And, strangely, neither is she."

"That doesn't make sense! She's shown me over and over that she has no use for me."

"It's not you." He hesitated. "Your mother has a problem. The basis of that problem is grotesque. Your mother believes in the transmigration of souls."

I felt the hair rise on the back of my neck. "W-who does she think I am? W-who am I supposed to be?"

He stopped pacing, stood in front of me. "Please understand, it has bothered me for years, your right to know. Now, I think it's time." He hesitated. "However fallacious this superstition, in her case, it cannot be denied. Your mother was brought up by ignorant peasants and well inculcated in this lore, she ... " He turned away, started pacing again.

"Please go on."

"She rarely speaks of it now, but you remember that at seventeen she went to Vienna to find her family?"

"I could repeat that story word for word."

"Yes. Well, during those moments of extreme emotional trauma when she was physically ejected from her mother's room, her mother's face–the eyes–became indelibly impressed on her mind. She relived that episode in nightmares for a very long time."

I was shivering, I sensed what he was going to say. Isabeau's eyes, my mother's eyes, *my* eyes ... were unreasonably alike. My grandmother's as well?

"At the time of your birth your mother went into shock; the melancholia that occurs in some women after childbirth. She was convinced,

376

because of your eyes, that her mother had been reincarnated in you."

"You're right, it's grotesque! But ... I must be a perpetual nightmare to her! Only who believes in reincarnation?"

"About two thirds of the population of the world. The Chinese peasant beats his horse with a good conscience: the animal is an evil person returned to earth in a lower form."

"That's shocking!"

"The whole thing is shocking. I was determined to stop that nonsense. There was no reason to believe her mother was not alive. Liza comes of an ancient and prominent family. I made enquiries through the British Embassy in Vienna." He stopped again.

"And?"

"Leeza's mother had died in childbirth about three months before you were born."

"God! Did you tell her?"

"And further alienate you from her? You know better. You must understand. This is an *idée fixé* with her and there is no logic that can erase it. Further, the fact that you were so different from the other children reinforced her belief."

I felt sick. "Different?"

"Precocious. You very early exhibited a mature discipline and independence. At the age of three you refused to believe Liza was your mother. At the same time you stopped crying. Liza could not control you and as a consequence you turned to me. I became your mentor and your confidante. As the one permanent influence in your life I must assume—whatever your moral character—I am responsible. As well, you are the only one of my children that I understand. To quote Sue," he smiled, "'I know what makes you tick.'"

"I took a deep breath. "Pa, Flora told me how you found out that Dick and I were no longer living together. Did you know I took a lover?"

"Your mother mentioned it. It seems she has looked quite closely into your affairs—without your consent."

"Do you think me obscene?"

"I know you are not."

"You are sure?"

"I would stake my life on it. I know you will make decisions without reference to convention, but you're no fool. You will have your reasons. I sense you have no shame and no guilt."

"And you don't condemn me?"

"No."

Tears in my eyes. For a moment I couldn't speak. "Thank you. But how explain your indifference to me–until now?"

"Ah, my indifference. Liza insists my ideas have wrecked your life, that it is because of me that you flout convention. Liza is aware that over the years her resentment of her mother has at times been unjustly transferred to you and she regrets it and blames herself. Now she insists she must deal with you herself, and I have no option but to support her. My 'indifference' is to indicate to you the depth of our displeasure at your scandalous behaviour. Liza is deeply concerned for your future. I trust that when she speaks to you, you will remember her guilt: the torture she has suffered for her aberration, and that she is fragile. I depend on you to do what you can to ease her mind."

I stood up. I could hardly breathe. Pa had just made me responsible for my mother's future happiness. I must leave. I had no intention of being instructed as to my future behaviour by Mother. I started out of the room.

"Philippa, wait! Will you confide in me? If you feel you can discuss it, I should like to know about your quarrel with Dick."

I hesitated, then turned back. I had come home to talk to him ...

In what turned out to be an all-night session; since he neither offered advice nor pressured me, and because of the rapport and love between us, we established a mature and solid relationship. He didn't want me to leave, but he didn't try to dissuade me, and he tried twice to give me money. I had no intention of taking anything from him.

At six o'clock, old George arrived to take me to the train.

Pa put his arm around me and walked with me to the door.

"When I've arranged my divorce, I'll come back and talk to Mother. I'll be in New York–the Plaza."

"Write to me."

"Yes."

"Drive carefully, George, she's a special child."

Old George tipped his cap. "Sir, I allus knowed that."

In New York, unwilling to make a final decision, I didn't phone Dick. Flora's poisonous attack haunted and enraged me. She would hasten to enlighten Geoffrey as to my scandalous behaviour. Sue had avoided me. I couldn't sleep. Shards of pain for Mother kept me awake and restless: if I divorced Dick, my reputation tarnished beyond repair, she would never believe I had been married; I could say a permanent good-bye to her, and except for Pa, to the rest of the family. I hoped against hope that Clay would rescue me: If Clay admitted that he loved me, whether or not he asked me to marry him, I would divorce Dick and go to him.

When his letter came I walked to Central Park and sat down on a bench.

Washington, D.C.
April

Nell,

Just a note to thank you for your belated report. It was damn meagre and I'm baffled as to what's going on and why. Without wanting to be nosey, may I ask whether you're still married. Just what is the status?

Would it be too much trouble sometime to swallow a cocktail or two with me on one of my rare trips to New York if I let you know I was coming? Have you a telephone?

Busier than blazes in Washington with the affairs of the nation—it's such a big nation despite it's large quota of small people.

Always, Clay

I didn't answer that letter.

A week later, ignoring the fact that I didn't love him, Dick persuaded me to marry him again. And so, in a private ceremony, in the presence of his mother and two cousins, our marriage—whether or not it had been before—was now legal.

My old Comtesse wrote that she had received my news with delight, and to my mother-in-law, Betty, that I must be a gem *précieuse*. She was right about that: to Bette, a great lady and a loyal friend, I was never "daughter-in-law," but always, "My daughter, Philippa."

At her own request Flora came to visit Dick and me in New York. She was concerned about our differences in the past. "We have to put that childish nonsense behind us. We're adults now."

Isabeau sent me a very beautiful emerald ring that had belonged to my grandmother. I had not told Mother about her and in the end it was too late.

Alex wrote. He was still living in France but concerned about Italy and Mussolini's blackshirts.

Mrs. Stevens came to lunch. She was "delighted" about our marriage and told Dick, privately, that she was astonished at how much I had changed.

Within the next few years, with Hitler beginning to dominate Europe and the subsequent falling off of tourism, the Volkhov's business began to

379

fail and, anticipating war, I persuaded Dick to settle them in New York. They had kept in touch with Clay so I had occasional news of him. I had not seen him since he'd left me near Munich and, although I no longer wrote to him, generally around Christmas or the New Year he wrote to me. These occasional letters, and my unrelenting need of him, tortured me.

> *Washington. D.C.*
> *January*

Nell,

> *My annual report: health good, but suffering on occasion from nerve-wracking work sessions that really have no place in this cockeyed existence.*
> *Mental attitude—unmentionable.*
> *Financila status—varies between thin dimes and plugged nickels.*
> *Marital status—free as the wind that blows, and glad of it.*
> *Possibilities—for anything, almost anything. What will the world offer a rank opportunist?*
> *Clay*

My unrelenting and desperate need of him tortured me. I burned with desire for him.

Dick said my night-fever baffled him, but he was glad he could make me well. In bed, when he put his hands on me the fever subsided: I turned cold.

We were in the "dirty thirties," that unyielding depression that cost the lives and happiness of thousands across the country. Dick was not affected by it, financially or otherwise. We were of that New York contingent who kept the nightclubs and theatres open. Flora, spending a week with us, was much impressed when, dropping into a crowded Sardi's after the theatre, the waiter greeted me by name and promptly seated us. Flora had become my best friend.

I had given up wanting to reform the world. In guilt, because of my lack of interest in him, I was determined to be the wife Dick wanted. That meant endlessly entertaining and being entertained. I was bored—but beautifully dressed. Three days before our marriage, Bette, visiting me at the Plaza, had relieved me of my worn Russia-Europe clothes: she threw everything I owned in the garbage. "That's that," she said. "Now a few things from the shops and then I think, Valentina."*

"She's high-handed!" Dick said, infuriated. He wanted me invisible

---

* Valentina: In the 90s: the present Valentino's mother.

and he didn't want me out of his sight. At parties he hovered at my elbow. He was drinking too much–unpleasant in bed.

We were now in the fourth year of our marriage. Isabeau was on a world tour and coming to stay with us. She wanted to meet Mother. She was killed in a plane crash coming out of India.

A few weeks later Alex wrote that my old Comtesse had died. She had just sent me a beautiful silver bowl. It was too late to thank her.

Dick's cousin, who played polo, invited me to join a riding class for ladies at the New York Armoury. I had left my boots, breeches and jacket to a girl in Moscow.

Dick said new riding clothes were too expensive.

I couldn't believe it. We had money for everything, for parties, the theatre, restaurants ... but not for what I wanted. Why did I submit to him? I'd hoped to make him happy, but the more I gave in, the more his need to dominate. I'd put up with it too long. If I didn't leave him now ...

He was sitting there, watching me. He had made a list, added up the cost of breeches, boots, jacket, fees, etc. "At the moment, Darling, I just don't want to spend the money. "You do see, Yabbit?"

"Quite." I turned away. I had to force myself to keep my face from falling to pieces. Let him win. I would divorce him.

I went alone to see Bette, to tell her. Improbably, she reproached me for being too kind to Dick. "But, Philippa, don't be hasty about the divorce. Other than that, at the moment, you need a change. What would you most like to do?"

I thought of the riding class Dick had refused me, of Abbie, and I couldn't speak. I wept.

"Never mind, you'll think of something. She went to her desk, came back and handed me an enormous cheque.

I stared in surprise.

"If that's not enough ... Don't you know, money cures everything." She was laughing.

I said, "Do you know Fay Romford? She keeps a stable of hunters in Connecticut, not far from New York."

"I know her mother. Is that it? You want to ride? There's the phone. Call her."

Three days later with Homer, her stable manager, Fay Romford and I took off for Virginia to buy horses. I bought three hunters. "Klim," because he resembled Klimenti Voroshilov, the Russian General's horse; "Rocket," (sky-rocket) because she jumped that way, and "Goosey," named by the stable hands because they had trouble getting near her.

I was in such misery over the deaths of Isabeau and my old Comtesse, my loss of Clay, and Dick's infantile behaviour that I half hoped to be killed on the hunting field.

I joined both the Watertown and Rombout Hunts. I rode, as a guest, at any of the several hunts within a radius of a hundred miles. If my horses weren't rested I rode and jumped recklessly any horse available. I thought, if I didn't get killed, the expense and my absence from home might force Dick to divorce me. But it may be true that absence makes the heart grow fonder. During my short and shorter times at home, Dick grew more possessive, more loving, more demanding–and very much more tiring.

Hunting ended with winter and keeping the horses in condition wasn't enough to keep me away from home. One day I drove to New Haven and arranged to enter the Yale School of Fine Arts. I was going to paint. I had ceased to worry about Dick. With my well-trained staff, I didn't care whether or not I made it home for dinner.

Inevitably, Dick found ways to keep me around: I missed classes, didn't finish my homework and at Yale, left my works of art in an empty closet where they disappeared. My grade at the end of the semester turned out to be zero and Yale removed me from its lists. In the meantime, I had learned a great deal about sizing and stretching a canvas, the chemistry of paints etc. I began to paint at home.

Unexpectedly one evening, for I rarely heard from her, my mother telephoned me. She was uneasy about Pa. I promised to come home, hung up and rang Dr. West. I threw a change of clothes into a bag, left a note for Dick and got into my car. Around nine o'clock the next evening I parked my car in front of our house in Edgeville.

I came in through the back door. Doors were never locked in Edgeville. I went through the dining room to the sitting room. Pa was lying on the sofa, reading. I said, "Where's Mrs. McCarthy?" Mrs. McCarthy has great ears.

Pa took his spectacles off, sat up and put his book on the table. "She's visiting her daughters. Are you alone? Where's Dick?"

"I traded him in. I need a drink. What about you?"

"For what, another horse? All right."

I found the cognac and poured us each a drink. Then I sat down.

He looked at me for a long time. "I'm glad you came. I couldn't make up my mind to call you. Who did? West? Did you have anything to eat?"

"I'm not hungry. Mother called me."

"But she's totally ignorant ... "

"She's uneasy. Isn't it best to talk to her? She'll think it's worse than it is. I talked to Dr. West."

"What did West tell you?"

"Exactly what he told you; it's your heart and he suspects a tumour, probably benign."

"Or perhaps malignant. That's what concerns me."

"Would you like another opinion? Would you come to New York?"

"That would terrify Liza. As it is, it's almost impossible to conceal things from her."

"Are you in pain?"

"Not yet. Tired. But if I'm in for a long illness, it will destroy her. I've been debating in my mind whether or not to talk to you. But now you're here I'll tell you." He hesitated. "I suppose you do know how to stop life, that is, without visible side effects."

"I do."

"I never thought I'd use a euphemism for killing."

"The word is euthanasia. I have no problem with it."

"I dare not ask it of you."

I stood up, approached him and kissed him gently on the cheek. "You don't have to ask. There is nothing in this world I would not do for you. I'll take care of it." I went back to my chair and sat down.

"I was sure of you. You understand, it's when I can no longer conceal my condition. You'll have to know when."

"I'll know when–through Dr. West." And I thought, Martha. Martha is no fool. "If I'm late–Pa, promise you'll call me."

"Yes, Philippa. Yes. That's a great relief. I'm grateful. I can't tell you *how* grateful! To see Liza in grief ... I'm not sure who this is for, her or me, I only know it's best for both of us. Thank you."

I said, lightly, "*Pas de quoi.*"

He looked startled. "Nothing? This has been on my mind for a long time. I realize, now, I must give you time to think."

"Pa, I don't need to think. You have my word. I promise you."

"Promise what?" Mother was standing in the doorway.

I turned from her to stare at Pa. "What do you think? He wants a book." I reached for my purse. "And just to make sure you'll get it, I'll put it on my shopping list."

Pa began to laugh. He stood up, took my hand and pulled me to my feet. "Gad, Liza, what an exceptional child."

34

The Lodge, 1947

I can't get that love-sick actress out of my mind. If she's as neurotic as reported, it must have been an intense affair. That ended when Johnathan met me? That he ended it abruptly should lead me to believe Lottie's estimate of him: in his relationships with women he is heartless. Yet I'm terrified of losing him and in an immediate panic when I hear his name associated with a woman's.

Fortunately, the panic doesn't persist. The basic fact is that the feeling I have for Johnathan is not simply sexual. To the contrary, that shock when our eyes met, that *coup de foudre*, that thunderbolt more powerful than thought or word that left us naked to each other and joined in some mystical way was for both of us, I know, as though an essential missing part had been restored.

Ever since I got here, writing, exploring my past, no matter what I am putting on paper, Johnathan remains immoveable in my mind. I shall have to face him soon and certainly, if he persists in wanting to marry me, I had better be prepared to talk.

Marriage? There can be no marriage without truth. How am I to confess my less than admirable past? How explain my marriage to Dick, that rich, spoiled, weak man I married to improve my wretched relationship with my mother. Someone once told me that love and money are the two most important things in life. Of more importance in my marriage were possession and lust: Dick wanted me dead, rather than divorced. And I submitted to his lust to get my own way.

How can I explain six months in a mental institution? If anything will distance Johnathan from me, it is the stigma of insanity. Not that I was declared insane. Under observation for three months the hospital informed me they couldn't hold me. It was my choice to remain a further three months. It is easy for me to see the series of events that led to my breakdown, but how make Johnathan understand? Perhaps if I jotted them down I could hand them to him and walk away.

Under stress since the day I was born, marriage had worsened my situation.

I had married to prove to my Mother what a great success I had made of my life. And from the early years trying to please Dick, to the later ones ignoring him, my marriage was a torturing lie.

My father's death shocked me into honesty. I saw my marriage as contemptible, and despite his near-lethal rage, I demanded a divorce from my millionaire, socialite husband. I took a studio alone and began seriously to paint. Added to the pressures of Dick's unhappiness; his insistence that we separate until the end of the war–take time to think–was my massive six-year effort to make up for lost time. I worked non-stop: I stood at my easel from first light until dusk. But when I divorced Dick I did not anticipate that–with the exception of Sue–my family would divorce me; that I would suffer again their hostility and rejection.

Within two years as a member of the National Association of Women Painters, in a group show of more than four hundred, Alden Jewel, art critic for the *New York Times*, named my painting "One of the three most creative."

At the end of the war, my divorce final, I left for Trinidad where I lived and painted for two years. Returning to New York, I discovered that my studio, with all my previous work, had been destroyed by fire. But the reviews for my Trinidadian canvasses in New York's prestigious art magazines, the *Art News* and the *Art Digest*, were solid and good. Sample excerpts show my work to be uniquely mine:

Flower paintings by Philippa Bentham, blooms that possess strangeness and beauty not of this world ... She offers an exotic view of the flowers, the jungle and the native women of Trinidad where she has been living for the past two years. Through the handling of light and composition alone, Miss Bentham suggests an almost surrealistic world: the mysterious jungle gloom, the fantastic vitality of coiling flora. When you look at faces and places through Bentham's eyes, you see beauty, terror and the pulsing cool heat of the jungle. A painter's brushstroke is his signature. Philippa Bentham's is absolutely Philippa Bentham. She needs no other signature.

With all the work over the years, when the light went, there were endless nights for parties, for wining and dining, for the theatre, movies, the ballet, men. Free of Dick, I lived as I pleased without regard for common sense or convention. In the end, what was left of my affairs were the echoes of romance; petty perhaps, but failures to me. As for money, I had thrown it away, and as I discovered, when, finally, I divorced Dick, except for Sue, the rest of my family. I was forced to accept a truth I have always known, the rest of my family tolerate me on one condition: "success."

But, I was in trouble: after my second show–in Trinidad–unable to retreat from my fast life, physically exhausted and with a persistent, underlying feeling of disquiet with my personal life, and no reconciliation with my family, I stored my remaining canvases in Sue's attic and began an unsuccessful search for a studio. I was desperate when Ala Storey of the American British Gallery suggested that I go to the Redfern Gallery in London. One freezing January day, with two Trinidadian canvases in my hands, I left New York and took ship for England.

The Redfern showed one of my pictures in a group show of the contemporary great painters and sculptors of England and France. Following that, my picture was one of forty from that group sent to the Manchester and Edinburgh festivals. My second picture was accepted by the Royal Academy for their large annual group show, but entered too late to be hung.

I had hit the top in my profession but it was a Pyrrhic victory. My triumph in the arts seemed to me petty. I had begun life expecting to be of some use in the world, but I had failed in Russia, failed in marriage and, in effect, sat out the war. The unexpected look of London destroyed me. I was in a city–unimaginable in New York–with ever-present grim reminders of Germany's barbaric air raids. Two years had not eradicated the brutal aspects of war. In almost every street blackened skeletons of burned buildings emitted acrid odours. One could not escape the devastation, or the fact that Britain, still on rations, was hungry. At the Savoy, when I ordered an egg for breakfast, the ancient waiter, hesitating, suggested cereal. I was sick at heart.

That I had done nothing to help during the war still haunted me. In the beginning, with a hundred other recruits, I had taken the examination for service in the women's army. I was told I was unsuitable, that I would not survive the long marches and the heavy work. At a loss, I settled for volunteer work where needed, and I gave lessons in painting to disabled merchant seamen. When the usual commendation for war services arrived from President Roosevelt at the end of the war, knowing I had done nothing to earn it, I destroyed it, but I could not destroy my guilt. I couldn't stay in London, I didn't want to go home, so upon the advice of a friend in the British Foreign Office, I went to the South of France.

In 1947 I was living in Menton on the French Riviera, in a magnificent, if slightly decayed villa whose owner had given his agent permission to rent it for next to nothing to keep it aired. The villa had suffered the German and Italian occupations, but looting had stopped with the back of the house. The service wing was stripped clean, but in the marble floored entrance hall, the glittering crystals still sparkled on the fine old chandelier, the wrought iron staircase curved gracefully, undamaged, to the floor above and throughout the house the carved marble mantels remained intact. Bedrooms and bathrooms were unscarred and there were still many handsome tables, chairs, bureaux and beds.

Outside, still beautiful in neglect, the acres of terraced gardens were surrounded by a high and intricate iron fence. One entered the grounds by an impressive gate.

I had been looking for some sort of hole-in-the-wall, with good light, where I could paint but I took it and hired a housekeeper. I took it compulsively out of an overpowering need to find a settled place–away from the sight and smell of family, of husband, of death. And the housekeeper to care for me because although I managed a public calmness, I was lost.

But in spite of a fabulous atelier and my triumphant entry into the world of great art, I had not been able to work. Canvas after canvas, begun in forced determination deteriorated into daubs. It was an exercise of will that got me out of bed and forced me through the day's routine. Body and mind rebelled against the slightest exertion. I had hit bottom and exhausted and revolted with my life, I had neither sufficient incentive nor strength to pick myself up.

When Sue wrote that she was coming to visit me I was appalled. What could I offer her? My finances were a muddle–I couldn't be bothered to look–my few acquaintances included the house agent and several old English, living out their remaining years in an agreeable climate. And of course Fish, the starved dog they insisted I buy, on the strength of my obvious affluence: the villa.

My only amusement that might not suffice Sue, revolved around Fish. Now happily fed, it was his habit to race up the garden path, take a running leap through the drawing room window and slide the thirty feet of polished parquet to the opposite wall.

Sue is blonde, blue eyed and very pretty. Devoted to Elliot, her husband, but with an eye for fun and men, she never steps over the traces but likes to pretend she might. Her conquests amuse her, but must finally resign themselves to being friends.

Sitting at the table under the chestnut trees, I forced a conversation. Everything at home, Sue repeated, was "fine." Her trip over was "fun." A man on board, "a movie magnate," wanted her to meet him in Rome but she had no intention of going there. Finally, in answer to my questioning– she had spent fifteen minutes looking at them–she expressed an opinion of my pictures. "I must say there's something wrong with your work," she said. "I can't imagine your state of mind. It must be chaotic for you to paint like that."

She was right, but emotion knows no reason. I was stricken. Should I tell her about my pictures in London? I wanted her approval, but I didn't want it through bribery. I wanted it blind, through faith in me. And then I realized that Sue knew: she had seen my weakness, my confusion. It was no longer necessary for me either to impress her or to cover up. She would help me. Tense in my need, the words came compulsively: "Yes," I said, "there it is. You've seen it. It's true. I'm in a fog. But worse, I've always despised people who won't stand on their own feet, who think the world owes them a living, but at this moment I find myself one of them. I simply cannot go on. I know this sounds fantastic, Sue, but I'm desperate. I need someone to take care of me."

Silence. Sue was staring at her feet.

Embarrassed, I looked away. Did she think I was trying to sponge on her? Why didn't she speak? Did she think I meant money? And then, in desperate earnest, I blurted the question that lies deep in every painter's heart. "Did it ever cross your mind that in painting I might be great? Can you believe that I could be?"

She spoke now: "I'm sorry, but I can't."

I murmured some excuse and left her.

Fish followed me, running and jumping through the garden, biting at my hands and dress, teasing me to play. I slapped him hard, slammed the kitchen door in his face and went up the back stairs. My studio was as I had left it when her letter came. A massive and unholy mess. A whole glass table-top, my palette, was covered with rigid and dirty paint. Unwashed brushes were everywhere, ruined probably. Bits of experimental canvas—colour on colour, or against colour—half tacked, falling off the walls, stepped on and scuffed on the floor. Bundles of stretchers, bottles, cans, varnish, oils, turpentine, used and unused tubes of paint, and my trademark, toilet paper—I use it instead of rags to wipe brushes—were in soiled and scattered heaps on the floor. I had never left it like that! Fire hazard ... It would take hours of labour ... Oh Christ!

I slammed the shutters together, cutting out the light. I latched the long windows. I went out of the room and shut the door behind me and turned the key in the lock. I stood, hesitating, the key in my hand. I wanted to hurl it over the edge of nowhere, I wanted it gone. I threw it to the top shelf of the unused linen closet.

The food was on the table and Sue was waiting to eat when I got back. I said: "Let's go away."

"Where?"

"Anywhere ... " (I could sell something–a bond.) "Egypt."

"Not Egypt," said Sue, "they don't like Americans there these days. What about North Africa? That might be fun. Let's have a party first. Who do you know?"

That afternoon, we went to a travel agency and arranged our trip to North Africa. Later, we called on my acquaintances, the old English, and asked them to the villa for a tea party.

Alone in my room that night, I stared at my reflection in the looking-glass. My shameful attempt at begging help had been brushed aside. Sue cared little for me and believed in me–not at all. Without her, there was no one left. No one left. Nothing left. Suicide. It had been in my mind for a long time.

Leave my dead body for Sue? A baby–in spite of her years–and on holiday? Horrible! And the rest of the family; I had no illusions about their feelings for me, but it would shock them. No. For the moment, I must go on and, as far as possible, give Sue her fun.

"How strange," I said aloud, watching my empty face in the glass, "How surprising. I had no idea it would end like this." And then, "Philippa," I told those witless eyes, "You are finished."

And beyond tears, past reasoning or hope, I could not support the torturing weight of pain. Lying on my bed, begging to be eased of it, senselessly praying for the one love that I had never doubted, I called on my dead father for help. And suddenly, in the blackness, I felt that he was near. The stillness that surrounded me was charged with life. My father was with me, but out of reach. The occult space encasing him–separating us–was stretched to the breaking point. It would need but little pressure to break it. Whatever that force, I must discover it. God would not, could not forsake me. He, Himself would give me my fairing.

And in that state of mind, my goal seemed reasonable. I did not anticipate failure. That there is in me a strange force whose origin I do not know is obvious to me. Long ago, I discovered that I have the gift of dowsering; a stripped willow twig in my hand will twist and turn down over water. Incidents of my childhood and early life, long forgotten and meaningless till now, crowded to my mind. Reviewed in this new light, they took on significance.

Our tea party was a success. Everyone liked Sue, admired her dress and made a fuss of her. The food was good and the conversation–pretending casual interest, I turned it to spiritualism–was absorbing. One old girl, who claimed she could make the spirits of the dead answer by moving the table, had us close the shutters and in the light-dimmed room arrange ourselves, hands outstretched and flat on it, around a small table. She asked questions and the table did move but so confused were our joint questions and the tapped "yes" and "no" answers, that we got nowhere. Still, I was fascinated.

It was Sue's idea, after they left, to make a kind of ouija board. We wrote the letters of the alphabet on small squares of paper and placed them in a circle on the table. We placed a small glass in the center of the circle and then, gravely, with hands conjoint and lightly touching it, we called our dead father to move it. The glass, faster than our following hands, slid across the wood, upsetting in its haste. But, adjusting to it and following it from letter to letter, writing each word as it came, we received our first message. Hypnotized, we read: "Man is bound to earth in time as by his earthly actions."

Two days later, mesmerized, spending all our time at our game, we left the villa to Clairette and Fish and took a plane to Casablanca. And some few hours later, lilting down to earth in that lazy, tropic-like city, we found it drenched in sun and its polyglot population, in their strange and varied dress, floating soundlessly through the wavering streets in liquid light. Enchanted, we arrived at our hotel. But here, what I had accepted for years as a normal atmosphere, now suffocated me. The hotel, just redecorated, smelled nauseously of paint. I refused to stay. And travelling in that ancient taxi, our baggage piled around us, searching fruitlessly in the increasing heat for rooms, the enchantment for Sue wore thin.

"Your idea of fun," she sulked. "After all these years, I can't quite believe another whiff of paint will kill you. Let's, for God's sake, go back to our hotel."

"I can't."

"There's no 'can't' about it! For some stupid reason, you won't."

My knees shook. How face the nightmare weakness that beset me at the smell of paint? "Yes," I said, "that's it. But, don't fret, my love. We can always sleep in the park."

"You silly, damn ass," Sue complained, "you haven't changed since you were born. You're still crazy!"

Late that afternoon, hot, dishevelled and weary, we returned to the airport where, by chance, we found sleeping quarters for one night in the hostel provided by the airlines. And the following day, consulting simultaneously the dead, the map and Sue's wishes—or rather her demand—for a "decent" hotel, we took off for Marrakech where there was a room for us at the Mamounia.

But our game, begun at my instigation–though neither of us could invoke them without the other–had become more hers than mine, for to my dismay I was not popular with the dead.

Openly baring their likes and dislikes, in brutal carelessness of the amenities, they were antagonistic and snubbing to me. Unanimously, they adored Sue. While the few who loved me tried to console me for the others, they rarely spoke. Cowed, or crowded out, by the multitude of Sue's clamouring admirers, they waited hesitantly to "come through." It was to Sue's blue eyes that Mr. Shakespeare wrote his sonnet. And though he detested me–"And if you live or if you die, see, Philippa, if I care"–along with Sue, I was dazzled.

What disturbed us greatly was Pa. He came frequently, but strangely with no other words than "Love me. Love me." Shocked and surprised, we assured him that we did.

Though the dead refused our repeated requests to tell our future, we did not move now without consulting them. Leaving our room, they would not be left behind and publicly demonstrated their presence and their strength. About to get up from dinner one evening, my ankles, not numb but simply not there, rolled under me. I fell forward on to the table. It was minutes before I could stand. Out of thin air, Sue began casually to quote them and she was startlingly right. "You'll win at golf today," she told the woman at the next table who hadn't won a game in fifteen days. The woman won–by one stroke.

We were so at home with them now, our dead friends, that lightly–never, of course, admitting their influence over us–we joked about them to acquaintances at the hotel. The guests, amused, came to us for advice and fun. Our dead had a sense of humour. They exposed secrets, foretold romances and were rudely bright.

And they had a sense of beauty, too. Back in our room, door and windows shut, we identified the changing odours around us, of roses, of gardenias, of incense. There were other scents unknown and exquisite that neither of us knew. The very walls exuded them. There too–outside we were more or less free of it–we were charged with or surrounded by an electricity in no way normal. Our clothes clung to us and had to be forcibly pulled away. Lifting a sheet on my bed in the dark, I must expect it to be followed by a crackling arc of flame. And in that blazing heat, inexplicably insulated from it, I suffered an invidious and paralysing cold.

With all my resting, I could not rid myself of fatigue and left to myself I would not have stirred. It was at Sue's insistence–"You can't spend whole days flat on your back! Let's get out of this room! There's nothing wrong with you!"–that I forced myself to get up. I was tired, tired, tired. And even in sleep, taunting me, the dead were there. Once, in shaking terror, their sardonic whispers echoing in space, I woke to fling myself at Sue's bed. She was in it but, dazedly, I wondered for how long? They loved her. They would take her. And so, concomitantly with the sights and sounds of Africa, the dead absorbed our lives.

Though it was her first time in Africa, Marrakech, for Sue, was coming home, but an ominous return. Knowing it without knowing it, she feared the desert, its dangers, its torturing heat and thirst. She would not step foot, nor ride on it. Though the rush hour on the New York subway did not faze her, in the market-place one short walk through the crowded souks left her physically ill. And then one morning back in our room, after a visit to an ancient cemetery, she slammed the door behind her and began, violently, to cry. "I saw my grave and me in it, with a golden necklace lying near my throat, but my head–just below the ears–severed from it!"

I seized her by both arms. Hysteria! When I was too exhausted to move. And the classic way to deal with it, slap her, shove her under a cold shower, but I am no classicist. I tried to comfort her. In spite of my inertia, a frozen disinclination to move, one thing was clear: I must get Sue out of Africa or risk the danger for her of a deep emotional upset. I hovered over her, disguising my lassitude with solicitous pats and phrases. When she was quiet, I picked up the phone and spoke to the desk.

"Get me two air tickets to Paris." With my free hand, I waved down her protests. "Tomorrow, if possible, or the next day. And would you be good enough to wire for a reservation? The Meurice–a double room. Two beds."

But my forced exertion on Sue's behalf was activated only by a life-time habit of protectiveness towards her. My concern was for myself. In increasing painfulness, I was concealing my hurt at her indifference and at the enmity of her dead, by a mask of, I hoped, casual insouciance. That mask covered a growing emotional chaos. It was almost impossible for me to think. Morbidly centered on myself, my channelled thoughts circled sluggishly in a maze of despair. In overwhelming lethargy, I neglected hair, nails and dress, yet to appear dowdily unkempt in public filled me with such bitter shame that I wanted to crawl away and die. If not suicide, what was to become of me? The dead refused to tell. But somewhere in this mysterious land–and, in desperation, I was determined not to leave without knowing it–there was someone who would reveal my future.

I picked up the phone again. "Sue, I'll have Mohammed take us to the best fortune teller in Marrakech. You'll see, once you're out of here, everything will be fine."

But late in the afternoon, facing the old man in his shabby room, I was jolted back to sanity by surging fear. In her present state of near hysteria I was exposing Sue to what? I jerked at her arm, my voice tense and hard in curbed fear, "It's all nonsense, Sue, I can't think why we came. Don't believe a word he says!"

"Ssh-h, he'll hear you!" Frowning, she pushed me aside. "You're in my way."

But the bearded old man spoke in Arabic, and Mohammed, haltingly, in his uneasy French must translate to me. Sue spoke no French so I was saved. No matter what he said, if it was bad, I would dissemble.

But obviously blessing and caressing her in his own tongue, the old Arab took Sue's hands in his. Then, gently releasing them, he drew from beneath his stained white robe a small and worn black book.

"Holy," Mohammed said, motioning towards it, "and old, very old."

"Your name?"

"Susan."

"Susan. Your happiness lies locked and secure in a familiar room far across the sea." He paused while Mohammed repeated his words. "I will show you." And suddenly, startling us, the old man shook his head in a familiar gesture.

"It's Elliot!" exclaimed Sue. "What did he say?"

"B-back to y-your husband." I stuttered, and I dared, at last, release my breath. "He's your good fortune."

He had love charms for her, bits of silky paper covered with a tight, black, unknown script. And directions for carrying them, bathing with them, chewing them, and swallowing them. Finally, reluctantly, their love fest ended, he turned to me.

"I am Philippa." I said.

And staring into those singular innocent and astute old eyes, nakedly exposed, I saw a grim and primal coldness replace the kindliness he had shown Sue.

"Philippa." Tentatively, he repeated it. Then he turned the pages of his book and twice he nodded as though the words he read confirmed his own deep knowledge of me. He would not look at me. He said, into space, hesitating, "One more bad break. Later ... When you learn death ... You have work. It will succeed. After that fête after fête after fête."

He shut the book. There would be no social chit chat. The old man couldn't wait to be quit of me. Since he refused to face me, I handed his fee to Mohammed.

"One more bad break for me," I said to Sue, as we pushed through the curtain to the narrow, dirty street, "and I'll be dead. It will kill me."

"Pill, really! Don't be stupid! What else did he say? I mean about me? Did you see him do Elliot? He's fantastic! What fun! And, he's right. Only six weeks till Christmas. I'd better get back to New York." That night we packed, and the next day we took the plane for Paris.

And there, nerves forgotten, Sue embarked on a shopping spree. Jealously watching and brooding on my own uncertain affairs—I had no letter of credit, the luxury hotels were ruinous for me—her careless spending for others tortured me. Married to Dick, I had never let Sue pick up a cheque but it was she now who had the money. I dared not pay the swank restaurants.

"It's all yours." I said one day in the Ritz dining-room, handing her the bill, "I have no notion what, if anything, I have in the bank."

Sullen with disbelief, Sue fixed her eyes on her plate. "What happened to your alimony?"

"I don't know. I ... "

"Well, I do! It's there! You've got it!"

"Sue, my alimony doesn't cover ... I don't know what I've spent ... By the time I pay the hotel, I'm not sure I'll have my fare back."

Silence.

Did she think I lied? Why try to force an interest that didn't exist? And her fun gone, she sulked. For our last four days, the weight of her depression was added to my own. Then, the night before she left, Sue had a dream. I woke to find her frowning down at me.

"W-what's wrong?"

"You have to stop!" she said. "Promise me you'll stop!"

"Stop frowning," I said. "You'll get lines. What have I done now? Stop what?"

She sat down on the edge of my bed and her innate goodness so long withheld shone in her eyes, came through to me in her clinging hands. "Oh, Pill, I dreamed the end! It's a sign to us! We both have to stop!"

"Stop what?"

"Listen, I dreamed we were in a race. I can see it plain as day. Many of us running for the prize and the prize a pure white dove. And it was I who caught it. But it withered in my hands to a yellow, rotten thing. You must promise me you won't go on. Promise that you'll stop talking to the dead."

The day before, lunching at Maxim's, I had run into an acquaintance, a New York painter who claims to paint from her subconscious, who told me that fasting increased psychic power and that often "in a trance-like state," her hand directed by an unknown spirit, she filled "copy books" with "automatic writing." I had every intention of trying it. But alone.

"I won't promise any such thing."

"You must! I'll worry!"

Worry? If she was so concerned for me why had she shut me out? She had as much comprehension of my state of mind as the man in the moon. Yet I saw the very real distress in her eyes. I forced a yawn, freed my hand and picked up the phone. "Oh, hum. Chocolate or coffee?"

"Promise me! Promise!"

Promise me! I mimicked soundlessly in sudden rage. "*Attendez.*" In a few hours she must leave for the boat train. I couldn't send her off in a tizzy. I turned to her and smiled. "Put your mind at rest," I soothed her. "I promise." "Chocolate?"

She nodded.

The automatic writing would have to wait till I got back to the villa.

35

I made it back to Menton with a couple of hundred francs to spare. Without Sue, I had not dared spend my sous for food or drink, but that was all to the good. I'd begun fasting.

The villa shone. Clairette had been scrubbing, but the money I'd left had not fed Fish. He was a skeleton again. And I had scarcely set foot inside the door when I must head off a welcoming committee: my old English. I greeted them with scant courtesy. "How kind of you to come! Forgive me if I don't ask you in. I'm about to fall into bed, uh, a bug I picked up."

I told Clairette to bring me an early supper, went upstairs, threw off my clothes and fell into bed. I meant to stay there; I didn't want to move for the rest of my life. My head felt dull and heavy–the fasting–I would get used to it. A match box, any small object, moved under my fingers, but slowly. Without Sue, it would be difficult to summon the dead. It would take fasting, patience, prayer. The writing was the thing. As soon as Fish was fed, as soon as I could be quiet and alone, I would try the automatic writing.

Clairette knocked, came in, put the tray on the table and left. I got out of bed. There were a few letters, wine, bread, cold meat and salad. I threw the wine down the sink, put the food on the floor and watched Fish gulp it down. He was still hungry. France was hungry. With Clairette out of the way, I could feed him. I threw on a robe, took fifty francs from my purse, rang, and met her at the door. "Clairette, bus fare. Spend the night with your family. I'll expect you tomorrow at ten."

Fish was under the bed scratching, trying to get to the empty plate he'd pushed out of reach. I would have to go to the market. I picked up my letters. Two from New York, a postcard from Marrakech, a letter from Flora. Why ... Mother? I tore open the letter and a newspaper clipping fell to the floor. Fish jumped at it, holding it with his paws, growling and biting at my hands. I shoved him away and picked it up. An overturned car. *X marks the spot where early this morning Dr. Geoffrey Jerrold was found some six feet distant from his wrecked car. Cause of the accident is still unknown.*

Dead? Was he dead?

Flora's sprawling script shivered in front of my eyes. "I hate to be the one to break it to you, but I guess you ought to know. They think Geoffrey may live, but he might lose his right hand."

A surgeon without a right hand? No!

My head! I put my head in my hands. My head was numb, swelling! I ran down the corridor and started down the stairs. Where was I going? I was naked. I slipped on the marble steps, knelt on them, holding my head. Geoffrey! I must write to him! I jumped up and ran to my desk. I found pen and paper, but the words were confused, wrong, crossed out. I must write and re-write the letter. I sealed it at last, put Fish on the leash and ran panting to the post office.

Breathless, gasping, following Fish's erratic chase back to the villa, in my giant head there was a growing dismay. The clipping! Why had Flora sent me the clipping? For in wavering horror, repetitiously jumping in front of my bulging eyes, super-imposed upon and bleeding into the earth, the trees, the sky, I saw the overturned car; the picture ... overdeveloped ... badly composed ... *X marks the spot where they picked up the body.*

The light was gone when I got back to the villa and in the shuttered dark, for I must relieve my eyes of the feeblest ray of the setting sun, I stumbled around my room. I could not lie down; I was suffocating. I had thrown off my clothes, but I put them on again. The market! I hadn't gone to the market. Fish needed food.

I found a small roast in the pantry, hacked it in two, threw half to him and waited while he gnawed it to the bone.

The moon was high when we ran through the grounds to the bottom garden. The wall was solid here and I was beyond the sight of prying eyes. Geoffrey! Recovered? Dead? In an agony of frustration, there was a surging, exploding energy in me that I must lose or go mad. Round and round, in the moon-shadowed night, I ran till I stumbled and fell. I had tripped over a hoe. I raised it above my head and threw it as hard as I could. Fish dragged it back to me. I took it and, with all my strength, I pounded the stubborn earth. I began to dig, lifting the heavy sod, straining at it in the dark. Flora! Flora! The clipping! Did it not shock you? Why send it to me? I am going mad!

My burning eyes are quite dry. I have no tears. It is the running sweat on my forehead that stings them. My brother: so beloved in his community that there was a public petition signed by thousands to prevent his leaving for the war ... *X marks the spot* ... Not that again! ... but in a semi-transparent screen against the blackness, whereever I turned, I saw it ... the overturned car ...

I leaned my elbows on the balcony rail and held my wrecked hands away from me. They were bruised black and blue, the skin broken and smarting, and they were swollen double up through my wrists. It was agony to wash. To numb my senses, I spent the nights digging. Geoffrey ... alive or dead? With his hand or without it? I'd had no further word from Flora. Nothing from Sue–from anyone.

The pain had gone from my head leaving a residue of cloud; a globe tight-filled with fog where half formed and fearful thoughts seethed and circled in endless futility. But one fact, solid and immoveable dominated that fog. I could no longer bear my life. And fighting the confusion in my head, I planned my death: an accident, but no embarrassing body left behind: a long swim out to sea.

The afternoon sun was gone behind a brooding mist. The light was a shy gentleness. *Coleur de tendre:* the 'colour of tenderness.'

I heard Clariette before I saw her. She was singing. She came through the great iron gate with Fish, pushed it shut and stooped to let him off the leash. Halfway up the drive she caught sight of me and stopped. She grinned, flung her arm above her head, waving her handbag to keep it out of his jumping reach.

"*Madame! Qu'il est terrible, ce Feesh I Il veut l'argent!* ... he's terrible, this Fish, he wants the money!

I nodded and smiled and shaking, stepped back to support myself against the wall. My spine was a string of lint. The bank had cashed my cheque.

At the animal hospital the Vet had talked to a couple whose dog had died of old age. I had written the letter that would allow them to take Fish. My jewellery and the housekeeping money were on my bedside table with a note for Clairette. "I've gone for a swim." I could leave the house now. And it was not fear of death that kept me hesitating. For days I had yearned for the soothing water; my need for oblivion, my desperate longing for rest, was bone deep. But I was lonely.

I picked up the pencil and put it down. The automatic writing. I hadn't tried it. Would anyone come? What if they came with hate? " *For if you live or if you die see, Philippa, if I care.*" I took the pencil again in my swollen hand and placed it on a clean sheet of paper. God, I prayed, send my father. With Pa, I could go easily to my death. And as I sat waiting, the pencil stirred and came to life. It moved, pulling after it my inert hand. Stunned, staring down at the paper, I saw, not my own, but my father's distinctive writing. I had no need to read the message. I felt the words through my following hand. "Death for you is a denial of love. Let be, Philippa, let be."

The shock of seeing my father's writing so many years after his death, threw me in to a paroxysm of weeping. But the message meant nothing; the sense of it didn't reach me. When my tears were gone, I felt a benediction in the space surrounding me. Pa had not deserted me. I picked up the letter for the Vet, jumped trembling to my feet and ran. I was halfway down the drive when the meaning of his words, repeating in my head, struck me. Pa had said, not death for me, but life. No! I stopped. No. He must know I had no more strength. I began to run again.

But I felt him with me, powerfully near: a weight of air pressed against my body that I must force myself through. Holding me! Demanding! I could not ignore him. I turned, went back to the villa and climbed the stairs to my room. I dropped my letter and picked up the pencil. And it was because, inexorably, he repeated that he would abandon a coward and a suicide that I did not die that night.

That night I slept. A heavy and a dreamless sleep.

I woke serene; lifted out of chaos into stillness and peace. The dead lived. This morning I would take a pencil and my father would talk to me. I got out of bed and stepped on to the balcony. The sun was up. Scented, green and filmed with dew, the garden lay quiescent; charmed into stillness by the sparkling light. Pa was with me. The two worlds were one. From now on I would live in both. In peace.

But as the day wore on, even for the simplest things, what clothes to wear, a question from Clairette, I couldn't think. I wandered around, my mind a blank–until it occurred to me that I need not try to think; I had but to pick up a pencil and the answer was there.

The pencil then was the medium through which many of the dead came to me. That much of what they wrote was vague and chaotic meant nothing, except that my contact with them was not fully established. And it was to increase my power to bring them closer that I continued to fast. But through fasting and weeping, for their love and tenderness brought me to uncontrollable tears, I was becoming excessively weak. I was in a state of physical and emotional exhaustion and I was aware of it, but I thought it a small price to pay for the greatest happiness of my life. Now, less and less did I move or go out. I sat endlessly in my room with pencil and paper and talked to the dead.

But there were constant interruptions. When Clariette brought my tray, she would not be dismissed, but stood stubbornly beside me until I swallowed a few mouthfuls of food. My old English, obstinate, demanded

Sue's address, demanded that I let her know I was ill. I gave them the wrong street. And much as I loved him, even with Fish, though I no longer had the strength to run and play, I must force myself to make sure he was properly fed.

It was Keats, bored with the interruptions, homesick for London, who persuaded me to leave. "Christmas," he said, "is the time to go." And over-riding my protestations that I had no strength, it was the dead, an inexhaustible electric force, who moved me. It was Keats who reminded me of the six-month's quarantine in England for dogs and who went with me to the animal hospital to find a heated kennel where Fish could stay until his new family claimed him. It was Vermeer who cleaned and packed my studio, discarded certain canvases, chose others, rolled and packed and tagged them.

Oddly, for I had no real interest in him, it was Vermeer who came most often. I was, he insisted, closer to him than any living painter. We were of the same stature, he said, and that accepted as second to Van Rijn. (He never called him Rembrandt.) Vermeer talked endlessly, not only of paint, but of the details of his life, none of which I knew. Later, in London, a brochure which, through vanity, he insisted that I buy, confirmed his story.

It was the dead who phoned my farewells, bought my ticket and closed the villa. And so, surrounding me, easing my contact with people, my loving company brought me, bag and baggage, to London.

I had ripped the worn parts from my old mink coat and resown it, but I could not button it for it was too small now across the front. It hung open over my summer clothes and I shivered under it, for London was freezing. But led and controlled by my dead, I took no heed of the penetrating cold. I walked in a dream.

From the London Station we went at once to an acquaintance, Arnold Mason, one of the ten members of the Royal Academy, who allowed me to share his Chelsea studio. And that Christmas, the happiest of my life, I went triumphantly back to work, for not only was I accompanied by Vermeer, there gathered around me other great dead painters. Of those who claimed spiritual kinship with me were Van Rijn and Van Gogh. There was no hesitation now, or indecision in my work; confident, swift, and decisive, the brush moved in my hand.

In the studio, at night with artificial light, we painted sixteen hours a day. It was they who choose subject matter, colour, contour. My own critical faculty lost or submerged in theirs, it appeared to my entranced eyes that the winding ribbons of scarlet, purple and gold that, at their direction, criss-crossed a floating landscape, were the apotheosis of great art.

400

And then, typical of me, a constant variance in the upward rhythm of my achievement, reiterated *ad nauseam* every time I neared the top, I was incapable of further effort. The day came when I could not lift my head from the pillow.

And they? How blessed and kind. They forgave me. "This," they said, "is part of the plan. For beauty has its roots in truth. Great painting has its roots in truth." It was my moral weakness that prevented my work from being great. They would uncover and destroy the false in me. They helped me from my bed and, again with pencil and paper, I sat at the rickety table, an eager and humble scholar while, one by one, exigent, they probed, questioned and tortured me. While, ony by one they seized hold of and dragged to light my endless sins. They said I must rid myself of greed. I would have no further need of "things" and it was a festive night when we wrapped and marked my jewellery, which was to be given anonymously to the poor.

I was slow-witted, but patient. They fed me the questions and the answers. Patient, they waited for me to learn.

I sat at the table and wrote and the ever-changing script was not my writing but theirs. For a week I did not leave my room. And I refused entrance to intruders, the maid, my snooping landlady. I had no time to wash or dress. My hair would not stay in place, it fell over my eyes so that I could not see to write. I hacked it off with my nail scissors, hastily, without looking in the glass. There were times when exhilarated at my progress and by their praise, I danced exuberantly with them, laughing with joy.

I did not eat:

> For he (who) on honey-dew hath fed
> And drunk the milk of paradise.
> Hath no physical hunger.

I hungered only for the rich and varied diet that they alone, people from a world infinitely more wonderful than my own, could bring me. A diet that fed the senses and the spirit.

What I had read with skepticism became clear to me. I knew the esoteric delight and the humble joy of the mystic, of those whose prayers and wanting had brought them closer to God. When the chill of my room dissolved in awesome mellow gold and shimmering light, in suspended stillness, in rapt ecstasy, I felt the presence.

Then my old world, oblique, obtruded on the new. Dismayed, one morning and with foreboding, I recognized Flora's writing on a letter thrust under my door, and I was tripped harshly back into my old life. "We have spent a lot of money on ourselves this year," Flora wrote, "more than six hundred dollars for a new radio—we have so little chance to hear good music—so I'm not going to send you anything. I'm sure you'll understand.

It had been some years since I had stopped sending presents to Geoffrey and Flora's children. In the face of the world war, the greed for gauds sickened me. I gave to those the war had made destitute, to orphans and refugees, yet I could not acquit myself of the family disdain. Still, Flora continued to send me her usual pair of gloves, handkerchiefs or stockings. "It's the thought that counts," she explained, "not the price." Now, breaking that lifelong convention, she repudiated my, to her, non-existent orphans, and destroyed the last shaky bond between us. I held the envelope upside down and shook it, hoping that, at least, a handkerchief would fall out, and when it did not, my knees would not support me and I threw myself on the bed.

And gravity went mad. It doubled. It tripled. The air above and around me, its weight an immensity; a black and gray, red-streaked and monstrous burden of crushing pain closed in on my defenceless body. I lay gasping under it. I had lost them! I had failed! Somehow, through my stupidity I had lost my family.

In all the years since we were born Geoffrey and Flora have been right. And I have been different.

A sailor once told me that to be different is to die. That once, to discover if English gulls would follow his yacht across the channel to France, he caught one and painted its breast with a crimson cross. He never found out. When he released it, the other gulls attacked and tore it to death. It was different.

"God," I shouted, "am I wrong and too petty to admit it? God," I said desperately, "I have tried and tried and I have failed." Safety lies with the mob. I have always known that and I have tried to conform. Yet how affected my efforts and how ignominious my failure. I have lived a full life and, from the outside looking in, a more than commonly successful one, yet it is only with animals that I am safe.

"God," I shouted, "Perhaps in your affairs you get confused. Is mine a soul that in transmigration lost its place? Should I be an animal? Flora and Geoffrey can love a dog. What they can't love is a snake.

" ... Am I a snake? God, am I a snake?" And, "no," I said, for even a snake has friends. I know, for once in Edgeville, " *Mid hushed cool-rooted flowers fragrant eyes ...* " I met a snake gliding along the dusty road with half a dozen little snakes; little dusty tooth-picks, sliding beside her. And when I came near, the big snake stopped and swallowed all the little ones. Were they her children or her friends? Children. Could she spit them up again or were they gone? I had wondered then, in sorrow, if accidentally, I had ruined that snake's life.

But I knew now. They were her children and she protected them. Who would protect me? If I were not protected now the pain would destroy me. If I could just turn into a snake, I thought, everything would be fine. Flora, with her self-preserving tongue, could beat me to death. And after death, peace. Silence. Silence to my pained, my desperate ears. My capable ears. Capable ...

" ... to his capable ears
Silence was music from the holy spheres;"

"Oh, John!" I called to Keats. "At last! Me! At last! I know now what you mean!" Silence! It's true! Heaven! And Flora, I thought, my teeth chattering, for I was deathly cold—the sharp and naked icicles of pain searing my wretched heart—the clammy sweat running on my face. Flora can listen to her radio till the cows come home. She won't know one note from another. Her singing voice is just off-key. And I couldn't help it, I had to laugh. I couldn't stop laughing.

Then I couldn't stop any of it, the laughing or the crying and the shaking. I was doing all of it together and frantically trying to get the blankets straight. And I could hear myself getting louder and louder, while I fumbled and fumbled. And I remembered that the walls were thin and they might hear me. People! They might try to get in!

I flung the heap of bedclothes on the floor. And to muffle my mingled screams of agony and my shrieks of joy, clumsily, I turned on the bed and shoved my face in the pillow. And lying there half-smothered, trying to stop, I began to think that at this very moment perhaps it was Christmas day. Or very near, and for all the love and charity I had for Geoffrey and Flora, my heart might as well be a stone. And thinking it, my body was gripped again in that excruciating and consuming pain. They were lost to me!

... Only who turned me into a snake in the first place? Them, or me? Who started it?

The whisper came in the space between my eyes. Was it John Keats, or his brother, Tom? It was Tom.

"It's the old story," Tom said. "The country puzzle—the chicken and the egg. Which came first? Flora will know. She's a country girl. Ask Flora at Christmas. Glorious Christmas. The place to be is at home with your loved ones."

Home. That's where I went that Christmas in 1945 ... the year the war ended ... the year I finally divorced Dick ... back to Otter to stay with Flora for, if I can help it, I won't see my mother. I phoned Flora to ask if I might to her for the holiday, and to tell her what, except for Betty–and at Dick's insistence–no one else knew: that having demanded a divorce from Dick five years before, I had separated from him when I took my studio, promising to do nothing further about it until the war ended. Now I intended divorcing him at once. And then, in a burst of confidence, sure of her support, I told Flora I had been seeing another man and that Dick knew about it.

At the station, when she picked me up, Flora barely greeted me. On the way home–those country roads are dangerous when it snows–absorbed in driving, she had nothing to say. I felt the dislike in her but it was not for me. Ever since my marriage we were very close. We had put away the childish feud, we were friends. But something had happened; was Edward drinking again? Pool Flora. When we stepped into the house I said, "I can't tell you how wonderful it is to be here." And I threw off my hat.

"Sit down." Flora commanded.

Flora is round and cozy-looking; warm hearted. She has small blue eyes in a pink face. Now her little blue eyes were full of disgust. She did not raise her voice, but the screaming was in her head. It dominated her foolish and useless talk.

I sat down at a card table by the fireplace, close to the glowing fire. I hadn't thought of it for a long time, now I remembered. By some God-given grace, Flora has all the facts. No need to be under the bed, ask questions, or investigate. She can tell by looking at me. And Flora believes in doing her duty. She does it well. But duty alone is dangerous, it blocks off the passage that leads from the mind to the heart–or the other way around. Duty should be weighted with compassion.

So there was our famous friendship that began when I married Dick, swamped in the swirling currents of Flora's uncompassioned duty: to stop my divorce. I wouldn't be Mrs. Richard Bentham anymore and the welcome mat she used for Mrs. Bentham had the old prefix–NOT–stamped on it again. So everything went back to the way it was before. Screaming ... screaming ... Flora screaming ...

In her most disdainful voice ... "Don't come to me for sympathy! Divorcing Dick! A fine man like Dick! You're the one to blame! Not Dick! There's nothing wrong with him except he's too good for you or he'd never have put up with you! Dick!

Dick! It was 2 a.m. but I left the light on. I was frightened to put it out. Since our visits to the psychiatrist, since I had left his bed and continued adamant about the divorce, Dick's silent rages, his bursts of anger and failing

404

attempts at reconciliation had produced such a deadly atmosphere in the house that even our servants moved around him in utter silence, as though fearing to be seen or heard. Dick! ... banging his way into my room and Sugar, our little dog—only he was big now—a great gray streak of Alsation, hurling himself at Dick's throat.

"Sugar!" I screamed. "Down!"

Dick, sideswiping him with his fist. Knocking him to the floor. And Sugar crouched, growling, all red sparks for eyes, ready; ready to spring again. While Dick sat on the edge of my bed quietly talking. The room was full of fear.

I could hear Flora's husky-bright little voice coming through her screaming. "You can't fool me! Dick will take you back, but he's a fool to do it!" Screaming ... How long has he stood for this? Since you took that studio? Since 1940?

1940. Almost a year after Pa's death when, looking for a letter addressed to both of us, I opened a desk drawer in Dick's study, picked up an inch thick batch of attached notes and saw that Dick had been doing research on poisons.

That was the year that Sugar intercepted a neighbour's child and in his haste to get away from me, a tooth broke the skin on her wrist. That was when—the following day—my neighbour came to me with tears in his eyes and Sugar's dead body in his arms. Terrified for his children, he had shot Sugar through the head.

1940. The year I buried Sugar and left the house and Dick for the last time.

"It doesn't matter to you, whose feelings you hurt!" Flora was ready to burst into tears. "You run around, stepping all over people, thinking you know it all when ... Dick's a fool to put up with your nonsense!"

Nonsense, I said to myself. Nonsense! We were almost there. "I know it's nonsense," I said to Dick. We were driving to Newport to tell his mother we would be divorced. "I know it's nonsense, " I repeated, "but I must say it. I've been terrified of you for months. I keep thinking—I kept thinking you were going to murder me."

Dick has eyelashes like a girl's, very long and black and soft blue eyes and his eyes followed the curves as we swung along and around them. He drives fast. He was looking at the road and his expression didn't change and he didn't change his position at the wheel. "I intend—to," he said. "I've been walking around night after night, torturing my brain for the way–the means–how to do it."

Intended? ... Intend? ... Which! I had to stop the confusion in my head, clear it, and try to remember the rhythm of his sentence ... Intend? ... Intended? ...

"And," said Flora, right through her screaming, "It's just as well for you that you sit there with your mouth shut, for no matter what you say–what you try telling us–we know enough not to believe you. You can't fool us in this family. We know too much about you."

"Flora," I said, "I know better than to try to deceive you. You don't need help for that."

"Much good it would do you, if you tried! You'd better reconsider!"

"Reconsider!" My mother-in-law said. "I beg you, Philippa, don't divorce him. Please reconsider. When you first married, I confess–not knowing you and all–I was worried. But now I think of you as my own daughter. My own child." I love her with all my heart and I would never hurt her. Intend? ... Intended? ... And without Sugar on the long drive back. If he did it on impulse, tried an accident, and got caught, it would destroy her. I glanced at him and he was looking at me, so I said it. "Tell your mother, Dick, what we were talking about on the way up. That you were ready to ... "

"Yes, Mama," Dick said. "Philippa won't change her mind. I have been wondering how to kill her."

"Children!" My mother-in-law said. "How can you talk such nonsense! Touch the bell, Dick, I'm sure Philippa would like a cup of tea."

... Still at the card table and I saw by my watch we had been there for more than an hour. And Flora, so wound up in her fortifying rhetoric that she forgot to offer me a cup of tea.

"Is that man keeping you? How Dick can trust you is beyond me! Poor Dick! Spending his money and cheating on him!"

I was shouting but my voice came faintly to my ears. "I should have lied to you, Dick! I'm a fool! I should have lied! That's the correct thing to do: conventional. I'll never learn!"

"I wanted to put something in your car." Dick said, "Time it! Blow you to bits on the highway! Make sure you never reached him! Some of those nights ... Christ! I was going crazy! But don't you ever dare lie to me!

I trust you. It's all right now, well, not all right, but I won't murder you. Not now. You bitch! I trust you."

He took my hand and gently held it. And that was rare with him. He only does it when he is frightened of losing me; if I'm going or gone. When I'm there he renews himself by destroying me. A parasite, he must kill what he battens on.

"What can I do, Dick? You know I can't stay."

"I know. But don't worry. It's all right."

"I'm sorry–for all of it."

"Tell me something about him. Will he marry you? Can he take care of you?

"No."

"That's too bad. Maybe you'll change your mind."

"No."

"But how will you live?"

"I'm not frightened of work."

"Kitten, I've been hard with you about money, but you still have my power of attorney. I won't revoke it until this is final. Use it as you see fit."

Dick's money! I was revolted. Once this divorce was final I would never touch his money again!

... I got the alimony for a silly reason. By mistake! Because ... A fact stated euphemistically to Dick is turned in his brain to some kind of fantasy that has no relation whatsoever to what has been said. His propensity for turning the ugly truth to a beautiful dream–that will leave him free of any kind of responsibility–is limitless. It was all settled that I would not come back. But he is used to me.

It didn't occur to him to stop seeing me. He walked in and out of my studio as though it were his own. He was hoping against hope that I would change my mind about the divorce and, to keep the peace, I didn't disillusion him.

In 1941, after Pearl Harbour, he enlisted in the Navy and spent most of his time in Washington, but he was often in New York when I would have lunch or dinner with him. I was preparing for a one-man show at the Norlyst Gallery one morning when he phoned and asked me to lunch. And accidentally that day, in anger, I hit him with a verbal axe. And in anger I took his unexpected money. It happened like this:

I looked around the elegant dining room and I was exasperated. I could live for a week on the money he was spending for our lunch. We had spent two hours, leisurely dining and I was boiling! The light was going. I wouldn't have much time to paint.

"There is nothing in this world I wouldn't do for you," Dick said, "you know that." Delicately, with a fork and knife, he was peeling a pear. I watched him take a fastidious bite. Hell! To hell with him!

"Hell!" I said, "Come down to earth Dick! There's 'nothing in this world you wouldn't do for me'–except protect me. You have never done that, unless I forced you to. Even then ... "

He put the napkin to his lips but they were clean. There was nothing to wipe. "You know I wanted to. I can't help the way I'm made!" Fastidious! Fastidious! The way he eats drives me crazy!

He looked at me reproachfully, for we both understand the way he's made. We have discussed it, and without anger, often. When he is– unpleasant–its because he can't help it: that's 'the way he's made.'

"Dick," I said. "The light's going. Forgive me for rushing, but I must leave."

"Not yet!" he said. "I've got the whole afternoon ahead of me, and I especially wanted to see you. Talk to you."

Ten minutes more and I would explode! "Dick," I said. "Your philosophy and your principles intrigue me but I'm tired of words. I'm sick of the bargain basement life you've forced on me; the cheapest price for all you can get. I don't have to remind you that you'd have plenty of money if you never did another stroke of work. If there's 'nothing in the world you wouldn't do for me' I'll accept your help. I hear I'm a genius in paint. You can support me."

He said, "Not that." He swallowed another dainty bit of pear. "Why should I give you alimony? You left me for another man. I'm the wronged one."

"Wronged! Wronged? I wronged you? The truth! How dare you! We've been married thirteen years, and in that time, which of us has wronged the other? The truth!"

He put down his napkin carefully. "Kitten," he said, "We have one thing and it's rare. And no one can take it away from us–ever. We speak the truth to each other. Frankly, you are the least selfish person I have ever known. You have helped me, taught me and given me more than you know. I have learned more from you than from anyone I have ever met. I owe you a great deal. But I won't give you a cent."

I said then through my unexpected and sudden furious tears–and it was my anger that bluffed him, for I never intended to do it, I would never have done it–"Really, Dick? Is that true? All the good I've done you? Then

408

I shall help you once more by bolstering up your fine and honourable principles. You shall pay your debt to me. And the way it hurts most. I'll fight you, in court, for money."

"Kitten!" he said. "Don't! Stop crying! Don't! It's true. You're right! Hush! What do you want? I'll give it to you. Hush!"

I couldn't find my handkerchief. I was using my napkin to shield my face from the hovering waiter. "Get rid of him!"

Dick told the waiter to go away. He took the napkin from my hand and gave me a clean handkerchief.

"Will you do me one favor? he asked.

"What do you want? I'll try."

"If you get what you deserve in paint, or whatever you do—and I think you will—you'll be famous one day. I'd like to think I had some part in it. Promise me that when this is over, no matter who you marry, that for your work you'll use my name.

I cried and cried. I couldn't stop crying.

"Vera," Flora screamed in her quiet voice, "Your Aunt Philippa has painted a picture for you."

Vera didn't like it.

Her face red with anger, Flora said, "Anyone who can't afford a present for a child at Christmas is beneath my notice, or anyone else's with any feelings at all."

I was stung at last to protest. "Flora," I said, "have you heard about the war? You can't set foot in this house without falling over Vera's presents. Sue cashed a bond for a thousand dollars for my refugees, the Volkovs. They depend on me. Dick refuses to help them. She gave me a hundred extra for ny fare, so I could come to you. I gave fifty of that to the Polish orphans. Really, I ... "

Flora turned her back on me.

"God,"I said. "that's enough." I can't endure it. I want to put the whole thing out of my mind."

God's voice rumbled back at me like an angry and jagged cloud. "I didn't like it either that day, when Flora's husband called you a shit."

"God," I asked, "How have I turned them into enemies?"

"Ho hum," God rumbled."

"What a voice! You're blowing straight through my head, and along with Flora's screaming ... "

"Perhaps," God roared, "she is screaming because you forgot your promise to her. In my opinion Flora has some fine qualities."

"You mean the Christmas Pa died?" I was jealous. "You mean You prefer her to me?"

"I judge ye," he said, "separately and privately. Comparisons are odious. Take a look, " he said. "There you are, you and Flora in Edgeville. *I'll be grateful to you for the rest of my life for taking care of Pa.*" He mimicked me.

"God," I objected. "Did Flora take care of Papa just for me? Must Flora always be paid?"

God made a wooshing noise in my ears, He sounded like a train letting off steam. "You told Flora you could never repay your debt to her and now," and He mimicked me again, " *I want you to put that whole thing out of my mind.*"

I was cornered, humiliated. "Dammit to hell!" I shouted. "You pay absolutely no attention to me for years, and now You intrude!"

"I can separate you head from your neck with a flick of My Thumb."

When God wants His Way He is lethal! The pressure was terrific! I was suffocating! I was terrified! "Get Your Thumb off my gullet!" But I couldn't even scream because he squashed my scream to a whisper. And whether or nor I wanted to, I was in for it: there I was, swearing my eternal love and gratitude to Flora. Swearing it over my father's coffin.

"Yes," God nagged. "Flora took care of him. You stayed away."

"God," I screamed, resenting Him. *You* ought to know! Once I promised to kill him, I didn't dare go anywhere near him! But Pa loved me! He loved me best! And he trusted me. It was *me*, he asked. In his final need, he came to me." I waited to hear if God would deny that, but He was gone. It was Tom Keats who was whispering to me.

"Oh, good!" Tom exclaimed. "Did you never wonder about that? Who else in the family would promise to end his life? To whom other could he have gone?

I lay shaking in the sudden and ominous stillness.

"Could he ask your mother?"

I was horrified. "Never! Anyway, she wouldn't know how."

"Sue?"

"Are you mad? He would not shock Sue!"

"Your beloved Flora?"

"For God's sake, Tom, be reasonable. Where Vera is concerned Flora would brave the gates of hell, But for Pa? Pa couldn't risk it."

"What about Geoffrey?"

"If Geoffrey were not a physician ... but there's his hypocratic oath. Geoffrey couldn't do it. Pa would never ask him."

410

"Well," whispered Tom, "Pa was right to ask you. And quite safe. For who, in that Canadian backwoods village, would suspect that you, your father's pet, as they so quaintly put it, would kill her father?"

"Safe! Safe?" I was in a blind rage. "You supercilious ass! Who cared? Who thought of safety? My safety never crossed his mind! Or worried him as little as it did me! And that was not all!"

... It wasn't my safety ... I could deal with that, but ... Would he wake up? Discover me? Would he understand? Forget he had asked me to do it? Would he shrink from me in horror? What if, too late, he had decided against it without telling me! Not euthanasia then but murder! Patricide!

"Pa! Pa!" I screamed, clutching at the pillow, and Flora's screams echoed with mine in the air. "Pa! Tell me it was because you trusted me! Not that I am the only one in the family who is ... " I said it at last ... "Unscrupulous."

"Love me! Love me!" Pa whispered.

And there was a great radiance around his voice so that I was happy—but annoyed. "Love me! Love me! Why do you say that, when you know I do!"

"Love him!" God roared. "Love him!" My father was speaking but God's voice blurred out his words. "Love him! He has need of it for only love can mitigate his punishment. It's time to consider his sin—to judge him for what he did to his favourite child, the child he loved best. Love him! Love him! Love him as much as you possibly can, for you shall bear witness against him."

Outraged—with violence—I shrieked my resentment against His despicable command. "What? What! Bear witness against my father? God! Are You mad? Hah! You're mad!"

"Love me," my father whispered. "Love me."

What transpired then to transform us all? ...

... It was not gold at all, his throne. It was constructed of living trees, great towering trees—were they oak? With saplings bent between them to support his back and bear his weight.

> ... *Set in the primeval wilderness where the*
> *wind howled and shook*
> *and the sun and the wind and the clouds and*
> *the sun*
> *the thunder and the great crashing streaks*
> *of blinding light*
> *over us, through, around, and over us*

... And at His right hand, in a smaller seat on a level with him, I was in my place.

I touched the white cotton robe that He wore and felt how the coarse and earthy and common stuff enhanced His Mightiness–silk on God would be tawdry. I felt that Giant and Muscular Arm that loomed above me and understood at last why my father came with the words "love me." God would impose penance on him for asking me to kill him. And only human love could ease that penance.

"God!" I shrieked again. "Don't be an idiot! Why blame Papa for something he–we–never did! He changed his mind!"

"It was the intent," God said. His voice booming in on the rolling thunder. "Not the act."

The heavens were riven and the lightning and the flood and my father at the judgement chair, kneeling. God towering above, and I between them. But I could not reach or touch my father.

"You haven't any rights over Pa!" In frustration and fright, I was hysterical. I clawed at His Indifferent, Impervious Arm. "Listen! Listen to me!" Could He hear in that howling wind? "Papa is an atheist! He never asked You–or any man–what to do! He just did it!" My heart exploded like withered straw to nothing. Pity flamed through it and touched it to dust. Pa is as good as God, any day in the week! And he was helpless! Caught!

God didn't even answer me. He was talking to Pa and I heard his words in hopeless disgust.

"You must beg Philippa's pardon! You have injured her!"

What a ... what a way to treat a guest! For, after all, we were in Heaven! And then I was angry ... and then amused–full of mirth. What nonsense! What sort of comedy? But I would not allow my father ...

"Pa," I said, hiding my impulse to howl with laughter behind forcedly sober and steady lips, (winking at him) and sarcastically, there's no need to apologize to me. I exculpate you."

"And who are you!" God roared, while everything shook in His Rage. "To mete out justice? It is I who shall decide. It is I who rule!"

"Pa," I shouted, furious again. "Don't do it! He's wrong!" And then, because I was afraid of the Fantastic Immensity of Him–His power–I bent down and whispered, "Ignore Him! Don't do it! He's wrong! There's no need."

But my father floated up to me and took my hand. "I tied the burden of my pain as a rock around the neck of a fledgling. I denied you peace and rest. I tormented you in the name of love. I have driven you in horror to madness. Forgive me, Philippa, I beg your pardon."

What was in my mind was to ask if anyone had made God beg Jesus' pardon! But the words faded away in stillness. There was a susurration of wings in the brilliance around us. Gliding, hovering birds crowded the breeze that tempered the ice on the sun. The breezes that cleansed and cooled our fever. And inexplicably then I began to cry: The person I loved and respected most, the person who had done more for me than anyone on earth, in his God-given wholeness and humility had come to beg my pardon!

"What an exhibition!" I said, trying to stem my tears, "Forgive me, Pa."

His hand was on my head.

"Be still, my child. Be still."

I put up my hand to cover his but there was only space. Yet against my hair I felt the pressure of his fingers. I lay in peace, secure, but haunted distantly by the echoes of a nightmare that was past and meaningless and could not touch me. I was drowsy.

"Be still, my child. I am here."

"Pa," I wept–the easy tears running sweet on my face. "Don't leave me, I want to talk to you. You talk to me."

... Talk? ... rigid, tense ... alert, talk? I pulled myself up on my hands and knees on the bed, crouched stiffly in my anxiety. Talk?

"Talk to me, Papa!" I whispered, "Talk!"

And there was his familiar voice, strong, and clear, sounding in my head, soothing me. Gently talking.

Talking!

I shot up in bed. "Pa! I can hear you! No pencil! I can hear your voice! Speak!"

And the others? And then I remembered. I had heard them all! I could distinguish one voice from another. God! Tom Keats! John! I had heard them! Heard their voices! No need of the pencil from now on! We could talk! I was free!

Still on my knees I lifted my hands, joined them, bent my head above them in prayer.

"God," I said, in awe, and the happy tears streamed down my face, "You have given me what I wanted most! I thank Thee."

And now they were with me, joyously demanding to be heard. But it was too much! There were too many! Their voices too clear! And who knew who might stop outside my door? Stop in the corridor and listen!

"Hush!" I whispered. "Hush! You who hate me to be loud or conspicuous! Must I caution you? Must I tell you that someone will come?"

I jumped out of bed and whirling blindly, I danced in joy, hugging myself–hugging them to me. I knocked over a chair and I tripped on the scattered clothes that were flung from it and I fell to the floor. I lay there hugging myself. Hugging them to me. Laughing. Glad.

After awhile I sat up. Serious now, happy, but sober.

"There is only one thing you have denied me, " I said. "I have asked for it over and over. Show yourselves to me. You know I am not afraid. Let me see you!"

"See yourself first," John Keats said. "There's a gift our Bobbie* wanted for the whole world. Few can do it, but that gift is granted now to you. Get up, Philippa, and look in the glass. See yourself as we see you–through our eyes."

"And after me?" I pleaded. "You? All of you?"

"That depends not on us but on Another. It depends on God," John said, solemnly.

"Ah, then I'll pray for it. He will grant me that too!" I was full of confidence that He would. It is true! God is Love!

I got up and picked up a towel to clean the neglected mirror. I must wipe the dust from it carefully and the circled smears of grease left by the hasty hands of the skivvy who did my room in ten fast minutes. When it was clean I placed myself in front of it and stared in shock. What had happened to me?

My charcoal hair was tangled in extraordinary beauty, shadowing my brilliant sapphire eyes. My white face had the subtle mystery, the bone-deep purity of a marble; of a sculpture from the hands of a master. Slender, graceful, despite the disarranged clothes, and I tore them off, for as with a piece of sculpture I must see, there stood before me a creature from another star. Hyperesthetically, I saw myself reflected in such beauty as I have never known, or had realized but dimly through the eyes of a lover.

That night ...

... the desert sand, the stinging red-hot smothering sand sifted down between us and cut me off. It filled my eyes, my nose, my mouth. It stretched into space beyond my weighted burning head, beyond my withered feet, beyond my charred hands. The chipped ice chinked against the frosted wet glass. It moved up and down. The chipped ice in the frosted water in the frosted wet glass moved beyond the aching ridges of stinging hot sand–out of my burning reach. It moved beyond my useless, my struggling, my hopeless reach ...

---

* Robert Burns: *Oh wad some power the giftie gie us, to see oursels as others see us!*

I woke alone.

The still, dark, bitter dampness of the London night, the London winter, oozed through my window. No moon, or it was hidden, but enough light to make out the shadowed clothes hung on a rack and the few sticks of furniture. I was alone.

Where were they?

I heard my voice, quiet at first, calling them.

There was no hurry. They could hear me.

There was no hurry. They would come.

There was no hurry, I assured myself, pleading with them to hurry.

Yet the night wore on and they were silent.

The room was heavy with silence. Dead silence. The air was lifeless, dull, blank with the relentless silence. The room was empty.

They were gone.

Gone!

And finally ... more helpless, more lost and more alone than I have ever been or dreamed of being, I knew in irresistible, in continuing, in uncontrollable and screaming agony, that if the dead, too, had found me wanting, denied me, deserted me, then God, Himself, had gone and there was nothing left.

It was that night that they forced their way into my room and—in coaxing trickery—took me to an institution for the insane.

36

J ust before they put me in the ambulance Gilbert Stuart in a high, thin, mocking voice came to torment me. "Yoo-hoo-Philippa, it's Gillie. You're not alone anymore, ha-ha-ha-ha-ha, Gillie's here and Gillie's staying."

I was astonished. Gilbert Stuart, the 19th century American painter had had a great success in London and Paris. I was familiar with his *Athenæm* (the left side of George Washington's face on an unfinished canvas), but, a picture of his I noticed, in London's National Museum, I had thought second-rate. Had I hurt his feelings?

Stuart rode with me through the night streets of London, and despite my demand that he shut up, he never stopped talking. When two burly attendants, each taking an arm, took me out of the ambulance, walked me through an icy court, unlocked a grimy metal door, ushered me through it, and locked it behind me, I knew in horror that rather than a "Nursing Home" I was locked up in an insane asylum! And Gilbert's voice, in triumphant glee, shrilled and darted and swooped through my head like a frenzied dragon fly.

The shock brought me sharply to my senses. Flat on my back on a stretcher in the admitting room, I had to force myself to shout to the Intern above his malicious chatter. "Please! My brother, Geoffrey Jerrold, is a doctor in Boston, Massachusetts. Please! Get him on the trans-Atlantic phone. He... "

"Just a second," the intern interrupted me. "Hold on. Do you see that, Nurse? The chest is practically paralyzed. Are you sure you've had no drugs, Mrs. Bentham? You didn't take anything? No one gave you a hypodermic? Can you take a deep breath? Try!"

"I don't feel like it," I mumbled. It was stupid to be uncooperative with the doctor, but I'd told him before I'd taken nothing and I'd used my available breath. Anyway, who cared about my physical condition? Not I. If I was insane, I might just as well be dead. I'd better get hold of Geoffrey. I'd seen too many dumb interns, blind to the patient, tied to the book ... This one, though, looked intelligent. And he was kind. I said, with all my breath, loudly, "Is there no one here with authority to place a telephone call for me? Call the trans-Atlantic operator! Call Dr. Geoffrey Jerrold in Boston. Let me do it! Get me to a telephone!"

"It happens to be after midnight, Mrs. Bentham," the Intern replied gently. "Do you know that? Do you get excessively tired? Not just lately, but as a general thing? Have you always had periods of exhaustion?"

All the time, I thought. I fought exhaustion daily, but I wasn't exhausted, I was lazy. I'd been so damned lazy all my life it was painful. But I ignored it. I worked around the clock ... If it was midnight in London it would be six hours earlier in Boston, a good time to ring Geoffrey. "They took my money with my clothes," I said, "but Geoffrey will accept ... "

"No sedatives," the intern interrupted me again. "There's something very wrong. One pupil doesn't react to light, her toes don't curl when I scratch the sole of one foot, her chest ... Her breathing is too shallow." He lifted the blanket and put it around my shoulders. "Get her to bed as fast as you can and try to keep her warm. Make sure she's covered. Get her on to a stretcher and keep her out of a draft, if that's possible in this ..." he turned away.

Why did the intern ignore me? I was in a rage. I was naked under the stained blanket and I clutched it around me, gingerly. I sat up and slid my feet to the floor. "Are you deaf, Doctor?" I shouted, caustically–to his disappearing back. "Can't you hear me? I asked for the trans-Atlantic telephone!"

"Geoffff–rr-ry'ss going to l-o-o-v-v-ve getting that c-ra-ra-razz-y call fr-rom his c-r-r-rz-z-zyy s-sis–ss-ter," Gilbert shrilled in my head.

"You fool!" I shouted at Gilbert, "get the hell out of my ... "

"Oh, Oh!" the nurse said. "Now you stop that. Don't you be rude to the doctor. He's got to go. But don't worry, Dearie, I'll take care of you. You don't need that old stretcher now, do you? Come along." She led me, barefoot, to a door, unlocked it and propelled me into a damp, dimly-lit bathroom.

I could hardly breathe and the stench of ammonia and rotting wood was suffocating. I gagged and started to back out, but the door slammed behind me.

"Now, now," the nurse pulled at my blanket, "Come along, now. Sit down. You're going to have a nice bath."

I took a look at the great dirt-rust-stained tub ... dripping water ...

"Oh yippee!" Gilbert howled, reeling through my head. "Personally, I'd shoot myself before I got into that."

"Shut up, you bastard!" I shouted at Gilbert, but the fool was right. The dregs of London's slums: the diseased, the insane, the drug addicts, the

417

prostitutes and the drunks had used that tub. I knew. I had taken my nurse's training in a city hospital. I jerked away from the nurse, turned, grabbed for the doorknob and stopped. It was gone. I couldn't believe my senses. I started running my hand up and down the door. Did we have disappearing doorknobs on the psychopathic wards in our hospital? I couldn't remember. I was trapped. "God-dammit," I panted, "where ... "

"Now you stop that language," the nurse said, firmly, "and quit trying to crawl through that door. It's locked. Locks automatically, it does, and someone else got the key." She held up two red, swollen hands to show me—no key—backed off, leaned against the wall, and pressed a bell. "I get so bloody tired of you, uh ... " she said. Then she added, coaxingly, "Don't be hard, Dearie, I got to bath you. It's routine."

I saw the work-worn hands, the sagging body and the dark circles under the eyes, and I hesitated, irresolute, because I, too, had known the endless fatigue of night duty. I would have to let her bathe me, I decided, but if I told her I was a nurse, perhaps she would allow me a token bath.

"What's goin' on 'ere!"

I turned in fright.

A heavy, coarse-faced woman in a blue uniform, fists swinging, obviously prepared for battle, was standing in the doorway. I took a step towards her—to stand up to her—I despise bullies. I said, loudly and I hoped firmly and contemptuously, "Nothing that concerns you. You may leave, you ... "

Gilbert circled, creaking through my head like a ratchet-wheel. "Pipe down, you nut!" he croaked. "They'll dunk you anyway. This is a well-run bughouse."

"You numbskull!" I shouted at him, "You vulgar ... "

"Now you watch your tongue!" the nurse yelled at me. She was running water into the tub. "I don't want no more out of you!"

Damn Gilbert! He flustered me. I shouldn't talk out loud to him, they would misunderstand. "N-not y-you, nurse."

"Not Mrs. Jones, either," the nurse upbraided me. "She's not to be talked to like that. She's a nice woman. You ought to be ashamed of yourself. Now you get over here and get in this nice water."

God! I thought, I haven't enough breath to explain and besides Gilbert kept ... "Look," I panted, surrendering my blanket to the nurse. "Look, I'll get in, but please let me stand up. I don't want to sit down. Look, I have to talk to my brother in America. Please listen, I ... "

"Oh no. Not again. Not the trans-Atlantic telephone again. Will you get in that tub? And sit down!"

418

All of a sudden I began to tremble. How could I forget? The nurse could do nothing but ignore the yammering of the insane. I stepped into the tub and–my knees wouldn't hold me–slid down into the water.

I spent the remainder of that night in a ward with about thirty other patients, huddled, head and all, under a thin blanket, sleepless. Although I was terribly cold it turned out to be a very happy night because Gilbert left (I never heard from him again) and John Keats and his brother, Tom, came and stayed with me until morning.

At daylight–a grim, cheerless dawn, in a grim, cheerless ward–the night nurse went off duty, and two attendants, student nurses I suppose, came on. They rattled and banged a heavy metal food cart down the ward, dealing out thick handleless mugs of tea and bowls of gluey gruel. A nurse will not eat from the patients' dishes, we know the diseases they might have– and the careless hospital kitchens. In any case, I had been fasting for a long time and I felt no hunger or thirst, so I refused to eat or drink. I was restless, tense, very cold and longing for a cigarette, but I knew it was useless to ask for one.

I looked at my neighbour, the trembling woman in the next bed– paralysis agitans, I wondered, who was smearing porridge on her face and dropping it down her neck in an effort to get the spoon to her mouth and I got out of bed in my bare feet and knee-length hospital gown to feed her.

The nurse snatched the bowl from my hand. "Get to your bed!" she shouted. "She's had enough!"

The patient, straining helplessly to reach the food, screwed up her face and began to cry.

I thought it over: a patient in a psychiatric ward, I was suspect. I got into bed. But when I saw the cart go round the ward in quick-time and the rest of the dishes, full or empty, slung on it, and these two Sairy Gamps* wheel it to the utility room and stay there, drinking tea and gossiping, while the patients groaned and moaned and called for them ... in a rage, I got out of bed again and stalked to the door and, cursing my hysterical voice, which I couldn't control, I shrieked, "You two hulking slobs, get back on the ward!"

To my surprise they jumped up like a couple of marionettes and ran to the door. But as I stood aside to let them pass, each seizing one of my elbows, they hustled me along a dark corridor, pulled open a heavy, barred door, and threw me into a padded cell.

---

* Sairy Gamp: a gin drinking, sluttish nurse: a character in one of Charles Dickens' novels.

A padded cell is the most comfortable place one could possibly imagine. And because they threw me, I landed in this one on my face and it was like landing on puffs of air. The floor and walls were upholstered in soft, tan-coloured leather, buttoned deeply in squares, about every six inches. It was warm and quiet inside and fairly dark. I was furious and then, because of my absurd position, spread-eagled on my face on the floor, I had to laugh. Then I thought, what an ass I am, if I'd known, I'd have raised hell last night, and succumbing to comfort, I lay still enjoying it.

Around four that afternoon, despite my protestations, they took me back to the ward and Dr. Ames, the resident, a slender man of medium height with blue eyes and sandy-brown hair came to visit me. I liked him at once. He sat down on my bed and took both my hands in his. "What's your name?" he asked.

"Philippa Bentham."

"Oh? So you admit to being you? Some people in here prefer to be someone else."

I laughed. "Like the virgin Mary?"

"Uh, well, she's not too popular, there are other candidates who ... Do you know where you are?"

"Yes."

"I see. And how did you discover that?"

"It came to me," I said, "suddenly, out of the blue–nothing to do with my surroundings."

"I see, you're bright. Has anyone done anything to harm you?"

"In the hospital? Certainly not."

"No one did anything to you here or outside?"

"Why, no!"

"Well, tell me how did you get in that padded cell?"

"Oh, that. I tried to get your staff to do a little nursing."

"By force?"

"I beg your pardon?"

"Uh–what kind of a try?"

"I suggested to them they were a couple of sluts."

"Really? Nothing else?"

"In a loud voice. That's all."

"You didn't attack them?"

"Attack those two hulking–do you think I'm craz-uh–" I suddenly found it hard to breathe. "I should have, perhaps."

"That's not their story."

I inclined my head, politely. "Probably not," I murmured. Why bother to try to prove I wasn't a liar? I'd tried that as a child and growing up, but the vindictive one–not me–always won. Wasted effort.

At this point Keats spoke in my head. "Say, Oxford University Press," he ordered.

"What?" I exclaimed, astonished. But I trusted Keats. I put my hand lightly on Dr. Ames' sleeve and looked into his eyes. "Oxford University Press," I said.

"What are you talking about?" he asked.

"I have no idea," I confessed. "Does it mean anything to you?"

"Not a thing."

"But it must," I insisted. "Why would Keats ... "

"Keep on saying it," Keats whispered in my head.

So I kept repeating it until Dr. Ames got up and left. "Damnation, Keats, what was that all about?" I protested. "I wanted to ask him to telephone Geoffrey!"

"You do as you're told," Keats replied, coldly. "We're running this show. And I told you before, stop calling me Keats, call me John, I'm sick of never hearing me first name."

I spent another freezing night on the ward and I was bitterly lonely. I wanted to talk to Pa and I called and called for him, but he didn't come. I kept remembering his death. My horrible secret. My horrible agony. Then I thought of Dick. More horror. I couldn't breathe; I was in agony.

"You're wanted in the office," the nurse said, shaking me. She pulled the blanket off my head. She was carrying a faded, cotton hospital robe and slippers. "Get up, Mrs. Bentham, the doctors want to talk to you."

Dazed, I got out of bed. "What time is it?"

"Ten o'clock," She helped me on with the robe, took my arm, led me to the front of the ward and ushered me into a small office. There were four men and a woman seated behind a narrow, scrubbed, deal table. Doctors. "Sit down, Mrs. Bentham."

I sat down on a high stool, facing them and the window. Daylight–I must have slept.

"Do you know where you are, Mrs. Bentham?"

"Yes, of course. An insane asylum."

"Is there anything we can do for you?"

What could they do? Nothing they could do would change the past. Or the future. If I was mad, I'd remain locked up. "No." I said, "Thank you, but no."

"Nothing at all?"

"Nothing."

"You don't want anything? We're willing to help you."

How could they help me? Everything was past. "My father was cremated," I said. "Burned to ashes, while Geoffrey ... " But Geoffrey's behaviour at that time was too shameful to be made public. Perhaps if they understood about Dick ... "Before I divorced my husband," I said, and stopped. I must never tell on Dick. Had I driven him to it? His innocent eyes, his tears, when he admitted to me, "I was going to put something in your car, blow you up on the highway, but Darling, I ... " Still, after I'd left Dick, there was the strange accident to our garage. It had blown up, burned to the ground with both cars before they could stop it ... I'd made my decision about that, I couldn't tell them anything. My throat was parched, I was dying for a cigarette. "All I want now," I said, "is a cigarette. Would one of you, please, give me a cigarette?"

No one moved. No one spoke. The nurse touched my shoulder. "Come along," she said, "we're going back to bed." She opened the door and we started down the ward.

God! I thought, I really am insane. I stopped. "I have to go back!" I exclaimed, "I forgot to ask them to telephone my brother."

"No, no, that's all, you've had your interview. They know all about your brother." She pushed me ahead of her down the ward.

At four that afternoon when Dr. Ames made rounds, he came and sat on my bed. "I talked to Dr. Jerrold," he said. "We're moving you."

Geoffrey, in his usual fashion, had been throwing his weight around: "Get her out of the ward," He ordered Dr. Ames, "if you have to give her your own office. And keep her under sedation."

Dr. Ames was impressed. He'd looked him up; Geoffrey had made a name for himself in medicine very early: he had been the first to institute early rising after surgery, in the U.S.A.; he was the youngest Fellow in the American College of Surgeons.

A few hours later I was moved to a private room: a store-room off the main ward that had been hastily cleared to make room for a cot for me. And that evening, I suppose because Geoffrey ordered it, the nurse brought me a full ounce of thick, black, liquid chloral-hydrate, and told me to drink it. I couldn't believe my eyes. A capsule of seven and a half grams was what we had dispensed to delirium tremens patients in New York. One gram is a knock-out drop: a "Mickey Finn." But while the nurse turned her head away and shuddered in revulsion, I drank it down, greedily. Between being talked to day and night by both the living and the dead, knowing I was

422

insane and likely to be locked up indefinitely, and worrying about my past, I hadn't had a moment's peace as far back as I could remember. I'd have drunk kerosene if it would have put me to sleep.

I woke in the middle of the night, badly hallucinating. By the light of a brilliant moon shining through the window at the head of my bed, I could see a jungle of moving leaves and animals shining on the ceiling. And that night I was afraid. A stranger's voice spoke to me: "You have a cloven hoof," he said. I put my hand on my foot and it was shaped like a goat's. I didn't dare lift the blanket to look at it, but I felt it as plainly as if I had.

I turned to look at the moon through the window. It rose above the iron bar of my bed and then it dipped below it. Philippa! Philippa! I reproached myself, stop moving your head. I hooked my chin carefully on the top bar of the bed and held my head steady with both hands. The moon kept rising and dipping, up and down, up and down. The hell with it.

I cuddled down into bed because I didn't want to waste the sleepy effect of the chloral-hydrate, though God knows, I didn't feel sleepy. And on the wall there appeared brilliant, round lights about the size of a silver dollar that I saw at frequent intervals. Where did they come from? They disappeared when I placed my hand over them–not appearing on the back of my hand, as they should, if the light came from an external source–and reappeared on the wall when I lifted my hand. That was ridiculous.

"Go stand in the corner and repent of your sins," the stranger's voice commanded.

I was wretched about my sins but too exhausted to move. I would have to repent of them in bed.

"Philippa, Philippa," the voice said, despairing, "you'll never get anywhere. You never improve. You never do the right thing."

I was glad when morning came.

Around ten that morning one of the charming duo who threw me into the padded cell–but who had been terribly sweet to me since I was important enough to rate a private room–came in and said, "Your sister is here, Mrs. Bentham. Gee, you should see her! She must be good and rich. I heard her tell Dr. Ames she's staying at Claridges. Are you rich, too?"

Claridges? Flora? It didn't sound like her. I took her to the old Ritz in New York for breakfast, just before I sailed for France, and she thought it was dowdy. She thought I looked dowdy, too. I was wearing an original Balman. "Why do you always wear such drab clothes?" she asked me.

Yet here she was. She must have flown over. Flora ... Before my divorce I introduced her, by telephone, to Alex, who had loved me for a long time and who had come from Paris to see me. He barely listened to her, then handed me the phone. "She doesn't approve of me," he said, mildly.

Flora disapproved of the illicit love affairs of others but, naturally, not of her own. A year later–still married to Edward–she came to my studio and beat her breast for three days about losing her lover. At the end of three days it occurred to her to ask about me. "Why don't you show me one of your paintings?" she said.

"There's one on the wall behind you."

"Oh, it's dull, isn't it? I guess," hesitating, "I guess it's all right."

"Leo Lerman of *Town & Country* thought it was very good."

"Really? That one? For heaven's sake."

Flora. In an emergency, she came out on top!

"I'm lousy, stinking rich," I informed Miss Gamp, "and I've got your name in my little book and my spies are watching you, so you'd better get back on the ward and do some work or I won't leave you my money."

"Do you really know my name?" the nurse asked. "And you won't forget me if you go away? You're not mad at me? Shall I write my name down for you–in case you forget it?"

"Don't bother," I said. "How could I forget you? Tell my sister to hurry up."

Flora must be looking very well. And she had flown to London to take care of me.

My heart melted. All my anger and disgust drained away and the love and admiration that glowed in me for Flora–whenever she allowed me her friendship–was renewed. After this, Flora and I would be friends, always.

The door moved. I opened my mouth to say, "Flora, how wonderful of you to come!" And kept it open, and silent, in shock.

Flora! I thought, you bastard! And Geoffrey–trust you to leave the dirty work to someone else. A doctor and a nurse, they understood the risks. How dared they send a lay-person to deal with insanity.

For it was my sister, Sue, covered from head to foot in black mink, who walked in, dripping tears.

"Well!" I said, sharply. "You've been telling me, for years, I'm crazy. And now that you find me in the loony bin you should be delighted to know you were right. Come here and give me a kiss."

"Why, Philippa Jerrold Bentham!" she said, and widened her big blue eyes at me. "There's nothing wrong with you at all. Thank God!"

"Nothing but a slight case of insanity," I said. And I wondered, again, what kind? Why couldn't I diagnose my own case? I had no idea.

Sue threw her arms around me and kissed me, laughing in relief. She started to take off her coat, hesitated, wrapped it around her, whirled like a model on one foot and said, archly, "How do you like my coat? Elliot gave it to me for Christmas."

"It's divine," I said, enthusiastically. "No wonder Miss Gamp fell flat on her face."

"You really like it?"

"It's superb. Elegant. I adore it. How come you're here? Where's Geoffrey? Or Flora?"

"Why, they couldn't possibly come," Sue said. "They're both busy. Everyone thought it was easier for me."

How true. Much easier.

" What about your pact with Elliot that you fly together or not at all? Did Elliot want you to fly the Atlantic alone?"

"Oh, well, an emergency. Aren't you glad I'm here?"

"I can't tell you how glad! Keep your coat on. It's cold here. What did Dr. Ames tell you? What am I? Schizo? Manic? Paranoid? What did he say?"

"It *is* chilly here. Aren't you cold?" Sue wrapped her fur around her and sat down. "Yes, I did talk to him and I don't understand because he told me you were very sick. You look fine to me."

"He didn't happen to give you a name for it?"

"Oh, you've only been here a few days. They wait before they diagnose these things."

I would have to be extremely careful, I thought, not to upset or frighten Sue, but one thing, I could talk to her, after our time with the ouija board, she would understand about the dead. The difference was that then we had struggled to have them spell out laborious messages to us, now they spoke to me directly, in my head.

What I could not tell her was that I was in terror lest someone evil oust my friendly and beloved spirits and taking over, control me against my will. For the spirits of the dead came with enormous physical power. If I had been living in the Middle Ages I would have said that I was possessed. At times, my movements submitting to an outside force, I had no free will. The air around me, invisible, or visible as heat waves, was as tight as a wide band of some unknown material. Encircled by it, I would be lifted bodily from my bed, Walking, it might control the direction of my steps and the speed. At times, infiltrating my muscles, my strength was increased beyond belief and praying for it to depart, I lay still, fearful of harming someone. The legendary strength of the madman is not fiction.

To prevent this power from being directed by malignant forces, I thought of primitive superstitions and I, repeatedly, made the sign of the cross at each orifice of my body, praying that no evil enter. This vigilance was horribly exhausting but I dared not stop.

However serious my disease, Sue paid no attention to it and with Dr. Ames' consent she took the plane to New York alone with me. Geoffrey, his face unnaturally strained, hatless as usual, met us at the airport. I noticed that his arm and fingers were held stiffly, but were not in a sling. I was in no hurry to greet him. Deliberately, I stared at him. Keats said, "Say soap, there's a soap factory near here."

I said it with a straight face, staring at Geoffrey. "Why did I say it, John?" I asked silently.

"Oh, nuts," he replied impatiently. "That's what you say in the backwoods of Canada. You're full of soft soap."

Geoffrey walked away from me.

Did he get it? I have no idea, but Keats' remarks generally sent whoever was talking to me in another direction.

Elliot arrived to meet Sue.

"We have two cars," Sue said. "Whom do you want to drive home with? Geoffrey or Elliot?"

To my astonishment and rage–for how could Geoffrey know I would not do something foolish in traffic?–Geoffrey took Sue in his car. Poor Elliot, I thought, forced to drive five miles with a madwoman. I had an almost irrational impulse to say "Boo!" But fear of the insane is not funny. I kept to my side of the seat and I was very quiet.

At Sue's insistence I stayed in bed for the first few days, but I got up when her doctor sent a specialist to examine me. When he informed us that if I stayed with Sue it would not be necessary to hospitalize me, I chose not to do so.

I made that decision for two reasons. I had no idea of the nature of my illness and my memories of psycho were still vivid. I was terrified of paranoia: my voices, now subdued, but still with me, had before controlled me, they might do so again. I could not risk the possibility of harming Sue.

The second reason was that the word asylum had assumed a very different meaning from its popular connotation. It appeared to me, and appealed to me, as an inviolable sanctuary. I had come to an horrific crisis in my life and I had drastic need for respite from outside pressures.

When Sue refused to sign me into an asylum, I signed myself into the Westchester Division of the New York Hospital. (I discovered later that this institution was known unofficially as the Millionaire's Country Club.)

When I was admitted to the hospital and given a room, Geoffrey came to see me. "If you don't like it here let me know and I'll have you moved."

Moved? I thought, ironically. No one would move me now without my doctor's advice or consent. I said, drily, blank faced, "Why should I move? I'm happy here, in fact I've never been so happy in my life."

Geoffrey stared, then he laughed. Then he walked away.

My beloved, brilliant brother, he would come back and talk to me, I thought. Flora would come, for this was the moment when deeply moved, in sympathy, we would talk; understand each other.

Six weeks later when my doctor asked if my brother had come to see me I said, "No."

"But that's ... " She looked startled.

I laughed. "That's normal."

Geoffrey sent flowers and I wrote and thanked him. Did I deliberately make my letter a little odd? His wife sent a picture postcard. Two eskimos rubbing noses. About the third month–the hospital had told me they could no longer hold me–Geoffrey flew in, in a hell of a rush because he had to fly back the same day. I broke down and asked him to talk to me.

"It's not my department in medicine," he said. "If you have anything to say about me or the family, tell it to your psychiatrist."

I told my psychiatrist that if she thought it best, I'd leave, but I didn't want to: I had no idea where I'd go or what I'd do if I left the hospital. In the end, and with the hospital's consent, I stayed another three months. It was during my first three months in the hospital that I met Alethea.

Eventually, Flora came to New York, but she didn't come to see me. She told my doctor she had always been unfailingly kind and generous to me, that she had been closest to me of anyone in the family and that she couldn't imagine why *I* was unkind to her.

Sue never missed a week, bringing me fruit, flowers and even a new lipstick called "psycho pink!" Because she never pulled her punches and behaved as natural and frivolous as ever–when it comes to putting people at ease, Sue has the brains in our family–we might just as well have been having lunch at the Plaza. I asked her if she had ever been frightened of me.

"Once," she said, "when you first came home and insisted that I turn off the light so I could see the pictures on the ceiling."

I remembered that. I couldn't see them in the light and I couldn't understand why Sue couldn't see them, or, for that matter, why she couldn't hear my voices.

The telephone was ringing ... I put down my pen and picked up the receiver.

Millie said, "My God! Philippa, it's about time! D'you realize I haven't heard from you in months? What's going on? What are you doing there? I thought the Lodge was closed. I talked to Lottie, she says you're writing a book. What happened to your painting? What ... "

"Oh Millie! How wonderful to hear from you, I ... " I stopped. I should have called her weeks ago.

"Yes? Well, go on. What are you doing?"

"At the moment? Uh, well ... I'm sitting here counting my thumbs. How are you? I meant to call you, but ... "

"I know. You're back from Africa because your mother died. I talked to Sue, but I couldn't get hold of her for weeks, either. I want to see you. Henry wants to see you. When are you coming to Boston?"

"Millie ... I want to see you, too. Let me think about things, I'll figure out a date and let you know. I'm in the middle of something here and not sure I should move. I have endless things to tell you, I should have called you before. It's not a book, I ... "

"Are you all right? You sound ... What's on your mind?"

I laughed. "At the moment? The Fulham General Hospital–in London."

"Jesus! You thinking of going back?"

"Not today. Look, the road's closed here. I can get out by helicopter but not now. I'll call you soon, or write–and lay bare my soul–or what substitutes for it. Are you all right? Henry? The children? Give them my love?"

"Do you need anything?"

"Just your love."

"All right, soon!" She hung up.

I sat back in my chair. Once out of Westchester, after leaving Sue, I had gone to Boston to spend a weekend with Millie and Henry. I'd ended up staying six weeks, while we dissected every minute that had led to my incarceration and every minute during it. They were my oldest and dearest friends, but until then it had never occurred to me to confide in them.

I left Westchester with no idea of the state of my finances. Dick had settled money on me at the time of our divorce, enough to live on, but I'd lost track. Sue and Geoffrey and Flora had paid my hospital bill and I would have to pay them back. I was still hearing voices when I left and the doctors knew it. I had never concealed anything from them. "You're a good patient, Mrs. Bentham."

I wanted to begin a new life away from everything familiar to me, and it was Graham Young, an old friend, who suggested Cape Town, South

428

Africa, and who provided me with the introductions that allowed me to establish myself very early in–what was for me–a new country.

Before leaving New York I had lunch with Dr. Burdick, chief of women doctors at Westchester. I asked if I should consult a psychiatrist in Cape Town. She said "No." I then told her that I had come to believe that I had brought the madness on myself. She said, "Oh, no."

My voices left me gradually over three years and never came back, but I have moments of precognition ... There was one strange incident before I left, I ... I glanced at the clock. Lottie's neighbours were flying over for dinner and I was late. I heard the helicopter. I had better change, stat.

37

I was in the largest greenhouse, talking to Abram, when we heard the helicopter coming down. It landed and Johnathan passed in front of it and opened the door for Alethea.

Abram said, "I'm always glad to see him safe on land."

"Yes."

"That's Lady Alethea, do you know her?"

"I met her after the war."

I had been running with Fish when Abram signalled me to come in. He was a handsome man, who had survived the German occupation of Paris by supplying the High Command with exotic plants and orchids. World renowned for his experiments in horticulture, by assuming an attitude befitting a country simpleton, both he and his supposed rustic employees, free of suspicion, had been allowed to come and go as they pleased. They had established a significant listening post for the Paris Resistance.

"Lottie is waiting for this." Abram wrapped a plant and placed it in my hands. "Tell her to water scantily."

I didn't move. I was suddenly breathless. Johnathan would be with Lottie. I looked a fright.

Halfway across the floor, Abram stopped to look at me. "My dear? ... It's not the moment." He came back and lightly touched my arm. "Leave it in the kitchen with Cook."

"Thank you!" I ran.

I gave the plant to Cook, plus instructions. I was still breathless. She started to tell me Johnathan had arrived, when I interrupted her. "Sorry to rush off, but ... "

Cook said, "Oh, you know. All right, run. He'll be on his way to the kitchen any minute now."

I tore up the back stairs. Johnathan here! I was terrified! I was in love. What if he took one look at me and ... What did I really know about him?

There was a note from Elsa on a stack of unopened letters on my desk. Sue kept sending them, but I couldn't think about anyone but Johnathan, so I hadn't looked at them. I opened Elsa's note. Johnathan would see me at lunch and asked that I would ride to the village with him directly afterward. Ride with him? … On a fool's errand? … to a fall? I threw the note at the desk and my hand hit the letters and knocked them to the floor. I got down to pick them up … a letter from Dick! Now what? I ripped it open.

Washington, D.C.
November 13th

Dear Philippa,

Your are most elusive. I enclose a letter sent to me from Paris to forward to you.

Where are you; how are you; what are you doing?

Mama is anxious. I told her you would undoubtedly write to her at Christmas. Please write to her. She has lost no feelings for you, and is as hopeful for your future as ever.

More anon and soon. Give me your address please! Via the enclosed envelope.

Must to bed now, as social business has been most distracting of late. Please give forth with a bit of news.

Cherrio and stuff, and
Love,
Your erstwhile.

Distracting! I could do nothing–had done nothing for days, waiting– worrying about what was going to happen when Johnathan finally came home.

I must telephone Betty!

I picked up a letter from Italy. Alex! I hadn't heard from him in ages.

Monselice
Padova
March 11th

Dear Philippa,

Do you remember me? I think so, even with no word of you. I write in hope.

As you see, I am at home in Italie after having spent four months in the lovely hills of Calabrie.

And you? What are you doing? Are you in New York? Paris?

Write to me. I await news of you.

As always
Alex

Just seeing his writing warmed my heart!

A heavy letter from Martha. ... The snapshots she'd promised me. I'd open it later. I shoved the rest of the letters together to put them away when *The Curator of the National Museum* caught my eye. My picture! I'd put my pictures in storage when I left Africa, but I'd completely forgotten the one in the Museum.

> *Cape town*
> *November 7th*

Philippa,

> *You never write? The group show was a success, but long gone. And your picture—did you intend giving it to us?—I suppose not—in my possession.*
>
> *A representative of Liverpool London Globe Insurance wants it. Let me know if it's for sale and the price.*
>
> *I miss seeing the new work and lunch at the St. James. The Cape is not quite the same without you.*
>
> *Let me know about the picture.*
> *When are you coming back?*
> *A bientôt!*
> *R*

We were on horseback. Johnathan, slightly in the lead, was trying to calm his over-active mount.

The luncheon had been hilarious; a reciprocal outburst of happiness at being re-united, but I had not had a chance to talk to Johnathan alone. I was grateful that he'd greeted me with no embarrassing show of intimacy, but having tried to prepare myself for this public meeting, I had not anticipated an elemental—transcendental—shock when our eyes met, nor a primal instinct to fling myself into his arms! Perhaps that stunned me, for I did nothing, but I felt my face on fire.

It was a joy meeting Alethea again. Beginning with our initial encounter in the hospital workshop, where I was re-creating a Corot landscape—which she recognized—there had been an instant rapport between us. She had never discussed the cause of her illness, but I knew now that for a long time she had been alone in the narrow confines of an attic in a German Officer's whorehouse, forced to listen to obscenities and drunken trivia while trying to sort out confidentialities relating to the war effort.

She had become both claustrophic and frightened into a state of psychoneurosis, and began to see people as mindless, therefore dangerous—this developed into seeing them, literally, as monkeys or gibbering apes.

Fortunately, she didn't see me in that light and together, despite our sad mental and emotional states, we found moments of peace and harmony.

Alethea left the hospital ten days ahead of me. At the last minute she came to say good-bye. She had been invited to stay with friends at Cap d'Antibes, and had just had a card from them: "Everything balmy here, too." Thinking back, I had to smile.

Johnathan, his horse under control, was riding beside me–staring at me." I hope that dazzling smile is for me."

I hesitated. "Is it dazzling? Actually, I'm feeling a little un-nerved. I... That is, Johnathan, I must thank you for the beautiful roses and, uh, your uh, ... constant attention. I've been overwhelmed, but ..."

"But?"

"But ... I ... The presumption that we would marry ... uh ... the haste of this affair seems to have convinced everyone that it's a predestined fact. Since the moment you left every eye on the place has been fixed on me."

"I've embarrassed you." He hesitated. "I hope they've been kindly eyes."

"Oh, more than kind. Why not? I suspect the entire company operates on a single mind. Yours."

Without looking at me–he hadn't looked me straight in the face since that first shattering eye contact–he said, "We're a close-knit family, but nothing could be further from the truth. Every man and woman on this estate has earned the right to his or her opinion, whatever it may be. I couldn't possibly influence any one of them. I'm glad to know they have accepted you."

In expectation of our first private meeting, I had intended loving kindness. Now I found myself attacking him. "In that case there's remarkable unanimity! How could you presume ... How could you be so sure I would ... The point is ... "

"My darling Philippa, I ... "

"The point is ..." I interrupted him, and stopped. It was the first time he had uttered my name. I held my breath. For a moment I couldn't speak. Damn it! I thought, I'm in over my head! "The point is, you assumed too much! We know nothing about each other! There are things in my past that would prevent ... "

He wasn't listening. He had pulled slightly ahead of me and was taking the trail to the right that led around the lake.

I began to have second thoughts. Was it I, now, who was presuming? Had he changed his mind? Had I lost him? I held my horse. "I thought we were going to the village."

He looked back at me. "Later," he said, and kept on going. We were out of sight of the Lodge and the outbuildings when he stopped.

He was off his horse and approaching me with outstretched arms. I leaned toward him. His touch sent a jolt through my heart that swept away reasoning and doubt. I slipped from my horse and into his arms and the world was obliterated.

We were in the "boathouse," an old mansion situated on the far side of the lake, miles from the Lodge. It had been reconstructed; the lower half scooped out to make room for boats and horses. The upper stories, refurbished, had been turned into a splendid apartment.

We had stabled the horses and were in the spacious second-storey sitting room overlooking the lake. The elegant high-ceilinged old room, gleaming in the afternoon sun, was spotless and warm. There was a fire in the fireplace, a bottle of champagne cooling in a silver bucket, glasses on a silver tray.

"It's lovely," I said.

"My home away from home. Let me take your things." He slipped my heavy jacket from my shoulders and I handed him my gloves and hat.

Except for that mad embrace–and that he'd held my hand when possible on that narrow trail–he'd said nothing. It didn't matter. It had all been said. He loved me. It was mutual, our love for each other! I was feeling it still; my first passionate response to him, and then that delirious, soft sweet, tender yielding ...

"Would you like a drink?"

"I think I need one."

He poured the wine and handed me a glass. "Philippa, will you drink to our future together?"

I hesitated, raised my glass to his. My hand shook. I tried to speak. This was lunacy! I dared not say yes to anything. When I told him about the asylum ... I felt the tears start to my eyes. Furious with myself, I turned my head away.

He lowered his glass, took my glass from my hand and set them both aside. He took both my hands. "Philippa, will you marry me?"

I tried to pull away from him.

He released my hands and I turned away trying to control my voice, my tears. I said, finally, "Johnathan, there are things in my past ..."

"My darling girl."

The brimming tears blinded me; the tender voice destroyed me. I couldn't speak.

He took me in his arms. "You want to marry me." A statement, not a question.

I caught my breath. I said sharply, shakily, through my tears, "You know I do!"

"Yes, I know. Shall I wipe your tears away?"

"Damn it!" I said, "I'll do it myself!"

He put his handkerchief in my hand. "Before we talk about your unhallowed past, I should like to … "

My unhallowed!… I pulled away from him. "I have to talk to you."

"Right. May I say something first?"

"Please do."

"If you think that by revealing your past you risk our future together, let me assure you that in disclosing my past, which I intend to do fully and scrupulously, I put it in far greater jeopardy. Will you sit down?"

I sat down.

"You have a strong stomach?"

"I believe I can take whatever you have to tell me."

"I hope so." He took the chair opposite me and lifting his hands, palms toward me, he said, "They are stained with blood."

I shuddered. "The war."

"The war. But for most the war was faceless. I killed in cold blood."

I felt my face twisting into a grimace of anguished horror.

"Ah, Philippa, my darling."

I stared into his eyes. His face was unreadable; expressionless and, then, without reference to any mental process, in an immediate transfer from his head to mine, I felt intense pain, rage, and a steellike determination to pursue justice! I shut my eyes, started to raise my hands to my head … it was gone!

"Can you forgive me?"

"Wait! Please wait!" I caught my breath. "There's nothing to forgive! If I had the courage, I'd have been with you."

"You realize what you're saying?"

"Yes." I had to go to him. I stood up. "Yes."

And then we were in each other's arms.

After awhile he disengaged himself. He said, "There's more."

"You don't have to…" My knees weak, I sat down. "Johnathan are you still involved?"

"Not that way. But because of my intimate knowledge of that time I am sometimes called for consultation." He was frowning, staring at me. "Philippa, you're pale. Are you all right?"

"You're not committed … ?"

"No. That's over."

All at once I felt wonderful; I felt an almost physical manifestation of his strength surrounding: holding me. It flashed through my mind that Holmes had had that same power, and that in the hospital, years ago, I had seen sick patients recover, almost miraculously, when certain doctors entered the room.

"What I want you to know is that because of those years there are consequences that exist and may persist for my lifetime that, as my wife, may cause you pain." He hesitated. "Do you know anything about The Fourth Arm? Have you heard of it?"

"No."

"The Fourth Arm was a hidden branch of the military services, a separate American, British, Canadian outfit committed to the destruction of Nazi criminals. I was an active member from the beginning. And because I had lived in a frivolous social atmosphere both in England and on the Continent–and had languages–I was slated for a role I despised: a role that gave me entrée to Nazi inner circles and to information essential to the Service." He stopped and picked up his drink. Then he put it, untouched, back on the table.

"Yes?"

"Uh … Well … There was an arranged courtship and marriage to a pro-Nazi bride, a girl I had known socially for years. She was no chaste virgin, but however revolting her beliefs and obsessions, she was a victim. She counted me a friend and was quite open with me. She married me to cover up her on-going affair with a married man. My wife's lover was a vicious, corrupt, high-ranking Nazi who murdered and plundered with immunity to satisfy an apparently insatiable greed. He was aware of the terms of our marriage–it was never consummated–believed it a cover for my perverted sexual habits and scorned me as her dupe; a weakling and a fool.

"He thought he was safe with us; an admiring audience–the idiot and the lover–so he bragged of his connections, his atrocious deeds, and gossiped about the secret affairs, political, financial and what have you of his superiors and friends. He was one of our chief sources of information and vitally important to us.

"Toward the end of the war he disappeared. At Nuremberg he was sentenced to death in absentia. A few years ago he surfaced; made himself known to me. There was an international conference. It was decided to carry out that sentence without the fuss and bother of going public … He is dead."

There was silence between us for a long minute. I said, "Your former wife, is she–do you still see her?"

"She's still around; a very high profile socially, and we're still friends, but I haven't seen her in several years. What I must tell you now is that following that wedding–during the war–I lived the kind of life, publicly, that proved me a conceited ass, a light-weight, a womanizer–or worse–and in a political sense, harmless. My visible image was that of a Nazi sympathizer and a fool. That reputation still follows me. Gossip dies hard.

"It may make it bearable for you to know that after the war the British honoured me with their Military Cross." He picked up his glass. "This will give you a chance to think what it would mean to be my wife. If you're still considering it." He paused. "It's your turn."

I took a deep breath. "I spent six months in a mental institution."

"The Westchester Division of the New York Hospital."

"What! How do you know? ... Alethea."

"No, of course not. I didn't know Alethea knew you until I told her about you in Paris. Is that where you met?"

"She didn't tell you?"

"Not a word, just that she'd met you in New York."

Protecting me. What a wonderful friend. ... "But how could you possibly know about Westchester?"

"Alethea had a rough war, her nerves were shot. Europe was in ruins, so was England. The Nazis had tortured and murdered her husband, she had lost most of her family. She couldn't sleep and became dependent on drugs. We had to get her out. When we put her in Westchester, because she might still be in danger, we did a complete check on everyone in the hospital who was not born in the United States. Your name was on the list. I asked for a report on you."

"Really! What did it say?"

"Nothing much–something to the effect that after three month's observation they couldn't hold you. Why did you stay another three months?"

"I had no place of my own; before I left New York my studio had been destroyed by fire. Sue and Elliot had set aside a suite for me in their New York house and I could have gone to them. But there was a large unanswered question in my mind. My doctor refused to name my illness and warned me not to start reading about it as "it would further disturb my mind." I had no intention of listening to him. I had to understand my illness, to make sure it would never happen again. I didn't want advice or interference. I had to be alone.

"I took an open cottage on the hospital grounds where, without supervision, I could come and go as I pleased. The first thing I did, through my old hospital, who knew nothing of my condition, was to obtain a card to a medical library. I took out every book I could find on mental illness. I diagnosed myself: Manic Depressive. I was appalled to read that in a typical case, such as my own, because the patient 'must live without obstacles,' at intervals, the patient was hospitalized again and again. I had to try to break the Manic Depressive syndrome, and I believe I did."

"You never went back?"

"No ... But in that respect ..."

"You have doubts?"

"Perhaps I should have." I hesitated, but he had better know. "Directly after leaving the hospital I went to Africa. I had six wonderful years. A one-man show in Cape Town and a picture in a group show in Africa's National Museum. In August my mother died and I went back to Edgeville, thinking I might stay there, but everything in that house, in my past, that was unbearable, hit me. I ran. I took a house in a slum near Bridgeport and withdrew from everyone and everything. I wasn't disturbed or melancholy, I didn't hallucinate, I didn't mourn my mother—I didn't think of her or of anyone else. I read interminably: novels, trash. I walked around mindless, rudderless. I might still be there if it hadn't been for the shock that brought me to my senses." I hesitated.

"Go on."

"One freezing night in November I needed coffee and food for Fish. I went out with no hat, no gloves, my coat buttoned six ways from Sunday, bare legs and, without noticing, I'd shoved my feet into high-heeled red satin evening slippers. An old Madam tried to pick me up. She thought I was a homeless whore."

He was laughing. "My exquisite girl! I can't believe it!"

"I couldn't believe it either until I stopped to look at myself in a looking glass on a corner drug store. What bothers me ... Why did it happen?"

"God! Combat fatigue! You think that only happened to you? It happens to all of us under stress. The mind can take so much. You came out of it because you had enough rest. I understand it very well, more perhaps than you would believe. If you survived that, you're safe. Anyway, you'll be safe with me."

I stood up and went to the window and he came and put an arm around me. Everything outside was brilliant with sun and snow ... the world renewed. My heart lifted. I turned to him and he took my head in his hands and gently kissed me. "My love, if you feel like talking, I very much want to hear more. You changed your life-style? Your philosophy?"

"I want to tell you. I'm not sure I know how. What happened was … an experience, rather than anything arrived at by rational thought."

We turned in unison and I went back to my chair. My glass was empty. He filled it and sat down opposite me. Waited.

"Just before I left Westchester I was in a strange state. I was still hearing voices. That was no secret, my doctor knew. They were no longer dominant or intrusive. I could call them or forget them. Still, I believe their presence removed the conventional boundaries that limit thought.

"I saw my life clearly and in a totally different light. And I understood that in accepting the mores of the world and my family as valid, I had allowed them to control me. That is, I had given up my personal control–or, in trying to adjust to the equivocal mores of the world, I was out of control–and had been for most of my life.

"I knew I could not go back to that and stay sane. I knew I could not again relinquish my personal control. I must identify with my true self.

"My true self? My identity? Who or what am I?" I hesitated, watching him. Was there a change in his expression? "Johnathan … do you think that ludicrous; a pursuit of the perennial half-wit?"

"I wouldn't dare."

We were both laughing. "I was never more serious in my life."

"Please, tell me."

"The ancient Greeks believed in duality in man: spirit and matter; dual control; divisible, separate. How not believe it? I had to accept that to discover my identity, if I place myself in reference or relationship to the world, I am automatically and coldly judged as to class, race, religion, colour, success, failure, or what have you. Conditions totally removed from what I am.

"According to the dictionary, Human … designates man; having human form or attributes.

"According to the world, 'I'm only human' is an excuse for weakness: for lack; either mental or physical or both.

"I refuse to be judged by the world's standards. That is not the truth of me.

"According to the dictionary, Being is … One that exists: specific: God:–with various qualifying adjectives such as, supreme, infinite, etc.

"And … Spirit: … The life principle, viewed as the 'breath' or gift of deity: hence the agent of vital and conscious functions in man: the soul.

"If I accept Spirit as my identity, to the exclusion of any other, I identify with Being: the creative force of life.

"When, at the end of my six months at Westchester, I recognized that, concurrently with that knowing, I stood immobilized in awe: *in a vacuum of silence–of omnipotent power!*

"What is this power? The invisible superhuman power that man, of whatever race or colour, since the beginning of time calls, 'The Presence of God': the Hebrew 'Shekinah': 'The earthly dwelling of God'?" I stopped.

After a long pause he asked, "And the application? It was all very new to you."

"I won't say my usual habits became immediately obsolete–more like obsolescent." I shrugged. "Old habits ..."

"Die hard. Yes."

"But it was so clear! I saw not only myself but everyone else in a new light. I understood at once how I could 'love my neighbour as myself' and very soon, however judgmatic my first impression, there was an immediate reaction against that; an immediate recognition of the Truth of Being. And my second thought was the correct one."

"Do those months, which I cannot imagine, haunt you? Have they left you scarred? Is it possible to talk of them without pain?"

"There are no scars and no pain. On the contrary. There was never a moment when I didn't know who I am, where I was, what was going on around me, and what I was doing. But that was incidental to the absolute joy of being in the presence of, and talking to, the dead people I had admired and loved all my life."

"Will you tell me about them? May I ask who they were?"

I nodded. "As an adolescent, to escape my everlasting unpopularity, I went to Keats, to the beauty of his verse and the study of his life. I have wondered ... Was that why he came to me? Did my voices, and particularly Keats' voice, send me out of my mind to protect me? I was desperately alone. I needed love and help; I needed sanctuary. Because of them I entered Westchester. Yet I was not certifiable. Within the next several months I was thankful *to them* for having been given sanctuary. It was my time, both with my voices and Westchester that brought me to my senses." I paused.

"Yes?"

"Well... Having said that, my mind, now, refuses to believe that I was actually in contact with the spirits of the dead. ...But how could all that have come out of thin air?"

440

"You think you were hallucinating?"

"I don't know. But how explain... Johnathan, something strange, beyond belief, happened shortly after I entered Westchester. It wasn't I, alone..."

"Darling, if it worries you ..."

"It doesn't. All right, here it is: Keats woke me. 'Get up, Philippa.'

"Half asleep, I stumbled out of bed. 'Face East. You will see two suns.'

"East? I turned to face the window. In the dull, gray, early morning light, through the bare branches of the trees, I saw two small, round, reddish suns.

"Keats said 'They will start to move closer to each other. When they coalesce you will be born again.'

"I stood, staring at the suns. They moved, merged: became one.

"Outside, I heard footsteps running down the corridor. They stopped in front of my door, and a breathless voice called out, 'It smells like Christmas! It smells like Christmas!'

"I ran to open the door. A woman stood there, facing me. I said, 'Mrs. Thompson! Good morning.'

"'Hi,' she said. 'It's the middle of February, but it smells like Christmas!'

"After a moment, she started off again, running down the corridor."

Johnathan said, "Many strange things happened during the war. Let me tell you a story. On one of the ships in a convoy running up to Murmansk with war material for the Russians, just before sailing, the old Captain died. Because of the shortage of experienced men, a friend of mine was hastily promoted to Captain and sent on board to take over.

"One night, in a violent storm, attacked by enemy submarines, his ship was hit and began listing heavily. Unable to right it, or keep it on course, it fell behind the convoy. He was certain they were lost. Suddenly, the ship righted itself, and the old Captain, standing beside him, said, 'That's O.K. son, we'll take her in.'

"They stood together during the long hours of the night and docked safely. My friend didn't notice when the old man left. He was unloading cargo when he went into shock. He had remembered, suddenly, that the old Captain had been buried before his ship left England."

Johnathan stood up. "My darling girl... " He turned away from me, took a few steps, turned back and looked at me. "Have I neglected to mention that I've been in love with you from the moment I saw you leaping on to that wild horse? I have never got that picture out of my mind. Later that morning when our horses collided, I was again enthralled. When you first appeared at the Lodge, I wasn't lying when I told you I'd been running after women, in the street, thinking they were you. But these past weeks in Paris have been hell." He turned away from me.

I was alarmed. What had happened?

He turned to face me, his eyes holding mine. "I was so hopelessly in love—and without hope. Why didn't you write to me? I'm not sure I'll ever forgive you for that."

"B'but ... I ..."

And then—obviously in despair of me, "Philippa! We've wasted enough time! How soon will you marry me?"

I stood up and fell in to his arms. "Is tomorrow too soon?"

Printed and bound in Canada by
Best Gagné Book Manufacturers